SHOIL

A Continuation of Jon Cornwall's Adventures

David Higgins

Strategic Book Publishing and Rights Co.

Strategic Book Publishing and Rights Co., LLC
USA | Singapore
www.sbpra.net

For information about special discounts for bulk purchases, please contact Strategic Book Publishing and Rights Co. Special Sales, at bookorder@sbpra.net.

ISBN: 978-1-68235-623-4

Book Design: Suzanne Kelly

PREVIOUS BOOKS BY THE AUTHOR

Read the trilogy and find out how it all began:

Jon Cornwall's Adventures—Part 1—Unofficial Secrets
(ISBN 978-1-47724-172-1)

Jon Cornwall's Adventures—Part 2—And Then
(ISBN 978-1-68181-551-0)

Jon Cornwall's Adventures—Part 3—The Revelations
(ISBN 978-1-950015-94-8)

PREFACE

Why bother?

It's a question I asked myself more than once while writing this fourth book. Why bother to write another book at all? I had completed my trilogy and successfully published them all. Ambition achieved; checkbox ticked. So why bother to sit down and write again?

I guess that in the back of my mind I never truly concluded my story and left the door open to continue it. It must have been about a year before I actually started writing again, deciding that I could not just leave Tampong and Shoil up in the air, both with unfinished business. I knew that the two had to finally face each other, although the ending changed several times while I was writing. There were several different versions of Terry's future too. In the end, I came to a decision and hope you enjoy the final meeting of two adversaries.

Is this the end? Will the survivors live happily ever after like some Disney movie? I have yet to make that decision. Who knows, maybe a fifth book will find its way onto my computer. What do you think? Feel free to let me know once you have finished this book.

Finally, I need to put on record my warmest thanks to my darling wife, my greatest supporter, and my greatest critic. Christine is my inspiration, and some of Terry's feelings expressed in this book are my own. Thank you, my lover.

David

THE GROUP MEMBERS—DEAD AND ALIVE

The Lower Middle Group

Aubril—Young female and Junior Guardian. Goes by the human name Tracey

Bilow—Young female and Second Guardian. Goes by the human name Anna

Catril—Young female and Third Guardian. Goes by the human name Maryanne

Dexter—Young male and Fourth Guardian. Goes by the human name Gordon

Elfon—Young female and Fifth Guardian. Goes by the human name Joanne

Foust—Young male and Sixth Guardian. Goes by the human name Stephen

Glib—Middle male and Seventh Guardian. Goes by the human name Peter

Jalip—Middle-aged male and First Lower Middle. Goes by the human name Jon

Deceased members:

Bilow—Killed in the London battle

Catril—Killed at the hands of Shoil

Dexter—Killed by Woul

Foust—Killed by Woul

Healt—Eighth Guardian who was betrayed and destroyed by Utter

Indi—Ninth Guardian and killed in battle

Kowp—Second Lower Middle and destroyed by Zelphur

Looud—Phantom and Third Lower Middle, destroyed by Youch

Moudi—Forth Lower Middle and Leader, betrayed and destroyed by Utter

The Higher Middle Group

Narib—Young female and Junior Guardian. Goes by the human name Joslin
Prowl—Young male and Third Guardian. Goes by the human name Steven
Shoil—Young female and Sixth Guardian. Goes by the human name Kara
Tampong—Young female and Seventh Guardian. Goes by the human name Katy
Viex—Middle-aged male and Ninth Guardian. Goes by the human name Ian
Woul—Veteran male and First Higher Middle. Goes by the human name Jack
Xtri—Middle-aged male and Second Higher Middle. Goes by the human name Stewart
Zelphur—Middle-aged female, the Fourth Higher Middle and Leader. Goes by the human name of Barry

Deceased members:

Narib—Killed in battle
Prowl—Killed in the London battle
Viex—Killed in the London battle
Woul—Killed in the London battle
Zelphur—Killed by Jon
Ottric—Second Guardian and destroyed by Jon
Queul—Fourth Guardian and killed in battle
Rasp—Fifth Guardian and destroyed by Jon
Utter—Eighth Guardian and killed in battle
Youch—Phantom and Third Higher Middle and destroyed by Looud

As in the initial trilogy, throughout the story there is a title reference to the group members' status, meaning whether they have transformed into their original forms, are starting that transition, or are still in a dormant form. Being dormant means that they are not aware of their powers and believe themselves to be ordinary human beings, albeit with some unique talents.

This transformation is called activation, which is achieved either through physical contact with another group member or by being in close proximity to any of the group members, be they Lower or Higher Middle. The higher up the order the group member is, the more sensitive they are to another member's presence. This can be an advantage as well as a disadvantage.

For my extraordinary and special wife, Christine, without whom none of this would have been written or even possible. She is my inspiration.

PREVIOUSLY IN THE ORIGINAL TRILOGY

Jon Cornwall had problems accepting who he is and his purpose in life. Even when his closest friends tried to convince him of his importance, he had difficulty accepting this. It did not help that whenever a woman started to develop a relationship with him, she met with a tragic end. During all these internal conflicts and emotional roller coasters, his enemies were closing in. They had unlimited resources, and it was not long before they tracked him and his group of defenders down, called the Lower Middle. The Higher Middle started to slowly eliminate the Lower Middle members, setting up various traps. It was not all plain sailing for the Higher Middle though, as some of the Lower Middle group had managed to escape, mainly because of Jon's unique skill to move around in his spiritual form—once he had transformed and accepted who he really was.

Two members of the other group, Shoil and Tampong, were experiencing vastly different emotions. While Shoil had designs on being the new group leader and was quietly building her strength through absorbing men, Tampong was having serious doubts about the group's purpose and her role in it. Shoil was not afraid to experiment, which, on one occasion, went terribly wrong when she tried to absorb a woman and was violently sick, while Tampong began challenging the sheer brutality handed out by other members of her group.

As the two sole survivors from the Higher Middle, they went their separate ways. Tampong headed north with a young boy, whom she had rescued from Shoil's wrath, while Shoil remained south, licking her wounds and determined to track down Tampong, whom she believed betrayed the group and almost killed her.

This is the continuation of that hatred.

THE HUNT CONTINUES

Date: June 2003
Age: Terry is 10
Status: Dormant

The sun was high in the Leeds sky and not a cloud could be seen. It was unusually warm for early June, not that Tampong complained. She hated the cold weather and was seriously considering moving to a warmer climate. The only thing stopping her was Terry. He was doing well at school, and she would hate herself if his schoolwork fell behind because she hauled him away to some foreign country. She was in deep thought as she drove the boy to school, subconsciously pulling up outside the gate, which she was surprised about, as the road was usually filled with cars dropping off children. She stopped the car, got out and walked around to the pavement to find Terry had already exited the vehicle. She kneeled down, pulled his rucksack straight on his back and combed her fingers through his hair.

He was looking at her with his head slightly tilted to one side, as if in deep thought.

'You are not my mummy, are you?' he blurted.

Tampong felt her heart skip a beat as she glanced into his clear blue, questioning eyes. She took a deep, calming breath.

'Why do you ask that now?' she questioned.

He tilted his head slightly the other way, suggesting he was puzzled as to why she should question him, but then simply shrugged his shoulders, deciding her question was worth answering.

'Well, at school yesterday all the kids were talking about their mummies and daddies and what they like and don't like about them. That was when I remembered my real mummy and daddy.'

Tears started to fill his eyes and run down his face, so she brought her hands to his face and wiped his tears away.

'We have spoken about this before. Remember?'

He sighed heavily.

'Then no,' she admitted, gulping down her guilt, 'no, Terry, I am not your real mummy.'

'She is dead, isn't she?'

'Yes, she is dead.'

'And my daddy, is he dead too?'

'Yes, he is dead too.'

'Did you kill them?'

His question turned her blood cold. She had had regular nightmares about that day and how that murderess Shoil brutally cut down innocent lives, including Terry's parents. She felt guilty. She always felt guilty, although she was not quite sure why. Could she have reacted quicker? Should she have anticipated Shoil's reaction? Should she even have been part of the Higher Middle? Almost two years had passed, but sometimes it felt like only yesterday when the horrors of that day happened. She shivered and held Terry by his shoulders. She had doubts whether these thoughts and fears would ever leave her.

'No, Terry, I certainly did not kill your mummy and daddy.'

'That's right,' confirmed Terry, clicking his fingers as if remembering, 'that big, horrible dog did, didn't it?'

'Yes, that big, horrible dog did.'

'Why?'

He must have asked this question a thousand times since she took him away from that bloody scene, and she always struggled to find the right words, opting instead to go with her usual response.

'Because it was an evil dog,' she finally answered.

It was her usual but completely insufficient answer. She had struggled to find the real reason. Historically the Higher Middle killed humans only to transform into their bodies as their own began to deteriorate, or when the Group was threatened. Shoil, however, took particular pleasure in killing and absorbing men, which she did on numerous occasions, for pure sport. Tampong never understood why Zelphur tolerated her behavior, but she did, so Shoil was allowed to continue with her person-killing quest.

Terry appeared to contemplate the answer, again, then shrugged his shoulders.

'Some dogs are really evil then,' he concluded, not for the first time.

'Correct, some dogs are unbelievably evil.'

He turned to look towards the school, and then back up at Tampong, who had stood up. She was anticipating his next move, holding him gently by his shoulders and steering him towards the school entrance.

'I have to go to school now. You will meet me after school as usual?'

'Of course, I will.'

She let go of his shoulders.

Terry started to walk towards the school entrance, then unexpectantly turned back and rushed into her arms, burying his head in her stomach. She stroked his hair gently and affectionately.

'I am glad you are my new mummy,' he whispered.

His words filled her heart with such warmth and happiness, she could hardly speak. Fortunately, she did not have to as he moved away from her and started to run towards the school entrance, waving to her as he did. She instinctively returned his wave, but he had already turned back towards the school, running towards the teacher who was hurrying the rest of the children inside.

She waited until he disappeared inside before turning to her car. She casually glanced at the other mothers. As usual, some were chatting amongst themselves, others were on their mobile phones, while others had already disappeared in all directions, but one stood directly opposite Tampong and was staring at her. She made eye contact, but the woman did not flinch, causing Tampong to go on the defensive. The woman walked up to her.

'Who are you?' asked the woman with menace in her voice.

She must have been in her forties and was well-dressed. She carried a Louis Vuitton bag and, what looked like, a string necklace of real diamonds.

'Excuse me?'

'I said who are you, exactly?'

'I don't know what you mean,' she replied defensively, pulling her car keys out of her pocket with the intent of opening her door.

She pressed the key fob and heard the reassuring pop of the locks disengaging. She gripped the handle and started to open the door.

'That was Terry, wasn't it?'

Tampong froze on the spot. The woman stepped closer.

'That was Terry, wasn't it?' she repeated.

'Yes,' she confirmed.

'So where is Karen? She loves that child and wouldn't leave him for a second.'

Tampong bit her bottom lip, stood up straight, and released the door handle.

'And who might you be?'

'I am Terry's auntie.'

'Ho.'

'Ho indeed, so just who are *you* exactly? I am not sure how many times I need to ask. I have seen you bringing him to school before, but not once have I seen Karen. I have tried contacting her, but she is not answering her phone. Nor is her husband answering his phone, which is all very strange indeed. I have even been around to their home, but no one answers. I have tried to get to you before now, but you always managed to avoid me.'

'My name is Katy, and if you really must know, Karen is dead,' she spat out.

'*WHAT!*' The woman screamed out disbelievingly while taking an involuntary step backwards in surprise.

Her hand instinctively moved to her heart.

'Right. Do you remember that attack in Fort Knox about two years ago?'

Tampong could see the woman's mind ticking through her memories.

'Yes, of course, in America, wasn't it? It was all over the news.'

'Well, Terry was there with Karen, who was unfortunately killed in the attack.'

'My god, and what about Paul?'

Tampong assumed that was the father.

'He was killed there too.'

The woman looked as though she was about to faint but managed to recover and compose herself.

'But that cannot be true, I am certain I have seen them both since then.'

'I doubt that very much as I have had Terry all the time since that awful day. He told me where he lived and which school he went to, so I moved here to be with him.'

'So, who are you, err, Katy, you said?'

'Just a friend.'

'So, you are telling me that his parents, Karen and Paul, were killed in that ghastly attack in America?'

'Sadly, yes.'

'Well, that's very strange indeed, and I now know you are not telling me the whole truth.'

'Really?'

'Really, particularly given that Terry's father's name is actually Robert and not Paul.'

'As I said, I am just a friend of Karen's and didn't really know the father all that well. I just assumed that Paul was his name.'

The woman shook her head.

'You cannot just take a child into your care like a lost dog. There are rules and regulations, social services needs to be informed, none of this makes any sense, and nor do I believe what you are—'

Tampong panicked. She grabbed the woman's arm.

The woman suddenly stopped talking the moment Tampong's eyes turned orange as she kept a firm grip on her arm. Tiny orange bolts of electricity shot from her arm into the woman's, whose own eyes now turned orange. Tampong looked around quickly, but no one was looking in their direction.

'You will forget all about Terry and his parents,' she said in a deep and echoey voice, 'all their memories will be erased from your mind. Now turn away and go shopping.'

She let go of the woman's arm, and both their eyes returned to normal. The woman said nothing but simply turned around and began walking down the street, shaking her head as if she was trying to remember what she was about to do. Tampong watched her walk away, then looked down at her key fob she was still holding and noticed her hand was shaking. She clenched her fist and the sensation disappeared. She opened the car door fully and slid inside. She hoped she would never have to do that again, but that was too close for comfort, and she realized she needed to be more careful in the future. It was the first time in nearly two years she had to call on her powers to rescue her from an awkward situation. Perhaps the idea of them moving away should be reconsidered.

Still, she got away with it, or at least she thought she had.

***

Shoil's eyes burst wide open, and she sat bolt upright in her chair. Her eyes locked straight ahead, although she was not looking at anything but absorbing the sudden sensation she now felt as her senses were on full alert as a result of the disturbance, and one she had not felt in a long time. Somebody had moved into their true form and created a ripple in their world. She knew who it must be. Tampong.

'So, you have finally revealed yourself, bitch,' she said, spitting the words out in contempt.

She knew it was not going to be easy to find her, but the faint disturbance suggested she was not close but must be in the same country for her to have been felt.

'Just move into your form again, bitch, and I'll be able to hunt you down.'

For the last two years she has hunted far and low for Tampong, but she had disappeared. She looked for signs in the news of anything unusual or unexplained, but nothing clicked. That was until now. Something must have triggered her to move into her true form. She had a sudden thought that perhaps the Lower Middle had found her and were taking her out, but she scratched that idea almost as soon as it entered her head. The disturbance was so short that it was unlikely that she was taken out. If she had been, then there would have been an abrupt end to the disturbance, but this felt controlled and deliberate. Besides, she wanted Tampong to be alive, wanted to be the one to finish her for the last time. Wanted her to pay for her betrayal.

She sat back in her chair and rested her head on her soft cushion. The disturbance had rekindled her desire to find her again. She had almost given up and for the last few months had even stopped thinking about her, but now she was at the forefront of her mind again. She knew she would have to widen her search pattern now, which would not be a problem in her animal form. She had been training hard since that failed attack. She recalled when she had spat at the spot where Zelphur's body exploded and urinated on the space where Bilow once stood. She smiled at the memory.

The Lower Middle had also disappeared off the face of the earth, but that would not be the first time that had happened. Whenever their group became dormant, then the Lower Middle returned to their human form quicker than the Higher Middle did, and they were only triggered when the two groups got very close to each other. How she longed for that to happen again. She was sure she was the remaining survivor of their own group, except for that traitor Tampong, and still found it difficult to come to terms with how they lost that battle. Even today, she wondered who those mysterious members were and whether that really was Jalip who became huge and monstrous, even when compared to Zelphur's own large size. She was never that close to Zelphur, so had no information on her network and resources, which she knew were extensive. She had to be content with continuing to work to pay the bills. The anger would always build up inside her at the thought of all that lovely money and available resources that could, and should, have been hers had she simply been part of the inner circle. Her one remaining hope was that Tampong was part of that inner circle, being slightly higher up the order than she was. If she could track her down and absorb her, then she would have all that information too. God, the things she could do with all those resources that would suddenly be available to her. If only.

She shook the thought away, got undressed and slipped into the shower. She washed herself vigorously, dried herself, dressed again, and then left her tiny apartment to make her way to the bus stop. She boarded the bus and moved to the back seats, as she always did. She glanced out of the window wondering what happened with her life. One moment she was full of optimism and looking forward to controlling this earth, the next she was going to work as a table server while her only means of travel was on a public bus. How quickly her world had changed. She felt depressed as she got off the bus and entered the small country restaurant, the King's Arm, her current place of work. The hotel come restaurant was in a small village just outside North London.

'Good evening, Kara,' announced the ever-enthusiastic manager.

'Good evening, Ken,' she replied, not bothering to look up.

'So how are you on this wonderful evening?'

'Now I am just on top of the world, mate, on top of the world,' she said sarcastically.

'That's the spirit,' he responded, not picking up on her sarcasm. 'Well, we are going to have an interesting night tonight. We have a local darts group coming in to celebrate their championship win. Wonderful news, isn't it?'

'Ho, yes, just wonderful,' replied Shoil, whose wish for a quiet evening had just gone out of the window.

'Get yourself changed then, girl, as we can expect them to start arriving in around thirty minutes.'

'How many exactly?'

'Should be thirty-five at last count.'

He rubbed his hands in anticipation of the income the evening would bring.

'Fantastic.'

She walked into the women's changing room and dressed in her ridiculous server outfit, which looked more like something a hooker would wear in some dodgy hotel. Her black dress stopped between her knees and thigh and had nine slips underneath, forcing the bottom of the dress out. She tied the piney to the front and stared in the mirror.

'What a perfect-looking whore,' she said aloud.

The push-up bra she had to wear forced the top of her breasts out of the top of her black dress. This was definitely designed by a man. A noise from outside forced her out of her depression and to turn and walk out into the main restaurant. Four guests had arrived and were discussing table settings with Ken. All four looked to be in their mid-forties, two men and two women. The men were dressed in suit and tie, while both women had opted for long, plaited dresses. Ken turned towards Kara as she entered.

'Perfect timing,' he announced, 'and this is Kara, who is one of our excellent servers and who will be looking after you all this evening.'

They all turned in her direction. The man in front adjusted his tie as he took in Kara's appearance.

'Good evening to you, Kara, and we look forward to you servicing us.'

In your dreams, thought Shoil, who clearly understood his sarcastic greeting and the words behind them.

'My pleasure,' she answered instead, giving him her best forced smile.

She was grateful that the door opened and more guests entered, stopping any further sarcastic comments from the man. She could see from the corner of her eye he was still looking at her.

This one is going to be a problem, she thought.

Her colleague then arrived behind the guests and walked quickly up to Kara.

‘Ho, my God, he is not making us wear these ridiculous outfits again, is he?’

Kara just nodded.

‘Why on earth?’

‘Apparently it was requested by some of the guests who are here tonight and have been here before.’

‘Guess it must one some of the men then.’

‘You guessed right,’ answered Shoil as she glanced across the room to see the man still staring at her. ‘Get yourself dressed, girl, as I don’t want to be the only one looking like a cheap whore.’

‘Great. What a long night it is going to be then. Be right back.’

She disappeared into the woman’s changing room, while Shoil moved behind the bar and started to clean a few glasses. The man eyeing her walked up to the bar.

‘Can I have a pint of your best local bitter please, Kara?’

His eyes seemed locked onto the top of her breasts.

She ignored his lecherous stare and glanced up at the clock.

‘I am afraid it is not quite time yet, sir. Could you please come back in fifteen minutes?’

He looked down at his watch, then back up to her.

‘So, what can I do for fifteen minutes then?’

She was tempted to suggest he shove something large and wide up his arse but was saved from the need to give any response as Ken came back out.

‘Not chatting up the bar staff already, are you, Tim?’

‘This one is as cold as ice, Ken, but no, I was actually just looking for a pint, but apparently I am too early.’

Ken looked up at the clock.

‘Ho, I think it is close enough. What is your poison?’

‘Thanks, mate, I’ll have a pint of your local bitter, please.’

He looked smugly across to Shoil, who simply shrugged her shoulders.

‘I trust I will not have call to complain about your service tonight, young lady. I am guessing this is your only form of income.’

Shoil just looked at him.

'I thought so,' he said quietly. 'Just remember that when I call upon you, and I *will* call upon you, you come smartly.'

Shoil said nothing but gave him her best submissive smile. She was tempted to suggest he enjoyed his last day on this earth, because if he were going to call upon her, then she would respond by consuming him very, very slowly. She smiled at the prospect, just when her friend walked back in.

Ken looked her up and down too, clearly pleased that he now had two sexy chicks to boss around.

Janet ignored the man.

'And what, pray, are you looking so happy about?' she inquired, seeing the smile on Shoil's face.

'Ho, just that tonight might not turn out to be a complete and utter wreck of an evening after all, Janet.'

Janet just gave her a puzzled expression and was about to ask for clarification, but Ken's hollering for them halted any further discussion.

'Kara, Janet, get your arses over here and start serving.'

They both walked outside to find the large table now full of chattering customers. Ken had poured thirty-six glasses of prosecco, telling his guests it was champagne, laying out twelve glasses on three trays. The girls each picked up a tray, while Ken scooped up the remaining one, and they marched towards the long table. Ken started at one end and the girls at the other, moving along either side of the table. As Janet leaned across the table to sit a glass down, a man grabbed her left buttock and squeezed hard.

She stood up promptly.

'Excuse me,' she demanded.

'You are excused, for now,' said the lecherous man.

His friends all laughed.

'Very nice butt,' he added as she moved away.

Shoil was opposite the man and leaned forward to place a glass on the table, giving the man the perfect view down the front of her dress. She looked across and saw his eyes were glued to her chest. As she suspected he would. He blinked once, then looked up to see her staring at him, so he looked down like a guilty boy. She knew the type, trying to be the big man in town, but in fact had little experience with women. As she walked down the table distributing the fake champagne, she glanced back down the table towards the man; he was looking at her again, so she smiled warmly at him, and he smiled back at her. His courage obviously lifted a little by her reaction to him ogling her boobs.

When it was time to collect the glasses, she deliberately moved to the other side of the table and brushed herself against the man. She heard him gulp in air. Another man was watching her from the other side of the table and was clearly jealous of the fact she was teasing his teammate and not him. He considered himself the best looker of the group and would never accept an attractive woman giving him the cold shoulder in favor of another team member. He thumped his fist on the table, causing the other guests to stop talking and turn in his direction. He pulled his tie tighter to his shirt collar as he stood up and cleared his throat.

'Ladies and gentlemen,' he began, 'we are all here tonight to celebrate a great victory, our first in seventeen years, in fact.'

This caused a ripple of applause while a few men cheered.

'We have shown the others that we have the skill and ability as a team to defeat all comers. That we can now move into the regionals next month.'

More applause and cheers.

'So, let us enjoy ourselves tonight; eat, drink and be merry.'

He looked at Shoil as he said the last words. She simply smiled at him as he sat back down. Shoil and Janet then disappeared into the kitchen.

'Did you see that man grope me?' she asked.

'I did, and next time you should say something.'

'Do you really think that is going to help? I have a little boy to feed and need this job, so I just have to swallow my pride and get on with it.'

'None of us should have to tolerate such abuse.'

'Right. When you are Queen of England, perhaps then I will take your advice. Let me know when that happens, won't you?'

Shoil was about to tell her that she would one day rule not just this country but the whole world. She nodded her understanding instead.

The girls returned to the table, this time with plates filled with food, lots of vegetables with very little meat, but the guests did not seem to object and started eating as soon as the plates were laid on the table. Janet had the misfortune to serve roving hands again, and he did not disappoint. His hand this time went up her skirt, and his fingers pinched her buttock, causing her to jump backwards. Shoil had a perfect view from the other side of the table, so repeated her move in front of him.

'What's your name?' she asked. Her eyes not leaving his.

'Colin,' he replied, 'what's yours?'

'Kara.'

'Well, Kara, it is nice to meet you.'

'And if you want to meet me again, you will keep your hands off my friend.'

'Are you jealous?'

'Something like that.'

'So, if I keep my hands off her, you will give me something else to put my hands on then?'

Clearly his full courage had returned now.

'If you are a good boy,' she answered.

He laughed.

Just then, the spokesperson grabbed her arm, pulling her closer to his face.

'And what about me then?'

'What about you?' she asked innocently.

'What do you see in him that I do not offer more of?'

'Hmmmm, let me think,' she said as she slowly and deliberately pulled her arm back up, despite his attempts to keep it pinned to the table.

His eyes widened in surprise, not sure he understood how such a weak-looking woman could have such strength. He quickly released her arm, looking down, now a little embarrassed.

'I like a man who acts like a man,' she whispered in his ear.

She then nibbled the bottom of his earlobe.

'What can I say,' scoffed Colin, 'you either have it are you haven't.'

'Go screw yourself, Colin.'

Colin just laughed again as his eyes followed Shoil around the room. Clearly he was now full of confidence and eager anticipation of the evening ahead. Better still, he had actually beaten Stuart to an attractive girl. He always seemed to win the hearts of girls around him, except tonight. He was going to relish the moment.

For the rest of the evening, he left Janet alone and kept his hands to himself, exchanging glances with Shoil instead all through the evening.

In the kitchen, the girls were scraping the last of the uneaten pudding into bins and preparing coffee. Janet looked across to Shoil.

'Are you going to bed that horrible man?'

'None of your business.'

'You are, aren't you?'

'I might.'

'But that large well-built guy sitting opposite him looks more your type.'

'What's my type exactly?'

'You know, large and muscular. Small brain, large penis, probably. And this big guy clearly has his eyes on you.'

'Do you think I am so shallow?'

Janet said nothing but gave her a knowing look. Shoil finally nodded her head in agreement.

'Well maybe, but at least you have been left alone by that pervert, haven't you?'

Janet stopped placing the cups on the table and looked directly at Shoil.

'Did you warn him, or offer him something to leave me alone?'

'I might have put a little word in his ear,' she admitted.

'You are playing a dangerous game, Kara, though I am grateful he has left me alone.'

'What is life without a few risks?'

'Men like that don't care what happens to the likes of us. It is not worth the risk, Kara.'

'I can look after myself, Janet, don't you worry yourself.'

'I hope you are right, girl, I truly do.'

Shoil said nothing else but carried out the tray of coffee cups into the restaurant. Some of the guests had already left, including mister muscles, much to her relief. She did not need a scene with two men coming after her. Colin was still there, of course, and watched her walk up to the coffee urn. She started to fill the cups and sensed him coming up behind her. He pushed himself against her buttocks, and she could feel his erection. She responded by wriggling her posterior against him in acknowledgement before standing straight up and turning to face him with a cup of coffee in her hand. She held it out to him, and he took it.

'Would you like cream with that?' she asked suggestively.

'I would indeed.'

She picked up the cream jug and slowly poured a little of the content into his coffee, her eyes never leaving his.

'And would sir like a little sugar?'

She licked the top of her lips as she spoke the words suggestively.

'I, I would indeed,' he stuttered.

'And would sir like a digestive afterwards?'

'What would you suggest?'

She moved a little closer to him to whisper. 'If you'd care to hang about outside afterwards, I can make you a few offers and give you a sample or two.'

'Cannot wait,' he whispered back.

He turned to rejoin a small group standing by the end of the table, but not before taking one final glance back towards Shoil. His friend nudged him in the ribs when he joined them, nearly knocking his coffee out of his hands.

'Have you clicked with that one?' his friend asked.

'You bet I have,' he said, sipping his coffee.

A knowing smile never left his face.

It was closing time, and Tim was settling the bill with Ken while Colin hung about outside the restaurant, pacing back and forth, impatient. He was waiting for Shoil. Waiting for the pleasures she was so clearly offering him all through the evening.

Ken walked out into the car park to see Colin pacing around.

'You not coming back into town then, Colin?'

'No thanks. I am waiting for the waitress to come out.'

'Ho, so you have scored with her then, have you?'

'I have indeed, yes I have.'

'Then I wish you a pleasant evening, you lucky sod.'

Colin just smiled and watched as Ken unlocked his car door, slid inside before starting the engine, then pulling away out of the car park. He continued watching until the car disappeared from view.

He then waited some more, glancing at his watch every minute, which seemed to pass like an hour.

In fact, it was only another twenty minutes before the front door opened again, just when he was beginning to think that she was never going to show. Out stepped Shoil, and she stopped in her tracks when she saw him.

'You still here?'

'What did you expect?' he replied, clearly puzzled by her question and now feeling a little frustrated.

'I got your message,' he explained.

'My message?'

'YES, your subtle woman's messages, saying you fancied me.'

Shoil could not resist bursting out laughing.

Colin now felt offended.

'Are you daring to laugh at me?'

Shoil stopped laughing and stared defiantly at him.

'Or what?' she challenged.

'Or I'll teach you a lesson of respect that you will never forget, little lady. Nobody makes a fool of me. My mates will want to know all the sordid details tomorrow, and I am not going to disappoint them.'

She started laughing again as she closed the restaurant door.

'Well, I've changed my mind, and I am no longer interested in anything you may have to offer.'

Something snapped inside him. He leapt towards her, intent on slapping her across the face, but she moved so quickly he only swiped clean air.

Her eyes turned orange, while her body quickly covered in hair, but all this was unseen in the evening light, as her teeth started to lengthen and her nose began to stretch out.

Colin collected his pride and turned around to challenge this nimble waitress but froze on the spot when she moved under a building light, and he could now witness the metamorphism taking place before his eyes. What was once an attractive-looking, sexy young woman was now a grotesque-looking animal wearing a dress.

'What the . . .' he started to say.

But a quick slash of her sharp claws silenced him as she ripped his throat wide open. He fell to his knees clutching his throat with both hands, but before he could fall any further, Shoil came up close to him, grabbed his face with both paws, forced his mouth open, then her long tongue entered his mouth and went down his throat. His body started to shake violently, so she had to hold him tightly as his skin turned orange and then transparent. She ignored the blood spurting from his neck but savored his life energy, which was being drawn into her mouth. His body began to shrink, and his face quickly turned skeletal. Shortly after a series of squelching sounds stopped, she sighed heavily, knowing she had completely absorbed him. She licked her long tongue around her face before allowing it to return to its normal human size, as she too returned to her human form. She stood up and looked around. No one was around to witness the attack. She quickly bent down, scooping up his blood-soaked clothing before walking up to the nearest bush and dumping his clothing behind it. She turned, but then hesitated, looked back, and returned to retrieve his trousers. She hunted through his pockets until she found a set of keys. She bounced them in her hand before throwing the trousers back to the ground. The keys had an electronic fob attached, so she pressed the button and heard a car horn beep twice, while its indictor lights flashed. She walked up to the brown Audi and slid into the driver's seat. She felt energized again, not sure when the last time was that she felt so good. She glanced into the rear-view mirror and noticed a spot of blood on her cheek. She wiped it away with her finger. She also realized that she could not return to this restaurant and would have to search for a new job—again. Still, he deserved what he got, and he would never threaten another girl. Anyway, she knew she had to widen her search for Tampong and would be moving on in any case. If Tampong had activated herself once, then maybe she would do it again. She licked her lips in anticipation. She glanced at the bushes where Colin's clothes were hidden.

She wound down her window.

'Tell that to your mates tomorrow, why don't you?' she shouted towards the bushes before winding the window back up.

The car pulled away up the driveway to disappear into the night. Neither would be returning to this particular place again.

***

He had just gone to bed and closed his eyes when they shot open again. They were completely blue. Gary lay still on his bed, frozen in place and incredibly quiet. All his senses were alert and fine-tuned to the disturbance he had just felt. Something had stirred in the night, something that could only mean a Higher Middle member had been activated, again, as he had just been. What this meant, he had no idea, only that nothing good would surely come of this event. It had been a long time since he felt anything like this, but the recent activations were unmistakable. He felt the body next to him move and looked down to see Tracey still fast asleep. She turned over onto her side to face him but was breathing slowly and still in a deep sleep. He took deep, relaxing breaths of air and felt himself calm down again, returning to normal. He had almost believed that the balance had been restored and the Higher Middle sufficiently depleted to deter any further attacks. This sudden awakening blew that hope right out of the water. Both sensations were sudden and did not suggest a battle with any Lower Middle member, nor did he have any sense of loss. However, something had clearly triggered the changes, and, for some unexplained reason, he concluded that it had to be Shoil on at least one occasion. The wild nature of the last feeling he experienced suggested a raw animal-type attack. He shuddered when he recollected how she had changed into a huge wolf-like creature, tearing into men and women with equal lust and disregard for life. Tracey stirred again, and her arm reached across his chest while her body moved closer to him, almost sensing his uncertainty. He stroked her arm, and it had the desired calming effect on her.

He continued to stroke her arm but could not avoid the tears forming in his eyes. He did not bother to wipe them away. The sadness he felt lay heavy on his heart. They had lost so many in such a short space of time, and he feared more losses if these sensations returned again and again. His biggest fears had been realized, and there were very few of them left to defend the balance. For two years he held onto the hope that the Higher Middle had become dormant following their defeat. The recent events confirm his worst fears. They were back in action.

He knew that no good would come from this. He kept stroking her arm and looked down at her.

'*I will defend you with my life, Tracey,*' he whispered.

He meant every word. She was his world, and if she were not in it anymore, he doubted he could carry on himself.

***

The following morning, Tampong was preparing breakfast when she heard Terry moving around upstairs. She recognized the sound of him jumping down from his top bunk and running into the toilet. It was always the first thing he did when he woke up. She continued to listen as the toilet flushed and the bathroom door opened.

'Wash your hands, please,' she yelled up the stairs.

Terry skidded to a halt and returned to the bathroom, turning the water taps on, took the soap, and rubbed it quickly into the palms of his hands, rubbing them together before rinsing them under the running taps. After turning the taps off, he reached over for the towel, dried his hands quickly, then threw the towel onto the rack—missing it but ignoring the towel falling to the floor as he headed back down the stairs. He entered the kitchen and slipped onto the highchair.

'How did you know?' he asked.

'How did I know what?' asked Tampong, already knowing the answer to his question.

'How did you know I hadn't washed my hands?'

'Because I know you so well now.'

He smiled, picked up his spoon, and started to eat his cereal.

She watched him eat and could not prevent the smile from appearing across her face. She never realized how much joy a human being could bring to your life. He meant the world to her.

After he finished his cereal, he drank the glass of milk sitting next to his bowl, wiped his mouth clean, and slipped off the chair.

'May I go outside and play with Joey?'

'Of course you may, but after you have brushed your teeth, and do not go any further than the playground, understood?'

'Understood, Auntie Tampong, err Katy, and thank you.'

He rushed upstairs and cleaned his teeth, insufficiently, she thought, before he rushed back down the stairs, ran outside and down the pathway. Joey was already bouncing a football in the park and waved to Terry when he saw him approaching. Tampong was about to call out to warn him not to run across the road, but it was too late, and he was already entering the park. She shook her head, knowing she would have to discuss the rules of the road one night with him. She collected the breakfast dish and empty glass and dropped them into the sink, turning the hot water on, letting it run as she picked up the liquid soap bottle and poured a little into the running water. As she washed the dishes, she casually looked out of the window to watch the two boys kicking the ball to each other. Joey was a skilled footballer and could do some clever tricks with the ball. She watched as he flipped the ball into the air and bounced it a couple of times on one knee, then switched it over to the other knee before flicking the ball into the air and passing it back to Terry. He tried to repeat the trick, and she knew this was not going to end well. He flicked the ball into the air and tried to control it with his knee, but he only succeeded in knocking the ball out of the park. It rolled into the street, so Terry started to run after it.

Tampong's had just picked up the glass when her senses suddenly went on alert. She quickly glanced outside the window and up the street, where she saw a speeding lorry coming down the road. She looked back towards the front door, through which she saw Terry, who was running fast to catch up with the ball.

'***Noooooo!***' she screamed, dropping the glass back into the sink and rushing out of the kitchen and out of the house.

When she reached the edge of the pavement, she heard the screech of the lorry's tires and the unmistakable thump of a body hitting the vehicle.

'***Terry!***' she screamed, while the lorry continued to screech its brakes before finally coming to a staggering stop.

Without thinking, she leaped over the garden gate and rushed over to the front of the lorry, where Terry was laying half under the truck, pinned in place by the front wheel. He was trapped. Tampong called on her abilities to move the truck away from the still body before carefully turning him over. The side of his face was covered in blood, and she could see a growing pool of blood on his shirt. She lifted his shirt carefully to reveal a deep cut in his side, oozing with blood.

The driver came running around to the side and gasped when he saw the body.

'My god, but he just came out of nowhere. I could not stop in time.'

'Call for an ambulance,' Tampong demanded, 'call for an ambulance now,' she shouted again, only this time louder.

The driver quickly turned and ran to his cab.

Tampong ripped the bottom of her top and covered the gaping hole in Terry's side. She brushed the hair away from his face. His eyes were closed, but he was still breathing, although taking quick, shallow breaths.

'Will he be alright?'

'What?'

'Will he be alright, miss?' asked Joey, who had run up behind her.

She never had time to respond when the driver came rushing back around.

'The ambulance is on its way. They said not to move him but keep him warm.'

Tampong ripped another strip of cloth from her top and wrapped it around his waist and over her temporary bandage. She checked it was tight before knotting it securely in place. The blood appeared to slow but still oozed out of his body. Suddenly her arm automatically lifted above his stomach, and she placed her hand over the wound. She understood what that meant, so closed her eyes. Unseen by the others, small electrical bolts entered Terry's body from the palm of her hand. His body tremored a little before she heard him sigh quietly, and he went still again. She felt his pulse, which was fast, but the blood flow had ceased. She looked down at her hand, which was still glowing orange. She quickly covered it with her other hand, pretending to push down on the wound. She then recollected Xtri's healing skills and realized that some of his healing abilities must have transferred to her. She silently thanked him before glancing down the road. Still no sign of the ambulance.

'Where's that bloody ambulance?' she screamed.

'It's on its way,' said the driver, trying to calm her, but with little effect.

Joey walked across the road to retrieve his ball, then held it tightly against his chest.

***

About fifty miles away, Shoil's eyes burned bright orange as she focused on the sensation, trying to gauge its distance.

'You are getting closer, my little bitch-friend,' she whispered.

She had widened her field of search and was now just outside Watford, moving slowly north in ever-widening circles, sensing that Tampong was more north than south. She was hoping that she would reveal herself again to help narrow her search field further and was pleased that her patience had been rewarded. She was moving in the right direction; the sensation felt closer.

She had taken temporary jobs while she searched for the traitor. Doing the odd restaurant stint or working behind a bar. There were never any problems getting temporary work, which helped tie her over. She kept up her consumption of men too, helping herself to their wallets and credit cards as a bonus. Every night she transformed into her animal form and searched the local villages and towns, hoping to find some sign of Tampong's presence or hear of strange things happening. Tampong had her total attention now, meaning that the surviving members of the Lower Middle were forgotten, at least until she had dealt with the unforgivable treason committed by that bitch. Nothing else mattered, and all she needed to do was find her and exact revenge. She licked her lips in anticipation while sniffing the air for any fragments of clues. So far, she had only felt the sensation of Tampong's activation, but she knew it was only a matter of time before she picked up her perfume and body scent. That day could not come quickly enough, but she knew she had to be patient and let her slip up a few more times. Allow the net to close in on her. She felt her heartbeat start to race as she anticipated the look of shock and horror on her face when they finally came face-to-face. What would she say? What would be her excuse? What would be her last words before her life ended?

***

The sirens of the ambulance could now be heard, while immediately behind was the wailing of a police siren. Tampong did not move, remaining close to Terry until a paramedic was leaning over her shoulder.

'OK, ma'am, we will take it from here.'

'He has lost a lot of blood,' she advised, her eyes never leaving Terry's face.

She stepped back, allowing the paramedic to examine the boy's body. He pulled the bandage away from the wound, which was now stitched up. He looked up at Tampong.

'Are you a first aider?'

'I have had some training,' she confessed.

'I'll say. Bloody good job with the butterfly stitches, ma'am, and you may just have saved this boy's life.'

'When in god's name did you do that?' asked the driver. 'I never saw you stitch the boy up.'

She said nothing as the paramedic completed his examination. His colleague arrived with the stretcher.

'Possible fractured right arm and right leg and puncture wound to the stomach. Let us secure his injuries and get him into the ambulance. He is going to need plasma.'

'Roger that,' acknowledged his colleague.

The paramedics worked diligently, securing his leg in a brace before placing a temporary cast on his right arm. Terry groaned when they raised his arm but did not wake up. They also placed a neck brace before gently lifting him onto the stretcher and wheeled him towards the ambulance, closely followed by Tampong.

Tampong went to enter the ambulance when the paramedic reached out to block her way.

'I am staying with him,' she announced firmly.

'Are you family?'

'I am his auntie,' she lied.

'Good enough,' acknowledged the paramedic, 'hop into the back.'

He lowered his arm, allowing her to slip in next to Terry. As the ambulance pulled away, Joey just stood there still hugging his ball tightly. He then turned to rush home to tell his mom.

The driver just stood there scratching the back of his head.

'How did she manage to stitch the boy up?' he was asking himself, still scratching the back of his head.

There were no medical tools or medical box that he could see.

He then walked around to the front of his vehicle and checked for damage. He saw none. At least that meant he didn't have to take the vehicle off the road but knew he had to report the accident in case the woman made any complaint to the company, although he was sure she had no idea who he worked for. He almost waved the incident away and was about to step up into his cab when the police officer indicated him to stop.

'So, sir, can you tell me in your own words what happened here?' asked the officer.

The driver explained the horrid series of events leading up to the policeman's arrival.

'You say you were puzzled by the fact the boy's cut had been stitched?'

'Right,' answered the driver, 'I was standing over her all the time.'

The policeman referred back to his notes.

'But didn't you say that it was you who called for the ambulance?'

'Yes, that's right.'

'From where exactly did you make that call, sir?'

'I have a phone in my cab. I called from there.'

'So you were not with the woman and child all the time then?'

'No, I guess not,' he conceded.

'That probably explains it then, sir. If she saw that the boy was losing a lot of blood, then she knew she would have to act quickly to save the child, which she appeared to have done.'

'And she just happened to have a medical box with stitches in it and everything?'

'I have seen stranger things, sir.'

'Guess so,' conceded the driver, 'is that all you need from me now, Officer?'

'Yes, thank you, sir. We have all your details and will contact you if necessary, although it looks like a straightforward accident, sad that it is, judging from your account and that of the boy's friend.'

'Thanks, Officer. I'd better be getting on my way then.'

The officer nodded to the driver, who then stepped into his cab, started the engine, and drove away.

It took twenty minutes before the ambulance arrived at the hospital's emergency entrance, where a doctor was already standing by. As soon as the back doors opened, the paramedic started his conversation with the doctor.

'Suspected fracture to the right femur and right arm with internal bleeding and large puncture wound to the stomach, temporarily stitched up by the lady,' informed the paramedic as he pointed towards Tampong, but her attention was fixed on Terry.

The doctor simply raised an eyebrow as he quickly examined his patient.

'Straight into surgical ward two, and we will prep for surgery. We need to be quick; this boy has lost a lot of blood and still possibly hemorrhaging internally,' observed the doctor.

He took the end of the stretcher and led them into the hospital, closely followed by Tampong.

At the door to the surgery, the nurse blocked Tampong's path.

'Sorry, but you cannot go any further. Please wait over there and the surgeon will come and see you as soon as he can.'

The nurse indicated the waiting room with her hand. Tampong said nothing and took a last worrying glance at the disappearing trolley before silently turning around and walking into the waiting room, where she slumped into a chair. She blamed herself for this accident. She should have been paying more attention to him. She would never forgive herself if Terry did not survive. Was this his fate? Was he meant to die at the hands of Shoil, and all she managed to do was delay the inevitable?

She sat there for two hours before the door opened again, causing her to look up. It was the surgeon, still in his blood-splattered gown.

'We have stabilized him for now, but he needs more blood and quickly. And that is the problem.'

'What problem?'

She sat bolt upright now.

'He has a rare blood type and something we do not stock at this hospital. You know his blood is AB negative, don't you?'

'No, actually I did not,' she admitted.

The surgeon looked surprised.

'Are you family?'

'I am his aunty.'

'Right. So how do we contact his family, his parents, for example, as one of them will surely have his blood type?'

'They are both dead.'

His shoulders slumped in disappointment.

'That is most unfortunate. We are calling around the local hospitals to see if they have any of his blood in stock.'

'And if not?'

'Then I am afraid his chances of survival are very slim.'

Tampong thought through her next words very carefully, but knew it was the right decision. The only decision.

'Take mine.'

The surgeon raised his eyebrows.

'Yours? Are you saying you are also AB negative?'

'I am.'

'Right, then come with me as we will have to confirm this. If so, you may have just saved the boy's life . . . again.'

She followed him into another room. The doctor had a brief word with the nurse, who indicated for Tampong to lay on the surgical table. The nurse tightly wrapped a strap around her upper arm before tapping her lower arm, looking for a good vein.

'Are you on any medication?' the nurse asked.

'No.'

'Do you have any history of any illness?'

'No.'

'Are you sexually active?'

Tampong raised her right eyebrow at the question.

'We need to know if there is a risk of any sexually transmitted diseases.'

'NO.'

The nurse then placed the needle into her arm and started to draw blood. Satisfied, she removed the needle and placed a cotton swab over the injection point.

'Hold this down please,' she advised.

Tampong complied as the nurse dropped the syringe into a bowl and left the room.

About ten minutes later, the doctor entered, closely followed by the nurse.

'Great news, your blood type does indeed match. The nurse here will take more of your blood, and we will begin the transfusion immediately.'

Tampong just nodded and lay back on the table, allowing the nurse to insert another needle in her arm. This one had a long rubber tube attached, which led into a plastic bag. The nurse handed her a small red ball and instructed her to roll it around in her hand. Her blood flowed quickly, and it took only forty-five minutes to fill the bag. The nurse removed the needle and sealed the bag, placing another swab on the point of insertion, before taking the bag into the room next door. She returned almost immediately.

'You need to rest for a while. Would you like a cup of tea?'

'Yes, please.'

'Milk and sugar?'

'Just milk please.'

The nurse nodded before disappearing outside, only to return shortly afterwards with a white paper cup.

'Careful, it is hot.'

'Thank you.'

She sat up and felt a little lightheaded. The nurse noticed.

'That will pass quickly enough. A good reason we tell people not to drive straight after giving blood. You have not really done this before, have you?'

'Is it that obvious?'

'It is to me. Seen too many patients and know the typical telltale signs.'

Tampong nodded her understanding, saying nothing more, choosing instead to sip her hot tea in silence. After a few minutes, she felt comfortable enough to sit up and was pleased not to experience any light-headiness.

Just as she finished her cup, the doctor returned. She looked up with expectant eyes.

'The transfusion was successful, and Terry is responding well to the new blood.'

Tampong felt like bursting into tears of joy and relief and could have hugged the doctor.

'We need to keep him in to monitor his injuries. He is a surprisingly tough little fellow, and I am sure he will soon be back up and running, but, let's keep an eye on him to make sure there are no other injuries.'

'Thank you, Doctor.'

'No, thank you. As I said before, you probably saved his life. The chances of finding such a rare blood group are incredible, and to have you not more than five feet from him is, simply, well, unbelievable. He must have a guardian angel looking out for him. Anyway, there is not much more you can do here, so you might as well go home and rest.'

'Can I see him?'

'Sure. He is asleep and will most likely remain that way for a few more hours. The nurse will show you to his room.'

'Thank you again, Doctor.'

'You are most welcome.'

'This way, if you please,' said the nurse, holding the door open, 'to your left, and it's the second door on the right.'

'Thank you.'

Tampong entered the small recovery room to find Terry almost completely covered in bandages. Wires protruded from his arm and led into a monitoring machine, which was slowly beeping. Her heart sank, filled with guilt. She slowly walked up to the side of his bed and took hold of his hand. Small orange sparks moved from her hand to his.

Then his eyes sprang open, making her jump. She let go of his hand and took a step backwards, because she was now staring at his eyes.

They were sparkling orange.

As soon as she let go of his hand, his eyes closed again.

'What have I done to you?' she asked aloud, not expecting a reply.

She took another two uncertain steps backwards, not sure of what to do next. Several different permutations were running through her mind. What if his eyes remained orange? Did he have her powers now? Had he changed in any way? Finally, she walked back up to the bed and leaned over the sleeping body. She carefully lifted his eyelid to expose his eye and felt the electrical connectivity between them, although the eye had returned to normal. She closed the eyelid back up before turning to leave the room. All the while she walked, she kept going through all the possibilities as she subconsciously got on a bus and made her way home.

She knew she would have to check up on him in the morning. She also knew she would have trouble sleeping. She was right.

***

Shoil was in the supermarket, buying her weekly groceries, when a new sensation hit her. This was different though, and her first reaction was that it must be another Higher Middle becoming active. She was certain it was not that bitch Tampong, but, if not her, then who could it be? She was also certain that all their other group members were killed in the various battles, but this was definitely different and even felt new. She kept her eyes down, knowing they would have changed to their original color, orange. Could it be a Lower Middle member? That would make more sense and could explain the strange sensation. Nevertheless, this was something she had not felt before, and it worried her. She did not like new experiences and not being able to explain a particular event. This was where she was right now. It was a very brief moment too; one second it was there, the next second it was gone. Whatever it was, she was closer to it now than when she felt Tampong become active.

Could these two events be linked? If so, how? She sensed that she was still heading in the right direction and knew that she now needed to discover the cause of this new sensation. Something had changed and the balance had shifted again, but in which direction?

She would continue her hunt and track down not only Tampong, but this new source too. Something had definitely changed, and this might be an opportunity too good to give up. She forced herself to take a deep, relaxing breath. As she passed a glass mirror, she risked looking up into it and was relieved to see that her eyes had returned to their normal state. Satisfied, she finished her shopping and headed home, all the time thinking about this new sensation. If felt innocent, almost as if it was a birth, but that was not possible. Tampong could not have given birth, surely! She didn't think that was possible with a human, and there were no male Higher Middle members alive to mate with, more to the pity.

She knew she had to keep heading north, as the sensation felt stronger than the last time. Her excitement began to grow inside her again. For now she needed to get back and ready for another night of table-waitressing. She hated it, but could not really do anything else, except shelf stacking, which she hated even more. Her mind drifted back to Zelphur and all that money she had stashed away somewhere. What she could do with all that cash. How her life could be so different, and better. The thought of all that money hanging around in various unknown accounts put her back in a foul mood. Which meant she would have to go hunting again tonight.

***

The following morning, Tampong arrived at the hospital, where she was greeted by the sound of laughter coming from Terry's recovery room. As she entered, two nurses were standing on either side of his bed, while Terry was sitting up and devouring his breakfast. He looked up and smiled when he saw Tampong enter. She was shocked at his apparent miraculous recovery. The nurses turned when they noticed him smiling towards the door.

'Ah, so this must be your mother then?' one of them asked.

'It is indeed,' confirmed Terry, scooping up another spoonful of cereal, not bothering to correct them.

'Then we will leave you two alone. Just press the button if you need us at all.'

They both nodded towards Tampong before leaving.

'Well, I must say you look a lot better than when I saw you yesterday.'

'I feel simply fine,' he replied, 'great in fact, but so very hungry.'

'So it would seem.'

'What happened to me exactly? The nurses said I was in an accident.'

'You were. Do you not remember?'

'No. I remember coming home from school, but after that, I woke up to find myself here, all wrapped up in these silly bandages.'

'I see. Well, you were playing football and ran into the street, and you were knocked down by a passing lorry.'

'Wow. Will I die then?'

'No, you will not die. You were in a bad state when you arrived in hospital, but the doctors have fixed you up nicely.'

'Did the lorry driver die?'

'No, he was not injured. Only you.'

'That's good.'

He scooped up another spoonful of cereal and was about to eat when he stopped and looked directly at Tampong.

'And you helped keep me alive too, didn't you?' he added.

'Why do you say that?'

'One of the nurses told me I had a rare blood type thing and that you gave me some of your blood.'

'That's true.'

'Thank you.'

'You are more than welcome.'

She sat at the edge of the bed.

'So, tell me, how do you feel?'

'Like a billion, trillion dollars.'

'Any pain?'

'Nope, none whatsoever.'

'Hmmm.'

'That's what the nurses said.'

'Did they say anything else?'

'Only that they have never seen someone recover as quickly as me. Does that mean I am a superman or something?'

'Or something,' she agreed.

Before she could say anything else, the door opened, and the doctor walked in.

'So, young man, the nurses tell me you are awake and very cheerful.'

The doctor nodded his greetings to Tampong as he walked up to the end of the bed and took hold of the clipboard, which he examined. He slipped it back onto the end of the bed and walked around to the side, opposite Tampong.

'Mind if I give you a quick examination, young man? I promise not to hurt you,' the doctor said.

'Sure, Doc, go ahead.'

The doctor placed his stethoscope against Terry's chest and listened.

'Breathe in for me and hold.'

Terry complied.

'OK, now breathe out slowly please.'

Terry complied.

The doctor gently lifted Terry's right arm.

'Does that hurt?'

'Nope.'

'Hmmm.'

He lowered the arm carefully back down onto the bed. He then lifted the right leg.

'And what about this, any pain?'

'Nope.'

'Hmmm,' repeated the doctor.

'I am a superman, Doc,' explained Terry.

'So it would seem, young man, so it would seem.'

He lifted the pajama top and gently pressed around the bandaged wound, but there was no reaction from Terry.

'Hmmm,' he repeated.

'Something wrong, Doctor?' asked Tampong.

'Quite the reverse actually,' answered a puzzled doctor. 'His body could be suppressing the pain, of course, but I have never seen anything like this before.'

'That's because I am—' began Terry.

'Superman,' said the doctor, finishing his sentence. 'I heard what you said. Well, young man, looks like you are doing very well. Amazing, in fact. Keep it up.'

The doctor twitched his head towards the door, which Tampong acknowledged.

'I just need to speak with your auntie for a few minutes. We will be right back.'

'Okey dokey,' responded a cheerful Terry, who resumed his breakfast.

Outside, the doctor closed the door and leaned towards Tampong.

'I have never seen such a reaction before.'

'What does it mean, Doc?'

'I am not sure. As I said, it could be his body suppressing all the pain somehow, but this should not be possible, given the extent of his injuries. Has he had any similar experiences, such as falling down and not feeling any pain?'

'Not that I can recall. He has cried when hurt, just like any normal little boy.'

'Hmmm. Well, I would like to keep him under observation for a few more days, just to be sure. I will arrange another X-ray to check how the bones are healing. I also want to do a scan to check on the other bones and his brain activity.'

'Really, is that normal?'

'No, but then these are not normal circumstances.'

Without thinking, she grabbed his hand, causing him to go into a trance. His eyes glittered orange.

'You will release the boy and clear him from the hospital and then forget about his speedy recovery.'

She released his hand and the doctor blinked twice, shaking his head to clear it.

'What was I saying?' he asked.

'You were saying that Terry was fit enough to go home.'

'Right, yes, I will sign his release forms, and you can take him home after we remove the cast from his arm and leg.'

'Thank you, Doc.'

She was uncomfortable about what an X-ray might reveal, and she had panicked. Given that some of her powers may have transferred to Terry, he might have been able to self-heal, and the X-ray would have revealed healed bones and raise unnecessary and unwanted questions. She decided that she did not want to expose him to such attention.

She returned to his room to find Terry finishing his breakfast.

'Good news,' she began, 'the doctor says you are well enough to come home today, and he is going to release you.'

'Great. That means I can get out of here then and get all these horrible bandages and wire things off me.'

One of the nurses then returned to his room. She had a puzzled expression on her face.

'Apparently the doctor says you can go home, Terry. I need to free you from your casts,' she said.

'Yes, that's what I have just been told.'

The nurse raised an eyebrow towards Tampong as she took hold of a pair of scissors and expertly cut through the two casts. She ran her hands over his arm and leg, looking baffled.

'I was speaking to the doctor, who told me he was OK to go home,' Tampong explained, now nervous about the all-too-inquisitive nurse.

'Well, I for one have never seen this happen before.'

'Seen what?' asked Terry.

'Such a speedy recovery and permission to leave the hospital so soon after major surgery.'

'Aha,' explained Terry, 'but you have not had a superman patient before, have you?'

'No, no I haven't,' agreed the nurse.

'Well, Terry,' interrupted Tampong, eager to get out of the hospital, 'let's get you dressed and home.'

'Okey dokey,' replied Terry, eagerly slipping out of bed.

The nurse moved in front of him, and Tampong thought she was going to try to stop him. She was ready to intervene, but the nurse simply took hold of his arm and removed the monitoring plugs.

'You will not want to be leaving with these still plugged in, will you?' she explained.

'Nope,' agreed Terry.

Tampong helped him dress before nodding her thanks to the nurse. When they left the room, the nurse stared down at the clipboard again. The readings did not make any sense to her, but then she shrugged her shoulders, dropping the clipboard onto the bed, deciding that the boy was clearly very mobile again and the doctor would know best in any case. Perhaps they were not fractures at all and the doctor was just erring on the side of caution. She shook her head. It was not her place to question doctors.

When they arrived home, Terry ran into the lounge and switched on the TV, flicking the channel over to watch cartoons. She followed him into the lounge and knelt down beside him.

'I'm hungry,' he announced, eyes fixed on the TV.

'But you have just had breakfast.'

'Did I?'

'Yes, but do not worry, I will fix you something. Do you fancy anything in particular?'

'Eggs, bacon, tomato, and sausages, please.'

'Have you ever eaten that before?'

'Nope, but I just fancy it now.'

'OK, but then that means I need to go shopping.'

'Oh, in that case, toast will be fine.'

'Toast it is.'

She walked into the kitchen but kept the door open so that she could still see him. She watched as he scratched his arm where the break should have been, showing no discomfort. She opened the bread bin and pulled the open bread bag out, extracting two slices of bread, which she dropped into the toaster, pulling the lever down to activate the heat. While it was cooking, she removed the margarine from the fridge and pulled open the lid, scraping some of the contents onto a knife. The bread then popped up from the toaster, so she spread the margarine over the toast, repeating to process with the other slice. She placed the toast onto a plate and cut them into two halves. She walked back into the lounge and placed the plate in front of Terry.

'Thank you,' he said, not taking his eyes away from the TV.

She glanced at the TV screen and noticed that he was watching Superman. She smiled to herself.

Returning to the kitchen, she sat at the kitchen table and tried to summarize the recent events but kept coming to the same conclusion. The blood transfusion had transferred some of her powers to Terry. The question was by how much and was he aware? Furthermore, would this change him in any way?

Terry entered the kitchen with his empty plate, disturbing her thoughts. He placed the plate into the sink and turned to face Tampong. She looked up and could see him staring at her.

'What's the matter?' she asked.

'Why did you tell the nurses and doctor that your name was Katy?'

'Sorry?'

'I said, why did you tell them your name is Katy?' he repeated, 'and the woman at school you were talking to.'

His eyes never left hers.

'Because that is my name,' she replied candidly.

She was now puzzled as to how he could possibly have heard their conversation at school. She had watched him enter the school before returning towards her car.

'No, it's not,' he said in a challenging tone, 'your real name is Tampong.'

Her blood went ice-cold.

'Where did you hear that?'

He thought about her question.

'I am not sure I heard it, but I just know it somehow. That is your real name, isn't it?'

'Yes, yes, it is,' she admitted.

'So, who is Shoil and why do you hate her?'

Tampong looked in shock and realized that not only must have some of her powers transferred to him, but some of her memories too. She beckoned him to sit down.

'Shoil is a bad woman,' she began.

'I know, it was her who killed my mum and dad, wasn't it?'

'Yes, it was.'

'But she was a dog then, wasn't she?'

'Yes, yes she was.'

'How come?'

His question made her stop and think.

'Actually, I am not so sure, but I think she absorbed an animal and became like it.'

'Makes sense,' he agreed in a matter-of-fact way.

She looked closely at him.

'What else do you know?'

'Hmmm,' he began, placing his finger on his bottom lip, 'well, to start with, we are the Higher Middle and the stronger of the two groups. Zelphur is our leader, or was, until she was killed during the Fort Knox battle. Only two of our group are still alive, you and Shoil, but you are not friends.'

She immediately picked up on his use of words such as 'we' and 'our', suggesting he considered himself to be part of the group.

'Anything else?'

'That Shoil is hunting for you.'

His simple statement shocked her. It was something she had assumed but had hoped she had left enough distance between them to prevent them from being tracked. She gulped down the growing nervousness.

'And why do you say that?'

'Because it's true.'

Tampong said nothing as Terry walked right up to her and took her hand. Electrical sparks leaped between their hands.

'And she will find you,' he added.

'And?'

'And one of you will die, maybe both.'

'How do you know this?'

'I don't quite know. It just popped into my head. What am I?'

'What do you mean, what are you?'

'Do I have powers like you and Shoil?'

'Like me and Shoil?'

'Yes. Shoil can mutate into other creatures and can eat men, which gives her super abilities. You can influence people by just touching them, and you have weapons, such as your fingernails, which can become long swords that cut through metal and concrete and stuff. All of our group have individual and different abilities, like the Lower Middle. So, what are my abilities then? Are they the same as yours?'

'Good question, Terry, but first I should perhaps tell you how you got these possible abilities.'

'Ho, that's an easy one to answer.'

'Really?'

'Yes. When you gave me some of your blood, you also gave me some of your abilities. Does that make you supergirl?'

'Somehow, I don't think supergirl is the right description for me.'

'Well, I think you are my supergirl.'

He hugged her, so she instinctively hugged him back.

'I'll protect you,' he whispered in her ear.

She pulled away from his face, her eyes filling up.

'You will protect me?'

'Yes,' he said, this time more confidently, 'I will protect you from Shoil.'

Tampong was lost for words and could only hug him tighter. She pulled him away again and stared into his innocent eyes.

'Guess we should find out if you do have any abilities then, other than knowledge.'

‘Is knowledge really an ability?’ he questioned.

‘It is one of the greatest abilities anyone can have. Now, show me your hands.’

He held out his hands, palms facing her but pointing upwards.

‘Now, imagine your fingernails are long blades.’

Terry closed his eyes and almost immediately all his nails transformed into long blades, shooting into the air. The sudden weight surprised him, forcing him to drop his hands down, causing the blades to crash to the floor.

‘WOW,’ observed Tampong, ‘just as well your fingers were not pointing towards me.’

His eyes were wide-open, staring down at the shining blades that were only seconds ago his fingernails.

‘Gosh,’ he screamed, ‘now I am a superman. But how do I control this as I cannot just simply drop my hands every time, can I?’

‘It will come with practice, Terry. Now listen to me carefully. You must not tell a soul about this, do you understand?’

‘Why can I not tell my friends, like Joey? They would be amazed.’

‘Normal people do not understand us, they may think you are strange and a threat to them.’

‘You mean they might put me away?’

‘Something like that, yes.’

‘But if they did that, then we can simply break free, right?’

‘We can try.’

‘Can you teach me?’

‘To break free?’

‘No. To use my special powers.’

‘Of course,’ she confirmed, watching as the blades gently retracted back into his nails.

He looked in awe at his fingers. Turning them over again and again.

‘I AM SUPERMAN,’ he shouted, rushing out of the kitchen and running around in the lounge.

Tampong watched in confusion, not sure whether this was a good thing or bad. He knew too much to try to change his mind.

That much she was sure. Anyway, her blood was now his blood and circulating in his system. She could not change that, and wasn't sure she even wanted to. She would have to train him to fight and to survive, particularly if he was right about Shoil. Perhaps this gave them an edge and could surprise any attacker. Could surprise Shoil even. A glimmer of hope shone in the back of her mind.

She followed him into the lounge. He stopped running when she entered.

'But for now, you must promise not to try and use these abilities. I will tell you when we can practice.'

'Is that because she can sense us when we move into our real form?'

'Do you know that she can sense us then?'

'Yes, she uses our abilities as a scent to track us down. So, we should keep our abilities quiet for a little while, until she passes by.'

'And will you know when that is?'

'Yes, I can tell she is currently moving towards us, slowly.'

'How do you know this?'

'I cannot explain it. It is just that I can connect with her and almost see her.'

'You can almost see her?'

'Yes, she is like a ghostly image which becomes clearer the closer she gets to us.'

'Then we need to be extra careful and not let her find us.'

'Ho, she will find us eventually, Tampong, that I am sure about.'

'Ok, then we will have to be ready and decide, if we can, where and when we meet.'

'We can play a game with her,' he suggested.

'We can try,' she countered, 'in the meantime, we must keep up our pretense to the rest of the world and continue to act like mother and son. Are you OK with that?'

'You bet, Mom.'

She smiled.

'Keep calling me Mum, please.

'No problem, Mum.'

He was about to walk out of the lounge when he stopped and turned towards her again.

'I can be like Clerk Kent,' he said.

'Like Clerk Kent?' she questioned.

'Yes. He has a secret because he is really Superman, but nobody knows that, except his silly girlfriend though.'

'OK,' replied Tampong, now understanding his chain of thought, 'you can be like Clerk Kent and only change when we say it is OK to do so. Agreed?'

'Agreed,' confirmed Terry, 'may I go outside and play for a little while?'

'Sure, but be very careful when you cross the street and keep within sight of the kitchen window.'

'Yes, Mom,' he said, running down the corridor and opening the door.

She watched as he walked up to the street, looked both ways, then crossed quickly. She smiled. He was learning quickly. She just hoped not too quickly.

***

A large animal was wandering through the woods. Its head was lowered, allowing its nose to sniff the ground. It was hunting, hunting for a scent. It suddenly stopped and lifted its head back up quickly.

That's it, keep it up, thought Shoil, *whoever or whatever you are, I will find you. And when I do, you will either join me or die by my hand.*

She continued to stalk around the woods, sniffing the air, now hunting out her next victim. Determined to top her abilities up to the maximum. Convinced she was going to need all her strength if she were to overpower whatever lay ahead.

She would be ready.

She had to be ready.

She soon grew tired of hunting for the day. Turned out it was a quiet night for men to be roaming the woods. She gave up and returned to her apartment. At the front door, she turned her head to look in both directions. There was no one in sight, so she focused on her inner self and transformed back to her human body and quickly entered her home.

Twenty minutes later she lay in the bath, allowing the hot water to relax her, as it always did. She preferred hot baths, ones that made her skin turn red as soon as she entered. For a moment, her whole body looked the same reddish color, that was until her body returned to its normal temperature and her burn marks down her side could clearly be seen again. She often rubbed the area and every time imagined Tampong raising her arms and firing at her. She would surely have been killed had she not been so strong and in her dog form. Her fur had taken most of the sting out of the bolt, enough that it did not kill her. She ground her teeth together and let out a deep menacing growl. If there were anyone else in the room they would have sworn there must be a dog in the bathroom with her.

She eventually stepped out of the bath as it had cooled down too much for her now. She leaned down, pulled the plug, and allowed the water to drain away. She dried herself then slipped on her knickers before stepping into the kitchen. She opened a bottle of red wine and poured herself a large glass, which she drank empty. She wiped her mouth with the back of her hand, then refilled her glass and moved into the lounge, where she slumped onto the sofa, not caring that she spilled some wine onto the carpet. She could not get her mind away from Tampong. Wondering where she was and what she was doing. More importantly, what is that new sensation she felt?

It was a mystery. She drank more of her wine.

THE NET CLOSES IN

Date: July 2004
Age: Terry is 11
Status: Semi-active

The disturbances came and went, but each time felt a little stronger.

More powerful.

More dangerous.

Gary felt uncomfortable every time the form, or forms, became active. What worried him even more was that it felt closer. He had never experienced this type of power before, and that worried him more than anything else. He hated surprises, but rather than try to ignore it, he tried to embrace it, tried to understand it, tried to learn from it. He thought about his last words.

'Learning,' he said aloud.

'Sorry?' asked Tracey, who was sitting next to him engrossed in her book.

'Ho, nothing, just thinking aloud.'

She placed her book on the coffee table and looked to his face. She saw those all too familiar worry lines. Her face changed.

'What is it . . . really?'

He sighed heavily.

'I have been having these sensations again.'

She gasped.

'Ours or theirs?'

'Not sure.'

'What do you mean?'

'It's just that I have not felt this sensation before. It felt, well, newer.'

'Newer? Like a newborn baby growing new?'

He looked into her eyes and could see her own worry mounting.

'I am not sure.'

He immediately raised a hand to stop her talking.

'As I said, I have not felt this kind of sensation before, this is new. This is something else.'

'Do we need to be worried?'

'You mean any more than we are already?'

'You know what I mean,' she answered, folding her arms across her chest.

'I really do not know, Tracey, I really do not know.'

'So, what do we do?'

'For now, nothing, because we do not know what or who it is. Let us just keep alert.'

'Should we tell Joanne?'

'No, let's not worry her as well for the moment.'

'Assuming she hasn't felt the same thing.'

'Assuming she has not felt the same thing,' he repeated quietly.

Like a newborn growing baby, he repeated her words in his head.

Had she just hit the nail on the head? Was this a newborn baby? It would explain the new sensation, and it did feel almost virginal. But was that even possible? He had never heard of a Group member becoming pregnant following sex with a human. The two just were not compatible. It would be like a goldfish trying to have sex with an elephant. Then why did her words strike him as so true? Have they been able to create something out of a human being? The very thought filled him with horror and dread. No, this had to be something else. He would have to keep his senses alert. He told the truth to her that there was nothing to be done for the moment. Only, what he didn't tell her was that he had no idea what to do next.

He suddenly felt very vulnerable. He shivered.

***

The days turned into weeks and weeks into months. During all that time the sensation did not return. Gary began to think that maybe he just got spooked and imagined the whole thing. He tried to tell Tracey as much but she was not impressed with his answer. So they both kept their guard up, both agreeing not to transform for fear of giving themselves away, but to keep themselves fit and healthy. Just in case.

Over the years they had slowly tracked down most of the Higher Middle's organizational support, using the knowledge Gary had absorbed from Zelphur before her body disintegrated. He had to admit to being impressed by her empire and how far it reached, and how high some of her members were in government. He also had all her bank account details but had not touched a penny, mainly because it was blood money. He had been tempted on more than one occasion, but just about resisted the urge, constantly reminding himself of who the money belonged to and how most likely she acquired it. He had not told the others about this wealth as they would want to use some of it, but he knew it was only a matter of time before he was forced to tap into it, particularly if any of the remaining Higher Middle were getting closer, or any of the Lower Middle were in danger. On that he would not hesitate.

PRACTICE MAKES PERFECT

Date: July 2006
Age: Terry is now 13
Status: Semi-active

Terry was now a fully-fledged teenager and had grown tall for his age. He had taken up football and developed quite a skill for the sport, his height giving him a distinct advantage over the other kids in his class. He had come a long way from his first practice with his friend Joey. He was also a very versatile member of the team, able to play in any position the coach deemed necessary. As a striker, he could tower over most defenders, as a result, he managed to score quite a few goals with the head. When he played as a defender, there were very few strikers who could out-jump him. His long legs also proved effective at stopping strikers from scoring. His speed and anticipation were equally impressive. He seemed to always be at the right place at the right time, causing the coach to ask if he had a twin brother on the pitch. He became a popular team member, and word of his skill soon reached the ears of a scout.

The team had reached the semi-finals of the regional cup tournament when the scout turned up to watch Terry. The coach had placed Terry as a striker for this game, mainly because his first-choice strikers were injured. The coach preferred to utilize Terry in defence, where he felt he was more effective. Plus the fact that whenever a corner was won by his team, Terry was encouraged to push up into the penalty area, where he scored several goals. Unbeknown to the coach, Terry had been training on improving his speed. Training on the track every day. His muscles seemed to respond to his demands for more power, and he quickly gained speed. During the match, midway through the first half, Terry raised his arm into the air, which was a preplanned signal for Peter, a midfield player, to cross the ball. Peter obliged, but the coach thought this was a wasted ball, which flew over the defence to land in the middle of their half in what looked like no-man's-land. Terry had already set off running, even before the defence had time to turn. The opposition keeper ran out of his box to intercept the ball, but Terry was too quick for everyone and reached the ball first. The coach's mouth dropped open in shock as he watched Terry dribble around the stranded keeper and score into an empty net. Halftime arrived, and his team entered the dressing room one nil up.

A delighted coach came into the dressing room.

'Great ball, Peter, but where on earth did that speed come from, Terry?'

'I've been practicing, Coach.'

'So it would appear. Right then, let's keep it tight for the first ten minutes and not do anything drastic. Let them come at us, which they are now being forced to do, and maybe we will get another opportunity to counter-attack. Terry, do you think you can launch a similar run again?'

'Just give the word, Coach.'

'Great. As soon as we win the ball back, cross it into the middle of the field for Terry to chase after. We might get lucky and kill off this game.'

The second half started as predicted. Terry's team was on the back foot with the opposition hunting for the equalizer. Two defenders were left to guard Terry, with one hanging back to cut off any run he may try to make and with certain instructions on how to stop him, not all within regulations. Terry sensed menace from the defenders and knew he would have to be cautious. Fifteen minutes into the second half, his team finally won the ball back and, once again, Peter launched to ball upfield for Terry to chase. He turned on a shoestring, leaving his first defender stranded. He began running towards the ball, conscious of the last defender bearing down on him.

The coach also saw the defender rapidly closing down on Terry.

'Look out, Terry, he is going to take you out.'

Terry never heard him and was in a world of his own. The defender was now only ten yards away, close enough that he could hear his heavy breathing. The angle meant that they would arrive at the ball at the same time, although the defender had no interest in the ball. They were no more than two feet apart when Terry sensed the defender's movement towards him. Instead of continuing his run, he suddenly leaped into the air, just as the defender moved his body to ram into Terry. Except all he did was run into empty space and lost control of his own momentum and was left tumbling around on the grass. Terry landed back onto the pitch with both feet and continued his run towards the goal, now with the ball at his feet. Their keeper had the sense to stay in goal this time and came out late in an attempt to block Terry. The keeper was big and knew his angles well, making an almost impassible obstacle. Terry had other ideas, though, and kicked the ball to the keeper's left, as if passing to someone, while he turned to the right of the keeper. The move completely fooled the keeper, who suddenly was stranded in the middle, undecided on what to do next. Terry ran past the keeper, avoiding his desperate flailing hand, and turned to recoup the ball, having just enough time to turn it into the goal. The second goal had a devasting effect on the opposition, with most of their heads dropping in defeat. Their coach made a couple of substitutions and brought on more strikers. Terry's coach reacted to this strategic change and instructed him to drop back into defence, and with most of their players now behind the ball, they made an impenetrable wall the opposition was unable to breach. Terry was able to head away most of the crosses that came thick and fast. The clock finally marked the end of the match, and the referee blew full time. They were into their first regional finals.

The celebrations were wild in the dressing room. Terry had been lifted into the air and bounced a couple of times. The opposition coach had raised a protest, saying that there was no way Terry could be the right age and wanted his team eliminated. The protest was quickly rejected by the league, who had seen similar protests before and had already investigated Terry's age.

In the other changing room the atmosphere was somber. One defender sat on the bench grinding his teeth. He had been left to look like a complete idiot by that tall striker's move. He could see the looks of his teammates, who were also wondering how he got by him so easily. He would not be able to live this down. He also knew a scout was watching, that this was his one-and-only chance of going professional, and that had just been blown out of the water. All because of that damned lanky kid. He will pay. He clenched his fists together, head bowed down, along with the rest of the team.

After he showered, dressed, and congratulated his teammates for the umpteenth time, Terry swung his knapsack over his shoulder and walked out of the dressing room, down the corridor, and out into the car park. He was only twenty minutes from home, so he didn't bother calling his aunt to come pick him up, deciding to walk home instead. He set off down the road and turned left into a quiet road. He was about halfway down the road when his senses alerted him to danger. He froze on the spot as his eyes searched left and right but he saw nothing. Just as he started moving again, the bushes to his right began to rustle and three boys stepped out to block his way. Terry instantly recognized one of them, the defender. He stopped walking and was now only two feet from the boys.

The taller of the three stepped forward. The defender. His mouth was half open in a sneer, while his eyes were half closed, as if concentrating on his next move, like a panther ready to strike.

'What do you want?' Terry asked.

He knew this was not going to end well, but he had to give them the benefit of the doubt.

'Your legs,' snapped the boy.

'My what?'

'You heard. We want to take your legs so that you cannot make a fool of anyone else like you did with me.'

'I am sorry if my skill offended you, but you were easy to read.'

His response only increased the boy's anger.

'Well, perhaps you can read my intentions now then.'

He clamped his hands together and moved one foot in front of the other in a hostile stance.

'Ho, I think so,' said Terry

The other two spread out on either side of Terry, blocking any attempt to escape. Not that that was Terry's plan.

The taller boy rolled his sleeves up in a deliberate, provocative move as he stepped closer to Terry.

'I don't want any trouble here,' Terry pleaded.

He was sincere in his wish. He did not want to harm these boys, but, at the same time, he was not prepared to let these boys hurt him.

'It's too late for that, lanky. You ruined my chance at going professional today with that clever stunt of yours. Guess the scout will pick you for his club now and not me. Except, you will no longer be able to walk, let alone kick a ball.'

The taller boy swung his arm up into Terry's stomach, forcing all the air out. Terry doubled up as he struggled to breathe. As he was bent over, the boy stepped even closer, intent on attacking again, to finish the boy off. He clenched his fist and was about to hammer down at the back of Terry's exposed head. However, Terry let out a high-pitched scream and grabbed the boy by the waist, intending to force him away, but the boy suddenly went rigid instead and gasped aloud. The other two froze and looked puzzled as the tall boy took an involuntary step backwards. He looked down and touched his hip and stared in horror as his hands came away bloodied. Terry looked down at his own hands, which now felt heavy. That was when he saw the blades, the tips still dripping with the boy's blood. He looked up at the boy who was now staggering backwards, trying to keep on his feet.

'Tony, what did he do to you?' asked one of the boys, wanting to help his friend but afraid to move.

Tony said nothing but just raised his blood-covered hands. He then closed his eyes as blood seeped from his mouth and collapsed backwards onto the ground. He lay still. Dead.

'What . . . what . . . what did you do?' stuttered one of the boys, still in shock.

'I . . . I . . . didn't mean to hurt him,' pleaded Terry, still staring at his hands as the blades slowly retracted back into his nails, unseen by the other two.

All they saw was the blood, a lot of blood, and it was enough to make them panic.

'You murderer,' screamed one of the other boys, who turned and started running away.

His movement knocked the other boy out of his trance, so he also turned and began to run as well.

It was Terry's turn to panic.

'**Noooooooo**,' he screamed and reached out towards the boys with his arms out straight, pointing his forefingers in their direction, simply wanting to stop them.

As if responding to his wish, small metal spears burst from each fingernail to shoot through the air and penetrate the back of each boy, sending them sprawling to the ground. He heard the thud, thud as the spears found their targets, burying deep inside each body. The boys were both dead by the time they hit the ground, having no time to scream out. They landed facedown on the ground. Both their eyes were still open, as were their mouths, but no noise came from them.

'No, no, no, no, no,' cried Terry.

Despair was in his voice. 'What have I done?'

Not knowing how this happened or what he should do, he sat on the pavement, put his head in his hands, and cried.

Tampong immediately felt his anguish and knew something horrible had happened. Without thinking, she rushed out of the house and into her car. She knew where he played, so quickly drove to the sports ground, only to find it locked up. She hurried around to the back and down the quiet street, the one she knew he always took when he decided to walk home. As she turned the corner, she saw him sitting on the pavement, his head buried in his hands. She quickened her pace even more and as she drew closer, she saw three bodies lying on the ground close to Terry. She rushed up to the first one, bent down and checked for a pulse, noticing the spear logged in his back. Nothing. She moved across to the next body and checked his pulse. Again nothing. Finally she walked up to the third body but intuitively knew it was pointless checking him. His eyes were open wide, while his pupils were dilated. He was dead too.

She slowly moved towards Terry and knelt down beside him. She took a deep, calming breath before she spoke.

'What happened here?' she asked quietly.

Terry slowly raised his head and looked up at her with tear-stained eyes.

'I don't know. They wanted to cause trouble, and this one,' he said, pointing to the taller boy, 'started to thump me hard and I screamed. The next thing I knew, my blades had come out and killed him.'

'And the other two?'

'I, I guess I panicked. They started to run away, and I wanted to stop them. I didn't mean to kill them, I just wanted to stop them from telling anyone about what they saw. I didn't mean to kill them.'

'Well, you certainly succeeded in stopping them.'

She remained calm, glancing around, but saw no one.

'What's going to happen to me?'

She grabbed him firmly by the shoulders, holding him in place.

'Now listen to me carefully, Terry. This was not your fault. They started this and you finished it. It is my fault for not training you properly. If anyone is the blame, it is me, not you.'

She stood up then brushed the hair away from his face with both her hands as she thought through their options. She quickly decided on a course of action.

'Right, my car is parked in front of the sports hall. You return to it and wait for me there. Here is my car key.'

'And what about these boys? We cannot leave them here. We have to tell someone what I did.'

'No, Terry, we tell nobody. They will not understand, and they will most likely put you away as some freak or worse.'

'But . . .'

'No buts, Terry. Go to the car and wait for me. I will sort this out.'

She dangled the key in front of him as a hint.

Terry said nothing. He reluctantly took the car key, rose to his feet, and walked slowly towards the car, keeping his head bowed down. Tampong watched him go. Once he was out of sight she looked around. Not much to be seen and no real opportunity to hide the bodies. There were a few small bushes and a hedge, but nothing that would hide a body for long, let alone three. Then she remembered passing industrial bins by the side of the sports hall. She looked up and down the street again, still saw nobody, so grabbed a leg from each of the boys and dragged them back towards the hall. Her strength made light work of the three trailing bodies, and she quickly reached the bins. She released the boys' legs and swung open the lid and was pleased to see it was already half full. She emptied some of the plastic bags out from the bin before lifting the three bodies into the large container. She pulled the two spears out of the boys' backs and placed them in her pocket. She then carefully covered the bodies with the plastic bags she had taken out. It wasn't perfect but it would have to do. She closed the lid and returned to the road where the attack took place to check it out one more time. There was only a little bit of blood on the pavement, not enough to cause any real attention or concern. Still, she picked up a handful of leaves and wiped most of the blood from the pavement, then threw the bloodied leaves into a nearby bush. Satisfied, she returned to the car to find Terry sitting in the passenger seat. He looked up when she opened the door.

'What's going to happen to me?'

'Nothing.'

'Nothing! But I killed three boys in cold blood. I am a murderer and need to be locked up.'

'**NO**,' she screamed, louder than intended.

Her reaction made Terry jump.

'You are now an active member of the Higher Middle, and these three were your first kills. An unfortunate event, but a kill all the same. It will not be your last kill, of that I am sure. You must, however, learn to control your abilities so that you kill only when absolutely necessary. Put this down as a lesson for both of us.'

He seemed to study her for a long time before responding.

'They are, after all, only human beings, right?'

'Right,' agreed Tampong reluctantly, 'although we do not just slaughter them for fun, but for a good reason,' she added.

'Only when it is necessary, such as the risk of exposing us?'

'Correct.'

'Then why doesn't it feel right. Why does it feel so very wrong?'

'As I said, you have not been trained properly, and that is my fault. We both must do better so that you can control your emotions and abilities. But it is good to have doubts about killing. That will make you question your next action.'

'What about the boys? Won't somebody be looking for them?'

He was looking through the window screen.

'Just because I was more skillful than he was at football, and just because we won the game easily. He was not happy about that. But as I said, people will be looking for them, won't they?'

'Sure they will, but these will not be the first boys to go missing. Some will assume they have simply run away, perhaps embarrassed by their defeat. Some will assume they have been abducted. Who knows?'

'What if they find the bodies?'

'Then at least the families will have peace of mind and closure. And before you ask, the police will be stumped by the cause of death and will be searching for a long, thin blade, one they will never find.'

'You removed the spears?'

'I did,' she replied as she pulled the two blades from her pocket and rested them in the palm of her hand.

Terry stared at the objects and his eyes widened as the blades became transparent and then liquified before they were absorbed by her hand.

He blinked twice.

'You are able to absorb my weapons?'

'Of course,' she said with a shrug of her shoulders. 'You have my blood, remember?'

'Right.'

He sat back in his seat when a thought suddenly struck him.

'And what about Shoil?'

'What about her?'

'She will have sensed my change and that will bring her closer to us.'

'Then we will have to be extra careful in the future, won't we?'

Terry just nodded. He knew he had just brought danger closer to them and to the inevitable battle.

'I am sorry for those boys.'

Tampong looked across to him and stroked his hair.

'It is good to feel regret. It means you are alive and have feelings.'

'Is that good? To have feelings, I mean?'

'Yes, it is good to have them, but you need to learn how to interpret them and when the right time is to react to them, and how you react. As I said, that will be my job to teach you. I have failed you in your teachings to date, but I will not fail you again. On that I promise.'

He nodded again, although not convinced that this was the life he was meant to live. Could he go around simply killing people who simply disagreed with him or tried to stop him doing something or, worse still, simply tried to make him do something he objected to? He was old enough to know good from bad, and this definitely felt bad. Could he ever get used to this? He doubted it, although something deep inside him was pleased with his actions. Pleased with the quickness of his defence and pleased with his abilities to deal with the threat.

Would that feeling come to the surface more? Somehow, he felt sure it would.

***

Shoil did indeed feel a disturbance and it did feel even closer this time. So she knew she was still heading in the right direction. That pleased her. The only thing she didn't understand was that this felt so new again, so different, raw even. It was like something had happened for the first time, uncontrolled.

This puzzled her.

This worried her.

The Higher Middle cannot have babies, but that was exactly how this felt. Like a baby had been born and was learning through its mistakes.

That was impossible.

She was now in Peterborough city center and had just purchased a hamburger. She sat in front of the cathedral, unwrapped her meal and began to eat alone but could not help smiling as she did so.

Just as she started devouring her burger, a man in his middle forties came out of the bank opposite and was just walking past Shoil when he saw her smiling. Misinterpreting her smile, he stopped directly in front of her. He looked her up and down and thought to himself that he had not seen such an attractive girl as this for a long time, and she appeared to be alone and smiling up at him.

'Are you enjoying that?' he queried.

Shoil swallowed her last bite and looked up at the man. He was not unattractive. He had chiseled cheekbones and confident brown eyes, although clearly had not worked out for a little while, judging from his bulging stomach, which was half covering his belt.

'I like the taste of meat,' she answered.

'Is that an Australian accent I detect?'

'It is, have you been to Australia then?'

'No, but it's one of those places I would love to visit. Besides, I watch a lot of TV and have a talent for accents.'

'Well, perhaps you should visit there one day.'

'Perhaps I will,' he answered as he sat down next to her. 'Don't mind if I join you, do you?'

'Not at all. I am not waiting for anyone in any case.'

She decided she would let him know she was alone.

'A pretty thing like you should not be on her own.'

'Flatterer.'

A snort of laughter escaped his lips.

'No, I mean it. Is there a special one in your life at the moment?'

'No,' she said simply.

'Well, that is incredibly sad. Listen, I have just taken some money out of the bank and feel in the mood to spend it. Would you like to keep me company this afternoon and, maybe later, I can take you out for dinner. I think I can do a little bit better than hamburger and chips.'

'I actually like hamburgers.'

'So it would seem. I am just saying I believe I can offer you something better in the way of food. That's all.'

'So what do you suggest we do this afternoon then, until dinner that is?' she asked suggestively.

She licked the top and bottom of her lip and could tell he was turned on by her.

He coughed in response to watching her tongue.

'Well, we could go back to my place if you like. Have a drink or two and enjoy each other's company. Work up an appetite if you like.'

'Hmmm, and where is your place?'

'Not far, I own a large house in the Orton's.'

'I have no idea where that is.'

'Ho, about a fifteen-minute car ride from here.'

'So you have a car as well?'

'Yes, it's a Porsche.'

'A Porsche you say.'

'A Porsche 911 Carrera 4S Cabrio to be precise.'

‘I have no idea what that it is, but sure sounds exciting.’

‘You should see how she moves.’

‘I could say the same about me,’ she suggested.

He gave her a beaming smile.

‘My name is Donald,’ he said, extending his hand in greeting.

‘Not McDonald?’ she quipped.

‘Aha,’ he replied through a laugh, ‘a girl with a quick wit. I like that, and I like you even more now.’

She smiled warmly at him and extended her hand to meet his.

‘Nice to meet you, Donald. My name is Kara,’ she replied, shaking his hand.

‘Then, Kara, allow me to escort you to my car. I am sure I can show you things this afternoon you have never seen before.’

‘Great, and mate, I can show you a thing or two that you have never seen before too, on that I can guarantee.’

‘Cannot wait. Shall we go?’

Shoil slipped the last piece of her burger into her mouth, squashed her wrapper into a ball, then tossed it into the bin beside the bench. She stood up, brushed her skirt down, and took a deep breath.

‘Let’s go,’ she said keenly.

He led them across the square and into the main car park. His black Porsche was on the second level. Hood already down. He opened the passenger door for her, so she slid into the seat, allowing her skirt to rise a little. She knew he noticed. Men were so predictable.

He shut her door and walked round to the driver’s side, opened it, sat in his seat, then he pressed a button to start the motor and the car roared into life. After he shut his door and buckled his seat belt, he put the car into reverse and backed the car out of the parking space, using the opportunity to take a glance at Shoil’s legs as he turned. Putting the car into first gear, he slowly drove out of the parking garage.

They drove over the bridge next to the rail station and passed the city hospital. When he entered the dual carriageway, he pressed on the accelerator, and the car responded by speeding up quickly, passing other cars in a blur. Her long hair was flowing in the wind, and it made her feel good. She pulled both arms up into the air and shouted out in glee. She always enjoyed speed.

They left the dual carriageway and entered a country road. Unseen by Donald, she unclipped her seat belt and turned her head towards him.

'So, how about you show me what this baby can really do, and if I am impressed, then I'll show you how best to ride me.'

'Pardon!'

'You heard correctly, matey.'

'Right you are, little lady. Prepare to be impressed.'

They entered a long straight stretch of road, so he put his foot to the floor and the car accelerated quickly. She casually looked around, as if taking in the scenery. They were the only car on the country road. She turned her head towards him and smiled. He turned towards her and smiled back.

Then her smile turned into a sneer. She quickly grabbed the steering wheel and jerked it to the right. The car careened out of control, zigzagged twice before bouncing off the road and into the air. Shoil leaped clear of the car as it tipped over. She heard him screaming in horror as she rolled over three times before landing on her feet. Moments later, the car hit the ground and rolled over five times before resting upside down in the field. Smoke streamed from its engine, while all four wheels still turned freely. She walked up to the car and was amazed to see Donald still alive. His seat must have broken free and had been thrown from the car. He was now lying in the field, next to his seat. The angles of his arm and leg told her they were both broken. He was groaning, unable to speak as pain ripped through his broken body.

She walked up to him and stood over him, her legs on either side of his head. He could see directly up her skirt, if he had been in any condition to enjoy the view, which he was not. He raised his unbroken arm.

'Help me,' he managed to cry out.

'OK,' she said simply.

She suddenly flipped up and backwards like a frightened cat to land on her knees, her legs on either side of his face. She then bent her head until her mouth was over his nose, ignoring his muffled cries of fear. Opening her mouth, she wrapped her teeth around his nose, clamping down and blocking his airway. His body suddenly went rigid and started shaking violently. He tried to breathe but was unable to. She placed her hands on his chest to hold him in place. His eyes shot wide open as he did not understand what was happening to him. He felt the air being sucked out of his lungs as his skin began to crinkle and crack, turning grey, before becoming transparent. He went silent and actually felt his own heart stop beating. She watched as his skin slowly dissolved and disappeared, followed by his muscles and finally his bones. She stood back up and looked down at the heap of clothing, all that remained of any evidence that physical Donald ever existed.

'Told you, didn't I? I bet you have never had a ride like that before.'

She knelt down and picked up his jacket and pulled his wallet out.

'One hundred and fifty pounds, is that all I am worth to you, you bastard?'

She looked over at the car and was amazed that it didn't look too beaten up. The side was all dented and one of the headlights was broken. Other than that, it looked OK. She picked up the driver's seat and walked up to the car, placed the seat on the ground as she quickly looked the damaged vehicle over. She closed her eyes and placed both hands on the edge of the car, felt its weight and heaved it back over. It turned easily, bouncing a couple of times before resting back on its tires. She pushed the start button, and after a couple of attempts it started, coughed a couple of times before the engine started to roar back to life.

'Well, well, these Germans certainly know how to build a car,' she commented aloud.

She lifted the seat and dropped it back into the car, then walked back to the bundle of clothing and picked up his jacket to retrieve his wallet. She searched through it until she found his driver's license. She hoped the address was his recent one and was confident it was when she noticed the Orton address. She dropped the wallet and searched his jacket for his house keys. She found them in his trouser pocket. After walking back to the car, she slid into the driver's seat, which wobbled freely. She was pleased to find a local road map in the passenger's glove compartment and quickly found his road. She then had to force the gear shift hard, it finally engaged, and the car limped out of the field and back onto the road. She passed a road sign indicating that Orton was only two miles away. She smiled.

Fifteen minutes later, she parked outside Donald's house. She turned the engine off and left the car still smoking from its accident. She tried three keys before she found the one that opened the front door. After stepping inside, she was impressed by what she found. He clearly had money and enjoyed the nicer things in life. A long white leather corner unit dominated the lounge. There was a large TV on a white unit. On the opposite wall was a well-stocked bar. Shoil licked her lips and poured herself a large scotch.

Just then the doorbell rang, causing her to almost drop the glass. Thinking quickly, she placed the glass on the bar before scratching her face with her nails. She then ripped the top of her blouse and scratched the top of her arm. On opening the front door she was greeted by an agitated man.

He swung around to face her when the door opened, clearly surprised by a woman opening the door.

'Where's Donald, what's happened to his car?'

'He's OK, upstairs fixing himself up. Had a bit of a bang on the head, but otherwise he is fine.'

'Ho, thank the lord for that. I told him that car would be the death of him.'

How true, thought Shoil.

'I am Kevin, his neighbor. I was just walking out with my bins when I saw the state of his car. He loves that car. Er, and who are you, by the way?'

'I am Kara and met Donald today. He was showing off in his car and, unfortunately, lost control and came off the road and hit a tree. He is quite embarrassed about it and sure he doesn't want to see you at the moment.'

Kevin immediately became suspicious but kept his calm.

'As I said, he loved that car and would never do anything stupid in it. I would like to check that he is OK, please. Just a quick word.'

'Fine,' she replied, stepping back to allow him to enter, 'please come in, and I will let him know you are here. Kevin, you said.'

She slowly closed the door, quietly turning the key in the door before extracting the key, then swiftly slipped the key into her pocket.

'Thank you,' he responded, 'he knows me very well, so no need for any formal introductions.'

Shoil led him into the lounge.

'OK, no problem. You are the neighbor, you said. Please help yourself to a drink while I let Donald know you are here.'

'That's very generous of you,' he replied. *Very generous with someone else's drink. Particularly as you have apparently only just met,* he thought.

He sat on the sofa while Shoil disappeared upstairs.

Five minutes had passed, causing him to tap his knees with his hands in frustration. Something was very strange about this mysterious woman. She seemed very much at home for someone who had only met Donald today. He was thinking about leaving and calling the police when he heard footsteps coming down the stairs and what sounded like heavy breathing. He stood up and walked out into the hallway.

He froze on the spot.

Coming down the stairs was the biggest dog he had ever seen. Its orange eyes oozed evil while the size of its paws and large claws looked menacing. Kevin glanced quickly towards the front door, knowing he did not want to confront this wild beast. As he took a step towards the door the animal gave a deep growl, shifting its stance as if to leap, anticipating his move. Kevin opted to stay still as the animal descended the stairs to stand directly in front of him.

He quickly thought through his opportunities to escape, all of which were limited. He knew Donald did not own a dog, so he assumed it belonged to this strange but attractive woman. He certainly saw why Donald would invite her back. He also knew that Donald would never allow a dog into his car. Something was very wrong.

'Hey, is this your dog down here, lady?' he called up the stairs. 'If so, I would be grateful if you could come down and put it on a lead or something. It doesn't look too friendly, if you ask me.'

He waited but there was no response, while all the time the animal paced back and forth in front of him, never taking its eyes off him.

'Hello, can you hear me?' he shouted out this time. 'Donald, are you up there?'

Still no response. The dog stopped pacing and stood directly in front of him, saliva dripped from either side of its mouth.

Kevin took an involuntary step backwards, but the dog immediately took a step forward, keeping the same distance between them. He glanced towards the door but was met with a warning growl from the animal.

'Is there anyone here?' he called out.

'No,' responded the dog.

Kevin's mouth dropped open. He thought he must be going crazy as he was sure it was the dog who responded, but that was not possible. He looked directly at the dog before he spoke again.

'You didn't just speak to me, did you?'

The dog said nothing but nodded its head in acknowledgement.

'Do you understand me?'

Again the dog nodded.

'What do you want with me?'

The dog seemed to consider his question as it leaned its head slightly to one side, licking its lips.

'To eat you,' it finally replied.

'**TO WHAT**!' exclaimed Kevin.

The dog said nothing but leapt into the air, reaching out with its large claws to land on Kevin's chest, forcing him to collapse onto the floor. He screamed in fear.

That was the last thing he did. Shoil slashed his exposed throat with her sharp claws, cutting through skin, muscle, and bone, like a hot knife through butter. He opened his mouth to try to suck in air, swallowing his own blood instead. Shoil chose that precise moment to extend her tongue, which entered his open mouth and plowed down his throat. His body started to shake violently as his skin turned orange, started to crack, and then quickly became transparent. She stood over the body until it was completely absorbed. Her tongue retracted back into her mouth as she stood and changed back to her human form, ignoring the pool of blood on the floor. She calmly walked over to her glass and finished her drink. She was now fully energized and felt powerful once again.

If only Tampong were here right now, she thought, *I could finish her off, finally.*

She placed the glass down on the coffee table and walked upstairs. She found fresh towels in the cupboard, so ran a bath. As she was already naked, she stepped straight into the bath to enjoy a hot, relaxing soak.

She closed her eyes as Donald's memories flowed through her mind. He had taken several young girls back to his apartment and had sex with them all, but his lovemaking skills were less than adequate, and she guessed all the girls left disappointed. The only silver cloud being that their bank accounts were a couple of hundred pounds better off. He had quite a bit of money in several accounts, one of them was a Swiss account. No doubt he was hiding money from the taxman. She now knew all his accounts and started to plan how to move the money. Perhaps she would buy herself a nice motor! She would not worry about property at the moment as she was on the road quite a bit, but at least she did not have to worry about money for a little while, nor did she have to look for a job either. She could be comfortable for a while. She slipped her head under the water and realized how fortunate it was to have met him in the city center. His loss, but her gain.

She would make full use of her new riches.

***

Terry's eyes shot wide open, he sat bolt upright on the sofa. Tampong jumped at his reaction and was immediately concerned.

'What is it?' she asked, not really wanting to know the answer.

'Shoil has killed again.'

'What! are you sure?'

'Positive, and not only once, but twice.'

'How do you know?'

'It was as if I was there with her. Seeing what she was seeing and doing. It was horrible.'

'Are you connected to her?'

'I am not sure. I do not feel her all the time, but usually only when she turns into that dog thing.'

'And she was that dog thing when she attacked?'

'Yes, at least for her last kill.'

'Is she close?'

'Closer.'

He turned to face Tampong. He looked worried.

'She is really powerful. I am not sure you can stand up to her now.'

'Then we will have to keep avoiding her until she weakens, or I am stronger, or we are stronger together, but I have to face her on my own. Keep you safe.'

'We *can* defeat her,' he announced.

'We?' she queried.

'Yes, we,' he confirmed.

'I do not want you involved in any combat situation with Shoil. Not just yet in any case.'

'You may not have any choice in the matter.'

'What is that supposed to mean?'

'I mean the situation where we all meet may be beyond your control. Our control, come to that. What if she finds me first?'

Tampong raised her eyebrows.

'Does she know about you?'

Terry contemplated her question.

'She knows something new has happened, but I don't think she quite understands what it is. Yet.'

'Then let's keep it that way.'

'If we can,' he countered.

'While we can,' she corrected.

She took his hands in hers.

'But I still need to understand how you are connecting with her. I never had that ability, and I am not convinced any of the other group members had that skill either.'

'Are you really sure none of the others who you absorbed had such abilities?'

Tampong thought about his question.

'As I said, not that I know about. If they were, then I should surely have been aware of these abilities too.'

Terry just shrugged his shoulders before involuntarily shivering, which was noticed by Tampong.

'What's wrong, Terry?'

'Just had a flash image of her killing those men again.'

'They are always men,' she responded.

'Why?' he asked.

'Not sure to be honest. Perhaps it is the female gene she cannot tolerate. Who knows?'

'Then she cannot absorb you then.'

'In theory, no. But I wouldn't put anything past that thing.'

'That might be a small advantage.'

'It might,' she agreed, 'but then we could lose that advantage if she captured and absorbed you.'

'I don't think she can.'

'What? Capture you or absorb you?'

'Absorb me."

'Why do you say that?'

'I think I have to be a man for her to absorb me.'

'You are a man.'

'No, I am still a boy. I have to have sex first.'

Tampong blinked twice quickly, taking in his last statement.

'You have to have what first?'

'Sex,' he replied simply. 'I don't think she can absorb male virgins.'

'Well, for your sake I hope you are right.'

'I am.'

'If that is the case, then we need to keep you away from women for a few years.'

'Is it good?'

'What, sex you mean?'

He looked a little embarrassed.

'Yes, sex.'

'Honestly, yes, it is a very nice experience. Especially if you are with the right person at the right time and in the right place and situation.'

'How do you know?'

'Because it will feel right, that's how.'

'Have you had good sex?'

'I think it is time we changed the subject. You are still too young for such conversations. Let's discuss this again when you are a little older.'

'OK, but I have a feeling you have had good sex. I look forward to experiencing this too. The boys at school all talk about sex with girls.'

'Really, and just what are they talking about exactly?'

'Well, it is more about the different kinds of sex you can have.'

'Really!'

'Have you tried different sex positions?'

She coughed in embarrassment.

'As I said, this conversation is now over.'

'OK, but we will come back to this in a couple of years.'

'If we are still able to,' she corrected.

'I hope so,' he answered somberly.

'You and me both.'

He simply looked up and smiled.

'In the meantime,' she added, 'we must continue with your training.'

'Practice makes perfect?'

'Practice makes perfect,' she confirmed.

Later that evening, Tampong walked into the room to catch Terry examining his hand. He was turning it around and clenching his fist.

'What are you doing?' she asked.

'What, ho, just looking at my hand.'

'What for?'

He didn't answer her question as he continued to stare at his hands.

'I am like Wolverine, don't you think?'

'Who?'

'Wolverine,' he repeated.

'Who the hell is this wolf person?'

'Wolverine,' he corrected, 'he is a character in this comic book I am reading.'

'Which is?'

She sat down next to him, so he passed her the comic book. She read the title.

'*X-Men*.'

'Yes. They are a group of mutants. All of whom have special powers, like us. Wolverine has these silver blades that come out of his hands, and he cannot be killed.'

'Mutants?'

'Yes, people who are not normal. This professor bloke has mind abilities and can find them all, all the good and bad ones. He brings the good ones to this special school and trains them to use their powers.'

'I see.'

'So, back to my question. Am I like Wolverine? Am I a mutant too?'

Tampong sat back on the sofa and thought about his question.

'Our kind have been around for thousands of years. Long before comic books like this ever came out. Perhaps the author had heard rumors about people like us and decided to write about them. Or perhaps he just has a really good imagination. Either way, we really exist, whereas characters like this are just figments of someone's imagination.'

'Very good imagination if you ask me.'

'True,' she agreed, 'perhaps, as I said, he had heard about us then. Who is the author?'

Terry flicked through the comic quickly.

'Actually, it looks as though there were several authors, Roy Thomas, Len Wein, and John Romita Sr.'

'Well, those names do not ring any bells.'

'Perhaps one of them saw or heard something, and the others just chipped in with ideas.'

'Who knows? Anyway, unfortunately, we can be killed.'

'That sucks.'

She looked at him.

'Where did you hear a saying like that?'

'Not sure. At school perhaps.'

'Hmmm,' she added, 'school sure was different in my day.'

'Are we good mutants or bad?' he asked.

'Does it matter?'

'Absolutely.'

'Well, some would say we are bad.'

'And you?'

She thought about his question.

'Yes, I was bad to start with, but then decided to try and change.'

'That's when you rescued me, wasn't it?'

'Yes, that's when I rescued you. I saw what Shoil was doing, and it just didn't feel right anymore.'

'Well, I am glad you changed.'

'So am I.'

'And I hope I am good.'

'You are, Terry, you are. Remember, you were normal first. It was my blood that changed you.'

'Like vampires.'

She laughed out loud.

'OK, yes, like vampires.'

They both laughed.

'But vampires are not real, either, are they?' he asked.

'Who said they are not?' She was looking at him seriously.

His puzzled expression made her start laughing again.

'You are teasing me, aren't you?'

'Just a little. But remember Shoil and the things that she does. If any of these so-called authors heard about her, then they would be creating another character around her, wouldn't they? And just how many people would believe it to be true?'

'Well, I know of at least two people, three, including Shoil.'

'True,' answered Tampong, 'very true.'

TIME FOR A DOG TO GO HUNTING

Date: July 2009
Age: Terry is 16
Status: Semi-active

Terry and Tampong sat in front of the TV half watching the news as they ate their Chinese takeaway in silence. Newsnight had just started, and the image of Jeremy Paxman appeared. He picked up a few sheets of paper and began reading the news headlines.

'Two bombs exploded in the heart of Jakarta yesterday, killing at least nine people. Jakarta police have issued a statement that two suicide bombers entered the JW Marriott and Ritz-Carlton Hotels and were included in the death toll numbers. They have further stated that fifty-three people were injured and hospitalized. No names have yet been released and will not until all the next of kin can be contacted.'

'The world has gone crazy,' Terry said to no one in particular.

'Sorry, what did you say?' asked Tampong.

'Oh, nothing of importance. Just that the world has gone crazy.'

Tampong looked up at the screen.

'Oh, you mean the bombings. Right, yes.'

'That and all the other things that are happening.'

'Such as?'

'Well, yesterday there was that air crash, in Iran, I think it was, where something like a hundred and sixty-eight souls lost their lives. Then earlier there were those riots in China where close to two hundred people died.'

Tampong placed her chopsticks down and looked at him.

'Since when did you become so interested in the news?'

'Ho, just taking a closer interest, for school and stuff.'

'And stuff?'

Terry just shrugged his shoulders and returned his attention to Jeremy Paxman.

'The largest hoard of Anglo-Saxon gold ever discovered has now been estimated to be worth 3.2 million pounds. Over 1,500 items were found near the village of Hammerwich in Staffordshire.'

'Wow, that's a lot of money.'

'It is.'

'What would you do if you inherited wealth like that?'

Tampong thought about his question and her memory immediately flashed back to Zelphur and her multimillions, if not more, which she must have hoarded in several places.

'Well, I try not to think about things that are not really likely to happen,' she finally answered.

'I bet the bloke that found all that gold thought the same as well.'

'Perhaps,' agreed Tampong, 'so, what would you do with all this sudden wealth then?'

Terry stared at the TV and then continued to stare blankly at the screen.

Tampong picked up on his change. She leaned forward and waved her hand in front of his face, but there was no reaction.

'Terry?' she queried.

No response.

'Terry, can you hear me?' she said louder.

Still no response.

'**Terry**,' she yelled.

He blinked twice, then slowly turned his head towards her.

'She's closer,' he whispered

Tampong's blood went cold. It always did when she heard that name. She shivered. She knew she didn't need to question his senses. Over the years he had developed his skills beyond even her understanding. She gasped in air, not realizing she had been holding her breath.

'How much closer?' she asked finally.

'My guess is within twenty miles, give or take a few.'

'Too close.'

'What do we do?'

'We have to leave and get out of this town as soon as possible. Get as far away as possible.'

‘You know she will still track us down, don’t you?’

‘Yes, but we need more time.’

‘You mean I need more time.’

‘No, I mean we both need more time. We leave in the morning. So pack your essential things and be ready for an early departure.’

‘You know you are only delaying the inevitable, don’t you?’

Tampong held him by his shoulders.

‘Listen to me very carefully, we have to plan when and where to take her on. It has to be on our terms and our way, otherwise we stand little chance, particularly if she finds either one of us on our own. The time is not right, not yet. You need more training if we are to have any chance of defeating this horrible woman, or dog, or whatever that damned thing is.’

‘Is she that good?’

‘Yes, she really is that good. I am sure she has absorbed a few of the Lower Middle and inherited their abilities. This makes her all the more dangerous.’

He nodded his head in acknowledgement.

‘Then we need to practice more often and harder then.’

‘Agreed, but without transforming into our true forms.’

‘That is going to be difficult, isn’t it?’

‘Yes it is, my dear, but it is something we will have to cope with. This is all new for me too, so we will learn together.’

‘And together we can beat her.’

‘Together we can defeat her,’ she repeated the words, although she was less than confident about the outcome.

They had been practicing regularly for the last couple of years. Every evening for a couple of hours Tampong would teach him all her combat skills. She was always impressed with how quickly he picked things up. They made sure they did not move into their true form. Terry soon became very proficient and grew in confidence with each lesson. It was not long before he could anticipate Tampong’s moves and counterattack. His reactions were lightning quick. On one occasion, Tampong moved to her left with the intention of attacking him on the right, but she feigned her move and double-checked her stance to attack Terry on his exposed left side. However, he quickly adjusted his posture and blocked her attack. In an instant he moved his right foot in between her legs and pushed his weight against her body, forcing her backwards and tripping over his leg. She landed with a smack on the floor on her back, but before her head struck the concrete floor Terry fell to his knees and his hand was under her head to prevent any harm.

'Wow,' she said, clearly impressed, 'nobody has been able to trip me like that before.'

'Well, you were quite easy to read.'

'Really?'

'Yep.'

'OK, cocky boy, help me up . . . please.'

'Sure thing,' he confirmed, offering his free hand, which she took eagerly and rose back to her feet.

'I think that is enough for today,' she announced, brushing herself down and straightening her hair. 'How come you were so lightning quick to stop my head from hitting the floor?'

'I just anticipated the movement and realized the danger, so I reacted more on instinct than anything else.'

'Impressive,' she conceded, still brushing herself down, more to hide her embarrassment than anything else.

Terry was watching her, and when she looked up she noticed.

'What is it?'

'How come you never married?'

'How do you know I have never married?'

'I just know, so?'

'Never met the right man I guess,' she answered quickly and honestly.

'I can understand that.'

'You do?'

She raised her eyebrow.

'Perhaps you can enlighten me then.'

'Sure, you are a beautiful, intelligent, and resourceful woman. It would take a special kind of man to handle you the way you deserve.'

Her eyes beamed warmly at him.

'My word, but that was a lovely thing to say.'

'Only because it is true.'

'I must have hit you once too many times in the head.'

'In your dreams.'

She laughed.

'I am going to run a bath and have a nice hot soak,' she announced.

'Well, I am going to train a little bit longer. Then I will be ready for my own bath . . . assuming you have finished with it.'

'Are you going to train for another hour?'

'Or longer.'

'Then the bathroom will be just about ready for you. I'll run another one once I have finished and give you a shout when it's ready.'

'OK, sounds good, and thanks.'

'For what?'

'For everything.'

She moved towards him and brushed his hair.

'You are worth it and a thousand times more.'

'Get going,' he announced, embarrassed.

She said nothing but turned and walked back into the house.

Terry watched her go and thought how lucky he was that she was around in his life and that he still had a life. There was no doubt that if Shoil had reached him then he would not be here today. Because of that, he was determined to train as hard as he could and be ready for Shoil. He was determined to help defeat the woman who murdered his parents. He was equally determined to defend and protect Tampong as best he could, even if that meant giving up his own life. He owed her that much.

He checked his watch; it was just after eight pm.

He started his warmup routine, bending his legs and moving his arms into the snake position. He closed his eyes and focused on his moves. He allowed his mind to take control of his body, as his senses became acute and aware of everything around him. He could now hear the slight breeze in the wind, insects working the ground beneath his feet, and could even hear

Tampong soaping herself in the bath. He straightened his arm, hand, and fingers so that they were parallel with the ground. All the insects close by suddenly went quiet, so Terry opened his eyes. Puzzled. He could still hear Tampong in the bath, but the creatures had gone silent.

He looked around until his eyes caught sight of a nail protruding from the wooden beam directly in front of him, it was shaking as if trying to free itself. He stared at the nail, and it responded by shaking even more, slowly extracting itself from the wood. Finally, it freed itself and shot across the patio and into Terry's forefinger. He panicked, thinking he had just impaled himself, but he felt no pain. He lifted his finger slightly for a better view. The head of the nail had indeed embedded itself into the tip of his finger, but instead of blood pouring from the wound, his finger started to turn metallic. Fascinated, he watched as his whole finger turned metallic grey. He moved his hand closer to his face for a better look and could see that the metal was slowly but purposely moving down his hand. He tapped his finger against the fence and heard metal hitting metal. He reached over with his other hand and felt his finger. It was cold and hard, just like the nail.

His finger had turned metallic, just like the nail.

He pinched the nail with his other hand and pulled it away. He was surprised it came away with little resistance. He raised his hand and saw that it was still changing. He placed his finger on the tip of his metallic finger and watched as metal was replaced with skin and bone again until his whole hand had returned to its normal state. He turned his hand over and over to check for any other change but could see no metal.

'Interesting,' he said aloud.

A few years ago such an event would have freaked him out, but now it was going to take a little bit more than his skin changing to unsettle him. Still, this was a new development in his abilities. He knew from what Tampong had told him that some members of their group had the ability to transform into any object that they touched, so he assumed he had inherited a similar gene.

The sound of insects resuming their work returned and he relaxed a little, knowing he had to give this new development some more thought.

'Terry, your bath is ready,' Tampong shouted from inside, breaking him free from his thoughts.

'So soon? OK, I'll be right there.'

He checked his watch, and sure enough, just over the hour had passed. It was now a little after nine pm.

Had that adventure really taken an hour? he thought.

He took one final look at his hand before he turned and entered the house.

'How was your training?' she asked as he walked into the house.

'Ho, OK,' he answered absentmindedly, looking down at his hand.

'Did you hurt yourself?'

She noticed him looking at his hand.

'No, surprisingly no.'

'Surprisingly?'

'Yep. I hit a nail, but not only did it not hurt but there was no blood either.'

'I guess this means that you are getting stronger then.'

'Guess so,' he answered, again absentmindedly.

She watched him go, confused by his sudden change of mood, but then shook the uncertainty away, assuming he was just surprised and relieved he had not cut or hurt himself.

He marched promptly upstairs, taking two steps at a time. Quickly undressing, he stepped into the bath and was pleased to be rewarded with the water still hot. Tampong knew he liked a red-hot bath, one that turned his skin red the moment it hit the water. He slid under the water to immerse himself. He counted to twenty before slowly raising his head above the water. He placed his hands on either side of the bath and closed his eyes. He again focused on his senses and immediately felt his hands changing. He opened his eyes quickly in time to see his hands molding into the bath's porcelain. He raised both his hands to find them completely white and solid. He placed them on his chest where they returned to their normal state.

'Really interesting,' he said, smiling.

This was something else he knew he would have to practice and fine-tune.

This might come in very handy, particularly should he come face-to-face with Shoil. He doubted she would have any idea of his new abilities, any more than Tampong did. He would keep this a secret and surprise them both when the occasion called for it.

Until that day, he would just relax and enjoy his bath.

FORCED INTO A CORNER

Date: August 2010
Ages: Terry is now 17 / Shoil is 1,161
Status: Semi-active

They had settled down in a small house in the middle of York City, having decided it was no longer safe to stay in Leeds with Shoil in close proximity. Another year had passed and, fortunately, it had been a quiet year, with no activity from Shoil. Terry sat at a table in McDonald's, eating his double cheeseburger, his favorite, when he casually glanced around the restaurant. That was when his eyes met another pair of crystal-blue female eyes staring right back at him. He blinked twice, looked down to take another bite of his burger before looking back across the room. She was still staring at him.

He smiled at her.

She smiled back.

Their eyes locked.

They shared a 'special' moment which was suddenly terminated when a large body moved between them. Terry watched the boy sit down deliberately in front of the girl while dumping his food tray noisily on the table. He looked across to Terry and raised his middle index finger at him before turning to face the girl. His face was red with rage and jealousy.

He leaned towards her.

'Hey, you are with me, girl, right?' he reminded her.

'I am not *with* you, we are just here at the same time,' she corrected.

He pointed his finger close to her face.

'You agreed to meet me here, so, the way I see it, we are together right now, so stop looking at other boys.'

'You mean I was forced to meet you here, so that you would leave my little sister alone.'

'And you better believe it too. It's you or her. She is really interested in me, you know?'

'No, no she is not,' she said, deliberately raising her voice, 'you were blackmailing her into dating you. She told me so.'

He glanced nervously around, but nobody was looking in their direction. Relieved, he leaned across the table.

'Keep your voice down, Karen. I was not blackmailing her. She really wants a piece of me, and I am tempted to give her what she wants.'

'Don't you dare touch her. She is only fifteen.'

'Well, you *are* old enough. So don't make me choose.'

'Old enough for what?'

'You know, a piece of me.'

He looked down towards his crouch.

'In your dreams.'

'Well, I'll make Tina's dreams come true instead then.'

He leaned back in his seat, picked up his burger, and took a big bite, all the time staring at the girl with an evil grin across his face.

Terry's fine hearing picked up every word, but he never looked up, never raised his head in their direction, but kept eating his meal. He was about halfway through his fries when he took a gulp of his Coke, taking the opportunity to take a sneaky glance towards the girl. She was clearly distressed and uncomfortable being with this guy. The boy, in Terry's opinion, looked to be your typical large-town bully. He was muscular and confident.

She, on the other hand, was quite beautiful. He could not remember seeing such a naturally beautiful girl like her before. She glanced in his direction again, but the boy noticed. Turning quickly, he glared towards Terry, who continued eating his fries.

The boy dropped his burger back onto his tray, stood up, and marched purposely towards Terry's table.

'Stop it, Stan,' the girl pleaded, 'leave him alone. He hasn't done anything to you, so don't hurt him. Please.'

He ignored her pleas and walked up close to Terry.

'What the fuck are you looking at, boy?'

His voice was filled with venom.

Terry looked up at the boy. He was well-built and obviously worked out quite a bit. He was therefore very confident of his own abilities and intimidation too. Terry, on the other hand, was slim and his height made him look even skinnier. This only built the boy's confidence up.

'Nothing,' he replied calmly.

'Nothing! You were checking out my girl, weren't you?'

'I thought I heard her say she was not your girl.'

'So, you were listening in on our conversation too, you fucking eavesdropper.'

'Kind of difficult not to overhear your conversation. I think the whole restaurant heard you arguing with the lady.'

'Listen fuck-head, keep your fucking ears to yourself, your fucking nose to yourself, and your fucking eyes off my girl.'

'You know you swear a lot.'

'Go fuck yourself.'

'Difficult, if not impossible.'

Terry knew he was winding the boy up, but he was growing tired of this bully, despite his imposing size.

'So, you think you are a fucking wise guy or something, eh?'

Terry went to pick up his Coke and finish it off, but the boy swiped it off the table and it crashed to the floor, spilling its remaining contents across the floor.

The boy laughed and turned to return to his table. As he walked back, Terry looked across to the girl, who was looking at him with sad eyes.

He stood up, picked up the Coke cup and took it with his empty cartons to the bins, popped them inside, and calmly walked out of the restaurant.

I guess I must have one of those faces that attracts the bad sort, he thought.

The other boy was watching him leave, so followed him outside, deciding it was time to teach this skinny boy a lesson about keeping out of other peoples' business, and confronted him in the car park.

'Where the fuck do you think you are going, boy?'

'I was going home.'

'A cocky little fucker, aren't you?'

'Listen, I don't want any trouble, I just want to go home.'

'I don't give a fuck what you want, it's what I am going to do to you that you should be worried about.

The girl rushed outside. Her face was wet with tears, streaming down her face.

'Stan, Stan, stop this madness.'

'Get the fuck back inside, bitch. I'll deal with you later.'

His remarks caused Terry to look up at the boy, then across to the girl, who was shocked.

'What did you just call me?' she screamed.

'You heard, bitch.'

She said nothing but turned around and stepped back inside the restaurant, more to hide the new tears running down her cheeks than anything else.

'That was rude,' remarked Terry.

As he talked calmly he reached out with his left hand and held onto the metal lamppost. He felt the cold steel wrapping around his fingers, so embraced it.

Stan swung around to face Terry. He could almost see the veins popping out of the boy's forehead.

'I don't give a running fuck what you think, you little shitface.'

Stan clenched his fist into a ball and moved his arm back. His intentions were all too clear, threatening, and all too obvious.

Terry did not move but continued to grip the post tightly.

'That won't save you,' Stan spat out, phlegm flying into the air. 'I am going to fuck your face up, boy, so that no other girl will ever give you a second glance.'

'Oh, but I don't think so,' replied Terry calmly.

Stan said nothing else. He pulled his arm back as far as it would go, then launched it forward with all his strength, straight towards Terry's exposed face.

Terry did not flinch, did not move an inch, and allowed the fist to hit his face.

There was a clunking sound like a fist hitting metal. Stan froze for a second, not sure what had just happened, then screamed out in pain. He wrapped his damaged hand under his arm, trying to ease the pain shooting up his arm.

Terry was unmarked. His skin was the same gunmetal grey color as the lamppost. He took two steps towards Stan and grabbed the belt of his jeans, lifting him easily into the air. Stan's eyes were now wide open, not understanding what was happening to him. Terry brought him closer to his face.

'Now listen to me, you little creep. Never try a stupid stunt like that with me again, got it?'

Stan just nodded in fear, still holding his broken hand.

'And another thing. Never bad-mouth that lovely girl again. Got that too?'

Again Stan simply nodded.

'And one final thing, if you don't leave her sister alone too, then I will hunt you down and break more than just your stupid hand. Understand?'

Stan nodded his head quickly, eager to get away from this mysterious little boy, who had inhuman strength.

Terry finally lowered him back to the ground.

'Now you had better get yourself to hospital, as you have several broken bones in your hand.'

Stan said nothing but simply nodded and stumbled off down the street.

Terry watched him go and was about to leave when he remembered the girl. He turned and reentered the restaurant. She looked shocked when she saw him, so quickly stood up, looking a little panicked.

'Did he actually let you go then?' she asked, looking back towards the door, half expecting him to rush back inside after this boy.

'No,' he replied simply.

'No?' she repeated, again looking towards the door.

'He will not bother you again.'

'What, why, when . . . *what*?'

'I said he will not bother you again. Believe me.'

She just stood there, staring at him, clearly hearing what he said but not really understanding its meaning.

'Do you want to sit down?'

She said nothing but instantly sat down. Her eyes never leaving him. Her mouth dropped wide open as if she wanted to say something but couldn't find the words.

He sat down in front of her and just watched her. Her eyes were darting from left to right as if trying to sum up what just happened. Finally she snapped out of her shock, taking another frightened glance towards the door.

'Where, where is S . . . Stan now?' she stuttered.

'On his way to the hospital, I hope.'

'The hospital!'

'Yep.'

'What happened?'

'He tried to hit me.'

'He *tried* to hit you. Do you realize he is actually a professional boxer? If he really tried to hit you, then it would have been *you* going to the hospital and not him.'

'Well, what can I say. He tried. I dodged, and he hit the lamppost instead.'

'He hit the lamppost. He hit the lamppost?'

'Yep.'

She started laughing uncontrollably, then got herself under control.

'If I were you, mister, I'd get the hell out of here and this town and hope he never catches up with you again.'

'Oh, I don't think I have anything to worry about.'

'You don't, eh? Well I do.'

'And he won't be bad-mouthing you or your sister again either.'

'He won't what?'

'He won't be bad-mouthing you or your sister.'

She stared at him hard, making him feel uncomfortable.

'Who are you?'

'Aw, right, sorry. Terry is my name. Pleased to meet you.'

'That's not what I meant.'

'I know.'

'Ho. OK. Well, I'm Karen.'

'I know.'

'You know? How do you know?'

'I overheard him calling your name during your somewhat heated discussion.'

'What else did you overhear?'

'Just that you were protecting your sister, that's about it.'

'You heard all that?'

'I did.'

'Wow, you must have superman hearing then.'

'Not required most of the time. He was not exactly subtle, was he?'

'True.'

She smiled at him.

'You should smile more often,' he remarked.

'What do you mean?'

'You have a beautiful smile. Your whole face lights up when you smile.'

She smiled again, broader this time, then looked down at her watch.

'Oops, I have to go.'

'Date?'

'Work.'

'What do you do . . . if you don't mind me asking?'

'I am a waitress in the restaurant just down the road.'

She indicated the direction with her finger.

'Do you mean the Red Lion?'

'Yes, have you eaten there then?'

'No, but I have passed it, and it looks expensive.'

'It is. Overrated and overpriced if you ask me. That's if I still have a job after today.'

'Why do you say that?'

'Because Stan's father owns the restaurant. When he finds out what has happened to him, due to me, he will most likely fire me.'

'It wasn't due to you.'

'Yes, it was.'

'Why do you say that?'

'Because you were looking at me.'

'And?'

'And I was looking at you.'

'I see.'

'Listen, I really appreciate what you did today, but I must go now. If there is the slimmest of chance that I keep my job, I cannot be late.'

'No, right, you go, but before you do, can I trouble you for your number? Perhaps I can call you and, maybe, I can take you out for dinner or something.'

She stared at him for a little while as if trying to decide, then took hold of his hand and turned it over. She pulled out a pen from her coat pocket and scribbled her number across his palm.

'It isn't the number for the local cemetery, right?'

'No, it's not. Call me.' She then stared at him for a little while. 'Haven't I seen you at school?'

Terry clicked his fingers. 'Yes, I believe we have art together.'

'Right,' she confirmed. 'That's probably where I have seen you.'

She turned, left the restaurant, and started running down the road. He watched her go and realized for the first time that his heart was pumping fast. He took deep, relaxing breaths to calm himself, just like Tampong had trained him. It had the desired effect. He felt a little lightheaded as he walked out of the restaurant and almost skipped all the way home.

As soon as he entered the lounge, Tampong grabbed his arm and swung him around.

'OK, what has happened to you?'

'What do you mean?'

'You are all flushed in the face.'

'Ho, right. I met someone today.'

'What's her name?'

'What makes you think it's a girl?'

Tampong simply placed her hands on her hips and gave him a knowing look.

'OK. Karen, her name is Karen,' he admitted.

'So, tell me everything. What's she like? Where did you meet? How old is she?'

'Er, well, she is beautiful, we met in McDonald's, and I don't know her age, but I'd guess similar to me.'

'And?'

'And nothing else. We just talked a little and she gave me her number.'

'She gave you her number?'

'Yes, why, is that strange?'

'Nope, just means she must like you.'

His eyes widened.

'She likes me?'

'Why else would she give you her number on your first meeting. It was your first meeting, right?'

'Yes,' he confirmed, trying to keep the excitement out of his voice but failing badly.

'Well, there you go then. She must like you. Make sure you call her. Girls hate it when they give their number to a boy and he never calls.'

'Ho, don't worry, I am going to call her.'

He turned to go upstairs.

'Hey,' called Tampong as he got halfway up the stairs, 'it's your birthday soon. Any ideas?'

'I would love a mobile phone,' he answered.

'Wow, those things are expensive.'

'You're right, sorry, anything will do then.'

'Well, how about a nice meal in a restaurant?'

He stopped at the last step and thought about Karen.

'Excellent idea,' he responded, a little too quickly.

'OK, do you happen to have one in mind?'

She placed her hands on her hips, guessing this Karen is going to be linked to his answer, if her instincts were correct.

'Well, I have often passed the Red Lion and it looks really nice . . . if that is OK with you? But I have been told it is a little bit expensive.'

'Sure, why not? The price is no problem as it is your birthday present after all. I'll call them and make a reservation.'

'Perfect.'

He ran the rest of the way upstairs and launched himself onto his bed. He had met his first girlfriend and he was going to call her for a date. His first date with a girl. He was surprised how calm he had been during the whole time, but much was because of his conflict with Stan. If he ever met Stan again he would have to thank him for bringing Karen into his life. He closed his eyes and thought about all the things they could do together.

Karen spent the rest of the day smiling to herself. She liked Terry and he seemed to like her. He appeared genuine and not false and braggy like Stan. She was surprised about the outcome and thought about contacting Stan to find out exactly what happened between the two of them, but immediately decided against it as he would only get the wrong idea. She silently hoped that Terry would indeed call her. Just then her phone rang, making her jump. She reached down and picked it up, only to see it was Stan calling.

Her heart sank.

'Hello, Stan,' she said hesitantly.

'Karen, listen, I have been stupid and want to apologize to you for the way I acted earlier on.'

'Really?'

'Yes, really. And also sorry for the things I said about your sister too.'

He seemed really sincere, sounding genuine in his regret.

'It's in the past now, Stan.'

'Good, so there is no need to speak bad about me to your new boyfriend then, is there?'

'My new boyfriend?'

'Yeah, the guy who I, er, spoke to at the restaurant.'

'Oh, that boyfriend.'

If only, she thought.

'What happened between you two outside?' she asked instead.

‘I’d rather not talk about it. Just promise me you will not bad-mouth me to him, and I’ll promise to leave you and your sister alone. Deal?’

‘Deal,’ she replied spontaneously.

‘Good, thank you, Karen. Goodbye.’

He hung up.

Karen just stared at the quiet phone, unable to fully comprehend what had just happened. One moment he was very threatening, using her own sister as bait, then he was as nice as pie. Something definitely happened between him and Terry, and she was determined to find out what it was. Stan was the regular school bully and had the muscles to back it up. Terry, on the other hand, did not look well-built, so, unless he was skilled in martial arts or something, then he found some other way the scare Stan away. She had to admit she was extremely grateful. Not just for her but for her sister as well, and, if she was honest with herself, she found Terry quite attractive. She shook her head, realizing that this was only their first meeting, and she might never see him again.

Then her phone rang again, snapping her out of her thoughts and making her jump. Perhaps it was Stan ringing back to tell her that it was all a joke and that he was going to bed her sister after all unless she agreed to bed him instead.

‘Hello?’ she said nervously, not recognizing the number this time.

‘Hello, Karen, it’s me, Terry.’

‘Ho, hi Terry.’

She desperately tried to hide the excitement in her voice.

‘You OK?’

‘Sure, just had a surprise call before you.’

‘Everything OK?’

‘Sure, sure, everything is just fine, so what’s up?’

‘Nothing. I was just following up on our conversation and was, er, wondering whether you would like to go to a movie or something?’

‘Er, sure, when were you thinking?’

‘How about Friday night?’

'Ouch, that doesn't work for me as I am working at the restaurant that evening.'

'Ho, OK, no problem, how about Saturday evening then?'

'Sure, that does work for me.'

'Great, then I'll meet you outside McDonald's, say at seven pm?

'Sounds good, Terry. See you then.'

'Fantastic. Look forward to seeing you then.'

'Me too.'

And she meant it.

'Bye for now.'

'Goodbye, Terry, and thanks for calling.'

She ended the call and placed the phone against her lips. Two positive calls on the same night. Must be her lucky day.

Terry was also feeling like he was on cloud nine. He never imaged himself going out with someone as beautiful as Karen. He was thinking about what he was going to wear when the phone rang. His heart sank, thinking it was Karen calling back to say she changed her mind. Tampong had reached the phone in the lounge first.

'Terry,' she called up the stairs, 'it's Colin for you.'

Relief washed over him as he swung across his bed and picked up the receiver.

'Got it,' he called to Tampong.

He heard the click of the receiver downstairs being replaced. Colin was his best mate and the first person he had gotten to know since he arrived at his new school. They hit it off straight away and spent a lot of time together.

Putting the phone to his ear he began talking.

'Hey, Colin, what's up?'

'Hey, you want to watch the World Cup final with me?'

'You bet. It's Spain versus Netherlands. Should be a great game.'

'I think so too. So come on over to my place. My parents have a big new wide-screen TV.'

'How big?'

'Forty-two inches.'

'Wow.'

'Right.'

'Hold on. What day is the final on?'

'Sunday, why?'

'Ho nothing. It's just that I have a date on Saturday, so that works out perfectly. Two exciting events in one weekend.'

'Wait one, you have a date?'

'I do.'

'Who is she? Do I know her?'

'I don't think you do. Her name is Karen.'

'Not Karen Wright? The girl big Stan keeps chasing after?'

'So you do know her.'

'Man, if I were you, I would keep a million miles away from her. If Stan finds out you are going out with her, he is going to squash you like a bug.'

'Don't worry. I have already sorted that out with Stan, all is cool.'

'Sorted out with Stan. Are you crazy? That guy is an animal and not too smart either. To top it all, he is a pro boxer as well, mate.'

'Like I said, it's sorted.'

'Jesus, I hope so for your sake. She is a real stunner though, mate.'

'Thanks.'

'Hey, if your date goes well on Saturday, why don't you invite her to join us as well?'

'I don't even know if she is interested in football.'

'From what I have heard, she might be. No harm in asking her, is there?'

'Guess not.'

'She might surprise you.'

'OK, mate. You will know if I turn up with her.'

'OK, mate. See you then. Either alone or with your new bird.'

He hung up.

'Hmmm,' Terry muttered.

He had never tagged her as a possible football fan, but then he did not really know anything about her. Hopefully, that would change after Saturday evening.

He couldn't wait.

Saturday seemed to take forever to arrive, but finally it did. Terry had opted for a simple white turtleneck jumper, black jeans, and blue blazer. Tampong had assured him he looked really cool. He hoped so. He had turned up about forty minutes early, not wanting to be late, and was pleased to see that the threatening rain had held off. Just as well as he forgot to bring an umbrella and now really hoped he wouldn't need it. Every five minutes he checked his watch, at times wondering if the damned thing had actually stopped. The church clock struck seven times, indicating that the time had arrived. No sign of her yet. Panic started to build up inside with each passing second. Perhaps she would not arrive.

'Hey,' said a female voice from behind him.

He jumped and turned around. Karen was standing there.

'Sorry,' she said, holding out her hands, 'didn't mean to startle you.'

'Ho, no, no, it was just that I was expecting you to come from that direction.'

He indicated down the road with his hand, then shrugged his shoulders and felt foolish.

'For some completely unknown reason.'

'OK,' she replied uncertainly.

'Stupid really,' he admitted. 'Glad you came though.'

'Did you think I wouldn't?'

'Well, I didn't think I could be so lucky as to go out with someone as beautiful as you.'

She smiled.

'Those kind of lines will get you a date with just about any girl.'

'OK,' he said nervously, 'so what do you fancy watching tonight then?'

'Actually there is this new funny movie that has just been released. I would love to see that. It's a bit childish but looks like a lot of fun.'

'OK, why not? What's it called?'

'*Despicable Me*.'

'Ho, I've heard about that. Actually, it is showing at the Odeon just down the road.'

'Perfect.'

Terry glanced at his watch. 'We just have time to see the seven thirty showing.'

'Again, perfect. Let's go.'

She slipped her arm through his and they started walking quickly down the road towards the cinema. Terry's heart was beating fast. He liked the closeness of her body, the smell of her perfume.

'You smell really nice,' he remarked.

'Thank you. It's J'adore by Dior.'

'Very nice.'

'And I have to say you look very handsome too tonight.'

'Why thank you, madam. Do you know the storyline to this movie?'

They carried on walking quickly down the road as they talked.

'Well, from what I have read, it seems that this guy called Gru has a secret basement where he invents all kinds of different things, mainly for criminal activity, and is supported by an army of little yellow minions, who look a bit like yellow Tic Tacs.'

'Yellow Tic Tacs!'

'Right. Anyway, this Gru is a master criminal, and he invents a shrinking weapon and plans to steal the moon.'

'So, not farfetched at all then. A criminal with an army of Tic Tacs looking to swipe the moon. Cannot wait.'

She laughed.

'We can always watch something else if you like. As I said, it is a little far-fetched.'

'Ho no, you have whet my curiosity with this one. Let's go.'

They quickened their pace even more.

They were fortunate when they arrived as they were the last two allowed into the theatre. It was full.

'Forgot this was its first night. So lucky to get in,' Karen said with relief in her voice.

'Must be popular then,' commented Terry.

They found their row and squeezed their way past people, most of whom stood up to allow them to pass and get to their assigned seats. They sat down.

'Blast,' announced Terry in a quiet voice, 'I forgot to get any popcorn and drink for the movie.'

'I'll forgive you this time. The movie only runs for about ninety minutes, so I think I can survive until then.'

'Perhaps we can go for dinner afterwards then?'

'Wow, two dates in one day. How lucky can a girl get?'

'I'm the lucky one,' he corrected.

'How so?'

'Every second I am with you is a second I will cherish.'

'Where do you get all these wonderful lines from? Did you swallow a book of romantic quotes or something?'

Fortunately, the darkened room hid his blushes.

'It's straight from the heart, and I mean every word,' he whispered.

She squeezed his arm affectionately, then they went silent as the lights dimmed. They were greeted with clips from upcoming movies, then a number of adverts. Finally there was a warning that this was a nonsmoking cinema and anyone with mobile phones should now switch them off. The movie started.

Terry had to admit he enjoyed the film. It was funny and fast-moving. The minions were great characters. You couldn't really understand what they were saying, but could guess, except for bananas, which they loved apparently. He enjoyed being with Karen even more, and she appeared to enjoy his company as well. He was grateful that Tampong had given him her credit card and it was she who suggested that he ask her to dinner afterwards. She would make a great matchmaker. His thoughts were disturbed when she took his hand in hers. He stroked her hand with his thumb, and she reacted by placing her head on his shoulders.

After the movie, they walked out hand in hand. They stopped outside.

'What do you fancy?' he asked.

'Well, what a leading question,' she replied.

'Pardon?'

Terry wasn't sure he understood.

'I'm pulling your leg. Actually, I would really love a pizza right now.'

'That's easy enough. There is a pizzeria just around the corner.'

'Then what are we doing standing here for? After all, we didn't get any popcorn in there, did we?'

'OK, OK, point taken. Let's go.'

It only took them another ten minutes to reach the restaurant. They were greeted by your typical Italian waiter.

'Buanasera signara e signore,' he said with a strong Italian accent, which was followed with a sweep of his arm in a welcoming gesture.

'Good evening,' responded Karen, 'table for two, please.'

'Certamente. Seguime per favore.'

'What did he just say?' whispered Karen to Terry.

'He wants us to follow him.'

They did, and he took them to a quiet table in a corner of the restaurant.

'Va bene cosi?' he asked.

'Perfetto. Grazie,' replied Terry, which prompted a surprised look from Karen.

The waiter handed them each an exceptionally large menu card then walked off to serve another table.

Karen lowered her menu and leaned towards Terry.

'Do you speak Italian?'

'A little,' he confessed, although in truth he had no idea where his knowledge of Italian came from.

'Impressive,' she said.

The waiter returned to their table.

'Cosa vorresti bere?' he asked.

'What would you like to drink?' Terry translated.

'A Coke, please.'

'Due Coke per favore,' Terry said.

'You a specka the good Italiano,' the waiter said, clearly impressed.

'Ho, you are just being generous.'

'No, no, I speaka the trutha.'

Terry simply felt a little awkward, opting to glance down at his menu.

'Well, I am ready to order,' Karen announced.

'Certamente signora,' replied the waiter.

'A pizza Royale for me, please,' she advised.

'Sounds good, make that two.'

'Certamente. Buona scelta.'

He scribbled on his notepad and walked away.

'What did he say?' she asked.

'He thought we had made a good selection, but then again, he says that regardless of what we order, trying to get a decent tip perhaps. Either that or he owns the place and thinks everything on the menu is great.'

'Are you always this skeptical?' she asked.

'No, not really.'

They went quiet for a few minutes, so Terry decided to break the silence.

'I have to admit I enjoyed the movie a lot more than I expected to.'

'Me too,' she agreed, just as another waiter brought their Cokes, first placing one in front of Karen, and the second in front of Terry.

'Here's to a great evening,' she added.

'Here's to a remaining great evening,' he confirmed.

They made small talk, mostly about the movie until the pizzas arrived, then ate in silence. Terry ordered a second Coke, while Karen declined. He couldn't wait until he was old enough to order a beer or something stronger next year. He loved the taste of beer as he was allowed to drink one last Christmas.

After the waiter collected their plates and both declined dessert, Karen placed her hands together on the table.

'So, tell me about yourself, Terry,' she asked, her eyes wide and alert.

'Not much to say, really, I was born down South, both my parents were killed, and my aunty took me in, and I have been with her ever since.'

'Ho, my god, that's terrible. I am so sorry. How old were you?'

'Eight or nine, I think.'

'Jesus. How did they die?'

He looked down and she could see he was uncomfortable.

'I'm sorry, I didn't mean to bring up bad memories for you.'

'It's OK, it's just that I haven't thought about them in such a long time. Does that make me a bad son?'

She reached over and placed her hands on his. They felt warm and inviting.

'No, not at all. I think it just means you are trying to move on.'

'Right,' he agreed.

'So, different subject. How many girls have you dated?'

'Including you?'

'Yes.'

'One.'

'No seriously, how many?'

'Seriously, one. You are my first date.'

'Ho, come on, you must be pulling my leg.'

'God's honest truth.'

'Ho my god,' she said, placing her hand against her chest.

'So, is that a good thing or bad?'

'Incredible. I would never have guessed.'

'So, if it is not too personal a question, how many boyfriends have you had?'

'Including you?'

'Yes.'

'And Stan, although I never thought of him as a boyfriend, but he did.'

'Yes, including Stan.'

'Then fourteen.'

Terry's mouth dropped open.

'Just kidding,' she said reaching across the table and poking him in the ribs with her fingers. 'In all honestly I have been out with only one other guy. Kirk was his name. Bit of a bore to be honest. Kept talking about bees. He loved bees. I went out with him twice, but then finished it and suggested he take a bee out instead next time. He did not quite understand what I meant.'

Terry laughed.

'So you have been on twice as many dates as I have.'

'Does that make me a terrible person then?' she fluttered her eyelids at him, an obvious show of being hurt.

'Not at all. I am kind of pleased I am not competing with your ex-boyfriends, except the bee lover of course.'

It was her turn to laugh.

'Believe me, there is no competition.'

The waiter then arrived with their bill, so Terry placed the credit card on top of the bill, then the waiter left to run the card through the machine.

'You should always check the bill, Terry.'

'Really?'

'Really. Take it from a waitress who has seen several customers going ape when their bill arrived, although usually most without justification, and probably just hoping to get a reduction for being quiet.'

'Point taken. I will check it when I sign it and add the tip.'

The waiter returned quickly, bid them a pleasant evening, thanking them for their custom before leaving them alone again. Terry glanced at the list of charges and was pleased to see it all looked correct. He looked and nodded to Karen, who nodded back, then wiped her mouth with her napkin. He signed the bill, leaving a good tip, and they got up and left.

They had been walking while making more small talk and the time passed quickly. Too quickly for Terry. They arrived outside her door.

'This is me,' she advised.

'Right, well, thank you for a lovely evening, Karen. Perhaps we can do this again.'

'I would love to.'

Her words were filled with warmth and sincerity.

Their eyes met and locked. Instinctively they both moved closer to each other. He placed his arms around her waist, and she moved even closer until their bodies touched. They both closed their eyes, and their lips came together. Terry felt a surge of electricity rush through his body as her lips touched his. But this was the power of love and desire, nothing else. As they embraced, he let his emotions take over and he pushed against her lips. She responded by pushing more against his.

His senses then went on alert, forcing him to open his eyes. A woman was passing them on the other side of the street where she suddenly stopped, as if hit by some invisible force. For some reason, Terry instinctively knew who it was.

Shoil.

Karen felt his change, so pulled away and looked puzzled.

'Something wrong?' she asked.

'No, not with you. You were perfect.'

'OK.'

She then turned her head in the direction Terry was looking.

'Do you know that woman?'

'Not sure,' he lied, 'she looks familiar though.'

'Do you want to go and speak with her?'

'***NO***,' he said louder than intended, 'sorry, didn't mean to sound like that. Let's forget her and concentrate on us.'

She turned back towards him and smiled.

'Sounds good to me. So, when do we see each other again?'

'How about tomorrow evening?'

'Wow, you do not believe in letting the grass grow under your feet, do you, but unfortunately I am working again tomorrow, and every night next week.'

'Saturday again?'

'Saturday would be simply fine, but you can call me in the meantime.'

'Don't worry, I will.'

He turned to leave then clicked his fingers and turned back towards Karen.

'Do you like football?'

'Football? Are you suggesting we play a game of football?'

'No, nothing like that,' he suppressed a giggle, 'it's just that I am watching the World Cup final with my best mate tomorrow afternoon and wondered if you would like to watch it with us?'

'Thanks for the offer, Terry, but I need to get myself ready for work tomorrow, but enjoy the match. You can tell me all about it when we see each other next.'

'That's sad, but I am looking forward to the final. Should be a good match, and I'll certainly tell you all about it, if you are sure?'

'I am sure. I do like football but prefer to watch it live.'

'Got it. Maybe we can make that another date in the future then?'

'Hopefully, so until our next meeting then. Thank you for a lovely evening, Terry. I really enjoyed it. Goodnight.'

As she walked up to the front door she glanced quickly across the road and noticed that the woman was looking around. She seemed to sniff the air, then started walking up the street again.

'Good night, Karen.'

He watched her go inside, gave a final quick wave, then started walking up the street in the opposite direction to Shoil. He felt a shiver run down his spine. He could have been wrong, of course, but all his instincts told him that it was indeed Shoil. He quickened his pace, wanting to get back home and inform Tampong of this latest unwelcome development.

Shoil froze on the spot. She had sensed a presence, something new was close and immensely powerful. Her eyes had turned orange and she almost turned into her dog form, ready to attack or defend against this latest threat. She was barely able to control herself. Her eyes expertly scanned the immediate area. The only people around were a young boy and girl kissing in the street. They looked innocent enough, so she assumed whoever or whatever the presence she felt was inside one of the houses. She sniffed the air for any clues but was none the wiser

For the last year, Shoil had been searching intently for Tampong, but she never moved back into her true form in all that time. This was a disturbing development for Shoil, and she wasn't sure what to make of it. Either she has been fully occupied with something or someone, or she had deliberately kept herself in her human state. She hoped it was the former and not the latter, as otherwise this suggested she was aware she was being hunted and kept herself invisible, making it all but impossible to be tracked.

She had been watching the news intently while scanning the internet for any strange articles or unexplained events. The closest she came was when three boys from a local football team went missing in Leeds and had still not been found to this day. They were the reason she was now in the area. Nothing else seemed out of the ordinary. Having visited the small football stadium and after absorbing the local police officer, she learned little more except that the trail had gone cold, with the police assuming the boys ran away after a confrontation with a player from the opposition, the one who was the main reason they lost the final. She read numerous articles about revenge attacks. Seemed young boys did not take defeat very well. She understood their anger. Just reading about their situation brought back painful memories for her.

She was just about ready to move onto the next town or village when her senses picked up a threat nearby. So she was right to be here after all. She doubted it was Tampong; the sensation did not feel the same, but it could be one of the Lower Middle keeping a low profile . . . or trying to. Or else, and more likely, it was this new sensation she felt earlier. Everyone in both groups knew that when one member of a group was in close proximity to a member from either the same or the other group, then their senses went on alert. That was exactly the sensation she felt today. She knew Tampong and knew when she was around. This was something else, something new and something definitely threatening. She was determined to track the source down, starting tonight.

Meanwhile, Terry was so nervously excited he almost ran into the house, forcing Tampong to stand up quickly when he entered.

'What is it?' she asked, worry dripping from her voice.

'She's here.'

'***What***!'

'She's here,' he repeated.

'Are you sure?'

He leaned his head to one side as if the say '*seriously*?'

'You are positive it was her?'

'My senses picked up on her, and she picked up on me.'

'But she didn't know it was you?'

'No, she looked over but only saw me kissing Karen.'

'You kissed Karen!'

'Seriously! You want to discuss my love life right now when Shoil was on the other side of the street!'

'No, no, of course not. What did she do exactly? Shoil I mean.'

'Well, she must have been walking down the road when she suddenly stopped, I assume that would be when she sensed my presence. She looked around and then started walking back down the street again.'

'Okay, okay,' said Tampong.

She was now pacing back and forth.

'So she sensed someone but did not know who it was. She would know me as much as I would know her, so she knew it wasn't me.'

'Could it be someone else from our group?'

'No, they are all dead. We are the last.'

'Except for Shoil,' he corrected.

'Except for her, of course.'

'Could she think it was one from the other group?'

'Possibly,' Tampong agreed, half thinking, 'but whatever she thinks, it means she will not be leaving any time soon. She will immediately start hunting for the source.'

'Meaning?'

'Meaning we may have to leave tomorrow morning.'

'And go where?'

'As far away as possible.'

'No, I am not running away again. She will only track us down.'

'We need more time, Terry. You need more training and need to be stronger.'

'No, we are not running. Not this time. I sensed fear in her.'

'Fear?'

'Yes, fear. I am something new, and she doesn't know what or who I am. We can turn this to our advantage.'

'I think your head is being ruled by your heart right now.'

'No, no it's not. Let's stand and fight if she wants to. Let's finish this once and for all.'

'You don't know what you are saying. You have no experience of battle and have no idea what she is capable of.'

'And she has no idea of what I am capable of either.'

'I cannot argue with that.'

'Then let's do it, let's stand our ground.'

Tampong could see the determination in his eyes. She knew he was still very young, but she was actually younger when she had her first battle, one she only just survived. He was right as well. They couldn't keep on running. Eventually Shoil would catch up with them, and perhaps it was better to know where she was than be surprised by her. The very fact she was here in York meant that she had a very strong sense of smell and had been able to track them here. She sighed.

'Ok, we stay, but we do this my way, OK?'

'You got it, boss,' he replied enthusiastically. 'Ho, by the way, I was planning to go around to Colin's tomorrow. It's the final of the World Cup and his parents have just bought a large TV. Is that alright?'

Colin lived just around the corner, and she knew his telephone number.

'Fine,' she reluctantly agreed, 'but you call me when you arrive and when you leave. Agreed?'

'Agreed, and thanks.'

Terry rushed upstairs with Karen still on his mind. He couldn't wait for Saturday to come. Today had been one of the best days of his life, and he had never felt so alive. He was so lucky to have found her. The only blip during the whole day was Shoil suddenly showing up, but she didn't know he was the one she sensed. If she did, he very much doubted if he would be standing in his bedroom right now. He had to be careful and knew that, providing he did not move into his other form, he would be shielded from her. The only risk was if she was in close proximity to him, then they would sense each other, and he couldn't chance another encounter. She would surely click that it was either him or Karen that was the source of the sensation. He could not risk putting her in harm's way. Still, there was not a lot he could do about that today, and besides, he was not seeing her again until Saturday, so she would be safe until then.

***

Shoil sat on her tiny sofa in her tiny apartment in a foul mood. She had consumed three men that afternoon, but it did nothing to change her mood. She knew she was close, but still no sighting. There was clearly something she was missing. She recapped her steps for the day and recalled all those she saw. When she felt that presence the only two people around were a young couple kissing on the other side of the road. She focused on the two of them, trying to picture them again. She only saw the face of the boy because his eyes were looking at her.

She sat bolt upright. His eyes were looking at *her*!

If it was a lovers' embrace, then his eyes should have been closed, not open. Why would a boy be looking across the street if he were kissing his girlfriend? Either he was not really interested in her and just looking to bed her, or something else caused him to look towards Shoil. She knew she was not unattractive to men, but this was something else. Could it have been her presence that caused him to open his eyes, no, forced him to open his eyes? Was he the source, after all?

How could she have missed such an obvious trait? But this did not make any sense. If he *was* the source, then *where* did he come from? She guessed he must have been in his mid to late teens, so that ruled out any recent sexual activity by Tampong. He could have been the result of a Lower Middle having sex with a human. That would explain the alien sensation she felt. Yes, that must be it. If he was indeed the source, then he must be the spawn of a Lower Middle, perhaps an unwanted or unexpected child. If so, that means there must be a Lower Middle member close by as well. She licked her lips in anticipation. She just needed to track the boy down again and follow him around until he led her to the Lower Middle member, most likely the mother. She would then take them both out, making sure that whoever gave birth to the boy would be the one to watch him die before her own life was taken by Shoil. She then cursed herself for letting the boy go but felt sure she could track him down again in her dog form. She would return to the point where she last saw him and see if she could sniff him out. That would work.

She had a plan. It had been a full year since the source had revealed itself to her, and now it was very close. She would not let this one slip by so easily. This time she would find it and deal with it.

It was a good plan.

***

About a hundred miles away, Gary also sensed the change both Terry and Shoil initiated as a result of their close proximity. He was also puzzled by the alien sensation and was also pondering the possibilities. This was definitely new, but stronger this time, as if the new contact was actually growing.

'Actually growing,' he said aloud.

Tracey looked across at him.

'What's growing?'

'Ho nothing, I was just thinking aloud.'

'Don't give me that, Gary. I know you all too well.'

'OK. Listen, I felt a new sensation some time ago and felt it again this morning, only this time it felt different, stronger even.'

'As if it was growing.'

'As if it was growing,' he repeated.

'What do you think it is?'

She knew better than to question his judgement. He was fine-tuned to any unusual disturbances, and the group had been saved on more than one occasion because of this.

'Not sure. Growing would suggest a child.'

'A child?'

Tracey sat up straight.

'Whose child could it be?'

'Again, not sure. We know that Shoil escaped the battle and, most likely, Tampong too.'

'Neither strikes me as a motherly kind,' Tracey remarked.

Gary nodded in agreement, then stopped.

'Unless desperation forced them into this move.'

'In order to increase their numbers?'

'Right.'

'But if they had intercourse with a human male, there is no guarantee that the child would inherit the woman's abilities, right?'

'As far as we know, yes. But let's consider the possibilities that the child did inherit the mother's abilities—and more if she had absorbed any members—which seems more likely given these strange sensations I am having.'

'That's a scary thought.'

'Tell me about it. But let's play this through. If the child of the Higher Middle did exist, then it could be even more powerful than its mother, once it reaches maturity.'

'Which is when?'

'Puberty.'

'So, what do we do then?'

'We need to track the source down and kill it.'

'Can you really kill a child?'

'I would not see it as a child but as a member of the Higher Middle, an enemy.'

'Would you really?'

'I hope so, for our sakes.'

There was no conviction in his voice.

'Should we contact Joanne to let her know?'

'No, not for now. Let's see what we can find out and, if necessary, call for reinforcements then.'

'But if it is indeed a child, then surely the mother will be close by.'

Gary nodded.

'True.'

'Then we do need reinforcements, particularly if it is Shoil we are up against and any bastard child that she may have produced. You haven't forgotten how she changes into that monster dog, have you?'

'Of course I haven't. Here is what I suggest. We track it or them down and then call for reinforcements when we identify the source and the players involved, and we know what we are up against.'

'Assuming they don't track us down first.'

'They won't.'

'God, I hope you are right.'

'So do I, Tracey, so do I.'

'Do you know where they are?' she asked.

'I have a vague idea of their general location. We should head for Yorkshire.'

'Yorkshire? Really?'

'Really. We start there.'

***

After lunch on Sunday Terry stood up, gave Tampong a quick peck on the cheek, then turned towards the front door.

She placed her hand on the cheek he kissed.

'What was that for?' she asked.

'Just because,' he answered, shrugging his shoulders.

'OK, then thanks! Enjoy the match,' she called after him.

'I will, see you later.'

He swung his arms through his coat, closed the front door and leaped over the fence towards Colin's house. It took him only minutes to arrive, banging his fist on the door for attention. Colin opened the door.

'No need to bang the door down, you know.'

'Didn't want to miss the start.'

'You need not rush. It doesn't start until this evening.'

'Really? You never mentioned that little piece of important information.'

'Oh, sorry, but I thought you would have been listening to the match commentators, like I was.'

'OK smart-arse. Can I still wait with you?'

'Sure. You can tell me all about that cute little bird you pulled.'

He looked back over Terry's shoulder.

'She's not with you then?'

'Nope. She has to get herself ready for work tomorrow.'

'Shame.'

He looked genuinely disappointed.

'As we have some spare time, then perhaps we can play football on your PlayStation 2.'

'OK, but you are definitely going to tell me how you and Karen got on. You are still together, right?'

'Yep. We are still together. As I said, she just does not have the time to watch the game with us. But you were right though. She does like watching the game. Now, about this PlayStation game?'

'What about Stan? What has he said about all of this? Does he even know you went out with her?'

'You ask a lot of questions, mate, but Stan is ancient history now, so let's play.'

'OK, but I am going to be England this time.'

'Fine, then I'll be Germany.'

'OK, hopefully we will not have the same result as in this year's World Cup tournament.'

'Yeah, tell me about it. Four to one was a bit of a hammering.'

'Don't remind me.'

Colin closed the door behind them. They did not know they were being watched. Tampong had kept a discreet distance from him, following Terry to make sure he arrived safely. She knew she needed to get back quickly as he promised to call her as soon as he arrived. The second she put her foot through the front door the phone rang. She picked it up.

'Checking in,' said Terry, 'arrived safe and sound. By the way, the game does not start until this evening, so I will not be back until late.'

'How late?'

'Maybe around eleven pm, particularly if the game goes into extra time and penalties. Anything is possible.'

'Ok. Back by eleven thirty then. You have school tomorrow. Enjoy the game.'

'Will do.'

The boys settled down in front of the TV. Colin had prepared a large bowl of popcorn, together with two large bottles of Coke. He placed a cassette into the PlayStation console.

'Right,' he said, switching on the TV and PlayStation, 'let's get this party started.'

They were quickly emersed in the game and lost all track of time. They were into their third match, the previous two being drawn, when Colin glanced at the wall clock.

'Jesus!' he exclaimed, 'it's just after eight pm, the match has just started.'

'Crickey! Where did the time go!'

'Time passes quickly when you are enjoying yourself, mate. Let's hope the evening continues in the same spirit with the real match.'

He switched the TV channel, and the match was into its fourth minute, still goalless.

They sat in silence and watched the first half, munching their popcorn and taking swigs from their bottles. Halftime arrived and the two boys looked at each other.

'More like rugby than football,' commented Colin.

'You can say that again,' agreed Terry, 'Webb has already dished out loads of yellow cards. I am surprised there are still twenty-two men on the pitch.'

'Holland are definitely targeting Xavi and Iniesta. They are out to stop Spain playing at all cost. Mind you, Robbins had a couple of decent chances. Should have done better on at least one occasion.'

'I hope the ref puts a stop to all these fouls. Somebody is going to get injured if it carries on like this. Anyway, changing the subject, how was your date with Karen? We never got to talk about her.'

'Great. We got on really well.'

'Seeing her again?'

'Of course.'

'Did you kiss her?'

'A gentleman never tells.'

'Bollocks. Did you kiss her?'

'Yes.'

'And?'

'And what?'

'Did she make you horny?'

'Mind your own business.'

'She did, didn't she? You had a hard-on.'

'I said mind your own business. Hey, the second half will be starting soon.'

'Did you talk about sex?'

'On a first date?'

'Of course. Girls like to know how experienced their date is.'

'Really?'

'Of course.'

'What if they have no experience?'

Colin raised both eyebrows in surprise, and he nearly dropped his Coke, just managing to put it back on the table.

'You're a virgin!' he barked.

'Mind your own business.'

'Wow, you're a virgin. Don't worry, girls like that.'

'How would you know; you are the same age as me.'

'Believe me, I know. I have been with girls too. Well, one to be honest, but we did it a couple of times.'

'You have had sex! What was it like?'

'Fantastic. The girl I was with was definitely not a virgin and knew her way around a man's body.'

'Does it hurt?'

'Not for us guys. Apparently for the girl it hurts the first time you penetrate her, but once she gets wet, then it just slides in and out nicely.'

'She gets wet?'

'Her pussy does once she is turned on. Smells a bit too, but you get used to that.'

'Wow, I never knew it was so complicated.'

Colin laughed and nudged Terry.

'It comes naturally, mate, once you are with a girl who wants you.'

'How do you know?'

'You just do. Hey, the second half is starting.'

They settled down to watch the second half, which followed the same pattern as the first half, with Holland trying to kick Spain off the pitch. Spain continued with their slick passing game, despite Holland's multiple attempts to stop them.

'Holland will not beat Spain playing like this,' announced Colin after thirty minutes.

'Agreed,' said Terry, 'they cannot get their playmakers like Sneijder and Robben into the game. They have hardly touched the ball.'

Full time arrived and still no goals.

'Going for a quick pee,' remarked Colin.

He rushed upstairs. Terry reflected on their conversation about girls and was interested to know how it felt to have sex with girls, particularly with Karen. He knew he was currently underage, but that didn't stop Colin. Perhaps he should talk with Tampong . . . or perhaps not.

Colin returned with another two bottles of Coke, passing one to Terry, who refilled his glass and took a long, refreshing gulp of the fizzy pop. The second period of extra time started and still no breakthrough, although Spain was taking control of the match. Both boys stood to their feet when the ref awarded a goal kick for an obvious corner.

'Corner ref,' they both shouted.

'He must be blind,' remarked Colin.

'Blinded by all the yellow cards he has been dishing out,' added Terry.

The inevitable red card arrived after 109 minutes when Jonny Heitinga was sent off for an early shower after picking up his second yellow card.

'Looks like this is going down to penalties,' observed Colin.

No sooner did he say that when Spain scored. Since coming on as a substitute, Fabregas had been bossing the midfield. It was his through ball to Iniesta that freed him up and he struck the ball well.

'***GOAL***,' the boys screamed out together.

They hugged each other in celebration.

'No more than they deserved,' said Colin.

Terry just nodded in agreement.

The game ended and Spain became the first team to win the World Cup after losing their opening game of the tournament.

They watched the trophy presentation when Terry glanced at his watch.

'Wow, I'd better get going. It's late.'

'OK, I'll call your aunt and let her know you are on your way.'

'Thanks, mate. Turned out to be a good game in the end if you forget the first half.'

'Right. Holland is a good team and will win the World Cup one year. Not playing like that though.'

'You said it. See you, mate.'

'Yep. See you.'

Colin closed the front door and moved to the phone to dial home for Terry.

'He's on his way back,' he said when Tampong picked up the phone, almost immediately.

'Great, thanks for letting me know, Colin. Enjoy the match?'

'Yeah, turned out not too bad in the end. I am off to bed now. Have a good night.'

'You too.'

She returned the phone to its cradle and went to the window. She waited for five minutes until she saw the silhouette of a boy turning into the street. She sat on the sofa and picked up her book, pretending to read.

Terry walked in and saw her. He was not fooled.

'Pretending you are reading then?'

'I don't know what you mean,' she replied in her best innocent voice.

'Sure. Well, I'm off to bed.'

'Good night,' she shouted as he disappeared upstairs.

'Night,' he replied.

He brushed his teeth, got undressed and slipped into bed. He didn't think about football but of Karen and what it might be like to be in bed with her. He went to sleep very quickly with a smile on his face.

At two in the morning a large dog could be seen skulking down the street. It sniffed at every gate and lamppost. It trotted past Colin's house but stopped. It sniffed the gate and the pavement around it. Its orange eyes glowed brightly in the night, like cats' eyes reflected by the headlights of a car. It looked around and growled, then moved on down the road.

The smell was different but not what she was looking for. Tampong had a unique scent, and she would know it instantly. This was most likely the boy who had recently passed. He would have made a quick meal but smelled too new, untouched, uneatable. It was the latter realization that made her growl.

Both Tampong and Terry opened their eyes simultaneously. Both rushed out of their bedroom, almost colliding into each other.

'Did you sense her too?' she asked nervously.

Terry gulped down phlegm. 'Yes.'

'You stay right here. I am going to check through the window.'

'Be careful,' he pleaded.

She slowly moved to the edge of the window, pulling the curtain very slowly open. She expertly scanned the road up and down.

Nothing.

She closed her eyes and reached out with her senses but felt nothing. Terry walked up behind her, almost making her jump.

'Anything?' he asked.

'No, nothing.'

'Good, but it was definitely her.'

'Agreed. She is hunting for us, so we need to be extra careful.'

'Right,' replied Terry, half listening as he too was looking down the road.

At the same time, Colin was staring out of his bedroom window and watched as the biggest dog he had ever seen was walking towards his house. He could not sleep, and a noise stirred him from his slumber. He held his breath when the animal stopped right outside his gate and appeared to look right at him. He continued to watch as the animal began to trot down the road. It was the eyes that really frightened him. They were orange and exceptionally large. He had never seen an animal with orange eyes before, and these seemed to light up in the night, like torchlights. They also looked evil. He dared not move a muscle in case the beast saw him. It eventually turned its head away and continued walking down the street. He walked back to his bed and slid under the covers, pulling them up to his neck.

He was not going back to sleep. His ears were listening now in case the monster returned.

He hoped not.

***

The next morning, Shoil was in yet another foul mood. She had lost the scent. The trail had definitely gone cold. She wished she had the foresight to follow the two lovers when she first saw them. Now it was like looking for a needle in a haystack. Why didn't her instincts kick in? Could they have been the link back to Tampong? Just thinking about her name brought even more rage. She stalked down the road, looking down and not noticing the man coming towards her until he was remarkably close. He walked past her, giving her a pleasing look up and down. That was when she noticed him.

'What are you staring at?' she snapped.

'Pardon me?' he replied.

He was tall and extremely black. His white eyes shot wide open by her surprise rebut of his stare.

'I said, what are you staring at, mister? Never seen a girl before?'

'Well, not a white one as pretty as you I haven't. Not for a long time, man. And particularly not one walking down the street in her birthday suit.'

'*Birthday suit*?' she repeated the words to herself, then looked down at her body.

She was naked.

She forgot that she had been prowling for Tampong in her animal form, and when she transformed, she was naked again. Her nakedness did not really bother her, so she straightened her body up and turned to face the man.

'Like what you see then?'

'Well, I was just admiring you. Nothing wrong with that, is there?'

'Looking for more?'

'What you are saying, woman?'

She looked up and down the road. All was quiet.

'You heard me, or are you both deaf and stupid?'

'Hey, listen up, missy, I ain't about to take no crap from a naked snowdrop.'

'Snowdrop?'

'Yeah, snowdrop. What, is you deaf and stupid too?'

His white teeth were clearly visible. To any normal young woman, this man would be quite intimidating. But Shoil was no ordinary woman.

He waved a hand in her direction, indicating that the conversation was over and went to turn and walk away.

'Nice titties though, for a snowdrop,' he remarked.

She felt her fingers harden. With the speed of lightning, not giving the man a chance to react, she thrust her fingers into his stomach and buried them deep. The man's mouth dropped open in shock and he took a sudden involuntary intake of breath. Shoil's body began to change. Hair quickly appeared all over her skin as her face slowly stretched out. Her body started to hunch over, forcing her onto all fours, her fingers still buried in the man's stomach. His body started to shrink, forcing his clothing off and to fall to the floor as she completely changed into her dog form. The man started groaning, so she silenced him with a quick snap of his throat with her bare teeth, then dragged him around the corner onto a quiet road. She was still full of rage and decided to take it out on this now still body. She started to plunge her claws into the man's diminishing body. Blood spurted from his new wounds, but she ignored it and quickened her attacks. He was long dead, but this didn't stop her as she continued to rip into the man's body, taking large chunks of flesh in her mouth and swallowing them whole. She kept swiping and ripping the body until all that was left was a bloody mess of bone and clothing. The man was unrecognizable now. She stepped back, snarled one last time at the man, then trotted off down the road.

What she didn't know was that there was a street camera bolted onto the post right opposite her, and it was activated by movement, their movement, and it was filming the attack.

When she reached her temporary apartment she had changed back to her human form, still completely naked, although mostly covered in the man's blood now. She realized she had lost control again and allowed her dog form to take charge. She couldn't allow that to happen anymore and needed to control her rage better. She was going to have to buy herself some new clothes as she had no idea where she left her original outfit. This hunt was beginning to get expensive.

She ran a bath and slipped under the hot water. She felt calmer now, so she sunk her head under the water to wash to blood off.

***

The train rolled slowly into the station. Gary watched from his seat window as the sign indicating York passed his window. He nudged a sleeping Tracey and her eyes blinked open.

'We have arrived?' she asked, rubbing sleep from her eyes.

'We have,' he confirmed.

He did not want to bring her with him as he knew this was going to be a long and possibly dangerous trip, but she could be very stubborn, and he knew it was going to be just about impossible to convince her to stay.

'If you are going into danger, then so am I,' she had told him earlier.

From her look of determination, he knew that arguing would be useless.

Tracey stood up and pulled her rucksack from the overhead shelf then slipped her arms through the handles. Gary pulled the small suitcase down off the rack, and they both stepped out of the train.

'Where to now?' she asked.

'Out of the station, and our hotel should be just around the corner somewhere.'

'Which is?'

'The Hilton Hotel,' he informed her.

'Wow,' she answered, clearly impressed, 'it should be a nice place then.'

'One of the nicest in York for the price, so I am told,' he advised.

'Could you not get something cheaper?'

'Not a lot to choose from at the last minute, and we got in at the Hilton because they just had a cancellation.'

'Lucky us, then,' she said, 'do you know where it is exactly?'

'Downing Street, which, as I said, should just be around the next corner if my memory serves me well.'

Tracery knew better than to question his memory. She guessed he had memorized the city map in minute detail and was confident he knew exactly where he was going.

'Not number ten by any chance?' she quizzed.

They both laughed. Neither realizing just how much they needed to laugh. It broke the tension both had been holding back, so they immediately held hands as they walked down the street.

They walked around the corner and Tracey gasped when she saw the facade of the impressive building. Long white pillars dominated the front of the building. As they entered the hotel, they were greeted by beautifully engraved wooden floors with backlights lighting up all the walls. There were multiple reception desks, all with wood paneling façades and numerous potted plants completing the luxurious ambiance. They walked up to the first free reception desk and were greeted by a cheerful young man. Gary guessed he must be in his early twenties, but brimming with confidence.

'Welcome to the Hilton,' he began, 'how may I be of assistance?'

'We have reservations. Mr. and Mrs. Hardgrove.'

He heard Tracey give a quiet snort of surprise but did not turn his head.

'Yes, here we are. We see you have reserved a double room. Unfortunately, we do not have any such rooms available at the moment, so we have upgraded you to one of our Executive King bedroom suites. We trust that you find this acceptable.'

'Most acceptable,' replied Tracey before Gary could respond.

'These are the most luxurious suites we offer our guests, with amazing views of the city. We also offer complimentary drinks from six pm onwards.'

'Ho, so we have missed that opportunity then?' asked Gary.

'Certainly not, sir,' countered the receptionist, 'I have arranged for a welcome drink for you both in your room.'

'Very thoughtful,' he replied, 'is there any extra cost for the upgrade?'

'Absolutely not, sir. This is our problem, not to be able to accommodate your first choice.'

'That's nice,' he answered.

Gary handed over his credit card. The receptionist swiped it quickly and handed it back. He then made a few notes on several pieces of paper and finally handed Gary their room key.

'You are on the top floor sir, room 815. Do you have any bags, sir?'

'No, thank you, we are travelling light.'

'Might do some shopping tomorrow, though,' added Tracey as she slipped her arm through Gary's.

The receptionist had seen this all before and guessed that when they checked out, they would do so with one or two suitcases.

'Very good, sir. Allow me to escort you to your room. If you will follow me.'

He stepped out from behind the reception desk and indicated them to follow him to the elevator. He pressed the shiny gold button and the doors silently opened. After they all stepped in, he pressed the eighth-floor button. The elevator was noticeably quiet and smooth, with gentle piano music playing in the background. The doors opened, indicating they had reached their floor, and the receptionist stepped out and walked quickly down the corridor. They followed him. He stopped outside a large door and held out his hand for the key card, which Gary passed to him. He touched the door lock, and a click could be heard. As he swung the door open, he stepped aside to allow them to enter. They were greeted with a spacious bedroom boasting a king-size bed. The receptionist followed them in.

'At the side of the bed you will find the remote control for the curtains, TV, and heating. If you need anything at all, just pick up the receiver.'

'Great, and thank you.' Gary handed him a twenty-pound tip.

The receptionist looked pleased.

'Thank you, sir. I wish you and madam a very pleasant evening.'

He closed the door behind him.

Tracey raised her arms over her head and fell backwards into the bed.

'This is heavenly,' she remarked.

'It is, but just remember why we are here. This is *not* a holiday trip.'

'Spoilsport. But we can still enjoy the stay here, can't we?'

Her pleading eye could melt butter, he thought.

'Sure,' he added, 'why not?'

'Great. Then I am off for a shower.'

'Then we go hunting,' he countered.

'OK, OK,' she reluctantly agreed, 'but only after we have eaten, OK?'

'OK,' he agreed.

He had to admit that he also felt hungry, as they hadn't eaten all day.

'I'll book the restaurant downstairs,' he called after her, but she never heard him.

Fifty minutes later they arrived outside the restaurant and a waiter quickly confirmed their reservation before ushering them to their table. They sat opposite each other. Gary had the view of the entrance. He preferred to see who was coming and going, while Tracey had the view of the long bar, complete with TV. Gary ordered a sirloin steak while Tracey opted for salmon. The waiter arrived with two salads, and they ate in silence. When the main meal arrived, Gary decided to break the silence.

'I thought we could start looking down the quieter streets,' he began. 'Shoil is not one who likes to parade herself to the public.'

He looked up, but Tracey was not listening to him. Her fork was raised in the air as if to eat, but her face was fixed to a point directly behind him. He turned around to see what she was looking at but only saw three people sitting at the bar.

'What is it?' he asked nervously.

'The TV,' she whispered, 'look at the TV.'

His eyes fixed on the TV. It was showing the end of a brutal attack by an exceptionally large dog. He couldn't tell what the animal was attacking, but it looked large and quite dead. He slipped out of his chair and moved closer to the bar, his eyes never leaving the screen. As he moved closer, he could make out the end of the TV commentator's news.

'The police have now begun a search of the area and warned all local inhabitants to be vigilant and report any sighting of this strange and dangerous beast.'

The barman noticed Gary watching the screen.

'That's some creature, isn't it, sir?'

'Sure is,' agreed Gary, 'do you know what happened?'

'Apparently this big dog-like monster, more like a small horse if you ask me, was picked up by a street camera dragging a body around the corner. Then it just started to maul the poor soul and eat it.'

'It ate it?'

'Right, the police said it must have taken large chunks of the man's flesh and eaten it. This is something right out of a horror movie. Never seen anything like this before. Definitely staying inside until this thing is caught.'

'Wise, very wise,' agreed Gary.

He turned and walked back to his table. He looked down at his half-eaten meal but pushed the plate away.

'I suddenly don't feel hungry anymore,' he said.

Tracey lowered the fork she was still holding.

'Me neither.'

When the waiter returned, he asked if everything was OK. Gary just explained that they were full but that the meal was very nice. He signed for their meal and they returned to their room, not saying a word until they closed the door. Gary picked up the remote and switched the TV on. He flicked the channels until he came across the local news. The headlines arrived and the presenter introduced himself.

'We start with a horrific attack by an incredibly large animal in the heart of York City yesterday evening, made all the more incredible as it was captured by a city security camera. What we are about to show you is very disturbing, so we recommend those of a sensitive disposition and young children do not watch the next couple of minutes.'

The image changed to a camera view of a street. It obviously had movement sensors and switched on as soon as the large animal appeared from a corner, dragging what looked like a large body. Gary and Tracey recognized the beast. It was Shoil. Tracey placed her hand on his shoulder, and he in turn placed his hand on hers. They continued to watch as Shoil needlessly started to attack the still body. Slashing at the abdomen, legs, and head. It was a frenzied attack. The beast lowered its head at regular interviews, apparently taking large bites out of the body. The frenzy continued until the image was phased out to be replaced by the presenter again, looking slightly paler.

He coughed.

'The attack took place in Duncombe Place, and this morning local police are warning nearby residents to be vigilant and not go out at night unless absolutely necessary. Police were able to identify the victim only because his wallet was still in his jacket pocket. No motive has yet been suggested, although police have not ruled out a racist attack. And now for other news . . .'

Tracey and Gary stared at each other.

'Well, at least we know her last whereabouts now,' she said.

'Right, but I wonder what caused that frenzied attack.'

'God knows. Perhaps she is changing more and more into that animal thing, rather than the woman she is or was.'

'God, I hope not. She looked bigger than before, and even stronger.'

'Agreed. So I assume we start looking around the park.'

She clicked her fingers, causing Gary to look up at her.

'Hey, just a minute. If she moved into her true form, how come you didn't sense her?'

'I have been wondering the same thing. I can only think it is because none of the group members were close to her.'

'Could be,' answered Tracey unconvincingly.

Gary didn't believe his own words either, which worried him more than anything else. He shook his head, knowing he needed to do something, but not sure what. He had felt her changing before. Could he have been too distracted to have noticed? Somehow he doubted that. If she was able to cloak herself from him, then she had just upped her game to a whole new level. This scared him more than anything else.

'Right, where is this place then, Duncombe Place?' he said instead, trying to shake the nasty thought from his mind.

Tracey stood and moved towards the dressing table. She pulled open the drawer and rifled through its contents and pulled a city street map out. She opened it up and quickly scanned the index for the street. She then tapped the map.

'Here,' she said, turning it around to face him.

She had her finger still pointing at the street.

'It's a street map of York City,' she informed him.

'Perfect.'

She tapped the spot again, so he leaned his head closer.

'Duncombe Place,' he announced, 'just off of the park. It is about a ten-minute walk from here.'

'OK, then what are we waiting here for?'

'You seem keen to find her.'

'I am keen to see an end to this, one way or another.'

He didn't like the way she finished her sentence, meaning it was either them or her.

Tracey turned to face him, concern etched across her face.

'Do you think we should try and contact Joanne now, let her know what we know?'

'Maybe.'

He was having the same thoughts.

'Hey,' snapped Tracey, 'you don't think that Shoil actually had a pup in that animal form of hers, do you?'

'Somehow I doubt it, mainly because that would mean she would have had to have mated with another dog.'

'Wouldn't put it past that bitch,' countered Tracey, tapping her bottom lip, 'particularly if she lost control like she did during that horrible video.'

He had to concede that she had a point. That would certainly explain these new sensations he had been feeling. If so, god help them and the world. If the Higher Middle had taken to animal sources for soldiers, then this marked a major turning point in this conflict.

'Perhaps you are right. Perhaps we should inform Joanne about what we have learned and seen here, just in case.'

'You mean just in case she finds us and takes us out.'

'Something like that, dear, something like that.'

'So, do you know how to contact her then?'

'We need to get back to London for me to do that. I think a face-to-face is necessary. Don't want to talk over an open line, nor send any electronic message.'

Tracey looked around the room.

'Sure do like this hotel and will be sorry to leave it.'

'We can always return. In fact, we will have to if we all agree to continue the hunt for Shoil.'

'Not sure I want to return here, now that I have just seen her attack again, but you are right, as usual.'

'Let's take a quick look around the area she was last seen in and see if we pick up any trail or scent. Then we can definitely decide on our next move.'

'OK, you're the boss.'

He just smiled. Inside he did not feel as though he was in charge of anything. Too many strange things were happening, but they could only deal with one problem at a time and, for now, it was a case of seeing if they could pick up Shoil's trail. He did not feel optimistic as she tended to be very good at hiding her tracks. His only hope was that she was not so careful in her frenzied animal form. He would find out soon enough.

'So, are we still going hunting now or not?' Tracey asked, snapping him out of his thoughts.

'What, ho, yes, I think we should still see if we can locate her. The more information we have the better.'

'If you say so, boss.'

Tracey's shoulders mentally sagged. She was not looking forward to any face-to-face with Shoil and felt sure they would be better prepared if Joanne was with them. However, she knew that Gary would never expose her to unnecessary risk, so she felt safe as long as she was close to him.

***

Terry did feel Shoil's change though. He was staring blankly out in front of him. Tampong looked up from her book and noticed.

'What is it?' she asked.

'She's killed again,' he answered simply.

'And?'

'This time it was different. She was angry, terribly angry. She attacked a man with such violence, not thinking about what she was doing, no attempt to absorb the man, just pummeling him to death. Taking large bites from him, leaving him a messy, unrecognizable lump in the road.'

Tampong dropped her book and slid across to Terry. She opened her arms and he leaned into her chest.

'It was horrible,' he added.

She stroked his hair to calm him. She could only imagine the horrors he saw, could only imagine the pain he must be feeling, but he wasn't shaking. He was quite calm in fact.

'It was incredible. Such strength, such power.'

She looked down at him.

'Why do you say that?'

'Because it's true. Shoil has immense power.'

'She is very dangerous,' Tampong added.

'Of course she is. All powerful things are considered dangerous. Anything you cannot control is labelled dangerous, by the weak.'

'By the weak?'

'Yes, by the weak.'

'Do you consider me weak?'

'If you say she is dangerous, then yes.'

She didn't like the direction this conversation was going, nor the way he was speaking. It was like he was being influenced by Shoil, being seduced by her power in some way. Perhaps she was impressing him, trying to persuade him to reveal himself to her. She could not allow that to happen.

'OK, then I guess I am weak,' she admitted.

'Good that you accept that,' he answered plainly, 'but I don't consider her that dangerous, just a little lost at present.'

'Lost?'

'Yes, she needs to find her way back into the group.'

'The group is all but gone. Only you and I remain of the Higher Middle.'

'Right, but if we all came together, we could defeat the Lower Middle that take our rightful place as rulers of this earth.'

She pulled him away from her and looked into his eyes. They were searching hers, looking for a response, looking for an answer.

'Why would you say that?'

'Because that is our purpose, our objective, our way of life.'

She clenched her teeth together, taking a long inhaling breath.

'That is not the way anymore.'

He leaned back, examining her almost with contempt. She had never seen him look at her this way before. It felt like a stab straight through the heart.

'It is the way of the Higher Middle,' he continued, 'we are destined to rule these pathetic human creatures. To do with them as we so please.'

'That's Zelphur talking,' she snapped.

He blinked twice on hearing the name and suddenly his expression changed. The old Terry was back.

'No, that was me talking, but I don't know why I said that.'

He stood up and started to walk out of the lounge.

'Where are you going?' she asked.

'To my room. I need to be alone.'

'This conversation is not over, Terry. We will talk again.'

'Yes, I know. Something is happening to me. I am changing. I don't know if this is a good thing or a bad thing.'

'Whatever it is, we will get through this together.'

'I hope so,' he answered quietly as he began to walk upstairs.

She watched him mount the stairs, unable to stop a tear running down her cheek. She ignored it. This connection he had with Shoil was starting to affect him. Changing him. She hardly recognized the boy sitting right in front of her. His eyes looked evil, almost daring her to challenge him. He was another person. She shivered when she recollected who it reminded her of: Shoil. If only she had someone to turn to, someone who understood these things and could help her, and him. But there was no one left, only Shoil, and she would clearly either kill him straight away or completely seduce him into following her. No, whatever she needed to do, she had to do herself. She prayed and hoped that he would not turn into a fully-fledged Higher Middle. She had to be the one who understood the power it can bring, the sense of being in control and able to do just about anything, with anyone, to anyone, at any time. She was not that Higher Middle person anymore, not since the attack on the Federal Reserve Bank, not since she saved Terry. She sat back on the sofa. Had she saved him, or had he saved her? Could he have inherited her Higher Middle genes? Could this be a natural development of his skills and abilities? If so, what was she going to do? She couldn't allow him to turn into one of them, to be a plaything of Shoil's. No. She would kill him before she allowed that to happen. *Kill him.* That was the first time such a thought ever entered her head. It made her cry again.

Terry lay on his bed, reflecting on the events of the day. He turned his hand around in front of his face, making his nails turn hard, then letting them return to their normal state. He had full control and didn't even need to move into his Higher Middle state to do so. He felt himself changing, felt the need for strength and power. The desire to control and rule. He never felt like this before. He had heard people say that you change as you reach puberty. That certainly seemed to be the case with him, but there was something else, something much deeper and darker than just a normal generic change. He had a link to Shoil for a reason, one he didn't understand—yet. She seemed determined, fearless, powerful, and confident. All the things he decided he now admired in a woman. Karen was cute but the complete opposite of Shoil. Karen would be fun to have around for a little while. Perhaps he would lose his virginity to her, or perhaps to Shoil. No, that would not be possible—would it? Tampong said she doubted Shoil could consume him while still a virgin, but she said nothing about the two of them having sex. He let the idea feaster in his mind. It stirred up desires deep inside his body. He felt his underpants become tight, so he slipped them off, only to see his fully erect penis. This was his first, and it felt exciting and mysterious. He felt himself and was surprised at how hard he was. He smiled again and lay down on the bed. He let his mind wander into the dark crevasses of his mind. He thought about Shoil, focused on her, trying to picture her.

And there she was.

He could see her clearly as if she were in his very room. Her long, flowing, wet hair, the swells of her inviting breasts, which lay just above the water's surface, her slim waist being brushed by the water like the tide, and long desirable legs, half submerged. He continued to watch as she turned her head in his direction, and she smiled at him, clearly sensing his presence, but then her face suddenly changed. Gone was the smile, only to be replaced with an ugly sneer. Her teeth began to grow, protruding from her mouth. Blood started to drip from her huge, pointed teeth. Her nose slowly started to stretch out, forcing the mouth out underneath. Then her skin started ripping apart to expose fur. The pupils of her eyes changed from being round, bright blue girlie eyes to diamond-shaped orange cats' eyes. The transformed head glared at him with those deep, penetrating, all-knowing orange eyes. He wanted to end the nightmare, to close his own eyes and make her go away, but he could not move and was frozen in place. It was obvious she wanted him. She wanted his body. That much was clear. But not for sex. Not for the desires he wanted to experience with the sexy naked woman he first saw in the bath, but for power, for his blood, and for his very soul. She wanted all of him.

The head of a huge dog continued to sneer at him until it disappeared under the water, releasing him from his trance.

He rose quickly from his bed, sweating and scared. He checked around the room and was assured she was not with him. He knew in his mind that she couldn't be here, but he needed his eyes to confirm it. He lay back down, confused as to what this all meant. He silently cursed Tampong for giving him this link, giving him the ability to easily kill and see horrors that no boy of his age should witness. It was her blood that started this.

It would be her blood that ends it. Still, he could not stop thinking about the gorgeous, naked woman that Shoil was. He felt certain that Karen would look just as good naked and was determined to find out. Thinking about her calmed him a little, so he lay back down on his bed. Shoil was pure evil and full of every horror you could imagine. She had revealed her true form to him. Wanting him to see her both before and after. Perhaps she was trying to gauge which form he preferred. Well, now she knew.

***

Shoil slowly emerged from under the water. She wiped the hair from her face, which had now returned to its human form, and took a deep, invigorating breath. Something touched her mentally, something wanted her. Something was trying to contact her.

Something was in the room, watching her.

Something was very scared of her when she changed.

As soon as she sensed it, she had gone on the defensive but regretted it now. She showed this strange contact her true self, and it had been scared away. She could not feel it now. But it felt new, fresh, almost innocent. It appeared to know her and her skills. It appeared to enjoy watching her until she changed. It wanted to learn more about her. Wanted to touch her.

'It wanted to touch me,' she said aloud.

She stood up and reached for the towel before she checked her reflection in the mirror. This is what the contact was looking at. Checking out her body, wanting to investigate further, wanting to penetrate her body. Not just touch her as she first thought but wanted to actually penetrate her. She dried herself off before wrapping her dressing gown around her and headed for the bedroom.

'Who are you?' she said aloud. 'What are you?'

No response came, of course. The contact felt real, and she was certain it wanted her. She was now also certain the contact must be male and a group member, but how was that possible? Zelphur had prohibited any sexual activity between group members, except for herself, of course. Could it be that Zelphur had actually given birth to a human child? Could she have hidden such a birth from the rest of them? Knowing her, it was definitely possible. But then who did she mate with? It could not have been that old fart of a man, who was one of them in any case. As far as she knew, Zelphur had met him a few times and only for sex. Could she have mated with him just to give birth, or perhaps mated with an ordinary human male? Both possibilities were interesting. Could this new male now have reached an age that he is developing his skills and has talents similar to Zelphur? If so, then this could be a golden opportunity for her. She could seduce this male and bring him into her lair. Train him to do her bidding and, together, they could hunt down and defeat the remaining Lower Middle, as well as hunt that bitch Tampong. After that, they would then rule this pathetic world, with her as their leader. That must be it. There must be a bastard child somewhere close, trying to reach out to her, trying to be with her. Next time she would not be so quick to frighten it off but try to welcome it and connect with it. Let it think she wanted him too.

She was now in a good mood again, so she helped herself to a stiff drink of whiskey.

'Here's to you,' she said, raising her glass, 'whoever you are and wherever you are. I will find you and welcome you into my fold.'

She drank her glass empty.

'If not, I will kill you and absorb you.'

She thought about her last statement and the excitement inside started to build.

Yes, she thought, *if you are the bastard child of Zelphur, then perhaps you have the memories of Zelphur. That being the case, as soon as I absorb you then I will have all your memories, and hers. All those wonderful resources will then be at my sole disposal.*

She poured herself another large measure of whiskey. She smiled at her reflection. She had a plan.

She was on her way to finally being the one true ruler. The one person she was destined to be. The one person she deserved to be.

***

They had spent the last four hours walking around quiet streets, zigzagging the park, but there was no hint of Shoil. The only signs of life they came across were a couple of lovers walking hand in hand and two homeless men, who had no desire to talk to them but instead warned them off from their sleeping place. Gary stopped for a moment halfway down the street. He felt as though someone was reaching out, trying to make contact. It was not with him, that much he was sure, but with someone close. It could only be Shoil. His worst fears were starting to materialize. If this new source joined forces with her, then the Lower Middle, and the world as a whole, was in trouble. His thoughts were disturbed when Tracey placed her hand on his shoulder for support as she lifted her leg.

'My feet are hurting,' she complained.

She took hold of her foot, slipped her shoe off, and rubbed her heel.

'Right,' he said, looking down at her shoes, 'not exactly best suited for long-distance walking, are they?'

'No! They are designed for a night out in a nice restaurant, or a little dancing perhaps. Not for walking the streets for hours and hours in the dead of the night.'

'OK, let's go back. The trail is cold anyway,' he lied.

He knew there was no point worrying Tracey any more than he needed to. She was the lowest member of their group and, as such, would be the first one the Higher Middle would attack, if they remained true to their form.

'Great. Tomorrow I will buy myself some good trainers and we can continue the search.'

'Somehow I doubt we will find her around here.'

'Why do you say that?'

'Not sure. Just a feeling I guess.'

Tracey wrapped her coat tighter around her body as she slipped her sore foot back into her shoe, making a grunt as she did so.

'Well I for one have learned to trust your feelings, so what are we still doing here then?'

'Not quite sure. Looking for something, I guess, anything, but what that is exactly I have no idea. Right, let's get back to the hotel and discuss our next move.'

'I am right behind you . . . providing you don't walk too quickly.'

She winced with pain as she took a step forward. Gary instinctively came to her side, and she gratefully leaned into him, allowing him to take most of her weight. They slowly made their way down the street

Back at the hotel, Gary ran a bath for Tracey, who slowly undressed. She slipped into the bath and soaked her sore feet.

'Ho, yes,' she screamed out, 'ho, yes.'

Anybody in the next room would have been forgiven for thinking they were having sex.

'Ho yes, yes,' she repeated.

Gary walked into the bathroom.

'Feeling better then?'

'Ho, yes, what a relief that is.'

He turned to leave her in peace.

'Where are you going?' she asked, seeing him about to leave.

'I thought you might like to be alone.'

'Get yourself in here. It is nice and hot. Only my feet hurt, not the rest of me.'

'Yes, ma'am.'

He slipped off his bathrobe and slid into the bath to sit opposite her.

He immediately felt the soothing effects of the warm water on his body.

'Wow, I must admit, that feels good.'

He leaned his head back and slid a little further into the bath. Tracey lifted her legs above his. He instinctively placed his hands on her thigh and rubbed them gently. He also made sure no part of his body touched her still sore feet.

'Right,' announced Tracey in a firm tone, 'so what's our next move?'

'We initially said we would return, hunt out Joanne, and return in force.'

'That is an option,' agreed Tracey, 'except we have no idea where Joanne is, and, if we do go back and do eventually find her, there is no guarantee that Shoil will still be here.'

'So what are you saying?'

'I think we should stay here and continue the hunt. If we locate her, then we try and contact Joanne. Perhaps someone within the MRC knows where she went. If we take a watching stance but not an intervening approach, perhaps we can discover this other presence you are sensing. That way we will know exactly what we are up against.'

'Wow,' he said with eyebrows raised, 'perhaps you should have sore feet more often. It certainly helps clear your mind.'

She raised her legs and splashed the water, soaking him.

'It was meant to be a compliment,' he complained.

'I know,' she said, smiling. 'If I thought for one moment it was an insult, then I would have kicked you and not splashed you.'

'Fair point.'

Tracey's eyes looked towards the ceiling, and he knew she was not finished. He waited and was not disappointed.

'We have not spoken about Tampong.'

'What about her?'

'Well, could she be responsible for this new presence by any chance?'

'What do you mean?'

'Well, she was the one who disappeared from the battle in Fort Knox, was she not?'

'As far as we know, yes.'

'Just before Shoil received that nasty injury that had her scurrying off into the night.'

'Again, as far as we know, yes.'

'Well, one scenario could be that Tampong has had a change of heart and no longer wants to fight, at least against us, and has instead embedded herself with locals and perhaps has even had a child with one of them. That could be the strange presence you are feeling. Could it not?'

Gary thought about her scenario and decided on a guarded response.

'Well, at the risk of getting splashed again.'

She lifted her leg in the air but didn't bring it down . . . yet.

'Your scenario has some interesting points. Let's think it all the way through for a minute and assume she has had a change of heart and did indeed walk away from the battle. If she did have a child, then I imagine that the last person she would want to meet is Shoil. Tampong would, I assume, be very protective of the child, her being a mother. Your scenario would also explain the strange presence I have been feeling, because as her child it must surely have inherited some skills from the mother. I cannot believe it would escape none of her abilities. But that would make the child very young and would not be on its own, which is the sensation I have.'

'So that would rule out either of them having a child then,' surmised Tracey.

'That's what I think.'

'Then that brings us back to what this presence could mean.'

'Right. I think our priority is to try and locate this presence and determine whether it knows who or what it is.'

'So how do we go about that?'

'Sit and wait.'

'Sit and wait?'

'Right.'

'Here?'

'Right again.'

'So you believe this new sensation is also here?'

'I do.'

'Could Shoil have also sensed it and tried to track it down as well?'

'That's certainly a scenario.'

'So we need to find it first.'

'Correct.'

'So what are we to do about money if we stay?'

'Don't worry, I will take care of that.'

'Why am I not surprised you would say that?'

'Hey, just how old are we? Don't you think I would have the sense to put something aside for a rainy day?'

'Guess so, and that's why I love you.'

'Hopefully not the only reason.'

'No, not the only reason,' she confirmed, 'but it is all part of the man you are. The man I want to be with, and the man I am in love with.'

He smiled.

'Perfect response from the perfect woman. Tomorrow morning I'll extend our stay here and we start hunting for this new source.'

'Great. I was in no rush to leave this lovely room.'

'OK, just remember why we are here.'

'Spoilsport.'

She lowered her leg, but this time Gary caught it before it hit the water. He wagged his finger at her. She looked injured but quickly recovered, leaned her head back and enjoyed the bath.

So they at least had a sort of plan. Stay here and continue the hunt but focus on looking for this new sensation. They would not try to find Joanne for the time being but make contact only after they knew what they were up against.

***

Tampong could not sleep. She was worried. Worried about Terry and how he was changing. She knew she had to do something but had no idea was that was. She too had felt an alien sensation, like someone trying to reach out. She felt sure it was Terry. She prayed and hoped that he wasn't trying to contact Shoil. That meeting would not last long. As soon as Shoil sensed that he had Tampong's blood, she would destroy him. No, worse than that, she would absorb him.

'*Heck, no,*' she said aloud.

She could only do that once he had reached puberty and was no longer a virgin.

He had to stay that way for as long as possible.

It was now morning and, having given up trying to sleep, she prepared his breakfast, as usual. She heard him get up and go to the toilet, as usual. Then she continued to listen as he came down the stairs and into the kitchen. She held her breath, not sure what to expect.

'Good morning,' he said cheerfully, sitting down at the table to devour his cereal.

She let her breath out.

'Good morning to you. You sound cheerful this morning. Sleep well?'

'Very well,' he stopped eating and glanced up at her, 'but judging by your face, you did not sleep much.'

'No, one of those restless nights. You know.'

'Not having those dreams again, are you?'

'No, nothing like that. Just a lot on my mind, that's all. Anyway, what are you up to today?'

'School, of course,' he said matter-of-factly.

'Of course, school. And afterwards, will you be seeing Karen again?'

He thought about her question, deciding not to tell her straight away that they had agreed to meet this Saturday. He decided to keep her guessing and play it cool.

'I might, not sure yet.'

'I thought you liked her.'

'I did, I mean, I do. Not sure it is reciprocal, that's all.'

'Well, just ask her.'

'I cannot just walk up to a girl and ask if she likes me. Can I?'

'Of course you can, providing you tell her that you like her first. If she is honest and a decent type, she will tell you yes or no. Mind you, if she is a total bitch, then she will also tell you she likes you, hoping that maybe you will buy her some nice new shoes or something. Bitches are like that.'

'That doesn't help much.'

'No, sorry. Ignore me. You should definitely tell her how you feel though. You might be surprised.'

'OK, I'll think about it. What about you, what are you doing today?'

'Ho, as I am not doing anything this week, I thought I would start looking for another job.'

'Good, you don't like what you are doing anyway.'

'True.'

He stood up and put the bowl in the sink, finished his glass of milk and sat the glass next to the bowl.

'Off to brush my teeth, then get ready for school.'

She watched him go upstairs. He seemed himself again, the old Terry. Relief flooded through her. Perhaps his mood was just that, something teenagers go through, and something she would have to go through with him too. She turned and started filling the dishwasher. By the time she finished, Terry came back downstairs.

'Off to school now. See you later,' he called to her, waving as he disappeared outside.

She waved back but he had already gone.

Just then, the newspaper arrived. She heard it flop onto the carpet, so she went to retrieve it, then returned to the lounge and sat on the sofa. She started to flick through the job section when something caught her eye. She read further.

Terry was walking down the street when Colin caught up with him and patted him on the shoulder.

'What happened to you last night?'

'Nothing, why?'

'I thought you were coming over to play the FIFA game.'

'Ho, right. Problem with my aunt.'

'Really. Gosh, she is one fit bird that one.'

'Hey, that's my aunt you are talking about.'

'I know, but, my god, she is so fit. Besides, it is only your aunt. It's not as if she is your mother or anything. You must invite me around more often.'

'You trying to get it on with my own aunt?'

'I like them older. They come with experience. I bet she can show me a thing or two about sex. Probably got a few special positions as well.'

'Hey,' he replied, pushing his friend, 'cut it out.'

'Just kidding. Actually, I thought you stood me up because you had scored with Karen.'

'Fat chance.'

'Why not?'

'I am too young, for starters, and besides, my aunt would kill me if she found out I slept with her.'

'She doesn't need to know.'

'Ho, believe me, she would know. She has instincts about these things.'

'I hear you, friend. I hear you. Still, if she is gaging for it, and you don't want to help her, then send her in my direction. I would definitely bonk that piece of arse.'

'Again, watch it. First my aunt, now my girlfriend. What kind of friend are you?'

'Hey, did you just say girlfriend?'

'Maybe,' he answered defensively.

'You did, mate, you did. Anyway, I am only pulling your leg. I would never touch her as you are so obviously really interested in her. I wouldn't do that to you, mate.'

'Just as well. I would hate to have to kill my only friend.'

'In your dreams, mate, in your dreams.'

School was its usual mundane event, starting with English, followed by history and then geography before lunch. Afterwards, there was the more interesting art class, and it was there that he saw Karen. It was the only class they attended together. They searched for each other, knowing the other should be in the class. When they found each other, their eyes locked together, at the same time her eyes were smiling back at his—at least that is what it felt like to him. He would never have thought it possible to feel eyes, but he did. He felt warm inside and decided there and then that she must definitely like him. They didn't get the opportunity to talk as they were on opposite sides of the class, with too many classmates in between them, but when she noticed no one else was watching them, she lifted her hand to her ear with her thumb in the air and her little finger pointing outwards, indicating that he should call her. He nodded his understanding. His second favorite class followed. Games. It was originally his favorite, but not since he knew Karen and that they shared art together. He was further rewarded when the teacher informed them that they would be playing football today. His day was just getting better and better.

Later that evening, he picked up the phone in his room and dialed Karen's number. She answered almost immediately.

'Karen?' he asked.

'Yes, is that you, Terry?'

'Yes, it is. How are you?'

'I'm fine. And you?'

'Great, thanks. Listen, I was wondering whether you are still good to go out on Saturday.'

'Of course I am. Any idea where?'

'Yes.'

'And?'

'It's a surprise.'

'Great, I like surprises. What time then?'

'Around seven pm. Meet at the same place?'

'Sounds good to me. Look forward to seeing you then, unless I see you at school before, of course.'

'Likewise. It was great to hear your voice again. I needed that,' she said in a soft voice.

'Likewise. Have a great evening.'

He put the phone down. He had no idea where he was going to take her. He would have a chat with Tampong, she always had good suggestions. He walked back downstairs and into the lounge.

'I have just spoken with Karen, and we have agreed to go out again this Saturday, but I have absolutely no idea where to take her.'

'What about skating?' she asked.

'Skating! I have never been skating in my life. I would make an absolute fool of myself.'

'Do you know if she can skate?'

'I have no idea.'

'Well, if she doesn't, then you can learn together, holding onto to each other, falling together. And if she does, then she can coach you and guide you, again holding onto you to prevent you from falling. It will be fun and, maybe, even a little romantic.'

'Providing I don't land on my arse and break something, if nothing else than my pride.'

'Language,' she barked, but there was no anger in her voice, 'believe me, if she is half the woman you describe, she will love it. You both will.'

'I hope you are right.'

'I am. Trust me on this one. Then take her for a nice meal afterwards. What about the Red Lion?'

'God no. She works there.'

'Aha, so that's why you wanted to go there for your birthday.'

'Busted.'

She leaned over and brushed her hand through his hair.

'I think that is a lovely reason to go. Anyway, there are other nice restaurants in the city. I'll find you one and book a table. My treat.'

'You are too good to me,' he said.

And he meant it.

Saturday evening finally arrived, and smartly at 7 pm he turned the corner, only to discover Karen already waiting for him.

He looked at her nervously.

'Am I late?' he asked.

He looked down at his watch, wondering if perhaps the stupid thing had stopped.

'Not at all,' she replied, 'I just wanted to make sure *I* was not late this time. So, where are we going?'

'Follow me.'

He lifted his hand and pointed towards the main street. They walked for five minutes before stopping at the bus stop. They chatted together for a couple of minutes until the bus arrived. Terry allowed her to board first and bought their tickets. Ten minutes later he stood up and she followed. The bus pulled away to reveal the ice rink center opposite. Her eyes widened in surprise.

'Skating,' she said full of excitement.

'Yes. Is that OK for you?'

'Perfect. Can you skate?'

'Never been on the ice in my life.'

'That's OK. I'll look after you.'

He realized there and then that Tampong was right . . . as usual.

'Perfect,' he replied.

She gently took hold of his hand, and then they almost ran into the building. Terry paid the entrance fee and skate loan, they selected their skates, and then walked up to the edge of the rink, sitting down on the bench. It was when she took her coat off that he saw she was wearing a miniskirt. She saw him notice.

'Not the most practical clothing to wear skating, but that's OK. Professionals actually wear a lot less than this.'

'True,' he chuckled.

In his mind he was silently hoping she might have a little tumble. With such a short skirt, it would surely reveal her knickers. He quickly shook the naughty thought from his mind, but only after taking another pleasing look at her long, soft legs. She expertly tied her skates and was ready before Terry had tied his first boot.

'Here, let me help you.'

She bent down and started tying the laces of his second boot. As she bent towards him, he could smell her perfume and watched as her skirt rose up her legs a little, almost revealing her underwear. She had that same beautiful smell as on their last meeting. Perhaps it was a favorite of hers, or perhaps she simply didn't have many to choose from. He made a mental note to check with Tampong about popular women's perfumes.

'There,' she announced, standing back up, 'you are all ready now. Do they feel OK, not too tight?'

He stood up and balanced on his skates, which felt a little strange at first and he wobbled a bit, but the boots were comfortable, and his feet felt secure.

'Fine,' he answered.

'Great. Let's go.'

She took his hand and led him onto the ice. He placed his first foot down on the ice and it immediately slid forward, but Karen was there to support him. He leaned against her, enjoying the feel of her hand on his. She took his other hand and encouraged him to put the other foot on the ice, which he did. She then started slowly skating backwards, all the time holding his hand and he glided along the ice. His balance felt good, so he smiled at her.

'You sure you have never been on the ice before?' she queried.

'Quite sure,' he confirmed.

'Well, then you must be a natural. I am going to release one of your hands now so that I can skate at your side. OK?'

'OK,' he said nervously.

She slowly let go and he quickly corrected his balance. She moved to his side and slid one foot in front of the other. He followed. After a little wobble, he started to slide across the ice. She moved her next foot forward, so he copied her. Soon they were both skating slowly around the rink. They were about twenty others on the ice, with about half of them being couples. There were a few showboating types, one of whom deliberately got too close to Terry, making him a little nervous and causing him to hold Karen's hand a little bit tighter. She didn't mind but gave the guy a dirty look. After ten minutes he was feeling more confident on the ice, so they speeded up a little. She gave him a gentle nudge forward and let go of his hand, but he stayed upright and started skating on his own. He felt great but kept the walls of the rink close enough to grab, if needed. Karen started to skate around him. She moved in front of him and was skating backwards, encouraging him to follow her, which he did without hesitation. He kept a watchful eye on one of the showboaters, watching his moves, and noticing him eyeing up Karen. He stopped next to his friend, and they spoke quietly together, both watching Karen skating. Terry sensed they were about to do something, perhaps try to knock her over. He watched as they moved in opposite directions around the rink. One coming behind Terry, the other coming from behind Karen. He waited until the last second before the two boys reached them. He grabbed Karen's hands and pulled her towards him as the two boys started sliding towards them. They were surprised by the sudden move and their momentum sent them crashing into each other. Both landed on their backsides, legs spread out in front of them. Their plan backfired, and they ended up exactly where they thought Karen would be, spreadeagled on the floor.

'Hey, watch out,' she called angrily at the two boys.

Both were now embarrassed when other skaters started laughing as they passed. Karen was holding Terry tightly, and their faces were almost touching.

'Arseholes,' she said as she turned towards Terry.

Their eyes instantly met and locked together. The room around him seemed to disappear and all he could see was her. He intuitively leaned towards her, and their lips touched. She did not pull back but returned his kiss. She then blinked and the moment passed. They stayed hand in hand as they skated around the rink together. The two boys had risen to their feet and were sliding slowly towards the exit, brushing ice off from their clothing. One turned to give Terry his middle finger. Terry simply smiled but made a mental note of the boy's face. Should they ever meet again, he would show him exactly where he should stick his finger.

A buzzer sounded, and the color of their wristband was shown, indicating that their time was up. He could not believe their time was up already. Hand in hand they slowly skated to the exit. They sat down in silence, removed their skates, and returned them to the receptionist in exchange for their shoes. Once outside, Karen turned to Terry and kissed him firmly on the lips.

'Thank you,' she whispered.

'The evening isn't over yet,' he announced.

She leaned her head to the side and gave him a questioning look.

'Really? Are we now going zipping or something?'

'Nothing as crazy as that,' he replied, again making a mental note that perhaps it was something to do for their next date. 'Are you hungry?'

'Now that you mention it, I am starving. All that skating and holding you up has given me quite the appetite.'

'Ho come on now. You didn't have to support me *that* much.'

'Really,' she answered, her voice dripping with sarcasm.

He said nothing but laughed as he led her down the road. They turned the street, and the restaurant was just down the road. He had memorized the route.

Karen looked impressed.

'Wow,' she announced, 'I have never been here before.'

'Good. Neither have I, to be honest.'

'How on earth did you find this place?'

'I have to be honest again and say that my aunt found it for me.'

'Good for her.'

They entered through the double glass doors to be greeted by a thin man, wearing a tight-fitting suit that glimmered in the spotlights.

'Good evening and welcome to the Cave. Do you have reservations?'

'Yes,' confirmed Terry. 'Terry Armitage.'

'Armitage,' repeated the thin man, his finger running expertly down the leather diary on the desk, 'yes, here we are. Actually, you are a little early. Perhaps you would care to have a drink at the bar—assuming you are old enough—and I will call you when your table is ready.'

'That will be fine, thank you.'

Terry decided not to respond to his question about their age. With his height and her looks, they both could get away with being older than they were, although the thin man was clearly not fooled by his height.

The man stepped aside, allowing them to move into the restaurant. In the dim lights, they could just about work out the tables and negotiate past them. The bar, on the other hand, was well lit and easy to find. They sat at the bar and were immediately approached by the barman.

'Good evening,' he began, still drying a glass in his hands with a cloth, 'what would you like to drink?'

'I would like a dry white wine please,' announced Karen.

Terry decided to follow her lead.

'And I will have a beer, please.'

'No problem. What kind of beer would you like, sir?'

'Do you have a local beer?'

'Indeed we do. Would sir like to try our IPA? It comes highly recommended. It is made by the brewery just down the road.'

'Yes, that sounds good.'

He had no idea what an IPA beer was or tasted like. He felt Karen kick his leg under the bar. She was not fooled.

The drinks arrived promptly, so they picked them up and clinked their glasses together. Both took a sip of their drinks.

'Hmm, very nice,' commented Terry.

'Glad you like it, sir,' replied the barman, turning his eyes towards Karen.

She simply gave him the thumbs-up as she took another sip. He nodded his approval and moved down the bar to serve another customer.

Karen leaned closer to Terry.

'My mother would kill me if she ever learned I was drinking wine,' she whispered, 'but, ho my god, this tastes good.'

'Mine too and mine too,' he replied.

She looked puzzled at first, but then realized he was answering both her statements.

'I think I will take another glass with my meal. Thank you so much for bringing me here tonight. I am looking forward to the experience.'

'Glad you like it here.'

They chatted about skating and lost track of time. Both had finished their drink when the thin man came up to them.

'Your table is ready,' he announced, 'if you would follow me. Table twenty-four,' he announced to the barman.

Terry guessed it was to add their drinks to the bill.

'Would sir and madam care for another round, or would you prefer to look over the wine list first?' asked the barman.

'Another round at the table please,' replied Karen.

The barman simply nodded.

They both slid off their barstools and followed the thin man to the middle of the restaurant. They sat opposite each other at a round table. The man bowed his head gracefully, placed a large menu in Karen's hands, then one in Terry's before stepping away.

Karen glanced over the menu and her eyes widened in horror.

'Have you seen the prices here?' she whispered.

Terry had indeed noticed the prices, and his throat felt a little dry.

'Hey, we are here to enjoy ourselves. My aunt would not have booked this place without first checking out the prices, so don't fret.'

'Are you sure?' She obviously had doubts.

'Absolutely,' he answered, trying to sound as confident as he could.

In truth, he had no idea whether Tampong had checked the prices or not, but she had given him her credit card and told him to enjoy himself, that much was true.

'Please choose what you would like and do not be driven by the price, really.'

'OK, if you are sure,' she replied, returning her attention to the menu.

There was clear excitement in her voice, and he felt equally excited to be with her. His heart was filled with warmth as she was clearly enjoying herself.

The waiter arrived with their drinks, placed them on the table and opened his little pad indicating he was ready to take their order.

'I would like to start with the vegetable soup followed by the salmon, please,' said Karen.

'Very good, madam,' replied the waiter, jotting down her order.

'And I'll have the prawn salad and the sirloin steak, please.'

'Certainly, sir. How would you like your steak?'

'Medium rare, please.'

'Certainly. And have you selected a wine with your meal?'

'I would like to keep with the wine I had at the bar, thank you.'

'And I'll stay with my beer, too, thanks.'

'Certainly,' the waiter repeated.

He swiveled on his heels and headed for the kitchen.

Karen leaned across the table, her hand resting on the tablecloth.

'You sure this will be OK?'

'Quite sure,' he replied, reaching over, placing his hand on hers.

She didn't flinch and even appeared to welcome the touch. They chatted quietly for a few minutes until their first course arrived.

'Vegetable soup for madam,' said the waiter, placing the white bowl in front of her, 'and prawn salad for you, sir,' he continued, placing the small glass bowl in front of Terry.

'Would either of your care for some pepper?'

Both shook their head.

'Very good, then please enjoy your meals.'

They ate in silence. While they ate, another waiter appeared with a basket of bread, which he placed in the middle of their table, quickly followed with their drinks. He bowed his head briefly and backed away. No sooner had they finished than the first waiter was back at their table removing their now empty bowls.

'That soup was delicious,' announced Karen, wiping the side of her lips with her napkins.

'I enjoyed the prawn salad too,' agreed Terry.

Ten minutes later their main meal arrived. They lifted their glasses and clinked them together. Again, they ate in silence. Terry's steak was perfect and simply melted in his mouth. He could not remember the last time he had tasted meat as tender as this. Karen appeared also to be enjoying her salmon, closing her eyes as she chewed on the fish. All too soon their meal was finished, and they placed their knives and forks on the plate at the same time. Karen picked up her napkin and wiped the side of her mouth. Terry could not take his eyes off of her. The waiter retrieved their plates and returned with the dessert menu and stood in anticipation of their order.

Karen's eyes quickly scanned the selection and made her decision.

'Apple crumble with custard, please.'

The waiter nodded.

'Make that two, please. Sounds good.'

The waiter nodded again and backed away towards the kitchen. Five minutes later he returned with their desserts, placing two hot steaming bowls in front of them.

'Would you care for coffee with your dessert?'

'Yes, please,' they said in unison, smiling at each other.

'And can I interest you in a digestive?'

'Thanks, but not for me,' replied Karen.

'Me neither, thanks. Just the coffee.'

'Very well,' acknowledged the waiter, again swiveling on his heels and returning to the kitchen.

They were about halfway through their dessert when he returned with two coffees and a long white plate offering a small selection of chocolates.

Karen didn't hesitate. No sooner had she finished her dessert than she reached over and picked up a white chocolate and popped it into her mouth.

'I cannot resist chocolate,' she admitted.

'I need to remember that,' said Terry.

Another mental note. He hoped he remembered all this information by the time he got home.

She looked at the remaining chocolate.

'Are you going to eat that?'

'Go for it,' he said.

She didn't hesitate, and two seconds later she was chewing the sweet in her mouth.

She sat back and patted her stomach.

'That was really a nice meal, Terry. Thank you for bringing me here.'

'My pleasure,' he replied warmly, catching the waiter's attention and asking for the bill with his hands, which arrived promptly on a silver tray with yet another chocolate.

Terry looked across to Karen, who simply shrugged her shoulders and swiped her hand across the table to pick up the chocolate. He picked up the bill and noticed there was a line for a tip. He entered ten pounds and the new total before placing Tampong's credit card on the tray. The waiter efficiently removed the tray and moved towards the reception table. Terry held his breath, wondering what he would do if the waiter came back to say that the card did not work. The waiter returned with his card and a receipt, placing both in front of him, this time with two mints.

'Thank you very much, and enjoy your evening.'

He offered them both a cute bow before backing away.

They rose from the table and left the restaurant. Karen immediately slipped her hand into his.

'Unfortunately, it is time to get me home,' she said.

'Sure,' he acknowledged, checking his watch, 'there will be a bus along in five minutes.'

They walked hand in hand to the bus stop and waited for the bus. Karen turned towards Terry and leaned forward, closing her eyes. He did the same. He felt her warm lips and pushed against them, feeling her respond by pushing against him too. He held her arms in his hands.

He felt his hands changing, matching the material of her coat. He focused on his hands, willing them to penetrate her coat and feel her skin, which they did. He relished the touch of her skin but stopped himself from absorbing into her body. Their lips stayed together until they heard the bus arriving, both reluctantly pulling away. Karen rested her head on his shoulders, not noticing his hands slowly changing back to their original color. They boarded the bus. As they sat down, she slipped her arm through his and again rested her head on his shoulder. He leaned his head against hers. He wished this day would never end. He wished he could stay like this forever. If he could stop time, then this would be the moment to do it. He felt proud for some reason. Proud to be in the presence of this beautiful woman, proud that she liked him. Proud that she kissed him.

The bus arrived at their stop, and they stepped off and walked a further ten minutes, hand in hand, towards her house. They stopped and stared at each other. Terry brushed his hand down the side of her face, forcing her to close her eyes. He leaned forward and kissed her again. She returned his kiss, wrapping her arms around him. He matched her movement. They stayed like that, enjoying the physical contact of their lips, both rubbing against each other, wanting each other, desiring each other. A light came on in the hallway of her front door, so they again reluctantly parted from each other. Her front door opened.

'Is that you, Karen?' called out her mother.

'Yes, Mum,' replied Karen, 'just coming.'

'Good,' replied her mother.

'Thank you for a lovely evening, Terry. I really enjoyed myself and cannot remember the last time I had such a great time.'

'Well, I can honestly say that was the best night for me too, being with you.'

She gave him another quick kiss on the lips before turning and heading for her front door towards her mother, who stood there with her arms folded.

'Goodnight,' he called after her.

'Goodnight, Terry,' she replied without turning back. 'Call me,' she said when she reached the door. She gave him a little wave before disappearing inside.

He watched her enter the house. Her mother gave him a disapproving look and a sniff of discontent before closing the door firmly behind her. Nothing was going to ruin his night. He walked light-footed all the way home.

When he entered the house, Tampong was sitting in the lounge, apparently watching TV. She turned her head towards him when he entered.

'So, how did it go?'

'Perfect,' he replied, 'just perfect.'

'Glad to hear it. Did you kiss her?'

His face went red.

'None of your business.'

'You did, didn't you? Good for you.'

Terry then remembered the restaurant bill.

'Did you have any idea how expensive that restaurant is?'

'Yes, I did. But I assumed you would not be buying a bottle of wine or two, so guessed it would be OK to push the boat out a little bit. Impress the lady if you like.'

'Certainly did that. I don't know how to thank you. I'll pay you back.'

He pulled her credit card out of his wallet and handed it back to her. She nodded her thanks, placing it on the coffee table.

'Forget it. My pleasure. Get yourself up to bed now.'

He nodded and skipped up the stairs. He would be having a nice dream about Karen tonight.

Tampong watched him go upstairs. She felt happy that he had found someone nice. She returned her attention to the application form she had half completed when the darkness lurking at the back of her mind resurfaced. She knew she had to do this, but at what cost to her relationship with Terry? She continued filling in the application form, knowing his safety came first, even at the cost of their relationship, and his.

Would he ever forgive her? She doubted it.

***

After three weeks, Gary and Tracey had covered just about every street in the city. There had been no further sightings and no further sensations, of any type.

'This is hopeless,' concluded Tracey as they walked down yet another dead end.

'I tend to agree,' he confirmed, 'let's give it up and return home.'

'As much as I like this place, I have to admit I am ready to go back home too now.'

'Ok, it's decided then. Should I sense the presence again, then I will try and focus more on it and even try to contact it.'

'Isn't that a little risky?'

'Yes, but what choice do we have, assuming I even sense it again?'

'True,' confessed Tracey.

She was far from happy about the prospects, but he was right, and this was probably the only real way they were going to track it down. They nodded to each other and headed back to the hotel.

***

Shoil was having similar doubts. There had been no further sense of this strange male, and he hadn't tried to contact her again. She started to wonder whether he had moved on and was thinking she would do the same. This city was too boring for her in any case. The men only seemed to be interested in one thing, and that was this stupid football team. The whole city appeared to be seduced by the actions of this team. Apparently, they had just won promotion into the Football League (whatever that meant), yet all the local talk was about them playing Manchester United in the cup, although they were completely outclassed and thrashed. She had taken a reluctant interest in the ups and downs of the various football clubs as it gave her immediate access to men. They seemed surprised at her interest and knowledge, particularly when she expressed her surprise at their relegation from Football League. The fans were naturally completely seduced by her, and she fed well on their stupidity.

The only thing that was holding her back from moving on was Tampong. She was convinced she was still close by but perhaps keeping herself shielded from her. Recently her focus had been on this new male, but Tampong was never far from her mind. However, she began to have doubts that Tampong was still local as she had not felt her for some time. Could the two sensations be linked? She had often asked herself this question, but always came to the same conclusion. There was no way that Tampong could have born a child that was now old enough to be interested in women. No, the two could not have any connection, that much she was certain. She was equally certain that eventually Tampong would slip up again and move into her real form, thus allowing Shoil to sense her and locate her. She would have to wait and try to be patient. In the meantime, she would keep herself alert to this male. She felt sure he would try to contact her again. He seemed inquisitive, interested in her, the way a young male suddenly became interested in females for the first time. She had seen this all too often in the past. Males were predictable at best. Letting their lust blur their judgement. This was, in general, good news for women. The clever ones being able to manipulate this weakness to their advantage. Shoil needed no such reason. No man could resist her. Her accent had softened a little, and to the uneducated it was not obvious anymore that she had an Australian accent, although she could bring it to the surface if and when required.

She decided she would have to play the waiting game, again, and let one of them reach out to her.

She was certain that was going to happen.

It had to.

She had her fill of men recently too, and definitely had enough of this unsuccessful football team. How these men could ever follow a failed team was beyond her understanding. No, it was time to leave this city behind and move on to her next location.

Wherever that may be.

BAD NEWS TRAVELS FAST

Date: September 2010
Ages: 17 / 1,161
Status: Semi-active

Tampong was drumming her fingers on the coffee table. The letter she had been waiting for had finally arrived, but she was not sure how Terry was going to take it. He seemed so happy at the moment, and she was in half a mind to simply tear up the letter and forget all about it. She couldn't and knew she couldn't. It was a once-in-a-lifetime opportunity for both of them. She could not turn her back on it, would not turn her back on it. The question was how to break the news to him. That moment had arrived as the front door opened and Terry entered the lounge. He bent over to give her a little peck on the cheek.

'Nice evening?' she asked.

'The best,' he replied enthusiastically.

'So another evening spent with Karen then?'

'And Colin,' he added.

Tampong swung her head around and raised her eyebrows in surprise. He saw her reaction and laughed.

'Nothing sexual or anything like that. We were just playing computer games.'

'Aha,' she said unconvinced.

'Truly,' he answered, starting to head upstairs.

'OK, OK,' she conceded, 'listen, we need to talk. I have something to tell you.'

'Right ho. I'll just have a quick shower and I'll be right back down.'

'Have you eaten?'

'Nope.'

'Right. Then I'll fix us a pizza. Sound good?'

'Perfect.'

He disappeared upstairs. She carefully folded the letter and placed it in the middle of the coffee table, rose, and went into the kitchen to place the pizza in the oven. She had taken it out earlier, thinking that even if he was not hungry, she would need to eat.

Twenty-five minutes later, he came back downstairs and headed straight for the dinner table. She heard the oven bleep, so she went into the kitchen and pulled the hot pizza out of the oven. She sliced it into eight pieces, picked up two plates, and took them all into the lounge, where she placed the plates and pizza onto the table. Without any hesitation, he grabbed a plate and a slice of pizza and started eating. He was obviously hungry. She was not halfway through her first slice when he picked up a second piece. He looked up to her.

'So what's this news you have?'

'What, ho that. I received a letter today.'

'And?'

'It was a job offer.'

'For?'

'For a very good job in an eyecare company.'

'Good money?'

'Very good money.'

'Great. I am pleased for you. So when do you start?'

'That's the problem.'

'What problem?'

'The job is not in this country.'

He stopped eating and put his half-consumed pizza slice down on the plate.

'Where is it then?'

'Singapore.'

'***Singapore!***' he screamed. 'Singapore is the other side of the world?'

'Correct.'

'So, I guess this means that you aren't going to accept it then.'

'Why do you say that?'

'Because it will mean you leaving the country.'

'You mean it will mean *us* leaving the country.'

'You expect me to go with you?'

'Of course.'

'Why? Why would you do that to me? I am happy here. My friends are here, my girlfriend is here. My life is here.'

His voice got louder and louder as he spoke.

Her greatest fears were being realized.

'Because,' she began hesitantly, 'because we would be safer there.'

'You mean you would be safer there.'

He stood up to leave. His pizza now forgotten.

'What do you mean by that?'

'It is clear that Shoil is hunting for you and not me. She is no threat to me. Only you. So I have nothing to fear from her. You are doing this for you and you alone. You don't care about my feelings. It's just about you.'

He was almost in a rage now. His eyes were wide open and angry.

'How can you stand there and say that? After everything I have done for you.'

'Yeah, right,' he replied, his voice dripping with sarcasm.

She felt her anger start to build up inside.

'Now just you listen to me, mister . . .'

She stopped talking when he suddenly raised his fingers towards her face. His nails hardened and long, thin steel rods shot towards her exposed face, but she had anticipated the move and swatted them away, sending them all crashing to the floor, where they disintegrated.

He looked down in horror at his hands, then down towards the floor. He clearly regretted his actions, but his anger was still boiling.

'I, I didn't mean to do that, but stop making me angry.'

'Stop making you angry?' she said with a raised voice, 'stop making *you* angry.'

She stood up and he instinctively took a step backwards. She spotted the slight movement and it told her that he was not yet ready to fully challenge her. She pointed her own finger in his direction and instantly saw the look of fear. He was thinking that perhaps she would respond to his attack with her own force, but she was just using her finger to emphasize a point.

'Your words cut right through my heart. I brought you here to protect you, and now it is clear that Shoil has tracked us down again. So it is time to move again, the further away the better. I am sorry you have found a girlfriend, but she will be in danger if she stays close to you.'

Her own words appeared to hit home, and he looked down towards the floor, in shame, but still defiant.

'So you simply expect me to drop everything, and everyone, and leave everything behind and go with you?'

'Yes,' she replied coldly.

She could see he was thinking about Karen. She hated having to do this to him but knew there was no other choice. She decided to change her approach.

'You don't want anything to happen to either Karen or Colin, do you?'

'Of course not,' he snapped, 'what kind of question is that?'

'Well, what do you think Shoil will do should she find you and spots you with either of them?'

'I won't let that happen, won't let anything happen to them.'

'You really believe you can prevent her from harming them?'

She could see the doubts crossing his mind, so decided to push her point.

'Moving away would protect both of them from Shoil.'

He looked up at her. Her words had again hit home.

'OK, OK, I get it, but I cannot just leave them both without any explanation.'

'Agreed, but you mustn't tell them where you are going. Is that clear?'

'So you are determined to go ahead with this move then?'

'I don't see any other choice, do you?'

'But moving all the way to Singapore! That's a little extreme, isn't it?'

'How far is safe enough with Shoil sniffing around?'

He shrugged his shoulders, not happy with the discussion but also not certain how he could change things.

'Guess there is nothing else left to say then. You have made your decision.'

He turned to walk upstairs.

'Terry, it is the only way to keep our distance from her. We have to keep moving. We have to keep one step ahead.'

He said nothing and disappeared upstairs. She heard him slam the door shut. She didn't blame him for being angry with her. She was angry with herself if she was honest. While he remained a virgin, she felt sure he would be safe from Shoil's absorption, but not from her wrath. She was certain that once she found out who he was, she would kill him without hesitation. She had to do this. She had to protect him.

Terry fell backwards onto the bed. His world was falling apart around him and there was nothing he could do about it. He understood her fears but felt sure they were for her and not for him. He felt as if he were getting stronger by the day and soon, very soon, he would be able to tackle Shoil on his own, if it were a dual she was looking for. He had doubts about that though. Perhaps he should try to contact her again? There are, after all, two sides to every story. He had no doubt that she killed his parents, but maybe she had a good reason. Maybe they were keeping him from becoming his true self, and now so was Tampong. He should at least give her the opportunity to explain herself. Didn't she deserve that much? He made his decision.

He focused on her again.

There she was.

***

Patience is indeed a virtue, she thought.

She never had much in the way of patience but didn't see any other way to detect this new male. Now he was trying to contact her again.

'Patience is a virtue,' she repeated.

She remained calm, although her heart was beating faster. She was sitting on the sofa, so sat up and smiled warmly at his presence, trying to embrace it, trying to welcome it. It seemed to be working. She tried to focus on the presence and a form started to take shape in her mind. It was the young male. His eyes were bright orange, proving him to be one of them, although his image was ghostly, and the only clear details were his eyes. She made her own eyes change and the contact strengthened. He appeared to be lying down. She reached out with her arms, and he did not flinch, did not back away from her approach but kept the contact.

'Can you hear me?' she asked.

No response came. Nor did his expression change. She kept her focus on his face. Searching out his details, the shape of his nose, his mouth, the length of his hair. The image appeared a little sharper. So much so that she was now certain it was the same boy she saw kissing in the street. If only she knew she was so close to grabbing him. Silently cursing herself, she remained still, waiting to see if he made a move.

He did.

Terry slowly sat up. This woman looked beautiful and sexy. She did not change into that horrible animal this time, instead she was smiling at him and looked to be even calling out to him. He felt sure she was trying to speak to him. He could see her lips moving and he sensed something at the back of his mind but could not bring it to the front. Perhaps he could make verbal contact with her.

'Are you Shoil?' he asked.

She saw his lips moving and knew he was asking her something. There were no words though. She decided to try something and started to unbutton her blouse. She could see his eyes immediately moving down towards her chest.

A typical teenager, she thought.

She continued to unbutton her remaining buttons before pulling her blouse open to reveal her satin white bra. She then stood up, unzipped her skirt, allowing that to fall to the floor. She then slid her blouse off and stood in front of the lounge mirror in just her bra and panties. He was watching her carefully. She could see the excitement in his eyes. He wanted her to continue. She had him trapped. Rather than undress further, she gestured with her hands for him to come to her. She saw him lean his head to one side, clearly not understanding her message. She took one of her hands into the other and placed it gently on her breast, then started to slowly rotate her hand, caressing her breast.

He will surely get the message now.

He did.

'Wow,' he gasped to himself, *she wants me to have sex with her.*

He could not take his eyes away from her. She was an incredibly sexy lady and knew it. She seemed to like him and wanted to be with him. He was not sure how he was going to find her but knew he had to try.

Tampong felt the contact. She looked up towards the bedroom in fear, stood up and rushed upstairs. She burst into his room and saw his bright orange eyes glowing. There was a ghostly image of a half-naked Shoil standing at the end of his bed, inviting him to come to her, trying to seduce him.

She grabbed hold of Terry and shook him.

'Terry, come back, **come back,**' she screamed the last words.

The contact was suddenly broken. He blinked twice and his eyes returned to their original form. Shoil's image faded away. She let him go, and he slumped back onto the bed.

'Why did you do that?' he asked, looking up at her, anger glaring in his eyes.

'What do you think you were doing?'

'I was just trying to contact her.'

'Trying to contact with that, that animal? Are you serious?'

'I want to know what she wants. If she wants me.'

'Terry, if she finds you, she will kill you.'

'You don't know that.'

'Believe me, I do.'

'How can you be so certain?'

'Because I was like her once too.'

He looked up at her, investigating her face. Trying to determine if she was telling the truth or not.

'I am nearly an adult and can make my own decisions,' he answered defensively.

'Firstly, you are not yet an adult, and, secondly, we make the decisions as they affect both of us and not just you.'

'That's what you say.'

'What is that supposed to mean?'

'Nothing,' he answered with a hump.

'No, not nothing, tell me what you mean by that.'

'Well, it could be she is just hunting you and will leave me alone.'

'Do you really believe that?'

'It could be true.'

'Shoil is all evil. She will do anything to find us both. And she will kill us both if she does and is given the opportunity. We cannot allow that.'

'I thought you said she cannot absorb me if I am still a virgin.'

'Cannot absorb you, no, but that won't stop her from killing you. Did you speak with her?'

'No, I could not hear her, only see her.'

'And what she was doing was obvious. You must not be fooled into believing she wants you. She is just trying to entrap you. Keep away from her.'

He had had enough of this conversation and turned onto his side, away from her. She was about to turn him back but decided to leave him to his thoughts. Instead, she turned and left his bedroom. The sooner they were out of the country the better. She never felt so worried as she did now. He had deliberately contacted her, risking their detection, risking their lives. They had reached a delicate crossroad in his development, and she was not sure which direction she should take. Uncertain on which direction he was going to take when given the choice.

This was a dark development, and she was not sure how to manage it. Suddenly, Singapore now looked like a priority.

***

Shoil felt the contact break. It was not of his own accord. Rather, something or someone disturbed him, forcing him out of his lock with her. She had him in the palms of her hands and he slipped away, again. She clenched her fists as her anger built up. She let out a high-pitched animal cry and punched the mirror with all her might. It shattered into a million pieces. The glass falling around her feet. She concluded that it must have been Tampong who interrupted them. She must be with him and might have seen him in his trance and guessed he was contacting her. At least that told her, if true, that they were together. Which was both good news and bad. Good in that when she finds the boy then she finds Tampong too. The bad news being that she needed to deal with Tampong first in order to get to the boy. She also sensed a physical barrier between her and the boy. This was a new development and needed some further analysis. Once more, her enthusiasm had been renewed. Her hunting instincts brought to the surface again. Tonight she will go out looking for the boy. She now knew his face and that he was close. She intrigued him. He had made the initial contact, so maybe he will try again. She hoped so. He had reached a level of maturity where he was questioning things. Perhaps he didn't understand his abilities, perhaps Tampong was keeping the truth from him, and he wanted to know more. She could help him, right up until she absorbed him and took all his memories.

Doubt then started to fill her mind as she dressed herself. If he *was* with Tampong, then it was unlikely he was the bastard child of Zelphur. He could of course be with one of the Lower Middle though. This would make more sense. They would not understand his abilities but that he was in a trance. This could also explain the strange physical barrier she felt. Could it be that the Lower Middle had shielded him for so long, but his growth had weakened that shield, allowing him to break free and try and contact one of his own? Perhaps he was calling out for help. This made even more sense to her and kept the faint hope that he was the son of Zelphur. A child full of her memories but unable to tap into them. She knew how. She felt drunk with the sudden possible power that would be available to her, making her even more determined to find him. She would return to the point where she last saw the two lovers. See if she could pick up the scent of either one of them. Find the boy and she would find the one protecting him. Failing that, by finding the girl, she would surely find the boy.

She had another plan, so removed all her clothing and placed them on the end of the bed. She needed to be in her true hunting form but didn't want to lose any more clothing as a result.

***

Terry couldn't stop thinking about Shoil. The way she looked at him, the way she undressed for him, the way she moved her hands over her body. It was so erotic, so real. She wanted him. He in turn wanted to touch that body for real. Wanted to feel her soft breasts and caress her fantastic body. He was certain that he would start the evening with her as a boy and end it as a man. Then he started to think about Karen and a guilty pain stabbed at his heart. An older woman had just thrown herself at him, and he was melting like butter. Karen also liked him, that much he knew, although he was less certain whether she was physically attracted to him. He was sure she would have just as good a body as Shoil, but, even better, it would be young and firm. Nor could he stop thinking about sex and what it must be like. He heard the warning from Tampong, but she might just be trying to scare him into staying a virgin for as long as possible. He was seventeen now, and many of his friends had slept with girls already. Even Colin had scored. He sat up and reached over for his phone, tapping Karen's contact details.

'Hello?' came her voice over the phone.

'Hey, you,' he began, 'I was just thinking about you in bed, so thought I would give you a call. I need to speak with you.'

'You were thinking about me in bed with you?' she said, taunting him.

'No, no,' he felt awkward, 'that's not what I meant.'

'It's OK,' she said in a calming voice, 'I was only teasing you. You said you wanted to speak with me? About what?'

'Can we meet?'

'When? You know I work during the week.'

'I know, but this cannot wait. Can we meet after you finish work?'

'Terry, are you OK?'

'Not really. That's why I need to see you.'

'OK then. Let's meet at the back of the restaurant on Monday night then. Let's say eleven?'

'Great. See you then, Karen.'

'Are you sure you are OK? You sound strange.'

'I'll be fine once I see you,' he lied.

'Right then. See you Monday, Terry. Goodnight.'

'Good night, Karen.'

He placed the phone down. He had decided he would tell her everything. Let her know how he felt about her and hope that she felt the same way about him. All being well, they could find a quiet place during the weekend and make love. He smiled at the prospect.

***

Gary felt the contact too. It worried him. There was no hostility this time, almost welcoming instead. What was happening? Had the Higher Middle become aware of their presence here? Were they planning a trap for them? There were too many variables in this equation. Too many. He had a change of heart.

'Let's get the hell out of here.'

Tracey looked concerned.

'What is it? Have you felt the presence again?'

'Yes, and it bothers me.'

'How so?'

'It seemed to be searching for someone. It's as if it wants to be found.'

'Really? Did you try and contact it?'

'No, mainly because it felt like I had spied on a party line.'

'A what?'

'You know, listening in on someone else's telephone conversation.'

'Could you make out what they were saying?'

'It wasn't that kind of contact. This wasn't physical, although I cannot help feeling that they both wanted it to be.'

'Meaning?'

'I'm not sure. It cannot be good though, for us that is.'

'Then, as you say, let's get the hell out of here.'

They both finished packing their rucksacks, took one last look around the room, closed the door and entered the lift at the end of the corridor. On reaching the reception, Gary checked out and they left the hotel. As they walked down the street, Karen was walking in the opposite direction. As they passed, she brushed shoulders with Gary.

'Oops, pardon me, ma'am,' he said.

'No problem,' she answered and carried on walking.

Gary froze on the spot. Tracey didn't notice straight away and had walked on a few feet before she stopped and turned around to see Gary watching the girl walk down the street. She walked back and held his arm. His stare never left the girl. Tracey looked back at her as she continued to walk down the street.

'What is it?' she whispered.

'Not sure,' he said, more half to himself.

He shook his head.

'Probably nothing.'

'I know you and your probably nothing,' she scolded, 'tell me.'

'It's just that when I brushed shoulders with that girl, it felt as though I had contact with a group member.'

'You mean, you think she is one of the Higher Middle. Perhaps Shoil or Tampong in disguise?'

'No, not that. If it were either one of them, then the reaction would be violent. No, this felt almost innocent.'

'Innocent!'

'I know it sounds strange, but that's what it felt like.'

'So what do you want to do?'

'Not sure. Let's follow her for now. Just to see where she goes.'

'OK,' she replied, although she was full of doubt.

They started walking quicker to close the gap to Karen, who continued walking down the road, completely unaware she was being followed. She was thinking about Terry and how nice he was and how lucky she felt. She was looking forward to their date again. He seemed different from the other boys. Kinder. Gentler. He didn't try to force himself upon her or do things she felt uncomfortable about. Maybe she had discovered a rare jewel of a male. If so, she intended to hold onto him for as long as possible. She wondered what news he had for her. He sounded a little nervous, and she hoped he was not having second thoughts about their relationship. She walked around the corner and opened the side door to the restaurant, disappearing inside.

Gary and Tracey watched her enter the building. He indicated with his finger for Tracey to stay where she was. She nodded her acknowledgement. He moved slowly towards the door he saw the girl disappear through. There was a name on the door, and as he moved closer he could work out the words: The Red Lion Restaurant. Employees entrance only

He returned to where Tracey was eagerly and impatiently waiting. She was nervously biting her nails but stopped when he approached.

'Well?' she asked.

'It's a restaurant. I am guessing she works there.'

'What now?'

'Well, we can wait here all evening until she comes back out, or we can go inside when it opens and have a meal and wait inside. We can watch her more easily that way. Who knows, maybe this strange presence will turn up.'

Tracey didn't need to think about her response.

'Definitely the second option. Who knows, maybe this strange presence will indeed turn up inside as well, if not already be there.'

'OK, let's go around to the front and find out what time it opens.'

She nodded, so they walked around to the front door. The restaurant opened at 7 pm and closed at 10:30 pm. He tried the door and it opened, so he walked inside. A man behind the bar noticed them enter, so stepped out from behind the bar.

'Can I help you?' he said in a pleasant voice. 'We are not actually open at the moment.'

'Yes, I know. I was just wondering whether it would be possible to book a table for tonight.'

The man nodded his understanding.

'Let me check. It is usually quiet on days like this.'

He walked up to the counter and flicked the large diary open.

'No problem. What time would you prefer?'

'Eight pm please. Table for two.'

'No problem. Can I have a name please?'

'Hardgrove, Gary Hardgrove.'

'Mr. Hardgrove,' he repeated, scribbling down the name in the diary, 'table for two at eight pm. You are all set, sir.'

'Thank you,' replied Gary, 'we look forward to seeing you tonight.'

'Likewise, sir,' he replied, escorting them to the front door.

Once outside, Tracey felt it was safe to start talking again.

'So what's the plan?'

'I don't have one actually.'

'What! No plan. I don't believe it.'

'No, really. I am just going on a whim here. See where it takes us.'

'You really think this girl can lead us to the source?'

'I do, I really do.'

'Then I guess we stay close to her. See where she lives, who she meets, that sort of thing.'

'I was thinking the same.'

'So you do have a plan then.'

'If you call it that.'

They walked back to the hotel in silence. Then Tracey suddenly stopped walking, causing him to turn to look at her.

'Where are we going now?' she asked.

'Back to the hotel of course.'

'But we checked out.'

He clicked his fingers.

'You're right. I had completely forgotten that. Still, I'm sure they still have rooms. The restaurant guy said it was quiet, so maybe it's true for the hotel too.'

'I hope so. I have no desire to sleep on the street tonight.'

'Don't worry, my love, I will keep you warm.'

'Nice try, but no comfortable room, then no comfort. Got it?'

'Got it.'

He shrugged his shoulders.

On reaching the hotel he went straight up to the reception. The man appeared to recognize him.

'Hello again, sir. Did you forget something?'

'Not really. Our train was cancelled, and we are stranded here. I was wondering if you have a room still available?'

'Of course, sir. Actually, your old room has just been cleaned and has not been reserved yet. Would you like that one?'

'Yes, please,' answered Tracey before Gary could speak.

The receptionist looked at Gary, who simply nodded in agreement.

'For how long this time, sir?'

'Let's make it a week, please.'

'No problem, sir, the same room is available for your entire stay.'

The receptionist expertly tapped the keyboard of his computer. Sheets of paper started pouring from the printer behind him. He turned and shuffled them together before laying them in front of Gary.

'If you would kindly sign here and here, please. And I will need your credit card again, please.'

Gary reached into his pocket and retrieved his wallet. He pulled his credit card out and handed it to the receptionist. While it was being swiped, he signed the registration form. The receptionist handed his card back, together with the room key. He checked the form and, satisfied, stapled two pages together, slipping them into the drawer in front of him.

'I assume there is no baggage, and you know where the room is, sir?'

'Correct,' replied Gary.

'Then I bid you a pleasant evening, sir.'

Gary nodded and they headed for the lift. Tracey took his hand in hers.

'Just enough time for me to have a bath before dinner then.'

'Just enough time for both of us to have a bath . . . together,' he added.

She smiled warmly at him as they entered the lift.

At 8 pm they walked promptly into the restaurant, both refreshed from their frantic lovemaking and bath. The man in the restaurant recognized them and bid them over.

'Nice to see you again, sir. Your table is this way.'

He led them to a small rectangular table covered in a white tablecloth, with two plates sitting on a white napkin. Silverware was laid on either side of the plates, and three glasses were aligned behind the plates. A small glass vase sat in the center with three roses laid professionally out, two yellow and one red.

'Good evening,' said the young female when she reached their table, 'my name is Karen, and I will be your waitress tonight. Would you be interested in starting with our house aperitive?'

'Good evening, Karen,' replied Gary.

He looked across to Tracey and raised his eyebrows as a hidden question.

She then looked up at the girl. 'Yes, please, that sounds nice.'

'Super, then I will get those for you. Meanwhile I will leave the menu with you and explain the specials when I return.'

She turned and headed for the bar.

Tracey leaned across the table.

'Well,' she began in a quiet voice, 'at least we know her name already.'

'Agreed,' replied Gary, equally softly, 'let's see what else we can find out about her.'

Karen returned with two flutes, placing one in front of Tracey, the other in front of Gary. 'This is prosecco with a little cassis,' she explained before taking a step backwards, 'in addition to our extensive menu, tonight we have the chef's soup of the day, vegetable. He also has his special steamed haddock, crab with lobster claws, or a tender slip of beef with all the trimmings.'

'Hmm,' replied Tracey, 'the steamed haddock sounds interesting. I'll have that with the tomato soup, please.'

'Excellent choice,' announced Karen.

'And I'll also have the soup followed by the beef please.'

'Another excellent choice, sir.'

Gary felt sure that whatever they ordered would have been an excellent choice, as seems to be the usual reaction of waiters/ waitresses in all restaurants.

'And I would like to see the wine list, please,' he added.

'Of course, sir.'

She reached over and took the menus before turning towards the kitchen. Gary took the opportunity to look around the restaurant. There was another young couple sitting in the corner. Their arms resting on the table and their fingers entwined together. Young lovers, he guessed. The only other presence in the room was the barman, who was currently drying glasses and placing them carefully on the shelf, and the receptionist who had spoken with Karen briefly, no doubt about their wine request. Sure enough, he came across to their table with the wine list tucked under his arm. He swept it out professionally and presented it to Gary, already open.

'If you have any questions about the wine, please do not hesitate to let me know,' he advised.

'Actually, I was going to ask if you have a recommendation?'

'I noted that madam is having the haddock and you are having the beef.'

'Correct,' confirmed Gary.

'Then may I suggest a white wine for the lady and a nice Coat du Rhone for you, sir.'

'Sounds ideal,' agreed Gary.

'Would you like a glass or bottle?'

'Bottle,' replied Tracey.

'Half a bottle of each, please,' clarified Gary.

The waiter nodded and left them alone again.

'Half a bottle!' she whispered, 'is that all I am worth to you?'

'We have to keep a clear head,' he argued.

'OK, mister sensible, right as always,' she lifted her flute, 'here's to a pleasant evening.'

'And a productive one,' he added.

She raised one inquisitive eyebrow.

'Have we not already been productive in the hotel?'

'Don't try to twist my words, madam.'

His eyes were smiling at her as he clinked his glass against hers.

Karen returned carrying their soups and placed them on the top plate next to the roses.

'Enjoy your meal,' she announced, turning around before they had the chance to reply, not that one was needed.

They ate their soup in silence. Gary watched the young couple out of the corner of his eye. The young man looked nervous. By contrast, the young girl looked confident, deciding on the dessert for both of them. This was most likely the young man's first date, and he was in awe of this girl, hanging on her every word and appearing to agree with everything she said. He then felt his shin being kicked. He looked up to see Tracey staring hard at him.

'Sorry,' he said simply.

'I should think so,' she replied, sitting back in her seat, 'we are here to watch this girl, not the others at the table.'

'Just keeping an eye out on everyone, that's all.'

'I know you all too well, Mr. Hardgrove,' she said with emphasis on his false name. 'You must learn to wind down now and then.'

'I will once we have dealt with the rest of the Higher Middle. All the while, even if one survives, then that one is a threat to this world.'

'I know, I know,' she pleaded, 'but killing yourself will not help us, or the world, come to that.'

He thought about what she said. Her words made sense, and for the last few years he had allowed himself to calm down a little, be his old self again. However, these recent experiences awoke all those previous painful thoughts, all the old fears came boiling back to the surface. He felt sure something was about to happen, just like it did all those years ago. It cost the lives of most of their group, but they were finally able to stop the Higher Middle. Or did they? Did they really stop them or just delay them? Were they waiting to recoup their losses, regroup for the final assault on their depleted group? He knew they had taken most of them out as well. That was when Jon was with them. He has passed on to the next world. He could stop them on his own, but he was gone and all he had to rely on was Joanne and Tracey. Tracey was the love of his life. It is ironic in some way that she should survive the numerous battles. Which made him think. Did they deliberately spare her life and focus on the others, knowing that the final battle would leave his group all the more weakened? He had no doubt that Tracey would fight well, but she stood little chance on her own against either Tampong or Shoil. He shook his head, not sure why such thoughts entered his head now. As long as he kept her close, then he could protect her as best he could. Joanne was a fifth guardian and should be able to look after herself, one-on-one. Given that Shoil appeared to be close by, that at least meant that Joanne was safe, for now. Perhaps Tracey was right, perhaps they should go back home and give up the chase. They should find Joanne and tell her what they know, particularly about this new presence. She needed to know, needed to be alert in case she came into contact with it herself. Throughout the history of their conflict, they seemed to have this knack for finding each other. As if they were drawn together by some unknown force. If this were true, then surely it would only be a matter of time before Joanne was drawn to them. God help her if she came across two of them together.

He then heard fingers clicking and he was snapped out of his thoughts.

'Earth to Gary,' Tracey was saying.

Her face was close to his.

'What, ho, sorry, I was in deep thought.'

'You can say that again.'

There was worry in her voice.

'Three times I called out your name before you acknowledged my existence.'

'Again. Sorry.'

'What were you thinking so much about this time?'

'Our future,' he said simply.

'And what does it look like?'

'Foggy.'

'That is not very reassuring.'

'Sorry, but I cannot give you a better answer, except I think you were right all along, in that we should return home and try and find Joanne.'

'What has brought on this change of heart?'

Before he could answer, Karen brought their main course and sat it in front of them. She was also carrying their wine.

'Enjoy your meal,' she said, walking around to the side of the table and pouring a little of the wine in Gary's glass.

He picked it up and sipped the wine.

'Very nice,' he announced, placing the glass back on the table.

Karen nodded and topped up his glass. She left the bottle on the table and picked up the white and repeated the process. Tracey smiled and gave a positive nod. Karen topped her glass up before leaving her bottle on the table too. She then turned to leave the two to their intense discussion. She saw them leaning close to each other and talking quietly. It wasn't a lovers' exchange, she had seen enough of them to know, but more of a concerned exchange. She also noticed them consciously seating back when she approached. An obvious sign she was not meant to listen to what they were saying, not that she had any interest. She just liked to study people and try to gauge what they were like. Judging by these two, they had been together for a long time and were comfortable in each other's presence. She admired them for that and wondered if she would ever experience such comfort with a male partner. That made her think about Terry again. Perhaps he was the one. She thought that maybe she would ask him this evening. Perhaps take the next step in their relationship. Her eyes then caught sight of the young man trying to catch her attention, indicating with his hands that he wanted the bill. She smiled and nodded her understanding.

As she walked behind the bar, Tracey leaned forward again.

'Well?' she asked.

'Hmm, this meat is delicious,' he replied, chewing.

'I was not asking about your meal,' she snapped.

He took a deep breath and lowered his knife and fork.

'I know,' he admitted.

He looked at her and could see her eyes trying to penetrate his. Looking for answers to questions she did not understand.

'I was just thinking that we should definitely inform Joanne, once we find her that is, and alert her to this new presence, just in case she should stumble upon it herself.'

It was Tracey's turn to lower her cutlery.

'Do you think that is likely?'

Gary did not answer straight away as Karen passed their table and headed towards the other couple, where she laid a silver tray down with a piece of paper and two chocolates in front of the young man. Gary assumed the paper was their bill. The young boy immediately pulled out his wallet and put his credit card down on top of the piece of paper, not even bothering to check it. The boy seemed very keen on leaving now. Perhaps he was on a promise. Karen picked up the tray and began walking back, but she stopped at their table

'Is everything to your liking?' she asked.

'Delicious,' they both replied in unison.

She nodded and walked up to the bar to process the credit card. Gary knew she would pass them again, so picked up his knife and fork and started eating. Tracey copied him. Karen walked past their table and laid the tray in front of the boy, indicating him to sign one copy of the credit card receipt. He did. After a few quick exchanges of words, the young couple got up and left. Karen started to clear their table. Stacking the dessert bowls and placing the glasses on a tray before returning to the kitchen.

They were alone in the restaurant now.

Gary could feel Tracey's eyes boring down on him, demanding a response.

'Listen, our group has a history of finding each other. It is like we were meant to be drawn together.'

She nodded her understanding.

'So I think it only fair to track down Joanne and warn her about this new presence. The fact that we have located Shoil, and the fact that she is active again.'

Again she nodded.

'Perhaps the three of us would be better closer together. Safety in numbers. That sort of thing.'

She didn't nod her head this time but shook it.

He looked puzzled.

'What is it?' he asked.

'I thought that the more of us there were together, the more of a ripple we create, which could be felt by the Higher Middle.'

'True, but only if we move into our true form. If we remain as humans, then we should not be detected.'

'Should not?'

She clearly picked up on his doubt. He should have known better. She was smarter than that. He needed to be more careful with his words.

'Nothing is guaranteed,' he said defensively, 'we should be OK as long as we are not in close proximity to them.'

'Hmmm.'

She was unconvinced by his reply.

'Still, what you say about warning Joanne makes a lot of sense. We can always go our own way afterwards, if splitting up truly is the safest way. Perhaps we can leave a way of contacting each other.'

'No,' he said a little louder than intended.

He quickly looked around, but the restaurant was still deserted.

'If we leave the slightest of trails, then that can be found if either one of us is absorbed.'

Tracey opened her mouth, realizing the stupidity of her statement. She placed a piece of haddock in her mouth and forced herself to chew on it, closing her mouth again.

They sat in silence for a few minutes, mainly to finish their meals. Gary took a large swig of his wine. He suddenly felt thirsty. He finished his glass, so topped it up again. He looked across and saw Tracey finishing off her glass, so he took her bottle and topped her glass up. She smiled warmly at him. He felt a pang of guilt pierce his heart. He had never loved anyone as much as he loved her. He would do anything for her. He would die for her. He would do so without hesitation if it protected her. She seemed to sense what he was thinking as she reached over and stroked his hand gently. It was a reassuring touch. A touch of love. Small electrical bolts ran up his arm on their touch, but he never flinched. Instead, he embraced the feeling, knowing that she was experiencing the same. She moved her hand away when Karen came back into the restaurant.

'Are you all done?' she asked when she reached their table.

'Yes, thank you. Our compliments to the chef,' said Gary.

'I will tell the chef straight away. Meanwhile, can I interest you in dessert and/or coffee?'

'Dessert sounds interesting,' announced Tracey with renewed excitement in her voice.

'Just coffee for me please,' replied Gary.

'And coffee for you too, madam?'

'Yes, please.'

Tracey looked around the restaurant.

'Is it always this quiet?'

Karen sighed.

'Yes, unfortunately. Our most popular nights are Thursday and Friday. Otherwise it is fairly dead here.'

She then looked directly at the two sitting at the table.

'Are you visiting here? I only ask as I am a local girl and haven't seen you around before.'

'Yes,' confirmed Gary, 'we heard about this interesting city, so had to come and see for ourselves.'

'Where are you from?'

'London,' he answered.

'London! Well compared to the capital, this is a graveyard.'

Gary and Tracey laughed.

'Surely it cannot be as bad as that. We have enjoyed our trip so far.'

'For a few days, yes, the city has a lot of history and some very nice buildings, but in all honestly, if you are not a football or university fan, then there is very little to keep you here.'

'But you stay here,' said Tracey.

'That's because I am a local girl. Give me a good reason and I'll be on the first train out of here.'

'Like a boyfriend perhaps?' asked Tracey in all innocence.

Nicely done, thought Gary.

His eyes glittered at Tracey, so she smiled back at him.

'If he was not a local lad, then yes, absolutely.'

'Aha,' said Tracey, raising one finger in the air, 'so there is someone keeping you here.'

'Maybe,' was her simple guarded answer, filled with a little bit of embarrassment. 'Let me get your dessert menu for you.'

'No need,' replied Tracey, 'do you have any ice cream? If so, I would love a scoop of vanilla and a scoop of chocolate.'

'Of course. A woman after my own heart.'

Karen's words were sincere, with Tracey guessing she also had a love of ice cream.

'I'll be right back.'

After she left, Gary silently applauded Tracey.

'What?' she asked innocently.

'You should be a detective.'

'Ho, it was just a girl thing. Something you men will never understand.'

'Amen to that,' he said.

Karen returned and placed a large bowl of ice cream, containing four scoops of ice cream. She then set a small tray down containing two coffees, a milk jug, sugar, and four chocolates.

'Enjoy,' she said, walking away.

'Clearly you have a fan there,' remarked Gary, looking in envy at her full bowl of ice cream.

He licked his lips wishing he had opted for the same now.

'Perhaps she is actually a lesbian,' said Tracey quietly.

'Doubt it. Probably just looking for a bigger tip.'

'Always the cynic.'

Gary laughed.

'Enjoy your dessert.'

He picked up his glass and finished off his wine.

As she ate, a large animal was slowly walking past the restaurant. Shoil had returned to the place she saw the two lovers kissing and was now tracking the scent back to the restaurant. As she passed she picked up a strong scent of the female. It was obvious she must have used this route often as her scent was still fresh. She had followed it one way until the scent faded, so she returned to walk back up the street in the opposite direction. She kept her nose close to the pavement, sniffing all the time. She ignored anything else around her, focusing all her attention on the scent trail. Two men were walking towards her when they noticed the large animal, one that looked horribly familiar. They quickly crossed the road and hid in a shop entrance. The animal completely ignored them and walked past. They both sighed, quickening their pace to put as much space between them and the animal as they could. They walked as quickly as they could, daring not to burst into a run, just in case it caused the animal to look in their direction. As soon as they disappeared around a corner they started running, never looking back.

Shoil never noticed them, keeping her nose close to the ground. As she came up to the restaurant, the scent was almost overpowering. She stopped and raised her head. Only two people were sitting in the restaurant, and both looked familiar, but she couldn't place where she had seen them. Just then, the girl came in, and Shoil's attention immediately turned to her. It was the girl.

She had found her.

Just as Gary placed his glass back on the table, he was about to ask Tracey for a taste of her ice cream when he noticed her eyes.

They were completely blue.

He knocked the glass over, causing Tracey to look in his direction. Her mouth dropped open. His eyes were completely blue too.

Karen was walking up to their table, behind Gary and directly in front of Tracey. She stopped when she noticed her bright blue eyes. Her first thoughts were that her eyes must be playing tricks on her, but as she started walking again it was clear those eyes were genuinely blue. She had never seen eyes like that before. They were almost as bright as a torchlight. Tracey saw Karen staring at her so looked down. Gary intuitively knew what that meant but also knew he couldn't do anything about it right now. He slowly turned his head towards the front door. He saw the large animal with glowing orange eyes. He indicated the door with his eyes. Tracey turned in the direction he was looking. She saw Shoil. Her spoon was hanging in the air. She watched as the animal slowly lowered its head and walked past the restaurant's main entrance. Tracey's ice cream slipped off her spoon to splash onto her plate. It was ignored by both.

Karen came up to the table.

'Would you like anything else?' she asked.

'No, no thank you,' answered a still shaken Gary, 'just the bill please.'

'Certainly, sir,' she went to turn but paused and returned her glance towards Tracey, whose eyes had now returned to normal.

'Excuse me for asking,' she began, 'but are you wearing special contact lenses by any chance?'

Tracey looked across to Gary. Seeing that his eyes had returned to normal, she guessed hers had too, so she risked lifting up her head towards Karen.

'Yes,' she lied, 'why do you ask?'

'Well, as I was walking towards your table, I could have sworn your eyes glowed blue like lamps.'

'Aha,' said Gary, 'we are trying out new contact lenses for an ophthalmic company, but they are not perfected yet. In certain light, they appear to glow. I noticed her eyes too and we will inform the company.'

'Wow, whatever will they think of next?'

She turned and appeared to accept his explanation. She quickly returned with their bill, placing the silver tray in front of him. He casually checked over the bill before putting his credit card on top, sweeping up the chocolates and passing two to Tracey. However, she had suddenly lost her appetite, so slipped them into her pocket. Karen took the tray, processed his card, and returned with his receipt. He added a generous tip, signed the slip, and picked up the copy. He slipped the copy and credit card back into his wallet. He rose and Tracey followed his movement.

'Thank you and have a pleasant evening,' announced Karen.

'Thank *you*,' replied Gary.

When they reached the front door, Gary indicated to Tracey to hang back. He opened the door and slowly leaned his head out into the street. He looked both ways but there was no sign of Shoil. He made a subtle gesture with his hand, so Tracey followed him outside. They slowly walked down the street, both alert and both extremely nervous.

Karen watched them leave. She thought it strange he checked the street before leaving. It was as if they were hiding from someone. She shrugged her shoulders, deciding it was none of her business. She looked at the receipt and noticed the tip. She nodded her approval.

Best tip I've had for a long time, she thought.

Shoil watched the couple leave the restaurant. She had transformed and was now standing naked in a doorway. They definitely looked familiar and that troubled her. Now she was of two minds. Did she follow these two or wait for this girl to finish for the day and follow her home? She decided to wait. This new source was her priority. She needed to find the male. She decided she would track the other two later. She moved back into her animal form and trotted up to the front of the restaurant. She stopped where the two strangers had stood and took deep breaths, registering their scent. She knew she could track them down later.

She turned and was about to start walking back to the doorway to confront the girl when her world suddenly started to whirl around inside her head. She briefly felt dizzy before losing control of her legs. She blacked out.

The pest control officer lowered his dart gun. He had shot the beast in its hind with his first dart. There was no immediate reaction, so he fired a second shot into the animal. He was rewarded when he saw it stagger, then collapse into the path. He packed his weapon away, stowed it in the back of his truck before calling to his colleague, who was standing ready with a trolley. They walked up to the sleeping animal, and the two of them just managed to lift the beast onto the trolley.

'Jesus, this is one heavy son of a gun,' remarked one of the officers.

The other officer puffed out his cheeks in exertion.

'This one certainly fits the description of that monster who ripped that man apart. We best be careful with this one. Perhaps put another dart in it for good measure.'

'Agreed,' confirmed the other officer, 'I don't want this bugger waking up in our vehicle.'

He returned to his cab and pulled out a pistol from the glove compartment.

He loaded a dart and placed the weapon against the neck of the sleeping beast. He shot the dart into its neck.

'Done,' he advised, 'let's get this beast back to the pound and then notify the authorities who will best decide how to dispose of it.'

The other officer nodded, keen to get rid of this dangerous animal. They loaded it onto the truck, closed the door, and entered the cab.

'Have you ever seen anything like that before?'

'Never,' confirmed the other officer, 'it's as big as a lion, bigger even, but looks like a dog. Not one I have ever seen before though.'

They drove away.

At ten thirty that same evening, the lights of the restaurant went out and Karen stepped out and made her way home. She had no idea she was being hunted. No idea that she was being followed. Gary and Tracey had kept a discreet distance from her. Gary was an expert trailer and knew exactly how to keep out of sight. Tracey had the sense to follow his lead, knowing all too well his skill in this area. They followed her home, catching the same bus, watching her go inside her home. They turned and nodded to each other. Tracey turned and walked away. She knew that Gary was going to wait all night to see if anyone else turned up. She was a little nervous about leaving him, particularly as they had seen Shoil so close. She also was nervous about being alone, if she was completely honest, and walked quickly back to the hotel, locking the door when she arrived.

Shoil woke up feeling cold. She was shivering. It was the cold that had woken her from her slumber. She was human again, and naked again. She looked around the small cell. Strange smells filled her nostrils. She realized she was not alone. Other dogs and cats were also in the room but in different cells. All were cowering from her. Dogs had their tails between their legs and had backed away as far as they could. Cats were spitting in fear at her. She looked at each animal in turn. None were a threat, so she looked around again. Her neck and rump felt tender. She rubbed her neck not understanding what had happened to her. She became aware of voices in the other room. She listened intently.

'Glad you could come so quickly,' said the voice.

'No problem. Where did you find the beast?' said the voice of another man.

'In the high street close to a local restaurant. It took two high-dose darts to bring it down.'

Shoil then realized she must have been knocked out by animal darts. Her anger started to rise deep inside. She released a deep growl, causing some of the dogs to howl in fear, and others joined in. Their howling was heard by the voices in the other room.

'I'd say the beast is awake already, judging by the sounds of those dogs.'

'That's impossible,' replied the other voice. 'I initially put two into the beast then followed up with a third in the neck for good measure. It should be out until morning.'

'Then let's check. Bring the weapons to be on the safe side.'

She heard the lock turn in the door, so stood up.

The two men entered the room and froze on the spot. Their eyes were open wide in shock. Standing in the cell was a beautiful, naked woman.

'What the fuck, Jack?' announced one of the men, who could not take his eyes away from the beautiful creature, 'I thought you said you captured the beast. Is this some kind of nice joke? It isn't my birthday, you know, not that I am complaining. This beast is one fine specimen.'

The other man shook his head and looked around at the other cells before returning his gaze to Shoil. They both walked closer to her cell, eager for a closer look. Shoil said nothing but slowly placed her hands on the cell bars.

'Where is the beast?' asked the animal inspector, griping his weapon nervously.

He was sure he placed it in this cell, although he had his doubts now. Where this naked woman came from though was a complete mystery.

'Right here,' replied Shoil, breaking the man out of his thoughts.

'How did you get in here?' asked the other officer.

'He put me in here,' she said, pointing at the man with the gun.

He simply shook his head in defiance.

'He paid me to be in here. He said I was to wait here for you. To be ready for you. A special gift. So, do you like your gift?'

She raised her arms into the air so that he had a full view of her figure. He looked her up and down several times.

'You bet I am liking.'

He licked his lips in anticipation.

'You cunning old dog. Not sure why you did this, but man, what a nice surprise.'

'Nothing to do with me mate, honest,' said the inspector, confusion sounding in his voice.

He then noticed the other animals' stances for the first time.

'What's up with these creatures?' he asked, 'they look and sound nervous. Scared even.'

'Who gives a shit,' answered the officer.

He could not take his eyes away from Shoil and was oblivious to anything else going on in the room.

'So are you coming in for some playtime then or what?' she asked, taking an inviting step backwards, lowering her hands slowly to her side.

'Give me the keys, Jack,' he asked, still not able to take his eyes off the girl.

He was unable to wait for the pleasures she was about to give him.

'It wasn't me,' he pleaded again, taking an involuntary step backwards.

Something wasn't right here. The strange, large animal had disappeared, and in its place was this naked woman. Nothing made sense. He was almost wondering whether he had spiked himself with one of his darts.

The other man's groin was making his brain go dull. He reached over and removed the keys from Jack's belt and started to move towards the cell. His eyes remained fixed on her body. It had been a long time since he had seen such a young, firm, welcoming body. Her full breasts, slim waist, and inviting groin. She parted her legs a little as if knowing where his eyes were looking, willing him to come for her. He wanted her so badly.

'No wait,' pleaded Jack.

He went to grab his friend but was shoved violently onto the concrete floor.

The man turned the key and started to open the cell door. Before his lecherous smile could leave his face, a long sharp tongue burst from Shoil's mouth to wrap around his neck. She tightened her grip quickly, decapitating the head almost immediately. Dogs howled even louder at the smell of fear, while cats darted around their cell trying to find an escape. Jack's brain wouldn't believe what his eyes were telling him, but his training kicked in and he started to rise off the ground still gripping his gun. He instinctively fired a dart at Shoil, which struck her firmly in her right breast. She screamed with rage, shooting orange darts from her eyes. They hit the man's face at the same time and his head exploded on contact. His body staggered for a few seconds before falling to the ground. She cursed her luck. Firstly she had ripped one of the men's heads clean off from his shoulders, the other one she had blown to pieces. Neither would help her if she absorbed them. Still, she thought there was nothing to lose, so she placed her hand inside the nearest man's neck, digging her fingers into his exposed spine. There was a guggling sound before his body started to shake violently. His skin started to break up as he was slowly absorbed. She repeated the act on the other body. Soon only two piles of their clothing were left on the floor, the only evidence of two lives suddenly snuffed out. She looked around the room.

'If only animals could talk,' she said aloud, 'what stories you could tell.'

She sneered at the pathetic creatures.

The dogs were still cowering in their cages. A couple had peed themselves, while cats frantically tried to gnaw their way through metal bars, succeeding in only breaking their teeth in the process.

Shoil then remembered the girl. She had no idea how long she had been unconscious but decided to go back to the restaurant in any case. She pulled the dart from her breast and threw it to the ground. She bent down towards the nearest pile of clothes, picked them up and slipped the trousers on. They were too big for her. Fortunately, the man wore a belt, so she tightened it up. She then slipped into his shirt, which was also a little big. The cuffs covered her hands, so she rolled them back. As it turned out, the man had small feet and she slipped into the black trainers easily, ignoring his socks and underpants. She left the room, much to the relief of the frightened animals. As she walked past the main office, she noticed a local map on the wall. She ripped it down and studied it. The animal shelter was marked with a red circle. She soon found the restaurant and was pleased to see that it was just two streets further down. She folded the map and placed it in her top breast pocket, then walked quickly out of the shelter and down the road, back towards the restaurant, rubbing her chest where the dart had struck. It felt numb and she was a little lightheaded.

She turned the corner to find the restaurant in total blackness. She screamed aloud, causing a dog in the distance to bark.

'Tomorrow then, bitch. Tomorrow.'

She turned and walked back down the street. Not for the first time, she was in a foul mood.

***

Back in the hotel, Gary and Tracey were staring at each other, looking for inspiration. Nothing came.

'So what do we do now?' she asked, breaking the uncomfortable silence.

'Not sure,' admitted Gary.

'Not helpful.'

'I know, I know.'

He stood up and started pacing around the room.

'Right, so what do we know so far?'

It wasn't really a question to her, although she responded as if it was. She also stood up and started to pace around the room in opposite directions to Gary.

'Well,' she began, 'we seemed to have found the girl and know where she lives. It seems as though Shoil has also found the girl, so there is a good bet she also knows where she lives. The question is, do we approach her, follow her, warn her . . .'

Gary stopped walking and turned to face her.

'Warn her?

Tracey thought about her earlier comment.

'Yes,' she confirmed, 'she may not know what she is walking into. We should warn her to keep away from the strange presence and Shoil.'

'Do you really think that is going to help?'

'It might.'

'Just think that through. What are you going to tell her, that the presence she is seeing might actually be out to kill most of the humans on this planet and rule the rest, while the large animal is really a woman also set on world domination?'

'Well, we don't have to put it quite like that,' she said defensively.

'No, we have to face facts.'

'Which are?' she asked.

'Now that Shoil has discovered the girl, we can assume that her life expectancy is extremely limited. If Shoil was indeed searching for the girl, then maybe that was because she does not know where the other presence is either.'

'So?'

'So maybe we can find it before she does.'

'And what about the girl?'

'As I said, she is as good as dead.'

'WHAT! You cannot simply leave her to Shoil.'

'What else would you have us do?'

'As I said, warn her.'

Tracey knew deep down that his words made sense, although she could not bring herself to believe that there was absolutely nothing they could do to save her, or at least try to save her.

'Tell her to get the hell out of the city. To disappear and never contact the presence again.'

'Do you really believe she would do that?'

Tracey sighed.

'No, I guess not. Not if it is true love.'

She looked across to Gary, her eyes filling with water. She felt hopeless. He moved towards her and opened his arms, which she gratefully fell into. He closed his arms around her.

He spoke quietly.

'I know sometimes I sound like a hard and even evil man, but I am only doing what I think is best. Best for the world as a whole. Sometimes we have to make sacrifices to save this planet. I believe this is one of those occasions. It is never pleasant, particularly when you get to know the person or persons involved.'

She tightened her grip around him.

'I know,' she admitted, 'if only there was a way to stop Shoil.'

'Don't forget about Tampong. She might be around as well.'

'Don't remind me.'

They stood together for a little while, not wanting to part. Gary gently stroked her hair, while she rested her head on his chest. He then gently pulled her away, clearing the hair from her face.

'OK, this is what we do,' he began, 'we go back to her house tomorrow and watch to see if she leaves during the day. Who knows, maybe we will get lucky, and she will take us straight to the source.'

'And if not?'

'Then we continue the search.'

'What about her, Karen?'

'Fate will decide,' he answered simply, not wanting to tell her what he really thought.

'And what about Shoil? What do we do about her?'

'That's a tricky one,' he admitted, 'let's cross that bridge when we come to it.'

'Well, I hope that is not a bridge too far.'

'Was that actually a reference to a film?'

She smiled. The first time she had smiled for a little while.

'Maybe,' she said simply.

Then she looked serious again.

'Not sure why I should think this, but I get the impression this presence you feel is a boy and could even be the boy she referred to as the reason she was staying.'

'Makes sense,' he conceded.

'Maybe,' she began, 'just maybe, if it is a boy and they are in love, that the boy can protect her, or at least stop Shoil from killing her or harming her.'

He kept stroking her hair.

'That's a positive thought,' he admitted, 'keep hold of that thought and maybe, just maybe, it will come true.'

She kept her head against his chest. If she had raised her head she would have seen his tear-filled eyes.

He was almost certain he knew the girl's fate and it made him sad.

***

'She's active again,' Terry said.

His tone was cold but calm.

Tampong looked up from the magazine she was reading, not sure she heard him correctly.

'You mean Shoil is active again?'

'Correct,' he confirmed, 'she has taken another two lives. Not for absorption though, but to escape from somewhere.'

'Escape?' repeated Tampong.

'Right. I sense a lot of animals around, in addition to her, of course. She was not a dog this time.'

Tampong lowered her magazine, resting it on her knees.

'Well, if she was escaping, that would suggest she had initially been captured. If so, I would love to meet the people who captured her and learn how they did it.'

Terry was not really listening to her.

'There is something else, something different is happening.'

'Different? Tell me more?'

'Well, I'm not sure, to be honest. Another presence perhaps.'

'Another presence?'

The conversation was interrupted when the telephone rang. Tampong was tempted to tell him to ignore it, but he was already standing up and heading for the phone.

'Hello?' he asked.

Tampong listened intently.

'Hey, Karen. Nice to hear from you.'

Tampong picked up her magazine, pretending to read it again.

'Sure, we are still on for Saturday. Did you have another boring evening at work?'

'Wow, that's a big tip. Were they rich then?'

She continued to listen.

'What was strange about them? Blue eyes? Nothing strange about blue eyes, is there?'

Tampong dropped her magazine.

'All of her eyes were blue! You mean the whites of her eyes were actually blue too? Contact lenses, wow, technology today is incredible. Yep, look forward to seeing you on Saturday then. . . . Same time, same place. . . . You too. . . No, no, I'll talk to you when I see you. I can wait, and we can forget about tonight now. No problem. You get some rest. Goodnight, Karen.'

He put the phone down and turned to see Tampong looking like she had just seen a ghost.

'What's up?'

'Blue eyes,' she said.

'Yeah, can you believe that? This woman in the restaurant had these amazingly blue eyes. When Karen asked her about them, she said they were some new contact lenses they were trying out. Apparently they had a few glitches, which she said caused the glow.'

'Blue eyes,' she repeated.

Terry walked up and knelt in front of her.

'What's wrong?'

She looked deep into his eyes as if searching for answers.

'You said earlier that you felt something different.'

'Yes, and?'

'It's them,' she said simply.

Her eyes were wide open in shock.

'Who?'

'The Lower Middle.'

'The Lower Middle. That's impossible. How could they possibly know you or Shoil are here?'

'They feel us when we activate ourselves. Like we feel them. Like you do.'

He sat back on his heels.

'But why would they be in the restaurant then?'

They both looked at each other.

'Karen,' they said in unison.

'But why would they be searching for Karen. She has no abilities. Has she?' he questioned, with concern etched across his face.

Tampong did not answer straight away. She too was wondering the same thing.

'Perhaps they have somehow found a link between her and you, or me.'

'Then we have to warn her straight away.'

He went to stand up, but Tampong immediately held both his hands to hold him in place.

'Wait. Let's not do anything hasty.'

'But she might be in danger. They may try to harm her.'

'I don't think so. It is not their way.'

'Not their way. What is that supposed to mean?'

'They are here to protect humans, not harm them.'

'Protect them! From whom?'

'Us.'

'You mean from Shoil?'

'No. I mean from us, the Higher Middle.'

His eyes widened in surprise. He took a step backwards, so she kept hold of his hands tightly. He tried to pull away, but she was too strong for him. He looked up at her, confusion written all over his face.

'I would never harm Karen, nor indeed anybody else. Not deliberately. You know that, don't you?' he said pleadingly.

'I know,' she said, 'but then I don't understand any of this either.'

She sighed heavily. The day she had been dreading for so long had finally arrived. She motioned him to sit down on the sofa. He did so reluctantly. She moved closer to him.

For the next two hours, she told him everything about the Higher and Lower Middle, their objectives, and the history between the two groups. She tried to cover everything, the good, the bad, the ugly, although deciding to conveniently leave out the harm she had inflicted on several humans. She had not been proud of what she had done in the past, but it was not something she could change, adding that this *was* something to learn from. He listened quietly, not saying a word until she had finished. He sat back and reflected on what she had told him.

'So, we are the bad ones, and the Lower Middle are the good ones,' he surmised.

'Not that simple,' she replied.

'Really, how so? We are trying to destroy humans and control the planet, whereas the Lower Middle are trying to defend humans and the planet. How does that not make them the good ones and us the bad?'

'OK. I can see why you would say that, and to some we would indeed be perceived as the bad ones in this argument.'

'Argument? You call killing people in cold blood an argument?'

'In all wars innocent people get injured or killed.'

'Not deliberately,' he countered.

She had to take a deep breath to calm herself down.

'Check your history. You will find some deliberate horrors have taken place without any help from us.'

'Such as?'

'Such as Hitler and his SS army, out to annihilate the Jewish population. That's just for starters. Then, if you go back even further in history, there were the crusades. A religious war purely based on beliefs.'

'That's different. Those were wars, one with an army being led by a crazy man.'

'This is also war. One that has been raging for thousands of years.'

He looked up to her.

'For thousands of years?'

'Yes. We have been around for most of mankind's existence.'

'So how can you be sure that you were not the reason for all these wars and battles then?'

'You had to be there. If you were, then you would understand.'

'And you were?'

'For the most part, yes.'

'How? You look no older than fifty.'

She almost slapped his face for the insult before realizing that to the young even people in their thirties must seem old to them. She had heard other children at his school expressing amazement that their parents could be as old as forty.

'Well, we switch bodies when the current one expires.'

'Expires!'

'Yes, become too old for us and start to lose their efficiency, particularly in the battlefield.'

'So how do you switch?'

'We find another suitable body and take it over.'

'What happens to the person the body belonged to?'

'We absorb the person, become that person. We have all their memories and thoughts as if our own.'

'Crickey! You murder them.'

It was a cold statement, but an honest one and she could not reprimand him for it. He had spoken the truth.

'It was them or us,' she replied simply.

'You had a choice. They didn't.'

Again his words rang true, and she started to feel guilty, although in her heart she knew they had no choice if the group was to remain strong and functional.

'True,' she simply replied, wanting to avoid any confrontation with him.

Terry then went silent. He was clearly thinking things through, so she left him to his thoughts. He nodded to himself.

'If this war has been going on for thousands of years, then the Lower Middle must switch bodies too, correct?'

'Correct,' she confirmed.

'Then in my mind that makes them no better than us. How can they claim to protect human beings if they murder them also in cold blood?'

'Not that I am trying to defend them,' she began, 'but if you put yourself in their shoes, they have little option if they are to be strong enough to try and stop us.'

‘I suppose so,’ he reluctantly agreed, ‘so what happens now?’

‘Well, we know that Shoil is around and now at least one of the Lower Middle, maybe more. We have no idea really why they are here. It could be because of me, you, or even Shoil.’

He clicked his fingers.

‘It’s Shoil,’ he replied excitedly, ‘they most likely saw the news report of that large dog attack and knew that it must be Shoil, so they came here to track her down.’

‘Makes sense,’ she agreed, ‘and given that they know all too well how powerful she is, there must be more than one of them. Most likely the man she was with. Otherwise he would have been equally surprised by the change in her eyes. So we can safely assume there are at least two of them here.’

‘Could there be more of them?’

‘If so, only one or two at most. We killed quite a few of them over the last decade. Sadly, they have taken quite a few of us with them.’

‘So let’s assume there are at least two of them. We can take them, can’t we?’

‘Not so fast, flyboy. I still remember the last battle with them. One changed into a huge giant, bigger than even Zelphur—she was our leader at the time and the most powerful one of all of us—he was able to crush her like a fly. No, if he is here, we will need all of us to tackle him, and that includes Shoil.’

‘Who, I suppose, will be less than keen on fighting with us,’ he surmised again.

‘Quite right. I am certain she would rather watch us be destroyed by the Lower Middle than come to our aide.’

‘Even as one of the Higher Middle. Would she really just watch us die?’

‘Her hatred for me runs deep. As for you, I have no idea. Maybe she will save you to help restore the balance.’

‘So if we cannot rely on her help and this giant shows up, what do we do?’

‘Run and hide, Terry, run and hide.’

‘That’s not the way of the Higher Middle.’

'No, it's my way.'

'Perhaps if I talk to Shoil, contact her, try to make her see sense. Show her I have special abilities too, thanks to you.'

'I doubt she would listen to you.'

'Worth a try, isn't it?'

'Too risky. Far too risky.'

'Then what about Shoil? What does she want?'

'Probably me. She is hunting me, but you know that.'

'There is something else.'

She looked hard into his eyes. He could not hold her gaze, which told her all she needed to know.

'What's happened?' she questioned, not sure she wanted to hear his answer.

'I think she knows about me.'

'How?'

He hesitated at first, then let out a long breath.

'Well, you know we have contacted each other with our minds.'

Tampong leaned closer to him.

'Yes, go on.'

'That's it. I was able to see her and felt sure she could see me.'

'Ho my god!' she exclaimed, leaning back against the sofa, 'you two can connect.'

'That's a good thing, isn't it? I didn't feel threatened by her, not the second time.'

She sat bolt upright.

'How many times have you made contact then?'

'Only twice, honest.'

He answered quickly, so quickly she knew he was telling the truth.

'Did you initiate the contact or did she?'

'The first time it just kinda happened. The second time I initiated it.'

'Why would you do that?'

'Because I wanted to try and contact her. Try to understand her. Try to reason with her. I was angry with you at the time.'

'And?'

'And nothing really. She just looked at me and smiled. That was it.'

'Just looked at you and smiled,' she repeated, although she was trying to digest what that actually meant.

'Yes, that's all.'

'Things are getting a little too close of comfort, Terry. Firstly, you are developing your skills very quickly and now you are able to connect with Shoil. Shoil of all people.'

'But that is a good thing,' he continued to argue, 'I can tell where she is and what she is doing.'

'And what if she can do the same with you?'

'I don't think she can somehow.'

'Can you be sure of that?'

'Not really, it's just a feeling, that's all.'

'We have to get out of here, and now.'

'Where?'

'Singapore.'

'Not that again.'

'Yes, that again,' she snapped. 'I have a job offer, and I now intend to take it. We will be safer there. The further away from here the better.'

'And what about me?'

'You will find new friends there.'

'No, I mean what about me and Karen?'

'There can be no you and Karen. She is better off away from you. This way she has a chance to continue living a normal life. Around you, she is certain to be found by Shoil, who will not hesitate to trap and finally kill her if she thought for one second it would bring you to her.'

'You don't know that.'

'Yes, Terry, yes I do.'

'You cannot do this to me. It's not fair.'

There were tears in his eyes now. He was shaking his head in disbelief.

'I am doing this as much for you as for me, Terry,' she replied softly.

He said nothing. Instead he just turned away and rushed upstairs, slamming his bedroom door shut again. She could hear him sobbing in his room, deciding it was best to leave him to his grief. Meanwhile, she had some planning and packing to do. She knew he was going to hate her for splitting him up with Karen. In time, he would understand that on occasions like this it was necessary to make hard decisions. At least, she hoped so.

Terry lay facedown on his bed. He turned over on his back and wiped the tears from his eyes. It just was not fair. He had found a girl he could fall in love with, if he hadn't already, and she said she really liked him too. They were good together. It was not fair. Perhaps Shoil should be the one he was with? Perhaps she could help him and make sure he stayed with Karen. Then he remembered the first time he contacted her, how she changed from being a sexy naked woman to that evil sneering beast. Could Tampong be right? Could Shoil just be luring him into a trap? He wished he were older, a little wiser. No, a lot wiser. He thumped his fist down against the bed. If he hadn't received her blood, then none of this would have happened. Then again, from what the nurses and doctors told him, he would be dead by now. Life just wasn't fair. Why did he have to go to Singapore with her in any case? He had done nothing wrong—had he? He then remembered the boys and how easily he killed them. How he got angry with Tampong and nearly harmed her. Could that happen with Karen? He felt sure he could keep it under control now, not like last time. The anger grew inside him again. Unbeknown to him, his eyes turned bright orange. He subconsciously raised his arms into the air and fired off sharp needles from his fingernails. Eight needles struck the wall opposite, penetrating deep inside the wall. The needle from his thumbs struck either side of the bedroom walls. He blinked twice, looking at the needles. He had no control. It just happened and he could not prevent it. He heard Tampong running upstairs.

'Terry,' she called out, 'are you OK?'

'Yes, yes I'm fine. I was just angry a little, but I'm fine now.'

'Can I come in?'

'No. I need to be alone now.'

'OK. I'll be downstairs if you are sure you are OK.'

'I'm sure,' he said quietly.

He then sensed someone trying to contact him and guessed it must be Shoil, who no doubt sensed his change like Tampong did. He didn't want to speak with anyone right now, so shut her out of his mind, and was surprised when she quickly faded away.

***

Shoil was staring at her reflection in the shop window. Her eyes were bright orange. There was also a hint of her teeth trying to protrude from her mouth. She forced herself back into her human form and watched as her eyes returned to their natural color, while her teeth retracted back into her mouth. She had felt his anger so reached out to him, but he recoiled from her advances. This was a new development. Had he been warned about her? She doubted it as she sensed no hostility from him, rather that he just wanted to be alone. She knew that feeling all too well. She had felt like that often enough. Since missing the girl, she felt the rage inside building up, but her attempt to contact him had calmed her a little. He still felt close, so that was good news. Nobody else was in the street, which meant that the Lower Middle could not be that close, as otherwise her change would have sent them running down the street. Today, she decided, was a day to forget. A bit like many others. Too many if she were completely honest. Tomorrow was a new day, and she would hunt for this girl again. She was certain that this girl would take her to this new source, this new male or whatever he was. It might even lead her to Tampong. She realized that she had not thought about her for some time now. She had done a good job of concealing herself, but she knew she would eventually slip up and reveal herself. She did not have the discipline that Shoil did. She could not control her natural instincts to change. That meeting day would finally come, and when it did, she would be ready.

***

It was Saturday evening, Karen and Terry were sitting in McDonald's eating a hamburger. Karen had been watching him carefully.

'You are noticeably quiet tonight?' she said.

'Am I?'

'Yes, definitely. What's wrong?'

He placed his burger down onto the tray.

'There is no easy way to say this, so I'll just blurt it out. I will be leaving here.'

She stopped chewing and gulped her food down.

'What! Why? When?'

She also lowered her burger onto her tray.

'My aunty has been offered a good job, but it means us moving away.'

'OK, but that doesn't stop us from seeing each other, right?'

'That's the whole point, it does. It's a long way.'

'Where?'

'I cannot tell you.'

'What do you mean you cannot tell me? How can you sit there and tell me you are leaving but not tell me where?'

'I just cannot.'

He could not lift his eyes to look at her.

'For how long?'

'I don't know that either.'

'So, you are just going to leave me here without any explanation?'

'I want to tell you where, but I cannot. I hate this as much as you do, but there is nothing I can do about it.'

'Of course you can. You are seventeen, Terry, almost a man. You can make your own decisions. Surely your aunt can go on her own.'

'No. I have to be with her.'

'So you are dumping me just like that then?'

'No, no, I am not dumping you.'

She didn't react to his last comment, almost as if she never heard him.

'And I thought you were different.'

'Believe me, I am.'

'No, no you are not. You are just like all the rest of them. You haven't gotten into my pants, so you are off looking for some other poor soul to bed. Well, sorry, I am not that easy.'

He finally looked up at her, seeing her eyes fill with tears.

'No, Karen. It's not like that. I really like you, really. If I had a choice, then things would be different. But I don't.'

'You always have a choice, Terry,' she said, standing up, 'and you have made yours.'

'Don't leave, Karen. Please. Not like this.'

'Enjoy your life, Terry. Look after yourself.'

'Karen!' he called out as she turned and stormed out of the restaurant.

He rushed out after her and caught up with her down the road, grabbed her arm, and swung her around to face him. She was crying. He brought her into his body and held her tight. At first, she tried to pull away from him, then relaxed and wrapped her arms around him. They stayed that way for a few minutes before she finally calmed down. As she lifted her head, he wiped the tears from her face. They leaned foreheads against each other.

'I don't want to lose you, Terry,' she said quietly.

'You won't.'

'But you are going away, and I have no idea where or for how long.'

'Look, all I can tell you is that it is abroad.'

'Abroad! You are moving abroad?'

'Yes.'

'Why can't you tell me where?'

'For your safety.'

'WHAT? my safety? You are not making any sense, Terry.'

'What you don't know can't hurt you.'

'That makes absolutely no sense. You are just talking in riddles now. How can we stay in contact and have any sort of relationship with you going abroad?'

'Listen. I have been reading about this new tool called Skype. You can use it to video chat with anyone anywhere in the world.'

'You are avoiding my questions.'

'I know. Please, you just have to trust me. I simply cannot tell you.'

'It's your aunty, isn't it? Is she in some kind of trouble with the law?'

'Not the law, no.'

'Who then?'

'Let's just say there are people who are looking for her.'

'Why, what has she done? Ho, wait, don't tell me, you cannot say, right?'

He simply shrugged his shoulders.

'God, Terry, I could thump you right now. You land this news on me but leave me completely in the dark.'

'I know, I know. You have every right to be angry with me, and I don't blame you. Believe me, if there was another way out of this then we would take it. I would do anything to stay with you.'

'What was this thing you said we could chat through?'

'Skype. If you go into your computer and search for it, you can download it. We can then see each other and talk to each other . . . if you want to.'

She moved her head away from his.

'Of course I want to stay in touch. I don't want you to go away but to stay here with me. I thought we had something special.'

'We do have something special. Listen, we might be able to take care of this thing quickly. Then I could fly back to you.'

'But we don't know how long that will be, right? It could be a week, a month, a year . . . never!'

He lifted her chin up.

'We will be together again as soon as possible. I promise.'

'You'd better had. I am not going to waste my life waiting for you.'

They kissed.

Tampong watched them walking slowly down the street together, hand in hand. She had seen Karen come running out of the restaurant, tears pouring down her cheeks. Watched as Terry ran after her and stopped her. She was proud of how he handled himself. They clearly had made up and she felt relieved. She turned to return home.

There were still a lot of things to do.

***

Just one week later, her appointment letter arrived, and she was to start in just two weeks. The first thing Terry did was to contact Karen and let her know. Not surprisingly, she was shocked.

'So soon?' she said disbelievingly.

'I am afraid so. I was shocked at the speed too.'

'Just as well I downloaded this Skype thing like you said.'

'I have too,' he confessed.

'I have been trying to prepare myself for this, but it still makes my heart go cold knowing you will be leaving soon.'

'I know. I feel the same.'

'So what do we do until then?' she asked.

'Enjoy as much time together as we possibly can.'

'Well, let's not enjoy ourselves too much, or otherwise the last day will feel much worse.'

'I don't care, Karen. The last day will be the worst day of my life even if we never saw each other after today.'

Her eyes warmed to his comments, so she leaned into him, and he held her tightly.

'I am so sorry about all of this, Karen.'

'So am I,' she admitted.

'But, as I said, I will return as quickly as possible.'

'You'd better.'

'Who knows? Maybe we can deal with this little problem sooner than expected, and then we can return home safely.'

'I'll pray for that.'

'Me too.'

'I am going to miss you, Terry.'

'And I am going to miss you, Karen.'

They kissed passionately for a long time. They kept their promise and met each other every day until departure day, even if it was just him meeting her after work and walking her home.

The last day was tearful. Both were crying as they kissed for the last time. He reluctantly watched as she walked back into her home, turning, and giving him a little wave goodbye.

His heart sank. Would he ever see her again in the flesh? He hoped he would, but something was nagging at the back of his mind, telling him this might be the last time he would see her.

He hoped not. He slowly walked home and tried to prepare himself for the long journey ahead. He knew it was not going to be easy.

THE LONG JOURNEY

Date: October 2010
Ages: 17 / 1,161
Status: Semi-active

'Are you all packed?' Tampong called out from her room.

No response.

'Terry, I said are you all packed?'

Still no response.

She stopped packing her suitcase and listened. She heard no movement. No sound. She stepped out of her room and walked slowly down the corridor towards his bedroom. She cautiously stepped inside and saw him just staring down at his two filled but open suitcases.

She walked up behind him.

'I said are you all packed up?'

'Just look at that,' he replied, pointing towards his cases with both hands.

'Look at what?'

'This represents my entire seventeen years of life. Two suitcases, mostly filled with clothes.'

'And?'

'That's it. That's all I have to show for my first seventeen years of life.'

She nodded her head. She now understood.

'Listen to me,' she said, turning him towards her, 'you are still young, and not many boys your age have much more than you do.'

'Really?' His eyes were searching hers for the truth.

He then appeared to see it.

She simply nodded.

'Hurry it along. The taxi arrives in fifteen minutes.'

She turned to walk out of his room, back to finish her own packing.

'OK,' he answered, looking around his small bedroom, 'I think I am just about done in any case.'

He sighed to himself as he zipped up his last bag. He carried both cases downstairs and placed them in the hallway. He then returned upstairs to help Tampong with her luggage. When he entered her room, she was just zipping up her last bag. She stood up and opened her arms out.

'Look!' she began, 'this is the contents of my entire life.'

He looked down at her four bags and two boxes.

'And I have a lot more years on you,' she added.

He nodded as he picked up two of her cases and carried them downstairs. She followed with two more.

They had just reached the corridor when the doorbell rang.

'That will either be the estate agent or taxi,' she said, walking towards the door.

'OK. I'll get the other boxes down.'

He disappeared back upstairs as she opened the door.

A young woman stood outside. She was slim and wore wide, round glasses while clutching a clipboard.

'Ms. Armitage?' the woman asked.

'Yes,' confirmed Tampong.

'Perfect. I am April from Nationwide.'

'Hello, April from Nationwide, please come in.'

She stepped aside and April walked in, looking around the corridor, up the stairs, and then in the lounge.

'We will take care of your house for you, have no concerns there,' she stated with as much sincerity as she could muster.

'Great. This house has a long family heritage, which is why I am renting it and not selling it.'

'Makes perfect sense, madam,' she said, only half listening, 'why not make the house earn you a little money while you are away, right?'

'Right,' confirmed Tampong.

Just then there was the sound of a car horn in the road outside. Tampong stepped through the front door and waved at the taxi driver. He waved back and parked up.

'If you just give me the spare keys, I will get out of your hair.'

Tampong said nothing but unclipped some keys from her keyring and passed them to April. She swept them up in her hand and headed for the door.

'Don't worry about a thing. We will take care of everything. Have a nice trip.'

'Thank you,' Tampong replied as Terry came back down the stairs.

'Is that the taxi?' he asked.

'Yep,' confirmed Tampong.

'Right, then I will take these boxes straight to the car.'

'OK. I'll be right behind you with some suitcases.'

On seeing them exit the house, the taxi driver stepped out of his car and walked to the boot and flipped it open. Terry slipped the boxes into the boot and returned to the house to collect two more suitcases. Tampong nodded to the driver as she slipped her cases into the boot. She pushed them towards the back, leaning forward as she did so. The driver leaned back to check out her bottom and was clearly impressed.

She returned to the house and passed Terry carrying two more cases. He too slid them into the boot.

'That your mum?' asked the driver, watching her enter the house.

'My aunty,' corrected Terry.

'Aha,' said the driver, still watching the house.

He did not have long to wait before Tampong emerged. She stopped at the front door, closed it, and locked it before picking up the remaining cases and walking towards the car. This time the driver felt obliged to help, so stepped swiftly towards her.

'Let me take those for you, ma'am.'

'Thank you, truly kind,' she replied, holding out the bags.

He took hold of them and grunted at the surprising weight.

'Wow, what have you got in here?' he asked.

'My life,' she responded.

He whistled before dumping them unceremoniously onto the top of the other cases. He slammed the boot shut before walking around to the side of the vehicle and holding the door open for her. She walked up to the door but then turned to take one last look at the house. She then turned towards Terry, who was also looking at the house, standing on the other side of the car.

'Got everything?' she asked.

'Not that that is much, but yep, I have everything.'

'Then let's get going,' she said, slipping into the back seat.

The driver shut her door and walked around and opened his own door to get in. Terry shrugged his shoulders as the driver did not bother to open his door and sat next to Tampong in the back.

'Heathrow is it, love?' he asked, adjusting the mirror so that he could see her.

'Yes, please, the British Airways terminal,' she confirmed.

'Right you are, love,' he said, putting the car in gear and pulling away.

Terry looked out of the window and watched his home pass by. His heart sank a little further when they drove past the Red Lion. He was already missing Karen. They had exchanged email details, and he promised to contact her as soon as he arrived, telling her that might be a couple of days, even a week. When she questioned why, he explained that they may have to install the internet when they reached their destination.

'Going on holiday?' the driver asked, glancing in his mirror at her.

'No. I am starting a new job abroad.'

He seemed saddened by the news, not that he had any chance with her.

'Ho. So where will that be then?'

'The other side of the world,' she answered deliberately vaguely.

'Aha,' said the driver, 'going to Australia then. I have a brother-in-law who immigrated to Sydney last year. He said it was the best decision of his life and suggested I do the same thing. Me. I am a Brit to the bones and cannot see myself leaving this beautiful island. That said, if I was offered a super job, then I might just be tempted to work abroad, but I would always come back home. Home is where the heart is.'

The driver continued to talk all the way to the airport. She learned about his desire to run his own cab business, to find the love of his life and have many children. She caught him glancing at her when he mentioned this. She simply smiled politely. After forty-five minutes, they finally arrived at the terminal.

'Here we are, love, British Airways terminal. Hold on and let me get you a caddy for your luggage.'

He stepped out of the car and rushed over to grab a spare caddy just before an old lady reached it. He ignored her grunts of disapproval as he wheeled it to the back of the car. Terry already had the boot open and was just lifting the first bag out. He placed it on the caddy and proceeded to load up the others as Tampong paid the driver in cash, giving him a decent tip. He was delighted.

'Have a great flight, madam,' he called out.

'Thanks,' replied Terry sarcastically, clearly a bit miffed that the driver had ignored his very existence the whole trip.

The driver watched the two walk into the terminal before he pocketed his fare and walked back to his driver's seat.

When they were inside, Terry leaned a little towards her.

'That driver fancied you.'

'I know,' she replied quietly.

'You know, if you had offered him a kiss or something, we might have got a reduced fare, or even free.'

'What sort of girl do you take me for?'

'A practical one,' he answered.

She laughed.

'Perhaps you should have suggested that before we got out.'

'Next time I might just do that,' he said, smiling.

He had to admit, he was quite excited about the trip and was now looking forward to it.

They walked up to the counter and were relieved to see only three other passengers in front of them.

'Either this flight is nearly empty, or we came at the perfect time,' he whispered.

Tampong simply nodded her head briefly in agreement. The check-in person waved the next passenger forward and they were pleased to see that the three passengers were together. Almost immediately they were called over to another counter. They stepped forward.

'We are flying to Singapore,' she said.

'OK, passports, please,' requested the young woman behind the counter.

Tampong handed them over and both were swiped through the computer.

'How many bags are you checking in?'

'Six bags and two boxes.'

'Fine. Please place them one at a time on the belt.'

Tampong did as requested. The woman tapped her computer then reached over and pulled the baggage slip out. Opened one end and slipped it under the baggage handles, pushing the two ends together. She then picked off a bar code from the slip, placing it on the side of the bag. After she finished with the luggage tag she pushed a button and the case started to roll onto the main carousel. She repeated the process with the other cases and two boxes. When she had labelled them all, she stuck the little baggage slips on the back of Tampong's boarding pass, then checked the details before placing them in their passport, keeping them both open, presenting the documents to them.

'We have changed your seats,' she suddenly announced.

'OK, any reason for doing so?' asked Tampong, hoping they had not been pushed to the back of the aircraft.

'Yes, madam. You have both been upgraded,' she replied.

There was a big smile beaming across her face.

'Enjoy your flight, and thank you for flying British Airways.'

'Wow,' remarked Terry.

'Thank you very much,' replied Tampong, equally impressed.

As they walked away, she passed Terry his passport and boarding pass.

'Crickey,' he began, staring in disbelief at the boarding pass, 'we are flying business class.'

'Apparently. And I didn't have to kiss her or anything.'

Terry looked back at the young check-in clerk, who was now busy attending to the next passengers.

'Perhaps she is a lesbian. She looks like she could be a lesbian.'

'Hey, she looks nothing of the sort, but a perfectly normal, polite young lady. Anyway, if we got these upgrades because she fancied one of us, then I have no problem with that.'

'Ah,' he remarked, raising his finger, 'I never considered the fact she might have fancied me. Now that makes more sense.'

She poked him playfully in the ribs, and they both started laughing as the security officer beckoned them forward. He gestured with his hands for their passport and boarding pass, opting not to say a word. They dutifully handed over their documents. He placed each boarding pass under the scanner, and they heard a reassuring bleep, and a green light flicked on. He stamped their boarding pass, initialed it, then handed back all their documents before indicating them to join the short queue on their left. He then beckoned the next passenger forward. They walked up to the security belt, took off their coats and slipped off their shoes, placing them all in a plastic tray. Tampong placed her handbag in a separate tray, so Terry placed his rucksack next to hers.

'Any liquids?' asked the security officer standing on the other side of the belt.

'None,' answered Tampong.

'Any laptops or other electricals?'

'Nope,' she replied.

'OK. Please step up to the security gate and walk through when requested.'

Terry obediently pulled his laptop out and placed it in one of the trays.

Terry stood behind Tampong, and they only had a minute to wait before the security officer on the other side of the gate waved his fingers, indicating Tampong to walk through. She did and the officer nodded and gestured with his arm to collect her bags and stuff. Terry followed her through and got the same response.

As they waited for their bags to pass through the X-ray machine, Terry leaned towards Tampong and talked quietly.

'They don't like to talk much, do they?'

'I guess they do enough talking when something goes wrong or doesn't go right,' she said in an equally quiet voice.

She watched as her coat and tray appeared, so she swept her coat up and picked up her bag and shoes. Terry did likewise, not forgetting his laptop, which he placed back in his rucksack. They both sat down on the grey bench to slip their shoes back on. Terry stood up before placing his rucksack over his shoulders, then he looked around.

'Where to now?' he asked.

Tampong looked down at her boarding pass.

'Well, we are travelling business class, so I guess that means we can use the business lounge.'

'But isn't that for business travelers?'

'It's for anyone travelling business class, I think. Let's go and check it out. What's the worst that can happen? They decline us entry. We have three hours before we start boarding, so if we can use the lounge, then it gives us a chance to freshen up, grab a drink or a snack.'

'Great, so where is this business lounge thing then?'

Tampong looked up at the signs.

'Well, we can go either north or south of the terminal. Take your pick.'

'Let's go south.'

'OK, let's go.'

They turned right out of customs and security, walking past several perfume counters where young women and men were eager to spray them with their latest sample. They came up to the Fortnum and Mason bar, where several couples were sipping champagne and nibbling on little sandwiches. Terry licked his lips as he walked past. Tampong was beginning to think they had gone too far when she finally saw the business lounge sign.

It led them to an escalator. The lounge on the first floor was the first-class lounge, which she guessed they were not entitled to. There was another sign for the business lounge, which led them to another escalator. Once at the top they were greeted with a big black horse with a lampshade mounted on its head. They walked up to the center counter where a young woman in a British Airways costume smiled a greeting at them.

'Welcome to the business lounge. Boarding passes please.'

They handed them to her. She placed them under another scanner, and they heard a beep. She checked her screen, then handed the boarding passes back.

'Enjoy your stay,' she said.

A relieved Tampong took the passes back and they walked into the lounge. Terry's eyes widened as he looked around the lounge. He leaned closer to Tampong.

'Do we have to pay for anything we eat or drink here?'

'I don't think so. Let's check out what they have got and look out for any price tags.'

Terry nodded, so they walked around the lounge, watching people as they did. Many travelers were walking up to the bar and helping themselves to drinks and snacks. They walked around the corner and Terry's eyes widened even further.

'Hey, they have a champagne bar. Can we?'

'Well, strictly speaking, you are still too young, but heck, why not? Let's live a little. It's not as if you are driving or anything, is it? You find us somewhere to sit while I get us two glasses.'

'Great, and thanks.'

He turned eagerly away and went hunting for two spare seats. It did not take him long to spot two by the window. He placed his rucksack on one chair and sat on the other. Shortly afterwards, Tampong arrived with two flutes of champagne.

'Now don't you go telling anyone about this.'

'No, ma'am,' he replied, taking one of the flutes.

They clinked glasses and took a sip of the bubbly liquid. The liquid felt fresh as it bubbled its way down his throat.

'Boy, I could get used to this,' he remarked, admiring his glass, watching the bubbles rise to the surface.

'Don't get used to it too quickly please, and remember, you are still underage.'

He ignored her warning.

'I am going to check out what they have to eat. Do you want anything?'

'Go knock yourself out. I'll have a look once you return.'

He took another gulp of his champagne before placing the flute onto the table. He rose quickly and went hunting for something to eat. He wasn't disappointed when he arrived at the buffet. There were hot and cold choices, with plenty of sandwiches in another bar just around the corner. He opted to try the chili with rice, adding a bread roll to the side of his plate. He returned to his seat to find Tampong's glass empty. He placed his plate down next to his flute, then took another swig of his drink. It was almost empty, so he finished it off.

'Would you like another drink?' he asked.

Tampong looked at her glass, then at her watch.

'Why not. Thank you, Terry.'

'No problem,' he answered, picking up her glass while still holding his own, which did not go unnoticed by her.

She opted not to say anything. He was enjoying himself, and he was almost eighteen in any case. She was sure he was not the only underage drinker in the business lounge. Sure enough, when he returned, his glass was also full. He saw her looking at his glass as he passed her own back to her.

'Err, I couldn't resist,' he admitted, 'it tastes so good.'

'Well, I am just glad you appreciate some of the finer things in life.'

'This kind of life I can get used to.'

She smiled as she stood up.

'I'm off to see what goodies they have on offer. Keep an eye on my bag, please.'

'Yes, ma'am,' he replied, taking another sip of his drink.

Tampong returned with a plate full of salad and was met with a look of disapproval from Terry. He was not a fan of salad, arguing that this was food for rabbits rather than human beings. They chatted briefly as they finished their meals. Just then electronic chimes rang out:

'Attention customers for flight 0011 to Singapore. Your flight will be boarding in five minutes from Gate B31. On behalf of British Airways, we thank you for using our business lounge and wish you a pleasant flight.'

'That's us,' announced Tampong, standing up.

'So soon?' he asked, 'where did the time go?'

'Time always passes quickly when you are enjoying yourself.'

He stood up and slipped the rucksack over his shoulders. Tampong grabbed her coat, took one last look around, and picked up her bag. They left the lounge and descended the escalators, heading quickly down the hallway towards the sign indicating B Gates. They descended yet another long escalator and walked up to a train station.

'I thought we were *flying* to Singapore?' quipped Terry.

'Shh,' warned Tampong, who was getting a little nervous that they could miss their flight.

She shook the bad thought out of her mind, telling herself that they would never announce the flight departure and not give the business class passengers enough time to reach the plane.

The train arrived, and they boarded after the sliding doors opened. The train departed fairly quickly, taking only two minutes for them to arrive at the next station, where they disembarked from the train. This time they ascended two escalators before they saw the sign for Gate 31. They smiled at each other and walked up to the gate, which was surrounded by people, all appearing eager to board. A crew member behind the check-in counter brought a microphone close to his mouth.

'Flight 0011 to Singapore is now ready for boarding. We would like to invite our first-class passengers to board on the left. Would all remaining passengers please remain seated and keep the aisles clear?'

Tampong noticed that not one person moved away. If anything, even more passengers got up and gathered near the gate. After a few minutes, the crew member picked up his microphone again.

'Thank you for your patience. We now invite out business class passengers to board through the priority lanes.'

'Excuse me,' came the abrupt voice of a large man, pushing his way through the hordes of people waiting their turn.

Tampong took advantage of this man rushing towards the gate and moved directly behind him as he cleared a path for them. She grabbed Terry's arm and dragged him along with her. They reached the gate entrance, where she presented her boarding pass, which was once again scanned.

'Thank you, and enjoy your flight,' said the crew member, who returned her boarding pass.

She glanced behind to see Terry being ushered through directly behind her. They walked along the jetway up to the aircraft door, where another crew member greeted them.

'Boarding pass, please?' she asked in a friendly and calm voice.

Tampong handed her pass, which was glanced at expertly.

'Across the galley and on the right please,' she advised.

Tampong nodded her thanks and entered the aircraft. She sensed Terry was still behind her and he was excited. She found her seat at the back of the business class section. She had the aisle seat and Terry had the window seat. She placed her bag in the overhead bin, followed by her coat before picking up the pillow and blankets, placing them on the floor and sitting down in the seat. Terry was already sitting facing her in the other seat.

'Wow, all this just for me,' he remarked, 'look at the size of this TV.'

She smiled at him and watched as he excitedly opened drawers and cupboards. He found the earphones so slipped them over his ears and turned the TV on. He started searching for a film to watch.

'Aha, fantastic. They have *Red*. I am going to watch that,' he said, lifting his earphones away from his ears.

'Enjoy,' she replied, but he had already placed his earphones back over his ears.

She decided to switch on the TV as well and see what else they had to offer. She selected *Resident Evil*, a film she could relate to personally. As she settled down to watch, she became aware of a presence standing beside her. She looked up to see a crew member holding a tray of drinks.

'Would you care for a little refreshment before we take off? I can offer you water, orange juice, or champagne.'

'Champagne, please.'

'Certainly,' she said, pulling out a small tray from the side and placing the drink on it.

She then walked around in front of her seat and tapped Terry on the shoulder, repeating her request.

He also selected champagne. Tampong's eyebrows rose but she said nothing. He just shrugged his shoulders, took a sip, then continued to watch his movie. Five minutes later, another crew member came along with a selection of newspapers and magazines. They both declined. Yet another couple of minutes later the first crew member handed out menu cards. Terry pressed pause on his movie and glanced at the menu. He removed his earphones, placed them around his neck, and leaned across towards Tampong.

'The service here is terrific. I can see now why businessmen fly so often. They make you feel like a prince.'

'Except they certainly seem to enjoy interrupting you at frequent intervals,' she remarked.

'Just making sure you have everything you need. I think I am going to have the chicken.'

'I am opting for the veggie,' replied Tampong.

Sure enough, another five minutes later, another crew member came to her seat and kneeled down.

'Have you selected your meal, Ms. Armitage?'

'Yes, I would like the vegetarian meal please.'

'Certainly. And would you like to be woken up for breakfast, or would you prefer to sleep through until we land?'

'I'll take breakfast, please.'

'Certainly, and thank you.'

She stood up and walked around to Terry's seat, no doubt going through the same list of questions with him.

The TV screen then went blank briefly before the British Airways logo appeared and the safety video began. Terry removed his headphones, although the audio could still be heard throughout the aircraft. He watched as the use of the seat belt and lifejacket was explained. He waited patiently until the video and advertisement finished. The screen then went blank again briefly before his movie reappeared, allowing him to continue watching. He stopped when he felt the aircraft jerk a little. He glanced out of the window to see the aircraft moving backwards. It stopped for a little while, which he guessed was to unhook whatever was pulling it. The engines then began to rev up and the aircraft moved slowly forward. It rolled for about five minutes before coming to a halt. Then the pilot spoke on the PA.

'Ladies and gentlemen, this is your captain speaking. We are second in the queue, so we should be taking off in the next few minutes. Please ensure your seat belt is securely fastened. Now sit back and enjoy this long-haul flight to Singapore. I will speak to you again with more information about our flight once we have reached our cruising altitude.'

Terry dutifully checked his seat belt. He heard the engines start to rev up again, then the aircraft jerked forward and sped down the runway. They were on their way to Singapore.

To a new country.

To a new life.

He got about halfway through his movie before the cabin crew arrived with drinks and peanuts. He opted for a Coke this time, prompting a nod of approval from Tampong, who, herself, opted for a glass of red wine. Just as his movie finished, the cabin crew started to move through the cabin with hot meals. Terry sat up and could smell the aroma, making his stomach growl in protest. When the crew reached their row, they placed a tray in front of Tampong, then passed his tray across to him.

'Would you care for something else to drink, ma'am?' asked the pleasant crew member.

'I'll have a white wine please,' she replied.

'Certainly, madam. We can offer you French or Italian.'

'French please.'

He took her glass and replaced it with a clean one, topping it up before passing it to her. He looked across to Terry.

'And for you, sir?'

'Another Coke please.'

'Certainly,' the crew member replied, kneeling down to pull a red can from the wagon, opening the can by pulling up the tab, and passing it over to Terry, who nodded his thanks.

His meal was steaming hot, so he decided to wait for a minute before eating, opting instead to find another movie to watch. He leaned across to Tampong.

'This is the way to travel, isn't it!'

'Absolutely,' she agreed.

Her meal was surprisingly delicious. She had put her movie on hold, deciding to watch it after her meal.

After he ate dessert and his tray was collected, he also selected *Resident Evil.* When it finished, he looked across to see that Tampong had lowered her seat and was fast asleep. He suddenly felt tired too, so found the button that lowered his seat. He had to unclip his seat belt to lower the footrest. He unwrapped the blanket, wrapped it around his body, raised the privacy partition, then clipped the seat belt together again. He settled down, closed his eyes, and quickly fell asleep.

He then suddenly opened his eyes, and everything was different. The roof of the aircraft was gone. He could see dark menacing clouds, with the sound of thunder in the background. He became aware of a hostile presence close by. He looked across and suddenly saw Shoil. Her eyes were locked on the body lying in front of her. He lowered the privacy screen and could work out Tampong's body, but she was not moving. He went to get up but could not move. He tried to call out, to warn her, but no sound came from his mouth. He looked back up to Shoil, whose own eyes shifted from Tampong to him. She sneered at him as her eyes turned completely orange. Long fangs started to protrude from her mouth. She raised her arm and he watched in horror as it transformed into a long silver spear. Her eyes returned to Tampong, who still had not moved. He then heard a deep, evil-sounding voice.

'I have hunted for you for such a long time, Tampong. Now that I have finally found you, you will not escape me again. This time, bitch, there will be no escape for you. This time I am ready for any trick you try.'

Still Tampong did not move. Terry tried to raise his head, his movement causing Shoil to look at him again.

'Do not worry, boy. Your time will come,' she said, her voice dripping with hatred. 'I don't know who or what you are, but you smell of this bitch, so that is all I need to know.'

Terry struggled against the invisible bonds keeping him in place. He called on all his energy, but no matter what he did, the bonds held firm. He tried to scream out again, but his throat felt as though something unseen was pressing down on it. His eyes moved back to Tampong, and he wondered whether she was experiencing the same restraints as she was not moving, not defending, not attacking.

Shoil raised her spear arm directly over Tampong. She looked across to Terry, giving him an evil smile before plunging her spear arm down into Tampong's body. Her eyes never leaving his. He could only watch in horror as Tampong jerked when the spear penetrated her chest, then she went still.

'Noooooo,' he screamed in his mind.

Suddenly his bonds were broken, so he rose quickly from his seat intent on defending himself against Shoil, but she was gone.

He blinked twice.

The aircraft was dark, with the glow of a few TV screens providing the only light. He looked back down, expecting to see the dead and bloodied body of Tampong. Instead, she was still wrapped in her blanket. Asleep. He wondered whether Shoil had wrapped her up to hide her death, then he watched as she turned over and sighed. Her eyes then burst open.

She looked up to see Terry hovering above her.

'What's up?' she asked.

'Nothing. Bad dream I guess.'

'Was it about Shoil?'

'Yes, why do you say that?'

'Because I was dreaming about her too.'

'Tell me,' he suggested, sitting back down in his seat.

Tampong raised her seat.

'Well, I am not sure where we were, but we were trapped, she had us cornered. I tried to protect you, but I couldn't move. I had to just stand there and watch her walk slowly towards you. Deliberately slowly, making sure I suffered as much agony as possible for as long as possible. I could only watch helplessly as her arm changed into an ugly spear and held it against your neck as she turned to sneer at me, knowing exactly what she was going to do, and not being able to do a thing about it.'

She stopped talking.

'And, what happened?'

'That's when I felt your presence close by and you woke me up. What about your dream?'

'Similar to yours, except we were in this aircraft, and it was I who could not move and could only watch as Shoil attacked you. I also saw her arm change and plunge her spear into your chest.'

'And?'

'That's when I screamed and must have woken up, because I looked over and saw you sleeping. What can it mean?'

Tampong shook her head.

'I am not sure. Perhaps it is a warning to be careful.'

'Or perhaps it's a glimpse into the future, telling us that Shoil will eventually find us and attack us. Killing at least one of us, if not both of us.'

'Well, it is no good us trying to figure it out right here and now. Let's just be careful and watch each other's back.'

'Amen to that,' he answered as he sat back in his seat.

'I need a drink,' he said aloud.

'I do too. So let's have one.'

'Really?' he looked puzzled at her agreement to allow him to consume alcohol again.

'Really,' she said simply, looking down the aisle and seeing a steward coming towards her.

She grabbed his attention by gesturing with her fingers.

'Yes ma'am?' he asked quietly when he reached her seat.

'Two glasses of red wine, please.'

'Two glasses?'

'Yes, please.'

'Certainly, ma'am. French or Italian?'

'French, please.'

He nodded, turned, and walk back towards the galley. Two minutes later he returned with two glasses and two small bottles of wine. He pulled her seat tray out and placed them on her tray.

'Would you care for anything to eat?'

'No, that will be fine, thanks.'

'I would like some crisps please, if you have them,' said Terry, poking his head over the partition.

'Certainly, sir. What flavor would you like? We have salt and vinegar, cheese, or plain.'

'Salt and vinegar please.'

'Certainly, I'll be right back.'

While he went back to collect Terry's crisps, Tampong opened one of the bottles and poured half into her glass. She decided to wait until he had given Terry his crisps before opening the second bottle and passing it to him. She did not have to wait long, and he returned almost immediately with two packs of crisps.

'Enjoy,' he said.

'How much longer before we land?' asked Tampong.

'We have another three and a half hours to go, ma'am,' informed the steward.

'OK, thanks.'

He nodded and resumed his walk up the aisle.

Tampong opened the second bottle and poured half into the second glass before handing it over to Terry. He reached over and took the glass.

'Your good health,' he said, taking a sip of the wine.

She watched him.

'Well, what do you think?'

'Hmmm, I can get used to this too,' he answered, taking another sip.

'Enjoy it because you will not have it every day.'

He just smiled at her, the nightmare gone from his mind.

'Time to watch another movie then before breakfast.'

'Breakfast, god, you do nothing but eat on this flight.'

'Must be the altitude or something,' he remarked, flicking through the film catalogue.

Tampong took another long gulp of her drink, the nightmare still very much at the front of her mind. She knew it must mean something, and her fear was that perhaps Terry was right, in that they may have had a glimpse into their future, what was left of it. Did that mean that despite their travelling halfway around the world, she still finds them and kills them? Was this all a complete waste of time and effort? She tried to brush the negative thoughts away, then noticed that her glass was empty, so she poured the rest of the wine into her glass. No, she decided, she needed to be positive. Moving away gives them more time. More time for her to help prepare Terry for the day he confronts Shoil. That day will surely arrive, that much she had no doubt. It was the way the Higher Middle worked. They had a knack of finding each other. He was getting stronger with each passing year, and he had already surprised her with his skill and strength. She felt he could even be a match for Shoil if he had more time to prepare and train. All she could do was provide as much guidance and training as she could. They would begin as soon as they reached Singapore. For her, that couldn't come quickly enough. She took another long gulp of her wine.

***

Shoil was standing outside the Red Lion restaurant. She had watched the girl go inside, so knew she was working. She also knew what time the restaurant closed, so settled down for a long evening. Her patience was rewarded when she saw the lights of the restaurant go out and ten minutes later Karen stepped out of the side door, slipped her arms through the sleeves of her coat, before starting to walk down the street. Shoil kept her distance, deciding to keep her human form. Her eyes expertly scanned up and down the street, but she saw no one. She increased her pace a little, closing the distance between her and the girl. Karen became conscious of somebody walking behind her, so she increased her pace a little, only for Shoil to further increase her own pace, closing the gap again. Karen took a gamble and glanced behind her to see a woman walking quickly towards her. She looked like she was a woman on a mission. Karen saw a bus coming up the road, so paced herself to reach the bus stop at the same time as the bus did. She timed it perfectly, and the bus stopped and opened its doors. She stepped inside, paid the driver, and started walking down towards the back of the bus. She glanced out of the window and saw the woman had stopped and was watching the bus. Karen's suspicions were right. The woman *was* following her. She watched as the woman suddenly knelt down.

Shoil snarled as she saw the girl jump on the bus, realizing she must have been found out. She crouched down and was about to turn into her dog form, which would allow her to easily follow the bus, when a group of girls walked around the corner. There were five of them, all in their early teens and all were giggling. One of the girls noticed Shoil on her knees, so rushed up to her.

'Are you OK, do you need any help?'

'No I'm fine, thanks,' replied Shoil, trying her best to keep her voice calm, despite the fact she was fuming inside.

She thought about taking the lives of these girls just for interrupting her, then decided against it. She needed to regroup and rethink her plan regarding this girl.

'Have you lost something?' the girl asked.

'Piss off,' snapped Shoil, wanting to be rid of this annoying girl, 'go back to your silly little girlfriends.'

'Well pardon me for trying,' quipped the girl.

She stuck her nose in the air in disgust and turned to rejoin her little group, all of whom had been listening to the short conversation.

'What's her problem?' one asked as the girl rejoined them.

'Gods know,' replied the girl.

'Perhaps she is menstruating,' suggested another girl, which prompted the others to burst out laughing.

The other girls all brought their hands to their mouths in a pointless attempt to hide their laughter.

They started to walk away, all the time glancing in Shoil's direction and giggling while huddled together.

Shoil was tempted to stop them and show them what was really troubling her. However, she guessed from their ages that they must be in their early teens and probably virgins. Being girls, she could not even absorb them. Instead, she stood upright and took one last look at the disappearing bus before turning in the opposite direction to the girls and headed back to her apartment. There will be other days and other opportunities. She needed to be more careful now as she was certain the girl realized she was being followed, which would explain her sudden change of pace when she stepped onto the bus, which was going in the opposite direction she came from this morning.

Karen shivered, despite it being a balmy night. There was something creepy about that woman, although she could not put her finger on what it was exactly. Her thoughts then turned to Terry. She was already missing him and could not wait for him to contact her again. She recalled him talking about this Skype thing. She had asked her manager whether he knew anything about it. He told her it was a new video platform that was free of charge so she downloaded it. Apparently, you could see the person at the other end in real-time. That excited her. Thinking about Terry put the woman out of her mind. She stood up and rang the bell, glancing back down the street, which was now empty. She decided she would catch the other bus back home. She would also keep a wary eye out for this woman. She didn't know why, but her instincts told her this woman was bad news.

***

Meanwhile, the plane had almost reached its destination when the aircraft's PA system burst into life again.

'Ladies and gentlemen, this is your captain speaking. We have just started our descent into Singapore airport and will be landing in approximately forty-five minutes. If you need to use the toilet, please do so within the next twenty minutes, after which the toilets will no longer be available. The weather in Singapore is an agreeable eighty degrees and sunny. We trust you have enjoyed the flight. It has certainly been our pleasure having you onboard. I will leave you in the capable hands of our expert cabin crew and will speak to you again shortly after landing.'

'Wow, eighty degrees,' remarked Terry, 'what is that in Celsius?'

'Let's see,' answered Tampong, making a quick calculation in her head, 'that would be around twenty-seven degrees.'

'Wow, that's hot.'

'Yep, glad I brought some sun lotion,' said Tampong.

'Never touch the stuff.'

'So I have noticed. You should be careful and consider using the stuff. Too much sun is not good for your skin, and there will be lots of sun in Singapore.'

'Bring it on,' he said proudly, 'the more sun the better.'

'You won't be saying that when you are rolling around in agony because you are all sunburnt.'

'We will see, we will see.'

He just shrugged his shoulders, and they both carried on watching movies until they were interrupted by a video explaining how to proceed through Singapore's customs and immigration.

Terry watched the video. When it finished, he popped his head over the privacy panel.

'It says we may need a visa. Do we? If so, what kind do we have?'

'We do not need a visa; we have a British passport. Singapore used to be ruled by the British.'

'Aha,' he replied, not understanding what a visa was in any case.

After twenty minutes, the seat-belt sign was switched on and the PA burst into life.

'Ladies and gentlemen, we will shortly be landing at Singapore international airport, and the captain has now switched the seat-belt sign on. Please bring your seats to the upright position, fold away any seat rests, and for our guests in first class and business class, please ensure the area around your seat is completely clear. The cabin crew will be coming along the aisle for one final check and handing out your immigration card. Please note you should enter UK in the box for country. Thank you for flying British Airways.'

Both Tampong and Terry flipped their footrests back into their original position and pressed the button to straighten their seats. Tampong folded her blanket and stuffed it behind her to act as a second pillow. She stretched her legs out, realizing she had been sitting for too long and was now feeling a little stiff. She rocked her head back and forward, then side to side. Terry rolled his blanket up, then stuffed it down the side of his seat. He raised the window screen and had to blink a couple of times as the bright sun shone through. He looked out, but all he could see was cloud. The cabin crew then came through the aircraft distributing immigration cards, which they duly completed.

'Cabin crew, thank you very much. Seats for landing,' announced the captain, although Terry noticed they were already sitting.

A couple of minutes later the tires touched the tarmac and the aircraft slowed quickly as the captain put the engines in reserve and touched the brakes, forcing Terry into his seat belt. The plane turned off the runway and it seemed to take an age before it finally stopped close to the gate. The cabin crew had already unbuckled their seat belts and were busy unclipping doors and taking out coats.

'Doors to automatic and cross-check,' said the captain.

A couple of passengers had already gotten out of their seats and were opening the overhead bins.

'Please stay in your seats until the seat-belt sign has been turned off,' announced one of the cabin crew over the PA.

One of the passengers ignored her and just shrugged his shoulders in defiance, pulling his luggage from the bin, and placed it in front of his seat. Unbeknown to him, the plane was not quite at the gate, and the plane suddenly jerked forward, causing the man to lose his balance and crash into the toilet door.

'**Sit down**,' came the voice of another steward, only this time much louder and firmer.

The man was now red-faced, so swept up his bag and quietly sat back in his seat. Tampong looked across to Terry and raised her eyebrows. She could imagine some of these businessmen acting as if they owned the airline, thinking they could do what they liked.

Eventually the seat-belt sign went off, resulting in a sudden burst of activity, as passengers looked as though they could not wait to get off the plane now that it had arrived. There was already a queue by the exit. A couple of more minutes passed before the door was pulled open and the steward stepped outside, blocking the business-class passengers to allow the first-class passengers off first. There were not many, and soon the business-class passengers started to disembark. Tampong and Terry followed the signs to customs and immigration, taking the conveyor belt, then walking along the carpeted corridor, passing over the departure area. They were then greeted with a large hall divided off by electric straps and colored signs. They followed the sign indicating foreigners and queued up. Fortunately, business class had its privileges, and Tampong countered only seven people in front of her. The process was slow but there were four customs officers and soon it was her turn. She had her passport and immigration card. The customs officer took the passport and immigration card, checking the card quickly. He checked the photo before swiping her passport through his machine. He tapped the keyboard a few times.

'Reason for your visit?' he asked, glancing briefly at the immigration card.

'Holiday visit,' she lied, knowing that if she said she was working here then he would have demanded to see a working visa.

The company she was joining had told her there was not enough time to process all the documentation but that they would sort it all out when she arrived.

'Place your left four fingers on the panel,' he then said.

She obliged.

'Now your right four fingers.'

She obliged.

'Now both your thumbs.'

She obliged, noting there was not a *please* from this man.

He checked the screen one last time before stamping, dating, and initialing her passport, he then initialed the immigration card before handing them all back to her.

'Enjoy your stay,' he said, waving the next passenger forward.

Terry was already at another booth and was just about finished, so Tampong walked as slowly as she could as there were several signs stating 'no waiting'. Terry picked up his papers and walked quickly to catch up with Tampong.

'That was not too bad,' he said quietly.

'One of the benefits of travelling business class. You get ahead of the crowds.'

She indicated with her head for Terry to look back at the hall they had just left, which was now full of passengers. Two international flights had arrived at the same time. She guessed one must have come from India, judging from the outfits most of the passengers wore. She couldn't help noticing that half of the passengers appeared to need wheelchairs. There was now a long queue of chairs along the side of the customs hall. She was so glad they were now on this side of the customs hall.

They turned right into another hallway when she noticed a TV monitor on the wall directly ahead. She walked closer and saw that their flight was already on the screen, stating that their bags will arrive on belt 25. There was another sign with the numbers 1 to 25 pointing to another corridor on the left, with the other higher numbers pointing to a corridor on the right. So they turned left.

They passed several duty-free shops while following the signs, which were clearly marked, and arrived at belt 25, where they waited. Tampong checked the belt's information screen, which indicated that their bags would arrive in four minutes.

Not too bad, she thought.

After a few minutes, an alarm sounded, an orange light began flashing, and the belt started moving. The first bags marked with an orange priority label arrived. Tampong spotted her first bag, then her second. Then her last two appeared, together with the two boxes. Terry had to wait a little longer before his bags appeared. They then checked for the exit and found it by belt 20. They placed their bags on a trolley and headed for the exit and joined the queue. It took another fifteen minutes before they were beckoned forward by the immigration officer. Tampong handed over her immigration card. The officer scanned it and nodded for them to proceed. They left the immigration section and turned right into the main arrival hallway. Tampong checked the signs until she found one marked 'taxi'. She nodded for Terry to follow her. They were directed down an escalator and then had to queue again in the hallway for a taxi, so they joined the end of yet another queue. Both were feeling the effects of the long flight now and could not wait to reach the hotel. It was another fifteen minutes before it was their turn to walk up to the next available taxi. The driver saw their trolley so popped his boot open but did not get out of the car. Terry loaded the bags and boxes into the boot and was pleased to see they all fitted easily. He closed the boot and stepped around to the side of the car, opened the door and slid inside.

'Where to?' asked the driver.

'The Carlton Hotel, Bras Basah Road, please,' replied Tampong.

'The Carlton, right ho,' said the driver, slipping the gearstick into drive and pulling out of the taxi rank.

'How long until we get there?' asked Terry.

'Assuming the traffic is good, about twenty minutes,' informed the driver.

They both glanced at each other. Tampong shrugged her shoulders in resignations, then shifted in her seat a little to get comfortable.

Fortunately, the traffic was light, and the driver finally pulled into the hotel driveway after nineteen minutes.

'Twelve dollars fifty,' he announced.

Tampong took her purse out of her bag. She had the good sense to buy some Singapore dollars before they left, knowing she did not want to use her credit card unless absolutely necessary, thus avoiding large transaction charges and unfavorable exchange rates, plus any internet footprint. She handed him a ten- and a five-dollar note. He nodded his thanks and popped the truck open, again not bothering to get out. She assumed his tip was not good enough to warrant him getting out of his car. A hotel porter came towards them with a hotel trolley and took over unloading the bags, much to her relief and surprise.

'Welcome to the Carlton,' said the porter. 'I will take care of your bags while you check in, ma'am.'

His accent had a distinct Asian twang.

Tampong said nothing, instead she turned and headed for the check-in counter. A pretty young blonde girl greeted them with brilliant white teeth.

'Hello, madam and sir,' she began, also with a strong Asian twang, 'welcome to the Carlton Hotel. My name is May-Sue, and I will be assisting you today.'

'Thank you, May-Sue,' replied Tampong, noticing that Terry's mouth had dropped open at the sight of the beauty on the other side of the counter, 'our name is Armitage, and we are checking in.'

She handed over her passport and nodded her head to Terry for his. He duly obliged.

'Thank you, Ms. Armitage,' she replied, taking their passports, opening them up before leaning forward to start typing.

Terry could not help but look down at the young woman's ample breasts, noticing that her top two buttons were open, revealing the top of her inviting bosom. Tampong caught him ogling the girl, so gave him a quick kick in the shin. He shot her a look of innocence, but his eyes moved back up to her face, which was also very pleasant to the eye.

'OK then,' said the receptionist, 'I have you in one of our classic deluxe rooms with separate queen beds. Is that OK with you?'

'Fine,' said Tampong.

'Very good,' replied the receptionist.

She glanced up at Terry and gave him a warm smile.

'Have you come far?' she asked.

'From London,' replied Terry quickly, not giving Tampong any chance to respond.

'London, wow, that is a long way. A city I have always wanted to visit.'

'You should,' he encouraged.

She smiled at him again before returning to her duties. She completed her typing and pulled two pieces of paper from the printer, placing them on the desk in front of Tampong.

'I just need your initials here and here, and your signature here,' she advised, pointing to the places with her pen.

Tampong dutifully initialed the two places and signed at the bottom before handing the papers back.

'Very good,' said the receptionist again, 'now, I just need a credit card to log the guarantee.'

Tampong handed her credit card, which the receptionist quickly swiped then handed back.

'Fantastic. You are all set. Your room is on the fifteenth floor, room 1525. Here are the keys to your room, and I wish you a wonderful stay here at the Carlton and in Singapore,'

She gave them another beaming white smile.

'Thank you,' replied Terry, giving her a returning smile.

'You're most welcome,' she replied, 'you will find the elevators on your left.'

'Thanks again,' said Terry.

'Most welcome. Have a great day.'

Tampong pulled at his arm, knowing this farewell could go on all night. He reluctantly walked away with her, taking one last glance at May-Sue.

When the elevator arrived, they entered and Tampong pressed the button for the fifteenth floor. As the doors closed, Terry turned towards Tampong.

'Are all Asian girls that beautiful?'

'Most are, I believe,' confirmed Tampong.

'Then I am going to like Singapore,' he commented.

Tampong smiled, giving him a little playful nudge. She decided it was probably best not to mention Karen as this would just make him feel guilty. She decided on a different approach.

'Just remember you are not quite eighteen yet, so keep it in your pants for a little while longer.'

Terry's face went bright red, causing him to look down in embarrassment. She gave him a little encouraging nudge again just as the door opened and the electronic voice announced the fifteenth floor. They stepped out and noticed the sign indicating their room was down the hall on the right. They entered their room, which was dominated by two queen-size beds. The wall on their left had floor-to-ceiling windows, through which they could see the skyline of Singapore. There was a forty-two-inch flat-screen TV on the wall opposite the bed and a luxurious granite full-sized bathroom, complete with towels, soaps, and toothpaste. The bedroom walls were plain but of a relaxing grey color.

'I think we will be quite comfortable here,' observed Terry as his eyes took in the room.

He walked over to the windows and pulled the curtains open.

'So that's Singapore then. Very impressive, isn't it?'

'Certainly not New York, but still very nice,' counted Tampong, 'and at least it will not be so noisy at night.

'True,' remarked Terry, although he had never been in New York, so could only imagine what it might be like.

He fell onto the bed closest to the window and picked up the remote. He switched the TV on as he glanced at the clock, which said it was nearly eleven in the morning.

'What time is it back home now?' he asked.

'Let's see, it's eleven am here, so that makes it three am in the UK, as they are eight hours behind us.'

'OK. Perhaps a little too early to call Karen right now to let her know we arrived OK.'

So, he is now thinking about his girl back home, she thought, glad that he had worked that out himself.

'She can wait until tomorrow. It's Sunday, after all, and I doubt she will be doing much, except waiting for your call. Remember, no mention of where we are, OK? It is safer for all concerned.'

'Got it. Well, I think I will have a shower then go out for a walk for a few hours to help clear my head.'

'Sounds like a plan. I'll have one after you. While you are in the shower, I'll unpack some of our bags, mainly for the essentials for tomorrow. We can unpack the rest tomorrow.'

He nodded and slipped off the bed and walked into the bathroom.

'Wow,' he said, 'this bathroom is huge.'

He closed the door, and she heard the shower water running. She placed one of the suitcases on the bed, unzipped it and began pulling out shirts and underwear. Whistling could be heard coming from the bathroom, causing a broad smile to appear on her face. As she finished unpacking, Terry emerged from the bathroom, wrapped in a bath towel.

'That was refreshing,' he said.

'Great. Hope you saved some hot water for me,' she quipped.

'Ha-ha, very funny. I am sure the hotel has more than enough hot water for you.'

'Hope so for your sake.'

She turned and walked into the bathroom, which was now full of steam.

'Hey, did you have a shower or a sauna in here?' she called back.

'Very funny,' he replied sarcastically, 'you know I like a hot shower.'

Tampong did not reply but started running the shower, so Terry reached over and grabbed his rucksack. He pulled his laptop out and switched it on. He was impressed with the speed of connection. He entered his family name and room number when prompted and was rewarded with access to the internet. He logged into his email account and sent Karen a quick message.

'Just to let you know that we arrived safely, and I will try and Skype with you tomorrow afternoon. Hopefully, it will work OK on your computer. If not, I will give you a call instead. I am off out for a walk now. Miss you already. Terry. xxx'

He pressed send before closing his computer and slipping it back in his rucksack.

***

Karen was half asleep, still feeling uncomfortable about that woman following her. She could see her face clearly in her mind and felt sure she had seen this woman before. Perhaps she had been following her for a little while now and yesterday was the only day she realized it. She heard her computer ping, announcing new mail. She reached down and opened her laptop, instantly smiling when she saw the email was from Terry, although puzzled as to why he would be writing so early in the morning. She read his mail, smiling all the way through until she came to the last sentence of his mail.

'Going out for a walk now!' she repeated aloud. 'Why would he be going out for a walk so early in the morning? Where the hell is he?'

More questions started to pop into her head, but she decided there was nothing she could do about it now. He said he would call tomorrow in any case, so she could ask him then. She yawned, closed the laptop, placed it back on the floor, laid her head on her pillow, and closed her eyes. She slept almost immediately, with all thoughts of the mysterious woman erased from her mind.

She slept well that night, dreaming of Terry.

***

Terry, by contrast, could not sleep that night. He looked at the clock, not for the first time. It said four forty. It felt like four hours ago when it was only four o'clock. He quietly slipped out of bed, pulled his laptop out of his rucksack, and headed for the bathroom, where he quietly closed the door, taking a quick peek at Tampong, who was sound asleep. He sat down on the cold marble floor, rubbed his eyes, opened his laptop, and switched it on. He blinked twice as the bright light from his screen appeared. He guessed it must be close to five now, so that made it eleven in the UK. A perfect time to call, so he logged onto the internet. He clicked on the Skype icon and was pleased to see Karen's picture and name listed in his short number of contacts. She managed to download the app then and had accepted his invitation. He clicked on her icon and heard the electronic telephone calling her. He waited patiently and was about to give up when her image appeared on his screen. She was smiling, grinning from cheek to cheek in fact, exposing her brilliant white teeth.

'Hey you,' he said.

'Hey, Terry.'

'Wow, this Skype thing is good. I can hear and see you very well.'

'Same here,' she agreed.

She then paused for a moment as she took in his image and his clothing.

'Are you in your pajamas?' she asked.

'Yes. I could not sleep, so I gave up trying and thought I would see if you were online,' he said quietly.

'Why are you whispering?'

'Because my aunt is asleep in bed.'

'Asleep already! but it's not quite eleven pm.'

'Not here,' he said too quickly, regretting it the moment he said it, but unable to take it back.

'OK, so where are you then?'

'You know I cannot tell you that.'

'Why not exactly?'

'Because I promised my aunt I would not tell anyone.'

'I am not anyone,' she retorted. 'Your voice sounds a bit funny, echoey. Are you in a bathroom?'

'Yep,' he confirmed.

'Why?'

'So that I don't disturb her,' he replied as if it was the most obvious thing in the world.

'OK, so you only have two rooms then. Does that mean you are in a hotel?'

'Yes, but it is only temporary until our house is ready.'

'And how long will that be?'

'Not sure. My aunt will find out more on Monday when she starts work.'

'It all sounds a bit cloak and dagger, Terry.'

'I know, sorry about that. Hopefully not for too long.'

'But if your aunt is starting work, and you are moving into your own home, that sounds a bit permanent, if you ask me.'

'It might be for her, but not for me. As soon as I am eighteen, I am my own person and can do what I like. My plan is to return home and be with you again.'

'I'd like that. So what's this place like even though you cannot tell me where?'

'I don't really know, to be honest; we arrived only yesterday and came straight to the hotel, unpacked and then ate. Perhaps we will go out and tour for a bit today.'

Karen's mind started to work in overdrive. They only arrived yesterday, and he did not sleep very well—all the signs of jet lag. Also, it was either very early or quite late when they arrived. He is awake now, but Tampong is still asleep, also a possible sign of jet lag.

'Do you have a nice view outside your window?' she questioned.

'We can see the bay,' he answered honestly.

So, you are close to water.

She wondered what else she could ask.

'How did you get there, to the hotel, I mean?'

'By taxi.'

'Oh. Was the journey long?'

'You are digging, Karen,' Terry suggested.

'Not at all,' she said in her best innocent voice, 'I am just interested in your journey. I miss you already.'

'I miss you too,' he said warmly.

'I will see you again, won't I?' Her eyes started to tear up.

He moved his head closer to the screen.

'You will see me again, I promise,' he answered quietly.

'But when?'

'Not sure. As soon as I know more, I will let you know, OK?'

'OK,' she said reluctantly, 'thanks for your email, by the way. Made me feel better knowing you arrived safely, wherever that might be.'

'I told you I would write as soon as I could,' he looked deeply into her eyes. 'You look beautiful, by the way.'

She blushed, pushing a strand of her hair back behind her ear.

'Stop it,' she warned.

'I mean it,' he said warmly, 'my heart beats faster whenever I see you.'

She smiled warmly at him.

'Listen, I will have to sign off now but will contact you again in a couple of days. OK?'

'Must you go so soon?' she pleaded.

'I must. My aunt may wake up soon, and I don't want her to catch me talking to you.'

'OK, if you must. When can we do this again?'

'How about Wednesday?'

'Not before?'

'If I can, then I will drop you a line, but we have lots of things to sort out here.'

OK then, Wednesday it is. What time?'

'After you finish work, if that is OK with you?'

'That works for me. Let's say eleven thirty then.'

'Eleven thirty it is. I will see you then.'

'Take care of yourself, Terry.'

'You too. Miss you.'

'Miss you too.'

'Bye Karen.'

'Bye Terry.'

Her screen went black briefly, only to be replaced with his contact picture. She sniffed back a tear, then clicked Google and typed in Carlton Hotel—which she noticed was written on the towel hanging behind him. A list appeared. They were all abroad and most were in exotic places. He did not realize that the angle of his screen was pointing slightly upwards, allowing her to also view the small bottles sitting on the shelf. When she focused on them, she worked out the words Carlton Hotel again. So she knew he was telling the truth about being abroad, but not much else. He had clearly just gotten out from bed, so that meant it was early morning where he was, which didn't help, as he could be both west and east on the globe. She adjusted her search to add in the word bay. It didn't help much, and there were too many Carlton hotels to pin it down. Frustrated, she logged off and sighed to herself. She was a little closer to knowing where he was, but not by much. Perhaps he will reveal more on Wednesday.

Terry also logged off and closed his laptop. He gingerly got back to his feet and suddenly felt tired. He crept back into the bedroom, slipped his computer back into his rucksack and slid back into his bed. He closed his eyes and slept.

Tampong opened her eyes and had to squint as the bright sunrays shone straight into her eyes. She blinked a couple of times until her vision adjusted to the light. She looked across to

Terry, who was sound asleep. She pulled the sheets down and stretched her arms in the air. She then glanced at the clock and was surprised to see it was nearly eleven. Her bladder forced her out of bed and into the bathroom. When she returned to the bedroom, Terry was also stretching his arms and yawning.

'Good morning sleepyhead,' she joked.

'Good morning,' he replied, 'you slept for a long time then.'

'Must be this jet lag.'

'Guess so. Took me ages to get to sleep, but when I did I slept like the dead. Feel OK now.'

'That's good to hear.'

Terry glanced at the clock.

'Do you think we are too late for breakfast?'

'I am guessing so. Check the menu card on the desk and see if there are any opening times. I am off for a shower.'

'OK,' he said, slipping his feet out of bed.

He yawned again as he walked across to the desk and picked up the menu card.

'Typical,' he said to himself as he turned towards the closed bathroom door, 'just missed breakfast. Closed at ten thirty already,' he shouted.

Tampong opened the bathroom door a little and poked her head out.

'OK, not really a problem as is it nearly lunchtime in any case. How about you make us a nice cup of coffee for now?'

'OK, I can do that, but I need water first.'

'Right. Pass me the coffee pot and I'll fill it for you.'

He nodded, walked across to the coffee machine, and picked up the pot. It only took him three paces to reach the bathroom, where he handed her the pot. She nodded before closing the door. He waited briefly before the door opened again and she passed him the now filled pot. He walked back to the machine and poured the water into the top of the machine, plugged it in, found a small bag of coffee, which he opened and slipped into the machine. He then switched it on when he heard the shower running. He returned to his bed, picked up the TV remote and started to zap through channels.

He stopped when the daily news channel appeared, so he decided to watch.

Twenty minutes later the bathroom door opened and Tampong emerged wrapped in a large bath towel.

'Wow, that felt good. Highly recommended. What are you watching?'

'Just the news. All about America really. Think I will have a shower now.'

OK. How's the coffee doing?'

'Just about ready. I'll have mine when I have had my shower.'

'Sounds good.'

Terry disappeared into the bathroom, so Tampong picked up her unopened suitcase and searched for her underwear and fresh clothes. She glanced at the news. Apparently, there had been another shooting in Oklahoma. Two people had been shot along with the shooter, who was taken out by the police. She got dressed and walked over to pour herself a large cup of coffee. She sat on the edge of the bed and sipped her hot beverage.

Fifteen minutes later, Terry came out, dressed in the same clothes he had travelled in.

'You are not going to wear those things again today, are you?'

'Yeah, why not? I only used them once, to travel here.'

'Exactly.'

He stood there looking puzzled.

'You surely must have fresh clothes in your case?' she suggested.

'Of course I do, but why waste perfectly fresh clothes when all we are going to do is go out walking. It is extremely humid out there, so I will be sweating in a matter of minutes. We are going out, aren't we?

Tampong shook her head in resignation.

'Yep. I think the fresh air will do us both good.'

'Right. So I'll fix myself a coffee, then we can go out for a walk and perhaps find somewhere to eat.'

'Are you hungry?'

'I'm always hungry. You should know that.'

'Right. Growing lad. Got it. Silly question. OK, drink your coffee, but at least brush your teeth before we leave.'

'Yes, boss,' he said jokingly, walking across to the machine and pouring the rest of the coffee into his cup.

He tasted it and immediately screwed his face up.

'It's not that bad,' remarked Tampong.

'Not exactly strong coffee, is it? More like colored water.'

'Don't grumble. It comes with the room.'

'Huh,' he said, noticing a small packet of biscuits, which he picked up.

Tampong caught sight of them too.

'Hey, share please.'

He shrugged his shoulders, then threw her one of the biscuits, which she caught easily. They ate in silence then finished their coffee.

'Right. I'm off to clean my teeth, then will be ready to face the world.'

'OK, but will the world be ready to face you?'

She threw her towel at him. 'Cheeky.'

She spun around and disappeared into the bathroom. Terry tidied up by placing the cups next to the machine and folding the wet bath towel. By the time he finished, Tampong entered the bedroom.

'All yours,' she said.

'Thanks,' he replied, walking into the bathroom.

It did not take long to brush his teeth and they left the room, switching the sign over to let the cleaning staff know the room was empty, then took the elevator down to the first floor. On exiting the elevator, Tampong headed straight for the concierge desk.

'Yes, ma'am, and how are you this fine morning?' he asked in the welcoming Indian tone, his head nodding slightly from right to left.

'I'm fine, thanks.'

'Very good,' he replied before she had time to continue, 'how may I be of assistance this fine morning?'

'I was wondering whether you have a local street map of Singapore?'

'Of course, ma'am,' he confirmed, reaching down to pull a map out from under his desk.

He spread it out in front of her and drew a circle around a building.

'That's the Carlton,' he explained, pointing out the red circle on the map, 'you will see it is fairly central and easy to find. The bay is right here.'

He pointed to the spot with his finger again.

'Perfect. Thank you.'

'You are most welcome, ma'am.'

She folded the map and tucked it under her arm.

'Have a wonderful day,' he called after her.

'You too,' she replied.

'Most kind,' he said.

When they were out of earshot, Terry leaned closer to her.

'Do you realize they always have to have the last word?'

'I did notice that, yeah. A little bit weird if you ask me.'

'A little too polite, but I guess that's their nature. Anyway, where are we going?'

Tampong suddenly clicked her fingers together.

'Hey, were you not supposed to let Karen know you arrived safely?'

'I did. I sent her a text message.'

'When did you do that?'

'While you were having your shower,' he lied.

'OK. So I thought we could walk down to the bay and then walk back up and find a restaurant for lunch. If we turn left out of the hotel, turn right at the Swiss hotel, and walk along Esplanade Drive, we can follow the bay all the way around, cross over at the river walk, which will lead us into Clarke Quay, where we can stop for lunch. Afterwards, we walk up Clemenceau Avenue and onto Orchard Road. There are lots of shops on this road, which turns into Bras Basah Road, and that's where our hotel is. All this should take most of the day to do. Sound good to you?'

'You memorized all this in that short space of time with the concierge?'

'Comes with years of practice,' she answered.

'Very good, ma'am,' he replied, imitating the concierge, but clearly impressed.

She nudged him gently in the ribs.

'Don't you start that,' she warned, but her eyes were smiling.

'If we walk down Esplanade Drive, we should pass the Marina Bay Sands Hotel. Apparently it is very modern and has an interesting feature on its roof, looks like a ship.'

'Do tell,' encouraged Terry as they walked out of the hotel and turned left then right into Bras Basah Road.

'OK, so what's so special about this hotel thing then?'

'Aha!' exclaimed Tampong, wetting her finger and pointing it in the air.

'Follow me.'

'OK, OK,' he replied in resignation, 'this ship thing had better be worth the trip.'

As they walked up to the bay, they reached the DNA bridge.

'Wow, that is some construction,' remarked Terry, clearly impressed by the bridge.

'This is the Helix Bridge,' she informed him, having memorized most of the tourist sites from the guidebook to Singapore she found in their room, 'it allows you to cross the bay and see all the sites at the same time. There are four different inner spirals, or platforms, where you can view the Marina Bay Sands Hotel, the bay, and other sights.'

'Did you swallow a Singapore guide or something?' he quipped. 'OK, let's do it then.'

He sounded a lot more enthusiastic now and quickened his pace, forcing Tampong to quicken her own pace and catch up with him. He walked onto the first platform and looked around.

'So where is this impressive ship thing of yours?' he asked.

She placed her hands on his shoulders and slowly turned him around, then pointed up with her finger. He followed the direction she was pointing. His jaw dropped open when he saw the magnificent structure perched on top of the three-tower hotel.

'Ho my god,' he said finally, 'can we go up there?'

'Sure. We have to pay, but that's not a problem. Just need to change some more money for Singapore dollars and we are all set.'

'I bet there is a cash machine inside that large shopping mall on the other side of the bridge.'

'We can do that,' she agreed, 'after all, I have no idea where a currency exchange shop is.'

They continued to walk over the bridge and into the shopping mall, enjoying the fresh air-conditioned environment as soon as they entered.

'Ho boy, that feels sooo good,' he said, feeling the cool air on his face.

'You are not wrong,' agreed Tampong, who was looking around for signs, finding one on the post. 'OK, there is an ATM machine on the first floor.'

'How could you possibly know that?' he quizzed.

She pointed at the post.

'Ho right. That will do it,' he conceded, reading the sign. 'Hey, they have a casino here.'

'Nice try, but you are too young,' she said simply.

'Spoilsport,' he joked.

They went down the escalator and followed the sign to the ATM machine. Tampong slipped her card into the machine, tapped in her code, then the amount. The machine warned that her bank could charge for this withdrawal, but she confirmed it in any case. After a few seconds, the machine spat out her money, followed by a receipt. She placed it all in her purse.

They found the escalator to the top. Having paid their twenty dollars, they entered the elevator, which quickly rose. They stepped out and were greeted with a panoramic view of Singapore. Terry walked up to the edge.

'Wow, this is amazing,' he remarked.

'Sure is,' she agreed, feeling the welcoming breeze on her face.

They walked around as far as they could. They could not walk across to the other side as they had to pay to enter the swimming pool. Having finished with their deck tour, Tampong turned back to face Terry.

'Right, let's get back down into the street and make our way to this Quay place.'

They descended the lift and had walked for about another hour. Their T-shirts were saturated with their sweat and both were feeling thirsty. They passed under a bridge, welcoming the break from the sun, so stopped at a beer garden, sitting at one of the free tables. She ordered two large local beers. They each drank half before placing the glasses back on the table. Terry wiped his mouth with the back of his hand.

'Man, I needed that.'

'Me too,' she agreed, picking up the glass again and taking another refreshing gulp of the cool liquid.

'I have to admit, it is very nice here,' he said, 'very modern.'

'Lots of money here too,' she added.

'Really?'

'Yep, once the Brits gave Hong Kong back, a lot of banking and financial companies moved from there to here.'

'It does look ultra-modern,' he agreed.

They finished their beers. Having paid, they got up and continued their walk around the bay, finally walking into Clarke Quay.

'I am getting hungry,' remarked Terry, rubbing his stomach.

'Now there is a surprise, about you being hungry, I mean. Well, we have arrived in Clarke Quay, and you can just about pick the type of meal you want to eat. Chances are they have it here.'

'Actually, I fancy some chicken wings.'

'OK. There is a Hooters restaurant with all-you-can-eat chicken wings just along here and by the river.'

'What's Hooter's?' he asked.

'A restaurant where the girls dress quite sexily for their customers.'

'Sounds perfect. Why do they call it Hooters, do they have lots of owl themes?'

She smiled at his innocence.

'No. Hooters is slang for boobs.'

Both his eyebrows raised almost into the top of his head.

'So what are we waiting for?'

She didn't reply but turned around and walked along the road a little before turning into Clarke Quay. She had memorized the route and was confident she could find the restaurant. She was not disappointed. After only ten minutes walking, she spotted the restaurant on the right of the street. Terry spotted it at the same time, so increased his pace. She had to speed up a little to keep up with him. There was an outside section next to the river, and she guessed he would opt for that.

She guessed right. As soon as they arrived at the restaurant, he immediately turned left and walked onto the wooden platform They entered the garden restaurant, which was full of tables, but most were still empty.

'Hi there, welcome to Hooters,' said the cheerful waitress, dressed in a white low-cut T-shirt and very short orange shorts, 'how many?'

'Two please,' replied Tampong.

'Please follow me.' The waitress picked up two large menus and led them into the rear of the platform and pointed to a table right next to the river.

'Will this suit you?'

'Perfect,' replied Terry, sliding into a high seat.

'Great,' replied the waitress, 'can I get you a drink to start with?'

She placed the menus on the table as she spoke.

'Two local beers please,' replied Tampong, 'large ones.'

Terry scanned the menu.

'Wow,' he remarked, 'it is not expensive here, is it?'

Tampong nodded her agreement when she sensed a presence close by. She looked up to see their waitress returning, carrying two large beers.

'Here you go,' she said, 'are you ready to order?'

'Yep, we are ready,' said Terry. 'I'll have the all-you-can-eat chicken wings, please.'

‘Bone in or not?’

‘Bone in, please.’

‘And what sauce would you like with that?’

‘BBQ.’

‘OK. You get one side with your chicken. Would you like coleslaw, fries, or potatoes with your chicken?

‘Fries, please.’

‘And I’ll have the same, please,’ said Tampong.

‘Super,’ replied the waitress, ‘I’ll get that order in for you and will be back shortly.’

She spun around and walked back towards the kitchen. Terry leaned back in his chair to check her out. She had a very nice rear, but his stare was rudely interrupted by a quick kick in his shin by Tampong, who was giving him a disapproving look. He shrugged his shoulders and looked around the quay instead. Lots of people were walking in both directions. The restaurant itself looked like it was suddenly half full already. He was surprised to see quite a few families inside, having imagined this kind of restaurant being a magnet for young men, coming to ogle at the young waitresses with their push-up bras and high-cut shorts. There were a couple of tourist boats moored. He watched as one loaded up with expectant passengers. It cast off, moving slowly down the river. He had just about finished his scan of the area when the waitress arrived with their chicken wings and fries, which she placed on the table.

‘Ketchup?’ she asked.

‘Please,’ confirmed Terry.

She reached over to the next table, picked up the bottle of ketchup, and placed it on their table. She noticed their beers were almost empty.

‘Can I get you another drink?’ she asked.

‘Yes please,’ they said in unison.

They smiled to each other before finishing their beers and placing their glass back on the table.

She picked up their empty glasses and headed for the bar. They each grabbed a wing and took a bite. The meat came away from the bone easily.

'Hmmm,' sounded Terry, 'these are delicious.'

'I cannot disagree with you,' she said between bites.

The waitress returned with their second beers.

'How are the wings?'

'Excellent,' remarked Terry while still munching on his wing.

'Super. Let me know when you are ready for second helpings.'

They both nodded.

'Super,' she said again before turning away and heading for the kitchen.

They had just picked up their last wing when she returned to their table. Terry put his thumb up, saying they were ready for the next plate. They both licked their lips and fingers clean.

Five minutes later she returned with another plate full of wings. Terry immediately reached over and took two new wings, while Tampong opted to take her wing directly from the plate, one at a time. They ate in silence and were on their last wing when the waitress came back.

'Ready for another helping?'

Both shook their heads.

'I'm stuffed,' said Terry

'OK,' she replied, taking up their plates, 'room for dessert?'

'I certainly have,' said Tampong, wiping her mouth with a serviette.

'Very good. I'll fetch the dessert menus.'

She turned and disappeared.

'You really have room for dessert?' questioned Terry, rubbing his stomach.

'Yes, and don't tell me you don't.'

'I didn't say that, just surprised you were game for dessert.'

'Well, in fact, there is not a lot of meat on those wings, delicious though they were.'

'True,' admitted Terry, still rubbing his stomach, 'although you did also eat half of the fries.'

She just raised her shoulders, trying her best to look like an innocent, hurt girl.

The waitress returned and handed them both the large menu.

'I'll give you folks a couple of minutes to glance at our selection. I can recommend the cheesecake, it's awesome.'

She left them alone again. They glanced over the selection.

'Not much of a choice,' noted Terry, 'but I think I might go for the strawberry delight.'

'And I will have the chocolate mousse.'

Sensing they were ready, she returned with pen and paper ready. 'What will it be then, folks?'

'I'll have the strawberry delight, please,' replied Terry.

'And I'll have the chocolate mousse, please.'

'Both super choices. Actually, the chocolate mousse is my absolute favorite. Would you like a coffee with that?'

'Yes please,' they said in unison, smiling again.

'Super,' came the inevitable response from the waitress. 'I'll get that order in for you folks. Be right back.'

'Everything is super with this girl,' remarked Terry.

Tampong nodded her agreement.

'I think it is just their way here.'

'Could be worse,' he added.

'True.'

Before they could talk anymore, the waitress was back with their desserts and coffee.

'Will there be anything else for you folks?'

'No, that will be it, thanks,' said Tampong.

'Super. Then I will just leave this with you. Take your time and enjoy.'

She placed a silver tray on the table with the bill and left.

'Wow, they are quick with the bill here, aren't they? Back home, you almost have to pry it out of the server,' commented Terry, reaching over and grabbing his strawberry delight.

He was impressed by the size of the glass.

Tampong was equally impressed with her dessert, which tasted delicious and slid easily down her throat. She passed one of the coffee cups to Terry and he added sugar and milk, while Tampong preferred hers black. She picked up the bill and was pleasantly surprised by the total. Her first thought was that the waitress had made a mistake, but when she checked the items, all were accounted for correctly. She reached down for her bag and pulled her purse out, placing three twenty-dollar notes on the tray. Terry watched.

'That's a generous tip, isn't it?'

'I read that around fifteen to twenty percent is the going rate here in Singapore.'

'Really! Perhaps I should think about getting a job here then.'

'It really is all about the service tip in this country as the basic pay is minimal in a lot of places here, so the staff really rely on good tips.'

'Aha, perhaps not such a good place to work then, unless you work really hard.'

'Not so much hard as being pleasant and making your clients feel at home and cared for.'

'Keeping them super you mean.'

Tampong laughed as the waitress returned.

'Are we all done then, folks?'

'We are,' replied Tampong, handing her the silver tray.

She looked down at the notes lying on top of the bill.

'Will you be wanting change, ma'am?'

'No thanks. All was great.'

'Super. Then I wish you a wonderful day and come back real soon.'

Tampong smiled, finished her coffee, and rose from her chair. Terry took a final sip of his coffee before following her out of the restaurant.

'That was . . .'

'Don't say it,' warned Tampong, stopping him from finishing his sentence.

'Say what?'

'You know.'

'Ho, you mean super.'

He dodged the swipe of her hand.

'Actually, I *was* going to say delicious,' he answered.

'Liar,' responded Tampong.

Terry laughed as they walked down the street. He was in a happy mood. It had been an interesting day and he now felt a little bit tired.

'Where are we going now?'

'Well, if you remember, we were going to walk to Orchard Road, but I am feeling quite knackered and thought we could walk back to the hotel instead. I feel like a nice long hot bath before preparing myself for tomorrow.'

'Ho right. I forgot. You have your first day at work tomorrow.'

'Right. So what are you going to do with yourself tomorrow then, while I am working?'

'Not sure. I might go for another walk. Later I will call Karen as I would like to speak to her.'

Tampong went to open her mouth, but Terry put his finger up in the air to stop her.

'Yes, I know, I must not tell her where I am. Got it.'

'It's for her safety as much as ours.'

'I know, I know,' he said sadly.

She felt sad for him.

'It won't be forever, Terry. We will eventually get rid of Shoil and be free to move around without watching over our shoulder.'

'I hope so,' he said, although there was no conviction in his voice.

They walked slowly and quietly back to the hotel. When they arrived back in their room, Tampong walked straight into the bathroom and began to run a bath. Soon the bathroom was full of steam. She looked over to Terry, who was zapping through TV channels. She guessed he was thinking about Karen, and she wished she could help him in some way, despite all that had happened. All said and done, she knew that deep down this was the right thing to do, for now at least. She sighed to herself and quietly closed the door and started to undress.

Terry was indeed thinking about Karen, what a beautiful woman she was, so kind, so gentle, so easy-going. He wondered if he could ever find another girl like her. Did he want to find another like her? Why was he thinking in the past tense now? It was as if he had already written her off. Perhaps she would find someone better than him. If so, he wished her well and a life full of happiness. He was not sure he could promise her that himself, not with Shoil hunting them in the shadows, not with his special abilities, which he could not control yet and, therefore, she would be at risk of being hurt, or worse, should he lose control one day and she was in the way. Perhaps Tampong was right. She was better off away from him, away from them, away from Shoil. He was still flicking through channels but stopped when he saw *Superman*. It was one of the original movies, the ones he preferred. So he stopped zapping, placed the remote on the bedside table and leaned back on his pillow. He was pleased to see that the movie had just started, so he settled down to watch, knowing that Tampong would be in the bath for a long time. She liked it hot and would stay in the water until it cooled. He must have watched about fifteen minutes before he closed his eyes and slept.

Forty-five minutes later, Tampong opened the bathroom door and came out wrapped in a bath towel. She saw Terry sound asleep, so tiptoed over to the bed, picked up the remote, and switched the TV off. She carefully wrapped the blanket around him, then got into her nightclothes before getting into bed. She set the alarm, stretched her arms in the air, yawned, and five minutes later was also fast asleep.

***

Beep, beep, sounded the alarm. Tampong blinked open her eyes, reached over and switched the alarm off. She felt refreshed and was pleased she had a solid night, sleeping straight through. She looked across to Terry's bed, and he hadn't moved, so she guessed he had a good night too. She slipped out of bed and quietly moved into the bathroom, closing the door gently. After she freshened up, brushed her teeth, and got dressed, she noticed the small notepad on the bedside table, so scribbled a quick note for Terry before placing it on his bedside table. She picked up her bag, took one final look at Terry's sleeping body before quietly closing the bedroom door, making sure the 'do not disturb' sign was on the door handle. She walked down the corridor and turned left towards the elevators, got in and pressed the first-floor button. The doors closed and the elevator smoothly descended. She stepped out and walked straight over to the concierge desk. On seeing her walking towards him, the concierge gave her a welcoming smile.

'Good morning, ma'am, how are you this fine morning?'

'I'm fine, thanks,' she confirmed, 'could I please have a taxi?'

'Of course, ma'am. If you would just follow me, I'll take you to the cab rank. There are usually two or three cabs waiting outside in the morning.'

'Perfect.'

She followed him outside, where another hotel staff member, dressed in a long overcoat and top hat, immediately put his arm in the air, prompting a taxi to move towards the main door.

The hotel doorman opened the back door of the taxi for her, so she stepped inside.

'Where to, ma'am?' asked the driver.

'Smith and Wayman's Pharmaceutical company, please.'

'The one in the Business Centre?'

'That's the one.'

'Righto, ma'am,' he said, slipping the gear into drive and pulling out of the hotel.

It didn't take long until the taxi was on the highway. Tampong was casually staring out of the window. The driver tried to start up a conversation.

'First time in Singapore?' he asked.

'Aha.'

'Right. You will find it quite a bit warmer here at this time of the year. Actually, the temperature hardly changes throughout the year.'

'Aha,' she replied again.

'Yep, but it can get hotter than hell here during the summer, I can tell you.'

'Aha.'

'It's not far now, ma'am. We will be there in about another ten minutes or so.'

'OK.'

He finally gave up trying to make small talk, realizing this one was not the chatty type. He was right about the time. In another ten minutes, he pulled up outside the main building.

'Here you go, ma'am.'

'Thank you. How much, please?'

'That'll be fifteen dollars, ma'am.'

She handed him a twenty-dollar bill and stepped out of the cab, to be greeted by a large black security guard.

'Yes, ma'am, how can I help you?'

'Hi, my name is Katy Armitage, and I am starting work here.'

'Is that right? Just wait here if you please. Katy Armitage, you said. Do you have any ID with you, ma'am?'

Tampong handed him her passport. He nodded his thanks and disappeared inside his cabin. After a few minutes, he came back out and handed her passport back.

'Please pin this temporary badge on your lapel, ma'am, and keep it visible at all times. If you walk straight down the road directly in front of you, you will come to the admin section, use the first door on your right. Please go to the reception desk inside, they are expecting you, and welcome to S & W.'

'Thanks,' she replied, pinning her badge to her lapel.

She began walking down the road, grateful it was not raining. She felt the heat of the early morning sun on her face and could well imagine it being as hot as hell, as the driver put it, here during summer. She came to the admin building and pulled the large glass doors open. Opposite was a long wooden reception desk, manned by a young woman and an equally young man.

'Good morning,' began the woman, 'welcome to Smith and Wayman's, how may I assist you?'

'Good morning. My name is Katy Armitage, and I am starting work here.'

She handed over her passport.

'Welcome, Ms. Armitage. I will notify HR that you are here. Please be so kind as to take a seat.'

Tampong turned around and dutifully sat down on a comfortable light-brown leather sofa. She did not wait long before a side door opened, and another young woman came walking up to her.

'Katy is it?' she asked.

'Yes,' confirmed Tampong.

'Would you follow me please?'

Without waiting for a response, she turned around and headed back to the side door. Tampong followed her. The woman led her down another long corridor. She turned right at the end, and they walked down another equally long corridor. There were glass doors on either side of the corridor, and all seemed to be occupied with people focused on their computer screens. The woman finally stopped at the last door on the right, opened it and beckoned Tampong inside. An elderly woman stood up from her desk and extended her hand in greeting.

'Welcome to Smith and Wayman's, Ms. Armitage. Please take a seat as we have quite a few papers to complete. I will then take you to your manager.'

'Thank you,' said Tampong, conscious of the air-conditioning and feeling a slight chill running down her back.

Her heart sank when she saw the pile of papers the woman placed on the desk. The HR woman noticed.

'Don't worry,' she said calmly, 'it is not as bad as it looks. Most of it is just reading material, which you can study later at your convenience.'

'Phew, that's a relief,' admitted Tampong.

For the next hour and a half, the HR woman explained the general setup of the company, its key objectives, and key rules, the first of which being never to reveal any details of any work going on within the walls of the building to outsiders.

'Why is that?' questioned Tampong, 'it's not as if we are doing work for the secret service or anything . . . are we?'

'It's the competition,' explained the HR woman, 'data is a valuable commodity, and sometimes our rivals would do just about anything to get their hands on our data, which is why we insist that you sign this confidentiality agreement.'

'I see. Makes sense,' lied Tampong, 'and I have no problem signing the agreement.'

'That's great, because if you hadn't, then we would have to terminate your employment immediately.'

'OK,' said Tampong in surprise.

'You will of course be on six-months probation, but I doubt that that will create any problems for either you or the company.'

Tampong signed the agreement and handed it back to the woman, who immediately placed it in her file.

'Do you have a Singapore bank account?' she asked.

'Not yet.'

'Then you must get one as soon as possible. Most of us use the Standard Chartered Bank. There is one just down the road. Very convenient for our staff and provides good service.'

'OK, I'll take care of that.'

'Great,' said the woman, handing over another form, 'once you have opened your bank account, please fill in this form and return it to me. We pay every two weeks directly into your account. The next cycle is not for two weeks, so you have some time to open an account. Our payroll people usually need at least a week's notice to make any payroll changes.'

'Got it.'

'Fine, then I think we are done for now. I will just give you the rest of these papers, which are for information and guidance, the most important one being our health and safety policy and our discrimination policy, which we take very seriously.'

'Thank you,' replied Tampong, taking the papers from her.

'Right, please follow me.'

The woman stood up and made her way to the door, so Tampong followed her, placing the papers in her bag. They walked back down the corridor to the elevator, where she pressed the button and the doors opened almost immediately. They stepped inside, and she then pressed the fifth floor.

'Your floor,' she explained.

They stepped out and walked to the end, then turned right into an open-plan office. The woman ignored all the desks and walked directly towards the office at the end. She tapped the door twice before opening it. A man in a grey suit and matching tie rose from his desk, with a big white teethy grin on his face.

He extended his hand in welcome.

'Welcome to the research center of Smith and Wayman's.'

'Thank you,' replied Tampong, shaking his hand, realizing it was a strong grip, one which he held slightly longer than necessary.

His eyes never left her face.

'Thank you, Silvia,' he said to the HR woman, who just nodded and closed the door.

'Please take a seat,' he said in a friendly voice, sitting back in his chair and crossing his legs. 'So, we have been looking forward to you joining us. You come with extraordinarily strong references, and we are delighted you have chosen to join our company.'

'I am excited to be here,' she answered, putting as much enthusiasm into her voice as she could muster.

He struck her as a bit of a ladies' man, and she hoped this was not going to be a problem going forward.

'And we are excited to have you here too, myself in particular. So what did Silvia tell you about our work here?'

'Not much really,' answered Tampong, 'she just went through the company policy and key objectives, pointing out I need a bank account ASAP.'

'We can help you with that. There is a good bank just down the road. I can take you there this afternoon. The sooner you get that done the better.'

'Thank you very much, that's very kind of you.'

'My pleasure,' he answered, looking her up and down.

The first warning signs started to flash in the back of her mind.

'Well, let me give you a quick overview of what we are about. We are trying to find cures for certain types of illnesses, such as rare cancer. We are also trialing a new, very promising drug that could extend life expectancy by up to twenty years.'

'Wow, that is exciting.'

'Right. A potential blockbuster.'

'A what?'

'A blockbuster. Any product with annual sales greater than one billion is classified as a blockbuster. All companies are searching for such products, which can make or break a company.'

'I see, and this extended life expectancy is one such product?'

'Correct. I am actually taking the drug myself. I am really fifty-six years old.'

Tampong's jaw dropped open.

'Just kidding. I am not that old. I am guessing you cannot be much older than twenty-five, not that I am really allowed to ask such questions.'

'HR mentioned something along those lines,' she said, having deliberately avoided answering the question.

'Quite,' he said nervously, 'let me introduce you to the rest of the team, then we can discuss getting you to that bank.'

He stood up, so Tampong followed his lead.

He opened the door and stepped through, not waiting for her.

'Everybody,' he said in a loud voice, 'your attention please.'

The room went quiet as heads turned in his direction.

'Let me introduce you to our new team player, Katy Armitage. Please make her welcome.'

There was a round of applause and one man at the back cheered. Tampong nodded her head in embarrassment.

He walked along the rows of desks.

'This is Su-Ellen, who is my private assistant.'

'Hi there,' said Su-Ellen.

Tampong gave her a friendly nod.

'And this is Woing, our technical expert.'

'Hello,' he said, not bothering to look up, so Tampong didn't even bother to acknowledge him.

'Kristin, our PR guru.'

'Hello,' she said with Colgate-white teeth.

'Hi,' replied Tampong.

'Roger, our key sales rep.'

He just nodded but seemed friendly enough, so she nodded back. She guessed it must have been him who cheered.

'And this is Samantha, who will be taking care of you and showing you the ropes.'

'Hello,' said Samantha in a not too friendly manner.

'Play nicely,' he warned.

'Hello,' replied Tampong, who turned to face the man, 'and you are?'

'Oops, did I not tell you?'

'Nope.'

'How remiss of me. I'm Brad.'

'Hello, Brad.'

He nodded, gave Samantha a warning glance, then headed back to his office. Just before he closed the door, he poked his head outside and called out after her in a loud voice.

'Let me know when you are ready to visit the bank.'

He then closed his door.

'So, he's taking you to the bank, is he?' queried Samantha.

'Yes,' said Tampong, sensing some hostility in the woman's voice.

'Cannot say I'm surprised. Watch yourself with that one.'

'Pardon me?'

Samantha ignored her question for clarity.

'This is your desk, and here are your temporary passwords. Log onto the main screen and change your password to something only you will remember. Once you have done that, there are some files you can start reading that will give you background information on what we are doing. I will then go through your routines, once you have been to the bank.'

'Thanks, Samantha.'

'Call me Sam, everyone else does . . . except him.'

Her eyes looked toward the closed door.

Tampong sensed some history between the two of them, but now was not the time to probe that little problem. She duly logged into the computer and quickly found the home screen. She clicked the password icon and entered a new password. Once she confirmed it, she was redirected to the company home page where an envelope was flashing at her, indicating she had mail. She clicked the icon and ten documents appeared on her screen. She clicked the first one and began reading. It was all about the age-enhancing trial. They were in Phase III trialing, whatever that meant, and were recruiting patients to test the drug on, although some would be getting the placebo and not the active drug. She stared at the words, then look across to Sam.

'May I ask you a question, Sam?'

'Sure, that's what I am here for.'

'If the drug is so effective, why bother with giving some patients a placebo?'

'That's standard trial protocol. Some patients react, thinking they have received the active drug, when in fact they have nothing more than an aspirin or something similar. It's called the placebo effect and helps establish the effectiveness of the real drug.'

'OK, thanks. That's helpful.'

'No problem.'

Sam then looked down at her watch.

'Hey, you had better get going if you want to make the bank today. I'll fetch the boss.'

Without waiting for a reply, she stood up and marched over to Brad's door. She knocked once and walked inside, closing the door behind her, which Tampong thought was strange. She could hear raised voices coming from inside the office and distinctly heard Brad saying, 'Keep your voice down, will you?'

There was a brief silence, and she noticed that everyone else had their heads down, pretending to look occupied. The door then opened, and a red-faced Sam emerged and stormed back to her desk, slumping down into her chair. Brad came out and adjusted his tie nervously. He walked over to Tampong's desk, glancing across to Sam, who kept her head down, obviously not wanting to engage in any further conversation with him.

'Samantha says you are ready for the bank trip.'

'Right,' she said, standing up, which prompted Sam to look up.

'Always log off your computer before you leave your desk. It's a security requirement,' warned Sam.

'Ho right, sorry.' Tampong sat back down and logged out of her computer before standing up again and reaching for her coat.

'Right, let's go,' said Brad.

When he led Tampong out of the office, all heads lifted up and first looked at the door they just passed through, then all turned to look at Sam, whose face was staring hard at the door, her eyes squinting a little.

She was not very happy about Brad leaving with the new girl.

***

Terry opened his eyes and glanced at the clock; it was nearly 7 am.

'Crickey,' he said, grabbing his computer, switching it on, and pressing the Skype icon.

He was relieved it was not quite 7:30 am yet, so he was not late. He did not have long to wait either as the screen changed to reveal Karen's face. She looked initially pleased, but her smile suddenly disappeared.

'Wow, you look tired,' she said, her voice sounding worried.

'Yeah, sorry about that. Long night. Catching up on some lost sleep I think.'

'So, what were you up to yesterday then?'

'Ho, just out and about, checking local sights out.'

'I see,' replied Karen, although she had no idea what he was talking about, 'so, are you settling in OK?'

'So far, so good. My aunt is at work now but will be back later this evening, and then we will grab something to eat.'

Later this evening? She repeated his words in her head.

He sounds like he has just woken up, yet his aunt has already gone to work. This was further proof to her that he must be in the

East somewhere, but where? He appeared to be in the hotel still, but there was no indication from his background to help her.

'Going anywhere nice today?' she asked instead, trying to lure him into giving away some little detail, no matter how small.

'Not sure,' he said, 'I may go out for a walk around the bay if it is not too hot. No doubt I will find a local restaurant while out, if not, then maybe even a takeaway tonight.'

She nodded, thinking about what she could ask to help gauge his whereabouts.

'So how has your day been?' he asked, knocking her out of her thoughts.

'Oh, you know, the usual. Boring day at school, and equally boring day at the restaurant, with just a handful of customers all evening.'

'Few customers, huh? Makes the evening drag out, right?'

'You can say that again.'

She went quiet and looked down. When she looked back up she spoke quietly, 'I miss you so much.'

Terry moved closer to the screen.

'And I miss you, Karen, so much.'

'How long can we keep this up?'

'Keep what up?'

'This distant chatting.'

'For as long as necessary.'

'But I need you here, Terry. I need to be able to touch you, to kiss you, to simply hold you.'

'I know.'

'Do you? Do you really?'

'Yes, I think so.'

'I don't think you do. You have no idea what it's like being here alone. I have only just gotten to know you, and now, all of a sudden, you up and leave me.'

Terry sighed, not sure how to answer her.

'It will not be for long, Karen,' he said finally.

Tears ran down her face, and he now suddenly felt extremely lonely and guilty.

'Listen,' he began, 'let me talk to my aunt, and maybe she will let me come back home for a brief while.'

'Do you think that is possible?'

'All I can do is try, but I will try my best. I promise you that much.'

'OK. Let me know as soon as you have news, good or bad.'

'I will.'

'Thanks. I will have to sign off soon as I need to get my head down. I have school tomorrow, you know, and Mum will go mad if she hears me talking to you.'

'You're right, as always. I'll let you go, but know my thoughts are of you, always.'

'I hope we can be together again soon.'

'Me too.'

She blew him a kiss then signed off. His screen returned to the Skype home page. He switched his computer off and slowly lowered the lid. He was not sure how he was going to approach Tampong about possibly travelling back. Even if she agreed, how on earth was he going to be able to return to the UK? He was not only going to need her agreement, but her money too. This was not going to be easy.

***

Tampong signed yet another form at the bank and handed it over.

That's fine, ma'am,' said the bank clerk as he gathered all the papers together, 'we will have a temporary chequebook ready in a couple of days, and we will ring you when it is ready. We will need a small deposit if you want a credit card.'

'Do I need one?'

'Yes,' answered Brad, 'just about everything is paid by card here in Singapore. You will find life difficult without one. Cash is accepted in many places, but it is much safer to use a card.'

'OK, then I guess I better have one.'

'Great. I would propose a Singapore three-hundred-dollar deposit to get you going. It will be refunded after three months, providing your credit remains good, of course.'

'Of course,' confirmed Tampong, pulling out her purse and handing the clerk 300 Singapore dollars.

'Fantastic. We will get that processed for you as well. Should be ready in a couple of days too.'

'Great,' answered Tampong, 'are we all done here?'

'We are, ma'am, have a great day.'

'You too.'

Brad nodded to the clerk, and they walked out of the bank. He walked around to the passenger side of his car and opened the door for Tampong. She nodded her thanks and slipped into the passenger seat, aware that he was standing closer than necessary. She was sure she heard him sniff her as she passed. He slowly closed the door, but not before checking out her legs, not that she noticed.

He walked around to his side and got into the driver's seat, started the engine, and pulled the car out of the bank driveway.

'So, where are you staying?'

'At the Carlton Hotel.'

'Nice.'

'It's comfortable,' she admitted, not liking the direction this conversation was going.

'Do you have time for a bite before I drop you off at the hotel?'

'Are we not going back to the office?'

'No, it's just after five pm, and I am the boss, after all.'

'I see. Thanks for the offer, but I need to get back to the hotel and eat with my nephew.'

'Your nephew? He came with you?'

'Yes, and yes. Why do you ask?'

'Ho nothing really, just surprised to hear you came with someone. What about his parents, do they mind him being with you?'

'No. Mainly because they are both dead.'

'Dead!' he repeated, looking directly at her in shock.

'Keep your eyes on the road please,' she said nervously, worried that he was not paying attention to where he was going.

'Don't worry about me, I'm a great driver.'

He started to speed up as if to make a point.

'So how old is your nephew then?'

'He will be eighteen in a couple of months.'

'I see. So he is old enough to look after himself then.'

'Meaning?'

'Meaning we can still have that dinner, and I'll take you back to your hotel later . . . much later.'

He gave her a knowing smirk.

'Thanks, but I'd still rather go straight back to the hotel.'

'Don't be such a fuddy-duddy. It was not a request, in any case. I am your boss, you know.'

'At work maybe, but not outside the office. I am my own person.'

'Listen, newbie, I don't take no from anybody. Ask any of the girls in the office. They know they need to be nice to me if they want to keep their jobs. You should too.'

'Is that a threat?'

'Of course not. It is just a matter of fact. If you want to keep your job, then you need to be nice to me. Very nice. You are a long way from home, you know. There is no one to look after you here.'

'Thanks, but I'll pass.'

He braked hard, and she felt pushed against her seat belt.

'Listen, bitch, if I say you do something, then you do it, right? I'll take no shit from a little piece of arse like you—nice though your arse is, which is mainly why I am allowing you to spend the evening with me. All I want is to see you up close and naked and for us to have a little bit of adult fun, if you know what I mean.'

'What did you call me?'

'A little piece of arse.'

'No. Before that.'

'Ho, you mean bitch?'

'Right, you dare to call me a bitch?'

'Well, just don't prove me right and just spend the night with me. You will not regret it.'

'You might.'

'I'll take my chances.'

Tampong thought through her options, which were limited, so she decided to change tactics.

'So what do you suggest?'

'That's better,' he said, relief clearly in his tone. 'I have a small condo not far from here. We can go there.'

'And what about dinner?'

'You are on my menu tonight.'

'I see.'

He slipped the gear back into drive and drove quickly down the road. He reached over and placed his hand on her thigh. She didn't move, so his hand went further up her leg, disappearing under her skirt. She held his hand in place before he went any higher.

'Concentrate on the road, Brad. There will be plenty of time for that.'

'Great. I am so glad you have come around to my way of thinking. The moment I saw you I knew I had to bed you. You have a great body, you know.'

'I know,' she confirmed, looking straight ahead.

'And I bet you know how to please a guy with that body as well.'

'I have had no complaints so far.'

'I bet. We will soon be there, and then you can show me all your tricks.'

'Ho, I'll show you my tricks all right,' she said quietly.

He turned the car off the road and onto a dirt track. They bounced along the road for a few minutes until he turned off again. She could now work out a small building straight ahead. Brad stopped the car at the side of the building, turned the engine off, and quickly slid out of the car, almost running towards the door while searching for his key. He found it, opened the door, and turned towards Tampong as she stepped out of the car, deliberately slowly, then walked slowly towards the door. All the time he was beckoning her to come quickly, waving his hand frantically and excitedly. When she passed by him, he placed his hand on her rear.

'Boy, I am looking forward to having that tight arse.'

She said nothing but walked inside and turned around, waiting for him to close the door. He did, turning the lock and slipping the key into his jacket pocket.

'We don't want to be disturbed now, do we?'

'I guess not,' she answered, certain that he did it to keep her locked inside.

'Now, missy,' he began, licking his lips, 'let's see what you have got under those clothes.'

'Why don't you come closer and undress me yourself?'

'I'd like that,' he said keenly while he began walking towards her.

On reaching her he immediately placed his hand up her skirt, intent on feeling her, but was surprised by her sudden speed. She reached down, stopped him in his tracks, and, instead, pulled his hand up into the air. Her strength was similarly surprising as she seemed to pull his hand as if he was a child.

'Hey,' a now surprised Brad said, 'what's your game?'

'No game, Mr. Bossman. I am going to show you my best tricks.'

He laughed nervously, conscious that he could not release himself from her grip. He looked up and could only see her hand holding his.

How is this possible? he thought, *she is just a slip of a girl, but her strength is superhuman.*

'Wondering how I am holding you up like this?' she guessed.

His eyes betrayed his mouth.

'No, just not sure of what your trick is.'

'Well, let me show you.'

Her eyes turned orange while one of her fingernails turned into a long thin needle, which she plunged into his stomach. His eyes bugled in surprise, and he gasped for breath.

'Now listen carefully to me,' she said, although her voice now sounded deep and threatening, 'you will never force another woman to have sex with you. In fact, you will never go out with another woman.'

His face was frozen, but his head nodded in acknowledgement.

Another idea then popped into her head.

'In fact, you have decided you actually like men, big black men. Ones who love to ram their dick up your arse, your sweet little piece of arse, lots, and lots of times. For now, though, you will simply drive me back to the hotel.'

She was about to pull her blade out when another thought struck her.

'And when you get back to the office tomorrow, you will realize that you did not offer me the right salary, and you will double it as well as double my bonus.'

She pulled the blade out and he slumped to the floor, whimpering like a little boy. She waited for a few minutes, then folded her arms.

'Have you quite finished?'

He stopped blubbering and slowly stood up.

'Yes, yes, ma'am. I am good now. Isn't it about time I took you back to your hotel?'

'Yes, yes, it is.'

He walked to the door, removed his key from his pocket, opened the door, and held it open for her, rubbing his stomach with his free hand, not certain why. The last few minutes were a complete blank to him, except he had an urgent need to take her back to her hotel. She calmly walked past him and up to the car door and waited. He quickly walked up to the car and opened the door for her. She slid into the car seat. He slowly closed the door and quickly walked around to the driver's side, sat inside, and started the engine. No other words were exchanged between them until they reached the hotel and he stopped outside the main door. The doorman came to the car and opened her door and she stepped out. Before leaving she bent down and lowered her head toward Brad, who was staring straight ahead.

'Thank you for driving me back to the hotel, Brad. See you in the office tomorrow.'

Without turning his head he answered her.

'See you in the office tomorrow,' he replied.

As soon as the doorman closed the door, he drove away. She watched him go. When his car was finally out of view, she nodded her thanks to the doorman and walked into the hotel.

When she entered her room, she was greeted with an agitated Terry, who was still pacing back and forth across the room. He stopped when she entered.

'What happened?' he asked worriedly.

'What do you mean?'

'I felt you change, so what happened?'

'Ho, you felt that, did you? Well, I was having some trouble with my new boss.'

'What sort of trouble?'

'He tried his luck with me.'

'He tried to bed you?'

'Right.'

'So what did you do?'

'I fixed him so that he will never harm another woman again.'

'You killed him!'

'No, nothing like that. I just put the thought into his head that women are to be worshipped and not used as some unpaid hooker. I might also have told him he is gay now.'

'You told him he is gay now!'

'Right.'

Terry started laughing, but then suddenly stopped.

'You know that if I felt you, then there is a good chance that she did too.'

Tampong slumped onto the bed.

'You're right. Boy, how stupid am I? I didn't even think about her.'

'Why would you? Some jerk was coming onto you, and he would have had no idea of your skills. I would like to have seen the look on his face when he found out.'

'Not much to tell really. He was more in a trance. It will be interesting to see how he reacts in the morning.'

'Who knows, given that we are so far away, perhaps she didn't sense you. It wasn't for long, after all.'

'It only takes a second, but you could be right. We might be far enough away.'

'Let's hope so.'

***

Shoil's eyes shot open. It was brief and faint, but it was definitely her. Her eyes turned orange as she tried to focus on the sensation, but it faded almost as quickly as it arrived. This time it felt different, as if she had moved further away. There was no doubt about it, it was definitely Tampong. She had been activated for some reason, probably dealing with a human threat most likely. Why did she seem so far away? Could she have tried to escape? If so, did the boy go with her? She would need the girl after all and was glad she did not end her life straight away, as was her original plan. She was sure that the boy would keep in contact with her, no matter where he was, so she was her best lead to finding him, and Tampong.

Then she could enact her revenge.

***

Gary dropped the book he was reading. He felt the faint sensation too, then another one, but much closer. The closer one he was sure was Shoil. The other one he concluded must have been Tampong, but she had moved away, which was not a bad thing. He sensed that Shoil was still looking for her and, perhaps, would pursue Tampong, which would put more distance between them and the Lower Middle, which was also a good thing. Or so he thought. The one thing nagging at the back of his mind was whether this was all some cunning plan of theirs, luring him into some false sense of security. He looked down at Tracey, who was fast asleep. He would not let his guard down, would not stop watching, and would protect this precious woman, even with his last breath.

CLOSING IN

Date: November 2010
Ages: 17 / 1,161
Status: Semi-active

The next day, Tampong arrived early in the office and was the first one to arrive. She switched on her computer and opened her files and started reading through more of the documents. She heard the door open and hesitated to look around, but it was Sam, and she did not look happy. She slammed her bag on the desk and slumped into her chair, forcing Tampong to swivel around in her chair.

'Bad night?' she asked.

'The worst,' sulked Sam. 'I was stood up. Can you believe that? **Me**! Stood up.'

'Boyfriend?'

'Ex-boyfriend.'

Tampong said nothing, preferring to return to her reading, except Sam was not finished.

'Did he say anything to you last night?' she demanded.

'Who?'

She turned to face Sam again and could now see tears forming in her eyes.

'That bastard, Brad, who else?'

'Ho right. Well no. He drove me to the bank and then returned me to the hotel.'

It was Sam's turn to swivel around in her chair to face Tampong.

'Back to your hotel. Did he come to your room?'

Her face was glowing red with anger.

'Absolutely not. He dropped me outside the hotel then drove away. I assume he went home but don't know for sure.'

'You would not be lying to me now, would you?'

'No. I am not lying. He dropped me off and drove away. You can ask the doorman at the hotel if you don't believe me.'

'Huh,' she said, returning to her computer screen and switching it on, 'then I guess he must have gone straight home then.'

She was more talking to herself than Tampong.

Just then, the main door opened, and Brad walked in. Both girls turned. Sam was about to rip into him when her jaw dropped open. Brad was wearing a rose-colored suit, purple shirt, complete with silk cravat. He almost skipped into the room. He was swinging his hips from left to right, with one hand on his left hip.

'Good morning, ladies,' he said in a high-pitched voice, 'what a blissfully lovely day it is today.'

He sounded different, he looked different. He acted differently.

'Are you OK?' asked Tampong, doing her best to suppress a smile.

'Simply divine, darling, simply divine.'

He skipped over to her desk and leaned forward, placing one elbow on her desk and rested his head against his hand.

'I must say, I am loving the color of your shirt, Katy, absolutely you,' he observed.

'Are you for real?' asked Sam, completely puzzled by his change of attire and voice. 'Where were you last night?'

'Last night, last night,' he said tapping his finger on his cheek, 'ho yes, after I dropped this lovely lady off at the hotel, I drove over to Gap and bought a whole new wardrobe. Just had the urge to go on a spending spree.'

'And what about our date last night?'

'Date!!'

He looked her up and down as if sizing up a piece of meat.

'Date! I really don't think so, darling. You are so not my type.'

Before she could respond, the main door opened again, and Roger walked in.

'Morning all,' he said cheerfully.

Brad looked him up and down,

'Now that's so my type.'

'What!' exclaimed a shocked Sam, 'Roger?'

'Roger by name and I suspect roger by nature . . . if only.'

He turned and skipped into his office, leaving Sam staring after him, her jaw still wide open in shock. She then turned to Tampong.

'Did you hear that? He likes Roger . . . a man!'

'So it seems. That would explain why I didn't feel threatened by him last night, he was as sweet as pie.'

'Yeah, minced pie.'

Tampong laughed and soon afterward Sam joined her.

'Who would have thought it? Brad is gay. Well, that at least explains why I was stood up. I never guessed. Never had any idea.'

'Who knew?' lied Tampong.

'And now I know why he didn't bother with me all the time I was here. I was the wrong sex.'

'Obviously.'

Suddenly the two hit it off and Sam was now very friendly with her, at least for the rest of the day.

Back at the hotel, Terry was restless. It was too early to call, so he was at a loss as to what to do with his spare time. He decided he would go for a walk to help pass the time. He had read that there was a lion statue in Singapore, so thought he would check that out. The hotel guide said the statue was a Merlion, symbolizing Singapore's humble beginnings as a fishing village. It was actually half lion and half fish. They must have walked right past it yesterday, but neither of them spotted it, so it cannot be that big. He pulled out the local map and found it easily enough. He understood why they missed it as they cut through the park. He decided he would walk around in the opposite direction, stopping at the Merlion, after which he could get something to eat. He picked up his rucksack and dropped a couple of bottles of water into it, along with the map, opened the door and flipped the sign over before closing the door and heading out of the hotel, turning right this time. He had a good sense of direction and never felt lost. He slowly made his way down the road, turning left when he sensed the need to and carried on walking until he reached the river, which he now knew led to the bay. He followed the river, crossed over a white-painted metal bridge before coming to the bridge they stopped at yesterday. He pulled out one of his water bottles and drank half of its contents, putting the rest back in his sack.

He found the Merlion, but unfortunately it was being refurbished and covered in scaffolding and tarpaulin. Even the water was turned off, so nothing was sprouting from its mouth.

Disappointed, he decided he felt a little hungry so looked back at the row of small restaurants under the bridge. He decided to walk back to the place where they stopped yesterday for a beer. It seemed nice enough.

'Good afternoon,' said the pretty receptionist, 'for one, is it?'

'Yes, please,' he confirmed.

'Great. Follow me please.'

The woman grabbed a menu and headed down the open restaurant with Terry following.

'Will this do?' she asked.

'Perfect.'

'Super. Your server will be right with you. Enjoy.'

She gave him a big smile, turned, and returned to her station.

'Hello, how are you doing?' asked the waitress, almost making him jump as she was so quick.

'Fine thanks, and you?'

'Very well, thank you. My name is Sandi,' she pointed to her name badge on her chest, 'and I'll be taking care of you today. Can I start you off with an appetizer?'

'What do you have?' he asked.

'We have chicken wings, onion rings, onion soup, crab fingers, pâté . . .'

He put his finger in the air to stop her talking. It worked.

'I'll start with the pâté please.'

'Pâté it is. And something to drink?'

'Do you have Tiger beer?'

'Of course. This is Singapore after all. I will need to see your ID first though.

'Ho, what age can you drink here in Singapore?'

'Eighteen, sir.'

'OK, then I'd better have a Doctor Pepper. I am not quite there yet.'

'Not quite there yet?' she asked.

'No. I am eighteen in a couple of months,' he explained, feeling a little embarrassed at being found out but having felt the need to be honest with this girl. He certainly didn't want to get her into any trouble selling beer to an underage customer.

She leaned a little closer to him.

'That's close enough,' she whispered before standing back upright again. 'I'll get that going for you while you glance over the menu.'

She turned gracefully and headed for the bar.

He watched her go, enjoying her form and the fact she pointed out her ample breasts, which her badge was pinned to. Then he felt guilty and thought of Karen. He looked at the menu and spotted a burger menu meal that sounded delicious. Sandi returned with his drink and placed it in front of him, leaning forward a little so that he could see down the top of her blouse, which he managed to avoid doing . . . just. She straightened up and took her notepad and pen out of her front pocket in her pinnie.

'Are you ready to order, sir?' she asked.

'Yes, I am. I'll have the cheeseburger menu, please.'

'Super. You have two sides with that.'

Again she leaned forward and indicated the place on the menu.

Terry's eyes would not obey him this time and looked at the tops of her inviting breasts.

'Erm,' he said with a slight cough, 'I'll have the fries and coleslaw, please.'

'Great. I'll get that sorted for you and find out about your pâté.'

'Thanks.'

'You are most welcome.'

She disappeared into the kitchen, so Terry took a long gulp of his drink. It was cold and refreshing, so he took another swig.

The kitchen door swung open, and Sandi stepped out with a plate, which she placed in front of Terry, again deliberately leaning forward a little.

'Enjoy,' she said.

She was about to step away when she stopped and turned back to him.

'If you don't mind me asking, have you just arrived here in Singapore?'

'Is it that obvious?'

'Well, you have a European accent to start with, and you don't know the drinking age here, plus you are so white at the moment. Most European tourists who have been here a couple of days look like boiled lobsters. This sun can be deadly if you don't look after your skin.'

He laughed at her reference to lobsters.

'OK, you got me.'

'Been here long?'

'No. Just arrived yesterday actually, from the UK.'

'Did you come on your own?'

He thought she was getting a little bit personal, but didn't mind the conversation, particularly as she was a beautiful woman.

'No. I am here with my aunty, who has just started working here.'

'Aha, so you will be here for a little while then.'

'Most likely.'

'Great, so we may see you here again then?'

'Most likely.'

She smiled warmly at him before heading back to the kitchen. He watched her go, having the distinct impression she was flirting with him. He liked it. He took a bite of his pâté, which tasted slightly spicy. He ate in silence, sipping his drink in between bites of his toast. It was not long before he was on his last piece and had just taken a bite of it when Sandi came back with his cheeseburger. He waited for the inevitable leaning forward motion, and he was not disappointed. She stayed in that position for a little longer than normal, forcing him to again look down her bra. She seemed pleased when she noticed his eyes ogling her.

'If there is anything else you need, just let me know,' she said teasingly.

'I will, thanks, Sandi.'

'You're most welcome. Enjoy your meal.'

She then noticed his empty glass.

'Would you like a refill?'

'You do refills here?'

'Most of Singapore does.'

'Then, yes please.'

She took his glass and left him to his meal, but before walking off with a little enticing wiggle.

He sliced through his burger, which was so tender his knife cut through it like a hot knife in butter. He slipped it into his mouth and savored the flavors. Sandi returned with his refill and sat it next to his plate.

'How's the burger?'

'Fantastic.'

'Great. Continue to enjoy. Don't hesitate to let me know if you need anything.'

She left him again. He felt strangely disappointed. For some reason he wanted her to join him. Perhaps sit in the chair opposite. Then he felt silly. It was probably just her warm hospitality, which was sending him mixed messages. Whatever it was, he was going to enjoy his stay here and would definitely return to this particular restaurant . . . and hopefully be served by Sandi again.

He was halfway through his meal when she returned to his table.

'How's it going? Ready for another drink?'

He took another gulp of his beer and handed her the nearly empty glass.

'So are you a local girl then?' he asked.

'Born and bred.'

'So you know the local area well then.'

'Like the back of my hand.'

'Great. Are there some places you can recommend me to visit?'

'Absolutely. You must go visit the Raffles Hotel for starters. Used to be an officers' mess during the war and is famous for its drinks. For example, the Singapore sling is a must-have drink.'

'I've heard of that one,' he replied.

'Well, I'd be surprised if you hadn't?'

'Wow, sounds awesome. Is it far?'

'Where are you staying?'

'At the Carlton Hotel.'

'The Carlton! Then it's right next door to your hotel. Couldn't be closer.'

'Ho right. I'll take a walk there then and have a look after lunch.'

She chuckled.

'You'll need to take your aunty with you, because of your age. I had to go with my mother when I first went there.'

'Really?'

'Really.'

'OK. Then maybe I will ask my aunty to take me there at the weekend.'

'Great. Then of course there is the Marina Bay Sands Hotel. One of the most modern hotels in the world.'

'I have seen that, and the ship on top.'

'OK. You were quick out of the blocks then.'

'Excuse me?'

'Ignore me, I am just being silly. Then there is the Universal Studios. It's on a little separate island, but you can get there by cable car.'

'Cable car. They have that here too?'

'Right.'

'Is it far?'

'About a forty-five-minute walk from your hotel, so not too far.'

'Anything else?'

'Well, there is a very nice garden theme park which is lots of fun. It also takes about forty-five minutes, and then of course we boast two casinos here in Singapore if you like to gamble.'

'You don't?'

'We have to pay two hundred dollars just to get into the place. There is also a little question of age as well.'

'Wow, does everyone have to pay an entrance fee to get in?'

'Nope, just us Singapore folk. It's a kind of local tax and a good way of discouraging locals from gambling.'

'Hey, Sandi, there are other tables needing your attention,' interrupted the receptionist, believing their conversation was going on too long.

'Excuse me,' she said, nodding to the hostess and moving across the room to the new customers.

Terry resumed his meal after having an enjoyable, albeit short conversation with Sandi. She seemed easy-going and he liked her. No harm in having a friend in town who just happens to be a girl, and a beautiful one at that. He hoped he would get the opportunity to talk more with her.

He had nearly finished his meal and his drink when she returned to his table. She glanced nervously towards the door, but the hostess was engaged with other customers. She smiled at Terry.

'Sorry about that. She can be a bit of a tyrant at times, but harmless enough.'

'No problem, and sorry if I got you into trouble.'

'Not your fault. I see you have nearly finished. Would you like dessert?'

'Yes, please. I am in no rush today.'

'That's good,' she said, rather too quickly.

She blushed a little.

'I'll get you the menu card. Would you like another beer?'

'Why not? It's hot here outside, but I'd rather the heat than the cold.'

She smiled as she took his glass, quickly returning with another beer and menu card, which she handed to him. He took hold of the menu and their fingers brushed each other. They looked into each other's eyes, and they were locked together for a few seconds. She blinked and the moment passed.

'I'll give you a few minutes to mull over the menu,' she said, leaving quickly, clearly embarrassed by what just happened between them.

Just before she entered the kitchen, she glanced back at Terry, who was still watching her. She smiled at him. He returned her smile before looking back down and glancing over the menu.

He placed the menu down and waited, tapping his fingers impatiently on the table.

'Have you decided?' said the strange female voice from behind him, making him jump.

It was the hostess.

'Er, yes, I'll have the apple crumble, please.'

'Good choice, and would sir be having coffee or something else with that?'

'Coffee please.'

'Coming right up, sir.'

She took the menu and headed for the kitchen.

His heart sank, thinking that Sandi must have been warned off him or something. He resigned himself to not seeing her again today. Shame, he was getting on well with her, and they appeared to click.

He was gazing out across the bay when his dessert arrived and was placed in front of him. He turned to say thank you and was delighted to see it was Sandi. His face lit up, and she was clearly pleased with his reaction.

'And your coffee.'

'Thank you, Sandi, thank you very much.'

'You are more than welcome. Will there be anything else for you today?'

'No, thank you, I think I am done.'

'Great, then I'll just leave the bill here for you. Absolutely no rush.'

He was not surprised this time, assuming this was typical protocol here in Singapore: to hand over the bill as soon as the customer is finished. He wished the UK would follow such procedures as it always took ages to get the bill there. He checked his watch. It was just after 2 pm, so still plenty of the day left. He checked the bill; it was twenty-two dollars. He calculated that a 20 percent tip would be around four forty, so he placed a twenty-dollar note and a ten-dollar note on the top of the bill.

It was not long before Sandi came back to his table. She looked down at the two notes.

'Would sir like change?'

'No, that will be fine, thank you, Sandi.'

'Then thank you very much, sir.'

'Terry, my name is Terry.'

'Then thank you, Terry, and I wish you a fantastic day and hope to see you again.'

'Me too.'

'You should keep hold of the receipt,' she added.

'Really?'

'Really,' she said, smiling at him.

He picked it up, folded it and slipped it into his wallet. He finished his coffee and stood up. He wanted to say goodbye again, but she had disappeared back into the kitchen. He walked out the front gate.

'Have a great day, sir, and we hope to see you again real soon,' said the hostess.

He nodded and left the restaurant, deciding to make his way back to the hotel. His mind was in turmoil. He definitely liked Sandi, and she seemed to like him, yet there was Karen, whom he thought he had genuine feelings for, but she was miles away and he was beginning to doubt himself and their relationship. He tried to convince himself that Sandi was just being polite, and he would probably never see her again. Their eyes did lock together for a moment, that much was true, but it was just a moment. He started whistling as he walked back to the hotel. As he walked down the street, he spotted a tourist shop, so stopped and walked inside to take a look.

'Good afternoon, sir,' said the salesman standing behind the counter.

'Good afternoon.'

'Is that an English accent I detect?' he asked.

'It is,' he confirmed.

'Then welcome and feel free to look around.'

'Thanks, do you know how long the Merlion will be covered up for?'

'They have not started yet, so a couple of more months, I think.'

'Wow, OK, thanks.'

'Looking for anything in particular?'

'No, just a souvenir of sorts.'

'Well, our most popular purchase is the Merlion statue, a Merlion T-shirt or jacket.'

'OK, then I'll purchase a T-shirt for now then.'

'Great. You look like a medium to me, sir. I'll just pop into the back and see if we have one in stock.'

'Thanks.'

The man turned and walked through a door, leaving Terry alone, so he walked around the shop. There were lots of bobbleheads of sports personalities, none of whom he knew. He picked up a football, which seemed more like a rugby ball to him. He placed it back on the shelf when the man returned carrying a T-shirt in a plastic bag.

'Yes, we do indeed have one. Would you like to try it on, sir, to make sure it fits you?'

Terry nodded and walked up to the man, who ripped open the plastic and pulled the T-shirt out. He shook it briefly before opening it up for Terry to slip his arms through. The man stepped back.

'Perfect fit, sir.'

'Great, I'll take it.'

'Great, sir. How will that be?'

'By card please.'

'Perfect.'

He tapped the keyboard of his cash machine a few times, entering the amount, before turning the machine towards Terry.

'Just present your card when you are ready, sir.'

Terry slid his card into the machine, watched as a circle whirled around a few times before he was prompted for his code, which he entered. The machine then spewed out a receipt, which the man ripped off and pressed a button on the machine again and another receipt was printed. He placed one copy on the desk.

'If you would sign this, please.'

He did, and the man took the receipt and placed it in the cash till. The other receipt he placed in a bag, along with the T-shirt, and handed it over to Terry.

'You are all set, sir.'

'Thank you, and have a great day.'

'You too, sir. Have a super day. Try to stay out of the sun this time of day. It is at its burning worst.'

He nodded and walked out of the shop, pleased with his purchase. He continued to walk down the street swinging his bag. He arrived at the hotel and went straight to his room. He placed the bag at the side of his bed and waited for the right time to Skype.

***

At the same time, Karen was looking at the clock, which seemed to have stopped moving. There had only been six customers all evening, so time dragged by. The owner was in a foul mood as well.

'Don't know why I bother to open during the week. It is as quiet as a graveyard.'

'So why do you bother to open then?' she asked.

'Because you never know. Perhaps a busload of tourists will stop, and we will have a great evening.'

'Yeah, and maybe pigs will fly,' she joked.

'Cynical,' he mocked.

She laughed and looked at the clock again. He noticed.

'Listen, you might as well go home. No one will come in now.'

'You sure?'

'Yeah, go and I'll see you tomorrow.'

'Thanks, Toni. See you tomorrow.'

She took her pinnie off and walked into the back room, grabbed her coat, placed the pinnie on the coat hook, and walked outside. She suddenly stopped, looked around but saw nothing, so started walking quickly towards the bus stop, keeping her eyes and ears on alert. She made it safely to the bus stop, waiting nervously for the bus to arrive. Two people, a man and a woman, also stopped at the bus stop, and she felt relieved and a little bit safer. She was not sure why she felt so vulnerable, but she had that woman on her mind and did not want to come across her again. She looked up and saw the bus arriving. She smiled.

***

Shoil checked her watch. It was time to leave. The restaurant would be closing soon, and she did not want to miss the girl coming out. She grabbed her coat and walked out into the night. She walked quickly, having memorized the route. She knew it would take only ten minutes to reach the restaurant and had found a perfect hidden spot with a clear view of the side door from where the girl would exit. Having arrived, she noticed that the lights were still on, so that assured her she was not too late. She stepped into the shop doorway, away from view, and waited. It was another twenty minutes before the lights of the restaurant went out. Her heartbeat increased as the excitement mounted. The side door opened and, ready to pounce, she bent her knees and was about to leap when a man walked out the door. She just managed to halt her intended leap and waited. The man fumbled for something in his pocket, finally retrieving his keys.

He locked the door.

She stood there, confused, uncertain of what to do next. She blinked several times, unable to believe her eyes. Her mind raced through several options. Finally, she stepped out of the doorway and walked towards the man, who was now putting his keys into his pocket. He saw Shoil approaching and froze on the spot. She recognized his stance, so raised her hands in a gesture of peace. He took a couple of steps backwards. It was late at night and some strange woman had suddenly appeared out of nowhere. This was not normal.

'Excuse me, sir,' she began in a friendly manner, not wanting to freak him out anymore, 'but I wasn't expecting you, but someone else, my friend.'

He seemed to relax a little.

'Ho, you mean Karen.'

So that was her name, she thought.

'Right. Karen. She works here and I was going to walk her home.'

'I see. Well, she left earlier this evening. It was quiet, so I let her go early.'

'You let her go early!' she tried to keep her voice calm, but she was boiling mad inside.

She just about controlled the temptation to rip this idiot's head right off his shoulders.

'OK, so I've wasted my good Samaritan time here tonight then,' she replied instead.

'I am afraid so, but I am sure she will have appreciated the gesture. Who shall I say was here to meet her?'

'OK then, mister, sorry to have bothered you. Good night.'

She turned and started to walk quickly away, ignoring his question.

'Hey,' he called after her, 'who shall I say was here to meet her?'

The woman disappeared around the corner. He shrugged his shoulders and walked to the car park.

Shoil was almost at breaking point and couldn't believe that the girl had escaped her, again. Did she have some guardian angel or similar protecting her? No one can be that lucky to escape her traps unless it was Tampong herself. She needed to take her anger out on something or someone, and soon. As she turned a corner, a drunken man was staggering down the road just ahead of her, so she quickened her pace and caught up with him. He was still holding a bottle in his hand and waving it around uncontrollably, muttering to himself, words she could not make out, not that it mattered.

She quickly checked her surroundings. No one else was around.

He never felt the blade pierce his back; he just had enough time to watch in horror as its point punched through his chest. She swiveled him around, opened his mouth and forced her tongue down his throat, just as he vomited . . . all over her face and chest. She didn't think she could get any madder, but this was the final straw. She let out a high-pitched scream of frustration and started stabbing the man with her free hand, keeping him pinned to the spot with her speared hand impaled in his chest. The man dropped the bottle, which smashed into a thousand pieces when it hit the pavement. His whole body shook violently as his skin began to crack then splinter. His eyes went into the back of his head as all his energy was sucked into her body. It was not long before she absorbed him, so lowered her blade, with his shirt and jacket still hanging on it. She watched uninterestingly as the bloodied clothing slowly slipped off the blade to flop onto the ground. Her hands then returned to normal, so she picked up his shirt, which did not have too much blood on it, and wiped some of the vomit off her face before throwing the shirt back to the ground. She stormed off, her anger still there, albeit subdued a little after her meal. She would have to be even earlier tomorrow.

She would trap that girl one way or another. She was the key to finding the boy and Tampong, and nothing was going to prevent that. For now, she desperately needed a shower to get rid of the alcoholic vomit that filled her nostrils.

***

'What is it?' asked Tracey, seeing Gary's eyes turning blue.

'She has attacked again.'

'Shoil?'

'Right. This time it felt like pure rage. As if something had gone terribly wrong and she was as mad as hell.'

'Perhaps she is also looking for this other sensation and lost it, or something.'

'Or something,' he replied, but more to himself than to her.

'Can we do anything about it?'

'Not at the moment. We have to be patient and let this play out.'

'If you say so.'

He just smiled at her. He felt uncomfortable not understanding what was going on. There were more players involved than he cared to admit, and that worried him. There should only be two of the Higher Middle left at most, but he felt a third presence and was sure it was not one of their own. Who could it be? What could it be? He needed answers.

He had to find answers.

***

Back at the hotel, Terry was resting on the bed, thinking about Sandi of all people. He checked the clock on the bedside table. It was nearly time to log on. He sat up and reached for his jacket. He pulled his wallet out and took out the receipt. It was to remind him to tell Karen what he had for lunch. He went to place it on the bedside table, but it dropped onto the floor, facedown. When he reached to retrieve it, he noticed a number on the back. He picked it up and brought it closer to his face. It was a telephone number. Sandi's telephone number. He smiled when he realized what it was. She was definitely interested in him then, enough to give him her number. Just then his computer burst into life as the ringtone for Skype sounded. It was Karen. He pressed the video icon, and her smiling face greeted him. He smiled back as he folded the receipt and placed it carefully on the bedside table.

'Sorry to call you at such a strange time, but I needed to hear your voice, needed to see you,' she began.

'No problem,' he answered, 'glad you did.'

'So, what have you been up to today?' she said in a cheerful voice.

He wanted to tell her about Sandi but was not sure what he could say and how he really felt.

'Ho, not much,' he began, 'walked outside for a bit and had something to eat, then got myself ready for our Skype call. You look good. How was your day?'

All throughout their conversation, he was only half listening to her. Sandi was on the front of his mind now. He felt confused. Should he come clean with Karen, or should he keep mum? He decided on the latter. Nothing happened anyway. Sandi was a waitress who served him at lunchtime. If that was all, then why could he not tell Karen?

Perhaps he wanted more.

Perhaps he needed more.

'Earth to Terry!' prompted Karen, 'are you even listening to me?'

'Sure, sorry, just missing you,' he lied.

'Great, now let me tell you all about my boring day.'

***

Tampong had just finished another electronic file and was feeling a little tired. Her eyes were heavy, and she felt a headache coming on, so she stood up and headed for the coffee machine and poured herself a mug. Not the best remedy for a headache, she told herself, but would help her make it through the rest of the day and yet more file reading.

Brad's door opened, and when he got her attention, he beckoned her over to his office. She walked over, shrugging her shoulders at Sam as she passed her desk. Sam just raised her eyebrows, but there was no hatred in her face now.

'Be a sweetie and close the door behind you,' he said when she entered, so she duly obliged.

She did not see the eyebrows being raised by others in the office.

'Please take a seat,' he continued.

She sat nervously down, still clutching her mug of coffee, wondering if he remembered what had happened last night and she was about to be fired.

'It seems we have a little problem with your contract, sweetie,' he continued.

'Really, what kind of problem?'

'Well, not to put too fine a point on it. I screwed up.'

'You did what?'

'I totally screwed up. Looking at your qualifications and experience, I made a gross error with your salary, which I intend to correct straight away.'

She relaxed a little.

'In what way correct?'

'I am going to double your salary and raise your grade from a four to a three. I just don't know what I was thinking. I hope you can forgive me, sweetie, and that we can move on from this horrendous error on my part.'

'Of course. Thank you for your honesty, Brad. I appreciate it.'

He placed both his hands on the desk and leaned forward while lowering his voice.

'To be perfectly honest, sweetie, if HR found out they would probably eject me from the company for gross incompetency, and I cannot say I'd blame them. If we can just keep this between ourselves, you would be saving my arse.'

'Well, we cannot have anything happening to your arse, now, can we?'

He giggled like a girl, waving his hand playfully at her.

'Ow, sweetie, you are such a laugh.'

She just shrugged her shoulders.

'Now then,' he continued, 'let's just pop this old contract into this conveniently located shredder and say bye-bye to that.'

He paused for dramatic effect.

'Bye-bye,' he repeated as the contract disappeared into the shredder.

He playfully waved goodbye to the disappearing papers before turning back to Tampong.

'And here is the correct contract with your correct grade, and if you would be so kind as to just sign both copies and leave one with me, then we can forget all about this little error. OK, sweetie?'

'OK, fine with me, Brad,' she replied, signing both copies and handing him one.

He scooped it up and placed it in her file, which he then placed in the filing cupboard, closing it.

'I will inform payroll of your revised salary and authorize the increase, then we are all set.'

'Great, thanks, Brad.'

'No problem. I can rely on your absolute discretion about this, can't I?'

'Absolutely.'

'Awesome, sweetie.'

He stood up and walked around his desk and opened his office door, bowing as she passed by.

'By the bye,' he spoke quietly, 'your new grade comes with an upgraded bonus package too. Isn't that just a hoot?'

'Quite the hoot,' she agreed, using all of her control to stop herself from bursting into laughter.

Back at her desk, Sam came rushing around and sat on the corner of her desk.

'So, spill the beans, what did she want?'

'She?'

'OK, it. What did *it* want?'

'Ho, apparently there was an error with my contract, and I am actually being regraded from a four to a three.'

'Shut the fuck up. Seriously?'

'Seriously.'

'You lucky cow. It has taken me nearly ten years at this stupid company just to get to a four. You are here for just three seconds and already you are a three. That really sucks.'

'What can I say? It was a mistake.'

'You are so lucky. Tell me truly, what did you do, blow him?'

Tampong stared up at Sam, whose eyes were wide open and fully alert, looking daggers at her.

'I don't think he would appreciate a blow job from me.'

She looked across the office.

'But Roger, on the other hand, now that is someone who Brad would welcome a blow job from.'

Sam continued to stare at her, then burst out laughing. They both laughed, causing others in the room to turn and stare. Brad's office door swung open, and he marched out.

'What's going on out here, a party or something?'

'Sorry,' said Sam, doing her best to suppress another giggle, 'just having a private joke.'

'Then you should share your jokes with the rest of us, sweeties. A little light relief never hurt anyone.'

He gave Roger a wink.

Roger's looked at him in total shock as Brad swung around and went back into his office, swinging his hips.

'Who turned the grouch into Santa Claus?' he asked aloud.

The two girls just turned to each other and smiled.

The rest of the day passed uneventfully, and when Tampong got back to the hotel, she found Terry still Skyping with Karen. She walked quietly around the bed and waved him hello. He waved back, which was spotted by Karen.

'Is your aunty back?' she asked.

'Yep. Just turned up.'

'How long have we been Skyping for?'

'Just over two hours.'

'Jesus. I need to do my homework. And I still have school tomorrow.'

'OK. Can we do this again tomorrow evening?'

'Not tomorrow. I really need some sleep. How about Friday evening as I don't need to get up the following morning?'

'OK, if I have to wait until then. Friday it is.'

'Great. Till Friday then. Miss you. Don't forget what we talked about.'

'I won't. Miss you too.'

He blew her a kiss and she signed off.

'So, how was your day?' Tampong asked.

'Great. Went for a walk, saw the Merlion, had lunch, and then came back to the hotel and Skyped with Karen for a couple of hours.'

'Wow, packed day. What's a Merlion?'

'It's an historical landmark, depicting the days with this island was nothing more than a fishing village.'

'Wow, have you been on a history hike or something?'

'Something like that. So how was your day?'

'Great, in fact. I got a pay rise and promotion.'

'What, all in your second day?'

'Seems there was an error with my contract.'

'Good for you.'

He fidgeted a bit and hesitated.

'Listen. Now that you seem to be establishing yourself here, I was wondering whether I could pop back home for a little while. Spend some time with Karen.'

Tampong sat down on the corner of the bed.

'What's brought all this on?'

'Nothing really. It's just that I miss her. It hurts even more every time I see her on Skype. Seeing her but not able to touch her, to feel her, smell her perfume . . .'

'Wow. You have got it bad.'

'I have,' he admitted.

'But it's not as though you can just hop on a bus and go visit for the weekend.'

'I know, but I really need to see her. I need to be with her.'

'I feel for you, Terry, I really do, but it is just not possible.'

'Why not?'

'I need to keep you close to me so that I can protect you should . . . should she turn up.'

He bowed his head.

'Will I ever be able to go back home?'

She stood up and walked over to his bed and sat next to him. She stroked his hair.

'You will, one day. I promise.'

'Sure. When we are both old and grey and she has long forgotten me.'

'Not that long . . . I hope. Let's take it one day at a time. Who knows, maybe you will find someone even nicer.'

He suddenly thought about Sandi.

'Maybe,' he said reluctantly, 'looks like we have no choice, do we?'

'Not at the moment. No. Sorry.'

He sighed.

She looked at his face.

'I have to say, you are taking this really well.'

'That's probably because I realize our options are limited.'

'Gosh, you are certainly growing up.'

She stroked his hair again then stood up.

He said nothing, but instinctively touched the table where the receipt was.

'I am off for a shower, then I'll be ready for some TV. How about you?'

'Nope. I think I might go for another walk. Clear my mind a little.'

'Good idea. Are you hungry?'

'Nope. I had a big lunch, so I am good.'

'Me too. OK. I'll see you later then.'

'Right.'

She started to unbutton her blouse as she got up and walked into the bathroom. Terry waited until he heard the shower running, then he took the receipt from the table. He turned it over and there was her number. She had given him her number! He thought for a second, then picked up the telephone and dialed the number on the back of the receipt. The phone rang three times before it was picked up.

'Hello,' said the female voice.

'Hi, is that Sandi?'

'Yes. Who is this please?'

'It's me, Terry, from the restaurant today.'

'The English guy?'

'That's the one. I was wondering whether you were free tonight.'

'Well, yes I am actually.'

'Great. I was wondering if, perhaps, you could show me some of the local sights, if that is OK with you and only if you are not doing anything else.'

'No, I have nothing planned, so sure thing. I assume you are without wheels.'

'Right.'

'OK. I can use my mom's car. Let's meet outside your hotel—the Carlton, right?'

'Right.'

'Right. Shall we say in thirty minutes?'

'Sounds good.'

'See you then.'

She hung up, so he replaced the receiver.

Mixed thoughts were going through his mind. He had feelings for Karen, but the chances are he would never see her again, judging by what Tampong had just told him. Whereas Sandi was clearly interested in him, and he was definitely attracted to her. She was here, and he may not have many more opportunities than this. Mind made up, he changed his shirt and was going to put some aftershave on but gave up on that idea as that meant going into the bathroom, where Tampong was showering. He would have to buy another bottle tomorrow when he went shopping.

'OK, I'm off out now,' he called through the door.

'Have fun,' she answered back.

He smiled.

'*Hope so*,' he said to himself.

He walked out of the bedroom, took the elevator and walked outside, where he waited. It dawned on him that he had no idea what car she would be driving, but there cannot be too many vehicles arriving at this time of day. A few taxis came and went, dropping passengers off and picking up new clients. He checked his watch. Thirty-six minutes since he contacted her. Perhaps she was not coming!

A blue Chevrolet Cruze then rolled into the hotel drive and stopped outside the main entrance in front of where Terry was standing. The passenger window lowered.

'Hey there. Hop in,' encouraged Sandi.

He opened the door and sat in the passenger seat.

'Thought I wasn't coming?' she asked, slipping the gear into drive.

'Not for a second,' he lied.

'Sure.'

She smiled at him and drove the car out of the hotel parking lot and up Bras Basah Road, turning right at the bottom and heading towards the bay.

'You know, we will not be able to drive along this part of the road soon.'

'Why not?'

'They are closing this section to traffic and getting ready for the military parade, which takes place every year.'

'Wow. So when do they plan to start work?'

'Ho, starts next week, I believe.'

'OK, so no problem coming back tonight then.'

She laughed. He looked at her from the corner of his eye. She was wearing a noticeably short blue dress, emphasizing her slim, long legs. She had a deep v-cut front, revealing nearly half of her breasts. She was clearly someone who had no problem showing off her assets, which he thought were indeed worth viewing.

'So, where are we going?' he asked.

'I thought I would take you to the Gardens. We have missed the daily shows, but still worth a visit.

They drove past the now familiar Marina Bay Sands Hotel and crossed the river. They drove for another fifteen minutes before she turned the car right into the Garden's car park, driving slowly across the cobbled stones until she came to the end of the road, where she turned left into the car park. She parked and switched the engine off. As she opened the door, Terry watched as she got out of the car. She straightened up and pulled her dress down a little. Terry got out and closed his door.

She pressed the car remote and locked the vehicle, walking around to the front where Terry was waiting.

'Let's just walk around and I'll explain a few things along the way. We can then go for a drink. Sound good?'

'Sounds very good,' he answered keenly, and was only too glad to be in her company.

She slipped her arm through his and they walked together. She pointed out the old trees, explaining that millions of tiny lights were strung along all the trees, which looked like stars when they shone at night. There were a number of souvenir shops and a restaurant at the top of a tree-like building.

'Is it always so hot in the early evening?' he asked.

'Yep. Here in Singapore the heat keeps climbing until around five pm, then starts to tail off. I must admit, you do look a little warm.'

'Not used to the heat.'

'You will. Let's grab a cool drink.'

'Fantastic.'

She laughed and led him into a restaurant, where the receptionist recognized her immediately.

'Hey, Sandi, how are you doing? We haven't seen you here for a while.'

She nodded her welcome to Terry, who nodded back.

'I'm great, thanks, Sally. Table for two, please.'

'You got it.'

She picked up two menus and escorted them to a window table.

'Here you are.'

Sandi sat down. Terry opted to sit opposite her.

'Hi there, folks, and welcome. My name's Todd, and I'll be looking after you this evening.'

'Hey, Todd. I'll have a Doctor Pepper.' She looked across to Terry and he nodded keenly. 'Make that two,' she added.

'Any appetizers?'

'Got any wings?' asked Terry.

'You bet. What flavor sauce would you like?'

'BBQ.'

'Right, and will that be for one or two?'

'Two,' answered Sandi.

He nodded and left.

'So you know quite a few people around the island then?'

'Yep. This is not a massive island, and the restaurant circle is quite small, so you get to know most of the staff working in places like these.'

'But the waiter didn't appear to know you?'

'Nope. He must be a newbie. Staff rotate quite quickly in a joint like this. They are mostly students looking for a tie-over until college starts again.'

'And what about you?'

Her head dropped and Terry realized he had hit a delicate subject.

'Sorry, didn't mean to pry.'

'No, no problem. I had dreams of becoming a lawyer, but then my dad became sick, so I had to drop out to look after him.'

'Ho, I'm sorry. Hope your dad is better now.'

'No,' she replied quietly, taking a deep breath, 'he's dead actually.'

'Ho . . . heck, I just keep falling into one big hole after another.'

Todd arrived with their drinks.

'Your wings will be along shortly,' he advised.

They both took a refreshing swig of the cool beverage. Sandi wiped her mouth with the back of her hand.

'Didn't realize I was that thirsty.'

He smiled and she smiled back at him.

'You have a lovely smile,' he said cutely.

He felt slightly embarrassed and wanted to change the subject.

'Why thank you. To be honest, I think you have a lovely smile too.'

He blushed a little.

'Do you have a girl back home?' she asked.

It was Terry's turn to drop his head.

'Oops,' she said, 'looks like I have just fallen into a big dark hole now.'

'No, it's fine. I had a girlfriend but, you know, long-distance relationships never work. I am sure she will find someone better than me. And what about you, any guy in your life?'

He was keen to get the subject back to her.

She looked down at the table for a long time before answering.

'Nope, no one serious and haven't had a boyfriend for . . . wow, four months now. I never realized it was that long.'

'Saving yourself for Mr. Right?'

'No. I don't think Mr. Right is truly out there. Mr. OK will do for me.'

'Any guy would be lucky to win your heart.'

She stopped drinking and looked at him again. There was warmth in her eyes. He watched as her lips parted slightly, as her nostrils flared a little, suggesting she was breathing more quickly now.

'That's so sweet of you, Terry.'

'It's the truth.'

She placed her drink down and was about to say something when Todd arrived with their wings, which he placed in front of them.

'Enjoy,' he said, then headed toward the front door to greet new customers.

'So, can I ask, how long since you lost your father?'

She seemed to think about the question.

'Let me see, it must be nearly two years now.'

'Wow, you were quite young then.'

'I was. What about your parents?'

Terry took a deep breath. 'They are both dead too.'

'Ho my god. I am so sorry to hear that. Was it an accident?'

'No, they were killed.'

'Killed!! My god, Terry. When was this?'

It was Terry's turn to think this time.

'It must be around eight years ago now.'

'Crickey, you were really young then.'

'Really young.'

'And how did you come to be with your aunty?'

'She has been looking after me ever since my parents were murdered.'

'It must have been awful for you.'

'It was. But I am just about over it now. My aunty has been awesome. What about your mother?'

'Ho, she mourned for about six months, then found another guy. She moved in with him, telling me that his apartment was a little crowded for three people.'

'Really! She actually told you that?'

'Right. Still, they gave me some money to find a place, which I did. I now share an apartment with a flatmate.'

'Gosh, you have had an interesting and difficult life so far too.'

She just shrugged her shoulders.

'Not as difficult as yours though.'

They ate in silence, looking at each other between wings and when drinking. They both accepted the refill offered by Todd. Still, they never spoke, but a hidden language seemed to pass between them. They smiled knowingly at each other. Finally, Sandi finished her last wing and dropped the bone onto the plate. She picked up her napkin and wiped her face clean. Terry finished his and wiped his mouth also.

'So . . .' she began, sounding hesitant.

'So!' encouraged Terry.

'Are you in a rush to return to your hotel?'

'Not at all. I am really enjoying being with you.'

He sounded sincere and his answer appeared to melt any further hesitation. Sandi hesitated for a second, then made her decision.

'Would you like to come back to my place?'

'Yes,' he answered without hesitation.

He hoped he didn't sound as if he answered too quickly. He wasn't sure if this simply meant going to her place for a coffee or something, but he would settle for that if it was. He was really enjoying her company.

Todd arrived with the bill, understanding that they had finished. Terry grabbed the bill and handed his card over to Todd, who nodded his thanks.

'Thank you,' said Sandi warmly.

She rested her hand on the table, so Terry reached over and placed his hand on hers. She turned her hand over and their fingers entwined. Todd returned with the credit card slip, which he placed in front of Terry.

'Many thanks, and come back again real soon.'

Terry reluctantly let go of her hand, added the customary 15 percent tip, signed, and left the receipt on the tray. They both got up and walked out of the restaurant. Outside Sandi took hold of his hand, which he keenly held tightly. They walked back to the car, where he held the door open for her. She slipped inside and started the engine as he ran around to the other side and got in. She drove away a little faster than when they arrived. They never spoke all the while she drove. It took them forty minutes before she drove into an underground car park and parked the car, turned off the engine, then got out. Terry followed her to the elevator, where she pressed the seventieth floor. The elevator moved quietly and swiftly with its two occupants standing side by side. Terry reached over and took her hand. She closed her fingers around his. They turned to each other and smiled. He was just thinking about moving towards her and kissing her when the elevator stopped, and the doors opened. They stepped out, Sandi indicating her apartment was on the right. He again followed her. She stopped at the fourth door and pulled her keys out of her pocket, opened the door and they walked in.

Terry was greeted with a very modern apartment. All the furniture was white, even the single bookcase. There was a large flat-screen TV hanging on the wall. The room was dominated by a large white corner unit sofa, which he guessed was leather, or at least a type of leather or look-alike.

'Not much, but it's home,' she said as she slipped off her coat and hung it on the white coat hook.

'Are you kidding! This is super.'

'You think so?'

'Really. If I have my own apartment, I am going to furnish it just like this.'

'Right, but truth be told, I do share this with another girl, and we go halves on most things. She is an air stewardess with American Airlines and is currently on her way to Mexico. Not back until tomorrow evening. So the place is ours tonight.'

'Nice,' he said simply.

He looked at her as she stood in front of him. Taking a couple of steps towards her, he placed his hand on the side of her face, gently running his fingers down her cheek. She closed her eyes, so he lowered his fingers to her neck. He heard her quick intake of breath, suggesting she was aroused by his touch. With his other hand he gently moved it around her waist, pulling her gently towards him. She came willingly. He could now feel her breath on his face. Her eyes were still closed, so he moved his lips closers to hers and kissed her gently. She responded by kissing him back, only firmer. He moved his fingers lower, instinctively caressing the top of her breast. Her breathing became quicker. He felt himself being aroused too, so slowly moved his fingers to the buttons on the front of her dress, and started to unbutton them, one by one. He reached her waist where he felt her buckle, so he unhooked that, then continued to unbutton her dress until he could not reach any more.

Sandi moved her hand down to his crouch and felt him hard, so she stroked the top of his trousers, sending wave after wave of erotic electricity up his back. He shivered in response, which was clearly what she was expecting as she started to speed up. With her other hand, she started to unbutton the top of his jeans, slipping her hand inside his pants, finding him easily. She started to move her hand up and down his erection. His breathing was rapid now. Needing no further encouragement, he slipped the dress off her shoulders. It immediately dropped to the floor. He quickly moved his hands behind her back and unclipped her bra strap. He also pulled the straps over her shoulders, and that too fell to the floor. She was also slowly undressing him now and had his jeans and pants down to his knees. Their lips remained glued to each other as he slipped his hands down her back into her knickers and grabbed her buttocks. She gave a sigh of pleasure, so he moved one hand around to her front and between her legs. He felt her warm and moist. He had never touched a woman there before, but this seemed a natural thing to do, and she certainly was not complaining. Their lips finally came apart and she looked into his eyes.

'Let's go into the bedroom,' she whispered.

He just nodded, so she took his hand and led him to her bed, which was high and large. Her dress and bra lay on the carpet in the lounge, forgotten. They both had to climb up onto the bed. She turned over onto her back and, raising her legs, she slipped her knickers off and threw them onto the floor. Terry also moved onto his back and finished taking his trousers and pants off, throwing them next to her knickers. She pushed him on top of her and opened her legs.

'I want you to know that you will be the first,' he said quietly.

He was about to kiss her again when she pulled her head back sharply.

'Are you serious? Are you telling me you are a virgin?'

'Right,' he confirmed.

'You sure you want to do this with me, now?'

'If I am going to lose my virginity, then I cannot think of a better person than you to lose it to.'

She gave him a warm smile.

'It that case,' she said, pushing him off her and onto his back, 'then I need to make this an incredibly special occasion for you.'

She raised up and sat across his waist, with both hands on his chest. He looked up at her perfect breasts and could not resist reaching up and cupping them in both hands. She rocked her head back.

'I don't have any protection,' he added reluctantly.

'It's OK, I'm on the pill,' she said as she lifted up slightly before lowering herself onto his penis and feeling him enter her.

He closed his eyes and enjoyed the sensation of entering her. She moved up and down his erection. Slowly at first, but then started to gradually speed up. She kept her head leaning back, while he kept hold of her breasts, enjoying the feel of them, enjoying her hard nipples pressing against the palms of his hands. He wanted to be even deeper inside her, so arched his body, which triggered her to speed up even more. She started to groan, but it was one of pleasure. It was not long before he too was groaning as the pleasure built up. It felt so good, magical, uncontrollable, unstoppable. Both were sweating now. He pushed himself quicker and quicker inside her, while she rode him quicker and quicker. Suddenly his whole body started to quiver violently. Despite his eyes still being closed, he could see stars. His whole body began to jerk, and he then came inside her. It felt fantastic. She also screamed out in pleasure, as she too reached orgasm. She flopped on top of him. He just had time to release her breasts, so wrapped his arms around her instead. They stayed like that for a couple of minutes. Eventually Sandi raised her head and gave him a firm kiss on the lips. He returned her kiss.

'I need a bath now. Fancy joining me?'

'You bet,' he said full of encouragement.

She slipped off of him and walked towards the toilet, ignoring the fluid running down the inside of her legs. Terry lifted himself onto his elbows to watch her walk away. He originally thought she had a nice rear, and now he knew that for sure. She was perfect in his eyes, and what's more, he had just made love to her. He flopped back onto the bed, realizing he was now a man and no longer a boy. He had no idea how he compared to other men and was afraid to ask her. For his part, he thought she was amazing, seemingly knowing how to please a man and how to bring them to orgasm. He heard the bathwater running, so slipped off the bed and walked into the bathroom. Sandi was leaning forward in the bathtub swirling some bath foam in the water. Her legs were slightly apart, and he could see her vagina, beautifully pink and inviting. He felt himself harden again, so walked quickly towards her, placed his hands on her hips and thrust himself into her. She grunted as he entered her but did not move away, instead she pushed herself towards him. He felt the need to speed up, unable to stop, not wanting to stop. He got quicker and quicker and yelled out in pleasure as he felt himself come again.

'Boy, you do have some stamina,' she said, turning off the taps before turning around and placing both hands on his shoulders.

'Now I need to clean up again.'

She tapped his nose playfully with her fingers.

'Why don't you get into the bath. I'll be along shortly.'

'OK,' he said simply, again watching her leave.

He could never get tired of watching her. He slid into the hot bath, the water coming up to his chest. After a few minutes, Sandi entered the bathroom, still naked but carrying two glasses of wine. He wasn't looking at the glasses but at her body. He wanted to fix every detail of her body to memory just in case he never had the opportunity to see her naked again.

'I know we are underage, but I thought that as this was a special occasion, we could enjoy a glass of wine in the bath.'

'Great idea,' he agreed, watching as she stepped into the bath, turned her back on him, then lowered herself into the water, resting her back on his chest.

She then held her hand out into the air with his glass, which he took. With his other hand he rested over her shoulder and across her breasts. She placed her free hand over his, telling him she was more than happy he was holding her.

'Cheers,' he said.

'Cheers,' she replied.

They both took a sip of the cold fluid.

'Hmm, nice,' he remarked.

'Glad you like it. Another first for you I think.'

'I am liking all these firsts with you.'

She chuckled.

'Well, I have to say you were going like an experienced lover.'

'Is that good?'

'That's exceptionally good. I'll be honest and say that not many men were able to bring me to a climax like you did.'

'I think you did all the work.'

'But I needed the tools to work with . . . if you know what I mean.'

She pressed her buttocks down against his penis in case he didn't get it.

'Glad I wasn't a disappointment.'

'Quite the opposite. I was getting a little tired of these little men . . . again if you know what I mean.'

'If you don't mind me asking, when did you lose your virginity?'

'Hmm, let me think. I must have been seventeen I think.'

'Seventeen!! Wow, that's young.'

'Tell me. I was naive and allowed the quarterback to seduce me into believing that everyone was doing it today at my age.'

'What happened to him?'

'Ho, he banged me then dropped me like a used condom.'

'Ugh. If I were here at the time, I would kill him for treating you like that.'

'That's sweet, but you did hear me say he was the quarterback, right?'

'And?'

'So he is full of muscles and has lots of teammates with even bigger muscles.'

'That wouldn't stop me. I can look after myself.'

'Hey, remember I have seen you naked. And while you may have a nice body, you are not exactly overburdened with muscles now, are you?'

'Muscles are not everything.'

'True, but they certainly help and can be very intimidating. Anyway, that was quite a few years ago, and I have moved on from that bad experience.'

'Have you had other bad experiences?'

She went silent for a minute, and he thought he had stepped over the line.

'Well,' she then said, 'yes, there have been a few other painful experiences. It seems most of the men I like just want to bed me and leave me. Just to put another notch on their rod.'

'So, no one special then?'

'Not yet, but I remain hopeful and decided that I will decide who to bed and when.'

'Good for you,' he encouraged.

'Good for you,' she corrected.

He laughed. They both took another sip of their wine, then went silent as they just enjoyed each other's company. She finally finished her glass, lifted herself up, and turned to face him with a serious expression on her face.

'You know I like you, Terry, don't you?'

'I do, and I really like you too.'

'So this will not be a one-off as well then?'

'I certainly hope not, Sandi. I want to see you as often as I can.'

'And what about your girlfriend back home?'

'As I said, she is on the other side of the world, and I am unlikely to return there anytime soon. Anyway, I am with you now and want to stay with you. If you will have me?'

She didn't reply but leaned forward and gave him a long, hard kiss on the lips.

'The water's getting cold, so let's get out.'

He nodded, so she stood up. Her breasts passed awfully close to his face, so he kissed her nipple as they passed. She stepped out of the bath and wrapped herself in a bath towel. She then held one open for Terry to walk into, wrapping it around him. She then leaned back across the bath and pulled the plug to allow the water to run away. They dried themselves, walked back into the bedroom, retrieved their clothes, and got dressed again. She looked at the clock on the wall and raised her eyebrows.

'I'd better get you back to the hotel before your aunt has the police out looking for you.'

'Wow, is that the time? Can I use your phone and call the hotel to let her know I am on my way home?'

'Sure, it's over there in the corner.'

He walked over, took the hotel bedroom key out of his pocket, dialing the number on the back.

'Carlton Hotel,' said a female voice, 'how can I assist you?'

'Room 1525 please. Ms. Armitage.'

'Just one minute, please. Transferring you.'

'Hello?' said Tampong.

She sounded agitated.

'Hi Aunty, it's me.'

By referring to her as 'Aunty' told Tamping he was not alone.

'Where the hell are you?'

'Sorry. I am with a friend, and we lost track of time. Just calling to let you know I am OK and on my way back.'

'A friend! Right, we'll talk when you are back.'

She hung up.

He looked at the phone briefly before returning the receiver.

'Not happy then?' asked Sandi.

'She'll get over it, but I have stayed out longer than I intended.'

'No regrets I hope.'

'None whatsoever. I just wished we had more time.'

'Tomorrow is another day.'

'I hope so, although I am afraid I am going to be grounded.'

'Ouch. Sorry about that. You have my number, so just let me know how it goes.'

'You bet.'

'OK. Let's get you back to the hotel before she really freaks.'

'Thanks, Sandi. Today had been simply magic.'

She looked at him, her head leaning slightly sideways.

'What?' he asked, puzzled by her expression.

'We will make a Singaporean out of you yet.'

He laughed.

They quickly rushed out of her apartment and back down to the garage parking. She drove quickly. Her speed made him feel a little uncomfortable, especially as she passed cars going around corners. One car sounded his horn in annoyance, but this only prompted her to give him the middle finger. Fifteen minutes later she came to a skidding halt at his hotel.

She turned to look at him. She had a serious expression on her face again.

'I will see you again, won't I?'

Her eyes were searching his.

'Are you kidding? Of course you will. As soon as I placate my aunt, we will see each other again. I promise.'

He leaned over and kissed her firmly on the lips.

'Good, because, as I said, I really like you.'

'And, like I said, I really like you too. Thanks again for the lift home.'

'Anytime.'

Her eyes were now watery, so she wiped them clear with her hand. She really hoped his words were true. This would not be the first time she was promised a second date, only to never hear from him again. Maybe Europeans were more respectful of women than others were. She hoped so. She moved the gear into drive and drove out of the hotel driveway.

Outside the bedroom door, Terry took a deep breath, opened the door, and walked into a storm.

Tampong swung around to face him. Her face was red with a mixture of rage and worry.

'Where were you?' she demanded.

'I met a girl and spent the day with her. We were having a great time and completely lost track of time. As soon as I realized, I called you.'

'A girl. What girl?'

'Her name is Sandi, and she works in a restaurant where I ate lunch. We started talking and just hit it off.'

'Just hit it off. You know nothing about her. She could be a trap. Designed to lure you into her net.'

'I really think you are being a little paranoid.'

He regretted the words as soon as he said them.

Her rage moved into fury. Her eyes turned orange and she physically lifted him into the air, throwing him against the bedroom wall, where he was pinned but still able to talk.

'Tampong, calm down, you have changed.'

She blinked twice as his words hit home. She relaxed and released him, causing him to crash onto the floor. Her eyes returned to normal as she sat on the corner of the bed.

'I am sorry, so sorry. It will not happen again. I promise,' he said in a pleading voice.

She softened her tone.

'Terry, honey, I cannot be with you every second to protect you.'

'I know, but you would sense it if I was in trouble, wouldn't you?'

'True,' she admitted.

'And you never sensed anything wrong today, did you?'

'No, but that doesn't stop me worrying about you.'

'I know, and I love you for that too.'

She held out her arms and he got up and gladly walked into her arms. They hugged for a little while before she pulled him away.

'So, what this girl like, Sandi?'

'Magic. So full of life and interesting.'

'Wow, sounds like you have been bitten by the bug.'

'Not sure I know what that means, but if it means I like her, then yes, I do.'

'And does she like you?'

'Well, she gave me her number and invited me back to her place.'

'Wow! You seem to have a gift for getting girls to give you their phone number.'

He puffed out his cheeks.

'What can I say!'

'OK, Romeo, but don't let it go to your head. So are you going to see her again?'

'That depends.'

'On what?'

'You.'

'Me, why?'

'I thought, maybe, you might ground me or something.'

'Huh?'

She placed her hand under her cheek as if in thought.

'I hadn't actually thought of that.'

She saw him fidgeting uncomfortably on the bed.

'But I have to admit, you are almost a man now, so I have to give you some freedom I suppose.'

He was going to say something, but she put her finger in the air to tell him she had not finished.

'That freedom comes at a cost though.'

'Which is?'

'That you let me know where you are going at all times and that we set the time when you have to be back. One you will keep to. Agreed?'

'Agreed.'

'What about Karen?' she questioned.

'What about her?'

'Well, you are now seeing this other girl. Don't you think you should say something to Karen?'

His shoulders noticeably slumped.

'I guess you are right. As you said before, she is probably safer without me. I'll tell her on our next call.'

'Do that, but don't forget . . .'

'Yes, I know,' he interrupted, 'don't tell her where I am.'

'Right. Even more important if you are going to dump her.'

'I'm not just going to dump her.'

'OK, then what?'

'Just tell her that I cannot come back, and that she would be better off moving on and forgetting me.'

'So, in other words, you are dumping her.'

'NO!'

His voice sounded hollow though. He knew her words were true but still found it difficult to accept.

'I'll just tell her long-distance relationships never work.'

'Long-distance!'

'OK, long absences.'

'That's better. Right, let's get some sleep. I have work tomorrow.'

'Right. I am going to brush my teeth and then get myself to bed.'

She looked at him.

'Are you OK?'

'Super. Why do you ask?'

'It's just you seem different. I don't know, all grown up or something.'

'Just happy perhaps.'

'Perhaps.'

She stood up and walked over to him, and as she brushed her fingers through his hair, she quietly sniffed him. He smelled of a woman's body scent, her sex scent. She looked down at him but said nothing. He already had a difficult life, and she doubted many boys his age would have experienced the horrors he had and still grow up a relatively normal boy. He was nearly eighteen in any case, and she would be a hypocrite to scold him as she lost her virginity at only sixteen, not that she would ever admit that to him. She brushed his hair once again, and when he looked up, she kissed him on his forehead.

'What was that for?'

'Just felt like it,' she answered honestly.

He stood up and, unexpectedly, hugged her.

'What was that for?' she asked.

'Just felt like it,' he said, turning for the bathroom to brush his teeth and freshen up a little.

It did not take long, and he was soon back in the bedroom, so Tampong got up and entered the bathroom. He knew she would be longer, although he never quite understood what women did for so long in there. He got undressed and slipped into bed. His thoughts were of Sandi, reflecting on their marvelous day together, especially their time together in her apartment. He was smiling when Tampong came back into the room, but his face was silhouetted by the lights outside, so she could not see his expression. She slipped into her bed and lay her head against the pillow. She looked up at the ceiling.

'Terry,' she said quietly.

'Aha.'

'You know I would never deliberately hurt you, don't you?'

'I know, but if truth be told, you did frighten me earlier on when you had me pinned to the wall. I didn't realize you were so powerful.'

'I know I did, and I am terribly sorry. It won't happen again.'

'OK. I forgive you. Good night, Tampong.'

'Good night, Terry.'

She looked at the clock, which said it was exactly midnight.

They both closed their eyes and were quickly asleep, both lost in their own dreams.

***

Shoil was also looking at the clock, which was telling her it was 7 am. She sighed heavily. Another restless night, only this time she was disturbed by a faint sensation. It was sudden and violent. It was also uncontrolled, so whatever triggered it, she assumed must have surprised the bitch, and she was not easily surprised, except by her.

Today she was determined not to let that other little bitch of a girl escape her claws again. This time she would wait all afternoon and evening, if necessary. She got out of bed and walked naked into the bathroom and ran the shower. She stepped in and began soaping her body, concentrating between her legs and under her breasts. She grabbed the showerhead and brought it closer to her body to help wash the soap away. With her free hand, she wiped the water and soap from her body. She replaced the showerhead and turned the water off. She reached across for the bath towel, wrapping it around her body as she stepped out of the shower. She rubbed herself dry, then looked at herself in the mirror. Age was beginning to tell on this body. There were now lines across her temple, and she was sure her nipples had dropped a little. Still, she knew this body was still attractive to men, even though everything was starting to head south. She wondered how long it would be before she had to find a new host. She had grown fond of this particular body, and it would be a sad day when she has to give it up. But all good things come to an end, even though she would live on, hopefully long enough to take her revenge on that bitch Tampong. The very thought of the name turned her eyes orange and she had to force herself to calm down again, allowing her eyes to return to normal. She had to keep that under control, difficult though it was. She did not want anything to spoil her surprise when she finally tracked her down, and the girl would help her to that end. On that she was sure.

It was only a matter of time. Meanwhile, she would have to learn more tolerance. And patience.

She decided to call in sick at work so she would have more time to watch the restaurant, just in case that stupid manager gives her the whole evening off this time. She walked into the kitchen and prepared herself some cereal and a cup of tea. She had grown fond of the English tradition of tea in the morning, even going so far as to poke her little finger out straight as she took a sip of the hot liquid. She placed the China cup on its saucer, picked up her spoon and began eating her cereals. Halfway through she paused for another sip of tea before finishing off her cereals. She drank the last of her tea, thought about making a second cup, but decided against it, dropping it into the sink instead. She grabbed her coat as she walked down the hallway and stepped out into the street, taking a deep, refreshing breath. Walking down the pathway, she turned right and headed down the street into the park. She liked to be close to trees, found them peaceful and reassuring. Perhaps it was linked to her animal form. She wasn't sure, but at least she didn't have the urge to crouch down and pee next to one. She smiled at herself. Two young men were walking in the opposite direction and caught her smiling, wrongly guessing it was for them. They smiled back but she ignored them. They looked at each other, puzzled.

'Hey, you,' the one on the left called out, his anger directed at Shoil.

His voice pulled her out of her thoughts.

'What?' she said bluntly.

'Not good enough for you or something? You were the one initiating the contact. We were just being friendly, so no need to blank us.'

'Blank you?'

'Yeah, you heard.'

'You mean kill you, don't you?'

'What!' they said together.

Shoil turned to face them, her eyes turning orange as she raised her fingers towards the two boys, firing two wafer-thin blades. Each one struck its intended target. The blade from her left finger hit the first boy dead center in his forehead, penetrating his brain and exploding out of the back of his head. He was dead yet still standing up, as his body had not registered his brain being destroyed. The second blade penetrated the other boy's eye, burying itself deep inside his head. The momentum forced his head backwards, lifting him off the ground to land twenty feet into the bushes. The first boy's body rocked back and forward a couple of times before collapsing facedown on the ground.

Shoil's eyes returned to normal, and she nervously looked around. Seeing no one, she walked up to the first dead boy, lifting him up easily, before tossing the boy into the bushes to join the other dead body.

'I really must learn to control my anger,' she said and started laughing to herself again.

She stopped laughing almost immediately, looking, still no one was around. She felt angry with herself for not absorbing them. A top-up was always welcomed. She walked up to a large tree and sat on the ground, leaning her back against the tree. She closed her eyes to mentally connect with the trees and all things around, the grass, the insects, the animals. Any normal person would embrace this sensation, but she only despised their weakness, the inability of some of them to move, to defend themselves. She only felt pity for them, being glad she had the human form at least. Only a few other living beings were more powerful than humans on a one-to-one basis on this little planet, but even those were prey to human weapons, such as the mighty elephant, the powerful lion, and the sheer size of a whale. All had been almost eliminated by mankind. Still, very few had witnessed her ability, and those that had did not live to tell anyone about it. She set the alarm on her watch, covered herself with leaves, then slept.

Karen had finished another boring day at school and was walking home. Not sure why, but she could not shake this feeling of being alone. She shivered and was at least grateful she would be working tonight, which would help take her mind of this strange, lonely feeling. She couldn't wait to see Terry's face and hear all his news. Perhaps she would tell him about these feelings she had been having. Who knows, he may be experiencing the same, or even worse. The thought of him feeling alone too perked her up a little, although she immediately felt a little guilty, wishing he felt lonely. It was just after 4 pm, so she had enough time to get home, shower, eat, and relax a little before she set off for work. She did not have any homework today, so could afford to relax a little.

The alarm woke Shoil up. She glanced down at her watch. It was 4 pm. She sat up to find that the sun was already setting. She stood up, brushed the leaves off from her clothing and then began to walk quickly out of the park, down the street and towards the restaurant. She took up her usual place in the shop doorway.

She waited.

It was just after 6 pm when Karen left the house. She caught the bus, getting off at her stop as usual. When she stepped off, she had a premonition, so decided to go into the front of the restaurant rather than the side, as usual. She intended to knock on the glass but found that the front door was unlocked, so she walked in.

'Hey, what are you doing coming through the front door?' questioned Toni, surprised to see the front door open, 'and I don't remember unlocking the door!'

'Just thought I would surprise you, Toni, and I was also surprised it was open. I was all set to start banging on the glass.'

'I must be going senile in my old age.'

'Not you, Toni, not you.'

'Anyway, glad you are here. We have two groups coming in tonight. Both made late reservations this afternoon. Can you believe it?'

'Great. Helps the time pass by. How many?'

'One group of ten and another group of six.'

'Wow, more than the rest of our clients put together this week.'

'No need to remind me. I have asked Sally to come in as well. We will need reinforcements tonight.'

'Good idea. I'll go into the back and change. What time do they arrive?'

She liked Sally. They were good friends, both joining the restaurant at the same time.

'First group will be here any minute. The second, smaller group, arrives at eight.'

He sounded excited and she was pleased for him.

Shoil checked her watch and brought it to her ear to check it was still working. She heard the ticking. Puzzled, she glanced across the street and saw the restaurant lights come on. She was about to leave, cursing her luck for missing the girl yet again, thinking she really must have a charmed life, when she saw a young woman walking down the street. She stepped back into the shadows and watched. The young woman turned into the alleyway and walked into the side door of the restaurant. Shoil watched but was confused. This was not the girl she was waiting for. Did she switch evenings? Did she have any idea that Shoil was watching her? Just then a small coach stopped directly in front of the restaurant and several passengers got off, walking straight into the restaurant. She quickly stepped out of the doorway and walked around to the main street, now opposite the building. Her attention was attracted to movement inside. She looked through the window, and there she was, inside, greeting the people that had just arrived. How did she do that? How did she miss her? She felt her anger building up again, having to swallow hard several times to control herself.

'So, bitch, think you can avoid me, do you? Think again.'

She moved to the corner of the building opposite, where she could watch both doors. She'd not make the same mistake again.

The evening passed quickly for Karen, much to her delight. Added to which, the girls received good tips. So, all in all, not a bad evening's work. She held the door open for the last remaining customers.

'Good night,' she said as they passed.

'Good night and thank you,' replied the last person, an elderly lady, as she left.

Karen closed and locked the door, switching the open sign to closed. Toni was at the cash register, looking incredibly pleased with himself.

'If only every night could be like this,' he said as she walked towards the bar.

'You can say that again,' she agreed.

Sally walked into the main restaurant and up to the bar to join the other two.

'So, how did we do tonight?' she asked expectantly.

Toni handed her a large wad of notes. Her eyes popped open wide.

'All mine?'

'All yours,' he confirmed, 'thanks for coming in at short notice and for doing a great job.'

'No problem. If you have more nights like this, then don't hesitate to call me.'

'I won't, and only wish we had several more reservations like this.'

'Be patient,' suggested Karen, 'it is the middle of the month and our quietest period. It will pick up once people receive their monthly salary.'

'I hope so. Always the positive one, aren't you?'

She shrugged her shoulders in a matter-of-fact way.

'OK, you two. Off you go and enjoy what's left of your evening. See you tomorrow, Karen.'

'OK, boss. Have a good night. Let me grab my coat and I'll walk with you, Sally.'

'OK,' replied Sally, who stood by the back door, waiting.

Karen turned and went into the back, collected her coat, waved goodbye to Toni, and left the restaurant with Sally by the side door.

Shoil saw the door open and watched the two girls step out. She recognized Karen, not really caring who the other one was. She waited until they turned into the main street, knowing Karen was heading for the bus stop. She stepped out of the doorway and walked parallel to them on the opposite side of the road, quickening her pace so that she would get ahead of them. Halfway up the road and ahead of them, she crossed and started walking back towards them. They were in deep conversation and not paying any attention to their surroundings.

'Cannot believe the tips we received tonight. I'm going to treat myself with this,' said Sally.

'Right, but we worked our arses off to get this.'

'True, but I would do it again for this kind of reward.'

'I hear you, girl.'

They both started laughing when Sally casually looked up the street. She saw the woman coming towards her. What made her stop were her eyes, which looked like orange traffic lights, enhanced by the evening light.

'What the . . .' she said, making Karen look up.

'What . . .'

She stopped talking as the woman was now within five feet of them.

'Hello, bitches,' snapped Shoil.

'Say what now?' demanded Sally.

'Deaf as well as stupid, are you?'

'How dare you . . . and what kind of contact lenses are you wearing?'

'None of your damned business, bitch. I am not interested in you but your friend here.'

Karen suddenly felt nervous. Panic started to build up inside her. She took an involuntary step backwards and was tempted to run and would have done so but for the defiance of Sally.

'Just who the hell do you think you are calling bitch? I've a good mind to teach you a lesson. I am a black belt in karate.'

Karen had no idea whether she was telling the truth, but her courage kept her in place. Two against one seemed like good odds to her.

'I've not the patience for your melodramatics, bitch.'

She was done talking, so raised her finger and fired a dart straight into Sally's chest. It penetrated deep into her body, with only the tip still visible. It happened so quickly that Karen did not even see the dart, just heard a whizzing noise and a thud. It was Sally suddenly gasping that made her look at her friend. Sally stood frozen to the spot when Karen then saw her chest turning red—red with Sally's blood. Sally's eyes rolled into the back of her head before she crashed backwards onto the payment. Her eyes were still open but now vacant. Dead.

Karen could only watch in horror, paralyzed by fear, unable to move.

'That's better,' said Shoil, 'that bitch was becoming truly annoying. Now, where was I? Ho yes, you are the one I am interested in.'

Her words snapped Karen out of her trance. She looked up at Shoil.

'What, what, what have you done?'

'To her?' she queried, pointing at Sally's body, 'why killed her, of course.'

'You . . . what . . . killed her!'

'Do you want to join her?'

'What!'

'Do you have a problem with hearing or something?' she said, stepping closer. 'I said,' she was speaking deliberately slowly now, 'do . . . you . . . want . . . to . . . join . . . her?'

'What, what do you want with me?'

'That's more like it. Information, that's all.'

'But I don't know anything.'

'You leave that to me, but not here.'

Before Karen could answer, Shoil swiped her hard across the forehead, knocking her unconscious. Before she collapsed onto the floor, Shoil caught her, not wishing to damage her prize. Not yet in any case. She laid her carefully on the pavement, then grabbed Salley's ankles and dragged her back down the alleyway. She opened one of the industrial bins and threw

Sally's body inside, then closed the lid. Just then Toni walked out of the side door, surprising Shoil.

'You again!' he said, recognizing her.

'Me again,' she acknowledged before slicing his neck open.

He opened his mouth in shock, giving Shoil the opportunity to extend her tongue into his mouth. His body shook violently, turning orange as his skin dried and started to crack open and shrink. His aura was being sucked into Shoil, who held her arms out wide, eyes closed, welcoming the new sensation. She opened her eyes when the sensation passed, and the only evidence of Toni was a pile of clothing in front of her.

'Pity,' she said, 'you don't know anything about the boy. Aha, but you do have a vehicle, which would be very handy right now.'

She bent down and searched his jacket then trousers before finding his car keys. She then pulled his wallet out and tucked that into her own pocket. She pressed the car remote and was pleased to hear the beep-beep of the car's horn close by. She looked around and saw the car's indicator lights flashing. She quickly walked back into the main street, picked Karen up and swung her over her shoulder before walking to Toni's car. She popped the boot open and dropped the unconscious body into it, then closed it back up. She opened the driver's door, got inside, turned the ignition, and drove off into the night. By absorbing Toni, she also absorbed his memories. He actually fancied both of the girls and had erotic dreams about the two of them and him, together. Pathetic. On the brighter side, he had an extremely healthy bank account, something she could make good use of. She now also had Karen's contact details just in case the bitch managed to avoid her again. She smiled at her good fortune. Now she had some resources at her disposal.

More importantly, now she had the bitch Karen.

***

'**Karen**!' he called out, terrified.

'What! Terry?' whispered Tampong, swinging around to stare at her phone in alarm.

She caught her reflection in the computer screen and immediately noticed her eyes were orange, a telling sign that Terry must be in distress, so she deliberately looked down at her desk.

'**Karen**!' he called out again.

Tampong still sensed his distress, so picked up the phone and dialed the hotel, asking for the receptionist to put her through to their room.

He picked up.

'Terry, it's me. What's happened?'

'She's in trouble,' he said simply.

'Karen?'

'Yes, Karen,' he said in annoyance, 'who else?'

'Sandi,' she replied sharply.

He swallowed hard, knowing her words to be true.

'Ho, right, yes, sorry, it's Karen.'

'What about her?'

'Something bad has happened to her.'

'How do you know?'

'I just sensed it.'

'Do you know what kind of trouble?'

'No, just that she was there one moment and gone the next.'

'I don't understand how you sensed this. She is not one of us.'

She carefully looked around the room, making sure no one was listening to her conversation.

'I cannot explain it, just a terrible feeling.'

'Could it be guilt?'

'What do you mean?'

'Well, you have gone out with this other girl, Sandi, and I understood you were going to end it with Karen.'

'I was. I mean, I am.'

'So?'

He thought about what she said. It made sense. He was feeling bad about having to break up with her, but there was something special about Sandi, and he felt closer to her than to any other person before, even Karen. He was half dreaming, half thinking, so perhaps she was right. A shiver ran down his spine and his body shook, which was also sensed by Tampong.

'Are you OK?' questioned Tampong, sensing his change.

'Yes, yes, I think so. You could be right. I don't feel anything anymore, and it was just a brief moment I sensed her distress. You are right, I cannot be attached to her like we are, and Shoil, come to that.'

Her name triggered something lurking at the back of his mind, as if she too were active at the same time. It must be a coincidence. There is no way she could know about them. Their meetings were few and infrequent.

'I feel OK now, it has passed.'

'Good,' she said. She sat back against her seat and drew a deep, relieving breath.

'Stay in the hotel for the rest of the day, and we'll speak again when I get home.'

'I wanted to meet Sandi later.'

'We talk first, then you can meet her. By the way, when were you planning on talking with Karen next?'

'Friday.'

'OK, that's just tomorrow. You could find out if anything happened to her then, right?'

'OK, but don't be late tonight, please.'

'I'll be there as soon as I can.'

She hung up, staring at the phone for a long time. He didn't sound like himself when she first spoke with him, almost as if he were in a semi-trance. She needed to find out what was wrong with him. She closed her file and looked at the clock. It was four thirty. She got in early this morning, so thought it should be OK for her to leave now. She was about to get up when she saw Sam get up and start packing her things away. She had arrived later than her, so guessed it must be OK to go home now.

'Good idea,' she said aloud, causing Sam to look up in her direction.

'I'm going home too,' she explained.

'Right,' Sam answered, 'you get no bonus here for working all the hours god sends. Doing anything interesting tonight?'

'Nope, just a quiet evening with my nephew, and you?'

'Actually,' she continued, now sounding excited, 'I have a blind date.'

'A blind date, eh?'

'Right. My friend set me up. Apparently, he is great, well-built, good-looking, and will be a good distraction from him.'

Her eyes moved toward Brad's office door.

'OK, just you be careful, my girl.'

'I will.'

'Look. Let me give you my mobile. If you feel it's not going well, just call me or text me, let me know where you are, and I'll come and get you.'

'That's so sweet. Thank you. I'm sure it will be OK, but good to have a backup plan, just in case.'

'Just in case.'

Tampong gave Sam her number, which she entered in her phone.

'Have fun and be safe,' said Tampong.

'I will,' she replied confidently, slipping her phone into her bag before waving goodbye.

Tampong knew it was risky giving her number to Sam, but she would never forgive herself if something happened to her. She quickly finished clearing her desk, locked her drawer, grabbed her coat, and headed out the door and down into the car park. She waived towards a waiting taxi, which pulled up in front of her. She threw her bag onto the passenger seat, then gave the driver her address, adding that if he was quick she would give him an extra twenty dollars. He put his foot down and drove out of the garage, fast.

Terry picked up his phone and texted Sandi, deciding it must be his guilty conscience playing tricks on him and that Karen was really OK.

'You free 2 nite?'

Almost immediately he received a response.

'U bet.'

'Meet me outside the hotel. 7pm?'

'Okay dokay. Not grounded then?'

'Nope.'

'Perfect. See you soon. xxx'

He smiled when he saw the three kisses and put his phone back down.

Tampong arrived at the hotel in record time, paid the taxi driver as promised, and rushed into the elevator, stepping out as soon as she had room to. She opened the bedroom door to find Terry lying on the bed. He sat up as soon as she entered. She dropped her bag and rushed up to him, holding him by the shoulders.

'Look at me,' she demanded.

He did, although not sure why.

She sighed heavily.

'Good. Your eyes are normal. So what happened earlier?'

'Just a strange feeling. Perhaps I was daydreaming. I am not sure.'

'And you have not felt anything or sensed anything since?'

'No, nothing.'

'Then it must have been a bad dream, albeit a daydream.'

'Are those real?'

'Daydreams? Why yes, of course they are real. People can also dream while awake.'

'No way.'

'True. Your subconscious can play tricks on you, make you imagine things even if you are awake.'

'Wow.'

'Right, wow. So I guess we put it down to a daydreaming event then.'

'Guess so.'

'So, you are definitely sure about this Sandi girl?'

'I'm sure.'

'And you are definitely going to end it with Karen?'

'Yes, I am going to end it with her, although not sure how I am going to do that, exactly.'

'Just be honest with her, she deserves that much.'

He gave her a 'really' look.

'About your feelings,' she explained, 'not your location.'

'Ho, right.'

'And when do you plan on seeing this Sandi again?'

'Actually, tonight.'

'Gosh. You are not letting the grass grow under your feet, are you?'

'I'm not sure I even know what that means. You talk in riddles sometimes.'

'Just be careful and be back home by ten pm.'

He gave her another look.

'OK, eleven pm, but no later.'

'Agreed.'

'So, have you eaten?'

'Nope. My plan was to have dinner with Sandi, if that's OK with you?'

'What, you mean I am not invited?'

She put on her best 'hurt' face.

'Just kidding. You go and have a good evening. I'll grab some room service and treat myself to a long hot soak in the bath.'

'Now there is a surprise.'

'What?'

'You and your long hot baths. I'm surprised you don't sprout gills, given the amount of time you spend in the bathtub.'

'A girl has her pleasures, you know, and we like to stay clean.'

'Right, whatever. Well, before you hug the bathroom, I am going to freshen up for my date tonight.'

'So it is a date then.'

'Yes, it's a date.'

She nodded her understanding as he walked past then slammed the bathroom door shut, indicating that the conversation was over. Tampong reached over and picked up the in-room menu card and started studying it. She had just decided when the bathroom door opened, and Terry emerged smelling of Boss aftershave. A lot of it. She coughed when he passed her, pinching her nose.

'What?' he asked.

'Bit heavy with the aftershave, I'd say.'

'You think.'

'Well, if you want to keep her away from you, then that will work.'

'Hey, that's not helpful.'

'I was being constructive.'

He sniffed himself.

'OK. I'll change my shirt.'

'Good idea.'

He quickly unbuttoned his shirt and threw it at her. She caught it easily, although the aroma hit her nostrils like a thunderbolt.

'Jesus,' she exclaimed, 'did you empty the bottle over your shirt.'

'Again, not helpful.'

She threw his shirt back at him, but he ignored it, allowing it to fall onto his bed. He opened his top drawer and pulled out a T-shirt, which he slipped over his head.

'Better?' he asked.

'Much better,' she agreed.

He looked at the clock. 'Right. Time I was off.'

'OK, enjoy yourself, and remember . . .'

'I know, back by eleven pm.'

'That's my boy.'

He poked his tongue out at her playfully. Picking up his jacket, he waved her goodnight and walked out of the door.

She watched him go and was in half a mind to follow him, but then almost immediately decided against it. Instead, she picked up the phone to order in-room service. She suddenly had a craving for a nice steak and a glass of red wine.

***

Karen's eyes flickered open. That was when the pain from her arms shot through her body, forcing her to look up. She was hanging from a wooden pillar, secured by large metal brackets around each wrist. She looked around at what looked like a large barn. She smelled compost and then saw the pile of excrement in a corner, on top of which looked like her clothes. She blinked twice then looked down at her body. She was completely naked. She wanted to cry out, but a dirty cloth had been tied tightly around her mouth, preventing any sounds coming out. She was cold and frightened, not knowing where she was and why she was here. Her wrists throbbed badly. When she tried to change position, she was met with a sheering pain down her arms, forcing her back into her original hanging position. She cried as the pain rippled through her fragile body.

Just then she heard the barn door opening behind her, but she couldn't turn around to see who it was. She was suddenly filled with hope that this was someone here to rescue her. The barn door closed, and there was the sound of feet shuffling through the dirt floor, feet that were coming towards her.

'So you are awake, finally,' said Shoil as she walked around to face Karen.

Karen stared at the familiar face. Her eyes wide open in fright.

'Aha, so you do recognize me then.'

Karen nodded, wanting to speak, but still gagged.

'Ho right, you cannot speak, can you? Let me take this gag away and give it back to the cows.'

She raised her little finger into the air as her nail transformed into a long, thin blade. She dangled it menacingly in front of Karen's face before she used it to cut the gag away. It fell to the dirty floor.

'That's better. Now you can answer my questions.'

Karen spat dirt out of her mouth and looked up at the woman.

'What do you want with me? Why am I here?' she asked.

Shoil's reply was physical, quick, and brutal as Karen felt a fist thump heavily into her stomach, forcing all the air out of her lungs. She rocked to and fro, causing even more pain around her wrists. She cried out while trying to get air back into her lungs. She desperately wanted to double up but was left hanging and simply had to endure the pain from her wrists and now her stomach.

'I'll ask the questions,' Shoil warned, 'you just give me the answers. Clear?'

Karen just cried, so was met with another thump to her stomach.

'I said clear?' demanded Shoil.

'Y. . . y . . . yes,' stuttered Karen.

Her mind was cloudy, and she just wanted the pain to stop.

'Good. Now let's start. Where is he?'

'W . . . w . . . who?'

'Your boyfriend, of course, who do you think, Santa Claus?'

She clenched her first again but did not strike this time. She relaxed her hand, instead caressing Karen's body from her neck down to her crouch.

'You know, you really don't have a bad body. I can see why the boys would like you, although I suspect you are still a virgin. If you don't answer my questions, I will mark your face and body so badly that you will stay a virgin.'

'I don't know where Terry is,' she answered nervously.

Shoil stared at her hard. So his name is Terry. Karen's eyes were petrified, and she doubted she had the strength to lie.

'You must have some idea,' she added, only a little softer this time.

'I . . . I . . . I think he is in Asia.'

'Asia? Why do you say that?'

Karen tried to think clearly, but it was difficult. She couldn't take any more pain at the hands of this woman, so would tell her all that she knew.

'It was just the way he dressed and some things he said.'

'Go on,' encouraged Shoil.

'He had just gotten up, having slept for a long time, and I could see daylight coming through his bedroom window, yet it was eleven thirty pm here.'

Shoil digested this new information. What she said made sense and would explain why she felt the last sensation was so distant. So Tampong and the boy had done a runner across the other side of the world.

'What's Terry's surname?'

'Armitage.'

'And where in Asia is he exactly?'

'I don't know, really, I don't know. He said he could not tell me.'

That made sense, concluded Shoil. The girlfriend could have been tracked down by her and forced to reveal their whereabouts.

Clever bitch, she thought.

'So you are in communication with him, Terry?' she continued.

'Yes, by Skype?'

'Skype? What's that?'

'It's a free computer app. You download it and can video call a contact.'

'Right, so when are you Skyping with him again?'

'Friday night.'

'Tomorrow, eh? Right, you will keep that meeting and find out exactly where he is.'

'But he will not tell me.'

'**MAKE HIM**,' she screamed, 'or I will show you what real pain feels like. I will tear your body apart bit by bit, making sure you are still alive when I rip your heart out and make you watch it stop beating. Do I make myself clear?'

She nodded frantically.

'Good. Now let me show you a sample of the pain you will suffer should you fail me.'

'No, please, no,' pleaded Karen.

Shoil ignored her pathetic pleas, instead she watched as her small fingernail extended into a thin blade again. She picked up a stool sitting in the corner and placed it next to Karen's hanging body. Standing on it, she forcibly grabbed the girl's hand, bending her fingers painfully back. She then placed the tip of her blade directly under the nail of her middle finger before jabbing the blade into her flesh under the nail.

Karen screamed in horror as excruciating pain shot up her arm. She felt sick and dizzy and wanted to pass out. Shoil pulled the blade out, releasing her hand.

'Remember that pain, bitch. That's just a teaser. If you don't deliver, then the next pain you will feel will be worse, much worse.'

Karen's head flopped onto her chest as she passed out.

'What a weak bitch you are,' she snapped, spitting at her before turning and leaving her hanging.

However, as she walked up to the door, she stopped and turned back. With the blade still formed, she cut through the chains holding the body and watched with disinterest as the body crashed to the floor. She hissed at the unconscious form, turned, and this time walked out of the door, locking it behind her.

It was twenty minutes before Karen finally regained consciousness, immediately feeling her throbbing finger. She rolled onto her back, realizing she was no longer hanging, and her arms were free. She sat up and rubbed her arms, looking around as she did. It was indeed an old wooden barn with the only window too high to reach. She looked at the double door, so gingerly stood up. Her legs felt a little wobbly, so she staggered up to the door, tried to pull it open but it was locked tight. Tears ran down her cheeks. She felt hopelessly lost, hopelessly vulnerable. She had absolutely no idea what this woman wanted with Terry. Whatever it was, she was desperate to find him, doing anything to do so . . . even kill. She had no doubt that this woman would kill her if she didn't help find him. Would she let her go afterwards? She had her doubts. Looking around for any form of cover, she found nothing, not even a bucket, and right now she needed to pee. She then heard a key enter the lock and start to turn, so she stepped backwards, covering herself as she did. Her bladder needs quickly disappeared, to be replaced by fear. The door opened and Shoil stepped in.

'So, you are finally awake again then.'

Karen said nothing as Shoil looked her up and down.

'No need to try and hide yourself, girl, I have seen all you have to offer. And I've seen better, like in a mirror.'

Still Karen said nothing, not sure how to answer this woman, not wishing to anger her again, incurring her wrath again. Shoil took a step forward, making Karen instinctively take two steps backwards. Shoil smiled at her in contempt.

'I hope for your sake that tomorrow you find out where the boy is, I really do.'

Still no words came from her mouth. Shoil threw a piece of paper and pen onto the floor in front of Karen.

'I need you to write down your address and where exactly your computer is. I will retrieve it so that you can keep your meeting with the boy. Do you understand me?'

She nodded and bent down to pick up the paper and pen. Despite her hand shaking, she wrote her address down, explaining that her laptop was on her bedroom sideboard. She held the paper out. Shoil stepped forward, snatching the paper from her hand. She read the address and instructions. She turned to leave.

'Please,' said Karen softly, 'I need to use the toilet.'

Her stomach started to ache from holding on.

Shoil turned toward her.

'Pick a corner,' she snapped, walking out of the barn and locking the door behind her.

Karen slumped to the floor and cried. She cried for a good fifteen minutes until another bout of stomach cramps forced her to her feet. She walked slowly to a corner in the room, where she squatted down to relieve herself. It felt so degrading and humiliating. She slowly rose back to her feet, avoiding looking down at what she had left. Now she felt thirsty and hungry and wondered if she would ever eat again. More tears flowed down her cheeks. Not understanding what was happening, or why, she felt utterly useless and powerless to fight this evil woman. One who knew how to shame someone and make them do things they would never dream of doing in normal circumstances, but these were not normal circumstances. She tried to be positive. If this woman wanted her to talk with Terry tomorrow, then that is what she would do. It even meant that she must surely be given some clean clothing and allowed to freshen up before facing him. So she just needed to survive for a day at most, then at least she would be out of this room, if only for a little while. She had to convince Terry to tell her where he was. This was not going to be easy, but she had to try. She was sure her life depended on it, and no one was worth her life.

Shoil decided to leave her to stew for the evening without any food or water, hoping this would make her more susceptible to her demands. She sensed a determined spirit in the girl and intended to take advantage of this. Once she had what she needed, she would dispose of her quickly, then track down the boy and, finally, Tampong. She licked her lips in anticipation.

The night was one of the longest in Karen's living memory, but finally she managed to get to sleep, only for the sun's rays coming in from the high window and hitting her face, waking her up. For a second, she thought she had been in some terrible nightmare until she looked around, seeing that she was still in the barn. Her heart sank. She sat up and leaned her naked back against the cold barn wall.

She had quite a sheltered life. Her mother kept her close to her and away from most trouble. She never really needed anything and had a happy, content life. That was until this horrible woman crashed into her life, turning it upside down. Would she ever have a normal life again? Somehow she doubted it. At the back of her mind, she couldn't help thinking that Terry was to blame for her current predicament. Had she not met him, not gotten to know him, then maybe this woman and she would never have crossed paths.

It was all his fault she was in such a predicament, so why should she try and protect him?

***

Terry was fidgeting again, not being able to keep still. He hopped from one leg to the other, glancing at his watch every ten seconds. His thoughts were of Sandi and wanting to be with her. He glanced at his watch for the umpteenth time when suddenly the now-familiar Chevrolet Cruze appeared, coming up the hotel driveway. Sandi flashed her headlights at him, so he waved enthusiastically back. The car rolled to a stop, so he eagerly opened the door and stepped inside, to be greeted by a smiling Sandi.

'Hi, y'all,' she greeted him.

He leaned over and kissed her firmly on her lips. She pushed against his lips in response. He placed his hand on her exposed thigh as they kissed, enjoying the smooth texture of her skin. Their lips finally parted, much to the relief of the doorman, who was trying to usher her car away with both hands. She noticed him so waved her apology and drove out of the hotel driveway.

'So, what do you fancy tonight?' she asked.

He just looked at her.

'I mean to eat or see something.'

He just looked at her again.

'I mean something other than me,' she then noticed the disappointment on his face, 'as you can have me anytime.'

He immediately brightened up.

'Surprise me,' he said, looking her over. 'You look great by the way.'

'Thank you. Reckon we might mosey on to downtown and grab us a bite to eat. Does that work for you?'

'You bet.'

'Great, because I'm fixin' to treat y'all tonight.'

'To a meal!' he clarified, with a silly smirk on his face.

'Yes,' she scolded him, 'to a meal. I've booked us into a nice restaurant.'

He looked nervously down at his attire.

'Is this alright?' he said, waving at his T-shirt and jeans.

'No problem,' she confirmed, 'just as long as you don't rock up in swimwear, Singapore is quite an informal town. Anyway, it is just up the road from here.'

He then stared at her for a long time, making her feel a little uncomfortable.

'What's with the stare?' she asked.

'What's with the cowboy accent all of a sudden?'

'Aha. Well, I was watching this documentary on Texas and the special drawl they speak. I was trying it out.'

'Doesn't suit you. Seems strange hearing that coming from an Asian girl.'

'Singaporean, if you don't mind, but I guess you are right. I should not try to be what I am not.'

As she spoke, she turned left, drove up the road a little until she found a parking space, which she pulled into.

'Great. It's after six pm, so no charges.'

'Cool,' he said, getting out of the car, walking to the front of it.

Sandi turned the engine off, grabbed her small bag and slid gracefully out of the car, closing and locking the door. She straightened her short dress, trying to pull out the wrinkles as she walked around to the front to join Terry.

He whistled when he saw her. She was in a short yellow dress with matching shoes, carrying a gold handbag. Her long blonde hair draped over both shoulders, resting on her ample chest. The V-neck of her dress had a deep plunge, revealing her cleavage. She looked amazing.

'Wow, you look fantastic,' he said as she slipped her arm through his and guided him down the road to a building on the corner.

'Thank y'all kindly, sir,' she acknowledged.

He gave her a stern look of disapproval.

'Oops, sorry, enough of the Texan drawl for one night.'

She steered him up a ramp leading to double glass doors. He held one of them open for her, so she nodded her thanks as she walked inside. He followed her and had to adjust his vision as it was so dark inside. The receptionist was a pretty young woman with jet-black hair and matching black dress. She showed them a full set of gleaming white teeth as they walked up to her.

'Welcome y'all to the Capital Grille. Y'all have a reservation?'

'We do,' confirmed Sandi, 'in the name of Pickford.'

'Fantastic. Please follow me. You are a little early, but your table is ready.'

'Awesome,' answered Sandi, strolling after the receptionist and grabbing Terry's hand, dragging him along.

The woman stopped at a small round table in the corner, placing a menu card on either side, then taking a step backwards to allow them to sit, which they did.

They picked up the menus and started reading through them. Terry noticed the prices.

'Wow, this place is not cheap,' he whispered.

'As I said, don't worry about the bill tonight. This is my treat.'

'I cannot let you pay for this all by yourself.'

'I hope you are not going all macho on me now,' she warned.

He shook his head and was about to answer when the table server walked up to them, wearing a grey jacket that looked two sizes too big for him.

'Hi y'all. Welcome to The Capital Grille. My name is William and I'll be taking care of y'all tonight. Can I start you guys off with an appetizer?'

'Hi, William,' Sandi began, 'and sure, let's start with lobster and crab cakes.'

'That's for two, OK?'

'Right, for two,' she confirmed, winking at Terry.

'Awesome. And to drink?'

'I'll just have water.'

'Doctor Pepper for me,' said Terry.

'Awesome. I'll get that going for you guys.'

He turned and left them alone, giving Terry the opportunity to look around, not that there was much to see. The restaurant was too dark. There were portraits hanging on all the walls. Most of the tables were occupied with a particularly noisy group in the far corner, seemingly celebrating something. His reconnaissance was distracted by Sandi when she placed her hand over his. Her hand felt warm, soft, sensuous, and inviting. He never realized that his body could be turned on by a simple hand gesture. He coughed to clear his throat.

She saw he was nervous, so patted his hand assuredly.

'Think of this as a thank you.'

'A thank you?'

'Yeah, thanks for giving me your virginity last night.'

Her timing could not have been worse as the waiter returned with their drinks and heard her response. He also coughed nervously as he placed their drinks on the table, quickly leaving them again.

'Oops,' she said, 'guess that was a little too loud.'

It was Terry's turn to take her hand in his, wrapping his fingers around her hand.

'It is I who should be thanking you.'

'For what?'

'For making me a man last night.'

She laughed, picked up her drink with her free hand and sucked the water through her straw, her eyes never leaving his. He picked up his drink and did the same. He felt her foot slide up and down the inside of his leg while she continued to suck on her straw very suggestively. He felt himself harden, nervously looking around to check nobody was looking. He needn't have worried; it was too dark for anyone to see anything. The waiter returned with their appetizer and placed it on the middle of the table.

'Are you ready to order?' he asked, seemingly a little embarrassed to be there.

Sandi looked up and gave him a little wink, making him place his fingers in his collar to clear some room for air.

'I'll have the porcini-rubbed bone-in ribeye.'

'And how would you like that?'

'Medium rare.'

'And sides?'

'Baked potato and green beans.'

'Awesome. And for you, sir?'

'I'll take the dry-aged New York strip please.'

'And how would you like that?'

'Medium rare.'

'And sides?'

'Streak fries and cream corn.'

'Awesome. I'll get that going with the chef.'

He again turned and quickly left.

'I think you have made quite an impression on him,' observed Terry.

'Not sure it was the right one though.'

'Whatever.'

'So Terry, tell me, what are you looking for in life?'

'Love and happiness.'

'That's it?'

'That's it. Why?'

'Just that it's not much and will take resources, particularly money, to achieve that.'

'Not necessarily. What about you, what are you looking for in life?'

'Ho, to see the world, stay young, live in a big house with a big car, be happily married with lots of kids and loads of money.'

'Wow, that's some list.'

'A girl should have ambition.'

'Guess so. Not sure how you will achieve so much ambition.'

'Ho, you will be surprised. Anyway, I think I am doing alright starting with you.'

'Me!!' he said, surprised.

'Yeah. In my dreams I find this wealthy European, who gives me everything I need.'

'Oh boy, not sure where I come into this picture.'

'It's early days yet, Terry, it's early days.'

They went quiet as they started to eat their crab cakes, which he thought were delicious. Sandi finished her lobster, wiping a little bit of sauce from her lips and taking another sip of her water. As if on cue, William arrived with their main course, placing the plates in front of them and taking the appetizer plate away.

'Would you just check the steak is as you ordered?' he asked.

Both picked up their knife and fork and cut into the steak.

'Perfect,' they both said.

'Awesome, then enjoy. Would you like a top-up?'

Both nodded, so he took their glasses away. Terry picked up his side order of fries and poured some onto his plate, doing the same with his corn. Sandi did the same with her sides.

'Bon appetite,' he said.

'Likewise,' she replied, taking a slice of her steak and slipping it into her mouth.

She closed her eyes as she savored its flavor.

'Hmm,' she moaned in delight, 'delicious.'

'Mine too, cooked perfectly.'

'I'm glad.'

He placed his knife and fork down and just stared at her.

'What?' she said, wondering if she had a piece of meat hanging from her lip or something.

'Ho, just thinking how lucky I am to have found you, and so quickly.'

'Meant to be I guess,' she replied, cutting another piece of her steak while smiling to herself.

'Could be,' he agreed, 'could be fate.'

'Do you believe in that sort of thing?'

'Fate? Well, I have never really thought about it before, but I guess so. You?'

'Ho absolutely. I believe there are certain things destined to happen.'

'Like us?'

'Like us.'

William returned with their top-ups.

'How's the steak turning out?'

'Perfect,' she replied.

'Delicious,' remarked Terry.

'Awesome,' said William, turning away to serve another table.

They continued eating, chatting in between about their hopes and dreams. He discovered her love for animals and her desire to be a vet, but college was too expensive, so she was looking at voluntary work in an animal shelter or something similar. She talked about how her father died when she was young. She had an older brother, but he was killed in a car accident, leaving her with a younger brother and her mother to care for. William interrupted their conversation when he collected their empty plates.

'Dessert?'

'Not for me,' said Sandi, 'just coffee please.'

'Me too,' confirmed Terry, 'just coffee that is.'

William nodded, picked up their side plates and balanced them on the dinner plates, then turned and headed back to the kitchen.

Sandi and Terry reached across the table and held each other hands. He caressed her hand with his thumb.

'Wow, you have had a tough start to your life, Sandi,' he whispered, stroking her hand.

'I can say the same thing about you,' she answered.

'Guess we are like two peas in a pod then.'

'I never thought I would feel this way about someone I've only just met,' she said softly, looking directly into his eyes, as if searching for any doubt or hesitation.

She saw none when he answered.

'Feel like what?' he asked gently.

'Like something special had happened. Like I need to be with you all the time. Want to be with you all the time.'

He gripped her hands just a little tighter.

'I could only dream of a girl like you saying such things to me. I feel there is something special about you too. I am very attracted to you,' he said quietly.

'You are?'

He did not answer in words but leaned across the table and kissed her firmly on the lips. Her eyes twinkled in response as she passionately kissed him back.

'A . . . hmm . . .' said William, making as much noise from his throat as he possibly could as he walked up to their table.

Get a room, he thought.

They reluctantly parted and sat back in their chairs while William served their coffees. He placed a silver tray on the edge of the table.

'Whenever you are ready,' he said, 'no rush.'

He diplomatically left the two alone. They smiled sheepishly at each other, neither regretting what just happened and what had just passed between them.

Terry popped two small sugar lumps into his coffee, then mixed in some cream. He stirred it all together, put the spoon down and picked up the cup to take a sip. It was still hot, so he placed it back on its saucer. His eyes never left Sandi's, who preferred her coffee black. She took a sip of her coffee, the heat appearing not to bother her.

'Do you know a Cher song called "Shoop Shoop," or something like that?' she asked.

'You mean, It's in his kiss?'

'That's the one. Well it definitely is,' she said, sounding satisfied.

He smiled, knowing that he would now have that song in the back of his mind for the rest of the evening. She took another sip of her coffee and finished her cup. She picked up the silver tray, wagging a finger at Terry, who was about to open his mouth, checked the total before pulling her credit card out of her purse and placing it on the tray. As if by magic, William appeared and picked up the tray with a nod of gratitude, disappearing behind the bar. He shortly returned with the credit receipt, which he placed in front of Sandi. Clearly he had observed who put the card down, either that or noticed the name on the card and guessed the male's name was not Sandi.

'Thank you for coming, and we hope to see you back here again real soon,' he said, sounding gracious enough, and the two smiled and nodded to him.

Sandi added a generous tip before signing and leaving the original on the tray, taking a copy for herself.

'Thank you for a lovely evening, Sandi,' he said, with so much warmth in his words that Sandi almost cried with tears of joy.

She just about managed to control herself.

'Absolutely my pleasure. Your treat next time.'

'Definitely. Not sure I can better this though,' he replied.

'Ho, there are many fine restaurants in Singapore. I have heard that even the restaurant where you are staying has an exceptionally good reputation and write-up.'

'Then it sounds like our next date is sorted then.'

She laughed.

'OK, Rockefeller, one day at a time.'

They stood up to leave. Sandi grabbed her bag and slipped her arm through his as they walked out of the restaurant, with the main glass door being held open by the receptionist.

'Thanks, y'all, and come back again soon,' she said as they passed.

'Thank you. We will,' replied Terry, and he meant it.

The waiter came up and stood by the receptionist, watching the two lovebirds leaving.

'How does a boy like that win the heart of a girl like that?' he asked aloud.

The receptionist just shrugged her shoulders.

'Money I guess,' she answered simply, 'this is Singapore after all.'

As the two lovers walked down the street, they heard the cathedral bells ring out several times.

'Was that ten pm?' he asked.

She looked down at her watch.

'Yep,' she confirmed.

'Jesus, where has the time gone?'

'As I have said before, always does when you are enjoying yourself so much. What time do you have to be back?'

'By eleven pm. We still have an hour,' he said eagerly.

'Right, and I have school tomorrow, so regretfully I'll have to take you right back to your hotel now.'

'Spoilsport,' he muttered.

She poked him in his ribs.

'Listen, I have after-school studies tomorrow, so I cannot see you, OK, but there is the weekend. We can do something special together.'

'Golly, a whole day without seeing you. Not sure I can cope.'

'You will, Terry, you will. Perhaps we can go to the amusement park I mentioned.'

'Disneyland?'

'Universal Studios,' she corrected.

'Right. Universal Studios, but I'm paying.'

'No argument from me there.'

He then realized tomorrow was Friday.

'It might be just as well we don't see each other tomorrow, as I have to have a heart-to-heart with Karen.'

'Your ex?'

'Right. It's not going to be any fun, but something I have to do. It's only fair to her and to you.'

She leaned over and kissed him gently on his cheek.

'I am sure you will be gentle with her.'

He was not so sure. He liked her when they first met, but with Sandi, it was so different. They clicked as soon as they met, as if they were meant to be. No, he would not beat about the bush but tell her straight that it was over between them. She would feel hurt for a little while, but she would get over it. They reached the car, and both got in. Sandi drove slowly back to the hotel, trying to delay saying good night for as long as possible. It wasn't far and was only ten thirty when they arrived, having walked very slowly to the car, hand in hand, and her driving was as slow as she dared. She stopped the car short of the driveway and turned the engine off. They leaned into each other and kissed for a long time. Both wanted time to stand still at that moment, both relishing the feel of the other's lips, the closeness of their bodies, and the mounting desire they both felt. Finally their lips parted, and they sat back in their seats.

'It would be nice to spend some quality time together alone at the weekend,' he said.

'Unfortunately not at my apartment. My friend is back, and she is bringing a friend to the apartment, so it's my turn to disappear.'

'Disappear?'

'Be out of the place so that they can be together. Do what we want to do no doubt.'

'Oh, right. I see. Then perhaps I can persuade my aunt to leave and give us the hotel room.'

Sandi turned towards him, hope filling her eyes.

'Do you really think she would do that?'

'I'll convince her,' he said, although not sure how exactly he would do that.

'That would be great,' she replied. 'I cannot wait to see you on Saturday then. Shall we say nine am here?'

'Nine am it is. Thanks again for a lovely evening.'

'You're most welcome.'

They kissed again before he unclipped his seat belt and got out of the car. He closed the door slowly, as she lowered his window down.

'Hope all goes well tomorrow,' she called out to him.

He waved his thanks and watched as she turned the vehicle around and headed off down the street. He continued to watch until she turned off and disappeared around a corner. He stood there a little bit longer before finally turning around and heading into the hotel.

When he reached his bedroom, Tampong was lying on her bed, reading a book. She looked at him above the top of her book.

'Hey, nice evening?'

'The best.'

'Wow. So what did you kids do then?'

'Sandi took me out for dinner.'

She dropped her book on her lap and turned to him.

'*She* took *you* to dinner?'

'Right.'

'Wow, either you have a strange power over this woman, or you have her hooked good and proper.'

'It was just her way of saying thanks.'

'For what?'

Terry hesitated to answer.

'For just meeting me.'

'Hmmm,' she replied, not convinced by his answer.

She picked her book up again and continued to read.

Terry settled down on his bed, content with life. He knew he was going to have a difficult day tomorrow when he Skyped with Karen, but knew it was for the best. Their relationship would never survive as he had no idea how long they would be staying here in Singapore. Besides, he was in no rush to leave now and had an excellent reason to stay. Perhaps he could find himself a job and, who knows, get a good career going, spending more time with Sandi and moving into their own place. Heck, was he really already thinking about moving in with her? They had only just met, but it felt as though he had known her for the whole of his life. He smiled to himself, closed his eyes, and dreamt about her.

***

Karen was still very cold and frightened. Her entire body was shaking from the cold, while her nose ran nonstop. She eventually gave up trying to wipe it. She felt totally lost, totally alone. She was going to die in this room, she just knew it. She folded her legs as close to her body as she could. The cold was eventually too much for her and she passed out, her head resting against the wall.

Forty minutes later the door unlocked and Shoil walked in carrying a bundle of clothes.

'Get into these . . .'

She stopped talking when she saw Karen unconscious on the floor. She dropped the clothes and rushed up to her, checking her pulse. She breathed a sigh of relief when she felt one, although it was terrifyingly slow, which was not a good sign.

'Damn you, bitch, you are not dying on me yet. I need you,' she yelled, picking up her body and carrying it out of the room.

She placed the unconscious body on a sofa, wrapping her in several blankets. She rushed over to her computer and typed in 'treating hypothermia'. She did the right thing in moving her into a warmer room and covering her with blankets. She placed some small towels in the oven and heated them before placing them on the girl's chest and back.

'Come on, girl, wake up,' she screamed out in frustration, shaking Karen's body violently.

She was her last link to the boy and Tampong. She couldn't lose her now, not being this close. She shook her again.

Karen stirred a little and Shoil almost cried in delight. She went into the kitchen to switch the kettle on, as apparently a hot beverage helps. After the kettle boiled, she dropped a lemon tea bag into a mug and poured the water over the bag. She stirred it a few times before removing the bag and returning to the room. On the dining table were several packets of crisps and some chocolate bars. Grabbing the chocolate, she returned to the sofa. Karen was mumbling to herself, incomprehensible words, but at least she was recovering. Shoil placed the mug and chocolate on the table and put her arms under Karen's shoulders and lifted her into a sitting position. Her eyes flickered open.

'Ouch,' she said slowly, 'what . . . what . . . a . . . nightmare.'

'Right,' said Shoil.

The sound of her voice forced Karen to open her eyes, fearing the worst. It was not a nightmare. Shoil said nothing, instead just picked up the mug and handed it to her, which Karen grabbed quickly.

'Careful,' Shoil warned, 'it is hot, so drink it slowly. You are suffering from hypothermia.'

Karen took the mug by the handle and sipped the hot beverage. She felt the heat run down her throat. Shoil then placed the bar of chocolate on the blanket covering her, got up and walked into the kitchen. Placing both hands on the sink, she blew out her breath heavily. She had so nearly lost her and all because of her own stupid carelessness. She needed to be careful in the future. Making them suffer was one thing, but killing them before she could benefit from them was simply a waste of time and energy. She made herself a coffee before returning to the room, just in time to see Karen stuffing the last of the chocolate into her mouth, desperate for some nourishment.

'So, you're back with the living then,' she said, trying to sound calm.

Karen said nothing, opting to take another sip of her tea instead.

'I could so easily have let you die, but I wanted to let you know that I have complete control over you, and your life is in my hands. Is that perfectly clear?'

This time she nodded. It was obvious this woman could kill again. She recalled the way she just murdered poor Sally without a blink of an eye, with no hesitation or regret. She realized that she had to do whatever she said, or she would end up like Sally.

'Now, do you want me to continue with your torture?'

She shook her head frantically.

'Good. And you will do as I tell you?'

She nodded her head.

'Excellent. I will go and retrieve the clothes I had for you, allow you to get dressed, and then we can talk about your meeting with Terry.'

'Can . . . can . . . I freshen up a bit please?'

'Yeah. You do smell like a badly used toilet. The bathroom is behind you, and don't think about trying to escape. There is nowhere you can go that I won't find you . . . and you don't want me finding you.'

Her frightened eyes gave Shoil her answer, so she turned and headed back to the barn, deliberately keeping the main door unlocked as a test. She returned to find the front door still shut, nodding to herself that the girl clearly got the message. When she entered the house, she heard the shower running, so she waited until Karen came out of the shower, wrapped in a bath towel. She looked a whole lot better when she reemerged. Shoil threw her clothes onto the sofa.

'Get dressed,' she demanded, turning, and leaving the room.

Karen took a deep breath, picked up the clothes and dutifully dressed, surprised that everything was her size, although not her own clothes. She shivered at the thought these could belong to another girl, perhaps one that was also dead now. She tried to shake the thought out of her head. She needed to stay alive, wanted to stay alive. She would do anything for that to happen and did not want to end up back in that awful barn again.

Shoil returned, this time carrying a coat, which she also threw towards Karen, landing a couple of feet short. She bent down and picked it up.

'I assume you will behave now and do exactly as I tell you.'

She nodded, slipping on the coat for the extra warmth.

'Right. I will drop you back at your house, where you will wait until you contact Terry. You MUST find out where he is if you want to stay alive. And you do want to stay alive, don't you?'

She nodded again.

'Good. And remember, I'll be watching you very closely. I know where you live, and I know where your family lives. I will not only kill you but every member of your family too. Do you have a father?'

She shook her head.

'Brothers or sisters?'

She nodded.

'Good. Should you not obey my every instruction, then you will watch me torture them all before I kill them, very slowly. I will make them suffer so much that they will all wish they were dead. Do you understand?'

She nodded quickly.

'Right. Go to the car outside and wait for me.'

Karen said nothing but walked out of the house into the waiting car. She could not even contemplate the idea of trying to escape. This woman was pure evil and had no doubt that she would do exactly what she said. No boy was worth her family, so she would have to convince Terry to tell her where he was. Her life depended on it. Her family's life depended on it.

Shoil closed and locked the front door, got into the car, started the engine, and drove away. They never said a word for the whole journey, something Karen was relieved about. She did not want to engage in any conversation with this killer.

It was an hour before Karen recognized where she was and that her street was the next road on the right, which Shoil took, parking right outside her house.

Shoil felt smug. She gained additional information from absorbing Toni, in particular the address and family details of Karen. He had a secret desire for her, watching her from a distance, wishing she fancied him. She almost threw up at some of his erotic dreams, mainly about this girl, but sometimes also with the other girl, Sally. She stopped the car and turned to Karen, who was looking down at the floor.

'Now you stay in your room until you contact Terry. As soon as you find out where he is, you come back outside into the street, no matter what the time is, and tell me. I'll be waiting and watching. Clear?'

She nodded, not looking up. She opened the car door and got out, walking gingerly towards the door. When she reached the front door, it suddenly opened, making her jump.

'Where have you been?' demanded her mum, 'you could have phoned and let me know you were staying out.'

She looked down the path towards the vehicle.

'And who is that?'

Karen reluctantly looked back towards the car.

'My friend I was staying with,' she lied.

Shoil waved politely before pulling away.

'Gosh, did you do an all-nighter? You look terrible.'

'Yeah. I am going to my room to rest now.'

'Cannot say I am surprised, girl. No more stayovers for you for the rest of the week.'

'As you say,' she answered quietly as she walked past her mother and up the stairs.

Her mother watched her walk up the stairs and was puzzled. She had just been grounded and did not put up any sort of fight or protest. Not like her at all. She then put it down to perhaps being just too tired to argue. She did not recognize the woman in the car either. She looked too old to be a friend. Perhaps she was the mother of her friend, which made more sense. She shrugged her shoulders and closed the door.

'Kids today,' she said.

Shoil drove around the corner, where she parked the car and turned off the engine. She got out, locked the car, then walked back up the street towards Karen's house. She leaned against the lamppost opposite and waited.

***

Friday arrived and Terry was nervous. He was not looking forward to this conversation one little bit. How do you end a relationship without hurting the girl? Simple, someone told him once, you don't, but over time they will get over it and move on. He hoped so for her sake. She was a lovely girl and deserved someone much better than he was. He checked the clock, it was 4:15. He would connect in another five minutes. The clock seemed to speed up, tormenting him and not giving him time to prepare properly. Tampong was not home yet, which was a good thing. He did not want her to hear this conversation. It was going to be painful enough with just Karen. He stood up and went into the bathroom, spraying water over his face and wiping his face dry with the towel, which he left next to the sink. He walked back to the bedroom, bent his fingers forward and switched his computer on. He left the bathroom door open.

Karen could not stop her hands from shaking. She would never recover from this ordeal, that much she knew. This was his fault. If she had never met him, then none of this would have happened. Why did he have to come into her life and bring all this horror with him? She knew he was a little strange but had no idea how much baggage he was actually carrying with him. She switched on her computer and clicked the Skype icon.

Terry accepted the incoming call, so the screen flickered a little, then her image appeared. His smile immediately disappeared.

'My god, Karen, are you OK? Did you have a bad night last night?'

'You could say that,' she answered cutely.

'Poor thing. You look really tired.'

'Thanks, just the sort of thing a girl needs to hear.'

'Sorry, just a bit of a shock I guess.'

'Well, I cannot say the same for you. Wherever you are, you look well and tanned even.'

'Yeah, well the sun is out, and it gets hot, so I am making the most of it.'

She squinted at the computer closer, noticing something in the background. She instinctively pressed the recording button so she could take a better look afterwards.

'Wherever that is,' she said.

He ignored her comment.

'So, what have you been up to since we last spoke?'

She wanted to tell him that her best friend had been murdered because of him, that she had been stripped naked and left for dead in a cold barn because of him, that her family was now being threatened because of him. Instead, she took a deep breath.

'Ho the usual, school and work. And you?'

'Ho, I've been touring downtown, checking out the local sights and eating out mostly,' he lied.

She decided this conversation was going nowhere, making a mental note of his description 'downtown'.

'Terry, we need to talk,' she said carefully.

'We are,' he said, sounding puzzled.

'No, I mean really talk.'

'About?'

'**About us**,' she said louder than she intended and was getting a little annoyed now. How obvious could it be?

'OK,' he replied, filled with doubt.

Did she sense he was about to dump her? Did women have an instinct for that sort of thing?

'I think we should stop contacting each other,' she said simply.

'OK,' he replied cutely.

His reply surprised her.

'Is that all you have to say?'

'What do you want me to say? We knew it would be difficult staying in contact being this far apart.'

'You said you would try and come back soon, didn't you?'

'I know I did, but that just cannot happen now. I am so sorry.'

'Why can it not happen?'

'Just because. It is difficult to explain, but I just cannot jump on a plane and come home.'

'Then I guess we have nothing left to say to each other.'

'Are you dumping me?'

'I think we both know that this relationship is one-sided. You will not tell me where you are, will not tell me why you cannot come home. Will not tell me anything. So what am I to think?'

'It's for your own safety, Karen.'

'For my own safety,' she spat the words out, 'so you are protecting me from whatever by being where you are, is that what you are saying?'

'Sort of.'

He did not like the direction this conversation was going.

'You have to believe me, Karen. It's for the best.'

'Best for you, you mean.'

'No, for you too.'

'Prove it.'

'What?'

'Prove it is best for me. Tell me how?'

He hesitated, looking around the room for inspiration, finding none.

'As I told you, there are people looking for us. These are not nice people and certainly not the sort you want to be associated with in any way.'

He was opening up a little, so she needed to squeeze him for some more information.

'I thought you said they were looking for your aunt. Whatever. So why are they looking for you exactly?'

He looked down at the floor, then back up to her.

'We know things about them, things that could get them into trouble.'

'And they want to stop you talking?'

'Right.'

'So you are running away and trying to hide, hoping they will simply go away.'

'Something like that.'

'And what if they find you? What if they find out you are associated with me, for example? Does that not put me at risk?'

She knew the answer to that question but wanted his reaction.

'You were one of the reasons I reluctantly agreed to come to Sing . . . here,' he corrected himself.

She caught the half word, making a mental note of it. She looked behind him, noticing an Asian picture hanging on the wall with a flag that looked like Turkey or something similar, but with stars. A red flag with a white moon crescent and several white stars to be exact. She checked she was still recording. She was.

'So what now then?' she asked, folding her arms. 'We cannot be together because apparently it is too risky, and you are not prepared to return home anyway. Where does that leave us?'

He sighed heavily.

'Then I guess it is as you say, the moment has arrived when we stop this relationship.'

'If you call *this* a relationship,' she snapped.

'It's not what I wanted, but it is best for both of us.'

'For you, you mean. Listen, I have had just about enough of this conversation, so I think it best we just end it here.'

Her eyes were watering.

'I don't want to leave with bad feelings between us.'

'Too late for that, Terry. Enjoy your life.'

'Wait, Karen, not like this.'

She disconnected her Skype call; her screen went back to her home page. She clicked on the icon again, realizing she was still recording, but it had stopped as soon as she disconnected. She pressed play and fast-forwarded the recording until she got to the point she was searching for. She pressed pause and the image stopped. She magnified the image. She was looking at his towel in the bathroom and stenciled on the towel were the words 'Carlton Hotel'. She opened up her Google search and typed in Carlton Hotel. Lots of options appeared, so she added 'Sing'. Her screen showed her the Carlton Singapore Hotel. She clicked on the website and made a note of the address: 76 Bras Basah Road, Singapore 189558. She then made another search, asking for the time difference between Singapore and the UK. Seeing it was seven hours ahead, she nodded, then noticed the flag. This all fitted with his attire. She had found him. She switched off her computer, grabbing the paper, she ran back downstairs, out of the door and into the street. As expected, the woman was standing on the pavement opposite, beckoning her over as soon as she saw her leaving the house.

When she crossed the street, she handed over the piece of paper. Shoil took it and read it under the streetlamp.

'They are in Singapore?'

'Right.'

'How can you be sure?'

'I saw a bath towel with the hotel's name, and he mentioned Sing, stopping short of saying apore as well. There was also a picture in his room with a flag, which turns out to be the flag of Singapore, which I also saw when searching for the hotel. It all fits.'

'You know that if this is some stupid little game you are playing, I will come back for you and your family.'

'It's true. I swear it. I would not risk my family for this boy.'

'Before I leave you, do you know his family name?'

'Yes, it's Armitage. Apparently, it's his auntie's name, but I told you this already.'

'Just checking,' she replied, only half listening, 'his aunty you say. Do you happen to know her first name?'

'Katy.'

'Right. You have been most helpful today.'

'So that is it now, have I told you all you need to know?'

'I suppose so, but just be warned.'

'So you will leave me alone now, please?'

'For now,' she answered coolly. 'I could kill you right now and be done with you, but if this is not true, then I will need to come back . . . but not only for you but your whole family too.'

She looked back at the house as if to emphasize the point.

'Thank you. You do not need to come back. I have told you everything. Can I go back in now, please?'

'Yes, and not a word about this to anyone, got it?'

'Right, not a word,' she said and meant it. 'I swear.'

Shoil knew the girl was frightened enough not to lie. She thought about killing her there and then but resisted the urge. Turning around, she walked up the pathway and turned into the main street. Karen just watched her go. She had never met anyone so terrifying as this woman before. She had skills that she had never seen, and she seemed afraid of nothing. She crossed herself and silently prayed that this was the last time she ever saw this woman.

Shoil arrived back at her apartment and sat down on the sofa. She recapped everything the girl had told her. She tapped her knee with her hand as she contemplated her options. She nodded to herself, got up and opened her laptop to search for the Carlton Hotel, Singapore. She found it quickly, making a note of the telephone number: +6563388333. She dialed the number and waited.

'Carlton Hotel. This is Sue-lee speaking, how may I help you today?'

'Hi Sue-lee. Can you put me through to Katy Armitage's room please?'

'Katy Armitage you say, just one moment please and let me check.'

Shoil held her breath as she waited. There was a click on the line as Sue-lee returned.

'Thank you for holding. Putting you through now.'

Shoil hung up.

'Got you, bitch,' she said aloud.

'Hello?' said Terry, picking up the receiver.

All he heard was static down the line. He shrugged his shoulders and returned the receiver to its cradle. He looked at the phone for what seemed ages. He wondered whether it was Karen trying to contact him and wanting to speak with him again, then realized she had no idea where he was. He shook the thought from his mind and continued watching the movie.

THE ISLAND OF SINGAPORE

Date: November 2010
Ages: 18 / 1,162
Status: Semi-active

'How much!' demanded Shoil, aghast at what she heard.

'Eight thousand and three hundred pounds, ma'am, that's return business class, as requested.'

'So, how much is economy premium then?'

'Sorry, ma'am, but there are no seats available on your preferred dates.'

'Economy?'

'Let's see.'

Shoil heard typing and guessed the woman was entering new details into her computer.

'I can offer you our main cabin for three thousand and five hundred pounds, also return,' she announced finally.

'No. I simply cannot fly economy. OK then. I'll take the business class option.'

'Very good, ma'am. These are excellent seats, and I am sure you will enjoy your flight with us.'

'I'd better,' she warned, giving the woman her credit card details.

The woman put her on pause, and she was left to listen to the British Airways theme.

She suddenly felt nervous, not sure if there was enough credit on the card, which belonged to Toni. But she needn't have worried.

The woman's voice came back on the phone.

'You are all set. I'll send you your flight information and confirmation by email, then you can be on your way.'

Shoil said nothing but was secretly pleased with herself that she took Toni's wallet and cards. He had collected several cards, and most of them were clear of debt, well, that was until she got hold of them, not that Toni was going to worry about that anymore. She would now go on a spending spree and buy some new clothes for the journey. It was hot in Singapore most of the year, so summer clothes were the essential thing. She did not have a lot to pack in any case. Back at the apartment she called the hotel again and made a reservation for herself. She checked her passport, completed the mandatory visa requirements, printing off the form just in case, then ordered some Singapore currency, which she could pick up on Saturday. Although US dollars were accepted just about everywhere in the world, she wanted some local currency to avoid too many questions about where she was from. She grabbed her bag and walked out to go shopping. Time to utilize his cards again. Nobody will notice or care until it was too late.

Unbeknown to her, somebody was monitoring the card's use. A silhouetted figure sat in front of a large computer screen in a dark room, watching line after line of data pass by. Suddenly there was a red line, so the operator paused the screen. Selecting the red line, he clicked it and more details appeared. The operator picked up the phone.

'Sir,' began the operator, 'the missing man's card has just been used to purchase airline tickets to Singapore.'

'Singapore?' said the voice at the other end.

'Roger that,' confirmed the operator.

'Do we have the passenger's name and flight details?'

'Yes, sir.'

'Then send them over to me immediately. We need to speak to this person. See who it is and, if not him, then what they know about our missing man.'

'The name suggests it's a woman, sir. Details are on their way, sir.'

'Thank you.'

The person at the other end of the phone replaced the receiver and looked over at his whiteboard. The faces of Toni, Sally, and Shoil were pinned to the board, along with two boys. The two boys were killed fairly close to the restaurant where the owner and two members of the staff had disappeared, and all in a short space of time. The boys were killed with a very sharp instrument, yet to be identified. The missing man and the young woman both worked at the same restaurant, so he was sure there was an obvious link here. The man's wallet and car keys were missing, so was his car, but his clothes had been found, DNA confirming that. His computer pinged, telling him he had a new message. He clicked the icon, and the information he asked for had arrived. He read it.

'OK, miss,' he said to himself, 'we need to ask you a few questions before you leave.'

He picked up the phone.

'I need the address of a potential suspect. I am sending you her name. I need her home address as soon as possible.'

He heard the acknowledgement at the other end, so replaced the receiver. He tapped the phone with the tip of his pencil.

'What are you running from?' he asked.

He dropped the pencil and picked up the phone again, dialing a number.

'Put me through to Heathrow's airport security,' he demanded.

Shoil was in a good mood. Shopping always put her in a good mood, and she did plenty of shopping today. She even splashed out on two new suitcases, nice ones. They were bright orange, a color she was instinctively attracted to, and which would help identify her luggage when she needed to collect it again. All was set.

***

Saturday arrived and she was excited. She walked into the bank and, sure enough, her currency was ready.

'Going on holiday?' asked the bank clerk.

'Yes.'

'Lucky you. Going anywhere nice?'

'Yes,' she said simply.

The clerk looked at her above her half-rimmed glasses. Obviously not a talkative person, and given the amount of money she was taking, not a woman without means.

The machine finished counting the money, so she popped it into an envelope, then passed Shoil a piece of paper.

'If you would just sign this receipt, you are all set.'

Shoil signed the receipt T. Hardrock and handed the form back.

'Thank you, Ms. Hardrock, and here is your ten thousand Singapore dollars, all in twenty-dollar bills, as requested.

'Thank you,' replied Shoil, taking the large white envelope and dropping it into her purse.

Turning, she walked out of the bank, patting the bag when she got outside. She knew the money would not last long, but hopefully long enough for her to find Tampong and the boy. Besides, if she needed more, then finding another wealthy man in Singapore should not be a problem. It was a small island filled with many rich men after all. All she had to do now was finish packing away her new purchases, then she would be ready for her flight tomorrow. Flying was not her favorite mode of transport, preferring to keep her feet—or paws—firmly on terra firma. Still, needs must, and she must get on this flight and get herself to Singapore, hunt down the bitch, finish her off, and take the boy. If he didn't come willingly, then she would finish him off too.

***

Back in Singapore, Terry was still puzzled over his conversation with Karen. Her turnaround was a complete shock, catching him off guard. At times it was as if he was talking with a different person, or someone not wanting to be near him anymore. His thoughts were disturbed when the bedroom door opened; Tampong had returned from work.

'Hey, you,' she said, 'how was your day?'

'Ho, so, so. And you?'

'Usual day at the office, hey, how did it go with Karen? You were talking with her today, right?'

'Right. Well, that is all over now.'

'So you managed to break it off with her then?'

'No, actually, she dumped me.'

Tampong stopped walking and just stared at him.

'Pardon me?'

'That's right. She dumped me.'

'I don't believe it.'

'Believe it.'

'What brought this on then?'

'Distance, I guess. She just could not deal with it anymore.'

'Anymore! Jesus, you guys have only been apart for a little while.'

'Tell me.'

'OK, well, then I guess that particular problem is solved, right?'

'I guess so. It was just so strange.'

'In what way?'

'She wanted me to tell her where I was, but of course I didn't. Then all of a sudden she dropped this clangor, and said it was over.'

'You are sure you never told her.'

'Positive.'

'Good. Well, she is better off where she is.'

'Yeah. I was all set to finish with her but wasn't prepared for her finishing with me.'

'Does it matter?'

'I am not sure. I should not be sad about the outcome; it is what I wanted, after all. It is just that she didn't seem herself.'

Tampong sat on the edge of his bed.

'In what way?'

'Well, for starters, she looked incredibly tired. I have never seen her like that before.'

'What did she say when you told her how she looked?'

'Nothing. She gave no explanation at all. Instead, she turned it all around and said I looked good, or something like that.'

'Romantically speaking?'

'No. Healthwise speaking.'

'OK, so what else?'

'She seemed distracted. Kept looking past me, at the background or somewhere.'

Tampong instantly became suspicious.

'She was looking at the room?'

'I think so.'

'Exactly where was your laptop when you spoke with her?'

'It was on the corner of the sideboard because I was sitting on the corner of the bed.'

She took his laptop and placed it on the corner.

'Like this?'

He stood up and adjusted it a little.

'More like this.'

She noticed the angle of the screen and looked straight ahead. All she could see was the wall, the picture, and the door to the bathroom. When she looked through the door she saw the bath towel draped next to the sink.

'Was that towel there before you started speaking with her?'

'Er, yeah, I freshened up before I spoke with her. Why?'

'Look.'

He looked toward the bathroom.

'What am I looking at?'

'The bath towel. It has the hotel name on it.'

'And?'

'If she saw it, then she will know what hotel we are staying at.'

'But there must be hundreds of Carlton hotels around the world. Even if she did happen to see it.'

She relaxed a little.

'Perhaps you are right. Maybe she was not looking at anything and could have just been distracted because of your conversation. It is probably just me being paranoid.'

'Most likely.'

'Right. In any case, we will not be here for very long.'

'Why is that?'

'Because I am working here, which means we need to find a home and not a room. You need your own space in any case.'

'That's true. So how do we go about finding a home then?'

'Not a problem, and I am already on it. There is a relocation specialist connected with the office whose purpose is to help relocate people like us. I am meeting her tomorrow to look at a few places.'

'Cool. It will certainly be nice to have a home again and, as you say, a room of my own.'

He also saw this as an opportunity to spend some quality time with Sandi tomorrow while Tampong was out house hunting. He felt sure that this would keep her occupied for most of the day. That just left Sunday to deal with.

'Hmmm,' she replied, not sure they were thinking about the same benefits and not knowing what he was thinking.

Still, she could not begrudge him a place of his own to bring Sandi to. After all, having him close by would be no bad thing. She was looking forward to doing a bit of house hunting. Colleagues at work told her not to bother buying because the property tax was really high in Singapore. There is no state tax apparently—whatever that is—so the state needed to rely on other sources of income. As was pointed out, renting would be more flexible as well, meaning they could move at a moment's notice, which might be a good thing. For now, she needed a shower, a bite to eat, and then relax in front of the TV.

***

'You have not sensed any activity for some time now, right?' asked Tracey.

'Correct,' confirmed Gary.

For the last hour they had been discussing the pros and cons of trying to contact Joanne again, with Tracey almost winning the argument.

'She is safe for now. Even we do not know where she is, so why not leave her where she is?'

'And what if we are wrong? What if the Higher Middle are planning some major offensive against us?'

'Why now?'

'Why not? Don't forget, they need us all out of the way before they can take control of this fragile planet and its inhabitants. We are all that stands in their way.'

'Major offensive!' she snapped, 'there are two of them at most, Gary. Are you even listening to yourself? We outnumber them for the first time since, since I don't know when.'

'Ever,' he informed her.

'Right. Ever. So what makes you think they will try and attack us now, when we have the upper hand?'

'Except we are only two as well,' he reminded her, 'and both of them are stronger than the two of use combined. Don't forget that.'

'But I thought you said the two seemed to hate each other.'

'True, but their mission may force them to put that hatred to one side, especially if it means taking us out.'

'There is still Joanne and Jon.'

'Jon?' He looked confused.

'We don't know what exactly happened to him, do we? Perhaps he is sitting in waiting, waiting for the right moment to show himself again.'

'God, Tracey, how I wish that were true. No, he is gone. I felt him disappear beyond the next realm.'

'You don't know that for sure.'

'Fairly sure. Enough to know we cannot depend on him.'

'Well, I for one will not give him up so easily and have faith that he will come and protect us, should it be necessary.'

Gary looked at her determined face, her stance. He admired her confidence in the group, and he was sure that nothing he said would sway her from that belief. He didn't feel the need to tell her that he did have some faint sensations suggesting that one or more of the Higher Middle was active again. It did feel faint, and he got the impression that whatever they were doing, or wherever they were doing it, they were moving away from them. He still could not shake off this bad feeling, a feeling that something big was going to happen. Where or when he had no idea. He decided he would search for Joanne himself secretly and not tell Tracey. She would only scold him in any case. He had to at least warn her that the others were active, to keep her guard up and trust no one. He knew he had to finish this conversation in such a way that satisfied her.

'I hope you are right, Tracey. I truly hope Jon does show up, if and when we need him.'

She leaned forward and kissed him.

'He will, Gary. He will.'

She got up and headed for the kitchen.

'Fancy a cup of tea?'

'More a glass of red wine,' he answered, feeling the need for a drink.

Tracey glanced at the clock.

'And it's only four pm. OK, I guess it is five o'clock somewhere.'

'Europe, for one,' he answered.

'One what?'

'One region where it is five pm now. They are an hour ahead of us.'

'OK then, so I guess we are drinking for Europe then.'

He smiled, thinking they were drinking for the salvation of mankind. Boy, did he ever need that drink now.

***

Flying day arrived. Shoil was packed, making one last check on everything. Passport, money, reservations, flight tickets, luggage. All was in place. She closed her second case, locked it before picking up the phone and calling for a taxi. Dispatch said it should arrive in twenty minutes, so she had enough time to make a final visit to the loo and check everything was locked away. She was in half a mind to just get rid of the flat, but she had grown fond of it, so decided she would keep it for now and make any final decision when she got back.

It was thirty minutes before she heard the car horn beeping, trying to get her attention. She struggled down the stairs with her two cases. The driver, on seeing her predicament, hopped out of the car and took the cases from her. She nodded her thanks, then opened the back door and slipped into the back seat. The driver closed the boot and dropped into his driver's seat.

'Heathrow Airport, right?'

'Correct,' she confirmed.

'Which terminal, ma'am?'

'British Airways, Terminal Five please.'

'Terminal Five it is,' he confirmed, slipping the car into first gear and pulling away.

It took another forty-five minutes before the car pulled up at the taxi rank outside Terminal Five. The driver had made small talk during the journey, and she was happy to engage in his conversation, as it helped to pass the time. He stopped the car and jumped out to take the cases out of the boot, placing them onto a free caddy. She thanked him, giving him a nice tip. He nodded his thanks.

'Have a great vacation,' he said, moving back to his driver's door.

She waved him away with a friendly gesture.

She walked into the terminal and quickly found the business class check-in. One of the counters was free, so she quickly walked up and placed her passport on the counter.

'Destination?' asked the friendly lady at the check-in counter.

'Singapore,' replied Shoil.

'Thank you . . . Ms. Hardrock.

She punched several keys, then looked up towards Shoil.

'Problem?' Shoil asked.

'No, no, just a seat reassignment. I will just be a minute. How many bags will you be checking?'

'Two,' she answered.

Shoil knew a lie when she heard one but said nothing as there was little she could do in such a busy airport. The lady picked up her desk phone and spoke quietly to someone at the other end. She nodded and placed the phone back down.

'All is in order, Ms. Hardrock. Here is your boarding pass, and you are welcome to use the fast track and business class lounge.'

She pressed a button and the cases rolled along the belt and onto the main track to disappear behind a rubber curtain.

'Thank you,' said a relieved Shoil, pickling up her boarding pass and passport.

She turned and placed her now-empty caddy along with the rest and moved towards the priority lane in security. There were two gentlemen ahead of her, and one of them was already moving towards the customs officer.

'Ms. Hardrock?' said a voice from behind her.

'Yes,' she confirmed, turning to see another two men standing behind her.

'Would you mind coming with us please?'

'I am about to board my plane,' she complained.

'There is plenty of time for that, ma'am, but you need to come with us.'

He flashed an airport security badge at her.

'Very well,' she said.

The man turned and led her to the elevator, with the other man stepping in behind her, no doubt to block any attempt for her to run.

They stepped into the elevator and the doors closed.

'Can you tell me what this is about?' she asked.

'Just need to ask you a few questions, ma'am,' the officer replied, not turning around.

'About?' she asked again.

He did not reply. The elevator stopped and the doors opened. The man gestured her to turn right, which she did. The other man stepped in front of her and walked quickly up to a glass door, which he opened for her. She walked inside to find another man sitting behind a desk. In front of him was an open folder.

'Ms. Hardrock?' he asked.

'Yes,' she said simply.

'Take a seat, please.'

She did so, noticing that the two men followed her inside and stood behind her. One closed the door.

The man sitting opposite glanced down at the folder, flicked over a few pages, then looked back up towards her.

'Do you know a Toni Blackwell?' he asked.

She blinked twice, which was noticed by the officer. She gave a nervous cough.

'Yes,' she said simply, knowing it was pointless to lie.

They had obviously found something on her.

'Really?' he answered, 'how so?'

'He owns a restaurant where my friend works.'

'Yes, you are right. He did.'

'Did?'

'Yes, Ms. Hardrock. Did. When was the last time you saw him?

'Err, well, I guess that must have been a week or ten days ago.'

'Right about the time he went missing.'

'He's missing!' she replied, trying to sound shocked.

'Yes, Ms. Hardrock, missing. He never returned home and has never been seen again.'

'What has this got to do with me?'

'That's what we are here to find out.'

She said nothing. She needed to find out what they knew or didn't know.

'How well did you know Mr. Blackwell?'

'Not well,' she said.

He leaned forward, placing his hands on the folder.

'Then can you explain how come you have been using his credit card?'

'Ho, that,' she said.

'Yes, that. You paid for your flight with his credit card and then went on a bit of a shopping spree as well.'

'OK, you have me cornered.'

'We have you more than cornered, ma'am. So, again, what are you doing with his credit card?'

'He gave it to me.'

She saw his eyes light up in surprise.

'He gave you his credit card?'

'Yes.'

'Now why would he do that?'

'Because we are lovers.'

He almost choked at her reply.

'You are lovers. Are you telling me you had a physical relationship with Mr. Blackwell?'

'Yes.'

'And he simply gave you his card?'

'Yes, as a gift.'

'A gift?'

'Yes. He told me to go and treat myself.'

'I would say a flight to Singapore in business class is quite a treat.'

'What can I say? I am very good in bed, and he was very grateful.'

She heard one of the men cough in embarrassment. She could sense him staring at her. No doubt wishing he were sharing her bed.

'Are you telling me you prostituted yourself?'

She tried her best to look shocked.

'Certainly not. I am a very passionate woman, one with lots of sexual needs. He had needs too, and I more than satisfied him. Do you not think I am attractive?'

He saw him flinch a little behind his desk, knowing she had hit a raw nerve.

'So, do you know where Mr. Blackwell is now?'

'I have no idea. He told me he had some business to attend to, that I should make myself pretty and go on a vacation, and that he would contact me afterwards when I returned.'

'And you expect us to believe that?'

'I don't really care what you believe.'

'OK, Ms. Hardrock, if that is your real name. We will be holding you here until we have investigated your story further.'

'On what grounds?'

'Fraud and attempted theft.'

'What!'

'You heard me, Ms. Now, I must ask you to wait here while I make a few calls.'

'I am afraid I cannot allow that,' she said, calmly placing both feet firmly on the ground.

'Excuse me?' questioned the officer, 'but you are in no position to make demands.'

'Oh, but I can, mister, I can.'

As he started to stand up, Shoil's eyes turned orange while she raised her hand slightly, firing a thin blade from her nail at the officer's exposed neck. She watched in morbid fascination as the blade disappeared into his neck. The officer gasped in shock, raising both his hands to his neck. His sudden movement caused the other two officers to look in his direction, which was their mistake.

Shoil did a backwards flip out of her chair to land in between the two officers. She lashed out with both hands, landing squarely on their chest, penetrating their hearts. Both men crumbled to the floor, dead.

The other officer was still choking on his own blood and finally collapsed onto the desk, then slowly slid off the table to crash onto the floor. Shoil walked over to his side, kneeled down, checked he still had a pulse and, satisfied, pulled his hair to lift his head up. She forcibly grabbed his chin and roughly pulled his mouth open. Her long snake-like tongue whipped out of her mouth and down the throat of the dying officer. His body immediately started to shake violently. She held him in place, absorbing him quickly, allowing his clothes to flop onto the floor.

'Well, boys,' she said, wiping her mouth with the back of her hand, 'you have been busy, haven't you?'

She flicked through the papers in the folder.

'You have been very busy indeed.'

Having absorbed the security officer, she now knew all the security access codes for the airport. She carefully opened the door and peered outside. Nobody was around, so she dragged the two dead officers along the corridor and dumped them inside a small cupboard room. She returned to the interrogation room, picked up the officer's clothes and dumped them on top of the two dead officers. She closed the closet door, breaking off the lock. Making one final return, she picked up the folder, placed it in her bag, then took one last look around before closing and locking the door. She straightened her skirt, then walked calmly back down the corridor, punching in the access code when she reached the door at the end of the corridor. She headed directly to the business lounge, having bypassed security and immigration without further interruption.

She needed a drink.

An hour and a half later, Shoil was trying to get comfortable in her seat. Business class seats were nice and wide, but her money belt strapped around her waist was digging into her ribs. She was about to pull her top up and adjust it a little when she noticed the guy seating in the chair opposite was leering at her. So, she would have to wait until she could use the toilet.

'Howdie, missy,' he said in a strong American accent.

She just nodded.

'So, do you go all the way?'

She felt physically sick. Do men have any other lines than these obvious ones, which was meant to come across as a mixture of funny and suggestive? She went to press the button to raise the privacy screen when a hand delicately stopped her.

'Sorry, ma'am,' the air stewardess said, 'but the privacy screen needs to stay down until we are in the air and the captain has switched off the seat belt sign.'

She then leaned back up and looked across to the American.

'Can I get you a drink before we take off, sir?'

'Surely can, little lady. I'll have a double bourbon on the rocks.'

'Sorry, sir, but the bar does not open until we are in the air . . . I can offer you water, orange juice, or champagne.'

'OK, little lady, then make it two glasses of the bubbly stuff and be quick about it. It is going to be a long flight.'

'You got that right,' she said quietly, although Shoil heard her, 'and for you, ma'am?'

'Orange juice will be fine, thanks.'

'Jesus,' he said, wiggly in this seat, 'these seats are so small there is no room to fart even.'

Shoil shook her head, placed on her headphones, and pretended to watch TV.

The air stewardess returned with their drinks, placing Shoil's orange juice on her tray, then reaching over and presenting the

American's two glasses. He took them without so much as an acknowledgement.

'Would sir care for a newspaper?'

'Do you have the *Tribunal*?'

'No, sorry, sir, just English papers.'

He waved his hand dismissively towards her.

'Don't want any of that English crap.'

She ignored his comment.

'Ma'am?'

Shoil took off her headphones.

'*Daily Mail*, please.'

She gave her a copy and Shoil nodded her thanks. The American had heard her talking for the first time.

'You an Aussie girl then?'

She just nodded again.

'So, how are things down under then?' he said suggestively again.

'I would not know,' she said simply, replacing the headphones.

'So you do go all the way,' then continued, 'to Australia I mean,' he clarified.

Again, she pretended not to hear him and kept her eyes fixed towards the screen. At least now she knew that this flight continued to her homeland after stopping at Singapore. Useful information to know for a later date.

He shrugged his shoulders in resignation, took one last look at her, then drank his champagne while peering out of the window, much to her relief. Just then the captain's voice could be heard through her headphones.

'Ladies and gentlemen, this is your captain speaking. Looks like they are just about to close the cargo doors and we will then be all set to go. We have a full flight today, so I would like to thank you all for boarding on time. We are just waiting for air traffic control to give us the green light to roll back. Heathrow is one of the busiest airports in the world, and it is not uncommon to have delays, but I am assured that we will depart on time, maybe even a few minutes early. I will let you know as soon as we have more information.'

'Let's get this tin can in the air,' barked the American.

As if responding to his request, the captain was back.

'Looks like the gods are with us today. We have just been given the OK to roll back. Cabin crew doors to automatic and cross-check.'

Shoil felt the slight jerk of the aircraft as it was pushed back from the gate. The aircraft was turned forty-five degrees before it stopped. She could see one of the ground crew through the aircraft's window. He crossed his orange sticks to tell the captain all was good and gave the thumbs-up when the captain must have acknowledged his sign. The engines started, and after a few minutes the aircraft started to roll forward. The American turned to see Shoil looking his way and assumed she was looking at him. She certainly was pleasant on the eye, even for an Aussie. He had heard they were as butch as the men and difficult to tell apart. This one was definitely all woman though. No mistake there.

'So, where are you bound for, little lady?'

She decided to play with him for a bit. If nothing else, it would help pass the time.

'Singapore,' she answered.

'Singapore you say. Well I'll be damned. That's where I live. Got myself a big spread with over five hundred head of cows and about the same in chickens. I breed them for restaurants and stores on the island. I had you pegged as going all the way to Sydney in this tin can. Guess I was wrong on that one.'

'Guess you were,' she agreed

She had no idea what he was talking about, except that he must have a lot of land to keep so many animals, and she read somewhere that land in Singapore was not cheap, given that there was not much of it. So it sounded as though he had money, but clearly not that much, as otherwise he would surely be flying first class, particularly someone as arrogant as he was.

As if reading her mind, he then leaned a little closer to the privacy screen and lowered his voice.

'Normally I would travel first class on these here little tin cans, but this was a last-minute change and, sadly for me, all the seats were taken—or at least that is what those bitches at the

Brit check-in told me. Bunch of crap if you ask me. So visiting family, are you?'

'No, just friends,' she lied.

'No partner or anything like that?'

'Nope.'

'We'll, I'll be,' he said, more to himself than her.

He was thinking he had a shot with this one.

She just lifted her chin up as if to say 'hey ho' when she felt herself being pushed into her seat as the plane gathered pace along the runway, finally getting up enough speed to lift off the ground. The aircraft shuddered briefly as the wheels became free of the runway. They were on their way, and arrivals could not come soon enough for her.

'At bloody last,' announced the man, also settling down in his seat, 'as soon as this bucket gets beyond the clouds, then perhaps the bloody cabin crew will start serving decent drinks, although I doubt they even know what a decent drink is, judging by the crap in those so-called champagne glasses.'

She just raised her eyebrows, placed the earphones back over her head and began watching her chosen movie.

***

'Miss Armitage?' asked a woman standing above Tampong in the hotel lobby.

'Yes,' confirmed Tampong.

'Great. I am Mary-Louis from relocation,' the woman explained.

'Right, great, pleased to meet you.'

'Are you ready to go?' asked Mary-Louis.

'Ready,' she confirmed, switching off her laptop computer and grabbing her coat.

'The drive is not far away,' Mary-Louis informed, 'and you can call me ML. Mary-Louis is quite a mouthful.'

'OK, ML it is.'

'We will be heading for a small, gated estate just off Orchard Street. This place is very conveniently located, close to the highway, shopping malls, banks, library, and schools.'

'Sounds perfect,' said Tampong.

It did indeed sound like a very good location to start life in.

They drove down the highway for ten minutes, ML pointing out a few things on the way and giving her some more information about Singapore. Of most interest to Tampong was the fact it was a growing city with lots of opportunities. It had become super-rich after the English gave Hong Kong back to the Chinese, with most of the large western banks and financial institutes opting to relocate to Singapore.

They turned off one highway and onto another. While she had no idea where she was, she knew it would only be a matter of time before she found her way around, and, besides, she had her trusty GPS once she got herself some wheels. ML turned right and parked the car.

'Here we are,' ML said needlessly.

Tampong doubted she stopped here for milk. Still, she kept quiet. The front of the building looked nice enough. They walked into the main building, turning right towards a desk manned by a thin man.

'Welcome,' he said, 'my name is Winston, how may I be of assistance?'

His wrists were slightly limp, suggesting to Tampong that he was probably gay, a point in his favor as he was unlikely to try to make a pass at her.

'Hi,' began ML, 'I'm Mary-Louis, we spoke on the phone about viewing a couple of units.'

'Absolutely. I have them all ready for you. Follow me, please, we will take the buggy. It is just parked out front.'

They walked back outside, and Winston slipped into the driving seat of the buggy. The two girls sat in the back seats. He drove towards the back gates, pressing a hidden remote in his hand and continued driving as the gates slid open.

'We have one available unit at the back of the estate and one on the lake. They are identical in format,' he informed them as he parked up the buggy in the driveway.

'This particular unit has an integrated garage.'

He opened the door, and they climbed the stairs to enter the lounge. There was a small kitchen in one corner, an open fireplace, and an L-shaped room housing the dining room and lounge, which led to a small balcony. Upstairs were two good-sized bedrooms and a cupboard for the washing machine. Both bedrooms had their own bathroom—another plus, thought Tampong. He then took them to the second unit, which, as he said, was the same as the previous one, except this had a separate garage, but the balcony had a wonderful view of the lake. He drove them back to the main building and they sat in the two chairs at his desk, while he walked around and sat in his chair opposite them.

'So then, any questions?'

'Just one,' began Tampong, 'when are they available?'

'Both are available immediately.'

'Wonderful. Then I would like to take the lakeside unit, please. Do they come furnished or unfurnished?'

'Either,' said Winston, 'although if you prefer them unfurnished, then it will take a couple of days to have the furniture removed. If you are ready to take the lakeside view unit as it is, then I just need a few forms to be completed and we can reserve the unit for you. When were you thinking of arriving?'

'As soon as possible. We are currently staying in a hotel, and the sooner we move out of there the better. Would Monday work?'

'Monday, why yes. The lakeside unit has just been cleaned. I will of course need a deposit as security and a month's rental upfront.'

'No problem,' she answered, digging out her credit card and passing it to Winston.

He passed her a few forms for her to complete, while ML left them to it and made herself a cup of coffee from the machine. Forty minutes later, Tampong rose from her chair and shook hands with Winston.

'So, we will see you on Monday then,' he said.

'Absolutely,' confirmed Tampong, pleased with her find. She was about to leave when a thought crossed her mind.

'Would it be possible to visit the unit again tomorrow? I would like to show my nephew,' she asked.

'Of course,' replied Winston, 'the office is closed on Sunday, but here are two sets of keys to your unit and two gate remotes. The left button operates the left gate, and the right button the right gate,' he explained.

'Got it,' replied Tampong, slipping them into her bag before thanking Winston again and heading out of the door with ML.

ML drove her back to the hotel, where she thanked ML for her help. She could not wait to tell Terry the good news, but then remembered him saying that he would be spending the day with Sandi in their room, so opted to do a bit of shopping instead.

By early evening she was all shopped out and decided to return to the hotel, where she found Terry lying on his bed, watching TV.

'Hey there,' he said when she walked in.

'Hi, how was your day?'

'Ho, quite good really. Sandi came over as planned, and we just chilled here for a bit. Then we went for a walk before she left to return home. I have been watching TV since.'

Tampong could not help but notice the unmade bed and two wet bath towels draped across the tub but decided to let that go as she was in such a good mood.

'So, aren't you going to ask how my day was then?'

'OK, so how was your day?'

'Brilliant,' she said excitedly, 'I have found us a new home.'

He sat bolt upright, now keenly interested.

'Really? Tell me more.'

'It's not far from here, overlooking a lake, close to shops, library, banks and things, AND, you don't need a vehicle to get to any of these places either, which is most unusual for Singapore.'

'Sounds perfect. Do I have my own room?'

'You do.'

'Awesome. So when do we move in?'

'That's the best part. Monday.'

'Monday! No kidding?'

'No kidding.'

'Awesome.'

'I think someone has been spending too much time with Singaporeans.'

'What makes you say that?'

'Awesome!'

'Really! Did I say that?'

'And not only once.'

'Wow. I didn't even realize. Sorry. Anyhow, I'll start packing my things away as I am assuming we check out of here Monday morning, correct?'

'Right. I have already informed reception that we will check out Monday. We have to do some more household shopping though, but it does have a sofa, beds, table, and kitchen appliances.'

'So what else do we need?'

'Things like some more cutlery, dishes, bed linen, towels, food, and other basics like that.'

'Ho, OK.'

'And best yet, the company has given me a generous allowance to help purchase these things.'

'Awe . . .' he began to say, but corrected himself, 'fantastic.'

'Better still, you can visit our new home tomorrow and see for yourself.'

'Cannot wait,' he answered enthusiastically.

He could not wait to see Sandi and tell her the news. It was also another huge step towards staying here for the long haul. Tampong would soon be getting a work permit and had made arrangements for him to receive one too, telling human resources he was her son and not her nephew. This meant he could soon start looking for a job himself and be that little bit more independent. He never imagined in his wildest dreams that he would warm to Singapore so quickly. A lot of that was down to Sandi, but even putting her to one side, he felt positive vibes about this place. He got up and rushed to the wardrobes, where he pulled his suitcases out, opened his drawer, and started transferring his clothes into his case.

Tampong smiled as she watched him. He seemed happy, which made her happy. She pulled her suitcases out and started packing too. Tomorrow was going to be a big day, and they were both looking forward to it.

***

'Ladies and gentlemen,' said the captain, 'we are starting our descent into Singapore airport and expect to be on the ground in approximately forty-five minutes. The restrooms will be available for the next twenty minutes. I will let you know if anything should change. In the meantime, I will leave you in the excellent care of our wonderful cabin crew.'

'About time too,' said the American, who pressed the call button then stretched out his arms.

The cabin stewardess came quickly.

'Yes, sir?'

'I'll have a double bourbon on the rocks before we land.'

'The bar is about to close,' she announced.

'You said "about", so it has not closed yet, has it, so be quick about it.'

'Of course, sir.'

She turned and headed for the galley.

'Can tell this is not American Airlines,' he muttered to himself but loudly, 'don't even have ice cream for dessert. What kind of cheap airline is this?'

Before Shoil could answer, the stewardess returned with his bourbon, which he grabbed in an unfriendly manner. Shoil then noticed the toilet was free, so unclipped her seat belt and got up and started walking behind the stewardess.

'I hope he chokes on that drink,' she said quietly to the stewardess.

'I don't,' she whispered back, 'I want him to drink it all . . . because we all spat in his drink.'

Shoil had to suppress a giggle. She reached the toilet just ahead of a man, pushing the door open and stepping inside, locking the door behind her.

After she freshened up, she unlocked the door to find the man still waiting there, looking a bit more desperate than he did before. When she returned to her seat, the American had already finished his drink, looking in disdain at his empty glass. He perked up a little when he saw Shoil return to her seat. She was now wearing a low-cut blouse, her white bra visible underneath. Her short skirt showed off her long legs. He was smitten.

'Hey there, little lady. Not long before we hit good old Singapore.'

She gave him an uninterested smile as she sat back down.

'You need a ride?' he asked.

His remarks forced her to turn her head towards him.

'Pardon me?'

He changed his language and tone a little.

'I mean, little lady, can I give you a lift to wherever you are going? I have a car waiting for me.'

Shoil thought quickly. This man might actually be useful after all.

'Well, I am staying at the Carlton Hotel in Singapore.'

'Know it well. Held many business dinner engagements there just last month. So let me drop you off there.'

'That's very kind of you.'

'My pleasure, little lady. Absolutely my pleasure.'

The seat belt sign was then illuminated, and the PA system burst into life again.

'Ladies and gentlemen, the captain has now switched on the seat belt sign as we will soon be landing in Singapore airport. Please now return your seats to the upright position. For our guests in first and business class, please make sure that the area around your seat is completely free. Please note that the toilets are no longer available.'

Shoil quickly checked around her seat. It was all tidy, so she settled down for landing. The crew came through the cabin to make a final check. When she reached Shoil's row, she stopped and leaned across to the American.

'Can you please put your seat upright, sir, for landing?'

'Does that really matter?'

'It's a safety requirement, sir.'

'Ho really,' he said reluctantly, sitting up and pressing his seat button.

Shoil rolled her eyes at the stewardess.

'Thank you, sir,' she said, moving on down the aisle.

'Think their little Hitlers,' he said when the stewardess passed.

Shoil ignored his sick humor.

The plane landed smoothly, although it took ages before it finally parked at the gate.

'Ladies and gentlemen, welcome to Singapore, where the local time is three forty-five and it is a balmy seventy-eight degrees. They are just moving the tunnel towards the plane, and you will soon be able to disembark. Thank you for flying British Airways, and we look forward to welcoming you back on another flight real soon.'

'Fat chance,' spat the American, who had already gotten out of his seat and opened the overhead bin, almost allowing his bag to drop as his eyes were pinned to Shoil's legs.

It didn't help things when she unfolded her legs, then leaned forward to get up, giving him a perfect view down her cleavage. Shoil never noticed as she got up but had to take a couple of steps backwards as he was too close to her, almost breathing down her neck, heavily. She went to get her bag, but he was too quick and grabbed it for her, handing it to her. She nodded her thanks, taking her bag. She turned around and headed for the exit and stood at the back of the short queue. He moved directly behind her, again too close for comfort. He leaned closer to her ear.

'I'll be going through the priority entry route, so I'll probably be through a lot faster than you are, so I'll wait for you after immigration and take you to the garage where my car is waiting. OK?'

'OK,' she replied simply, not bothering to turn around.

He slapped her gently on the bottom, making her jump a little. She bit her tongue, forcing herself not to retaliate, but decided he would pay for that later. The American misconstrued her silence as someone who enjoyed the little tap on her butt.

Think I am in here, he thought.

The aircraft's door finally opened, so the passengers started to file out quickly. Shoil followed the rest until she reached the large customs hall. She saw the sign for foreigners, so speeded up. Business class had its advantages, not least was being one of the first off the plane. There were only four people in front of her. She saw the fat American walk to the priority entry lane, where nobody else was. He walked up to a machine, tapped a few keys, placed his passport down, and then he was gone. It was her turn to use the machine. She was requested to place her passport down, then to give her fingerprints. She answered a few questions before a white ticket was printed out. She took it and placed it in her passport along with her immigration card. A customs officer waved her forward, so she gave him her passport.

'Business or pleasure?' he asked.

'Pleasure.'

'How long do you plan to stay in Singapore?'

'Three weeks.'

He stamped her passport, initialed it, then handed it back.

'Welcome to Singapore, Ms. Hardrock. Next.'

She took her passport and headed for the luggage belts. The screen informed her that the baggage for her flight was on belt twenty-four. She headed down the escalator and waited. An alarm sounded, a yellow light started flashing, and the belt started moving. She quickly learned another benefit of business class travel when her bags were ones of the first to arrive. She grabbed her bags, placed them on the caddy, and headed for the exit. There was another queue, but it moved along nicely, and she was soon beckoned forward by an immigration officer. She handed him her passport and card. He professionally scanned her card before handing back her passport and waving her away.

In the arrival hall, the American was eagerly waiting for her.

'Little lady,' he called out, getting her attention.

She saw him waving his hand in the air. She nodded and walked toward him.

'So, you were not that far behind me then. Thank the lord for that. Let's get to the garage. Follow me.'

She said nothing, but followed him out of the terminal, across the road and into the parking garage. The Singaporean heat and humidity hit her as soon as she walked out of the terminal. There was no getting away from where she was. Still following him, he led her to the VIP car park, where a large black Lexus's boot popped open, indicating they had arrived at his vehicle. The driver was dressed in a black suit, white shirt, black tie, and black hat. He saw them approaching, so got out and walked around to the back.

'Good to have you back home, sir,' he said, taking the American's luggage and lifting it into the car.

'Good to be back on terra firma, Bob. We are talking this little lady with us.'

The driver nodded and took her bags and popped those into the boot as well. He then smartly walked around to the passenger door and opened it for her. She nodded her thanks and slid inside to find the interior nice and cool.

The American sank himself into the seat next to her, again leering at her long legs in an all too obvious fashion. She was now regretting her decision to wear a short skirt, but the heat of this country told her this was a must, and she could not imagine walking around in jeans.

'Hey, little lady,' he began enthusiastically, 'how about I take you back to my place for a little welcome to the Island of Singapore drink and a little o' Texan hospitality. That's where I am from, if you hadn't guessed already.'

Again, she had to think quickly. It might be interesting to see just how much he was worth and, besides, she was in no rush to get anywhere at the moment.

'Why not?' she replied, 'and I thought you must be from the Southern States.'

He smiled and patted her leg. She was tempted to rip his arm out from its socket, but just about controlled her emotions . . . again.

'Home, Bob, as quickly as you can,' he instructed the driver.

'Roger that, sir,' replied Bob, 'there is cool water in the middle if you need it.'

'Water!' said the American almost in disgust.

'For your whiskey, sir,' the driver clarified.

'That's better,' replied the American, opening the middle, pulling out the whiskey bottle and pouring himself a large measure.

He offered the bottle to Shoil, but she politely refused.

'Water will be fine,' she clarified.

'Your funeral,' he said, adding a splash of water to his drink, then finishing the glass off in one session.

Shoil just rolled her eyes into the air and looked out of the window. He poured himself another large measure, making her hope he would be asleep soon. Those thoughts were dashed as she felt his hand rest on her leg again, only this time it stayed there. She looked down at his hand, which felt warm and sticky.

'So which part of Aussie are you from then, little lady?'

'Sydney,' she replied.

'Been there. Nice location, but the locals are too much like the bloody Brits for my liking.'

She said nothing, still looking at his hand as it moved up her leg a little. She bit her lip. She turned towards him to see him leering at her. His intentions were so obvious it could have been plastered right across his forehead in bold letters. Still, she would let him have his little bit of fun, thinking he had scored with her. He would feel her real wrath once they were alone.

'You know,' she began, 'I don't even know your name.'

'Lucas,' he answered, 'Lucas Colman Senior, but you can call me Luc.'

His fingers edged a little further up her leg and were now level with the bottom of her skirt.

Out of the corner of her eye she saw the driver glance into his rear-view mirror, suggesting the name was a lie. Not that it mattered to her.

'OK, Luc, so how far before we reach your home?'

'Ho not far now. You in a rush for something?'

'No. I would just like to freshen up a bit, have a shower, change my clothing, if that is possible.'

'Of course. I like my women smelling nice.'

The tips of his fingers disappeared under her skirt. Because she did not resist she knew she was inviting him further up her leg, and he didn't hesitate to accept the invitation. She felt his fingers touch the bottom of her knickers and start to push underneath and upwards.

'Soon be home now, sir,' announced the driver.

The driver's words stopped his hand, much to her relief. Luc leaned across his seat to whisper in her ear.

'We'll continue this later.'

His fingers gave one final sweep across the front of her crotch, stroking her pubic hair before pulling his hand back out.

The car pulled into a long driveway, passing through double metal gates that opened as the car approached. It stopped under a covered entranceway. The driver got out and walked around to Shoil's door, opening it. She stepped out. Luc got out himself and shoved the door shut with his butt.

'Will you be needing me anymore this evening, sir?' he asked.

'Yes, you'll need to drive the little lady to her hotel when we have finished.'

She saw the driver's shoulders slump in disappointment.

'Of course, sir,' he replied professionally.

His eyes turned to Shoil and seemed to say, '*please be quick with him.*'

'I'll leave her cases in the boot then, sir,' he replied instead.

Luc ignored the driver, opened the door with an electronic key and waved her inside. She stepped into a large hallway. Opposite were two circular stairways, with several doors upstairs. Luc closed the door behind him, waving the key again to lock it. He saw her watching.

'For our privacy,' he clarified.

'Right,' she said, unconvinced, 'bathroom?'

'Upstairs. Use the left stairwell, and it's the first door on the left. I'll fix us a drink and will be waiting for you in the lounge.'

He pointed out the lounge with his hand.

'Thanks,' she said, walking up the stairs, feeling his eyes watching her.

At the top, she turned left and went through the door suggested by Luc. He was right, and she entered a very large bathroom. In the center was a circular tub. To its left was a double shower and it looked inviting. She closed and locked the door, ran the shower water, and started to undress. She stepped into the shower and used the body gel to wash herself. There was some shampoo as well, so she used that and rubbed it into her hair. She suddenly stopped when she had a strange sensation, like she was being watched. She glanced at the door, which was still closed, so she looked carefully around the room but saw no one. Still, she could not shake this uneasy feeling away. She washed the shampoo out of her hair and replaced the showerhead when something glinted from just above its head. She looked closer and noticed a small black dot in the middle of the showerhead. No doubt this was a camera, and the pervert was most likely watching her. She kept the showerhead in its rack, but deliberately pointed it slightly upwards while she finished washing the gel off her body. Turning the water off, she stepped out of the shower and dried herself. She found some body lotion on the shelf, so used some of that, which felt good and refreshing on her skin.

Having got dressed, she took a deep breath, unlocked the door, and walked back downstairs and into the lounge. Luc entered the room from a door opposite, walked over to his bar and picked up two champagne glasses, one of which he handed to her. She took it and they clinked glasses. He downed his in one shot, walked over to the bar and refreshed his glass. He walked back over to her, putting his hand around her waist.

'So, you are nice and clean for me now then?'

'Yep,' she answered simply, placing her glass on the coffee table, 'although I was unable to change my clothing as my cases are still in your car.'

'I think clothes are overrated and prefer not to have them on my ladies. They just hide the treasures that await me.'

'Ho, I certainly have treasures for you,' she replied.

'Awesome,' he said as his other hand went to her breast, squeezing her firmly.

'Enjoying that?' she asked.

'Not really, too many clothes for my liking, but we can soon sort that one out.'

'Haven't you already seen me naked?' she said calmly.

His eyes shot towards her face in shock.

'Er, what do you mean?'

'You were watching me take a shower, weren't you?'

'I don't know what you mean. You locked your door, so how could I possibly see you?'

'If you were still down here, then how did you know I locked the door?'

'I . . . er . . . I. . . must have heard.'

He took his arm away from her waist and released her breast as he nervously finished his drink.

'Or you saw me,' she countered.

'Saw you!'

'Yes, *saw me.* You have a camera in the shower, don't you?'

'Don't be ridiculous. You are just being paranoid. Must be the long flight. Here, let me fix you another drink.'

He went to grab her glass, but she held firmly onto it. Her strength surprised him, and he looked up at her face.

'You want to fuck me, don't you?' she said matter-of-factly.

'Well, yes, that is the general idea,' he confessed, placing his hand back around her waist. 'Let's forget this stupid shower thing and just enjoy each other's company. OK?'

'OK,' she confirmed, 'close your eyes and open your mouth then.'

'What?'

Her hand moved to his crouch and was not surprised to feel him aroused. Her movement convinced him that she intended to start caressing him, so he closed his eyes and opened his mouth.

Her eyes turned orange as her tongue changed into a long, thin snake, which shot from her mouth into his open, inviting mouth and straight down this throat. He gagged as his eyes popped open in alarm. His whole body started shaking as his eyes rolled up into his head. She held him in place as she watched his skin start to go dry, turn grey and then orange before it started to crack and splinter. She felt his aura enter her body and continued to hold him until his body began to shrink and dissolve. The gases from his evaporating body moving into her mouth. Eventually her tongue became free, so she pulled it back into her mouth and licked her lips. When she opened her eyes, all that was left of Luc was his pile of clothing. She instantly knew his real name and that he had three cameras in the bathroom and had been watching her get undressed, showered, and dressed again, switching from one hidden camera in the mirror to another hidden in the light fitting on the ceiling.

'You dirty old git,' she said to the clothing.

Clearly he had had several young women in this house, and all were encouraged to use the same bathroom, where he filmed them, including her. She turned and walked to the opposite door, pressed a hidden switch on the bust of a Roman woman and entered his secret room. On the shelves were stacks of video cassettes. There were three TVs in the room, and Shoil now knew that one was for the bedroom and the other was for the toilet. So he was a sick fucker too. She saw the red blinking light on the video recorder, so rewound it a little before pressing play. She watched herself showering, stepping out of the shower, and drying herself. He had zoomed in on her breasts, then down to her crotch. She pressed stop, ejected the cassette, and threw it into the bin by the seat. She then collected all the other cassettes and threw those into the bin as well. Using her fingers, she fired a bolt of fire into the bin, setting the cassettes alight.

She walked out of the room and back into the lounge. Walking up to the large picture over the fireplace, she clicked a secret button on the bottom right of the picture frame and heard a releasing click as the frame swung open to reveal a large safe. She moved the dial clockwise to 21 then anti-clockwise to 17, then back clockwise to 27. There was another click, so she turned the handle and opened the safe. As she expected, it was full of cash. She moved to his desk and opened the bottom drawer, taking out the briefcase she knew would be there. She filled it with the cash, then closed the safe and returned the picture frame to its original position. She placed the briefcase on the desk and opened the top drawer this time, pulling out a wallet and placing that in the briefcase as well. At least he told the truth about being well-off. He was quite rich, and she was impressed by the size of his bank accounts. She shuddered at his memories, which were mainly of sex with young girls, some of whom were below the legal age, the ones he preferred. He only picked her because there were no younger ones on the plane. He had paid several local prostitutes, who came regularly. It was easy money for them as he didn't last very long.

'Weak bastard,' she said aloud, then remembered the driver was still waiting.

She picked up the bag and started to walk towards the door, stopping only to stoop down and collect the electronic key, which he had placed in his left trouser pocket.

Outside the driver was indeed still waiting, looking relieved when he saw her. He quickly got out of the car and moved to the side door, which he opened for her.

'Ready to go, miss?'

'Ready to go. Carlton Hotel, please.'

'Carlton it is, ma'am.'

He closed her door, walked around to the driver's side, got inside, and started to drive out of the estate. He looked at her in his rearview mirror.

'Pleasant evening, miss?' he asked.

'Very pleasant,' she said, 'and he gave me a present too.'

She waved the briefcase up in the air. The driver would not be surprised as he gave all his conquests a present. Hush money.

The driver just nodded and resumed his concentration on the road.

They arrived at the hotel, where he parked the car and, as usual, got out and opened her door. He then walked around to the boot and pulled her two cases out, placing them on the pavement, where a hotel porter immediately picked them up and placed them on the hotel trolley.

'Thank you, Bob,' she said to the driver.

As she started to walk towards the hotel's rotating doors, she stopped and turned back towards the driver, who was just getting back into his car. She just had a brain wave. She walked up to his window, which he wound down when he saw her returning to the car.

'Ma'am?' he asked, thinking that maybe she had forgotten something.

'Before I forget, I have a message from Robert,' she said, using his real name.

She could see this registered with him.

'He said that you can have that four-week vacation you have been nagging him for. Apparently he has to go into town for a little while on business, so will not be needing your services.'

She dug into her briefcase and grabbed a bundle of notes.

'And he told me to give you this, some holiday money.'

She dropped the dollar bills onto his lap.

'He said I could have my vacation?'

'He did. He said you might appreciate it coming from me rather than from him directly. It really wasn't his sort of thing.'

Again, she knew from his memories that he hated granting such holidays, thinking them a waste of time and money, and knew that the driver was aware of this weakness too.

'And immediately?'

'Immediately. You can keep the car as well as he has sorted out other transport arrangements.'

It was not uncommon for him to do this either, usually waiting until the last second to tell him.

'Great, well, thank you for this delightful message, ma'am. I wish you a pleasant evening.'

'You too, Bob, and happy holidays.'

He waved her goodbye and drove off. She watched him go, thinking that perhaps she should have killed him too, particularly as he had seen her and could easily recognize her. Still, she had had her fill of killing for one day and doubted that he could really pick her out from a crowd, given the number of women he had driven to that house. Besides, he was a genuinely nice guy, so why end his life for no reason? She simply patted her bag again and entered the hotel.

'Good evening, ma'am,' said the pleasant receptionist, 'welcome to the Carlton Hotel. Are you checking in?'

'Yes.'

'Passport and credit card, please.'

She hesitated a second before deciding on her next action. She nodded to herself and passed the woman her passport. She then dug into her briefcase and retrieved Robert's wallet, pulling out his gold credit card. She placed that on the desk and waited.

The receptionist went quickly about her business, tapping a few keys and filling in a few pieces of paper, one of which she handed across to Shoil.

'Please initial here, here, and here.'

She indicated the places with her finger.

'And sign here, please.'

Shoil did as requested.

'And you will be using this card?' she said, pointing to her credit card.

'Yes,' confirmed Shoil, 'I am using my husband's account.'

'Of course,' she said, thinking nothing of it.

It was not uncommon for young women to use a gentleman's card in a hotel like this.

She swiped the card, entered the amount, and waited. The machine blipped, so she turned it around for Shoil to enter the pin, which she did. He used the same first four numbers as his safe. So predictable.

The machine blipped again, so the receptionist turned the machine back, ripped off the paper and pressed a button on the machine to eject another piece of paper, which she stapled onto the receipt on the hotel form and placed it in her drawer. The other receipt she placed on top of the key card and handed both to Shoil.

'Your room is 1212, and the elevators are to your left. Do you have any luggage?'

'Thank you, and yes, my luggage is on the trolley,' she said, pointing towards the porter standing behind her.

'Very good, then enjoy your stay.'

The woman grabbed the porter's attention and beckoned him forward.

Shoil nodded, picked up her card and walked over to the elevator, pressing the 12 button when she entered, followed by the porter. As the doors closed, she smiled. Soon she would be face-to-face with Tampong and be able to deal with her once and for all. She could then deal with this Terry. He was only a boy, so should not be too much trouble. He would either join her or join Tampong in the next life. She didn't really mind which route he took.

She was so looking forward to tomorrow. When she arrived in her room, she tipped the porter then went straight to the bathroom and ran herself a hot bath. A long soak always made her feel better. She had new access to yet more considerable resources and was pleased to see her wealth building up nicely. Soon she would match Zelphur's power and resources. There might not be any Higher Middle left to boss around, depending on the boy's decision, but plenty of humans to meet her beck and call. This would be a day she had longed for. Tampong has no idea she has been found. The shock on her face would be worth the travel and miles.

Yes, tomorrow would be a great day. For now, she would enjoy a nice long hot bath.

As she lay in the bath, she sifted through all of his memories, his sexual encounters . . . and his illness. Suddenly her eyes burst wide open while her face exploded in rage. She sat bolt upright in the bath, now feeling physically sick. Robert was HIV positive and had been for the past seven years. Now she was HIV positive too, through his absorption. She could feel her body already slowly dying.

She let out a high-pitched scream, splashing the water with her hands in frustration. She screamed again.

***

'Did you feel that?' asked Terry.

'I did, and it felt close. Too close,' said a now worried Tampong.

'She has killed again too. What do you suppose this means?'

'That she has found us.'

'That's not possible. Not so quickly.'

'Anything is possible with Shoil, believe me.'

'But how?'

'She must have gotten to Karen, who in turn must have worked out where you are.'

'Again, but how?'

Tampong looked around the room. Her eyes settled on the picture hanging on the wall next to the bathroom.

'You said your laptop was sitting on the corner there, right?' she said, pointing to the desk.

'Yes,' he confirmed, a puzzled expression on his face.

'Then look at the picture.'

He looked but nothing registered.

'So what am I looking for?'

'The flag, Terry, look at the flag.'

He did.

'Ho shit.'

'Ho shit indeed. If she saw the flag and the towel, it would not take even an amateur Sherlock Holmes to work out where we are.'

Terry's eyes then bulged open in shock and worry.

'But that would mean Shoil found Karen and got her to talk.'

'It would indeed.'

'Which means she is probably dead now, right?'

'Not necessarily.'

'How can you be so sure? We came all this way to protect her, only for Shoil to find her in any event. She must be dead, and it's all my fault.'

He was not thinking straight as guilt filled his mind.

'Did you feel anything?' she questioned.

He was only half listening to her.

'What do you mean?'

'If she killed Karen, you would have felt Shoil change. She can only kill and absorb in her original form.'

'So, you are saying she could be alright?'

'She could be. Shoil may have spared her in case she needed her again should she lose your trail.'

'God, I hope you are right.'

'We cannot worry about her for the time being. Just as well we are checking out of this place. The sooner the better, for my liking.'

'Amen to that,' said Terry.

His thoughts were still of Karen. He hoped that Tampong was right and that she was indeed OK. It was true that neither of them felt Shoil change, but that was no guarantee that she didn't harm or even kill her in her human form, which she could have done without being detected by them. He needed to try and contact her as soon as possible to check for himself.

They went back to the unit, and Terry toured their new home, but neither was in the mood to celebrate, so they went back to the hotel. That evening he slipped under the sheets but had a restless night. The sensation they both felt might have been Shoil absorbing Karen, absorbing all her memories, knowing everything about him. Could she have possibly dragged Karen all the way here with her? Surely not.

He hoped not.

***

On Monday morning, Tampong headed straight to Toni's office, knocked on the door, and walked in without waiting for a response.

'Hi, Katy,' he said cheerfully, 'what can I do for you, deary?'

'I have found a place to live, and it is ready today. I was wondering if I could take the day off to move in?'

'Of course. Things are fairly quiet here at the moment, and newbies are allowed time off to relocate in any case.'

'Great, thanks, Toni.'

She returned to her desk and switched her computer off.

'Somebody on a promise or something?' called out Sam, who was watching her keenly packing her things away.

Tampong smiled back at her.

'Better. I have found a new home, and Terry and I are moving in today. I am taking the rest of the day off by the way.'

'Oh, OK, good for you. I look forward to receiving a house-warming invitation soon then,' she shouted after her.

Tampong had already left the office, rushed down into the main car park, and was grateful to find a taxi waiting, which drove her to the hotel.

***

That same morning Shoil's eyes blinked open. She looked around not quite sure at first where she was, that was until her senses quickly returned, as they always did. She sat up and stretched her arms into the air. The clock told her it was 9:30 am, so jet lag must have hit her a little harder than she expected. Still, no harm done. Getting up, she showered, got dressed, and went downstairs for some breakfast, not sure when she ate last.

She ate well, not realizing how hungry she really was, while downing four cups of coffee in the process too. She signed the breakfast receipt and headed back to her room to brush her teeth. She checked her image in the mirror. A woman with high anticipation and excitement looked back at her. Then she noticed a dark spot on her forehead. Leaning closer, she instantly realized it was the first sign of AIDS. She leaned back again, conceding that soon it would be time to ditch this body and find a new host. That made her feel a mixture of sadness and anger. She liked this body. It had served her well, but all good things must come to an end, if only sooner than expected thanks to that bastard of a man. He knew he was HIV positive and went around trying to infect as many women as possible before he died. What an arsehole and horrible man. There are now many women walking around with no idea that they had been possibly infected by this man, who made the point of avoiding the use of any condoms, convincing the woman that it was more enjoyable for him that way. He even promised many of them he would not cum inside them, but of course he did, claiming that the excitement was too much for him and he couldn't pull out in time. However, this wasn't the time to start thinking about that particular problem right now. First, there was a little matter of Tampong to take care of. Then she could concentrate on finding a new suitable host. She finished dressing, grabbed her coat and keys, then headed down to the reception desk.

'Good morning, ma'am, how may I help you?' asked the receptionist.

'Could you put me through to Ms. Katy Armitage's room, please? We were supposed to be meeting down here, but she hasn't shown up yet.'

'Sorry to hear that, ma'am. Of course, just let me check for one moment.'

He tapped his keyboard.

'You did say Ms. Armitage, right?'

'Yes, Katy Armitage.'

He coughed uncomfortably.

'Well, it appears that Ms. Armitage checked out this morning, ma'am.'

Tampong's eye's widened in surprise.

'She checked out?'

'Yes, ma'am, this morning. Could you have had the time wrong, or perhaps she will still meet you here?'

Tampong was only half listening, still in shock at the news.

'Ma'am,' he said, trying to interrupt her thoughts, 'is there something I can do for you? Call someone perhaps?'

'What . . . er . . . no . . . no.'

She turned and left the receptionist looking puzzled as he watched her walk away.

It is not possible, she thought, *it is simply not possible. How can someone be so lucky so many times? She must have a guardian angel.*

Once again Tampong had managed to elude her, this time by only a matter of minutes. She suddenly clicked her fingers as an idea came to mind, so she stopped walking, turned around, and returned to the receptionist.

He looked up when she arrived again.

'Did she happen to leave a forwarding contact address?'

'Sadly not, ma'am, and even if she did, unfortunately it is hotel policy not to divulge such information without a court order.'

'I see, so did she happen to say where she was going?'

'Sorry, ma'am, but I did not check her out. I can ask my colleague if you like?'

'That would be very nice, thank you. We have been friends for such a long time, and I'd hate to miss the opportunity to meet up with her again.'

She was amazed as to how calm she remained. Normally she would have ripped his head off after receiving such news. This did not stop the anger she felt deep inside. Somebody was going to have to pay for this later on. She folded her arms impatiently.

'Just one minute please.'

He walked into the back room and was gone for a couple of minutes. Eventually he reappeared.

'So sorry, ma'am, but my colleague has no recollection of her saying where she was going, except that she headed for the main car park with her luggage and son. Most likely to hail a taxi.'

Shoil said nothing, turning away again and headed for the elevator. The receptionist watched her go again, shook his head before returning to his paperwork. He had seen it all before. Some guests were extremely pleasant, while others, like her, were simply very rude.

Back in her room she started throwing things around. First the glass smashed against the wall, then a cup hit the TV, causing a large crack to appear from one side to the other. Using her strength, she toppled over the bed, ignoring the blankets and pillows flying across the room. She was mad, even angry, more with herself than anything else. Why did she not go straight to her room last night and finish her off, rather than waste time in a stupid bathtub? Her rage knew no bounds but was suddenly halted when the phone rang.

'What!' she yelled down the phone.

'Is everything OK, ma'am?' asked the concerned voice at the other end of the phone.

'Fantastic,' she sniped, 'why would it not be?'

'It's just that we have had a complaint about a lot of noise apparently coming from your room.'

'Oh, right. Yep, that would be me. I will try to be a bit quieter.'

'That would be very thoughtful, ma'am. Thank you for your cooperation and have a nice day.'

Shoil said nothing but slammed the phone down. What was she going to do now? She knew they had to be close, but how was she going to track them down? She could try moving into her animal form and see if she could pick up her trail, but that was unlikely as she most likely drove away in a vehicle. She could stalk the streets until she found them, but that could take the rest of her life, which was very limited now, thanks to the virus spreading quickly through her body.

'Think, Shoil, think,' she said, knocking her hand against her head.

A light suddenly came on at the back of her mind.

Go back to your original contact point and kill two birds with one stone.

She clicked her fingers.

'That's it. Get myself back to the UK and absorb that Karen bitch. This Terry is bound to contact her to check that she is alright.'

She realized that this meant distancing herself from Tampong for the time being, but hopefully only for a short time. Decision made, she picked up the phone that had ended on the floor in the corner. Fortunately it was still working.

'Reception, how may I be of assistance?'

'I'll be checking out tomorrow.'

'So soon, ma'am. Very well, we will be ready. Would you like a taxi for tomorrow morning?'

'Yes, I'll be going straight to the international airport.'

'Very good, ma'am. At what time?'

'Don't know yet. I'll let you know later.'

'Very good, ma'am.'

She pressed the phone to end the call. She retrieved her bag and pulled out Robert's wallet. His gold membership card had a number on the back, so she dialed it.

'Thank you for calling British Airways. How may I help you?'

'I need a flight tomorrow morning, it's an urgent personal matter.'

'Of course, ma'am. Can I have your membership number, please?

'22345279845.'

'Thank you. And for security reasons, can you please let me know your favorite movie?'

'*Star Wars*.'

'Thank you. You are looking for a flight tomorrow. We have one leaving tomorrow evening at eighteen hundred hours, nonstop to London Heathrow. Is that of interest to you?'

'Yes. Are there still business class seats available?'

'Yes, ma'am.'

'Then I'll take it.'

'Very good, ma'am. Will you be paying with your usual card?'

'Correct.'

'Then can I just have the security pin, please?'

'691.'

'Perfect. You are all set. Your confirmation number is NY97612. Is there anything else I can do for you?'

'No, that's all.'

'Then have a pleasant evening and thank you again for choosing British Airways.'

She hung up and called reception. As soon as the receiver picked up she started talking.

'I'll check out at three pm, so have a taxi ready to take me directly to Singapore International Airport, the British Airways check-in.'

'Very good, ma'am,' the receptionist replied politely.

She hung up again. This time she dialed Hertz and reserved a car at the airport. This was not what she envisaged and cursed herself for flying all this way for nothing. She spent the rest of the day rearranging the room. She looked at the broken TV, not sure what she was going to do about that. She opened the door slightly and saw the maid down the corridor. She took her key card and walked down the corridor. When she arrived at the trolley, she looked at the contents, deciding to sweep up all the coffee bags, and stuffed them into her pockets. Just then the door opened, and the cleaning maid stepped out. She jumped when she saw Shoil standing there.

'Ho, me goodness,' she said in a strong Mexican accent. 'You make a me jump, madam.'

'Oops,' said Shoil, 'I was just wondering if you have some more coffee. I am out and could really do with a cup right now.'

'Ha, si,' said the maid, looking down at her trolley, then scratching her head, 'strange, but I was sure I had some. No problem, I will just go to the stockroom and get some more. What room are you in, madam?'

'It's OK, I'll wait right here and guard your, er, trolley.'

'Si, si,' she said, turning and heading down the corridor.

Shoil waited until the maid turned the corner, then hurried back to her room, picked up her broken TV, which she carried into the now vacant room being cleaned. She picked up the TV in that room and ran with it back to her room. She turned to go back, then spotted the remote, so she grabbed that and rushed back to the room to switch them over. She just made it out of the room before the maid came back with a handful of coffee sacks. Tampong slipped the remote into her pocket.

'Madam,' she said, handing Shoil several coffee sacks.

'Perfect, thanks.'

She turned and went back to her room. Before she shut the door, she stuck her head back out into the corridor.

'By the way, I'll be working in here all day, so I don't need my room cleaned.'

'Do you need any towels or anything?'

'No, I'm good.' She smiled, putting the 'do not disturb' sign on her doorknob and closed the door.

She finished packing her bag, leaving enough clothing for tomorrow, then, feeling her stuffed pockets, decided to make herself a cup of coffee.

***

By the time they arrived at their new home, both were in a more positive frame of mind.

'So, what do you think?' asked Tampong after Terry had finished running up and down the stairs, looking into every room as his smile got broader and broader.

'This place is awesome,' he said, 'wow, and check out the view of the lake. How did you find this place?'

'You can thank relocations for that. I understand that quite a few of the company employees are usually relocated here. Most stay, but some move on and buy their own place.'

'You are not thinking about buying a place, are you?'

'No, the general consensus seems to favor renting rather than buying in Singapore, mainly because of the high property prices and all the taxes you have to pay to live here.'

'If you say so, but this place is . . .'

'I know, awesome.'

'Right. Do I get to pick my room?'

'You do.'

'Great, then I'll take the room in the front. Both have a huge bathroom, so really either one will be OK if you prefer that room.'

'No, I'm good with the back room.'

'Awesome.'

'So, what are your plans tonight?'

'Thought I would try and contact Karen, check that she is OK, then, assuming she is, then firm up my next meeting with Sandi.'

'Aha, were you thinking about Skyping with Karen?'

'Yes, why?'

'It's just there is no internet here yet. The guy comes tomorrow to install it.'

'Ho, right. Bummer. Is it OK if I try to call her then?'

'Sure.'

She passed him her mobile.

'I'll be quick.'

He took the mobile and headed upstairs for some privacy. Then he called back downstairs.

'Do you know the international code from here?'

'Yes, it's 000 44 then the number, ignoring the first zero.'

'000 44, got it, thanks.'

He lay on the bed and dialed Karen's number. It rang four times before switching over to voicemail. He waited for her message to end and for the beep.

'Hey, Karen, this is Terry. I am just checking in to make sure you are OK. I . . . I . . . had a bad dream, well, at least I hope it was a bad dream, so I am just checking in with you. Can you please text me or call me so I know you are OK? Thanks, and bye.'

He hung up, dropping the phone on the bed. He looked at the clock, realizing that she was most likely in bed still, as it was early morning there. So he had to wait until tomorrow before he was likely to hear from her or if he tried contacting her again. He retrieved the phone then went back downstairs to give it back to Tampong.

'And?' she asked.

'It went straight to voicemail. Maybe I will hear from her tomorrow, or I will try again tomorrow.'

Tampong checked her watch.

'Of course, she is most likely tucked up in bed right now. Does she normally turn her phone off?'

She kept her voice calm, not wishing to spook Terry any more than she had to.

'Not sure, but you are probably right,' he said simply, although doubts were lurking at the back of his mind too.

He would only feel better once he heard from her.

***

Karen woke up when the phone rang. She looked at the caller ID and saw it was Terry's aunt calling. She guessed it was probably Terry himself. She was in no mood to talk to him right now. She felt she should warn him about her contact and threat but dared not in case that evil woman found out and came back for revenge as she promised. Her eyes started to water, and she sniffed back a tear. She lay on her back and let the phone take the call. She would check in the morning to find out what it was he wanted. She wished she had never met him now. Sure, he was a nice boy, kind, very friendly, but came with too much baggage. She had already lost one good friend and could not risk losing any others or members of her family. She felt weak and helpless. It would be better for all if she never saw or spoke to him again. If the call was some feeble attempt to try and get together again, then she would ignore it and try to get her life back on track with some resemblance of normality.

She went back to sleep.

***

Shoil felt the aircraft shudder a little, so she opened her eyes. Fortunately, on this flight there was a young man in the seat opposite and he was either nervous of her, in love, or just wanted to be left alone, which was just fine by her. She wanted to be left alone. Needed to be left alone. She needed time to think, to consider her options, run the pros and cons of all the options. In the end, she kept coming back to the same conclusion: get to the girl as quickly as possible, not to wait this time. All being well, the boy had not contacted her yet.

The captain announced that they would be landing soon, so she got up and changed into fresh clothes, washed herself as best she could, casually glancing into the mirror and seeing another blotch had appeared on her forehead. She took out her makeup bag and dabbed over the spot. The virus was taking a grip. Returning to her seat, she waited for the plane to land. She brought no luggage with her this time, so she could get straight out and back to York as quickly as transport would allow. Driving should be the fastest way, and she had already hired a car at Heathrow.

The plane landed with a bounce on the tarmac as the engines roared in reverse to slow the aircraft down. Some passengers clapped as the aircraft landed. She never understood why people did that. The captain was well paid to fly the aircraft, and landing was just a natural part of that. Still, she guessed that it was probably relief more than anything else.

As soon as the seat belt sign went off, she was out of her seat and the first to the exit, impatiently waiting for the aircraft door to open. As the door started to finally swing open, she pushed past it and walked quickly down the jetway, following the exit signs that led her to customs and immigration. She used her passport at one of the free terminals and was through in seconds. Walk-running out of the arrivals, following the sign for the sky train, she skipped down the escalator, barging past people standing on either side and just caught the train before the doors closed. The car rental center was two stops away.

At the rental center she rushed into the Hertz rental shop and up to the gold counter. The board listed all the gold members' reservations, and she quickly found her name. She headed for bay twenty-three, opened the door, started the car up, and drove quickly to the exit. Her papers were checked, and she was cleared to proceed. Driving out of the rental center, she followed the signs to the M25. Not caring about her speed, she put her foot down on the accelerator. The car sped up, racing past other vehicles as it did. Once on the motorway, she decided to slow down to almost the speed limit, not wishing to attract too much attention and unnecessarily delay her journey. She had checked the route, and the A1(M) appeared to be her best route, taking her almost directly to York City. It should take around six and a half hours, meaning she should arrive late afternoon. Perfect. Karen would be finishing school but not yet going to work. Her stomach rumbled, telling her she hadn't eaten on the flight. She pulled into the next service station, grabbed a sandwich and a drink before returning to her vehicle, deciding to eat on route.

***

It was a restless night, she had been tossing and turning in her bed, unable to get comfortable. Finally she gave up trying to sleep and got up at five fifteen. Slipping on her dressing gown, she headed downstairs for breakfast, subconsciously picking up her phone as she walked out. It was an automatic thing for her now, and she did so without thinking about it. Downstairs she prepared some cereals and a glass of milk, which she was enjoying when her mother came downstairs.

'Ho, it's you,' she said, seeing Karen at the kitchen table.

'Sorry, did I wake you?'

'No matter, I was getting up in any case. Got an early start today. So what are you doing up so early, and on a school day too?'

'Could not get back to sleep, so came downstairs.'

Her mother walked up to the table and reached over to pull a strand of hair away from Karen's face.

'Is everything OK, dear? Are you worried about school or something?'

'No, just bad dreams.'

'My poor baby.'

'I'll be fine, Mom,' she said, gently moving her hand away.

'If you are sure?'

'I'm sure.'

'So are you working again this evening?'

'Yes.'

'Will Sally be there too?'

Karen went quiet, causing her mother to look at her face, which looked as white as a sheet now.

'What is it?'

'It's, it's Sally.'

'What about her? Have you two fallen out?'

'No, nothing like that. It's just that she . . . has left.'

'Left, ho right. I thought something terrible had happened. Don't worry. You'll find new friends.'

Karen didn't have the heart to tell her the truth. How was she going to explain the way Sally was killed? Nobody would believe her. She even doubted her own eyes and thought that it may have been just another bad dream, except she knew deep down it wasn't. She looked up and smiled pitifully at her mom. She had to keep her safe, had to protect her as best she could. It was just the two of them now, her father having died a few years ago from cancer while her younger brother had left for college and her sister was staying with friends. She raised her eyebrows instead of replying, her mom taking it as an affirmative.

'Right, I'm off to work. Have a great day at school and see you tonight.'

'Bye, Mom,' she said, still thinking about poor Sally.

She was not sure how she was going to explain her disappearance to Toni either. She shuddered. Better just tell him that she decided to stop working there, or that she moved away with her parents. Yes, that would work. Having finished her cereal, she went upstairs, brushed her teeth, dressed, and got ready for school. She had a strange feeling that something bad was going to happen today. She could not shake this bad feeling away. It kept nagging at the back of her mind. She picked up her phone and stared at it for a little while. Finally, she pressed messages and listened to Terry's voice. He sounded concerned and worried even. His voice made her own little warning voice in the back of her mind even louder. Perhaps she should Skype with him, just so that he could see her and know that she was OK.

Even when she got to school, that bad feeling was still there. It wasn't until she started concentrating on her lessons that she was able to push it to the back of her mind.

***

Shoil made good time, stopping only once to refuel the car. The sign for York told her she had only another fifteen miles to go. Her excitement started to grow, with the only doubt being that she got to the girl too late. Not much she could do about that right now. She got here as quickly as possible. Surely Tampong could not be that lucky! She bit her lip at the thought.

Twenty minutes later she parked the car in the high street. She would have to wait for her to arrive at the restaurant. She did not know the school she went to or what class she was in. Still, given that Singapore was seven hours ahead, the chances were that the boy was still in bed and would not try to contact her until this evening, when she finished work. That made sense. Now she had to play the waiting game. She coughed roughly into her handkerchief, noticing speckles of blood on the cloth. This illness was getting worse. She had to move soon and transfer into another body, otherwise she would waste away and never be able to transform into anything ever again. Having parked in front of a cafeteria, she walked inside and ordered chicken and chips, together with a coffee. She sat at a window seat, offering a perfect view of the restaurant. She ate slowly.

Later that afternoon, Karen waved goodbye to her friends as she walked out of the school gates straight to the bus stop. Checking her watch, she knew she had just a few minutes to wait. A couple of other girls walked up to the bus stop and stood behind her, chatting about boys, of course. School girl conversations seemed to be limited to boys, clothing, and makeup. Karen smiled to herself because she used to be a girl like that. She had grown up a little since then, knowing that there was more to life than how you looked and who looked at you. Fortunately, she did not have to listen to too much more as the bus arrived. She boarded the bus, opting to sit downstairs, guessing the girls would prefer upstairs. She was right. Just as the bus doors were about to close, three boys got on the bus, quickly following the girls upstairs, looking up their short skirts as they did so.

'Hey, Pauline, I didn't know you were into pink knickers,' one of the boys called up to the girl.

The girl turned sharply, bringing her hand around to her back and pushing her skirt against her buttocks, preferring not to respond to the boy.

The second boy nudged his friend.

'I heard she doesn't bother with them usually, as it wastes too much time.'

All the boys laughed.

One of the other girls had already reached the top of the stairs and leaned over to pour a little Coke over the boys.

'Hey, watch it, bitch,' one yelled, trying to wipe the Coke off his school jacket.

'Just trying to wash the filth out of your mouths, boys. Looks like you wet your pants, little boys.'

'We'll get you for that,' yelled one of the boys.

'Yeah, just try and see what happens if you so much as touch me,' she warned.

The third boy recognized her, so grabbed the shoulder of his friend, who yelled.

'Quiet, Steve, that's Mike Muscles' sister.'

The other boy gulped, going quiet as they walked dejected up the rest of the stairs.

'Oi,' barked the driver, looking back down the bus, directing this attention at the boys, 'get yourselves upstairs and sit down, or else get off the bus, which isn't moving until you do one or the other.'

'Sit the hell down, you brats,' screamed an old woman sitting in the back row and annoyed at the delay.

The boys realized they were outnumbered, so quietly climbed the rest of the stairs and sat down. Karen wondered if she was ever like that. She hoped not.

It took only ten minutes for the bus to reach her stop. She rang the bell and got up and stood by the door. When the bus stopped and the doors opened, she stepped out and walked down the road towards her house. A chill ran down her spine, forcing her to nervously glance behind her, but she saw nothing. She quickened her pace and reached her house without further incident. Walking straight into the kitchen, she opened the fridge to see what was on offer. Not much, so settled for a meat pie. She then opened the freezer and took the bag of frozen chips out, sprinkling a few on the tray, setting the pie next to it. She then slid the tray into the oven and switched it on.

Taking a glass from the cupboard, she filled it with tap water, sat at the kitchen table, and quietly sipped her water. The front door opened, and her mother came home.

'Hey, sweetie, so how was your day?'

'Ho, a normal school day, you know.'

'Right. What are you cooking?' she asked, seeing the light on in the oven.

'Just a pie and chips.'

'Not particularly healthy eating, is that?'

'Well, there wasn't a lot of choice,' she whipped back.

'Aha, right. I meant to go shopping yesterday. I'll go tomorrow as I am not working.'

'No problem. This will work for me.'

'Done any for me?'

No, sorry. Do you want me to add some?'

'No, it's OK. I'll grab a sandwich later. I had a meal at work, so that set me up well for the day.'

'Up to you,' she said, only half listening.

The oven beeped, so she got up and switched it off, waiting a few more minutes before grabbing a plate and placing it on the table. Slipping into the oven mittens, she opened the oven door, slid the tray out and placed the hot food on her plate. Sitting back at the table, she began to eat, just as her mother came back into the kitchen.

'Hmmm, smells good,' she remarked.

'Tastes good too.'

'Enjoy. Are you still working tonight?'

'Unfortunately, I am. Need the money.'

'Don't we all. Remind me, what are you actually saving for?'

'My own car.'

'And how much do you have so far?'

'Five hundred and seventy-five pounds.'

She nodded, impressed.

'You must be serious then, but have you taken any driving lessons yet?'

'Not yet. Thought I would wait until I got closer to my target.'

'Which is?'

'A thousand pounds. I can pick up a decent second-hand motor for that.'

'Well, you might get a little beaten-up runaround with that sort of money. Listen, if you get to your target, then I'll match it for you. Sort of an early birthday present.'

Karen looked up in surprise, her loaded fork hanging in midair.

'Are you being serious?'

'Quite serious.'

'You're the best mom.'

'Remember that when Mother's Day comes around.'

They both laughed.

Later that evening, a happy Karen bounced down the stairs, rushing into the kitchen. Her mother was now sitting at the table eating a ham sandwich. Karen walked up to her and planted a kiss on her forehead.

Her mother had a mouthful of sandwich, so just smiled at her.

'I'm off to the restaurant. See you later.'

Her mother waved her goodbye.

She almost skipped down the road, not believing her luck. A few more weeks of good tips, plus her salary, and she should reach her goal, which her mother would now double for her, meaning she should be able to pick up a nice little motorcar for herself. A few more weeks in the restaurant and she would have enough for driving lessons. She couldn't wait to be independent with her own wheels. She would most likely be the first girl at her school with wheels. She was thinking about all the things she would do and where she could go as she boarded the bus, got off, and was walking down the road towards the restaurant. She reached the side door and pushed to go in, but it would not budge. She pushed harder, but it still did not open. Puzzled, she went around to the front of the restaurant, when she noticed that all the lights were off. She tried to peer into the restaurant with her face almost against the glass. She saw nothing inside, but then froze when she saw the reflection of a woman standing directly behind her.

It was Shoil.

The blood drained from her face as she straightened up and turned to face Shoil.

'Good day, little bitch,' Shoil snarled.

'You, you promised to leave me alone,' she stuttered.

'I lied,' replied Shoil, sounding evil.

Her voice was deep and intimidating.

'What, what do you want? I told you all I know about Terry's whereabouts.'

'Has he contacted you since we last spoke?'

'What!'

'You heard, bitch. Don't make me repeat myself.'

'No, no, I've not spoken with him.'

Shoil could tell she was too frightened to lie.

'Has he tried to contact you?'

'Er, yes, he called me and left a voice message.'

'Saying?'

'He just said he needed to speak to me urgently, to check that I was alright.'

Karen now realized that Terry was most likely trying to warn her about Shoil.

'Very astute of him,' remarked Shoil, 'shall we go inside?'

'What, ho, we can't. Toni is not here.'

'We don't need Toni,' she answered, dangling his keys under her nose, which she had retrieved from his jacket just before she positioned herself on the doorway, pleased that the bins had not yet been emptied.

She placed the keys in Karen's hand, indicating the door with her eyes. Karen took the keys with shaking hands. It took several attempts to find the right key because her hands were shaking so much.

'Hurry it up,' snapped Shoil, getting impatient, looking nervously around.

She finally found the right key, turned the lock, and opened the door. Shoil pushed her through the door, eager to get out of the street. Taking the keys out of the lock, she closed the door and locked it again. Karen just stood there, unable to move, frightened beyond belief. Shoil turned to face her. That's when Karen saw the glow of her orange eyes, those same eyes she had seen before, but blue.

'Right, bitch, get undressed.'

'Sorry, what?'

Before she could react, Shoil's hand whipped through the air to slam into the side of her face. Karen staggered backwards, her face stinging from the strike. Her eyes watering from the pain.

'I said don't make me repeat myself.'

Karen slowly started to unbutton her blouse. The buttons seemed so small; her shaking hands could not grasp the small buttons. Shoil had enough, took two steps forward, grabbed her blouse, and ripped it off her. It fell in two pieces. Karen could not speak, dare not speak, so she just unzipped her skirt and let that drop to the floor. She stood there in her bra and knickers, not knowing what to expect next.

Shoil glared at her.

'Did I not make myself clear? I said undress.'

Tears rolled down Karen's cheeks as her hands went behind her back to unclip her bra, which she let drop into her hands before placing that on the floor. Reluctantly, she pulled her knickers down, stepping out of them. She now stood naked in front of this evil woman. She placed her hands in front of herself, trying to cover as much of her nakedness as possible.

'Are you still a virgin?'

'What!'

She wanted to challenge but saw Shoil take a step forward and feared another strike across her still tender face.

'Yes, yes, I am still a virgin,' she admitted.

'How come? You have a body men would want to fuck. So why not?'

She thought about the question for a second.

'Guess I was waiting for the right boy.'

'How old are you?'

'Nineteen.'

'And still a virgin. Jesus, what a waste. Any illnesses?'

'Er, no, nothing out of the ordinary.'

'Excellent, then you are the perfect match.'

'Perfect match! For whom?'

'Why for me, of course.'

'YOU! I had no idea you liked women, but I am sorry, but I am not into girls.'

'I don't want you sexually, you naive little bitch.'

'Then what?'

'Your body. I need your body.'

'So it is sexual then.'

Shoil said nothing, just stared straight at Karen. Karen looked at the strange woman in front of her, who also began to undress, ripping her clothing off as quickly as she could.

Ho my god, I am going to be raped by this woman, she thought.

Then she looked at Shoil's eyes, which appeared to be getting bigger, rounder, larger. She blinked twice, not sure she believed her own eyes. She continued to watch in horrid fascination as Shoil's skin slowly started to change color, turning orange, as her mouth grew wider and wider. Shoil's body started to shake violently. Cracks appeared in her skin. Karen was tempted to make a dash for it but suddenly could not move. She was pinned to the floor by some unseen force. She peed herself.

Shoil started to make inhuman noises, which sounded as though they came from deep inside her. She was muttering incomprehensible words, speaking in some strange dialect. A ghostly gas-like substance now encircled her whole body. She held her arms out parallel to the ground as her body floated into the air. She then let out an inhuman cry as her skin seemed to melt off her body while the gassy substance seemed to take a humanish form. She continued to float as her skeleton frame, with all her organs now visible, started to bubble. Her bones began to look like bubblegum, unable to hold her organs in place anymore, and they started to fall one by one onto the floor. Karen felt physically sick when she heard the squishing sound of her liver as it hit the floor, then her kidneys, intestines, and finally her heart. Karen could not take her eyes of the heart—it was still beating. Her eyes then fell out of their sockets, while her hair dissolved like water. Eventually all that was left was this gassy image of something that looked human but was not. It had a head, two arms and two legs, but no other features.

Karen's heart was beating twice as fast now. She could hear it beating in her ears. Her eyes widened as the gassy image started to drift towards her. Still unable to move, unable to scream, unable to do anything except watch. Watch as the gassy image came closer and closer. She wanted to pass out, but something was preventing her from even doing that. Suddenly she felt her own body start to lift into the air. Her arms were forced out to her side, matching the stance of the gassy image. It was now only a few inches from her, and she could have sworn she heard it talking to her, but her voice sounded like she was in another room, another place, yet she could hear her, although unable to understand what she was saying. It sounded like a chant in a foreign language. Then the gassy image covered her own body. That was when she felt the searing pain, like a million needles piercing her body. She went rigid as the endless pain seemed to grow, while the gassy image began to blend itself into her skin, as if she was absorbing it. The last thing she remembered was wishing she were dead, anything to stop this unbearable pain. Her world went dark, and her body crashed to the ground.

Shoil breathed in and out slowly, sat up and looked around the restaurant. It was still dark, and she was alone. Standing up, she looked at her body.

'Not bad, bitch, not bad,' she said to herself, realizing that she was no longer ill, and this body was AIDS-free.

'So now I am the little bitch, Karen. So be it. Could be worse I guess. And I am a virgin again too.'

She realized that this poor girl was terrified of her and was telling the truth about Terry, that she had not spoken to him since Shoil last met her. She felt guilty about the death of Sally and had no idea what had happened to Toni. What she did find strange was that she had no long-term memory. There was no recollection of anything beyond her first meeting with Terry.

'Right then,' she said aloud, 'time to get myself home and wait for Terry to call me.'

She would play the love-stricken little girl, one who misses her one true love, despite the miles apart. He was obviously concerned for her well-being and had even risked contacting her, no doubt against Tampong's wishes. She got dressed in Karen's clothes, picked up her own and bundled them into a ball. Karen was a size eight, so she was going to need a new wardrobe, but would wait to see what else she had in the girl's wardrobe that was worth keeping. She had her favorite little black dress and her white T-shirt and jeans, which she wore quite often, although nothing much in the way of sexy underwear. No wonder she was still a virgin. She would go out this week and buy some decent underwear and other clothing, replacing her old wardrobe. Tucking in her blouse, tying it up at the bottom as the buttons were now missing, and straightening her hair, she strolled out of the restaurant, locking it again, before throwing the keys down the drain. This restaurant would not be opening for business for a long time. By the time they worked out that the owner was still missing, presumed dead, she would be long gone. She walked down the road to the bus stop, then remembered that she was supposed to be working tonight. She would have to explain to her mother why she was back so early and didn't need that hassle just now. She then remembered the café she had used before, one where she and Terry had had a drink together. That would do for a little while, afterwards, she might go and see what was on at the cinema. Then she needed to feast, so would stalk the roads for a suitable meal.

***

Tracey and Gary both sat bolt upright on the sofa. They had been watching a movie. Tracey was resting her head on his shoulder. They felt the sensation at the same time. They turned to look at each other, confusion written all over their faces while their eyes were twinkling blue.

'What the hell was that?' she asked.

'I am not quite sure,' said Gary, now holding his chin in his hand. 'I can only remember one similar feeling like that in recent years.'

Tracey stared at him, not sure she wanted to hear the answer, but knew she had to ask.

'So when was that then?'

'When Jon turned.'

'When Jon turned? You mean when he became Jalip?'

'No, I mean when he turned into that ghostly giant and defeated Zelphur.'

'Could it have been Jon then, could he have returned?'

There was excitement in her voice now.

'No, this felt different, hostile, filled with pure evil even.'

Her shoulders slumped down.

'Evil! You mean to tell me you think that one of those Higher Middle things has become more like Jon. God help us if you are correct.'

'No, not like Jon changed. If I were a gambling man, I'd say one of them has transferred bodies.'

'What! Why would they do that?'

'Maybe their body was damaged, broken or something. It happens.'

'Great, so not only do we not know where they are, we now don't know what one of them looks like.'

'That's not an issue for us really.'

'How so?'

'You know where and who, because when they are close it causes a reaction from both of us. We will know when they are close.'

'Not very comforting. From what I could sense, this one was already very close.'

'That's what is bothering me more.'

'Why?'

'The fact you felt it so strongly too means at least one of them is closer than I expected. As you know, I am more sensitive to them than you are, so the mere fact we felt this at the same time does not bode well for the future.'

'So what do we do about it?'

'Not sure. There is not much we can do at the moment. No idea who it is or why it happened. All we can do is keep our guard up and tread carefully.'

'Again, not very comforting.'

Tracey leaned back on the sofa. Just when they thought they were safe, this goes and happens. Will they ever see an end to all this violence, the hiding, and the running? She folded her arms across her chest like a scolding child.

Gary looked at her and just smiled. He understood her concern and uncertainty. He felt the same, only he didn't react the same way of course. He needed to give some thought to this latest development. All interest in the movie was gone. Neither was watching, so Tracey switched it off. It was too early to go to bed, so she grabbed a magazine and started to browse through it.

***

At the same time, Tampong and Terry experienced the same sensation in Singapore.

'Did you feel that?' asked Tampong.

'I did. What do you think it means?'

'Not sure. This was something different.'

'Right. I didn't sense any anger or assault, or violence even, but she has done something completely different, and she seems different too,' he said.

'What do you mean?'

Tampong was watching him carefully. His head was leaning slightly to the right, deep in thought, as if trying to comprehend what had just happened.

'Her aura appears different, like she is someone else now.'

'Someone else?'

'I know it sounds crazy, but she doesn't feel the same as before. Anyway, whatever she is, she is gone now. Back into human form I suppose.'

'I don't like this.'

'You and me both.'

'She felt far away to me. Did you have the same feeling?'

'Yes. I think she is a long way from us.'

'That's one good thing, albeit little comfort.'

Tampong did not like this change of events. Shoil had done something terrible, on that point she was sure. She was up to something, and whatever it was, she was sure that they were her ultimate target. She needed to keep Terry close for the time being until she found out what Shoil was up to. Eventually, they would have to face each other. She doubted she would come out of the fight alive but knew she had to try, if not for her, then for Terry. She would still put her own life on the line for him. Terry knocked her out of her thoughts.

'And the internet guy comes tomorrow, right?'

'Right. Said he would be here about nine am. Apparently, he is the estate telephone representative and stays on-site so he can easily respond to requests quickly, like ours.'

'That's good, as I need to contact Karen and check that she is OK.'

'Have you tried calling her?'

'I did once, but it went straight to voicemail.'

'Do you want to try again?'

'Do you mind?'

'Of course not, if it will put your mind at ease, and mine, as I hate to see you this worried.'

'Is it that obvious?'

'Yes.'

'OK, thanks. I'd really like to speak with her.'

'Well, it's late evening there now, so she should have finished work and is probably waiting for you to contact her.'

'Crickey, you are probably right.'

Tampong threw him her mobile, which he caught easily and hurried up to his room. He jumped onto the bed and dialed her number. He heard the line connect and the phone ring. It rang four times before switching to voicemail, again.

'Karen, it's Terry again. I really need to speak with you and check you are OK. Please let me speak with you, if only for a couple of seconds. We have moved and I am waiting for our internet to be connected, which should be tomorrow. All being well, I'd like to Skype with you tomorrow evening, your time. If not, then I'll understand and leave you alone, but just please let me know that you are OK. Bye for now.'

He hung up. It was not like her to just ignore him. Surely she couldn't hate him that much! Guess he would find out tomorrow, should she bother to Skype with him.

He went downstairs to give Tampong her phone back.

'No luck?' she asked, guessing his response and judging from the glum look on his face.

'Nope. It went to voicemail again. It rang a few times before doing so, which means her phone must have been on, but she didn't pick up.'

'Maybe she was out or in the toilet, or something,' she said, trying to be more positive for his sake.

'I hope you are right, I really do.'

'So, are you still Skyping with her then?'

'I said I would connect tomorrow, assuming the internet is up and running. I guess I will know then whether she wants to talk to me or not.'

'I'm sure she does.'

Tampong thought it best to change the subject.

'When do you see Sandi again?'

He seemed to perk up a little on hearing her name.

'Actually, we have not set a date for our next meeting.'

'Then why don't you invite her over for dinner here?'

'Can I?'

'Of course. I would like to get to know her too. And I promise I will not pry or ask awkward questions . . . and I will leave you two alone after dinner.'

'OK, thanks, thanks again.'

He held his hand out, and she handed him her phone again so that he could text her. His face brightened and she judged him well. He was in a better mood now. As he ran back upstairs to text, she leaned back in her chair and started thinking about Karen. She didn't strike her as one who would simply ignore his calls. There had to be a reason why she did not talk to him. She had a bad feeling about this and began to wonder whether this was linked in any way to what they felt Shoil did. God, she hoped not. It didn't bear thinking about what Shoil might do if she knew about Karen and, worse still, found her. She too hoped that she would make that Skype meeting tomorrow.

***

Shoil lay on her new bed. It felt nothing like her old bed. This one seemed lumpier, but she would get used to it, had to. She checked the bedroom clock again and it was a little after midnight. Terry had not tried to contact her, and he was not online. Could he have felt her transforming into Karen's body? She dismissed the thought. He was too young and too naïve to understand what had happened, even if he felt her. No, there had to be another reason for him not contacting her. She had to play the waiting game a little bit longer. He was bound to contact her eventually if his voicemail message was anything to go by.

'Karen, are you home?' called her mother from downstairs.

'Yes. In my bedroom,' answered Shoil.

'OK, have a good night then. Sleep tight dear.'

'You too,' she answered.

Shoil could not see her mother's reaction, but she was looking upstairs with a puzzled expression on her face. She shrugged her shoulders, then walked into the kitchen to make herself a hot chocolate before calling it a night.

Shoil gave up waiting and switched her laptop off. He knew her number, so could call her again. She placed her computer on the sideboard, got undressed and slipped into bed. She moved around a little until she finally got comfortable. She now had a new identity, plenty of money to access, and a small lead to the boy. She smiled an evil smile, then realized she hadn't absorbed anybody since her transformation. That took a lot of her energy, and she needed a refill. Listening intently, she could not hear any movement downstairs, so slipped out of bed, got dressed again, then opened the bedroom window. She jumped down to the grass easily, landing on her feet. It was time to go hunting.

She had forgotten all about Karen's phone, which was still switched on and resting on her bedside table.

She walked slowly down the street, keeping close to the lamplights so that she could easily be seen. It didn't take long before she saw a young man walking in the opposite direction on the other side of the street. She was about to cross over when he waved to her and started to cross the street.

'Hey, Karen, long time no see. How are you doing?'

'I'm fine, thanks,' she had to dig deep in Karen's memory, but eventually found his name, 'how are you doing, Kevin?'

They had one date together about a year ago, but he never followed up with another date.

'Great, thanks. I was just in the neighborhood and thought about contacting you. I meant to contact you a long time ago, but I stupidly lost your telephone number. A friend told me you were working in Toni's restaurant, but when I went by there this evening it was closed.'

'Right. Toni is not feeling too good, so he did not open.'

'Ho, I hope he recovers soon. Anyway, I was wondering how on earth I could find you and, hey presto, here you are. What are the chances and at this time of night?'

'Indeed, what are the chances?'

'So, what exactly are you doing out this time of night?'

'Ho, I was bored, could not sleep, so just out walking a bit.'

'You need to be careful, there are some iffy folk out here this time of night.'

'Not to worry. I can look after myself.'

'Not so sure about that, but you are looking great. A little bit different even.'

'How so?'

His question worried her. She needed to find out and correct the mistake if she were to avoid other awkward questions.

'Well, you look more, how do I say, freer.'

'Freer?'

'Er, yes, your boobs?'

She looked down at her T-shirt, not sure what he was talking about.

'What about my boobs?'

'You are not wearing a bra.'

He felt a little embarrassed about mentioning it and awkwardly shunted from one foot to the other. It would be obvious to her that he had been ogling her chest.

'And?'

'Well, on our date I remember you saying that you could never imagine walking around without a bra. You said it was indecent, or something like that, but here you are. I have to say the look suits you.'

'Ho, well, I guess why not? If you've got it, flaunt it. Right?'

'Right,' he said, his eyes not leaving her chest.

'I'm up here,' she eventually said in a not too friendly tone.

'Yeah, right, sorry.'

'So, you like what you see?'

'What, ho, yeah, I do.'

'Want to see more?'

'Say what?'

'Are you deaf? I said do you want to see more of me, or shall I just go and find some other lucky soul?'

'Err, yes, yes, definitely. Definitely like to see more of you.'

He could not believe his luck. Not only did he find her again, but now she was basically offering herself to him. How could a guy be so lucky?

'OK, do you have a place in mind?'

'Er, yeah, I share an apartment with a mate. It's not far away.'

'Then what are we waiting here for?'

'Well, he is most likely at home now, given how late it is.'

'Not a problem for me. Is it for you? You don't share a bed or anything like that, do you?'

'Er, no, no, not at all. I have my own room, you know, and he is probably fast asleep by now in any case.'

'Perfect.'

She slipped her arm through his and they started walking down the street.

'My god, but you have definitely changed, Karen.'

'In a good way?'

'Yes, in a very good way. You seem more forward now. More confident. More outgoing. On our date you were quite shy and reserved. We didn't even kiss goodnight.'

'Well, we will have to make up for that, won't we?'

'Hmm. I like the sound of that.'

They started to walk more quickly, mainly due to his sudden burst of enthusiasm.

'My apartment is just round the corner.'

They turned right and he led them into the second door on the right. Unlocking the door, they climbed a set of stairs. On the first-floor landing there were three doors, he opened the middle door and held it open for her. She walked into a typical guy's apartment. Not much in the way of furniture, just a sofa and a small table with two chairs. There was a large TV on an old sideboard and the inevitable games console sitting on a chipped coffee table. He put his finger to his lips, indicating them to be quiet, then pointed to the closed door. Obviously, his friend was fast asleep in there. She just nodded and followed him into his bedroom. It smelt musty through lack of fresh air. The bed was unmade, and the sheets looked as though they hadn't been cleaned in a long time. Dirty clothing items were scattered around the room. He saw her looking around.

'Sorry about the mess. I was not expecting visitors,' he said, clearly embarrassed, scooping up items of clothing and stuffing them into a drawer.

'You don't say,' she said sarcastically.

'There, that's better,' he said, having collected his dirty laundry and hidden it. 'So, you said something about showing me more?'

'Cannot wait, can you?' she teased, pulling up her T-shirt to just below her bust.

'No,' he answered honestly, 'the things you said in the street have got me all worked up.'

'Are you horny?'

'Er, yeah.'

'Show me.'

'Show you?'

'Yes, show me how horny you are?'

'You show me something first,' he demanded.

She said nothing, but pulled her T-shirt over her head, twirled it around in her fingers before tossing it into the corner of the room.

'Your turn,' she said, deliberately looking down at his crouch.

His eyes were glued to her breasts, which were fully round and firm. Without taking his eyes off of her, he unzipped his jeans and struggled out of them. He then pulled his pants down and kicked them into a corner. His shirt was just covering him, but she could see his erection pointing out against his shirt. He was definitely aroused.

'Like what you see?' she asked, pushing her breasts together with both hands.

He just nodded.

'Want to see more?'

He nodded enthusiastically this time, rubbing himself as he did.

She licked her lips suggestively, unzipped her skirt, and stepped out of it. With both hands she pulled her knickers down, keeping her head up towards him. She took one foot out of her knickers and used the other one to toss them away. She stood with her legs slightly apart with her hands on her hips.

He looked her up and down. Never before had he seen such a beautiful woman, and one that clearly wanted him. He unbuttoned his shirt and allowed it to fall onto the floor.

She looked him over, staring longer than necessary at his penis.

'Do you like oral sex?' she asked.

'I don't know, I have never had oral sex before.'

'You know how to perform it though, don't you?'

'Yes, yes, of course. I have seen videos.'

'Well, this is the real thing. I like to give and receive.'

'Wow, this is going to be great. What do you do first?'

'Well, I think I will do you first . . . if that is OK with you?' She fluttered her eyelids like a little girl.

'Great, let's go. What do you want me to do, or what position do you want me in?'

She tapped her finger as if contemplating her next move.

'Sit on that chair,' she was pointing to the chair next to the bed, 'now spread your legs, close your eyes, and open your mouth.'

'Open my mouth?' he said, sounding confused.

'Yes, open your mouth, I want to stuff my boob into your mouth first, and then I am going to kiss your chest, your stomach, and finally I will go down on you and suck you hard like a hoover.'

'Wow, I don't think I'd ever live to have such a night as this.'

'I don't think you will, Kevin, I really don't think you will.'

He was thinking about the incredible sex he was about to experience with this amazing woman. He could not wait to tell his mates about this evening. Shoil, on the other hand, was quite certain he would never live to see another night like this one.

'Get ready and open wide,' she commanded.

His eyes widened in eager anticipation, so he sat, spread his legs, closed his eyes, and opened his mouth.

As soon as he closed his eyes, her own eyes turned orange as her tongue mutated into a long snake-like rope. She slowly walked up to him, sat on his lap, and felt his hands go around her waist. She leaned his head back a little, hearing him give a little squeal of excitement. She then plunged her snake-tongue down his throat. He immediately started to gag, thrashing around, trying to get her off his lap.

'What! Don't like deep throat . . . no wait, you are supposed to do that to me, aren't you? How silly of me.'

He continued to thrash, pulling at her, trying to scream, his eyes burst open in fright, and were now orange. His whole body shook like it was being electrocuted, while his nails began to dig into her skin, but she felt nothing. His skin became fluid-like, slowly dripping off his body to reveal muscle and bone.

The bedroom door behind her suddenly flew open, revealing an angry man.

'What the fuck, Kev, I am trying to sleep,' he screamed.

He then saw the naked woman sitting on Kevin's lap while Kevin's upper body was obscured by this woman.

'Can't you do that more quietly? I am trying to sleep?'

He never saw the silver needle shoot through the air and enter in the middle of his forehead. His body stood rigid for a few seconds, not registering that his brain was now dead before he finally fell backwards onto the carpet.

Kevin's body was still shaking violently as Shoil reached down to grab the hand of the now-dead flatmate, dragging him closer to her. By now, Kevin's body had disintegrated into a gooey mess as she began to absorb him. When she finished, she turned around and sat on the back of the dead guy, turning his head completely around. She heard the crack of bone as she forced his head into a full 180-degree turn. She then forced his mouth open and forced her tongue down his throat. She hoped she was not too late and was pleased to see his body start to shake, suggesting that the absorption would still work. It was a full five minutes before she had consumed both bodies and now lay on the carpet feeling rejuvenated. Taking a deep relaxing breath, she sat up and looked around the apartment before getting back to her feet. She slowly got dressed and walked into the kitchen to pour herself a glass of water. She then returned to the room, first going into the flatmate's bedroom. Finding his wallet, she emptied it of all his cash, taking his credit cards too. She then went into the hallway and found Kevin's jacket, emptying his wallet too. Taking one last look around, she picked up her handbag and calmly walked out of the apartment, locking the door before slipping the key under the front door.

She was recharged, refreshed, and ready for the hunt again. All she needed now was for this Karen to try and persuade Terry to reveal his whereabouts. She didn't need the money, but it seemed a waste to leave it behind, seeing as how the boys were not going to use it anymore. She skipped down the road, back towards Karen's home.

She had absorbed Kevin's memories, but not his flatmate's; no doubt she was too late, and his brain was already dead. Kevin was an out-and-out liar. He had had only one woman sexually before, but he was right about having no oral sex experience. He did not have any money in his bank account and lived off his salary checks, spending them almost as soon as he cashed them. Nothing else of interest with this one, so she pushed his memories to the back of her mind.

***

'She's killed again,' said Terry, dropping the book he was reading onto his lap.

Tampong had just arrived back from the office and had just sat down when she too felt the horrible sensation.

'Are you sure?'

'Yes, but this time it felt different.'

'In what way different?'

'I am not sure. It was as if someone else was doing the killing rather than Shoil.'

'I am not sure I understand.'

'You and me both. It doesn't make any sense, I know, but it just felt different.'

Just then, the doorbell rang, so Tampong got up, taking one last look at Terry, before opening the door. A man in light-blue overalls stood at the door holding a black toolbox.

'AT&T, ma'am,' he explained, 'I am here to install your internet and telephone.'

'Ho right, please come in.'

Tampong stepped aside to let him in.

Terry closed his book when the telephone engineer came in, who nodded to him. He placed his toolbox down and walked over to the wall, where he unscrewed a telephone box panel.

'Will it take long?' Terry asked.

'Nope. These units are already wired up for the internet. I just have to connect the box, activate the line, and you will be good to go.'

Tampong was not listening but thinking about what Terry had said earlier, trying to understand what it could mean. She considered all the possibilities but kept coming to the same conclusion, that Shoil must have transformed. All the pieces fitted together, the unusual sensation they both felt, the need to absorb males to replenish herself, and the fact that Terry said she seemed different. That must be it. So now they would have to be extra careful as they would have no idea what she looked like. Things couldn't get much worse, could they? The only positive out of all of this was that she still felt a long way away.

'All done,' said the technician, snapping Tampong out of her thoughts.

'Sorry?' she asked.

'The internet and telephone,' Terry clarified, 'they are working now. We are back in the twenty-first century.'

'Ho, great, and thank you.'

'You're welcome, ma'am. You both have a great evening.'

She showed him out of the door. By the time she came back into the room, Terry already had his laptop out and was trying to log onto the internet. He thumbed his fist into the air triumphantly.

'Yes, it's working,' he said, pleased with himself.

'Great, so now you can try and contact Karen, yes?'

'Yep. It's too early to call now as she will most likely still be at school, and I don't want to disturb her, but I'll send her a text message saying we can Skype tomorrow, which will be evening her time, if she is free.'

'I know you will feel much better once you connect with her.'

'Ain't that the truth.'

He switched off the internet, closed his computer, and picked up his book again. He would try again tomorrow, give her one more chance. He would text her one more time. The memory of Shoil had been pushed to the back of his mind, mainly due to the excitement of being back online again. He never realized how much he depended on the internet, not until he didn't have it. He could not imagine how people coped ten or twenty years ago when such things didn't exist. It was a wonder people ever had relationships, unless they were with local people, and they did not travel. As Tampong said, he would feel much better once he had talked to her and found out she was OK and out of any danger, at least for the time being.

He just hoped she would actually Skype, if only for his peace of mind.

***

Gary's eyes shone blue, like luminous lights in the night, their blue glow clearly visible to Tracey.

'What is it?' she asked nervously.

She was forced to look in his direction when she saw the blue glow coming from his face.

'There has been another attack.'

'Shoil?'

'I don't know. It felt different this time.'

'How so?'

'I am not sure, just so very different.'

'What do you think it means?'

'Again I'm not sure, just that whatever it is, it has attacked.'

Tracey looked worried.

'It's not Joanne, is it?'

'No, I am sure I would have felt her if that was the case.'

'Then some other poor soul has lost their life.'

'I am afraid so.'

'How many more?'

She said the words more to herself and then went quiet.

'If it wasn't Shoil, then who could it have been, Tampong?' she finally asked.

'It didn't feel like her, strange as it might sound. This felt new even.'

Tracey looked at him with a puzzled expression on her face, then sat back and slowly picked up her book. She tried to start reading again but had lost interest in it. She dropped the book on her lap and gazed blankly at the wall opposite.

Gary did not want to worry her any more than necessary. Didn't want to tell her that this was not just one attack, but two. It felt different because it *was* different, confirming his worst fears that one of them must have transformed. But why? Was the body damaged or diseased in some way? Was it disabled in an accident? So many questions, so many possibilities, and no answers, not yet in any case. Could the two girls have found each other, and one even killed and absorbed the other? He hoped to god that was not the case, because, if so, it would be just about impossible to stop whoever was left. This would be a challenge even for Jon. No, there had to be another explanation. Surely he would have felt both of them coming together. If he was wrong, then, again, god help them.

God help the world.

***

Shoil arrived back at Karen's house, opened the front door, and went straight upstairs to take a shower. She needed to wash the smell of dead men from her body. She went into her bedroom and started brushing her hair when she saw the mobile phone in the mirror's reflection. The little green light was blinking. She stood up and walked over to pick it up, noticing she had one new message. She listened to it.

'Shit,' she said aloud, checking the clock on her bedside table.

She quickly grabbed the laptop, switched it on and clicked the Skype icon. It finally loaded, too slow for her liking. She checked the last log-on and was relieved to see that there was no missed call, so he hadn't tried after all. Initially, she was pleased she hadn't missed him, then she began to worry, thinking that he would not bother to contact her again. She slammed the laptop's lid down and was almost tempted to throw it across the room but controlled herself on the off chance he would call again. She checked the mobile again to see if there was a number registered. Not surprisingly, the number had been withheld. Tampong being cautious, no doubt, and not that stupid. No, she would have to continue and play the waiting game, again. Wait for him to contact her—it was her only option to find him. Zelphur used to say that patience was a virtue, but this was a virtue that did not sit too well with her. For her, sitting around doing nothing was just a waste of valuable time, time that could be usefully spent doing other things. However, her options were limited, and for now she had to rely on him contacting her. She decided to use some of the waiting time by having a bath, so she walked into the bathroom, put the plug into the tub, and ran the water. A shower was not enough, and she needed to soak away those men. She poured some Radox into the running water, undressed, then stepped into the half-filled bath.

Her mobile phone was on the bedside table.

***

Terry lay on the sofa feeling a little bored. He picked up Tampong's mobile, which she had given to him to text but not call. He pressed contacts and selected Karen's mobile, pressing the text icon. He wrote:

We are back on the internet now and I really want to Skype with you tomorrow, 11 pm your time. Please connect with me. I need to talk with you, to make sure you are OK. I understand if you don't want anything more to do with me, but please just Skype so that I can at least know you are OK, if only for us to say one final goodbye. Hope to see you tomorrow. Terry.

He pressed send, and the screen disappeared. He truly hoped that she would connect tomorrow. He had this bad feeling about her for some time now and just needed to know that no harm had come to her, because of him. He could never forgive himself if that was the case. None of this was her fault. She was just in the wrong place at the wrong time, with the wrong guy, namely him. It was not as though they had history together. In fact, they had only been out on a couple of dates. He just wanted her to have an ordinary, happy life. Meet someone decent, someone who would love her and take care of her. He could do the first, but not the second.

His mind then turned to Sandi, and he began to wonder whether he was putting her at risk too. She had a much stronger character than Karen and was confident in herself. She knew what she wanted and went after it. He felt so alive in her presence and so at ease. He could not let this fear of the unknown rule his entire life. He nodded to himself as if deciding something. He put the phone down, got off the sofa and grabbed his jacket and walked out of the unit. Tampong mentioned that there was a large supermarket down the road and was walkable. It was called Marks and Spencer's, he seemed to remember. He could not believe that some of the British stores had made it all the way to Singapore. He would see if he could find it, or some other store, buy some fresh bread, ham, and tomato, then come back and make himself a nice ham sandwich. He shut the front door, locked it, and walked out of the estate, turning right down Bras Basah Road. He crossed over when the sidewalk ended. It was a lovely, sunny day, not too hot, and not a cloud in the sky. Perfect for walking. He was just beginning to think he must have walked the wrong way when he spotted a bank on the corner. After that appeared to be a large car park, which looked promising. As he entered the car park he saw the supermarket on the left. She was right, so he went shopping.

***

After a long soak, Shoil felt revived and refreshed. She wrapped her bathrobe around her and strolled into the bedroom, brushing her new hair. It felt different and she enjoyed the sensation. It was calming, relaxing even. Still brushing her hair, she noticed her phone blinking at her again. She dropped the brush and rushed over to the phone, picked it up and saw she had another missed text. She read Terry's message, and a broad smile appeared across her face again. He hadn't given up on her.

In fact, he would have Skyped yesterday but did not have any internet. She would definitely Skype with him tonight though. Today was turning out to be a great day after all. She heard a noise coming from downstairs, so guessed her mother must have returned home from work. She put her phone back down and went downstairs.

'Ha, you're home then,' her mother said, seeing her come downstairs.

'Of course,' Shoil answered, puzzled by the comment, 'where else would I be?'

'Ho, the usual place, your friends.'

'They are all busy tonight,' she answered.

Her mother gave her a strange look, which Shoil caught.

'What?'

'Ho nothing,' replied her mother, although something was clearly not right, leaving Shoil feeling a little on edge.

She needed to be careful, not slip up and make any stupid mistakes. Not this close to connecting with the boy again.

'Are you hungry?' her mother then asked, changing the subject.

'Sure.'

'OK, I'll put a pie and some chips in the oven. Good enough?'

'Good enough.'

Her mother looked at her again.

'Are you sure you are OK?'

'Of course, why do you ask?'

'Ho, it's probably nothing, pay no attention to me.'

'OK,' said Shoil.

That awkward feeling was building up inside her.

'I'm going to watch some TV until dinner is ready.'

Her mother watched her walk into the lounge, her eyebrows frowning together.

After twenty minutes, dinner was ready. Her mother placed two plates on the kitchen table and took the pie and chips out of the oven, putting one pie on her plate and one on Shoil's. She placed half the chips likewise.

'Dinner's ready,' she called out.

'Be right there,' answered Shoil.

She got up and walked into the kitchen, sat down, and sniffed the meal.

'Smells good,' she observed.

'Enjoy,' her mother said half-heartedly, still looking at her daughter.

Shoil began to eat. She had taken three mouthfuls when she realized her mother was staring at her.

'What?' she said, resting the base of the knife and fork on the table.

'Who are you?'

'What!'

Shoil's bad feeling was about to erupt.

'Who are you?' her mother repeated.

Shoil guessed she must have been found out. She was not sure how this happened, but her mother clearly noticed something different about her.

'Don't be silly, Mother,' she snapped, continuing to eat, trying not to make eye contact.

'Since when were you left-handed?'

'What!'

'You heard. Why are you eating with your knife in your left hand and not your right? Did you damage it or something?'

'Er, yep, that's exactly what I did. It happened at sports yesterday. The ball hit my hand really hard, and it hurts like hell now.'

'Must have interfered with your beliefs too.'

'What do you mean?'

'You always eat your chips first, leaving the pie till last. You always left your favorite part of the meal to last.'

Shoil looked down at her plate, realizing that she had been eating the way *she* used to, and not the way Karen did.

'Busted,' she said, gripping the fork tightly.

'So, what on earth has happened to you, Karen?'

'My body has been taken over by a superior being and my soul no longer exists.'

Her mother suddenly looked angry.

'Don't try to change the subject by making silly remarks. Tell me the truth.'

'I ***AM*** telling you the truth.'

Shoil's patience snapped. She flicked the fork across the room, headfirst, straight into her mother's throat. The head of the fork disappeared into her neck as soon as it made contact. Her mother gasped at the sudden impact, the force rocking her head backwards. Instinctively, she pulled the fork away immediately, dropping it onto the table. She spat blood from her mouth, staggering to her feet, making her way towards her phone. Shoil calmly rose to her feet, allowing her nails to transform into long, tiny spears. She blocked the door as her mother staggered towards it. As she went to push Shoil out of the way, Shoil brought her arms quickly up and jabbed her nails into both sides of her mother's neck. The thin spears had grown in length and burst out the other side of her mother's neck. Before her mother had a chance to react to this new attack, Shoil twisted her hands, pulling the blades across the exposed neck, severing it cleanly. She had to sidestep quickly to avoid the head dropping against her. It flopped onto the floor. The eyes were still wide open in shock. The body fell backwards, landing against the kitchen table, covering it with blood. Shoil looked around. This was not the way she had hoped her day would end. It was all going too well. Hey ho. She went into the garage and found some plastic sheets, which she laid next to the headless body. She rolled the body onto the sheet, then kicked the head next to it. Covering the body with the sheets, she then taped them up. After dragging the body feetfirst into the garage, she opened the boot of the mother's car and loaded the body into the back of it before closing the boot again. Returning to the kitchen, she filled a bucket with soapy water and mopped the floor and table, getting rid of the blood. She might need this place for a little bit longer, so she had to hide any evidence of her murderous act. Finished, she slid the rest of her mother's meal onto her own plate and placed it in the microwave. Once heated, she sat back down and began to enjoy the rest of her dinner, in peace. She looked at the clock. It was only 6 pm, so she decided to drive out later and ditch the body in the woods. Then she would return to the house and wait.

Wait for Terry to call and reveal his new whereabouts.

***

Terry shivered. He felt the murder, only this one felt close, not physically, but impacted someone he knew emotionally. He was sure it was not Karen, but it could be someone close to her. A friend perhaps. It felt quick, like there was no absorption this time. He didn't like not knowing what was happening. The sooner he spoke to her the better. He thought about just opening his laptop and trying to contact her, but then checked the time difference. She would be at school and private laptops were forbidden, and she would not have returned home yet. He would have to be patient for a little bit longer. To help pass the time, he decided to text Sandi and was pleased to get an immediate response from her.

'Hey you, what's up?' she asked.

'Missing you,' he replied.

'Sweet.'

'Are you still free Saturday?'

'Sure am. What did you have in mind?'

'How about watching a football game? Singapore are playing.'

'Are they any good?'

'Leading the league at the moment, and undefeated.'

'Sounds like a good team then, but I don't know where to get tickets.

'No problem. My friend has a couple of tickets going spare. I'll grab them from her. The game kicks off at six pm, so we can enjoy the whole day together before it starts.'

'Sounds perfect. Meet you at eleven am in front of the library then.'

'See you then. xoxo.'

He smiled when he read the xoxo at the end of her message, although he was not sure if this was better than three kisses.

Still, he would take it. Perhaps they could go back to her place after the game, grabbing something to eat on the way. That took care of part of the weekend, now he just had to finish nicely with Karen, and that would be the end of that particular short romance. He switched on the TV and started to watch *Friends*. That always helped pass the time.

Eventually, the time arrived, so he picked up his laptop, opened it, and switched it on. He took a deep breath as he clicked the Skype icon to load the tool. He hovered over the connect button for an instant. His instinct was telling him not to make the connection, but his heart was telling him the opposite. He owed it to Sandi to finish cleanly with Karen and just check she was OK. No loose ends and a clear conscience. He pressed the connect button and the call went through. It rang three times, and he was just beginning to think that she was not going to answer when her face appeared on his screen.

It *was* Karen, and she was smiling warmly at him. Relief flooded through his body on seeing her.

'Hey, you,' he began, not sure how best to start an awkward conversation.

'Hey, Terry,' she replied, sounding friendly, 'how are you doing?'

'I'm fine, thanks, and you?'

'Top of the world.'

'I am so glad to see you and that you are OK.'

'Of course, and why should I not be OK?'

'Ho, no particular reason. Just that we have not spoken for some time.'

'You mean since you up'd and left me?'

She put as much hurt into her voice as she could.

Terry coughed nervously.

'I deserved that, but I am genuinely glad to see you.'

'Well, here I am.'

She bit her lip. Getting hostile so early was not going to get her anywhere.

'Anyway, what happened is water under the bridge. Glad you are back on the internet. Did your move go smoothly?'

'Wow, I am so pleased you are taking such an adult view about this. It was not my ideal way of leaving you, but I had little choice and, yes, we moved into a nice house now.'

'So you booked out of the hotel you were in then?'

She knew the answer already but wanted to see how he responded.

'Right. It was quite quick in the end. My aunt found this place, so we checked out and moved in here. It is great, by the way.'

'It is?' she tried to sound excited, 'then tell me about it.'

'Well,' he began, 'it's a town house . . .'

'A what?' she interrupted.

'It's a house on three levels, thin, and connected to three other similar houses. That's why it's called a town house. Anyway, it has a garage on the first floor, the kitchen, dining room, and lounge is on the second floor, along with a study with its own toilet and shower, then upstairs there are two large bedrooms, both with their own bathroom, and a landing where the washing machine and dryer are located.'

'Sounds great. Near anything interesting?'

'Actually yes. We have a small balcony that overlooks a private lake.'

'A lake you say.'

'Right. And just down the road are all the shops, banks, restaurants, and stuff that you need. All within walking distance.'

'Wow, sounds like you are in love with the place already.'

'I am. You would love it here too.'

'If only.'

He bowed his head.

'Right, if only.'

She knew she had to keep him talking, so decided to change the subject.

'So what's the weather like there?'

'Oh, it's quite hot here and getting hotter. The summers I have been told can be roasting. We are so lucky to have a swimming pool here.'

'You have your own swimming pool?'

'Well, it's not ours, it belongs to the estate we are on. It's quite big. Looking forward to using it in a few weeks. It's a little bit on the chilly side at the moment.'

'So what other delights does this place have to offer?'

'Well, there is a modern gym, a reception area, and all within a gated community.'

'What's a gated community?'

'Ho, it's where there is a guarded entrance, and you need a code or remote to gain entrance through the gates.'

'OK. So does it suit your aunt too?'

'You bet. She is the one that chose this place, in fact.'

'She must like it too then?'

'Of course, and it is very handy for her work. It is only a twelve-minute drive to and from her office.'

'OK, that's really handy.'

'You can say that again.'

'So, any places of interest for you nearby?'

She was digging but wanted to see how far she could go.

'Yes.'

He seemed keen to tell her about this place.

'I can walk down the street, and there is a river that runs right across the town. If you follow it, it takes you to a new town where they have just built a casino and lots of nice shops and restaurants. It's a good hour's walk, but worth the trip. It's a great place to run too, so I am going to buy myself some running shoes and stuff and take up running. And there is a library just across the road. You know how much I like reading.'

'Wow, a new Terry. Never took you to be a runner. Are you aiming for anything in particular?'

'It's like you are reading my mind,' he said. 'well, yes, I would like to run the Marine Bay sponsored marathon that takes place around May of each year. I think I have enough time to train for that. If not, then maybe the half-marathon. It can be very humid here, so you have to get used to the climate to be confident of finishing the course.'

She made a mental note of Marine Bay.

'That's cool.'

'And what about you, what are your short-term objectives?'

She so wanted to tell him that she wanted to hunt him down and kill that bitch Tampong he was with. Then kill him if he did not join her.

'Ho, just to finish school and go to college,' she answered instead.

'Really?'

He sounded surprised. Shoil picked up on his change, knowing she must have said something wrong.

'Yes, why?'

'Well, I thought you hated school and wanted to leave as soon as possible.'

She flashed through Karen's memory. He was right.

'That's right. I do hate school, but that doesn't mean I don't want to finish empty-handed and not go on to college.'

'Guess not,' he agreed.

She gave a quiet sigh of relief. Got away with that one.

'So, what about us then?' she asked directly.

'What about us?'

'Is there still something between us?'

He looked away briefly, then slowly returned his eyes to the screen.

'Listen, Karen,' he began, sounding remorseful, 'the distance between us makes it almost impossible to have any sort of relationship. I think it is better we go our separate ways now.'

'Go our separate ways?' she tried to sound shocked and horrified, 'then why did you even bother to contact me this evening?'

'As I said before, to check that you were OK.'

'OK about what?' she demanded, raising her voice.

'Just that you were OK and that no harm had come to you.'

'Why should any harm come to me?'

'Well, life can be a bitch at times. You never know.'

'Did your aunty do something terrible while she was here? Is there someone hunting for her?'

She knew she was treading very close to the truth but wanted to see how he reacted.

'No, my aunty didn't do anything bad, as such, but, yes, there are people looking for her.'

'And has she put me in harm's way now?'

'No, no, that's why we moved here.'

'How do you know it was far enough away?'

'We believe it to be so, that's all I can say.'

'So we finish because your aunt is being hunted. Doesn't sound very fair, does it?'

'No, no it's not, but that's how it is.'

'So why can't you leave her there and come home?'

'I have to stay with her. To help her.'

'From whoever is hunting her?'

'Yes.'

'Do you think a young man like you can really help her?'

'I am not without my talents,' he snapped back, hurt that she thought he was helpless.

Good, it's working, she thought.

'How can you help her?'

'I just can, that's all I can say. We are stronger together.'

'Perhaps you are even stronger on your own then?'

She knew she was skating on thin ice but had to take the risk.

Terry stared at her for a long time, trying to work out what she actually meant by that last statement. Wondering if she had some idea about his abilities.

'You might be right,' he conceded, 'but I owe her and have to stay with her, until this is all over, that is.'

'And when will that be?'

'When that bitch . . . I mean once we locate the people hunting us and deal with them.'

'You are scaring me,' she lied.

She almost made him crack, almost made him reveal his true identity and purpose.

'Sorry, I didn't mean to.'

He looked at the wall clock.

'I think we have spoken for long enough. It warms my heart to see you well, and I truly hope you have a good life.'

'So you are just going to say goodbye, are you?'

'I think it's best, Karen.'

'What if I don't want to finish this way?'

'Karen . . . it just wouldn't work . . . it's too late . . .'

'Too late!'

The anger built up inside her again, more for Karen than for herself.

'Do you mean you have found someone else?'

He looked down. There was her answer, but she wanted to hear the words.

'Tell me,' she demanded.

He looked up again.

'Yes, I have met someone here.'

'You didn't wait very long, did you?'

'It's not like that, Karen . . . it just happened.'

'Just happened, JUST HAPPENED,' she screamed out the words a second time.

'Karen, please . . .'

'Go screw yourself, Terry. You were just using me. Just a plaything to pass the time away. You never wanted me, never loved me. You just used me.'

She wanted to really play on his heartstrings.

'Don't be like that, Karen. Let's not finish like this.'

'Ho, would you rather I wished you all the best and hope that you have found true love and live a long and happy life with this, this, woman?'

'No, nothing like that.'

She interrupted him.

'Did you know her when you were here? Is that why you went away?'

'No, no, she works in a restaurant downtown. That is where I met Sandi. She offered to show me around the island, and we just hit it off.'

'So, have you bedded her yet?'

She made a note of her name.

Terry looked away from the screen again, clearly embarrassed.

'So you have.'

He said nothing, but his silence was deafening, and he could not bring himself to make eye contact with her.

'You bastard. You couldn't have me, so you found some foreign bitch to bed instead.'

'I hardly call Singaporean foreign,' he argued. 'Look, this is getting us nowhere. I think I should go now.'

'And just leave me, just like that?'

Again she made a mental note of Singaporean, not that that helped any. She already knew the island he was on, but it might be helpful to know that his new bitch was a local girl.

'I don't see any other way, do you?'

'Just tell me where you are, that would help a little bit, knowing where you are.'

'It's too risky.'

'You told me I'd be safe here now that you have gone. Was that a lie too?'

Her eyes were wide open, her face going red with anger.

'No, no it's not a lie.'

He was confused, not sure how to deal with this almost hysterical woman now.

'Listen to me,' he began, trying to keep his voice calm, 'you will be safe as long as we both stay here on this island.'

He thought about telling her the community he lived in as well, as it could not hurt as he could be in any country.

So he was still on the island, living in a gated community with a private lake, close to shops, etc. He also mentioned a library just across the road.

'OK, that sounds like you are on the other side of the world. So will I ever see you again?'

She tried to make a tear appear, but it proved harder than she thought. Obviously, she wasn't that disappointed about finishing with him.

'Right and, no, I don't think we will be seeing each other again.'

'Then I guess all that is left is to say goodbye.'

'Don't be like that, Karen.'

'Goodbye, Terry,' she said and pressed the disconnect button.

His screen returned to the Skype home page, so he switched the laptop off and slowly closed the lid. Once again, it did not go quite as he planned. She seemed OK at first, then became very hostile when she learned about Sandi. Perhaps he should not have mentioned her, but too late now. She cannot claim he was not honest with her. No, it's better this way, out in the open, no secrets. Anyway, it's over now, she can move on, and Shoil can leave her alone.

Shoil immediately entered Marine Bay hotel in her search field. Several entries were found, indicating UK, Italy, and Singapore. She then typed in Marine Bay sponsored marathon, and this time only Singapore came up.

'Nearly found you,' she said aloud.

If nothing else, she could be there for the marathon and look for him. She then tapped her finger against her chin, thinking about what else he said. She then searched Singapore Library. Three hits came up: Singapore Central Library, Singapore City Library, and Singapore public library. She clicked on the map of the first two, but they didn't fit his description of the place. He mentioned one being just opposite his gated community. She clicked the map on the third hit and looked closer at the detail. Orchard Street ran along its front, and opposite were two estates, both backing onto a lake.

'That's it,' she yelled in delight, 'found you.'

She followed the road down, and it showed a bank and then shops. She nodded her delight. The conversation was indeed worth waiting for. She had found him. She made a note of the two estates and their addresses then saved the page before closing down her computer. She walked over to the sideboard and picked up the phone. She needed another flight to Singapore, only this time she intended to find him and Tampong, dealing with them both. She was determined not to return this time until her targets had been found and dealt with.

The next available flight was on Monday, so she booked herself another business class seat, giving herself a month there before opting to return. She might as well check out the place, once she had dealt with her little business, given that he seemed so impressed with the place, or it may be just because of this new girl. Ho, she hoped she found her too. If she absorbed the girl's body, then she would have all her memories too. If she knew where he lived, then she would know. It was going to be another long, boring flight, but the prize would be worth the trip. She went up to Karen's bedroom and looked through her wardrobe. She didn't have much in the way of nice clothes. She checked her mother's wardrobe. She had a few nice things, so took them out, throwing them onto the bed. She checked the chest of drawers, finding several nice knickers and matching bras. If nothing else, her mother liked to look good underneath. Having checked the size, she found they would fit her. She now wished she could have absorbed the mother but knew that that was not possible. Surely she would have a stash of cash hidden somewhere. Karen just had her savings tin, with little over a thousand pounds in it. That would do nicely as pocket money. Rifling through drawers and cupboards, she did find some cash under the mattress, nearly two thousand in fact. Obviously did not trust the banks. She stuffed the money down her bra before continuing her search. There was some jewelry and a nice watch, so she pocketed that. Satisfied, she took one final look around, then gave up looking, going back downstairs to make herself another meal. She suddenly felt hungry again

At the dinner table she looked over her small find. She had just over three thousand in cash, some jewelry, and the watch. Not much for two people's life inheritance. Perhaps her mother had more money stashed away somewhere, but this would have to do. She still had Robert's credit card and his bank account. She would withdraw some more cash from the ATM machine and buy herself some Singapore dollars with the money she had. For now, she decided it was time to go shopping. She dropped her dirty plate into the sink, not caring that it smashed on contact. Picking up her coat, she left the house, locking the door as she did so. She was whistling to herself as she walked down the street. Two boys were walking in the opposite direction towards her.

'Hey, it's Karen,' one said, pointing towards her.

As they got closer, her memory kicked in. The one on the left was called Robin, and the other one Trevor.

'Hey, boys,' she said in a welcoming voice.

'What happened to you today then?' Robin asked.

'What do you mean?'

'You skipped school. Reported as a no-show.'

'Ho, I wasn't feeling very well this morning, so Mom let me stay at home.'

'You look OK now,' observed Trevor.

'Yeah, it passed, so I am just getting some fresh air.'

'Well, Miss Pincher was asking after you. Nobody knew where you were.'

'Well, screw Miss Pincher.'

The boys looked at each other.

'Don't think Pincher will appreciate that.'

'Who gives a shit?' she was getting a little annoyed.

'Pincher does. She said she would phone your mother to check,' Robin said with a puzzled expression on his face.

'What's up with you?' asked Trevor.

She realized that she was not acting like Karen but like Shoil. She had to correct that.

'Sorry, just not feeling myself today,' she answered honestly.

'You can say that again,' said Trevor, 'never heard you cuss out like that before.'

'People change.'

'Not you, Karen. Not you,' answered Robin. 'Anyway, Pincher is on your case. You have never missed a school day before, and I think she is concerned. Said something about coming around to check on you.'

That caused a reaction from Shoil. The last thing she needed right now was someone nosing around at the house so soon, especially with a dead body still in the boot of the car.

'Thanks for the heads-up. I am going back home anyway as I have had enough fresh air for one day.'

'Ok, see you at school on Monday perhaps,' said Trevor as the boys started to walk away.

She just waved them away, picking up her pace to get back to the house. As she reached Karen's home, a woman was standing at the front door, knocking.

'Miss Pincher?' asked Shoil, walking up behind her.

She turned quickly, startled by the sudden presence behind her.

'Ho, it's you, Karen. What happened to you today?'

'Sorry, miss, but I was not feeling very well and stayed at home. Feeling much better now though and will be at school on Monday.'

'So it would seem. Why did your mother not call the school?'

'She must have forgotten.'

'Unlikely. I know your mother very well. She is a stickler for protocol. Where is she? She isn't answering the door. She must be home because her car is in the driveway still.'

She pointed to the vehicle in the driveway.

'*Shit,*' said Shoil to herself, she had forgotten all about the car.

'Perhaps she is upstairs and didn't hear you knock. I'll go and check and let her know you were here and get her to call you.'

She went to open the front door, but the teacher did not budge.

'Not good enough, Karen. I need to speak with your mother now, to check that you are telling me the truth and didn't just skip school. It is your first time, I know, but you will not be the first girl to do so.'

Shoil quickly ran through her options, which were limited.

'Ok then, why don't you come in, and I will fetch her for you.'

'That will do very nicely, thank you.'

Shoil opened the door, stepping aside to let her teacher in. Miss Pincher walked into the lounge and stood in the middle of the carpet, arms folded, waiting for her mother. Shoil went downstairs, and the teacher heard her open and close a door and thought she heard Karen talking, then the door opened again and Shoil walked back up the stairs and into the lounge, carrying a dead body.

Miss Pincher's arms dropped to her side as her eyes widened in shock and her mouth dropped open. The body was covered in blood, which was still dripping from her fingertips, as a woman's arms flopped by her side.

'Here she is,' announced Shoil, dropping the headless body onto the carpet at the feet of the teacher, who involuntarily took a step backwards. She gasped.

'What . . . what happened here . . . why did you . . .'

She stopped talking when she looked at Shoil. Her eyes were twinkling orange as she raised her arms towards the teacher.

'What . . . Karen . . . what are you doing?' she asked, raising one hand to her heart.

'Giving you what you want,' Shoil said coldly.

The teacher was shaking and could not control her hands. Her pulse was racing as she tried to take in all that was happening.

'I need to call the police.'

She dropped her hand to her purse, frantically searching for her mobile.

'I don't think so,' warned Shoil, causing the woman to stop in her tracks.

'What!?' she asked, confused.

Shoil said nothing, instead she fired two spears from her fingers, which flew across the room to puncture the teacher's chest. Miss Pincher was thrown backwards by the impact, crashing against the sideboard, causing ornaments to fall and smash onto the floor. She slid down the sideboard as her chest quickly turned red. Her hand was still in her purse. She mumbled a few incomprehensible words before her head fell forward against her chest. She was dead.

Shoil just stared at the teacher for a little while.

'Why could you not just mind your own business?' she said to the corpse, as if expecting a reply.

She walked up to the dead teacher, grabbed her ankles, and pulled her back onto the carpet next to her mother's body.

Wrapping both bodies in the carpet, she stood back to think. Clearly she could not stay in the house any longer. It would not be long before the teacher went missing. Those two boys knew where she was going, so it would not be long before the police came calling on her.

She carried the bodies upstairs, undressed them both, then placed them on the bed. Pulling the blankets away. She placed the teacher's head on her mother's chest, wrapping her mother's arm around the teacher's back. She then went back to the car to retrieve her mother's head, which she placed carefully back in place. She stepped back. They looked like lovers, lovers who had been discovered and killed. The mystery would be why the mother was beheaded and not the other woman. That should keep the police busy for a little while, at least long enough for her to get out of the country. She had no desire to return to this house in any case. Going back downstairs, she picked up the teacher's bag and searched through it. Her purse had forty-five pounds in notes and some change, all of which she pocketed.

'True what they say,' she said aloud, 'teachers really don't get paid very much, do they?'

She kept the mobile, checking she could access it. Miss Pincher obviously did not believe in safeguarding her information. There was no screen lock on her phone. Other than a small notebook, pen, housekeys, lipstick, and a few store cards, nothing else of interest was found. She contemplated keeping the keys but decided against it. She had no idea where the teacher lived, and it was probably wiser she was not seen anywhere near the woman's home. She went back up to her room to finish packing. She still had time to do some shopping. Going back downstairs, she picked up her mother's car keys, walked outside, opened the boot of the car, dropped her luggage inside, then closed it up again.

Unseen by her, the neighbor's net curtains twitched slightly, suggesting someone was spying on her. A grey-haired woman had poked her head out of the corner of the window and was watching as the teacher arrived, then the daughter, and the two disappeared inside.

Inside the house, Shoil slipped the keys into her pocket before leaving the house. She checked the front door was locked, then headed off to do some final shopping. She had the weekend to get through before she was back in the air again. She could not wait to leave this home of death.

All the time the net-twitcher watched.

***

Terry's eyes turned orange as he felt Shoil kill again yesterday. He finished off shaving and could see his eyes in the mirror's reflection; they still had small specks of orange in the corner, which he knew would fade. He wasn't paying attention and nicked himself with his razor, so dropped his razor and grabbed a tissue, dabbing at the blood.

'What are you up to, Shoil?' he asked aloud. 'You are being quite active for some reason. What are you planning?'

The blood stopped, so he finished shaving, washed the shaving foam from his face, then wiped his face dry with a towel. He applied some aftershave balm, which always made his face feel smooth. He checked himself in the mirror. He still hadn't quite got the hang of this shaving thing, although he only had one nick this time, which stopped as soon as his face was dry. He'd been shaving for a couple of years now. He had no father or brother to show him how it should be done, so it had been a bit of trial and error. The first time he looked like he shaved with a broken bottle. He was slowly getting better, but still felt he needed training. He slipped his white T-shirt over his head, tucking it into his jeans. He then opened the bathroom cabinet and selected some Aramis aftershave, which he dabbed on his chin.

'Ready,' he announced to himself.

He checked the wall clock, and he had plenty of time before he had to leave to meet Sandi.

Tampong was already in the kitchen, having made herself breakfast.

As he walked downstairs, he decided not to tell her about Shoil. No point in worrying her unnecessarily.

'Wow, look at you, all neat and glamorous.'

He waved her comment away as he sat on the sofa.

'So, did you speak with Karen yesterday?'

'I did.'

'And?'

'And it's really over, but she is OK. That's the main thing.'

'How did she take it?'

'Strangely, if I am honest. Our conversation started off OK, and she was quite friendly. She became hostile towards the end and just said goodbye and hung up.'

'So what triggered the hostility, any ideas?'

'I think it was because I mentioned Sandi.'

Tampong raised her eyebrows at the news.

'You told her about Sandi! No wonder she turned hostile on you.'

'I wanted to be honest with her.'

'There is honesty, and plain suicidal, and that, my dear, was suicidal.'

'I thought it was always best to tell the truth.'

'Sometimes ignorance is better.'

'Ho well, it's done now. She can move on from me now.'

'Guess so. So, where are you up to today?'

'We are going to watch a football game and then might go to the movies, but I haven't decided on the second option yet.'

'So what do you think you might almost watch?'

'Almost watch?'

'You don't do into a dark room with a pretty girl to actually watch a movie, do you?'

He smiled while his cheeks blushed.

'I was thinking about *The Tourist*, which has just been released.

'Aha. I heard about that movie. It stars Johnny Depp and Angelina Jolie, doesn't it?'

'I think so, Johnny Depp for sure.'

'Then you must tell me what you thought of it . . . assuming you see much of it. I might go and watch that myself.'

'On your own?'

'Of course.'

'Why don't you have a boyfriend, or a friend who is a boy at least?'

She seemed to contemplate his question.

'Guess I have not found the right guy yet.'

'I bet you have not even looked, have you?'

She simply shrugged her shoulders.

'It's not as if you are not bad-looking. You are quite fit for someone your age.'

She looked at him, not sure whether that was a compliment or an insult, deciding it was the former, as he didn't really have a nasty bone in his body.

'Thank you. I think.'

She went to brush her fingers through his hair, but he moved his head away, guarding his hair with his hands.

'Oops, sorry,' she said, 'don't want to mess you up. Particularly as you will be spending the day with a lady.'

He looked at the clock.

'Guess so, but I should text Sandi and see where she is. Are you going to be OK on your own?'

'I'll be OK. I can look after myself . . . for my age.'

He bent his head slightly to the right.

'Go,' she encouraged, 'and enjoy yourself.'

She threw him her mobile.

'Thanks. Have a great evening.'

'Wait . . .' she then said quickly.

He looked inquisitively at her.

She picked up her purse and took some money out and handed it over to him.

'What's this for?'

'A nice day,' she said simply.

'Thanks. You are the best.'

He grabbed his coat and placed the money inside his wallet, waved to her, and rushed upstairs. She watched him go. Her heart felt heavy, and she suddenly felt sad. She would soon be on her own again, and not for the first time either. She looked around, wrapping her arms around herself. She could not remember the last time she had company, the last time she was with someone as a couple. Would she ever find that again? Could she ever find that again? It would be difficult, if not impossible, to have a lover. He would age, whereas she would eventually switch bodies and continue with her life, and she would have to watch him get older and older, eventually withering away and dying. Still, that should not prevent a short-term romance. Should not stop her from having a physical relationship with someone. Heck, she needed that, wanted that. Perhaps she would follow Terry's lead and go out and find someone. How did he meet Sandi again? In a restaurant, she seemed to remember. She could do that as well. There were also these dating sites, but that was definitely not her cup of tea. Besides, there were lots of weirdos out there, too many, to be honest. Maybe a bar, there are always lonely men out there, drinking their troubles away. So what if they are married, would that really matter? If it was just sex she was looking for, then a married man would not try to tie her down, or look for any long-term relationship, which would be ideal for her. Right, then, no point in sitting around here looking glum and lonely.

Terry jumped on his bed and quickly texted Sandi.

'Hey, gorgeous, are you also free tonight?'

He waited a few minutes before he received her reply.

'What, cannot wait for me to arrive?'

'NOPE. Fancy watching a movie later on?'

'Do you have something in mind?'

'The Tourist.'

'Sound good.'

'Then we can go to a restaurant of your choosing afterwards.'

'OK, sounds perfect. Then let's do it. I'll book the restaurant and will pick you up around 11:00 am. See you soon. xoxo.'

He quickly rushed back downstairs to return Tampong's phone. She could see his eyes twinkling, so knew what that meant.

‘Guess that’s a yes for tonight then?’

‘It is. I will grab my coat and go now as she is picking me up soon.’

‘Enjoy yourselves,’ she called after him.

‘You try to, too. See you later.’

He was right. She slapped her thighs, stood up, went upstairs, undressed, and had a long, hot shower. She blow-dried her hair, put some sexy underwear on, then opened her wardrobe. Her options were limited. She really must go out and do some shopping for herself, now that she was earning decent money. She could afford to splash out a little on herself. She pulled out her short blue dress and put it against her body. It would have to do. The V front was cut a little too low for her liking, but she was wearing a push-up bra, so why not flaunt it a bit! She slipped into the dress and selected a blue pair of shoes, which had high heels. She looked at herself in the long mirror, hardly recognizing the woman that stared back at her.

‘Not bad for a woman in her second millennium,’ she said aloud. She got undressed again and slipped back into her comfortable jeans and T-shirt. She had time to kill so would do a bit of shopping.

All set, she picked up her handbag, dropping her purse and phone into it, grabbed her coat and car keys, then left the house, bound for downtown and some serious girl-shopping.

Terry was pacing back and forth outside the apartment, impatiently waiting as always. He hated the waiting, never knowing for sure if she would turn up or not, wondering whether he would be left waiting outside like a lemon, with perhaps her intended partner now in the corner of some club joking about the boy she left standing outside his own apartment. He knew he should have more confidence about himself, except when it came to women, he was still in his infancy, inexperienced and uneducated in the ways of women.

He needn’t have worried; five minutes later Sandi appeared from around a corner. She stopped the car and got out to greet him. She was wearing a short white dress with matching shoes. Her long blonde hair bounced easily against her shoulders while her bright blue eyes twinkled like stars in the night. She was truly a vision to behold, and this vision always took Terry's breath away. He just stood there opened-mouthed, unable to say anything. Sandi walked right up to him, placed her hands behind his neck, and pulled his head towards hers. She then planted a warm, firm kiss on his lips.

'Hope you haven't been waiting long,' she said, fluttering her eyelids.

'No, not at all,' he lied.

'Lier,' she said, seeing right through him.

He stepped back, holding her hands in his.

'You look amazing, like a picture, like an angel.'

'Well, I'm not sure about the angel bit, but I'll take it. Shall we go?'

'Ha, yes, of course,' he replied, opening the car door for her, watching her as she slid into the driver's seat.

It took only ten minutes to reach the stadium car park. He was surprised to find that the pitch was actually floating on the bay. Sandi's friend had good seats, and they settled down to watch the match, holding each other's hand. Singapore were too strong for their opponents and kept their winning streak alive, finishing 4–0. It was a good match, and both were screaming out their support. Game over, they returned to the car.

Sandi had checked the showings before she left, and they were fortunate to find a car parking place just around the corner from the cinema. She parked and they entered the cinema, again hand in hand. They opted the sit in the back row, which was almost empty. The movie started, not that either of them noticed. They spent most of the showing kissing. When they were not kissing, Sandi had her head resting on his shoulder, while he gently stroked her hair. The lights in the cinema suddenly brightened, indicating that the movie had finished, so people rose and started to leave. Sandi and Terry reluctantly got up and left the cinema. They walked still hand in hand back to where the car was parked.

'Did you enjoy the movie?' she asked.

'What movie?'

They both started laughing as he again held the car door open for her. They quickly drove down the street, turning right before she parked the car again. She nodded with her head towards the restaurant on the opposite side of the street. It looked small and cozy. Terry nodded his approval, so they got out and walked across the street.

They entered the restaurant and walked up to the reception desk, where there was a young man waiting expectantly for them with two menu cards in his hand.

'Good evening, and welcome to Saint-Emilion Restaurant. Do you have a reservation?'

'Yes,' replied Sandi, 'Price.'

'Ha, yes, we have your table ready. Please follow me.'

He walked out from behind the desk and led them to the far side of the restaurant, which was small with around fifteen tables, according to Terry's quick scan. Half of them were already occupied. The receptionist pulled Sandi's chair out. She nodded her thanks before sitting down. He then took the table napkin off the table, flicked it in the air before laying it gently across her lap. Terry suspected that he did this just to google her legs, which were long and exposed due to her short dress. She crossed her legs as Terry sat down opposite her.

'You server will be with you shortly, enjoy your meal,' he said, nodding to them both before stepping back and returning to his desk.

'Looks nice here,' she observed, looking around the restaurant.

'Let's hope the food matches the décor.'

'Wow, quite the pessimist, aren't you?' she said jokingly.

He just gave her a warm smile as a young woman in a white blouse and black trousers came up to their table.

'Bonsoir,' she began, 'my name is Yvette and I'll be your server for this evening. May I interest you in a house aperitive?'

'You may indeed, Yvette. What is it?'

'Tonight we are offering a crémant d'Alsace with a touch of cassis.'

'Sounds good. I'll have that please.'

'Me too,' replied Terry.

'Excellent,' Yvette said with a slight French accent, 'and will you be enjoying a bottle of wine with your meal this evening?'

'We will,' confirmed Terry, looking across to Sandi, who nodded her confirmation.

'Excellent, then I will leave this wine tablet with you. Just select the type of wine and use your finger to guide you through our extensive list.'

She turned away to get their drinks. Another waiter came up and placed a large board by their table.

'These are our specials for tonight. Yvette will be able to answer any questions you may have about these and any other items on our menu,' he explained, turning and walking away.

They both glanced at the board. The steak caught Terry's eye, while the salmon set Sandi's juices flowing. Just then, Yvette turned up with their drinks.

'Here you go,' she said, placing a drink in front of each. 'Have you had time to look over the menu? Any questions?'

'No, thanks,' replied Sandi, 'I am going for the salmon, please. I love salmon.'

'Excellent choice, ma'am, and for you, sir?'

'I'll have the steak, please.'

'Another excellent choice. How would you like that?'

'Medium rare, please.'

'Excellent. Have you had the chance to review the wine list?'

'Not yet,' admitted Terry.

'No problem. I'll get your order in and then return when you are ready.'

'Thanks,' said Terry, picking up the wine tablet.

Yvette left them to it, so they picked up their glasses, clinked them together, then took a sip. Sandi leaned forward towards Terry as he spoke quietly.

'Just as well they didn't ask for any ID.'

Terry nodded, conscious that he could look straight down the front of her dress. He guessed she was not wearing a bra, but it took all of his control to keep his eyes looking at her face. Finally, and much to his relief, she sat back up. If she was testing him, then hopefully he passed.

'So what do you fancy?' she asked suggestively.

'Say what now?'

'The wine,' she clarified, 'what wine to do you fancy?'

'Ho, the wine,' he replied.

He coughed a little in embarrassment.

'It's OK,' she said, reaching over and taking his hand, 'I was only teasing you.'

'So, what's it to be then? You are having fish, so that normally would be white, wouldn't it? While I am having the steak, which would suggest red.'

'A half bottle of each perhaps?' she suggested.

He clicked his fingers with his free hand, while his other still held hers.

'Great solution. OK, I've picked mine, now you pick yours.'

'Hand it over,' she demanded.

She took the tablet from him, placing it on the table and thumbing through the list.

'Got it,' she announced after a quick browse.

Terry raised his arm in the air to attract Yvette's attention, and she came right over.

'We will have half a bottle of cabinet sauvignon, and half a bottle of pinot noir, please.'

He pointed the selections with his finger once Sandi slid it back over to him.

'Excellent. I'll get those sorted out for you.'

She took the tablet and left them, still holding hands. He stroked her hand with his thumb. Her lips parted a little to suggest she was enjoying his caress. His heart was pounding in his chest and his breathing was rapid. He was in love, he was sure. He had never felt anything like this before. She seemed so natural, everything she did seemed right. He could only hope that she felt half the way that he did, but he dare not ask her, yet.

'Are you OK?' she asked, tilting her head slightly as if examining him, 'you look a little hot.'

'It's because of you,' he answered honestly.

Her head bent back quickly, surprised by his comment.

'Sorry?' she questioned.

'I mean,' he stuttered, 'I just love being in your company. It always makes me feel . . .'

'Horny?'

'Warm inside,' he corrected.

'Horny,' she repeated.

Her eyes were smiling at him.

'OK, horny,' he confessed.

'That's OK, because you make me feel special and warm inside too.'

'Really?' he said, gripping her hand a little more firmly.

'Really,' she said, leaning forward again, inviting him to do the same.

He did and their lips met. He felt a tingling sensation run through his whole body at her touch. She seemed full of electricity, or was it just the effect she was having on him? Whatever it was, he liked it. They reluctantly parted company, just in time for Yvette to arrive with a couple of starters.

'We would like to offer you these aperitives. Fresh foie gras set on a slice of toasted brown bread on a bed of salad. Enjoy,' she said, placing the plates in front of them.

Directly behind her a waiter arrived with their bottles. He placed them on the table and opened the white first, pouring a small measure into Sandi's glass. She picked it up, swilled it around a little before taking a sip.

'Delicious,' she said.

He nodded and topped her glass up. He then repeated the process with the red, this time presenting the wine to Terry. He copied Sandi, having no real idea what he was doing. He nodded his approval, so the waiter topped his glass up and placed the bottle on the table.

'Enjoy,' said the waiter.

'Thank you,' replied Terry, picking up a piece of bread, spread some foie gras on top, then popped it into his mouth.

'Hmmm, tasty. What exactly is foie gras then?'

'Goose liver.'

He almost choked.

'What?'

'It's goose liver, well normally. It can also be duck. They are force-fed twice a day to help make them nice and fat, then slaughtered for their liver.'

She popped her bread into her mouth and licked her fingertips.

'Delicious.'

'I sometimes think it is better not to know what you are eating.'

'You're not wrong there,' she said, poking her salad and popping that into her mouth.

Terry poured her some more wine, then topped up his own glass. He slid her glass across to her and she picked it up. He did likewise and they raised their glasses.

'Thanks for being here, Sandi. You are the sun in my day, the wind in my hair, and the beat of my heart.'

'Did you swallow a book of romantic poems or something?'

He looked embarrassed and she felt a little bit guilty now.

'No, really, those were lovely words, Terry, thank you.'

They clinked glasses and took sips of wine. Sandi placed her glass back on the table and she looked pensive. Terry noticed and his heart sank.

'What is it?' he asked, concern etched in his voice, 'did I go too far, say too much?'

'No, nothing like that.'

'Ho god, you are not dumping me already, are you?'

'No, silly, nothing like that either.'

'Then why the strange look?'

She looked up at him. Her eyes were watering.

'Did you mean the things you just said?'

'Of course, every word.'

She took a deep breath.

'It's just that . . . well . . .'

He took her hand to reassure her, and she seemed to welcome his touch, placing her other hand on top of his.

'It's just that I have never felt this way about anyone before. I cannot stop thinking about you . . .'

His heart was pumping even faster now as the excitement built up inside him. Sandi looked deeply into his eyes.

'I know we have not known each other for long, but I think I am falling for you.'

'Really?' he said quietly.

'Really,' she replied.

Just then Yvette arrived with their meals. The aroma reached his nostrils and his steak smelled delicious.

'Enjoy your meal,' said Yvette, who instantly turned away to serve another table.

Sandi and Terry never took their eyes off each other, both were locked in their own world, looking deep into each other's eyes. He gave a little cough to clear his throat.

'I am falling for you too,' he said quietly, 'in fact, I think I fell for you the moment I saw you.'

She raised her eyebrows at him.

'Really! How could you possibly fall for someone you don't even know?'

'I don't know. When I saw you for the first time, I knew I just had to get to know you better.'

'That's so sweet,' she said warmly, patting his hand gently, before looking down at her meal. 'Guess we should start eating this while it is still hot.'

'Right,' he agreed, letting go of her hand and picking up his knife and fork.

***

At the same time, Tampong walked into a cocktail bar and sat at the bar. The barman wiping the bar came up to her.

'Hi there, how are you doing?'

'Fine, thanks.'

'So, what will be your pleasure?'

'Not sure,' she answered, picking up the cocktail card, 'I'll have a tequila sunrise,' she decided.

'Coming up,' said the barman, 'would you like some bar nibbles with that?'

'Yeah, why not.'

'On your own tonight?' he asked, making small talk as he prepared her drink.

'Maybe, why do you ask?'

'Well, none of my business really, it's just that you look amazing, if you don't mind me saying so.'

'I don't mind you saying so,' she replied. 'I heard that barmen speak the truth.'

'We do,' he agreed, 'anyway, the way you look, I am surprised you are on your own.'

'Well, I am.'

'That's very sad.'

'Ho, I'm OK. Sometimes it is better being on your own, that way you are not disappointed.'

'I hear you, lady. I have seen a lot of things on that side of the bar and sometimes wonder on occasion how two people can actually stay together.'

She nodded. She could imagine the stories he could tell, but then again, she had seen more than her fair share of pain and suffering. The barman placed two bowls in front of her, one with nachos and the other had the sauce. She absent-mindedly dipped a nacho into the sauce and ate it. The barman placed her drink in front of her.

'There you go,' he said, knocking her out of her thoughts, 'one tequila sunrise.'

'Thank you,' she said, sipping the drink through the straw, 'delicious.'

'Of course,' he said modestly, continuing to wipe the bar.

As she was sipping her drink, a tall man walked into the bar and sat two stools away from her, dumping himself heavily onto the chair and dropping his bag onto the floor without a care.

The barman slid towards him.

'Hi there, Mr. Strider, how are you doing?'

'Like my world has just ended, Brad,' he snapped.

'OK.'

The barman gave Tampong a quick look, and she just shrugged her shoulders.

'What would you like, sir?'

'Give me two double bourbons on the rocks.'

'Coming right up,' said the barman.

He took two tumblers from under the bar, picked up the bourbon bottle, and poured two measures into both glasses. He scooped up some ice and dropped them into both glasses before sliding them in front of the man. The man said nothing, just picked up one of the glasses and emptied it. He then played with the second glass for a little while before picking that up and emptying that as well. He then clicked his fingers for the barman's attention.

'Same again,' he said, not bothering to look up.

'Bad night, sir?' asked the barman.

'Bad night?' he repeated.

'None of your bloody business, just serve the damned drink, will you?'

'Sorry, sir, just seeing you attack those drinks suggested you have not had the best of days, that's all.'

The man appeared to mellow a little.

'The bitch dumped me,' he said, still not looking up.

'Ouch, sorry to hear that, sir.'

'Found someone fitter and younger.'

'Double ouch, but you won't find any comfort in these,' he said, handing two more glasses.

'Maybe not, but at least these won't dessert me.'

Tampong could not resist a giggle, forcing the man to glance in her direction. It was the first time he saw her and clearly liked what he saw, although he was still in a foul mood.

'Something funny?' he asked.

She slowly turned in her chair.

'Yes, you are.'

'What do you mean by that?'

'You have been dumped, and all you can think about is hitting the drink, because it won't dessert you.'

'And?'

'But it can kill you.'

'Better the drink than a knife in the back.'

'Whatever,' she said, swiveling back around.

He took another swig of his drink, then looked at her again.

'So what would you do then?'

She took a sip of her drink through her straw, then turned to look at him. He wasn't unattractive, if a bit on the slim side for her liking.

'Well, love is like a bike. If you fall off, then rather than simply give up, you get back on and try again.'

'I would, but there are too many bikes out there with wobbly wheels.'

That caused another giggle from her. Even the barman had to suppress a giggle this time.

'What?' he asked.

'You are a funny man,' she explained.

'Well, glad you are having a good evening, albeit at my expense.'

She laughed again. Her laughter was infectious, and soon the man joined in too.

'May I buy you a drink?' he asked, moving into the seat next to her.

'Sure.'

'Whatever that is, barman, and one for yourself.'

The barman nodded his thanks.

'So why so glum earlier?'

'The truth?'

'Always.'

'Well, I caught my so-called girlfriend in bed with my brother-in-law.'

'Ouch.'

'Right, ouch indeed.'

'So, what did you do?'

'Apologized for disturbing them, grabbed my coat and wallet from the wardrobe, and told them to carry on.'

'That's it? That's all you did?'

'Well, I might have kicked her arse with my foot as she bounced her head up and down on the brother-in-law.'

'That sucks.'

'She did, quite well, actually.'

They both started laughing again. The barman placed her drink on the bar, her first one still only half finished.

'I'm Graham, by the way,' he said, holding out his hand.

She shook it.

'Hi, I'm Katy.'

'Pleased to meet you, Katy, and sorry about my foul mood earlier on.'

'No problem, history now. Water under the bridge, etc., etc.'

'So, what's a beautiful lady like you doing out on a Saturday night on her own?'

'Just waiting for the right guy to come along I guess.'

'Looking like that,' he said, moving his hand up and down in front of her, 'I'm surprised you don't have men queuing up outside to prove to be Mr. Right.'

She looked back towards to door.

'Nope, nobody queuing there.'

'I would,' he said simply, taking a large gulp of his drink, finishing off his third glass.

Tampong said nothing but took a long sip of her drink, nearly emptying her glass. He was clearly coming onto her, and she liked it, as long as he didn't keep drinking, otherwise this was going to be a very short evening. The barman brought some more nibbles and placed them on the bar. This time the bowls contained nuts and dried fruit. Tampong picked at the dried fruit.

'So, what do you do?' he asked, deciding to keep on safer ground.

'Me, ho I work for a pharmaceutical company.'

'Really? That must be interesting and rewarding work.'

'It is,' she agreed, 'and what about you, what do you do?'

'I run my own limousine company.'

'Really?'

'Truly.'

'That must be both interesting and challenging work.'

'You are right on both counts. Mind you, it has its benefits. For example, I can drink as many of these as I like and order myself a limo later on.'

She laughed.

'Have you eaten?' he asked.

'No, I haven't actually,' she admitted.

'So, would you care to join me here for dinner? I hear the food is very good.'

'It is,' chipped in the barman.

'Why not?' she replied, swiveling around in her chair to stand up in front of him.

He had a quick glance of her long legs and was sure he caught a glimpse of her white underwear. He wondered whether she did it deliberately.

'I'll put these on your tab, shall I, Mr. Strider?' asked the barman.

'Please,' confirmed Graham, 'all of them,' he clarified.

'That's very generous of you,' she said, clearly impressed.

He stood up then stopped in front of her.

'It was just the one drink before I arrived, right?'

'Yeah, just the one.'

'Not that it matters, of course,' he corrected.

She just smiled.

The barman waved to a member of the staff, indicating a table with his hands. A woman in her early thirties came over and escorted them to an empty table. Tampong decided that this was not going to be such a bad and boring evening after all. She intended to enjoy herself tonight and see where it went. If they ended up in bed together, so much the better. She would show him a good time and then some.

***

Terry was also having the time of his life. He had enjoyed a wonderful meal, washed down with a wonderful bottle of wine and, best of all, enjoyed such wonderful company with Sandi. They were just finishing off their cheesecake when Yvette brought their coffees with some candies on a small tray.

'Will there be anything else for you?' she asked.

'No, that's all, thank you very much,' replied Terry.

His eyes never leaving Sandi's.

She placed the small tray on the table.

'It has been my pleasure serving you. No need to rush, so please take your time.'

He reached over and took Sandi's hand again, still looking deep into her eyes. She seemed to anticipate his question, as her eyes twinkled in the candlelight.

'I really don't want this day to end,' he said quietly.

'It doesn't have to,' she whispered her response, caressing his hand with her hand, 'my friend is out tonight, so we will have the condo to ourselves, if you would like to stay.'

'If I would like to stay! Are you kidding me? I would love to stay over with you.'

'Will it be OK with your aunty?'

He thought for a moment.

'We can swing by my house, and I can leave her a note to say I am staying with you. I will have to leave her your address and telephone number. Will that be OK with you?'

'Sure, no problem. It's not as if she is likely to come rushing into the house and save me from you . . . is she?'

He laughed.

'No, as long as she knows where I am, that will be fine.'

'Then let's do it,' she said, now with even more excitement in her voice.

His eyes smiled at her knowingly. He placed money on the tray, while still holding Sandi's hand in his other hand. Yvette promptly returned to their table and picked up the tray. Terry never even noticed, as his eyes never left Sandi's. His world was her world. Everything else faded or blurred into the distance. All he could see was her. All he wanted to see was her.

'Please come back again soon, and have a pleasant evening,' she said politely, nodding to them both before turning and walking away.

They finished their coffees and cheesecake, wiped their lips with their napkins, then rising together and walked arm in arm out of the restaurant. Yvette was standing by the door and opened it for them.

'Have a great evening,' she said.

'Thank you,' replied Sandi.

Terry opted to just nod his thanks.

Outside, Sandi stopped at the car, turning towards Terry. She placed her hands behind his neck again, pulling his face closer to hers. She kissed him passionately on the lips. He returned her kiss, holding her firmly by the waist, not wanting to release her. They embraced for a long time before she finally pulled away.

'I love you,' she whispered in his ear.

His heart thumped heavily in his chest, almost hard enough for it to explode. He had dreamed of this moment, wished for those very words to be heard. He leaned into her, kissed her neck, then whispered,

'I love you too.'

'Let's go home,' she said quietly, opening the car door and slipping into the driver's seat.

He closed her door quietly, walked around to the passenger side and got in. He placed his hand on her thigh, it felt silky smooth as always. She patted his hand with hers before putting the car into drive and pulling out of the car park. Terry kept his hands on her thigh for the entire journey. She constantly turned towards him and smiled.

Tonight was going to be special, he just knew it.

***

Monday morning arrived, and Shoil sat down in her seat, not believing she was back on a plane so quickly, although excited about the prospects of finding the boy and Tampong. Dealing with them both would be ample revenge for Tampong's treachery. It had been many years since that dark day, a day that would live long in her memory, long after she defeats that bitch even. She settled down in her seat and felt pleased with herself. The air stewardess came up to her with a tray of drinks.

'Would you care for a drink before we take off?' she asked, lowering the tray.

'Yeah, I'll have a glass of champagne.'

'Ho, I'm so sorry, honey, but according to our manifesto, you are underage, so all I can offer you is orange juice, water, or apple juice.'

'Ho right, of course,' she said, shrugging her shoulders, 'worth a shot I guess. I'll take the apple juice, please.'

The steward looked around, then bent down to whisper in her ear.

'Have you had this before?'

'Yes, at my sister's wedding,' she lied.

'OK, then here you go. If anyone asks, it's fizzy water.'

She placed the glass of champagne on her tray before moving down the aisle.

Shoil thanked her, then took a sip of the champagne. Trust her to transform into an underage body. This was going to be a problem in Singapore because of their strict drinking laws and always requiring ID before giving any alcohol. She was in half a mind to find another body but could only transform if this one was damaged or diseased in some way. She would have to find a suitable companion to do her buying for her. She knew this body was attractive to men. She noticed quite a few of them staring at her at the airport as she walked through. Perhaps some of them had fantasies about bedding a young, fit girl like her. Maybe one of them would get lucky in Singapore. She smiled to herself at the prospect.

Just then the captain spoke over the aircraft's PA system.

'Ladies and gentlemen, this is your captain speaking. On behalf of British Airways, I would like to welcome you on flight one ninety-three to Singapore. We will be flying at a height of thirty-three thousand feet, and our expected flight time is eleven hours forty-five minutes. We are expecting a smooth flight, and I will turn off the seat belt sign as soon as we reach our cruising altitude. We have just received clearance from tower control and expect to start pushing back in the next minute or so. The weather in Singapore is a barmy seventy-five degrees and expected to be warmer by the time we land. We are not expecting any delays, but if that changes for any reason I will let you know. In the meantime, I will leave you in the excellent hands of our cabin crew and wish you a very pleasant flight. Thank you again for flying British Airways.'

Shoil glanced over at the empty seat and smiled. No annoying large American to spoil her trip this time. Just then the stewardess returned, checked her clipboard, then returned to economy class. Shoil guessed she must have just been checking the seats, but that hope was instantly dashed when she returned with another passenger. A large man squeezed past the gap and sat in the empty seat.

He looked over at Shoil.

'Hi, young lady,' he began with a strong American accent. 'Lucky me. I asked to go on the waiting list for an upgrade, and fortunately for me the passenger assigned to this seat was a no-show. How lucky was that?'

'Great,' said Shoil, who just slumped back into her seat.

Nearly twelve hours of this, she thought.

The thought occurred to her that she could just kill him now and be done with it, but that would cause too much attention to her and bound to hit the news, which could alert them to her coming. She could not risk that. Better to just try to occupy herself, watch TV and perhaps get some sleep. Just then she heard him fart in his chair and shortly afterwards the stink hit her nostrils.

This is going to be one hell of a long trip, she thought.

The stewardess came back to her chair, her nose wrinkled at the smell, but she put on a professional face. Obviously not her first time.

'Mr. Pickles?' she said.

'That's my name, honey, don't wear it out.'

'Sorry, but there has been a mistake.'

'What mistake? I have been upgraded, as I asked.'

'Yes, but you were in standard economy, so your upgrade should be in premium economy. If you could follow me, please, I'll show you to your proper seat.'

'I am just dandy right here, thanks.'

'Sorry, sir, but the plane cannot take off until all the passengers are in their correctly assigned seats.'

'Well, that is BA's error, not mine.'

'Again, our apologies, sir, but you must return to premium economy, or else this plane will not be able to take off.'

Her last words caused a stir of conversation from those seated around him. He clearly felt their animosity towards him.

'Fuck it,' he swore, getting out of his seat.

As he squeezed past Shoil, he farted again, only this time louder.

'Oops,' he said with a childish expression on his face, 'better out than in.'

'Better to keep it in during the flight, sir,' replied the stewardess.

She winked at Shoil as she passed while pinching her nose with her fingers.

Shoil smiled and settled down into her seat, trying to ignore the smell. Fortunately for her, for the rest of the flight the seat remained unoccupied, although she could hear the fat man constantly grumbling about the service in premium economy and that he should have been bumped up to business class, given all the air miles he had traveled with the airline and the fact it was their mistake to put him in the wrong seat in the first place. No one was listening to him, but he seemed willing to vent at anyone, even those who were just passing his seat to use the toilet. She was able to drown him out when she placed the headphones on and began watching the first of many movies.

THE REUNION

Date: January 2011
Ages: 18 / 1,162
Status: fully active

Shoil stepped out of the airport, doubting she would ever get used to the heat and humidity of Singapore. Her clothes immediately stuck to her as she stood in the taxi queue, waiting for her time. It took another twenty minutes before she was finally waved towards a silver cab with its boot open. The driver saw her approaching so rushed out of his cab and grabbed her luggage.

'I'll take that heavy thing from you,' he said, eyeing her up as he did so.

Would she ever get tired of men ogling her? Of course not. It was to her advantage that they were attracted to her like moths to a dangerous flame. A flame that would eagerly consume them. It was one of the reasons she chose Karen's body. It was young and sexy. The driver dumped the luggage in the trunk, shut it quickly, and rushed around to open the passenger door for her. She had no doubt he only did it to stare at her legs. She wouldn't disappoint, dragging her first leg inside slowly, ensuring her skirt rode up a little higher so that he would have the merriest of glimpses of her underwear. She saw his eyes flick to her waist. He didn't miss a trick. Just as she thought. How predicable can men be! He slowly closed the door before walking around to the driver-side and sitting in the seat, not bothering to attach his seat belt.

'Where to, love?' he asked, looking at her through the rearview mirror.

'Carlton Hotel, Bras Basah Road,' she answered, crossing her legs.

He immediately adjusted his mirror a little. It now pointed further down.

'Carlton it is.'

He started driving, and she was waiting for the inevitable question.

'So here on your vacation?'

'Nope, I'm here doing a little business.'

'A little business you say. What, is that for a school assignment or something?'

She looked at his eyes in the mirror.

'What makes you think I am still in school?'

'No offence, it's just that you don't look young enough to drink, that's all.'

'Ho, I do more than just drink.'

His eyes flicked towards her again, just as she expected.

'You have family or anything here then?'

There was the first probing question.

'Nope. I am here on my own.'

Another flick of the eyes.

'Your boyfriend must have been sad to see you go.'

What an obvious leading question.

'Nope, no boyfriend either.'

'A pretty thing like you with no boyfriend. That's criminal.'

'Ho, I am not interested in boys. I like men.'

Another flick of the eyes.

She uncrossed her legs, then recrossed them, switching legs over, doing what she called her Sharon Stone move. The difference being she was wearing underwear, this time. There was the eye movement again. She then realized she had to be a little careful. If this guy spent too long glancing into his mirror, they were going to have an accident.

'So, how long do you intend to stay here in good old Singapore?'

'Undecided, much depends on the outcome of my business venture.'

'What business would that be then?'

She thought about his question and was glancing out of the car when an idea sprung into her mind.

'I want to set up a hooker's house.'

She heard him cough and almost choke. He cleared his throat.

'Do you know that's illegal in Singapore?'

'That's what makes it all the more exciting, doesn't it?'

'Are you for real?' he asked, staring at her in his mirror again.

'Of course. Do you not think there are men on this island that would want to fuck a young thing like me?'

She raised her arms in the air to show him her figure.

He coughed again and pulled his shirt collar away from his neck.

'Right, but most men do not want to pay for it.'

'Nonsense. This way there is no drama, no long chats, and evenings out in the faint hope that he might get into her panties. This way, both parties know exactly what is going to happen. Besides, there must be many lonely businessmen visiting Singapore and looking for something or someone to do in the evenings.'

'As I said, that is illegal here.'

'It is if you demand a fee for sexual favors. My business would not. We would simply request that the man makes a gift of a donation to help with home maintenance, bills, and improvements, etc. If a woman shows her appreciation because of his gift, then that is up to her.'

'Wow, looks like you have this all worked out.'

In truth, she hadn't and had basically said the first thing that popped into her head, not that he would know that.

'Of course,' she continued, 'I have a good brain and well as a good body.'

'No argument from me there, missy.'

He went quiet for a little while. She wanted to continue with the charade. She leaned forward to take a closer look at his car badge.

'So what's your story . . . Dick . . . is that really your name?'

'Yep, Big Dick. That's me.'

'So, what's your story, Dick?'

She decided she was not going to refer to him by his nickname, not yet at least.

'Ho, I was born in Malaysia, but my parents moved here for work when I was four. Been here ever since. Didn't like school and hated college. Dropped out, then bummed around a couple of local islands for a few years before returning to Singapore and took up taxi driving. Been doing that ever since.'

'Ever been outside the country, Dick?'

'Yep. Went to my home country Malaysia twice. Didn't like it though. Speak funny there.'

She smiled.

'So you must have quite a few strange stories about some of your passengers then.'

'Not as strange as yours. I had a couple who spent the whole journey arguing with each other. Ended up in an almighty fight.'

'Was the girl badly hurt?'

'No, but the guy was. She beat the crap out of him.'

She laughed.

'Seriously?'

'I am being serious. That chick could look after herself. I had to stop the car and call the police out. She was still laying into him when they arrived. Literally had to pull her off him. And I didn't get my fare paid. Had to take the cab back to the garage to get all the blood out off the back seat.'

'So, anyone special in your life then?'

'Nope. I go with the flow. Love 'em and leave 'em, that's my motto.'

'My kind of client then.'

There was that look in the mirror again.

'I would certainly pay to get a piece of arse like yours.'

'We don't charge a fee, Dick.'

'No, of course not. I mean I would make a nice donation for some . . . special appreciation.'

'I see,' she said simply, leaving the thought in the air.

They continued to chat until he pulled up outside the hotel, parked the car and hopped out to open the door for her. She slid out, making sure he caught a glimpse of her underwear again. He had a sinister smile on his face. His thoughts were painfully obvious. He wanted her. He closed the door and walked around to the trunk and pulled out her luggage. The hotel porter arrived, so the driver loaded the luggage onto his trolley. He then pulled out one of his business cards, which he handed to her. She slipped it into her bra. His eyes followed the card's path. He licked his lips.

'So, you interested in making a large donation then?' she asked directly.

'With you?'

'Of course.'

'Then definitely. Yes.'

'OK, you can start by not charging me for the cab ride, then come to my room in about, say, an hour, to show me the size of the rest of your donation. Then I'll show you how much I appreciate your donation.'

'Ho right. I have seen this before. I leave and you disappear, leaving me short of a cab fare, which is also part of my donation, by the way.'

'Fair enough. I can see your point. Then park your cab somewhere unseen and come into the hotel with me. I'll wait in the reception for you.'

'You promise?'

'Cross my heart and hope to die. You will be able to see me through the glass window.'

She crossed her index finger in front of her chest to emphasize her promise.

'My god, but I am going to bang this bitch big time,' he said to himself as he got back into his cab.

He drove out of the driveway and parked the cab in a corner under some trees so it could not be viewed by any arrivals or departures. He would have parked the car here, anyway, not wanting it to be seen abandoned at this hotel and being reported to his shift manager. He needed this job. He liked his gambling nights with the lads, but there was a price to pay, and he was in debt, big time. This girl he guessed could not be any more than eighteen years old, but she seemed so confident for someone so young. He could not remember the last time he had a gorgeous young chick like her. This was going to be some wild ride. He opened his glove compartment and pulled out a black wallet, taking a wad of notes out before closing the compartment back up. Perhaps he could drive for this bitch and her bitches. Should be good money in that, with some additional benefits. He gave a lecherous smile to himself. He got out, locked the doors, and slipped the key into his pocket. As he walked towards the hotel, he could see the girl at check-in, no doubt getting her room key. As he passed through the sliding doors, she moved away from the reception and turned just as he entered. She wiggled her forefinger, indicating him to follow her, which he did. She led them to the elevator, where she pressed the call button. The elevator doors opened immediately, so they stepped inside. She pressed the twelfth-floor button and the doors closed. Dick was standing next to her. He reached out and put his hand on her cheek and caressed it. She did not move away, so he slid his hand under her dress and up into her knickers.

'Careful,' she warned, not turning around, 'there are cameras in this elevator.'

'So we can give them a show.'

'I don't want them thinking I am a hooker and forcing me out of the hotel already.'

'OK, I see your point. I can wait, but only just.'

He reluctantly pulled his hand away.

'We will be in my room soon enough.'

'Cannot be soon enough for me,' he said with clear excitement in his voice.

He was moving from one foot to the other, unable to keep still. He glanced at the profile of the girl, which looked as good as her front and back. This one had a body to worship, but he was going to give it hell.

The elevator stopped and she stepped out, so he followed her. Turning right down the corridor she walked to the end, taking her keycard out and swiping it against the lock. The lock beeped once, so she opened the door and walked in. He followed her inside. As soon as the door closed he wrapped his arms around her and grabbed both of her breasts, squeezing them hard. Shoil said nothing but reached behind her back and felt his crouch.

Not surprisingly, he was aroused, she held him and squeezed tightly. He let go of her almost immediately, trying to pull away from her grip, but her strength belied her slim form. She knew what she was doing. She turned slowly to face him.

'I'll tell you when we can start to play, right?'

He could only nod his head quickly as the pain was unbearable. She let him go, and he doubled up, going down on his knees.

'Go into the bathroom and sort yourself out. My luggage will be here soon, then we can play any games you like.'

He staggered to his feet, still holding his crouch, limped into the bathroom, and closed the door behind him.

Just as the bathroom door closed, her bedroom doorbell rang. She opened the door to find the porter standing there with her luggage. She stood aside to allow him to enter. He wheeled his trolley into the room and placed her luggage on the rack next to the TV. She held out a note in her hand and slipped it into his. He nodded his thanks and left the room, closing the door behind him. She looked back at the bathroom and made her decision. She unzipped the back of her dress and just stood in the middle of the room.

'OK, it's all clear to come out now,' she called out to Dick.

The door slowly opened, and Dick stepped out, no longer holding his crouch.

'Jesus, little lady, but that is some grip you have there.'

'You need to know how to look after yourself in my business,' she said calmly, 'now, do you want to play or not?'

'Not sure I am in the mood anymore after your vice grip of my dick.'

'Ho, but I think you will be,' she said, sliding her dress off her shoulders and allowing it to fall onto the floor.

She stepped out of it and stood in front of him in just her bra and knickers.

He looked her up and down, concentrating on the curves of her breasts, her slim waist, long silky legs, and inviting crotch. He went to move towards her, but she held her hand out to stop him.

'Remember, I need to see the size of your donation first,' she reminded him.

'Of course,' he said, 'business before pleasure.'

He took the wad of money out of his pocket and threw it across to her. She caught it easily, checked the amount before placing it on the edge of the bed.

'Nice donation,' said remarked, moving her hands behind her back, unclipping her bra.

She let it drop into her hand before placing that on the bed too.

'Nice rack,' he said, 'I like bush too.'

'Of course,' she said.

She moved her hands to her thighs, grabbing both sides of her knickers, she slowly slid them down her legs, taking one foot out after the other. She carefully placed those on the bed next to her bra. Then stood back up to face him.

'Your turn,' she said.

He licked his lips, although his throat felt dry.

'Man, am I going to bang you like you have never been banged before.'

'Like I have never heard that one before,' she said sarcastically. 'Now let's see your dick, Big Dick.'

He unbuckled his belt, unbuttoned his jeans, pulling them down to his ankles. He stepped out of them one foot at a time. He was not wearing any underwear. He unbuttoned his shirt, then slid that off his shoulders, not caring where it fell.

She looked at his erection. A sad expression appeared on her face. She decided it was time to stop playing around.

'What?' he said, clearly confused.

'Well, it may be Big Dick by name but not big dick by nature, is it?'

'*What!*' he shouted, clearly offended.

'Come on now. A more appropriate name for you would be chipolata, I would say.'

'You little bitch. I will show you just what I can do with this.'

He moved forward, filled with rage.

She let him come, changing her expression to one of fear. When he reached her, he shoved her hard onto the bed, grabbed both her ankles, then roughly pulled her legs wide apart.

'Prepare to be fucked hard, bitch,' he screamed.

Still holding her ankles, he quickly entered her, just as her eyes turned orange, unnoticed by him. He started to pump her hard and fast with an evil grin on his face. He would show this little bitch just what he could do to a woman, but just as he started getting into a rhythm, he felt himself being mysteriously pulled deeper inside her, finding it harder and harder to actually pull out of her.

'Keep going, little dick,' she screamed.

Her words simply enraged him even more, so he tried to forget the strange feeling and, instead, intended to force himself as deep into her as he could. He let go of her ankles as he reached up and grabbed her breasts, squeezing them painfully and deliberately. He snarled at her, but her head was back, and she seemed to be wanting more. After a while she did not even appear to notice what he was trying to do, the way he attempted her hurt her, make her feel threatened. Instead, she kept pushing herself up into him. He suddenly felt lightheaded, then aware that he was no longer in control of his own body. He tried to pull out of her, but she seemed to be sucking him back inside her. He let go of her breasts and pulled against her legs in an attempt to free himself, but no matter how hard he pulled, her legs would not move. He began to panic. This bitch was not normal. His body began to shake uncontrollably. He was losing control of his bodily functions; his mouth began to drool. He looked at his hands, which were still clinging to her legs. His hands looked like those of an eighty-year-old and appeared to be aging by the second. He was distracted by the woman now as her body seemed to change color, turning orange. Her strength was incredible, inhuman. Actually, she looked inhuman now . . . and it frightened him. His body felt strange, changing, aging quickly. All thoughts of sex had long disappeared, yet he could not stop pounding her. In fact, he was involuntarily speeding up. His body was shaking violently now, his breathing rapid and difficult. His chest appeared to shrink. He could see his ribs starting to push against his thinning skin. His eyes were glued to his chest as he watched in horror as his skin started to blister and crack. Blood oozed from several openings.

Still, he pounded her, quicker and quicker.

The cracks of his skin widened, enough for him to see his bones. His eyes were now clouding over, meaning he was unable to see clearly anymore, he tried desperately to step back away from this eerie body. No matter how hard he pushed, it was like trying to free himself from metal vices. He was getting weaker as well, the energy ebbing out of every crack in his body. He was finding it hard to think.

Still he pounded her, quicker and quicker.

His head felt like it was pushing against his brain. Fluid ran into his chest and up his throat. He choked, trying to clear his airway, but was unable to. He gagged, unable to breathe anymore. He stopped pushing against her, all his willpower had dissolved. His eyes rolled up inside his head. His world went black. He was gone.

Shoil slowly sat up.

'That was interesting,' she said to herself.

She had never experienced an absorption like that before. It felt invigorating, new even. She liked the sensation while it lasted. He did his best to try and hurt her, to cause her pain, yet he only succeeded in arousing her even more. He may not have been well endowed, but he lasted a long time and made her sweat a little. That was a first for her. She realized it was also a first for Karen's body. Perhaps that is why it felt so different.

She now had his memories, and he definitely wanted to fuck this little girl. It was one of his many fantasies involving young girls. He had a collection of young porn in his small apartment, jerking off while watching them. He was pathetic. Shoil stood up and walked into the bathroom. She badly needed a shower but felt reinvigorated as a result of the sex and absorption. If this was how future absorptions were going to be, then she was going to like this body even more. Sadly, the guy had no money and was, in fact, in debt to several casinos. She surmised that it was only a matter of time before one of the casinos had enough and beat him to death. So she had saved them the bother.

Having showered, she got dressed, walked over to his jeans, and removed his car keys. Picking up her room key card, she went downstairs and into the car park. The taxi was parked in the corner, so she unlocked the passenger door and opened the glove compartment, taking out the black wallet, which she emptied, placing the wallet back into the glove compartment before closing it. She locked the door then casually threw the keys into the nearest bush. She walked back into the hotel, suddenly feeling hungry. She walked up to the concierge's desk and requested a cab to take her to the Marina Bay Sands Hotel in thirty minutes, where she had heard they had a very nice restaurant. Time for a nice meal before the hunt began.

When she returned to her room, she bundled up the driver's clothing and placed them in a plastic bag. She carefully opened her bedroom door and peered outside. No one was around, so she quickly walked to the staircase and down to the basement. When she reached the bottom, she opened the door and was pleased to see several large industrial bins lined up against the hotel wall. She opened the first one and threw the plastic bag into it, closing the lid, and then returned to her room.

The phone rang. It was the concierge to let her know that her taxi was now outside. It took only ten minutes to arrive at the hotel. She walked through the large revolving doors and was immediately greeted with a large sign for the restaurant, pointing to the right.

'Welcome to the Signature Restaurant. Will you be dining alone tonight, madam?' the man asked with a strong Chinese accent as she walked up to the reception desk.

'I will,' she confirmed.

'Then please follow me. I can offer you a great table by the window. Your timing is perfect. The water show is about to start.'

'The water show?'

'Yes. The hotel has a world-famous water show set to music. Not quite at the same standard of the Bellagio in Las Vegas, but quite good all the same.'

He stood next to a small round table, sliding her seat out for her. She sat down.

'May I offer you an aperitif?'

'Champagne,' she answered.

'Of course. One champagne coming up.'

'Tell you what,' she said, raising her hand in the air, causing the waiter to stop and turn back to face her, 'make that a bottle.'

'Of course, madam. One *bottle* of champagne, coming up.'

She was pleased he did not bother to check her ID. Perhaps she now looked a little older after sex, who knew?

He turned away again, so she gazed out of the window where a crowd of people was gathered around the front of the hotel and the bay. After a couple of minutes, the water show began with a splash of color and music. Images of butterflies and other animals were created by lasers hitting the water. She was impressed by the spectacle. The waiter returned with an ice bucket, champagne, and a flute, the latter he placed in front of her. Opening the bottle, he quickly poured a measure into her flute.

'Gān bēi,' he said.

'Sorry?'

'That's cheers in Chinese,' he explained.

'Ho, right, thank you.'

'Xiè,' he replied.

'Thank you?' she guessed.

He nodded.

'Xiè xiè,' she repeated, causing the waiter to give her a beaming smile.

She took a sip of the bubbling fluid. It felt good going down her throat. She then realized she was quite thirsty, so took another mouthful of the delightful liquid. She then watched the show, which lasted for twenty minutes. The waiter returned halfway through to top her glass up. His presence knocked her out of her trance, so she picked up the menu and read through it. As soon as she placed the menu down, the waiter walked over with pen and pad in hand.

'Is madam ready to order?' he asked.

‘Yes. I’ll have the ala carte menu, the first item on every course,’ she said.

‘Excellent choice, madam. And would you care for some wine, or would you prefer to keep with the champagne?’

‘I think this is enough for one person for one evening, don’t you?’

‘Of course,’ he said, bowing his head.

He left her alone again. When she turned to look outside, the show had finished and the crowd had already dispersed. Outside it was now dark and the lights around the bay were on. A rainbow of color could be seen all around the bay. This was a rich man’s playing field, rich pickings for a girl like Shoil. Surely she could enhance her wealth here with the right contacts. She only needed one millionaire to find and absorb, then she would be set for life. She was smiling at the prospects when her first course arrived.

‘Freshly shucked French oysters with ginger flower and plum dressing,’ the waiter explained, ‘enjoy your meal.’

He bowed again, topped up her glass once more, then left her alone to her meal.

She started eating, not realizing until now just how hungry she was as well. Sex sure does give you an appetite.

The oysters tasted delicious.

***

Terry sat at the end of the bed, his eyes having just returned to their normal state, not a moment too soon as Sandi walked in from the bathroom wrapped in a bath towel.

‘Ready for you,’ she said.

‘Bathroom?’ he questioned.

‘That as well,’ she said with a cheeky grin on her face.

‘I’ll not be long,’ he replied, taking off his shirt and throwing it onto the chair.

He went into the bathroom, closing the door behind him. He was worried. Shoil had just killed again. That didn’t bother him as much as the feeling she was much closer this time. Could she have found them again? Was that even possible? He shook his head, trying to shake the negative feeling away. He turned the shower on, finished undressing, and stepped into the shower. The feel of the warm water on his body felt good, washing away any doubts he had. Instead he felt more positive and started to weigh up all the good things that had happened to him recently. More importantly, he had a beautiful woman waiting for him in the next room, so nothing was going to spoil this evening, not even Shoil. That is exactly what she would have wished for, so he was determined not to indulge her tonight. He washed soap over his body, washed his hair, then rinsed himself clean. Stepping out of the shower, he switched the water off and dried himself with the bath towel Sandi had left him. He noticed it wasn't a large towel like she had. It made him smile. He wrapped the towel around his waist and walked into the bedroom.

Sandi was already in bed. One arm tucked behind her head. She had poured two glasses of wine, both glasses were on her bedside table. She looked at the wine then at Terry, raising her eyebrows. He got the message and sat down beside her on the bed, picked up the two glasses and gave one to her. Their crystal glasses gave a delicate clink as they met. They both took a sip of the wine, savoring the flavor when Sandi placed her glass back on the table. She took hold of the bedsheet and flipped it across the bed to reveal her naked body. Terry nearly dropped his glass and quickly had to hold it tightly with both hands. Sandi noticed.

'Nervous?' she asked quietly, her eyes never leaving his.

'A little,' he confessed.

'You needn't be. I'll be gentle with you, this time.'

She patted the bed invitingly.

Terry didn't need a second invitation, dropping his towel, he placed his glass next to hers and lay down beside her.

'You are beautiful,' he said, stroking the side of her face.

'Why thank you, kind sir. And it's going to be a beautiful evening, for both of us,' she replied, pulling him closer to her.

Their lips met and Terry felt that explosion of emotions again. He pushed his lips against hers, forcing her backwards onto the bed. He moved his leg across the top of her thigh, but she stopped him and moved his leg back. For a second he was confused, worried that she was about to reject him, when her own leg slid over his body, followed by her whole body. She lay on top of him for a little while, pushing her hip against his. He brushed her fallen hair away from her face, pulling her closer to him. They kissed passionately. It was long and hard. He felt her tongue searching for his inside his mouth. They met and rubbed against each other as her body started to move a little quicker, gently pushing against his penis, making sure he was aroused. He was.

She sat up, placing her hands on his chest. He placed his own hands on her thighs and stroked them gently. Her eyes were closed, with her head rolled back. She lifted her body a little, found him, and gently lowed herself onto his erection. He entered her slowly and the pleasure filled his whole body with a mixture of warmth and electricity. She started slowly at first, moving deliberately up and down to feel all of him. He thought he was going to explode and felt himself pushing up as she came down on him. She gave a passionate sigh of pleasure as he did so, so he matched her movement and speed. She started to speed up, bit by bit. He matched her as his hands moved up her body to cup her breasts. This seemed to invigorate her further as she started to speed up even more, moving faster now and groaning in pleasure. Terry could not stop himself from letting out groans of pleasure too. It appeared to be the exact reaction she was looking for as she was now moving so quickly it almost looked like a blur until she let out a scream of delight. Her whole body started shaking, making Terry look up nervously, hoping he had not hurt her in any way. Then he felt her moist, realizing that she had climaxed, which in turn made him reach orgasm too as he felt himself explode and pumped himself inside her. She felt him cum and continued to ride him a little longer before collapsing on top of him, hot and sweaty. He didn't care and held her tightly, running his fingers down her back.

'I think we need another drink before we go again,' she whispered, getting her breath back.

'Before we go again?' repeated Terry, who was also breathing heavily.

She lifted her head and swept the hair away from her face.

'Don't think you are up for it?'

'Ho, I'm up for it, little lady. Just wanted to make sure I didn't hurt you.'

'Hurt me!! My god, but that was amazing. If that is hurting me, then please, god, oh god, hurt me again and again like that.'

'I think you were the one doing all the work,' he countered.

'Well, I trust you appreciated it.'

'I will show you just how much I appreciate it,' he replied, rolling her over and moving on top of her.

'So soon?' she asked.

He did not reply but sat up on his knees and picked up the wine glasses, handing her one. She sat up on one elbow and took the glass with her other hand. They nearly emptied their glasses before she handed hers back to him and he placed them back on the table.

'Now I'm ready,' he announced.

'So I see,' she said, looking down at him.

He smiled, wondering how many times he could manage it in one evening. He felt sure that she was up to whatever he did. She was truly fit and strong, while her body was amazing, and she obviously knew how to please a man. Not that that was difficult, He felt sure most men would cum just watching her undress. This was going to be a night to remember.

***

'Are you OK?' asked Graham, looking apprehensively at Tampong.

'What, ho, sorry, just miles away for a moment. Thinking about my nephew, if I am honest.'

'Do you have a problem with him?'

'No, quite the reverse actually.'

'Hmmm. Then I'd have to say you are pretty lucky to have a young teenage man with no issues.'

'I wouldn't go so far as to say that,' she replied.

Still, her thoughts were of Terry. Something happened to him this evening. Not in a harmful way, but he seemed to be ecstatic about whatever it was he was doing. She had mixed emotions. On the one hand, she was pleased he was enjoying himself, but on the other hand, she would like to know exactly what he was doing and what made him so happy. She knew he was meeting Sandi, and that would put him in a delightful mood, but this was different, this was something special. Perhaps she would bring the matter up with him when she saw him later this evening, depending on his mood.

'Would you like me to take you home or something?' asked Graham, clearly confused by her change of mood.

'What! Ho sorry, no, it's not you. It's me.'

'Ho right, so that makes it all OK then.'

'Sorry. You are right.'

She shook her head, trying to clear Terry from her mind. He was OK, that was the main thing.

'Would you like to come back to my place?' he asked.

'That's really forward of you,' she replied.

'Life is too short to waste time on small talk. I like you and would like to spend more time with you.'

'You are a fast worker.'

'As I said, life is too short. So is it a yes or no?'

'Yes,' she said without thinking.

'OK, great. Then let me get this bill sorted out and we can go.'

'OK,' she said again.

As he got up and moved towards the bar, she stared out of the window, wondering what she was doing. She had just met a strange man and agreed to go back to his place. Should she back out? Why? She wanted some 'me' time and now she was getting it. Terry was OK, so why not have some fun herself? It had been a long time, and she suddenly felt nervous. She smiled at herself, realizing she was acting like a little girl. She felt excited. She hadn't felt like this in a long time. She took in long, relaxing breaths of air as Graham came back to the table.

'All set. Ready?'

'As I'll ever be,' she replied.

He held out his hand, and she took it as she got up from the table.

'Have a wonderful evening, both of you,' said the barman as they passed.

Tampong nodded her thanks to him, which prompted a wink in return.

Graham led them out of the restaurant and down to an underground car park. He pulled out an electronic key fob from his pocket and pressed the black button. She heard a car horn beep twice and could see indicator lights flashing from a vehicle on the right. It was a white Mercedes. Graham walked around to the passenger door and opened it for her. She slipped into the passenger seat, the leather seat feeling welcoming and comfortable. Graham gently closed the door and walked around to the driver's side, opening the door, sitting in the driver's seat, then closing the door. He pressed another button on the driver's console, and the car's engine burst into life. He pulled slowly out of the garage and turned right onto the main street.

He looked across to her and smiled.

'My apartment is just at the end of this road and has a lovely view of the bay.'

'Wow, do you own the apartment?'

'I do.'

'Gosh, I have heard that apartments on the island are very expensive.'

'They are criminally expensive. But if you live on the island, then it is better to own rather than rent, which can be just as criminally expensive.'

'Right, so what do you do, Graham, that allows you to buy such a place?'

'When I am not running my limo service, you mean? Well, I'm a stockbroker, and a very good one.'

She smiled and nodded to him. Looks like he has made the right bet this evening. If anything he said was half true, then he had made a lot of right bets.

A HUNTER KNOWS HOW TO HUNT

Date: December 2020
Age: Terry is 19
Status: Fully active

Tis the season to be jolly, at least that is what the song said, although she was only half listening to the music playing in the shopping mall. Certainly did not feel like Christmas as she tried to pull her T-shirt free of her body once again, but failing, once again. The humidity was energy-sapping. She could not understand how locals put up with a climate such as this. She had spent the last few days and nights camped outside the gated community, but there was no sign of either the boy or Tampong. She had to keep herself out of view, just in case he stumbled across her and would, of course, recognize her as Karen. She looked down at her watch and decided it was time for a drink and maybe something to eat, so she headed for the shopping mall. At least the air was fresher once she entered the mall itself, the cooler air hitting her like a large refrigerator opening up in the middle of a desert. She looked at the people moving all around. She pitied their pathetic, insignificant lives. She began to wonder whether she would ever find those two, who were certainly elusive. It had crossed her mind on more than one occasion that perhaps they were not meant to be found. More than once they had managed to just slip her clutches, on one occasion by no more than a few minutes. Truly the gods of luck were with them.

She leaned on the rail and looked down at the multiple levels of shops, restaurants, and banks, which seemed to sum up Singaporean life. She sighed to herself, grateful that she only had to remain here until she found and dealt with Tampong, if that was ever going to happen, but that was her sole motivation for tolerating this oppressive heat.

After an hour she stood up, feeling a little stiff, when she sensed someone was watching her. She slowly looked around when her eyes fell on a young man who was watching her from the other side of the balcony. She caught his eye and smiled at him, but he immediately looked away, embarrassed to have been discovered. She smiled to herself and began to walk slowly along the balcony, keeping the young man in her peripheral vision. As she suspected, he moved along the opposite balcony, parallel with her. She paused in front of a dress shop and watched the young predator stop on the opposite side. When she slowly turned around, the man quickly turned to face the shop, unaware he was now staring at a window full of ladies' underwear. Suddenly realizing this, he quickly stepped away from the window to stare into the next window, which was a bookshop. He pretended to be studying a particular book. Shoil decided to walk across the bridge and stopped in front of the same window. She heard the man start breathing a bit quicker.

'Seen anything that interests you?' she asked.

She sensed the man was trembling. Not scared but nervous. Probably because of her beauty and the fact she had caught him watching her.

'Pardon, miss?' he said.

'I asked if there is anything that interests you?'

'Oh, well, just this book,' he replied, pointing quickly to a black book sitting on the shelf.

Shoil looked closer at the book, then turned to the man, who kept his own head looking towards the window.

'A hundred and one ways to please a woman?' she announced, 'interesting.'

'What, ho no,' he snorted, clearly embarrassed, 'no, I meant that one.'

He was now pointing to a completely different book.

Again she looked closer.

'Fossils and rocks of Singapore,' she read, 'wow, I think I would prefer the other book.'

He coughed, not sure what to do now, as she turned and leaned against the window.

'You were watching me earlier, weren't you?'

He still did not move his head.

'I don't know what you mean.'

She placed her hand on his shoulder and felt him flinch.

'You know it is rude to talk to someone and not have the decency to look at them when you do so.'

Her words registered with him, so he slowly turned to face her. She studied his face. He was definitely young, she guessed in his late twenties, but was not bad-looking, although nothing special. He was no Brad Pitt.

'You know exactly what I mean, and I am not mad.'

His eyes slowly rose to look at her face.

'It is just,' he began hesitantly, 'it is just, you are a very pretty lady, and I noticed you as soon as you entered the mall.'

'Well, that's nice of you to say so.'

His courage seemed to pick up a little. He straightened his body and took a deep breath.

'Most of the women around here are too Asian-looking for me, so when you came into the building it was like a breath of fresh air.'

She tapped her fingers against her arm, as if contemplating his remarks.

'Well, I have been called many things, but never a breath of fresh air.'

She paused for effect before continuing.

'But I like it,' she added.

He smiled, revealing brilliant white teeth. Obviously someone who looked after himself.

'So,' he continued, 'are you here with anyone?'

'That's a direct and personal question, isn't it?' she countered.

'Just wanted to know if you are alone or not. Didn't mean to sound too personal or anything.'

'And if I were, alone, that is?'

'Then I would ask if you would like to join me for a drink?'

Again, she delayed her response, making out she was considering his suggestion.

'I am indeed very much alone and would love to join you for a drink, if I am to know your name that is.'

'Ho right. I'm Roger. And you are?'

She almost gave him her real name but managed to control herself.

'Karen, my name is Karen, and I am pleased to meet you, Roger.'

She held out her hand, which he immediately shook.

'Shall we go outside then? There are quite a few nice bars along the bay.'

She was so tempted to say no, not wishing to go out into that sticky heat again, but this man intrigued her.

'Sure,' she replied, 'after you, Roger. Lead the way.'

He nodded and walked across the bridge that she had just crossed and up to the doors to exit the mall. She had to pick up her pace to keep up with him. Outside he turned left, following the bay until he came to an open bar, which he entered. She followed him and was pleased to discover that it felt nice and fresh under the fans. He sat at a high table, so she sat opposite him, placing her clutch bag on the table.

'What would you like to drink?' he asked.

'I think I would like to try a Singapore sling,' she replied.

His eyes shot wide open.

'Problem?' she queried.

He leaned across the table, so she matched him. He spoke in a quiet voice.

'I just need to check. The age limit to drink here is eighteen.'

She raised an eyebrow.'

'Only eighteen?'

'Yes.'

'Then I would say I am good.'

He sat back and looked pleased. At least he now knew she was not underage. He raised his arm into the air. A waiter noticed and walked up to them, nodding his greeting.

'Two Singapore slings please,' Roger requested.

'No problem. I just need to see your IDs to verify your age,' said the waiter.

Shoil turned to look the waiter straight in the eye.

'Do I not look at least eighteen?' she asked.

The waiter had clearly heard all the arguments before.

'Sorry, ma'am, but it's the law here.'

She shrugged her shoulders, reached for the bag, and pulled out her passport, which she presented to the waiter. He glanced quickly before nodding his thanks. Roger then showed his ID. Again the waiter nodded, then turned and walked towards the bar.

'They say Singapore is a fine place,' he announced.

'A fine place?' she questioned.

'Yes. With so many laws, they fine you for everything here.'

She laughed and he quickly joined her.

'You have a lovely smiling face,' he said, staring at her.

'Thank you, Roger,' she replied softly.

'So, how long have you been in Singapore?' she asked.

'Ho, for most of my life actually. My parents moved here from San Francisco when I was four. I am a Singaporean national now.'

'Wow, that's interesting. What do your parents do that warrant them moving from the States to here?'

'Dad's a stockbroker and used to travel a lot to Hong Kong and Singapore. We moved here so that he had less travelling to do. That was until the Brits gave the island back to the Chinese and most of the financial markets moved to Singapore.'

'So he was smart to move here before that happened then.'

'Right, he has a knack for catching things at the right time. Guess that is why he is so successful. He bought an apartment overlooking the bay when we arrived, and now it is worth millions.'

She mentally licked her lips. Roger had what sounded like a rich father.

'By successful, I assume you mean rich?' she asked.

'I guess so,' he conceded, 'although my dad keeps his financial affairs very quiet. He did tell me that I have an inheritance waiting for me once I come of age.'

'Once you come of age?'

'When I am twenty-five,' he clarified.

'Why that certain age?'

Before he could answer, the waiter came back to their table with their drinks, placing them on the table. He then presented a silver tray to Roger, who simply placed a gold credit card on top, not bothering to check the total. The waiter returned to the bar with the tray.

'Actually, I asked my father that very same question. He said it was when he was twenty-five that he made his first million.'

'So, does that mean you will receive a million when you come of age?'

He picked up his drink.

'Honestly, I have no idea.'

She picked up her drink and they toasted each other before sipping the liquid through the straw.

'So,' he began, putting his drink back on the table, 'what brings you to Singapore?'

'Ho, just visiting. I had heard many good things about this place, so thought I would check it out myself.'

'Right. It's not too bad here, although for a tourist it can get dull after a few days. There is really only eating and shopping here.'

'And also casinos, a beach, and an amusement park.'

'I see you have done your homework then. Have you visited any of these yet?'

'No, not yet. I ate at the Marine Bay Sands Hotel the other night and watched the light show.'

'OK, so you can tick that off your list. If you would like, I would be honored to show you some more of Singapore.'

'That's very kind of you, Roger, but don't you have to work or something?'

'No. I am on a break from college. Taking a year out to go and visit the world.'

'OK. So when do you start this little adventure around the world then?'

'Actually, I have booked a flight to New York next month. I hear it will be very cold there, but I am looking forward to a change from all this heat. After that I plan to visit Hawaii, then Japan. I will see where I go from there.'

'I hear you. It is certainly energy-sapping, and that's quite an agenda you have worked out so far.'

'You bet. As for the heat, you get used to it after time.'

Shoil doubted very much she could ever get used to this never-ending heat.

'So what do your parents think about you travelling around the world?'

'My dad is OK with it. In fact, it was he who suggested I got out and about before I settled down with a career.'

'Your dad sounds cool, but what about your mother?'

'He is. As for my mum, she divorced my dad several years ago because of his infidelity.'

'His infidelity?'

'Yeah, seems he likes the young hookers on the island too much, if you know what I mean.'

'Ho dear, how sad,' she replied softly.

She was actually thinking quite differently and now was keen to meet this rich man who had a liking for young whores. It wasn't as though she needed his money or anything, but still, what is it that drives the rich? Right, those millionaires want to be billionaires, and billionaires want to be trillionaires. Why should she be any different? After all, finding a rich man was one of her objectives, not realizing she would find one so quickly.

'She returned back to her home country of Taiwan,' he continued, pulling her out of her thoughts.

'Do you see much of her then?'

'Not really. About every couple of years I fly over to spend Christmas with her. But she has a new man in her life now and they have a baby, so she doesn't have much time for me anymore.'

'That's sad.'

'It's OK. So, what about you?'

'Me, ho my mother is still around and lives in the UK. My dad passed away quite a few years ago. Like you, I am between school and college at the moment, hence the reason I am here, spending some quality time with you.'

His eyes pricked up at her last comment, just as she had anticipated.

'So, going back to my earlier question, could I show you around some of the sights on the island?'

'That would be lovely, and thank you, Roger.'

'May I ask where you are staying?'

'At the Charlton Hotel. Do you know it?'

'Yes, of course. It is on Bras Basah Road. You have chosen quite a central hotel.'

'Not the best though,' she conceded.

'True, but it does boast a very nice restaurant.'

'Have you eaten there?'

'Several times, mainly with my dad.'

'So, what do you propose we see first then?'

'Don't know about you, but I am a bit hungry. Would you like to join me for something to eat? Then perhaps I can show you our wonderful gardens with their unusual trees.'

'Sounds delightful, as long as we eat inside.'

He laughed and was now completely comfortable in the presence of this beautiful girl.

'No problem. Do you like Japanese or Chinese cuisine?'

'Love them both.'

'Then I know just the place.'

He dropped some Singapore dollars onto the tray as a tip, stood up, and indicated Shoil to follow him, which she did. She followed him back into the mall, down two escalators, then along the hallway until they reached, what looked like to Shoil, a food hall. He turned left, and they came face-to-face with a Japanese restaurant. Just as he opened the door for her, his phone rang. He raised his finger in the air, asking her to hold for a second. She did. He talked briefly before placing the phone against his chest.

'It's my dad,' he explained, 'he is asking me to come to his club for lunch.'

Shoil thought through her options quickly. She could sound annoyed and insist he take her to lunch, or else she could act like the understanding type of girl. She opted for the latter.

'No problem. Go if you must, no hard feelings.'

He raised his finger in the air again, then resumed talking to his father. While he chatted, he looked towards Shoil. She guessed he was telling his father about her. She watched as he nodded, which she always felt was strange when talking to someone on the phone. He ended the call and put his phone away.

'He said I should come to the club and bring you with me. Would that be OK with you?'

'What is this club?' she asked.

'It's called the Tower Club, and it's one of the most illustrious private clubs in Singapore. It has an awesome view of Singapore upstairs too.'

'OK, then how can a girl refuse such a location?'

'Great. I'll hail a cab and we can go straight there. They have an extensive menu too, so there is bound to be something you like.'

Like your father perhaps, she thought.

'Sounds good,' she said instead.

He nodded. Taking hold of her hand, he led her outside, and she was surprised to see a line of taxis waiting outside the main entrance to the mall. Clearly, this was a popular destination for locals and tourists alike. He opened the door of the first taxi in line, and she slipped into the back seat. He closed the door and walked quickly around to the other side, where he got in.

'Where to?' asked the driver.

'Nine Raffles Place,' replied Roger.

'The Republic Plaza Tower?' questioned the driver.

'That's the one,' confirmed Roger.

The driver nodded, put the car into gear, and moved out onto the main road. As she sat in the back seat, she looked down at her attire, then across to Roger. He saw her looking.

'Problem?' he asked.

'I was wondering about my attire, given you said this was quite an illustrious club.'

He clicked his fingers.

'Right. Then we need to do something about that, don't we?'

She raised an inquisitive eyebrow.

'Driver,' Roger began, 'let's return to the Marine Bay Sands Mall, and I'll give you an extra two hundred dollars if you wait for us.'

'You got it, boss,' acknowledged the driver. Two hundred dollars was a lot of cab fares, so he was more than happy to wait and just sit in his car.

He smartly turned down the next road and headed back to the mall. He parked directly outside the main entrance, keeping his occupied sign on, much to the dismay of two clients who were about to get in after Roger and Shoil exited. Strangely, all the taxis had gone. Roger noticed Shoil looking at the now empty taxi stand.

'It's the time of day,' he explained, 'taxis know where to be at the right time to maximize their clients. After lunch the mall is almost void of travelling passengers, so the taxis move onto the restaurants and clubs. That's why I offered our driver an extra bonus to stay with us.'

'I see,' said Shoil, 'sure is good to have the benefit of local knowledge.'

He just smiled at her as they walked into the mall, where he stopped and looked at her. She leaned her head to one side, suggesting she was enquiring as to why he was looking at her in that way.

'I think you would look great in Chanel,' he explained.

'Whoa,' replied Shoil, putting both her hands out in front of her, 'not sure my credit card will cope with a designer dress.'

'It won't have to; it will be my treat.'

She looked at him with warm eyes.

'That's very generous of you,' she answered.

He just smiled as he opened the large glass door for her. She walked in and was immediately greeted by a young Asian woman wearing a short black dress. She had long black hair with dark eyes but brilliant white teeth.

'Good afternoon and welcome to Chanel's,' she said.

Roger had closed the door and walked up to the side of Shoil. The young woman recognized him.

'Aha, Mr. Strewmen, how nice to see you again, and with a young lady this time.'

'Hello, Kim. Yes, and this young lady needs a nice outfit for the Tower Club.'

'Of course. Would you mind following me, miss?'

Shoil nodded and followed Kim to a row of exclusive dresses.

'These will be your size, madam. Let me know if you see anything to your liking.'

'Thank you,' answered Shoil as she browsed through the rack of dresses.

She stopped when she noticed a ruby dress. It had a rounded top and glittered. She pulled it off the rack and held it against her body. Roger whistled.

'Nice,' he remarked.

'Would madam like to try it on?' asked Kim.

'Madam would indeed,' answered Shoil.

Kim swept her hand graciously towards the changing rooms, which Shoil promptly walked into. As she entered, Roger pulled his phone out of his pocket and called his father to explain their delay.

Ten minutes later, she emerged from the changing room. Roger's mouth dropped open when he saw her. The dress finished just below her knees and was figure-hugging, emphasizing all her curves. Shoil stood in front of the long mirror fixed to the wall and turned from side to side. She nodded her approval before turning towards Roger.

'Well, what do you think?' she asked.

'Definitely you. Definitely,' he replied.

She saw the price tag hanging from the sleeve of the dress, so grabbed it and turned it over. She raised her eyebrows when she saw the price.

'It's a little bit expensive,' she remarked.

'But madam looks stunning,' chipped in Kim, desperate for a sale today.

Roger was nodding as he continued to stare at the vision of beauty standing before him.

'She certainly does, Kim, she certainly does. We will take it.'

'Will this be on sir's account?'

'It will,' he confirmed.

Kim was never one to miss an opportunity for another sale, or a boost for her commission, and saw this heart-struck young man as easy bait. He clearly liked this girl, and she bet he was keen to impress her.

'Perhaps some shoes and a clutch bag would be good accessories with the dress?' she suggested.

'Absolutely,' agreed Roger.

'Absolutely,' repeated Shoil, who was enjoying herself and also saw Roger as easy bait.

'And some jewelry perhaps,' he added.

Both women raised an eyebrow; neither could believe their luck today.

Twenty minutes later they walked out of the mall with Shoil swinging several bags in both hands. The bags contained her old clothes, as she was now dressed from top to tail in her new outfit. The taxi was still waiting outside as promised. The driver looked relieved to see them as he had to refuse several other customers, and some were not too pleased to be shunted away. They got into the vehicle. The driver turned his head and quickly looked Shoil over before turning his attention towards Roger.

'The Republic Plaza Tower?' he asked.

Roger just nodded, so the driver turned back and pulled out of the taxi lane. Shoil looked out of the window to see puzzled expressions on several people, all of whom had been waiting for a taxi and were wondering what kind of influence this young couple had to secure their own taxi service. She then looked down at her new gold necklace, bracelet, dress, and shoes. If nothing else, this day had turned out to be quite rewarding, and it was not over yet.

After fifteen minutes, the driver pulled up outside a large tower block. Shoil could not suppress a whistle to show how impressed she was. Roger just smiled as he got out of the taxi and quickly walked around to the other side and opened the door for her. She took his hand and rose out of the vehicle. She felt like a princess. Roger handed the driver several hundred-dollar bills. The driver was more than pleased.

‘Do you need me to wait for you again?’ he asked expectantly.

‘No thanks,’ replied Roger, ‘I suspect we will be here for the rest of the afternoon.’

The disappointed driver nodded his reluctant understanding before pulling away towards the nearest taxi stand. Shoil followed Roger into the building. He went straight past the receptionist, who seemed to recognize him, and up to the elevator, where he pushed the button. The elevator doors opened, where she now saw a lift operator waiting on the inside as the two entered.

‘Which floor, please?’ he asked.

‘Penthouse,’ replied Roger.

‘Password please,’ asked the operator.

Roger leaned close to his ear and whispered a word, which Shoil could not quite make out. The operator nodded and pressed the top button after turning a key in the control panel. He popped the key back into his waistcoat.

‘Tight security here,’ she observed.

‘It’s to keep the riffraff and uninvited prostitutes out of the club,’ answered Roger.

She picked up on the word ‘uninvited’, suggesting this club met a lot of gentlemen’s needs. She was liking this place more and more. The elevator doors opened, and she was greeted with extensive wood-paneled walls, with matching reception desk, behind which sat two very attractive young women. Both looked up when the doors opened, and both smiled when Roger exited. Their smiles quickly disappeared when Shoil exited the elevator too. She had no doubt that both wouldn’t mind getting their claws into this young, rich boy and saw her as competition. They would be no match for her, so she gave them both a warm smile.

‘Mr. Strawmen, welcome back,’ said the one on the left.

‘Your father told us to expect you. You will find him in the Ba Xian restaurant. We will let him know of your arrival,’ said the other woman on the right, giving Shoil a professional nod while her eyes screamed ‘whore’.

As Shoil walked past the reception desk, she leaned closer to Roger.

'The Ba Xian restaurant?' she questioned.

'Chinese,' he replied.

'Aha, good, I thought so,' she lied.

They walked down a long corridor with wooden paneled walls on both sides. Roger took hold of her hand, then looked towards her and smiled. She smiled back before returning her attention to the end of the corridor, where a man in a black suit was blocking the door. As they moved closer, he obviously recognized Roger and stepped aside without saying anything. The door opened as soon as they reached it, and they were greeted with a long, dark room, filled with round wooden tables and high-backed seats with wooden edges, each with the emblem of the club engraved. The tables were made of highly polished wood, which looked more like a poker table than a dining table. She then noticed a man in the far corner waving to them. Roger spotted him too, so waved back and moved towards the table.

The tall man came towards them. He was well-built with a tanned complexion and warm, brown eyes. He looked every bit a Singaporean. He held out his arms, so Roger let Shoil's hand go and fell into his embrace.

'Hey there, son,' he said.

'Hey, Dad,' replied Roger, slowly pulling away from his dad. 'Can I introduce you to Karen, my friend?'

He looked Shoil up and down quickly.

'My word, when you said you were bringing someone, I had no idea it would be the goddess of beauty.'

Shoil did her best to blush. He then held out his arms towards her.

'Welcome, Karen,' he said.

She stepped into his embrace. He held her firmly, and she was sure he held her longer than his own son. He smelt good. Boss, she guessed. He then straightened his body out but still held her by the shoulders.

'So, where did you two meet?' he asked, not taking his eyes off her.

'In the mall,' Roger answered.

'Wow, I must go there more often then. Please, come and sit down,' he said, gesturing to a chair.

She sat down as he slid the chair under her. She noticed he opted to sit next to her, so Roger sat on her other side, opposite his father. She crossed her legs and immediately noticed the father's eyes flick down towards her legs.

Typical male, she thought, also realizing that what Roger had said about his dad was most probably true.

'My name is Arthur,' he announced. 'I thought you would like to know my name as you cannot go around calling me dad like my son now, can you, at least not yet,' he added, laughing.

'Dad!' retorted Roger, clearly embarrassed.

Arthur just shrugged his shoulders.

'So what brings you to Singapore, Karen?'

'Ho, I heard it was a beautiful island, so I thought I would find out for myself.'

'So you are here on your own then?'

'Dad!' repeated Roger, 'enough with all the third-degree questions please.'

'It's OK,' replied Shoil, 'and yes, I am here alone. That's how I like it sometimes.'

Arthur nodded, then clicked his fingers for attention. The attentive staff were at his table immediately.

'What would you kids like to drink?' he asked.

'I'll have a Coke,' replied Roger.

'Singapore sling for me, please,' said Shoil.

Both men looked at her. Roger looked shocked, while his father looked pleased.

'And I'll have a Singapore sling too, thanks, Lea.'

The waitress bowed slightly then turned on her heels and headed for the bar. The other waiter stayed at their table.

'Are you ready to start your meals?' he asked.

'We are. I think we will go for the chef's specialty today.'

'Very good, sir,' acknowledged the waiter, who also bowed his head slightly before heading off to the kitchen.

Shoil then felt Arthur's shoe knock against her own. She didn't move, knowing that was an open invitation for him to continue. Their drinks arrived. Roger looked at his Coke, wishing he had now opted for the sling too. They raised their glasses and toasted.

'Here's to all the pleasures Singapore has to offer,' announced Arthur.

'To Singapore pleasures,' said Roger.

'To pleasures,' said Shoil simply.

Her words did not go unnoticed by Arthur, who tapped his shoe against her shoe again, as if acknowledging her toast and words. Again, she did not move. If the first contact was deemed an accident, then the second contact definitely was not. She glanced at him and was met with a little wink, unseen by Roger.

'So, what do you kids plan to do after dinner then?' he asked.

It was Roger's turn to speak.

'I thought I would take Karen to Universal Studios.'

'Nothing like on the scale of the studios in the USA, or even Japan, come to that,' his father countered.

'But I have not been to either,' Shoil said, 'so I have nothing to compare it to.'

'In that case, you should enjoy yourself then,' he answered, taking another sip of his drink.

The first course of soup arrived, followed by another cute bow by the waiters before leaving.

'So how long will you be here, Karen?' asked Arthur.

'Ho, I have another two weeks before my flight is due to return, but I am thinking about extending my stay here.'

Both Roger and Arthur looked at each other. Both were pleased with the news.

'Well then,' continued Arthur, 'we will have to make sure that you get the most out of your stay with us, won't we, Ro?'

'Yes, sir,' said an eager Roger.

No sooner had the last spoon been placed back in the bowl, then the waiters returned to collect their bowls and hurried back to the kitchen. She could see both their minds working overtime. No doubt both were wondering what it took to get into her knickers. One would not be disappointed. The waiter reemerged from the kitchen carrying a tray holding several bowls, which they placed in the center of the table.

'A sample of Chinese delights,' informed Arthur.

'Not dead insects, I hope,' said Shoil, her words coming out quicker than she intended. Arthur just laughed.

'No, this menu caters for the Western palate. No dead insects here.'

She picked out what looked like chicken from one bowl and something, either beef or pork, she wasn't sure which as it was covered in sauce, from the other bowl. She then selected the noodles and some vegetables. She had to admit everything smelled delicious and tasted even better. She helped herself to seconds.

They chatted about different sights to see in Singapore, and both seemed intent on escorting Shoil to some, if not all of them. Roger was feeling slightly uncomfortable with his father now.

'Surely you have too much work to do,' he finally suggested. His words were a clear warning-off sign to his father. If his father understood the message, he chose to ignore it.

'Come now, Ro, you cannot have a monopoly on this beautiful woman. I am also allowed some free time too, you know.'

Roger looked daggers at his father, who was clicking his fingers for the waitress's attention. She quickly shuffled over to their table.

'Another round of slings please, Lea.'

He looked over to his son.

'Make that three,' Roger replied.

Lea bowed her head and shuffled off back to the bar. There was tension in the air now. Shoil, for her part, was enjoying herself, watching son and father trying to battle for her favors. For her, it was no competition; the father was the clear winner, so she decided to make that clear. She rubbed her shoe up the side of Arthur's leg just as he was finishing his drink. He stopped halfway through and glanced towards Shoil, who gave him a little wink of acknowledgement. He placed his unfinished drink down on the table.

'Funniest thing about stockbrokers,' he began, 'my colleague at work also ran into a beautiful woman the other evening. Must be the season or something.'

'So?' said a less-than-interested Roger.

'She is a Brit and has just started working here. She is not married but has her nephew here staying with her. My colleague said they are dating now, and he seems quite taken with her.'

Shoil almost choked on her drink, so quickly grabbed her napkin and wiped her mouth clean.

'Dating so soon?' she said, as if by way of explaining her sudden choking fit.

'I thought it was a bit quick too. He has only known her a few weeks. Still, his definition of 'dating' might not be our definition, if you know what I mean?'

'No, I don't know what you mean,' replied Shoil.

She was now running through several new options that had suddenly presented themselves. Perhaps her luck was finally changing.

'Well, he had just struck out with his last girlfriend, and this one apparently almost landed in his lap. So this might be a bit of a rebound thing, and maybe she doesn't see their relationship going in the same direction.'

'You mean, it might just be wishful thinking on his part,' she surmised.

'Exactly,' agreed Arthur.

Roger yawned loudly, causing the other two to look in his direction.

'All very interesting, Dad, but I don't really care what kind of relationship your colleague may or may not have.'

Shoil was thinking the absolute opposite. This sounded all too much like Tampong and the boy, and she was not going to let this opportunity pass her by, no matter how tentative a lead this might be. It was just a question as to how to get close to this colleague, which most likely meant getting closer to Arthur.

It was as if he was reading her mind.

'Perhaps I can show Karen around some of the sights too,' he suggested.

Roger was about to open his mouth, but Shoil spoke quickly before he had a chance to answer.

'That would be lovely. What did you have in mind?'

'Well, how about a tour around the island in my yacht tomorrow?'

'Tomorrow!' blurted out Roger, 'but I am playing football tomorrow.'

'That makes it perfect, you play your game, and I'll entertain this lovely lady while you do. We can all meet up afterwards.'

'But Dad . . .' he began.

'Sounds perfect,' interrupted Shoil again. 'I am not a football fan anyway, so could not imagine standing there for ninety minutes or whatever.'

'You know we are talking about real football, right? Not that American trash they play in the States.'

'I know the difference,' replied Shoil sternly. 'The UK has several football teams too, you know . . . and rugby teams. Some are quite good.'

'Rugby!' said Arthur in an exasperated voice.

'What's wrong with rugby?' she countered. 'It's a real man's sport. Not many divers, and no armored padding like American footballers.'

'No, no. I just never took you to be interested in rugby, that's all.

'Ho, I like watching all those muscular, sweaty bodies huddled together. OK, it's a bit strange that the only way to move the ball forward is to pass it backwards, but watching them tackle each other and grabbing each other in a scrum is quite a turn-on for a young girl like myself.'

Roger coughed uneasily.

'Footballers can be muscular too,' he said.

Shoil just gave him a gracious smile.

'OK, then that's settled. I will arrange for my driver to pick you up tomorrow, just after lunch. We can tour the island and then meet up with this little football star in the evening. He can tell us all about his game . . . just the highlights that is.'

Roger gave his dad a condescending look, while his father just raised his shoulders in defence before turning his attention back to Shoil.

'So, where does my driver pick you up?'

'At my hotel, I guess,' she answered.

'Which is?'

'The Carlton,' chipped in Roger.

'Then the Carlton it is.'

He looked down at his watch.

'Guess I must leave you kids to it now, as I have to get back to the office. I have an important call with the US office in fifteen minutes.'

'Must you go?' asked Shoil.

'Yes, he must,' replied Roger, a little too quickly.

'I really must,' he confirmed, rising from his seat, giving his son a stern look as he did, 'but I look forward to seeing you tomorrow, Karen. It was a pleasure meeting you.'

'The pleasure was all mine,' replied Shoil. *But I can be all yours for pleasure if you play your cards right*, she thought.

She watched him leave and licked her lips in anticipation that he could actually lead her to Tampong and the boy. She had struck gold finding Roger, then meeting his dad, Arthur. Unbeknown to her, Roger was watching her and followed her eyes towards his father.

'He cannot be trusted with young women,' he remarked, now also watching his father leave the restaurant.

His words knocked her out of her thoughts.

'Sorry, what?' she asked, not hearing him the first time.

'My father,' he clarified, 'he has a thing for young, beautiful girls.'

'Nothing wrong with that, is there? It is healthy for a man to desire young blood, isn't it?'

'It's creepy,' he answered simply.

She decided not to divulge him in this conversation anymore.

'So, how do we pay for this meal, now that your father has left us stranded here?'

'No problem, it just goes directly onto his account.'

'Ho, I see. Nice.'

'So, what do you fancy doing now then?'

'Actually,' she began, stretching her arms in the air, 'I'd like to go back to the hotel and rest for a while.'

His head dropped in disappointment, so she reached across and gently patted his hand.

'Don't worry, we will see each other tomorrow, right?'

He seemed to perk up, then consciously looked towards the exit door again.

'Be careful with my dad.'

'I can look after myself.'

'He has a cunning way of seducing young women.'

'As I said, I can look after myself.'

'I hope so,' he answered as he patted the table with both hands, as if making up his mind. 'OK then, let's get you back to your hotel.'

'Thank you, Roger. Today has been great.'

They stood up and left the restaurant. All the servers were at the exit and bowed as they left. Outside there was a row of taxis, so they slipped into the first one.

'Charlton Hotel, Bras Basah Road,' requested Roger.

The driver just nodded, checked their doors were closed, then pulled out of the taxi rank. Ten minutes later he pulled outside her hotel.

'This is me,' said Shoil, opening the door.

'Right,' said Roger quietly.

She moved towards him and gave him a gentle peck on his cheek. He blushed.

'Again, thank you for a lovely day. I really enjoyed myself.'

'Glad you did. Hopefully tomorrow will be even better,' he said.

He seemed to brighten up.

'Good luck with your match tomorrow.'

'Thanks. I will see you afterwards then.'

'Sure.'

She stepped out of the taxi, gave him a little wave, then watched as the taxi pulled out of the hotel drive. She intended to return to her room. It was time to start planning for tomorrow. Then she stopped walking, turned back around to make sure the taxi had disappeared, then turned away from the main entrance and walked down the street towards Orchard Road. She decided it was time to buy some more sexy clothes for her meeting with Arthur tomorrow. Her thoughts were focused on how she was going to entrap this stockbroker and give his whereabouts away.

***

Tampong was also thinking about the stockbroker, which brought a smile to her face, which was noticed by Sam, who put her papers down and slowly walked around to Tampong's desk, sitting on the corner.

'So what are you smiling about?' she asked.

'Ho nothing.'

'Don't try tricking a trickster. What gives?'

Tampong moved a little closer to Sam, speaking in a quiet voice.

'Well, if you must know, I've met this wonderful guy, and we are going out again tonight.'

Sam slipped off the table and kneeled by Tampong's chair.

'Wow. Tell me more. What's he like?'

'Tall, dark, and handsome.'

'Is he rich?'

'He's a stockbroker.'

'So he **IS** rich then. So, have you banged him yet?'

Tampong looked up in surprise.

'Don't play innocent with me, girl,' countered Sam. 'So, have you done the deed with him yet?'

'None of your business.'

'You have, haven't you?'

Tampong could not resist the smile appearing on her face. She just nodded.

'OK then. So what's he like in bed?'

'Amazing. Certainly knows his way around a woman's body.'

'You lucky girl. So, does he have any eligible friends?'

'I am not sure.'

'So are you going to let him ride you again tonight?'

'**SAM**, please!'

'Come on, girl, spill the beans.'

'We will see,' she said guardedly.

'Just a simple yes will do. Find out if he has any eligible buddies, will you?'

'I'll see if I can drag it into our conversation.'

'Thanks. Have fun.'

She stood back up and returned to her desk, where she started packing her things away.

Tampong closed down her computer and started packing away her stuff.

'So, what are your plans tonight?' she asked.

Sam tapped her finger on the bottom of her face.

'Probably curl up with a good book.'

'That's sad. Listen, if, and I say if, he does have a buddy looking for a nice young girl, then perhaps we can arrange for a meeting.'

'We can have a foursome,' replied Sam excitedly.

'I trust you are not talking about anything sexual?'

Sam just shrugged her shoulders.

'Whatever floats your boat,' she answered, waving to Tampong as she slipped her coat on and walked out of the office.

Tampong checked her watch, then quickened her speed and finished putting the rest of her things away before she too rushed out of the office, waiving to her colleagues as she did so. She was back home in fifteen minutes, almost a new record for her. Terry was lying on the sofa reading a book. He casually looked up when he saw her enter.

'You must have a date tonight,' he announced.

'What makes you say that?'

'The time,' he answered simply.

'The time?'

'Sure. You are never home this early usually, so I can only assume you have a date of some kind.'

'OK, clever clogs.'

'So who is he?'

'Just a guy I met in a cocktail bar.'

'Just a guy?'

'Just a guy,' she repeated.

'Just a guy you happen to like then?'

'Maybe,' she answered guardedly.

He watched as she dumped her bag on the floor, hung her coat lopsidedly on the hook, then headed for the stairs.

'Looking forward to meeting this guy then?'

'Of course,' she said, mounting the stairs two at a time.

When she reached the top, she leaned over the balcony.

'Have you got plans tonight?'

'Yep. Meeting Sandi again.'

'Might have guessed. OK. Hope you have fun tonight.'

'You too,' he answered as she disappeared into her bedroom.

It was another forty minutes before she reemerged and walked back down the stairs. Terry saw her and whistled. She was wearing a long white dress, but with one side of her dress open from the hip.

'You look hot,' he observed.

'Not too slutty, is it?'

'No, not at all. Very classy in fact. So, are you going anywhere nice?'

'Don't know, to be honest.'

He then checked the clock on the wall.

'Oops. I'd better get my skates on too. Don't want to be late.'

'OK, sweety. See you later.'

'You too.'

He waved her away as he rushed upstairs to quickly change.

Tampong walked outside the door just in time to see a car pull up. Graham got out and walked right up to her, giving her a gentle kiss on her cheek.

'You look amazing,' he said, looking her quickly up and down.

'Thank you, sir.'

He opened the door for her, and she sat in the passenger seat. He quickly closed the door then rushed around to the other side, getting into the driver's seat, buckling up, and then started the motor.

'So, where are we going tonight?' she asked.

'The circus,' he answered.

She swiveled around in her seat to face him.

'The circus? Am I dressed OK for a circus?'

'Perfect. It's a dinner circus. We are entertained while we eat.

'OK, sounds interesting.'

He laughed.

'Believe me. It is better than it sounds. The circus just arrived and is located on the sports pavilion in the bay. It is an all-human show. Not a single animal in sight.'

'That's good,' she answered, with relief in her voice. 'I am not a fan of caged animals being cruelly trained hours on end just for our entertainment.'

'Then I guessed right.'

He slipped the car in gear and pulled gently down the road. At the bottom of Bras Basah Road, he turned right, then the second left, pulling into a multi-story car park on the right. A security guard was standing at the gate but waved them through when Graham flashed his VIP badge. He drove up one level before being guided into a free space by another security officer. By the time he switched the engine off and got out of the car, the security guard was already at the side of his car, opening the door for Tampong. She accepted the hand he was holding out for her.

'Good evening, ma'am,' he announced with a strong Asian accent, 'welcome to the Cirque du Soleil.'

'Thank you,' she answered, giving Graham a quick nod of approval.

'I wanted it to be a surprise,' he admitted.

'It worked.'

He looked pleased as he walked around to her side and nodded to the security guard before taking her hand and leading her out of the car park towards a large tent. At the entrance there was yet another security guard, so Graham handed over his tickets, which were quickly examined by the guard, before he in turn handed them over to a young woman, who had heavy makeup and was dressed in what looked like a swimsuit, but with wings attached to her back.

'Would you please follow me,' she said.

They followed her up two flights of stairs and along a row of seats before she stopped in front of two vacant seats in the middle of the tent. Graham nodded his thanks, then noticed his colleague already sitting. He rose from his seat on seeing his friend arrive.

Graham shook hands, then turned towards Tampong.

'Katy, may I introduce Arthur to you. He and I work together.'

'Nice to meet you,' Arthur said, 'and his description of you does not do you justice.'

'How kind,' Tampong answered, slightly embarrassed.

'On your own?' asked Graham, noticing the seat next to him empty.

'Yep. Christie decided she wanted to go in another direction regarding our relationship.'

'Another direction?' Graham queried.

'Yep, away from me.'

'More likely she has gone back to school,' remarked Graham

Arthur just shrugged his shoulders.

'Still, I have seen this other little lady that I find very interesting.'

'Is she still in school as well?'

They were both laughing when a waiter came up to them. Tampong was not sure she wanted to know any more details, but clearly this Arthur had a liking for young girls. At least she should be safe from his attentions.

'Can I start you off with a drink?' he asked.

'You surely can,' answered Arthur. 'I'll have a champagne. Would Katy care to join me?'

'Certainly,' she replied.

'And I'll have the same,' chipped in Graham, nudging his friend playfully.

***

Terry was outside the compound waiting for Sandi to arrive. He didn't have long to wait before he saw the now-familiar headlights of her vehicle. He guessed she must have some Swiss blood running through her veins as she was never late.

'Hey, you,' she said as a greeting, winding down the window, 'hop in.'

He sat in the car, and she pulled away even before he had his seat belt fastened.

'Are we in a rush?' he asked.

'Just a bit,' she agreed. 'I managed to get these seats. They were the last two, but the show starts in ten minutes.'

'A show?'

'Cirque du Soleil.'

'Ho, I've heard about that. Lots of acrobats and things, right?'

'That's the one. Is that OK for you?'

'Sure is. Put your foot down, girl. We don't want to miss the start.'

She pressed the accelerator but kept her speed at a reasonable level so as not to attract any unwanted attention of the police. They arrived at the multistory car park. She flashed her tickets and was directed towards a ramp. She had to go right to the top before a security guard directed her into an empty space. They got out and rushed down the stairs. Music could be heard as they rushed up to the tent entrance. A security guard put his hand out to stop them.

'Tickets please,' he demanded.

Sandi eagerly passed her tickets to him, which he checked before handing them over to the young girl. She too looked quickly at the tickets before waving them into the tent. They could hear the presenter over the speakers.

'Ladies and gentlemen, welcome to Kooza, the Cirque du Soleil.'

The lights then went down, so the young woman instantly switched on a flashlight as drums banged loudly. She led them to a small round table at the back of the tent. They both sat down.

'Can I get you a drink?' the young woman asked.

'Yes please. I'll have a Tiger beer,' Sandi replied.

'And for me too,' confirmed Terry.

'Be right back,' said the young woman, turning and disappearing into the tent's darkness.

The evening began with acrobats sliding down a silk curtain, rapping themselves around the cloth before tumbling down towards the ground in circular motions. The crowd applauded, and some even gasped. It was halfway through the show when Tampong felt a presence close by. It wasn't hostile, that much was clear. When the lights came up for a break in the show, she scanned the tent, looking for the source. Her eyes then fell on Terry. He was also looking around and saw her at the same time. They both gave an innocent smile to each other. Graham noticed her looking towards a young couple at the back.

'Do you know them?' he asked.

'Yes, actually. He is my nephew.'

'Aha. Would you like them to join us?'

Tampong thought about his suggestion.

'Thanks, but no thanks. I think they would prefer to be on their own. They are on a date and don't think they'd appreciate sharing it with an aunty.'

Arthur also looked up to the young couple, and his eyes immediately rested on Sandi.

'Sure you don't want them to join us?' he challenged.

Graham knew his friend all too well.

'I think they are fine where they are. And she is safer there than here.'

'Safer?' queried Tampong.

'My friend here has a thing for young, attractive girls.'

'I see.'

'Just a healthy enjoyment, but nothing illegal I must add.'

'I should hope so too,' quipped Graham.

Arthur then stretched his arms into the air and yawned.

'Think I will call it a night,' he said, 'got an early start in the morning.'

'But it is your day off tomorrow, isn't it?' questioned Graham.

'Correct. I am going to show a young lady around the bay tomorrow morning.'

'Not Christie then?'

'No, she is water under the bridge, if you pardon the unintended pun. This is another young lady.'

'I hope she knows she could be entering rough seas.'

'I have the impression this one is coming with her eyes wide open,' corrected Arthur.

Tampong's instincts told her that this guy was only interested in young blood, probably virgins as well. If she had a daughter, he would be one of those men she would warn her about. She took a sudden dislike to this guy.

'I hope so,' replied Graham, knocking her out of her thoughts.

Arthur stood up.

'Well, it was a delight meeting you, Katy,' he said with a gentleman's bow of the head.

She just nodded back politely.

'I'll see you back in the office in a couple of days then?' asked Graham.

'You bet,' he replied. Gabbing his coat, he turned and left them alone.

Tampong watched him go.

'He is OK,' said Graham, as if reading her mind, 'he is harmless really.'

‘I hope so,’ she said almost to herself.

She would hate to have to teach him to some respect about women. She smiled to herself as she thought that perhaps she could create another gay man in Singapore.

‘Don’t know about you,’ Graham said, ‘but I am ready for bed.’

‘I am not tired,’ she remarked.

‘Neither am I,’ he replied.

She smiled knowingly. She glanced up at the top table and saw Terry and Sandi getting up to leave too. They caught each other’s eye again and both nodded to each other.

Both were going to have a bit of physical exercise in bed tonight. Both were going to sleep soundly in bed tonight as well. Safe in the knowledge that neither was at risk, for the time being.

SETTING THE TRAP

Date: December 2020
Age: Terry is 19
Status: Fully active

Shoil looked out of her hotel window. It was difficult to believe that it was winter back in the UK and almost Christmas. Mind you, this felt more like her home roots of Australia. It had taken her a little to adjust to the cold climate of the UK, but once she did, she liked the colder weather. She also liked the fact that there were four seasons there, rather than the two that existed in Australia: hot and cold. That said, Australia beat Singapore, which appeared to have only one season, sweaty and hot. She walked away from the view of the bay and stood in front of the long mirror. She was wearing a very brief orange bikini. She turned to her side and admired her firm, round rear. She nodded her approval and was about to finish dressing when her phone rang.

'Your car has arrived and is waiting in the driveway for you, madam,' the concierge explained.

'Thank you. I'll be right down,' she said before replacing the receiver.

She slipped on a short orange skirt, buttoned up a silk blouse, picked up her clutch bag and left the hotel room.

When she walked outside, she saw a long black limousine waiting for her. The dark-suited chauffer was standing by the rear door.

'Karen?' he asked.

'Correct,' confirmed Shoil.

'I have been requested to drive you to the marina,' he explained, opening the door for her.

She smiled politely to him as she sat in the back seat. The chauffer quietly closed the door, walked around to the front of the car, and sat in the driver's seat. The middle glass was up, so she could not see him, which was no bad thing and meant he could not see her either and would not attempt any side chat. She half interestingly gazed out of the window, watching as the white bricks of the Raffles Hotel passed, to be replaced with neon lights of the shopping mall. It had all been decorated for Christmas, which, somehow, didn't feel right in Singapore. Eventually the car pulled up outside the marina. The chauffer shut off the engine and got out of the car. Shoil waited for the door to open before she emerged.

'Straight ahead, and it is the last yacht on the right, madam,' the chauffer informed.

'Thank you,' she said simply.

She walked along the gangway, passing several expensive-looking yachts as she did so. One was occupied by several scantily dressed young women, most of whom were hovering around a middle-aged man carrying a tray of drinks.

'Ahoy there,' called out Arthur when he spotted Shoil walking towards his yacht. She was pleased to see that it was far from the smallest vessel moored in the marina.

His call prompted a couple of the young girls to glance in Shoil's direction. She was sure she sensed jealousy from the girls, no doubt because her man did not look nearly as old as the fossil they were with.

'So glad you could make it,' he said, offering her his hand.

She accepted his firm grip, and she walked gracefully across the wooden plank and dropped gently onto the deck. It took him a little bit longer than necessary before he released her hand.

'Welcome aboard. We will now set sail, and I will show you all that the bay has to offer a young woman.'

She looked around at the vessel.

'Very nice,' she remarked.

'Wait until you see inside her. Then you will be impressed.'

She nodded politely as he unmoored the ropes, then moved to the cabin to begin steering the vessel out of the marina. Shoil spotted two sun loungers at the front of the yacht, so moved to the nearest one and sat down.

'I will be with you as soon as we hit open waters,' he called out from the cabin.

She simply waved her acknowledgement. She was in no rush for a man to be at her side, although she was getting impatient about finding Tampong and the boy.

It was ten minutes before he arrived at her side, carrying two glasses of champagne, offering one to her, which she accepted. She looked around, seeing the land disappearing quickly into the distance. The sun was beating down from a clear blue sky. She took a large gulp of her cold drink. She almost finished half of it.

'So who is driving?' she asked.

'It's on autopilot now,' he explained.

'So it's just the two of us then?'

'Just the two of us,' he confirmed. 'Let me get you a refill while you make yourself at home.'

'Thank you,' she said, handing him her glass before leaning back on the sun lounger, sliding her legs up as she did so.

Arthur returned and passed her refilled glass back. She noticed that his glass was still half empty. So, his intention was to get her drunk and then have his way with her. She had other plans though.

'It is so peaceful out here,' she remarked.

'Peaceful and private,' he answered.

She took another gulp of her drink, then looked at him as if pondering a question. His head leaned to one side as if waiting for the question.

'Would it be too bold of me if I ask if it is OK to go topless? It is just that I hate suntan lines on my body and, as you said, it is quite private out here.'

He almost choked on his drink.

'Of course not,' he replied finally.

'Thank you,' she said gratefully, 'only if you are sure?'

'Of course I am sure. As I said, you should make yourself completely at home.'

'OK then,' she acknowledged, handing him her glass as she sat up slowly in front of him.

She slowly unbuttoned her blouse, slipping it off and allowing it to drop onto the sun lounger. She reached around to her back with her right hand and unhooked her bikini top, which dropped into her waiting left hand. She laid it gently on the end of the lounger before lying back down and reaching out for her drink. His hand was shaking and he almost spilled her drink as he passed it back to her. He took a large gulp of his drink, his eyes never leaving her chest. He then wiped his mouth with the back of his hand.

'You did say you didn't like suntan lines on your body, right?'

'Correct,' confirmed Shoil, knowing that he would pick up on that little piece of information.

'Well, if you would like to, you can undress completely here.'

Her eyes widened as she turned her head to look directly at him.

'Are you sure you wouldn't mind?'

'Of course not. My home is your home.'

'Well, I do usually suntan naked at home,' she said, 'and, as you said, it is quite private out here, isn't it?'

'Absolutely,' he confirmed, licking his lips in anticipation.

'Well, only if you are really sure?'

'I am quite sure.'

Shoil slipped her legs around to the side of the lounger directly in front of him. She then began to rise, slowly, keeping her chest out and moving it very close to his face. She could hear him gulp in air. She unzipped the side of her skirt and, with both hands, slid it down her legs, again, very slowly. She then pulled the bow at the side of her bikini bottoms to free the material from her body. She caught her bikini bottoms with her hand and laid them next to her bikini top. She then slowly sat back down before leaning back onto the lounger, lifting her legs back onto the lounger, then reached out for her glass. Arthur's still shaking hand handed her glass back.

He could not believe his luck with this girl, who was completely at ease with her nakedness, and what a sensational body she had too. He examined her from head to toe.

'Ahh, that's better,' she said.

Arthur just nodded his head, unable to say anything.

Shoil then took another sip of her drink, deliberately spilling some onto her chest. She looked up at Arthur with pleading eyes.

'Seems such a waste of good champagne,' she said suggestively.

He didn't need a second invitation. He leaned forward and started to lick her chest, covering a much wider area than necessary.

'Thank you,' she said when he lifted his head.

'Thank *you*,' he said in response.

She then looked at him for a long time, making him feel slightly awkward.

'Look, I feel a little awkward sitting here naked on my own. Why don't you join me? It would make me feel much better.'

'Sure, of course. First let me top your glass up again.'

She smiled as she handed him her glass. He stood up and returned to the cabin. She took a deep breath, looked around again to check that no other vessel was around, then Arthur returned with her glass, only this time he was naked too. He stood in front of her with a full erection. He handed her her glass, which was nearly overflowing.

'Wow, that's quite a mouthful,' she suggested as her finger slightly brushed against his penis as she retrieved her glass.

She dipped her finger in her glass, then stroked his penis with her wet finger. She heard him groan in pleasure.

'So you like it in the mouth, do you?' he asked

'I like it everywhere,' she added.

'Well, let's start with the mouth then.'

She said nothing but slowly placed her glass on the deck. She took hold of his penis and started to rub it slowly, back and forth. Her eyes never leaving his face. She watched as he closed his eyes and rocked back and forth.

'I said in the mouth,' he demanded.

'Patience.'

'Blow me,' he repeated.

'Fine, OK. Take all the fun out of it, why don't you?'

'The fun is when I feel your lips and teeth on my cock.'

'Get ready for a suck you will never experience again.'

'Ho boy, like I have never heard that before,' he said sarcastically.

She took another deep breath and felt herself changing. She closed her eyes, opened her mouth, and slid his erection inside. He groaned out loud.

'Oh yes, baby, oh yes. . .'

She then gripped him tightly with her teeth as her hands clutched his buttocks, pushing him closer to her. He stopped groaning as his body started to shake. Her nails started to push deeper into this skin, gripping his buttocks tighter and tighter, pushing him inside her further and further.

'OK, not so rough, girl . . .'

His whole body was shaking violently now, forcing him to drop his drink. The glass shattered into a thousand pieces on the deck. Still her grip grew harder and harder, eventually tearing his skin. He wanted to scream out. To tell her to stop, but he could not do either. He could not stop himself from pushing further and further into her. He could not understand how she could still be demanding more and more of him. She should be choking on him. Her grip was vice-like and hurting like hell. She had super strength as he could not pull away from her. He felt her bite down on his penis, felt his blood shooting from his now damaged membrane, but still she did not stop. He felt liquid entering his lungs and he started to have difficulty breathing. He was taking quick, short breaths. Nothing was helping though. His skin was shaking so violently it appeared to start cracking. The last thing on his mind was what kind of young girl could hide such violence and horror. It was another five minutes before Shoil wiped her mouth with the back of her hand. She reached down and picked up her drink, washing the man-taste from her mouth. She had all his memories now and was sickened by his desire for young girls. He preferred them untouched by another man and had even bedded a couple of schoolgirls, knowing them to be underage. She felt no pity for this piece of filth. She also had all his knowledge of the stock market and, more importantly, of his friend Graham and his latest girlfriend, Katy.

'Thank you, Arthur, you have been very helpful.'

She stood up, got dressed, then walked back toward the cabin, switching off the autopilot before swinging the yacht back around and heading back to the island. She would have to be careful when entering the marina and make sure nobody saw her leaving on her own. Having steered the vessel in the right direction, she bundled up Arthur's clothing, opened up a seat at the back, which she now knew contained diver's weights. She tied one of the weight belts around the clothes before tossing it into the sea. She opened the fridge to find a half-finished bottle of champagne.

'Shame to see it going to waste,' she said to herself, so topped her glass up again.

After she finished off the bottle, she tossed that overboard as well, then settled down for the yacht to arrive back at the marina. She knew he had a meeting with Roger this afternoon, but also knew he would not question the whereabouts of his father, as the two very rarely saw each other. If she had to get rid of him too, then so be it. He could be just a tasty treat, but she doubted she would gain much more information from him. As the yacht drew closer to the marina, she glanced nervously around, but nobody appeared to take any notice of yet another yacht arriving. Several vessels were leaving, and one pilot even waved to Shoil, who waved back. She tied up the vessel, then headed for the taxi rank to catch a cab back to her hotel. She would change and be ready for Roger's meeting.

***

'She has killed again,' Terry said simply.

The occasions were now so frequent that it no longer came as a surprise to him, although he always shuddered at the method she used to absorb her victims.

'And?' asked Tampong.

'Still very close,' he answered.

'What is she up to?'

'Looking for us no doubt,' he answered.

Tampong looked at Terry, who was in deep thought.

'This was more, wasn't it?'

'Yes,' conceded Terry, 'this felt planned and deliberate.'

'Like she needed information from this man?'

'Exactly.'

'We need to ask around and see if anyone we know has gone missing.'

'God, I hope that's not the case.'

'You and me both,' replied Tampong.

***

Shoil was waiting outside at their arranged spot when Roger arrived on his motorbike. Shoil looked surprised.

'We are travelling on two wheels?' she asked when he turned the engine off.

'My new toy,' he explained.

'Nice toy.'

'So how was it this morning with my father?'

'Ho, fine.'

'He didn't try anything with you, did he?'

'Nope. He was the perfect gentleman.'

'Really? Not sure we are talking about the same man.'

'Maybe he has changed,' she suggested.

'Unlikely. You cannot teach an old dog new tricks. Glad it went OK, that's all.'

It was more than OK, she thought.

'Enough talk of my dad. Ready?' asked Roger.

'Ready,' confirmed Shoil as she sat on the back of his bike, wrapping her arms around his waist.

'I think I like your new toy.'

'Thanks. It is a lot easier getting around the island on this thing.'

He switched on the engine, put the bike in gear, and roared out of the hotel driveway. She liked the feel of the wind blowing in her hair, although she now wished she had opted for trousers rather than a dress, which was quickly riding up her legs. She pushed herself against Roger's back, pinning her dress in place. Roger felt her pull closer to him and assumed it was a gesture of affection. He smiled to himself. He pulled up outside the cable car station. The cable car took them to Imbiah Lookout, where they boarded the Sentosa Express monorail, getting off at the Waterfront Station. They then walked up to the studio entrance. Roger had prepaid for the tickets, passing her a map of the studio, so they were able to use the fast-track lane and were quickly inside the park.

'So what do you fancy doing first?' he asked.

Shoil studied the map.

'How about we start with a couple of white-knuckle rides like Battlestar Galactica?'

'A woman after my own heart. Let's go.'

They quickly walked up the main street, turning right, following the signs to the sci-fi park and found the ride's entrance up on the right. There was only a five-minute wait, so they queued at the back of the line. The ride itself was quick but fun. There were two options, one marked Human, the other Cylon. They spent the rest of the day travelling around the park, visiting Ancient Egypt, The Lost World, skipping Far Far Away as it looked too much for little kids, then Hollywood and finally New York. That was when Shoil's stomach growled, which was heard by Roger. She patted her stomach.

'Hungry?' he asked.

'Starving,' she replied.

'Well, we are in New York, so there is Loui's New York Pizza Parlor?'

'Sounds perfect.'

He took her hand and led her down the main road. Loui's was a small restaurant where you normally required a reservation, but Roger knew the owner, who found them a table.

'You are lucky because this table was actually reserved for your father, but he was a no-show.'

Roger raised his eyebrows in surprise.

'My father never misses an opportunity to eat here. Are you sure he booked it for today?'

'Positive. He even mentioned that you might drop in with your lady friend here.'

'Trust my dad to try and outdo me . . . again.'

'I should phone to find out what happened to him.'

Shoil panicked.

'Don't do that,' she said quickly, causing both men to look at her.

She quickly thought through her options.

'Why?' asked Roger.

'Well, I promised I wouldn't say anything, but he told me he met a young lady this morning, and he had agreed to take her out on his yacht, as she was quite insistent apparently. It was a last-minute thing.'

Both men looked at each other, nodding their understanding.

'Now that sounds like my dad,' acknowledged Roger.

'And fortunate for you two too as you get to have his table,' answered Loui.

He turned to attend to new customers arriving, so they continued to eat in silence. Roger finished his plate and looked across to Shoil.

'You seem quiet,' he said.

'It's just that I feel I have let your father down. He told me about this girl in confidence.'

Roger reached across and placed his hand on top of hers to reassure her.

'Don't fret it. This is my dad. He does things like this all the time.'

'If you are sure.'

'Of course. Now, let's continue our tour of the studio.'

Shoil could not help hiding a smile. She was relieved that her knowledge of Arthur gave her some more valuable time, but she wanted this meeting over and done with so that she could get back to planning her meeting with Graham. She knew his address now, and he lived not far from her hotel.

'Would you mind terribly if you took me home now? That pizza has gone straight to my stomach, and I am not feeling too good.'

'Gosh, so sorry. I'll get Loui and tell him.'

'No, no, please. I don't want to cause any trouble. It's just my sensitive stomach. Probably a mixture of the sea air and stuff. Nothing a good night's sleep won't put right.'

'OK, if you are sure.'

'I am.'

He waved Loui goodbye, leaving a couple of notes on the table to pay for the pizzas. They were not far from the exit, and it didn't take them long to get back to the cable car, then down to his bike. She stood looking at the bike.

'Problem?' he asked.

'Not sure riding a bike in my condition would be a good idea.'

'Of course, silly me. Look, there is a taxicab just across the road. I will grab you a cab.'

'I can do that by myself,' she said.

'Nonsense, wouldn't hear of it.'

Without allowing any further discussion, he grabbed her hand and led her over to the row of waiting taxis, opening the rear door of the first taxi for her.

'To the Charlton Hotel please,' he announced to the driver.

He watched as she sat in the rear, then leaned closer to her.

'I hope you feel better soon. Perhaps we can do something tomorrow?'

'I'll let you know,' she replied, patting her stomach.

'Right. Look forward to seeing you soon then,' he answered, closing the door.

The taxi pulled away, so she let out a breath of relief.

'Change of mind,' she said to the driver, 'take me to the Tanjong Pagar Centre please.'

The driver glanced into his rearview mirror.

'Tanjong Pagar Centre?'

'Yes, you heard correctly.'

'Very good.'

The driver pulled off the autoroute and did a quick turnaround before reentering the highway but going the other way now. Ten minutes later he pulled outside the tallest building in Singapore. Shoil went to hand him a twenty-dollar bill, but he waved it away.

'The fare is taken care of,' he advised.

'OK, that's nice. Thank you.'

'Would you like me to wait for you?'

'No, that will not be necessary, thanks.'

'As you wish,' he said simply.

She got out of the car and stood in front of the impressive building, then entered through large glass doors. Two receptionists were sitting behind a long, high-polished wooden desk. One looked up as Shoil approached.

'May I help you?' she asked.

'Yes. I am here to see Graham Stockholm.'

'May I have your name please?'

'Karen Wright.'

'Thank you, Ms. Wright. Please bear with me.'

The receptionist dialed a number and had a short, quiet conversation with the person at the other end of the call. She looked up towards Shoil.

'What is this in connection with?' she asked.

'I am a friend of Arthur Blake's. He said to mention code fifty-three.'

Some more quiet conversation took place before the receptionist replaced the receiver.

'Thank you for your patience,' she began, 'please proceed to the elevator on your right and press the fifty-three button.'

'Thank you,' replied Shoil.

Arthur's memory had told her that on more than one occasion he had sent young girls to Graham's apartment. He was not sure what went on up there as Graham never mentioned them, nor did he ever see the girls again. She walked up to the elevator, which opened as soon as she reached the doors which, she assumed, had been operated by the receptionist. She entered the lift and pressed the fifty-third-floor button. The doors closed silently, and the lift gently began to rise. When the elevator stopped and the doors opened, she stepped out to find a half-opened apartment door with the silhouette of a man standing in the doorway. He beckoned her towards him. As she stepped closer, she recognized the man as Graham.

'So how much did he pay you?' he asked directly.

'Excuse me?' questioned Shoil.

'How much did that swine Arthur pay you to come and visit me?'

'I am not a prostitute, if that is what you think.'

'Really, then why did he send you?'

'We have a mutual friend.'

'And who might that be?'

'Katy. Katy Price.'

He blinked twice quickly.

'You know Katy?'

'I do,' she answered.

He stepped aside, allowing her to enter his apartment. It was luxurious. He closed the door behind her.

'So, how do you know Katy?'

'We come from the same part of the UK and, in fact, were on the same flight over.'

'I see. It's funny, because I do not recall ever mentioning Katy to Arthur.'

Shoil stepped from behind the sofa to face Graham.

'Really. Well, you know where she is living, right?'

'Excuse me?'

'I asked if you could let me know where she is living.'

'I thought you said you knew her?'

'I do, but I just do not know where she is living and need to contact her.'

'About?'

'It's a girlie thing.'

'Fine, but I need to go back to my original question and ask how you knew she knew me?'

'She must have mentioned you or something.'

'Perhaps I'd better check directly with her myself,' he said guardedly, walking towards the white phone sitting on the white sideboard.

Shoil stepped in front of him to block his path.

'We can do this the easy way, or the hard way,' she said.

'I don't have time to play games with little girls,' he barked, now losing his patience.

He went to brush past her, but she didn't move and was as solid as a block of concrete.

'I remember you from the circus. So it's the hard way then.'

She grabbed his arm with both hands and threw him across the room. He landed on the glass coffee table, smashing it. There were cuts on his forehead as blood ran down his face. Before he had time to recover, Shoil pounced on top of him, pinning him to the floor. With one hand she roughly pushed his head back against the floor, while with the other one she forced his mouth open. She then opened her mouth, allowing her long snake-like tongue to shoot out into his mouth and down his throat. Graham thrashed around, trying to free himself, but all was in vain. She was far too strong for him. It took a full ten minutes before she finished absorbing him, ending up kneeling on the floor on top of his clothing. She stood up and went into the bathroom to splash cold water over her face.

'Thank you, Graham, you have been most helpful,' she said, walking back into the lounge and looking down at the pile of clothing.

'So, you were meeting her tonight, were you? Well, we must not disappoint her.'

God, this guy was actually in love with the bitch and was going to buy her an apartment in the same building. Boy, is she ever going to be shocked when she finds out what happened to him.

She laughed at her good fortune. Never in her wildest dreams could she have imagined this order of events, one which ending up with her knowing the time and location of Tampong's next planned meeting. How she was going to enjoy telling her that she had destroyed everything that was important to her.

THE ENCOUNTER

Date: April 2011
Age: 19
Status: Fully active

'She's at it again,' said Terry, 'and she is very, very close.'

'Damn that woman,' cursed Tampong.

'I don't think you should go out alone tonight,' he said.

'Was it not you who said we cannot allow her to control our lives?'

'I know, but this is different. She is very close and getting closer.'

'Then we just need to be that extra bit careful.'

'Right, which is why I don't want you going out on your own tonight.'

Tampong's expression changed as she looked affectionately at Terry.

'That's so sweet of you, but I will be fine.'

'I will keep a safe distance and leave you two alone once he picks you up. I promise.'

She could see the look of determination on his face, realizing there was little chance of changing his mind.

'And who is going to look after you, because you will be alone tonight, won't you?'

'I'll be fine. As I said, I'll keep out of sight and, in any case, I can sense her long before you can.'

'True,' she conceded. 'OK then, but you must keep your distance and out of sight, agreed?'

'Agreed.'

'OK then. Let me get my coat and we can be on our way.'

They walked out of the apartment together. Just before they reached the football stadium, Terry moved across to the other side of the road. He kept a careful watch up and down the road, but he saw nothing out of the ordinary.

Tampong stood just outside the main entrance and glanced at her watch. She waited another ten minutes, but there was still no sign of Graham. She glanced at her watch again. It was getting dark now. Clearly something had gone wrong. She glanced across the street towards Terry, shrugged her shoulders in resignation, and began walking back up the street.

Terry suddenly felt a shiver run down his spine despite the warmth of the sun. He shivered not quite understanding why, so he carried on walking on the opposite side of the road, keeping parallel with Tampong. Tampong was walking quickly now and in deep thought, wondering what could have happened to Graham, when she suddenly stopped and, instead, began running across the road towards Terry, gripping him firmly by the arm when she reached him.

'Ouch,' he cried out, 'that hurts.'

'I sense something,' she said more to herself, concern etched in her voice.

She suddenly went on alert, forcing her eyes to change to her fighting color of orange, which also heightened her senses.

That was when Terry also felt the disturbance and wondered if that was the reason for his sudden feeling that someone had just walked over his grave. He now welcomed the reassuring grip of her hand. It felt safe and more secure.

Then her grip was suddenly gone as his body was ripped from her hand. He flew into the air and across the street. It was as if some hidden force had physically lifted his body into the air and tossed it away like a rag doll. He was floating quickly across the road, unable to react. He crashed into the wall of the stadium building. The impact of his head hitting the wall knocked him unconscious. His body flopped to the floor.

'**Terry**!' Tampong screamed as she started running across the road towards his still body.

She almost reached him when she felt a sharp pain in her side, forcing her to stop and collapse onto one knee. She placed her hand on her side, and it came away red with her blood. She looked down and saw a silver blade embedded just above her hip. Without thinking, she pulled the blade out, causing her to scream in pain. She felt giddy but her thoughts were of Terry and not her, so she didn't see the figure suddenly appear at her side and who kicked her sharply in her stomach, forcing all the air out of her lungs and physically pulling her backwards. She landed on the street on her back. Before she could move, a black boot rested firmly on her chest, pinning her to the floor.

Shoil stood above her, wearing a short black dress with long, black leather boots.

'Who are you?' spat out Tampong, puzzled by the strength of this stranger.

She looked like a young girl, but the weight of her boot crushing her chest belied her weak stance.

'You mean you do not recognize me, Tampong? Why, I feel quite hurt. Has it been that long?'

'**YOU**!' answered Tampong, recognizing the voice instantly.

'Yes, bitch,' she replied, 'it's me, back for my revenge.'

'If you have hurt the boy . . .'

'You will what?' challenged Shoil, 'kill me?'

'Yes.'

'I cannot believe how easy you made this for me. You have lost all your fighting instincts, Tampong. How could you possibly allow someone like me to sneak up on you?'

It was a question that didn't demand a reply, not that Shoil was expecting one. Tampong tried to run through her options, which were very limited. She could feel the blood oozing from her wound and knew it was a serious strike. Shoil also had her pinned firmly to the ground. Despite the fact she looked like an innocent young girl, the weight of her boot felt like a cement block on her chest. She tried to push up against it, but it was like hitting your head against a brick wall. It didn't budge a millimeter.

Shoil called the discarded spear back into her hand. It flew off the ground and landed in the palm of her hand easily as she knelt down on Tampong's chest, knowing it was going to be difficult for her to breathe.

'Well, well, well,' she began, 'looks like all the hunting for you has been worthwhile and finally paid off. You had me chasing shadows there for a little while, but I knew you would slip up eventually, although I really have the boy to thank for most of the slipups. He really did like the girl who had this body, or was it just the body he liked? Anyhow, I was able to track you down through him, and now I am going to finish you off, then take care of the boy.'

'Don't you dare touch him, Shoil,' Tampong demanded.

'You are in no position to demand anything, bitch. I will do whatever I please with the boy.'

'He hasn't harmed you or any of the Higher Middle. Let him go.'

'He smells of you, and he has abilities too, hasn't he?'

'I . . . I don't know what you are talking about.'

'Don't lie to me, bitch. I have contacted him through thought. He knows of me, of us.'

Shoil noticed a sudden change of look from Tampong, which told her all she needed to know.

'Aha, so I am right. What I don't understand is how he has these abilities in the first place. What did you do to him?'

'Nothing,' answered Tampong, still trying to wiggle free of her boot.

'**Liar**!' Shoil screamed.

She felt the blade in her hand, rolling it around in her palm as if deciding what to do.

'Did you transfer some of your abilities to him to try and protect him?'

Tampong did not respond.

'Tell me, bitch, or I'll make you watch me kill him slowly before I turn my full attention back to you.'

That got her attention. Shoil realized that Tampong had strong feelings for the boy.

'He . . . he has some of my blood, that's all that happened.'

'You gave him some of your blood? Why?'

'An accident . . . he needed blood . . . it was the same type as mine.'

She was now feeling weak and finding it difficult to concentrate and stay focused. She stopped pushing, accepting there was no way she could force Shoil off her body.

'So that's why he smells of you. He has part of you inside him.'

She turned to look at Terry's unconscious body.

'It is going to make it even more enjoyable to absorb him.'

'You . . . you . . . cannot . . . he is still a virgin.'

She coughed and spat blood out of her mouth.

'A virgin!' Shoil answered, almost laughing, 'how little you know about him. He has been fucking that little bitch he met here.'

Tampong's eyes shot upwards towards Shoil's.

'You didn't know,' said Shoil, the pleasure dripping from her voice. 'That makes your failure all the greater. Now I am bored talking to you.'

She raised her arm into the air before plunging the spear hard into the other side of Tampong's hip. The spear struck bone and slipped further inside her body, causing Tampong to jerk as a searing pain shot through her body. Shoil leaned close to her face.

'And now, bitch, you will die.'

There was a sudden wisp of air as a small metal blade hit Shoil in the side of her head, forcing her off Tampong and to collapse onto the street, lying next to Tampong. She hadn't noticed Terry climb to his feet, stagger over to the two women, and fire off a spear from his finger. He tried to reach Tampong before Shoil plunged the spear into her, but he never made it. He dropped to his knees, gently placing a hand under her head, lifting it slightly off the ground.

Tampong was barely conscious, but her eyes focused on Terry.

'You . . . you . . . are . . . alive,' she stuttered.

'Yes, yes, I'm still here,' he said with tears rolling down his cheeks.

'Shoil!' warned Tampong, 'you need to get away from Shoil.'

'She is here, next to you,' explained Terry.

Tampong slowly turned her head to where Shoil lay.

'Is she dead?'

'I don't think so.'

'Then kill her and get away from here.'

'I need to take care of you first,' he argued.

'It's too late for me, Terry. I am done for.'

'Don't say that. I need you.'

'No . . . no . . . you don't . . . not anymore.'

'I do. I cannot do this alone.'

His voice was filled with worry.

Just then Shoil started to move, causing both of them to look urgently in her direction.

Tampong grabbed his arm, pulling him closer to her so that she could whisper.

'The only possible way you can defeat her is if you absorb me.'

'Absorb you!' he cried out, 'are you crazy?'

'It's the only way, Terry. With my abilities and your own, you might be able to defeat Shoil, particularly as she is weakened a little at the moment.'

'I cannot, I will not,' he argued.

'You *have* to. I will be dead in a short while . . . so by absorbing me . . . I will always be a part of you, Terry. Together . . . we can . . . defeat her.'

Her head flopped backwards, and as she coughed, more blood dripped from her mouth.

'Please . . . Terry,' she begged.

Shoil slowly raised her arm to her head, feeling the spear that had embedded itself. She grabbed the shaft and pulled it out of her head. Her hair quickly became matted with her blood. She dropped the spear and lay back down on the ground.

Terry looked across to Shoil, then back down at Tampong, whose eyes were starting to close, while her face looked pale. She let go of his arm, and her hand flopped to the ground. Her lips were moving but no sound was heard, so he leaned closer to listen to what she was saying.

He understood, so leaned down and kissed her on the lips, allowing his tongue to enter her mouth. His whole body went rigid as their skin coloring changed to orange. Both bodies shook violently, causing Terry to grip her body even more tightly. He kept his eyes closed and missed the tear falling from Tampong's eyes as she looked up to him for one last time. She took her final breath, closed her eyes, and allowed the absorption to complete its work.

Shoil slowly sat up and took hold of the spear in her hand. She looked down at it and at the blood still dripping from its tip. Her blood. She bent the blade in her hand and threw it across the street in contempt. Her head felt tender and definitely wet with her blood, but her anger pushed away any pain. She quickly realized what had happened. She didn't keep an eye on the boy, and he must have woken and tried to save the bitch, but he was too late.

'You are going to pay dearly for that, boy,' she snapped, getting to her feet slowly.

She then looked around for Tampong, but there was no sign of her. The boy was sitting in the street with his back to her. He was holding something, although she couldn't tell what it was from her angle.

'Did you hear me, boy?' she said, louder this time.

Still no response.

'I am talking to you, boy,' she said, almost screaming now.

How dare this little rug rat try to defy her. She rocked her head around her shoulders, pleased that it moved freely. She clenched her fists and moved towards the boy. He didn't turn towards her. Didn't say anything. He didn't move an inch. Shoil hesitated slightly. Perhaps the boy was dead and left in a sitting position. She took a couple of careful steps towards him, moving as silently as possible. She was close enough to look over his shoulder. He was holding a pile of clothes. She blinked twice, realizing they were Tampong's clothes. So she was finally dead, but where was her body? Surely the boy could not have absorbed her. He wouldn't know how. His head was bent down, crying into the clothes. He looked pathetic. She moved her arms out by her side and focused on her fingers, feeling the blades emerge from her fingernails. She wanted to change into her animal form, but something or someone was preventing her from doing so. She brushed the puzzling thought out of her mind, focusing instead on the boy, watching his every move.

'So the bitch is finally dead,' she spat out, 'good riddance to that piece of filth.'

Her words caused a reaction from the boy. He lifted his head, still not turning towards her, but looking straight ahead instead. She didn't care. He had Tampong's blood flowing through him. He had her filthy blood, so he had to die with her. She raised her hands and pointed her fingers towards the boy's back. It was an easy target. One she couldn't miss. She focused her energy on the blades and released them at the same time. They flew towards the boy. Her aim was true, but the target was not reached.

The blades hit an invisible force field inches from the boy's back and disintegrated, leaving an orange dust balloon made up of millions of tiny orange stars. Shoil's eyes widened in shock. Her arms were still held out, so she made more spears appear and was about to fire again when the boy suddenly rose to his feet and turned around in midair to face her.

His eyes were a bright, dazzling orange. His skin glowed orange, and he now looked menacing.

Shoil stood defiant in front of him. Tampong was not the most powerful Higher Middle member, so even if he had absorbed her, he would still be no match for her. The small doubt niggling at the back of her mind was how her blades just disintegrated.

'How did you do that?' she demanded.

'Do what?' he asked, dripping with sarcasm.

'You know what,' she screamed, 'how did you stop my spears from penetrating your back?'

'Ho that,' he replied calmly, 'well, it seems that healing abilities can also be protective abilities.'

She kept her guard up as his confident pose troubled her.

'What do you mean, healing powers? That bitch never had any healing powers.'

'Well, Tampong did actually, she had Xtri's healing abilities.'

'Xtri!' she repeated, 'but that's not possible. How could she have his abilities, unless . . .'

She left the last words unspoken.

'Click,' said Terry, making a turning motion with his hand at the side of his head.

'Have your fun, boy, it will be the last thing you do today.'

She felt her rage building up, felt the change that was about to happen. Whatever had stopped her from transforming before was now gone or beaten. She watched hair quickly cover her entire skin. Her face began stretching out as her back arched, forcing her down on all fours. Her eyes turned orange, while her clothes tumbled from her transformed body, strangely leaving her knickers clinging to her waist. Terry would have laughed had this been any other occasion. Instead he stood his ground and waited for her to complete her change. He felt strangely calm in front of this ghastly beast. Shoil was now back to being a large, menacing dog. Her head slightly lowered as she moved from side to side, ready to pounce on her prey, waiting for her moment to strike. Still Terry did not move, watching the animal move quickly from right to left.

'Your days are finished,' growled Shoil.

Her voice now deep and threatening.

'I think not, Shoil,' he replied in defiance.

He slowly slid one foot in front of the other and checked his balance. He felt solid. That was when the idea came to him. He slipped his foot out of his shoe and felt the cold concrete of the pavement. He focused on the concrete, allowing it to enter his body, to fill him, to be one with him. All this was unseen by Shoil, who still paced side to side in front of him. He then remembered watching a martial arts movie, so lifted his arm towards her and beckoned her towards him with his fingers. A deep growl came from her throat as she leaned back on her haunches.

She leapt quickly and purposefully towards Terry. Her front paws raised in front of her, both with pointed claws, which were razor-sharp and would tear any human skin to pieces in seconds.

Except Terry was not a normal human and no longer had normal human skin. He had abilities that went back thousands of years. Ones that had been dormant until woken up by a combination of events, most of which were created unknowingly by Tampong. He did not move as the enormous animal flew through the air towards him. Waiting for the inevitable contact.

Shoil struck home. Both paws reached her target at the same time, but suddenly her world changed. As soon as her paws contacted the boy, her claws broke into a thousand pieces. It was like hitting a brick wall at a hundred miles an hour. Her paws then crumbled under her body, and her head struck his hand. It felt like a solid hammer hitting her. Her whole body's flight was suddenly halted in midair and then thrown sideways like a rag doll.

She lay stunned on the ground. The pain of her broken claws ripped through her body. She screamed aloud. Howling like a raged animal. It took all of her control to numb the pain. She rolled over and carefully stood back up on her hind legs, her front paws were too tender to put any pressure on them.

'What did you do?' she asked through painful breaths.

'I did nothing,' he said calmly. 'What happened, you did by yourself.'

She quickly looked around, half expecting to see a second person. Someone must have assisted him as he could not have resisted her on his own. However, she saw no one. She felt the anger build up inside her again, so embraced it, knowing it gave her power. Her eyes widened. She took a deep breath, then fired two bolts of lightning from her eyes. They hit Terry in the chest, knocking him over.

To her horror, he simply got back up, dusted himself off, then turned back towards her.

'Now it's my turn,' he said. 'I have to thank you for changing into your animal form. It makes killing you all that easier. I had doubts as to whether I could kill a human being, but then you are not a human, are you, Shoil?'

She moved her head slightly to the left, trying to understand his words.

Without warning, he raised both his arms and fired two thin silver blades from his fingers. They flew quickly through the air to plunge into her front paws, forcing her to collapse into her chest. She howled again.

Terry slowly walked up to the dog, no longer afraid of it, no longer running from it. He stopped just inches from her front paws; both were useless and limp in front of her. She forced her head up from the ground. For the first time, he saw fear in her eyes. He almost felt sorry for her, but only for a second.

He knelt down and lifted her head further off the ground, level with his face.

'You killed Tampong,' he began, 'but worse than that, you killed my parents. WHY?'

His face was red with rage now. He wanted answers. Wanted to know why this beast destroyed his family and changed his world.

Shoil was breathing heavily now. Her front paws were helpless, while her back paws were pinned under her body. She needed time to think. Needed to react quickly if she was to survive this encounter.

'They, they were human,' she stuttered, knowing she had to say something.

'**HUMAN**,' he repeated loudly, 'they were my parents. The loves of my life. The two that protected me.'

'Well, they didn't do a particularly good job then, did they?'

She knew she was taunting him, which was risky, but it appeared to be working.

He stared back at her in confusion. What she said hurt to the core, but it was also true. They were not strong enough to protect him. If it hadn't been for Tampong, then he too would be dead. Lying next to his parents. Half of him wished that had happened, while the other half was grateful he had his chance to revenge their deaths. He thought about Tampong again and how she had protected him with her last, dying breath. He owed it to all of them to kill this beast. Tampong had given him the ability to do so, and he intended to use it.

'I am going to finish you off now, Shoil. You will never take another human being. You will pay for the death of my parents and Tampong.'

He stood up and pointed his fingers down at her head. Her eyes were staring defiantly back up at him.

That was when she noticed his skin change from grey to pale flesh color, so she guessed he had mutated back to his original form, ready to strike her again. She took another risk and focused on her eyes, flashing two more jets of fire towards his face. He screamed in pain as the fire struck his face. He quickly covered his face, falling backwards on the ground. He was blinded by the jets of fire, while his whole face burned badly.

Shoil managed to free her back legs from under her body and stood up on her hind legs and hovered over the screaming boy. His hands still covered his face. She could see red blotches on his cheeks, realizing that his changed form no longer protected him from her attacks.

'Burns like hell, doesn't it?' she said, not expecting any reply.

The boy was still wriggling around on the floor, desperately trying to fend off the searing pain gripping his face. Deep in the back of his mind, he heard Tampong's calming voice.

'Focus on the pain, Terry,' she said softly. 'Let the healing abilities do their work, then finish the bitch off.'

It was difficult for him to concentrate on the voice. He wasn't sure whether it was real or not. The pain was unbearable, and he was still unable to see.

Shoil staggered towards Terry. She lifted one paw up and, with her teeth, pulled the blade out of her paw. She did the same with the other paw, dropping both blades to the ground.

'You were overconfident, boy. I have a thousand years of battle experience over you. Even with your added abilities, you are still no match for the likes of me. I will kill you, then absorb you, taking all your abilities for myself.'

She focused on her eyes again, took another deep refreshing breath, and was about to shoot a final lethal blast of searing fire down at the boy.

She never had the chance.

'**NOOOOOO**,' screamed a female voice as Terry's hands suddenly moved away from his face and two thin metal blades shot from his eyes.

He didn't have any time to aim and didn't even know what he was doing. It was as if he no longer had control over his own body. One blade penetrated Shoil's eye socket, while the other hit her in the chest.

She was forced backwards by the impact, falling heavily back onto the ground. Her whole body shook violently as her uninjured eye suddenly let out a burst of lethal fire, to shoot straight into the air and explode harmlessly high in the air. She knew she was dying, could feel her lifeblood leaving her body. Her heart was beating faster, trying in vain to replace the lost blood. With her good eye, she looked over at the boy. How did he beat her? Whose voice was that she heard. Her breathing was rapid now, as her body slowly changed back to her human form. The blades in her body suddenly went limp, dissolved, running down her body, leaving holes where the tips had penetrated. Her damaged arms flopped by her side. Her bloodied eye filled with more blood to pour down the side of her face, while blood continued to spurt from her chest.

Terry covered his face with his hands again, focusing on his eyes. He felt the smoothing flow of some invisible force. It diluted the pain, forcing it slowly from his body, until he was able to stand up again. He could now see blurred images out of his left eye, although his right eye was still shut tight. He staggered to his feet, walking over to the body lying in the street. He looked down at the naked girl. Even through his blurred vision, he was sure he recognized the body.

'Karen?' he said with a puzzled expression on his face.

Shoil coughed blood, spitting it out on the floor.

'She served her purpose, and now you have killed her too,' she answered.

'You took over her body, didn't you?' he demanded.

'What do you think?' she said, dripping with sarcasm.

'Why, why would you do that to her?'

'Another failure of yours,' she answered instead.

'**WHY**?' he screamed.

'Why not?' she replied simply. 'I needed some way of getting to you, and she was my best bet.'

'You bitch,' he spat.

A smile appeared on her face. She was about to die but took some pleasure in the knowledge that he had lost nearly everybody close to him.

He shook his head in rage. Not wanting to look down at the body anymore, but his eye would not obey him and locked onto the dying body. He watched as the body jerked a little as Shoil went into spasm. He could not watch anymore. Could not allow Karen to suffer anymore. He raised his hand and fired a bolt into her head. It penetrated her forehead and she died instantly.

He fell to his knees and took hold of her hand. 'I am so sorry, Karen,' he said as tears ran down his face. 'I never intended you to get hurt and end up like this.'

'She was dead a long time ago, Terry,' said the female voice again.

It sounded like it was inside his head. It was a voice he knew.

'Tampong?' he called out, looking around.

'I am with you, Terry, part of you now.'

'I . . . I don't understand.'

'You didn't kill Karen. Shoil must have absorbed her some time ago and used her body. That would explain the change I felt.'

'Well, this is definitely Karen lying on the ground in front of me. The body I just killed.'

'No, Terry, you killed Shoil. Now you must leave this place and return home to recover from your injuries.'

'I cannot just leave her naked in the street,' he cried out.

'No, no you don't have to. Watch.'

Terry blinked his good eye twice and looked down at the body, which began to glow orange, became transparent, and slowly dissolve into a million tiny stars, which drifted into the air and disappeared like bubbles in the heat of the day. Watching the body dissolve helped Terry accept that it wasn't Karen but Shoil. Still, he felt heartbroken that he had been responsible for her death, even if it wasn't at his own hand.

The orange stars rose up into the air, hovered above his head for a few seconds, before descending down fast to enter his body. It was like an electric current hitting him. He gasped at the energy entering his body and thought he was going to explode. His whole body shook violently, forcing him backwards. Lying on the ground, he had spasms after spasms. It took a full five minutes before his body went still again. He lay there breathing heavily, feeling strange, like something unnatural had entered him.

'Terry!" called out Tampong.

He just lay there.

'**Terry**!' she screamed.

His eyes blinked twice as his senses returned. He sat up and shook his head, trying to clear the dizziness. It didn't help much.

'You need to go, Terry,' warned Tampong.

He slowly stood straight up, took one last look at where the body was before turning and slowly walking up the street. He never looked back. His eye was still blurry, while his other one remained shut.

'What will happen to me now?' he asked.

'The future is yours to decide,' she answered.

'And what about you? Will you always be inside me?'

'Yes, I will always be part of you now, Terry, but you will not be hearing from me again.'

He stopped walking. 'What! Why?'

'I have to move on.'

'Where?'

'To my next life, to join the others.'

'But they will know what you have done here, won't they?'

'I don't think so, but even if they did, it would be nothing more than I deserve. I betrayed the Higher Middle.'

'What you did, you did to protect me.'

'They will only see that as a weakness and not a strength.'

'I cannot survive without you, Tampong. Stay with me.'

'That's not possible. I have to go. You will be fine on your own. I am very proud of you, Terry.'

'I cannot cope on my own. Where will I go, what will I do?'

'You have all my knowledge now, and all the resources I had at my disposal. They are now yours.'

He was suddenly aware of all her accounts and all the people she had killed to get them.

'This is dirty money,' he said.

'Do what you want with the money, Terry, but you cannot survive without any.'

'I need time to think,' he said.

'Of course. Take all the time you need. Now I must go, Terry.'

'No, please stay, Tampong,' he pleaded.

'Goodbye, Terry, and thank you.'

'For what?'

'For giving my life purpose and for being in my life.'

'I need to thank you, several times, for saving me.'

'Actually, you saved me, Terry, in a way you will never understand.'

'I will miss you, Tampong.'

'No, no you won't, because there will always be a part of me with you.'

'I truly hope so.'

'It's true, now go and enjoy your life.'

'Goodbye, Tampong. I love you,' he replied with tears in his eyes.

'Goodbye, Terry. And I love you too.'

He felt her leave. Knew that she was gone. It left a hollow lump in his heart. In one day he had lost both Tampong and Karen. He started walking again. He walked for hours around the bay, his head lowered towards the ground, wondering what was going to happen to him. He suddenly had all these new memories, all the things that Tampong had done, all the people she had killed and all the bodies she had absorbed. Still, it felt as though there was purpose to her killing. It was not just an insane lust, like Shoil, but she only killed when she had to. He was now a rich, young man. His right eye still stung like hell but felt a hundred times better than it did a few hours ago. He wondered why Tampong never told him to absorb Shoil's body, but then again, perhaps it was better not to know all the horrors that she had inflicted. He was not sure he could absorb her in any case, not as Karen. It wouldn't have felt right. He realized that for the first time they were no longer being hunted. He also now sensed that the Lower Middle had been activated. He could feel them for the first time. They were no threat to him for the moment and they were a long, long way from here. Perhaps they would keep their distance. If not, he knew he would have to defend himself again, and wondered whether Tampong would come to his aide. He hoped so. He then began to wonder about those orange stars that were all that was left of Shoil's body—or was it Karen's body? Did he in fact absorb her after all? He brushed the thought away. Surely if he had absorbed her then he would have all her horrid memories.

'Hey, kid,' said a man walking past, 'are you OK?'

His words knocked Terry out of his thoughts.

'I'm fine, thanks,' he answered without looking up.

'You need to take care of your skin. Looks like you have spent hours in the sun. Your face is the color of a lobster.'

'I will, thanks, mister,' he replied, still walking.

He realized he needed to get inside and out of public view. Give himself time to sort himself out. Time to heal properly. He needed to plan out the rest of his life, and he hoped that Sandi wanted to be part of that. The thought of her brought a smile to his face, which he instantly regretted as the pain returned as soon as he stretched his skin. He needed to work on his healing abilities and quickly. He quickened his pace, eager to get back home and complete his healing process.

***

Both Gary and Tracey were staring at each other. Both their eyes were sparkling blue.

'What the hell!' said Tracey.

'Not sure,' admitted Gary, 'but whatever it was, it was strong.'

'And violent,' Tracey added.

'And violent,' he repeated, more to himself. 'It felt as though there were several players involved this time.'

'What do you think it means?'

'Again, not sure, but it felt as though at least one of them is gone.'

'Gone?' questioned Tracey, looking worriedly into his eyes.

'Hard to explain,' he began, 'but if I were a betting man, then I'd bet that two of the Higher Middle have had some sort of disagreement.'

'And you think that one has been killed?'

Her voice sounded hopeful.

'That's what it felt like to me. First, there were several presences, then a sudden reduction and a change.'

'A change?'

'Difficult to explain, but the presence of one seemed to change.'

'Could it be Shoil mutating?'

'I don't think so. This was something different.'

'Good or bad?'

'Again, not sure. Whatever or whoever they are, they were a long way from us.'

'Which is a good thing, right?'

Tracey looked pleadingly into his eyes. She so badly wanted some good news about the Higher Middle.

'Might be,' he conceded.

'Just might be?' she challenged, slumping back into her chair.

'That's what I said. Listen, I don't have all the answers, and sometimes it is difficult to interpret the sensations I feel. They do not always make sense.'

'Like the last experience?'

'Exactly.'

Tracey sighed heavily.

'I am sorry,' she said softly, reaching over the table and taking his hands into hers, 'I didn't mean to push you and know you can only guess what is happening, but you are more often right than wrong.'

He smiled warmly at her.

'Thanks for that,' he replied, squeezing her hands gently.

His mind was somewhere else though. He couldn't tell her that it felt as though one of them had been absorbed, which was the worst possible scenario for them. A Higher Middle with the abilities of several of the group would be almost impossible to stop. This particular absorption felt almost deliberate. Not quite planned, but suddenly evoked, perhaps out of need or urgency. He just hoped that it wasn't Shoil who had absorbed Tampong. If that was the case, then nothing would be able to stop her. She would be too powerful even if all the rest of the group were together and combined their abilities to challenge her. No, something terrible had happened, but there was no point in scaring Tracey at the moment. Not if he was not sure. Not if he had his doubts.

Tracey had been watching him carefully all evening. She knew him very well now and he was not telling her everything. He was keeping something back from her, which meant that he did not want her to know what he knew, which could not be good news for her, or the rest of the group. How she wished she could contact Joanne now and talk to her. They were always able to talk freely with each other. They were almost like sisters. One evening she would bring up the idea of tracking her down again. Something at the back of her mind told her that they were going to need the strength of all three of them if they were going to survive this strange event.

***

Terry lay naked on his bed, his eyes closed, his breathing slow. He focused on his injured body and wanting to heal it. He almost gave up when he suddenly felt his body changing. His skin tingled all over, and he just about resisted the urge to sit up and wipe the sensation away. Instead, he embraced the feeling, let it surround his body. The force concentrated around his eye and over his face. He felt its soothing effects and smiled.

After three hours he felt energized so sat up and walked over to the mirror. Both his eyes were open again and he could see clearly through both. His face still looked as though he had been out in the sun for too long but no longer stung, nor did it look funny. He was pleased with the results. He turned to start dressing when his phone rang, making him jump. He walked over and picked it up.

'Hello?' he said.

'Hey, you. It's me,' announced the female voice at the other end. He recognized her voice instantly.

'Hey, Sandi. How are you?'

'Fine, thanks, but just checking in on you.'

'Why?'

'Because I miss you.'

'That's nice.'

'And?'

'And what?'

'Are you missing me?'

'Of course I am. You are always on my mind.'

'Good answer. So are we meeting up tonight?'

'Sure, would love to.'

'OK. How about a meal out then back to my place?'

'Sounds perfect, but let me pick the restaurant this time.'

'OK, you're the boss. Meet me outside my apartment, say at seven pm?'

'I'll be there,' he answered warmly.

'Perfect,' she answered before replacing the phone.

He held the receiver in his hand for a few seconds, listening to the humming of the telephone line. It felt strangely comforting. He realized that for the first time in a long time he didn't have to look over his shoulder anymore. Shoil was finally gone. He would never forget Tampong, and just the thought of her brought a tear to his eye, which he brushed away. She had saved him again, and he was determined not to waste this second opportunity. He also realized he now had access to some considerable funds, never realizing how rich Tampong was. She had kept a frugal lifestyle. He decided there and then that tonight he was going to celebrate his new life and opportunity. He picked up the telephone book and found the telephone number for Raffles and dialed the number.

'Good day, this is La Dame de Pic Restaurant, how can I help you?' said the pleasant female voice.

'Hello, I was wondering whether it is possible to book a table for tonight?'

'Tonight, gosh, that's very short notice, sir, we normally require at least three weeks' notice. Can you hold for a moment, please?'

'Sure,' replied Terry, feeling a little disappointed now.

He tapped his finger on the table while waiting for the woman to come back on the phone.

'Sir, thank you for waiting.'

'No problem,' said Terry.

'How many people would be dining?'

'Two.'

'Perfect. Actually we have just had a cancellation in our Elegance restaurant. Would that be OK for you, sir?'

'Perfect.'

'What time can we expect you?'

'Say seven thirty?'

'Seven thirty it is. And the name, please?'

'Armitage, Terry Armitage,' he answered.

'Thank you, Mr. Armitage. We look forward to seeing you tonight then.'

'Thank you very much, and goodbye for now,' he said, trying to hide all the excitement in his voice.

'Good day, sir,' said the woman as she hung up.

Terry replaced the receiver and swung around in his chair. Today was going to be a good day after all. The only cloud was the death of Tampong, but, as she said, she would always be part of him now, so she would never be gone completely. He held that thought and buried it deep inside his head. Now, he had to get ready for dinner tonight. First, though, he went to the bedside drawer, pulling it open he took out Tampong's purse. She had several thousand dollars in it, together with her credit cards, which he also took out and slipped into his wallet. He checked the clock on the wall. The shops were still open, so he had time to do a bit of shopping before coming back, having a shower, and be ready to meet with Sandi.

He almost ran out of the house and was soon standing in front of a jewelry store. Almost immediately a young woman came out of the store and stood in front of him.

'Are you looking for anything in particular?' she asked.

Terry looked at the young woman, who was very attractive.

'Actually, I am looking for a gift for my girlfriend.'

'Then you have come to the right place,' she answered, gesturing with her arm for him to enter.

He did so.

'Now,' she began as she moved to the other side of the counter, 'what does your girlfriend like?'

'I am not sure, to be honest,' he confessed.

'No problem. May I ask if your girlfriend is a Singaporean lady, or foreign?'

'Singaporean.'

'OK. Then may I suggest a brooch with a gold chain. Most local young girls are into these at the moment.'

She picked up a golden brooch and handed it across to him, placing it in his hand. It felt cold to the touch, but its slightly deformed heart shape looked warm. He felt the metal in his hand.

'It is actually a locket,' she advised, 'go ahead and open it.'

He did so.

'As you can see, there is room for two pictures, which can be either of the two of you, or perhaps her parents?'

'Maybe,' he agreed, deciding it was better not to mention the fact that the father was not around.

'OK, I'll take it please.'

'Would sir like it gift wrapped?'

'Yes, please.'

'Fine. Then I'll just get that sorted for you. Please take this slip to the cashier, and while you are paying I will get your gift ready.'

'Thank you,' he replied, taking the slip, walking over to the cashier, and passing it to her.

'That will be twenty-five hundred dollars please,' said the cashier.

Terry was shocked at the price but managed to hide his surprise. Instead, he opened his wallet and handed her one of the credit cards.

'Thank you,' said the cashier, slipping the card into the small machine sitting by the side of the till.

She typed in the price before turning the machine around towards Terry.

'If sir would not mind entering the code please?'

Terry took a deep breath before typing in four numbers and pressing the green button. The machine beeped once, so the cashier turned it around again, pressing another button, causing a little sheet of paper to shoot out of the machine. She ripped it off and pressed the same button, causing a second sheet of paper to sprout from the machine.

'Thank you, sir,' she said, placing one of the sheets of paper on top of the credit card and handed both to Terry.

He nodded his thanks before returning to the counter, where the woman was standing holding a bag in both hands.

'You are all set, sir,' she said, handing him the bag. 'Do come back again soon, sir, and have a wonderful evening.'

She bowed her head as a sign of respect as he took hold of the bag, placing both hands together as she did so.

'Thank you and good evening,' he replied, gripping the bag tightly and walking out of the shop.

He was swinging the bag gently and was not paying attention until he was aware that a young girl was walking alongside him. He looked across at the young, slim girl, whose blouse was unbuttoned almost down to her waist. She wore a very short red skirt with matching high heels.

'You buy me a drink?' she asked.

'Another time perhaps,' he answered.

'You like to fuck me?' she asked bluntly.

'Er, what?'

'You like to fuck me,' she repeated, keeping pace with him.

'Thanks, but no thanks.'

'Why not. You no like girls?'

'I like girls very much.'

'Then fuck me. I am very good, you know, and have a good body.'

She moved quickly in front of him and presented herself with her arms out wide.

'Thanks, but I am meeting someone tonight.'

'No problem. I fuck with girls too.'

'Again, thank you but no thank you.'

'You want a boy then?'

'No.'

'Then why you no want to fuck me? Look at me. I have good body, no?'

'Yes, you have a very nice body, but I am not interested. I have no money,' he lied.

That did the trick. She suddenly stopped walking, said something obscene (he guessed) in a foreign language before turning away to hunt for her next client.

He shook his head as he turned down the road and was soon back in the comfort and safety of his home. He had a shave and took a long hot soak in the bath. He thought that a hot bath in a hot country like Singapore sounded ludicrous, but it was refreshing. He got out, dried, then put fresh clothes on. He opted for a white shirt and black trousers. He first put on black trainers, then decided to wear black shoes instead, after all, they were going to a nice restaurant. He slipped his watch on, combed his hair, and generously splashed aftershave over his face. He opened the wardrobe and selected his black leather jacket. He stood in front of the mirror and was pleased with his reflection. He just hoped Sandi would like his effort.

He checked his watch; it was time to leave. He placed his wallet in his jacket pocket and picked up the gift bag. Locking the front door, he walked down the road to hail a taxi. He did not have long to wait, and it was only another ten minutes before the taxi dropped him outside Sandi's home.

'Can you possibly wait?'

'If I keep the meter running, I can wait as long as you like,' answered the driver.

'Fine with me,' replied Terry, 'we will be going to the Raffles Hotel.'

The driver nodded.

Terry jumped out of the taxi and stood at the bottom of the gate.

He waited another ten minutes before the door opened and Sandi appeared.

She looked amazing. She was wearing another short white dress. Her hair was bundled into a bun at the back of her head. She did not appear to be wearing any tights or stockings. If she did, then they were truly fine ones. She wore white high heel shoes and carried a white clutch bag.

She saw him looking at her.

'Am I OK?' she asked, concern in her voice.

'Heavenly,' he said simply.

She sighed in relief.

'Well, I have to say you have brushed up very well too.'

'Thank you.'

'And I see you have a cab waiting too, very impressive.'

'Nothing more than a lady deserves,' he answered, opening the door for her.

She nodded her thanks and slipped into the taxi. Terry tried to avoid looking at her long legs, but his eyes would still not obey him. She caught him looking at her and smiled warmly up at him. He closed the door and rushed around to the other side. As soon as he was settled, the driver pulled away.

'So, where are we going?' she asked.

'You will see.'

'Aha. Great, I like surprises.'

He took her hand while she laid her head on his shoulder.

It took the taxi only another ten minutes to reach the hotel. As soon as the taxi stopped, Sandi looked out of the window and gasped.

'Raffles?'

'Correct.'

'Ho my. I have always wanted to see inside this place.'

'You never have?'

'Well, once, a long, long time ago. With my mother, but I was very young and have little recollection.'

'Well, that's one more thing you can tick off your to-do list.'

He paid the cab driver, giving him a generous tip, jumped out of the car and ran around to the other side to open her door. She reached out with her hand, which he gladly took and helped her out of the vehicle. As soon as he closed the door, the taxi pulled quickly away. Terry guessed he had seen another potential passenger. Sandi just stood on the pavement looking up at the building.

'Beautiful,' she said.

'Yes, you are,' replied Terry, slipping his arm through hers and walking her through the main rotating doors.

'May I help you, sir?' asked a man in a tall hat and long green jacket.

'Yes, please,' answered Terry, 'we have a reservation at the Elegance Restaurant.'

'The Elegance you say, sir. Then please go straight down the corridor and turn right. You will find the restaurant on your right.'

'Thank you,' said Terry, leading Sandi down the corridor.

She was taking in all the decorations, looking at the fine porcelain statues, the decorated ceilings, and ornate carpets. They finally came to a halt in front of a reception desk, causing Sandi to brush against Terry, who looked pleased.

'Good evening, sir, madam. Your name please?' asked the well-dressed receptionist.

'Armitage, Terry Armitage,' he replied, feeling Sandi holding him tighter as she became even more excited.

'Mr. Armitage. Thank you. Would you follow me, please?'

The receptionist led them into the restaurant, which was quite dark, and they had to allow their eyes to adjust to the dim lighting. They moved to the far corner of the restaurant until the receptionist stopped in front of a small, round table.

'I trust this is acceptable?'

'Very much,' said Sandi, who freed herself from Terry's hold to slide around to the far side of the table.

She patted the place next to her, so Terry obliged and slid next to her, where she held his hand again.

'Your table server will be with you shortly. Enjoy your meal,' said the receptionist, turning away and disappearing into the dark restaurant.

'This is awesome,' said Sandi, looking around the restaurant.

Before he had time to reply, their server suddenly appeared at their table, almost making Terry jump.

'Good evening, my name is Whyyoume, which does indeed sound like a question but is in fact my name, and I will be taking care of you this evening, so welcome to the Elegance.'

She put her hands together and bowed her head. Sandi placed her hands together and bowed her head in return, so Terry copied her, feeling a little awkward.

'Would you like to start with an aperitif?' she asked.

'I have always fancied trying a Singapore sling here,' replied Sandi.

'When in Singapore,' replied Terry before looking up at the waitress, 'we will have two please.'

'Coming right up. Meanwhile I will leave these menus here for you to browse through and I will return to let you know our specials.'

She turned and, like the receptionist, disappeared into the darkness of the restaurant. Terry turned towards Sandi to see her staring at him.

'Something wrong?' he asked.

'Have you been out in the sun all day?' she asked.

'I have, but I am surprised you can tell in this dimly lit room.'

'I noticed the moment I saw you at the bottom of the gate. I have to say, the coloring suits you, but you should not stay out too long. The sun's rays here can be very dangerous.'

'Thank you and thank you.'

She leaned forward and their lips met. She forced his mouth open and kissed him hard. He was grateful that they had their own, almost private cubicle and were not overlooked by any of the other guests. He enjoyed the feel of her soft lips, which were rubbing against his own. He placed his hand on her thigh, feeling her soft, silky skin. At least he now knew for sure that she was not wearing any tights or stockings. She slowly moved her head away and stared into his eyes.

'You know, I think I am truly falling for you,' she said softly.

'That's the nicest thing anyone has said to me,' he answered straight from the heart, 'and I can honestly say, again, that I fell for you the moment I saw you.'

'Really?'

'Really.'

She leaned forward and kissed him firmly on the lips again. Just as she moved away, the waitress arrived with their drinks.

'Two Singapore slings,' she said, placing one in front of Sandi and the other in front of Terry. 'Now, for the specials we have the wild sea bass seasoned with seaweed and orange pu-er tea, or lobster from Brittany cooked over coals. I'll let you continue browsing and will return shortly.'

They both picked up their glasses, clinked them together, and drank.

'Hmmm,' announced Sandi, 'this is really nice.'

'Quite, surprisingly good,' said Terry in his best English upper-class accent.

Sandi giggled.

They had drunk about half of their slings while browsing the menu when Whyyoume returned.

'Any questions?' she asked.

'Nope, I think we are good,' advised Sandi. 'I am going for the amuse buche menu with amadai from Yamaguchi.'

'I will have the same menu but with the organic Welsh lamb, please.'

'Super. Let me leave this wine list with you. If you have any questions about the wine, I will have our wine expert come to your table.'

'Thank you,' said Terry, taking the wine list.

Sandi moved closer to his side to look through the wine list with him.

'Do you have a particular favorite?' he asked.

'Actually, I do like a Rioja wine.'

'Rioja it is then.'

He flicked through the list until he came to the Spanish wines. He ran his finger down the page until he found two bottles.

'Gosh. Their prices are a little steep,' she observed.

'Hey, this is a special occasion. Let's push the boat out a little tonight.'

She sat up and looked at him, slanting her head slightly to the left as if examining him.

'Are you sure?'

'Positive,' he replied, 'so, let's go for this bottle then. Roda.'

'If you are sure!'

'Quite sure,' he said, then almost jumped again when a person appeared next to him.

'Do you have any questions about the wine list, sir?' asked the man, his hands clasped behind his back.

'No, no thank you. We have settled for a bottle of Roda, please.'

'Excellent choice, sir. I will have that brought to your table. Enjoy your meal.'

He turned to disappear into the dark.

'These damned staff just keep appearing out of nowhere,' he whispered.

'Just as well we are not doing anything risky . . . yet,' she replied quietly, squeezing his thigh playfully.

Terry just coughed. He was saved from any further embarrassment when the waitress returned with their starters.

'Your starters are beef heart tomato, seasoned with geranium and pine nut pesto, glazed with mezcal and sage marinade. Enjoy.'

Sandi looked down at the array of cutlery next to her plate.

'Where do you start?' she asked.

'I believe you work from the outside in,' he advised, picking up the first knife and fork and cutting through the tomato.

Sandi copied him.

'Wow, this is delicious,' she remarked.

Terry nodded his agreement. They ate the rest in silence. As they were finishing, another waiter turned up with their wine. He presented the wine to Terry, who nodded his satisfaction. The waiter then pulled the cork and served a taster for Terry, who lifted his glass and drank the glass empty, causing the waiter to raise an eyebrow in surprise.

'Great, thanks,' Terry finally said on seeing the waiter standing still with the bottle in his hand.

He nodded and filled Sandi's glass before refilling Terry's. He then placed the bottle on the table and quickly left them alone again. Sandi brought her hand to her mouth to suppress a giggle.

'What?' challenged Terry.

'I think you were supposed to sniff the scent of the wine first, then take a sip to test whether the wine is good or not.'

'Right, of course. Hey ho.'

She patted his leg gently then lifted her glass, which Terry followed.

'Are we celebrating anything in particular tonight?' she asked.

'Why, yes, my independence and freedom.'

'Your independence and freedom?'

He clinked his glass against hers, took a sip, then placed the glass back on the table. He took a deep breath.

'My aunt has decided to return home.'

'What! Why?'

'It turned out the job was not for her, as she knew she would not be happy, so she opted to quit and return home.'

'And leave you here?'

'Right.'

'With nothing?'

'Not quite. She left me a bank account with quite a bit of money in it. Unbeknown to me, I inherited some money from another distant aunt. So my aunt gave these funds to me, knowing I did not want to return home with her.'

'And she was OK with that?'

'Not at first, but she understood how I felt.'

'About?'

'About you.'

'Me!' she said, almost dropping her glass.

Terry's reactions were fast, and he grabbed her glass before it could tumble from her hand. She never noticed his quick reaction and was still digesting his latest revelation.

'You stayed for me?'

'Yes. You mean the world to me, Sandi, and I could never leave you, not now.'

Tears formed in both her eyes, so he leaned forward and wiped them dry. She took his hands, then leaned forward and kissed him firmly on the lips. She then moved her head away quickly. There was a puzzled expression on her face.

'But what will you do?'

He laughed.

'I have absolutely no idea, but I thought that whatever it is, we could do it together.'

Her eyes twinkled and a broad smile appeared on her face. Just then the waitress returned and took their plates away, smiling at them both. They held hands and just stared into each other's eyes. Terry then broke the spell by picking up his glass again.

'So any ideas what we might do here on this small island?' he asked.

'Actually yes, I do have a few ideas.'

'OK, then let's hear them.'

'Well, I have always had a dream to open my own cocktail bar here on the island. I think there is a market for it. It is warm here all year round, and people are always thirsty and enjoy the outside life.'

'Interesting,' he remarked.

The waitress arrived with their main course, so they went silent until she left.

'Enjoy your meal,' said the waitress, topping up their glasses before leaving.

'You think it is a silly idea, don't you?' Sandi said with sadness in her voice.

'On the contrary,' he replied quickly, 'I actually think it is a great idea.'

'Really?'

Her eyes lit up again.

'Really,' he confirmed. 'Let's discuss it more over the coming days and see what's involved.'

'You would do that for me?'

'I would do anything for you, Sandi.'

She grabbed his hand again, brought it to her mouth, and kissed it.

'You are the best.'

They spent the rest of the evening discussing possible names and where the best location might be, whether to have a mobile bar or a fixed one. The evening passed very quickly, and the moment seemed to flash by when the silver tray was set on the table.

Terry checked his watch and was surprised to see it was just after eleven thirty already.

'Where did the time go?' he asked aloud.

'Always passes quickly when you are enjoying yourself,' answered Sandi.

'True,' he agreed.

He dropped the credit card on top of the tray and was not surprised to see it picked up almost immediately. After a couple of minutes, the tray was returned with the receipt.

'Thank you for your custom,' said the waitress, 'and we hope to see you back again soon.'

'Everything was perfect, thank you,' replied Terry.

The waitress smiled and moved away from the table. Terry looked around and noticed that only one other table was still occupied. They were also a young couple, who were just getting up to leave. Terry looked at the bill, added a generous tip, then signed the receipt.

'Ready?' he asked.

'Ready,' she replied.

As they left the restaurant, the staff were at the door, and all bowed as they left. They both nodded their appreciation.

Outside the air felt a little fresher and cleaner. They both took in a deep breath of fresh air.

'Let's walk home,' she suggested.

'Fine with me.'

They started walking up Bras Basah Road and had just passed the Carlton Hotel when Terry noticed three youths walking towards them. They were gesturing in his direction and laughing at each other. As they got closer, their faces turned to a serious expression and they blocked the path, forcing Terry and Sandi to stop. The three youths looked Sandi up and down.

'Problem?' asked Terry.

'Only if you make one,' said the taller boy standing in the middle.

'Meaning?'

'We think we will take your slut off your hands. She looks too much of a handful for you but might just be able to handle the three of us.

'What did you call me?' demanded Sandi.

'Shut the fuck up, bitch. We will deal with you later. I am going to check whether you are a real blonde or not.'

Terry took hold of her arms firmly and pulled her back, sensing she was about to launch an attack at the boy.

'I need you to apologize immediately to my girlfriend.'

'You need what?' challenged the boy standing directly in front of Terry.

He was taller and broader than Terry, who guessed they were rugby players or something similar.

'I need an apology,' he repeated.

'Leave it, Terry,' pleaded Sandi, 'let's just go.'

'You ain't going anywhere, bitch, unless we say so.'

'Again, stop with the insults.'

'Or what?' challenged the taller guy.

Terry said nothing, instead he kicked out at the boy standing opposite him, landing his foot directing into the boy's crouch. He then thrust out with his arm towards the taller boy, keeping his fingers straight, ramming them into the boy's throat. He then turned to the third boy, who took a step backwards, shaking his hands in surrender. The other boys collapsed onto the pavement. Terry then stepped towards the taller boy and placed his foot on the boy's neck.

'I did ask nicely for an apology. Now I am demanding one.'

He pushed his foot down on the boy's neck to emphasize his point. The boy grabbed his shoe but could not pull it away. He looked up in horror, coughing and choking.

'OK, OK,' he screamed through gasps.

Terry lifted his shoe off his neck a fraction.

'So?'

'I'm sorry,' the boy said.

'Not to me, to my girlfriend,' reprimanded Terry.

The boy looked towards Sandi.

'I'm sorry, miss, for insulting you.'

Sandi folded her arms.

'Fine, but remember my man here is more than all three of you put together.'

Terry looked at her and smiled. He released his hold on the boy and they began walking back down the road. Terry then looked back as the two boys slowly sat up.

'Next time you will not be so lucky,' he called out after them.

The boys said nothing. Clearly they were shocked and surprised by Terry's speed and strength.

'My hero,' whispered Sandi. 'I am so going to show you how much I appreciate you tonight.'

She leaned closer to him and nibbled on his ear.

'I cannot wait,' he answered enthusiastically, 'maybe you will let me take off your underwear?'

'What underwear?'

He looked at her face, so she blew him a kiss and winked at him.

'You mean to tell me you are not wearing anything under that dress?'

'Correct.'

'Ho boy. Let's get you home.'

They both laughed.

It was one in the morning and Terry could not sleep. They had made love nonstop for nearly an hour, but now Sandi was fast asleep next to him, lying on her side. He felt relaxed and content, not remembering when he last felt this good. He closed his eyes and tried to sleep.

Something began to change in him.

He felt different, light, almost floating. His senses seemed acute, and he was convinced he could control them. That was when he felt a distant presence. It was faint at first, but as he focused on it, it came closer and began taking shape. It was a man. He recognized the man, not sure how, but he did. The man had sensed him too and was now looking directly at him.

'Who are you?' asked the man.

'I am the Higher Middle,' answered Terry.

'Not possible,' challenged the man, 'only two are left, and both are female . . . unless you have transformed.'

'No to both statements. Shoil and Tampong are both dead.'

The names registered with the man, who was puzzled as to who Terry was.

'How do I know you are telling the truth?' asked the man.

'You know. You sensed their departure.'

'I sensed something, true, but could not tell for sure what it was.'

'At least that is an honest response,' said Terry, impressed with the honesty of this man. 'Are you Lower Middle?'

'I am,' replied the man.

'How many are you?'

'That's for me to know, and for you to find out.'

'I can do that,' remarked Terry.

'Then you do not need to ask the question,' taunted the man.

'True,' Terry conceded.

'What do you want?'

'To warn you to keep away.'

'Or what?'

'Or I will destroy you the same way I destroyed Shoil.'

'I will not be hunting you, on that you can be certain.'

'Good. Then we have an accord.'

'Fine with me.'

'But take heed,' continued Terry, 'should any one of you try to hunt me down, I will find you all and kill you all.'

'You can try,' retorted the man.

'I will succeed,' replied Terry, who then cut of the contact with the man.

He leaned back against his headboard and looked down at Sandi. He stroked her hair gently. He had found a new life and happiness and didn't want anything to spoil that. He reached out to the other group to warn them away and let them know that both Shoil and Tampong were gone. He now understood his immense power and ability and was confident he could deal with anything the Lower Middle threw at him. Hopefully, they would be wise to his words and stay away. He had no argument with them.

***

Gary sat on the edge of his bed, sweating heavily and breathing rapidly. The boy had been able to make direct contact with him, warning him away. Could it be true that both Shoil and Tampong were dead? It felt too good to be true. In his experience, if it sounded too good to be true, then it probably wasn't true. However, the boy seemed confident in his abilities. Perhaps he had absorbed one or both of the girls. That was a worrying thought and would make him extremely powerful. That said, he sensed no menace in the boy's voice, who genuinely appeared to warn them to stay away. He had the impression he was not alone, so this was either a heartfelt plea to keep clear, or an awful trick of the Higher Middle, which would not be the first time. He slid back onto the bed and slipped under the covers. Tracey stirred a little, placing her arm across his chest. He looked across to her sleeping body. Could the boy be experiencing the same love that he was? If so, then keeping away would suit them all, allowing them to make the most of the rest of their lives in peace.

If Shoil really was dead, then the threat to the planet and its occupants was all but gone. He hoped and prayed that he was right. He stroked Tracey's hair, unaware that Terry was doing exactly the same thing at the same time with Sandi.

They were like two peas in a pod.

If only.

***

Terry got out of bed, unable to sleep anymore. This man was playing on his mind. Why did he contact him? Was it his destiny? Is this how it was meant to be between them? Doubts filled his head. He was not a killer, but could kill if required, as he had proven several times now. He sat on the window ledge and peered out onto the bay.

Sandi stirred from her sleep and slapped her arm against the sheets. Her eyes blinked open, and she realized Terry was not in bed. She turned her head and saw him sitting at the window.

'Are you OK?' she asked.

Terry turned his head towards the bed.

'Sorry. Did I wake you?'

'No, not at all. I just realized you were no longer with me and panic rose up inside me.'

She slipped out of bed and walked towards him.

'Something on your mind?'

'No, not really.'

'You must be missing your aunt.'

'True. I am.'

She wrapped her arms around him as she stood behind him. He placed his hands over hers.

'It's beautiful here,' he said.

'It is. And we can stay here, together.'

He slid around to face her.

'You are right. We can and should. I am going to spend the rest of my life making you happy.'

Her eyes welled up.

'I love you,' she whispered.

'And I love you,' he answered.

He turned back towards the window and they both looked out. Their heads leaned together while he held her hands tightly. This was going to be his life now, here with Sandi, and god help anyone who tried to change that.

THE END

AUTHOR'S NOTES

This book is primarily located in York and Singapore. The former is a delightful city, while the other is a beautiful island with many friendly locals. While York is steeped in history, Singapore is indeed very modern, and many of the places described by me are true and based on my several pleasurable visits to the city and the island. For example, the Marina Bay Sands Hotel does indeed exist, complete with its ship on the roof. Most of the apartment blocks mentioned in this book exist as well, although I have taken liberties with some of their occupants and locations. I have no idea what the inside of these places look like, but I have maximized writer's privilege and imagination in describing some of them.

The history of the Singapore sling is accurate, and it is quite a nice, refreshing drink. Many of the roads mentioned exist, as do Universal Studios, the cable car ride, and the casinos.

As I mentioned at the beginning of the book, several different endings were going through my mind as I began writing, but I finally decided to kill both characters off but leave several key characters alive so that should I have the urge to continue the saga, then I have enough ammunition to go with. After all, perhaps Terry takes up the Higher Middle mantle and goes after the surviving Lower Middle members. I am not sure why I did not bring Joanne into this particular story more, other than some side mentions. Perhaps I am keeping her in reserve. So watch this space.

Review Requested:

We'd like to know if you enjoyed the book. Please consider leaving a review on the platform from which you purchased the book.

CPSIA information can be obtained
at www.ICGtesting.com
Printed in the USA
LVHW110723260422
717138LV00005B/33

9 781682 356234